THE
MAGIC
FISH

THE
MAGIC
FISH

Trung Le Nguyen

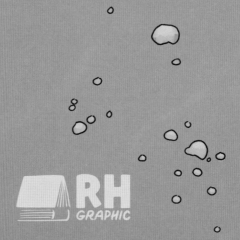

The first 168 pages of this book were drawn traditionally on card-stock printer paper with a combination of Micron fine liners and Staedtler pigment liners. The remaining pages were drawn using a Cintiq tablet in Adobe Photoshop, and subsequent colors were also applied in Photoshop.

Cover art, text, and interior illustrations copyright © 2020 by Trung Le Nguyen

All rights reserved. Published in the United States by RH Graphic, an imprint of Random House Children's Books, a division of Penguin Random House LLC, New York.

RH Graphic with the book design is a trademark of Penguin Random House LLC.

Visit us on the Web! RHKidsGraphic.com • @RHKidsGraphic

Educators and librarians, for a variety of teaching tools, visit us at RHTeachersLibrarians.com

Library of Congress Cataloging-in-Publication Data
Names: Trung, Le Nguyen, author. I Title: The magic fish / Trung Le Nguyen.
Description: First RH Graphic edition. I New York : Random House Graphic,
[2020] I Audience: Ages 12 and up. I Audience: Grades 7–9. I
Summary: "Real life isn't a fairy tale. But Tiến still enjoys reading his favorite stories with his parents from the books he borrows from the local library. It's hard enough trying to communicate with your parents as a kid, but for Tiến, he doesn't even have the right words because his parents are struggling with their English. Is there a Vietnamese word for what he's going through? Is there a way to tell them he's gay?" — Provided by publisher.
Identifiers: LCCN 2019043692 I ISBN 978-1-9848-5159-8 (paperback) I ISBN 978-0-593-12529-8 (hardcover) I
ISBN 978-1-9848-5160-4 (library binding) I ISBN 978-1-9848-5161-1 (ebook)
Subjects: LCSH: Graphic novels. I CYAC: Graphic novels. I
Coming out (Sexual orientation)—Fiction. I Identity—Fiction.
Classification: LCC PZ7.7.T79 Mag 2020 I DDC 741.5/973—dc23

Designed and lettered by Patrick Crotty

MANUFACTURED IN CHINA
10 9 8 7 6 5 4 3 2 1
First Edition

A comic on every bookshelf.

For my parents

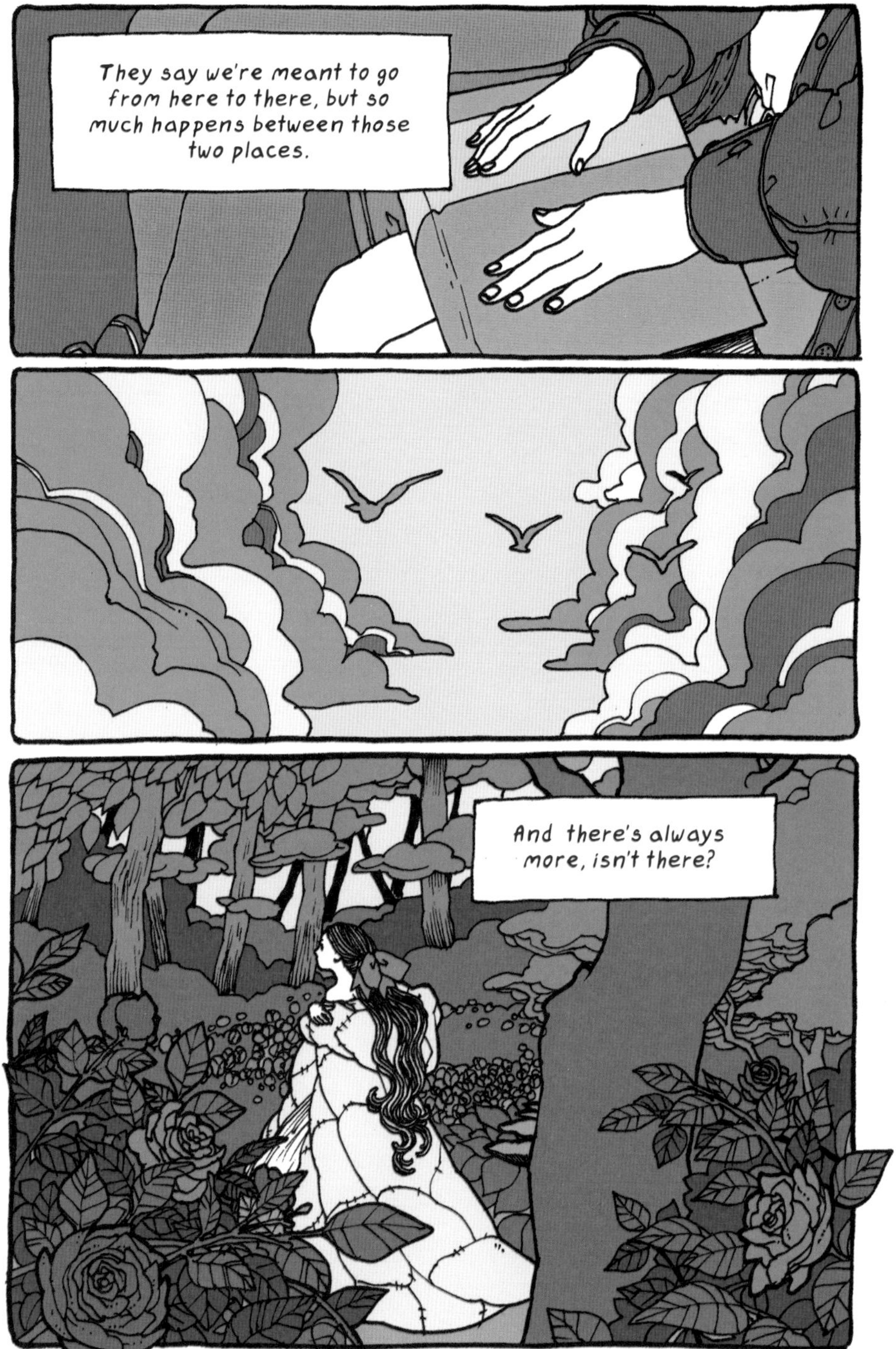
They say we're meant to go from here to there, but so much happens between those two places.
And there's always more, isn't there?

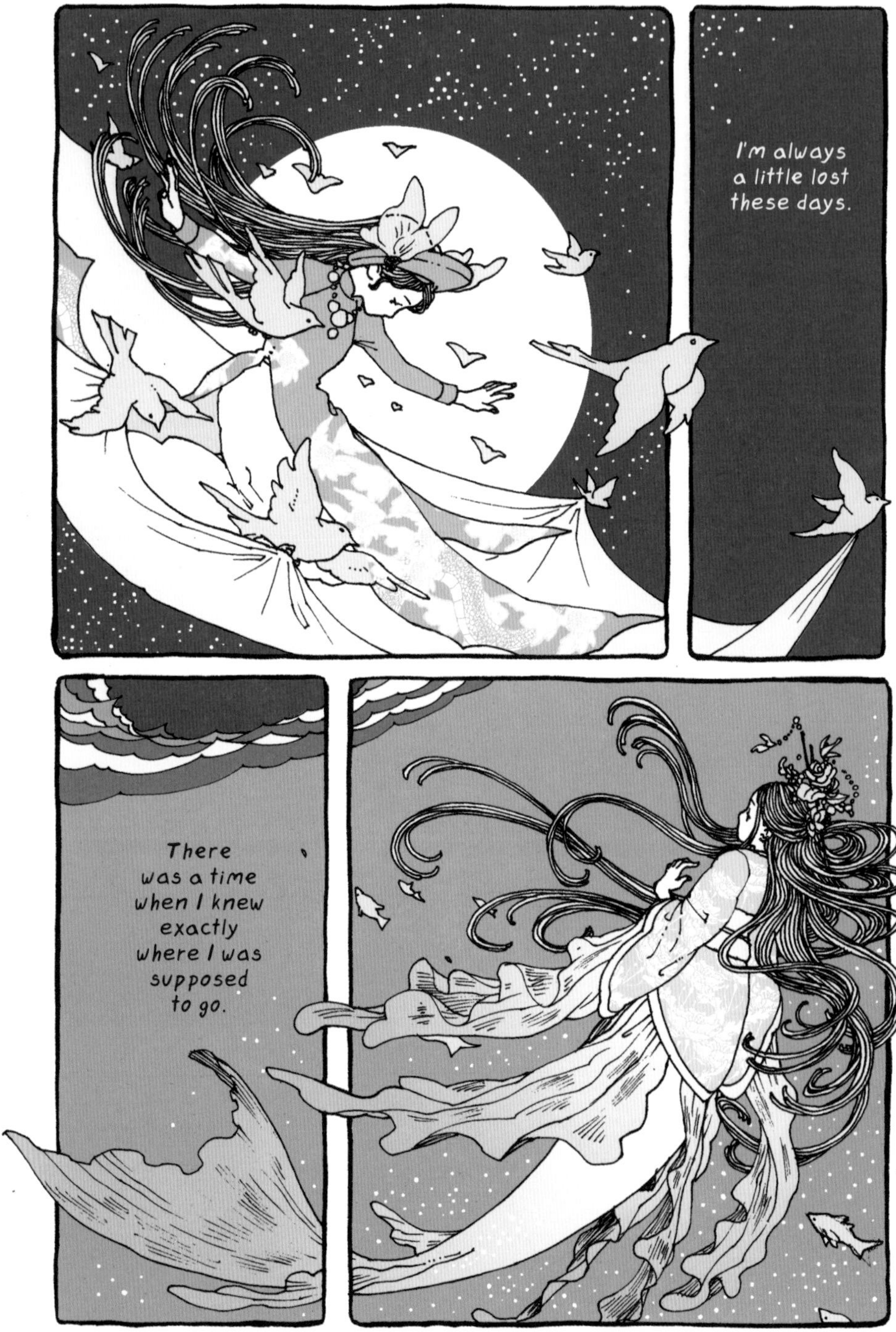
I'm always a little lost these days.
There was a time when I knew exactly where I was supposed to go.

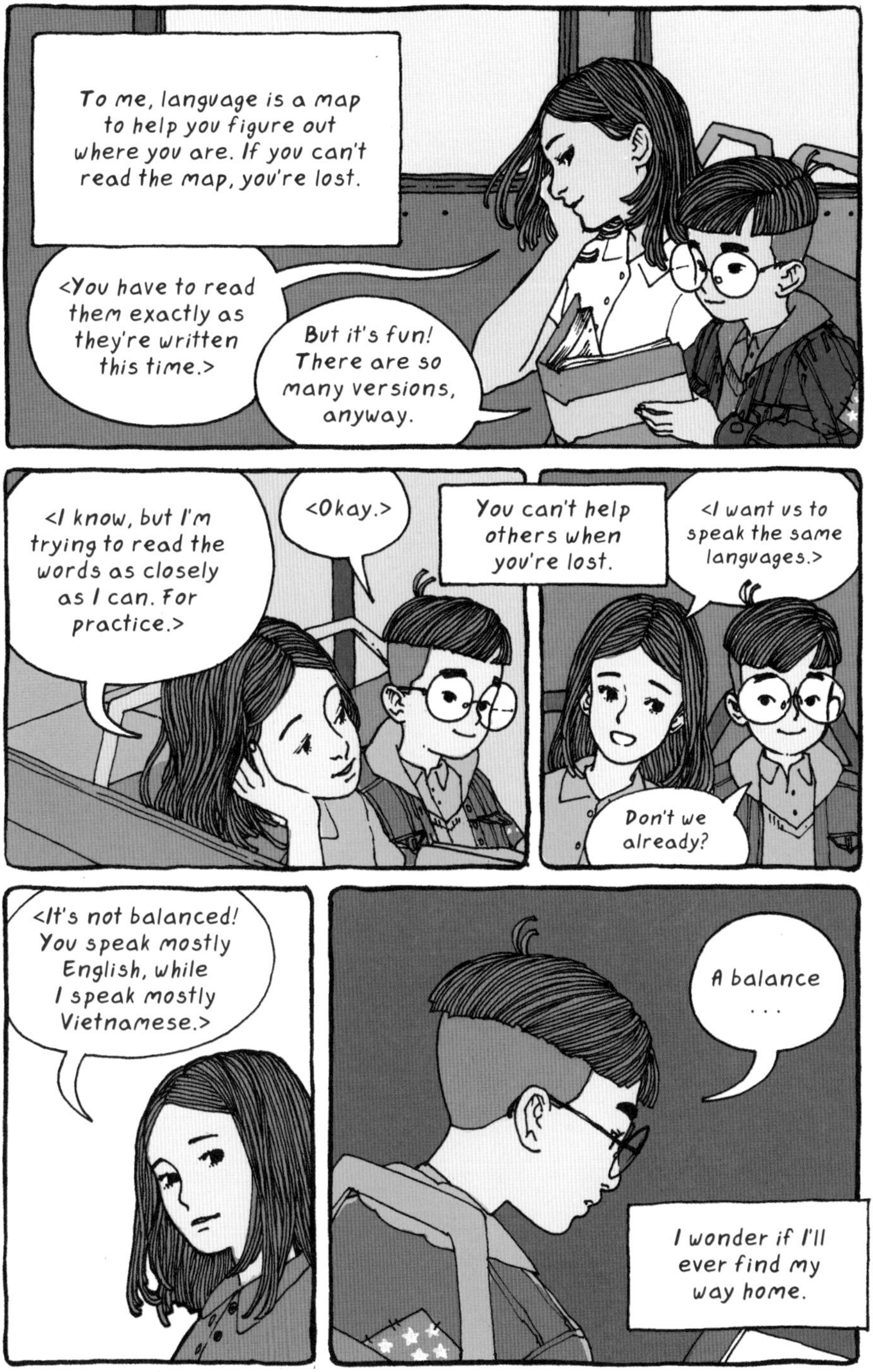
To me, language is a map to help you figure out where you are. If you can't read the map, you're lost.
<You have to read them exactly as they're written this time.>
But it's fun! There are so many versions, anyway.
<I know, but I'm trying to read the words as closely as I can. For practice.>
<Okay.>
You can't help others when you're lost.
<I want us to speak the same languages.>
Don't we already?
<It's not balanced! You speak mostly English, while I speak mostly Vietnamese.>
A balance . . .
I wonder if I'll ever find my way home.

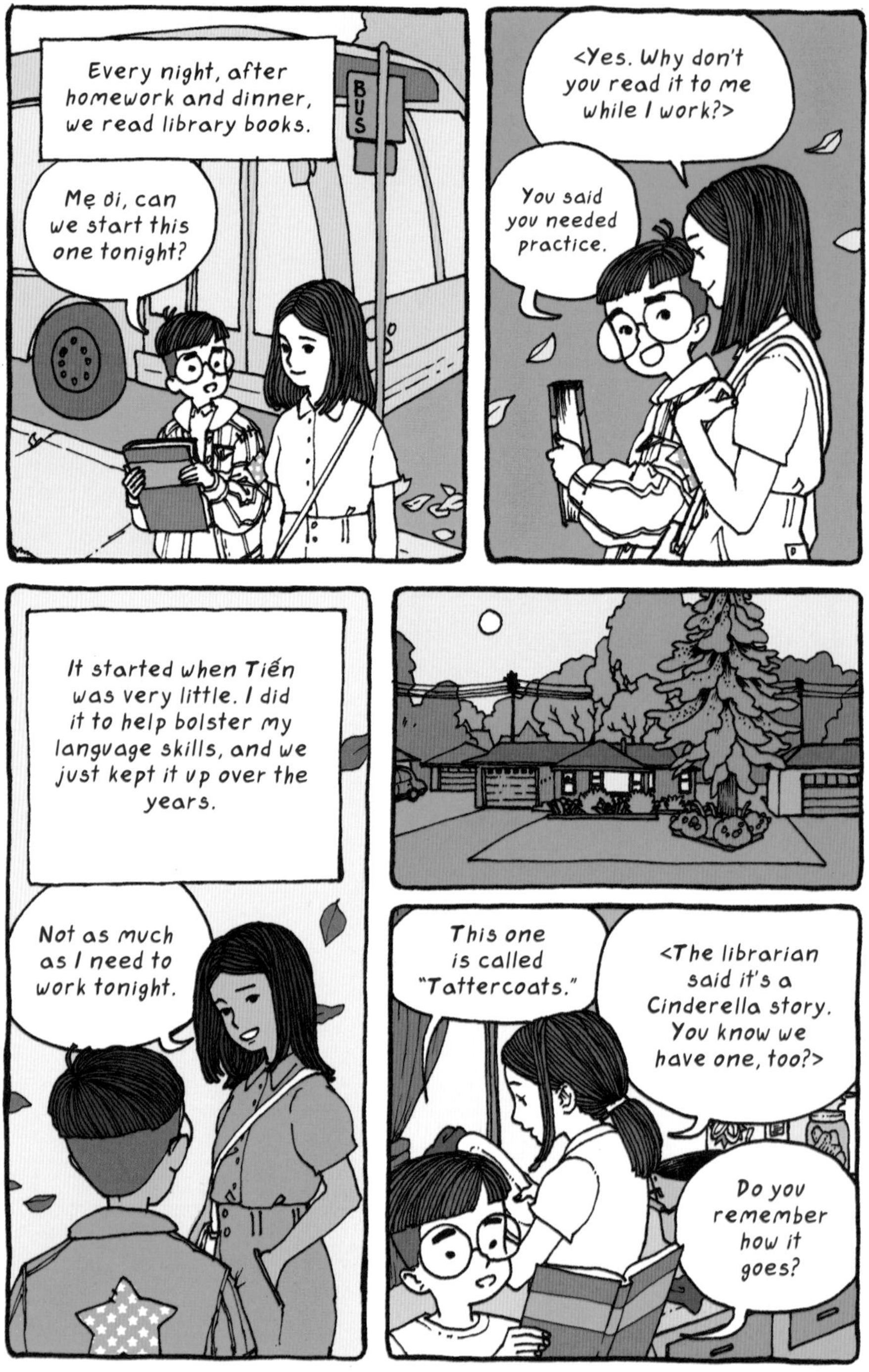
Every night, after homework and dinner, we read library books.
BUS
Mẹ ơi, can we start this one tonight?
<Yes. Why don't you read it to me while I work?>
You said you needed practice.
It started when Tiến was very little. I did it to help bolster my language skills, and we just kept it up over the years.
Not as much as I need to work tonight.
This one is called "Tattercoats."
<The librarian said it's a Cinderella story. You know we have one, too?>
Do you remember how it goes?

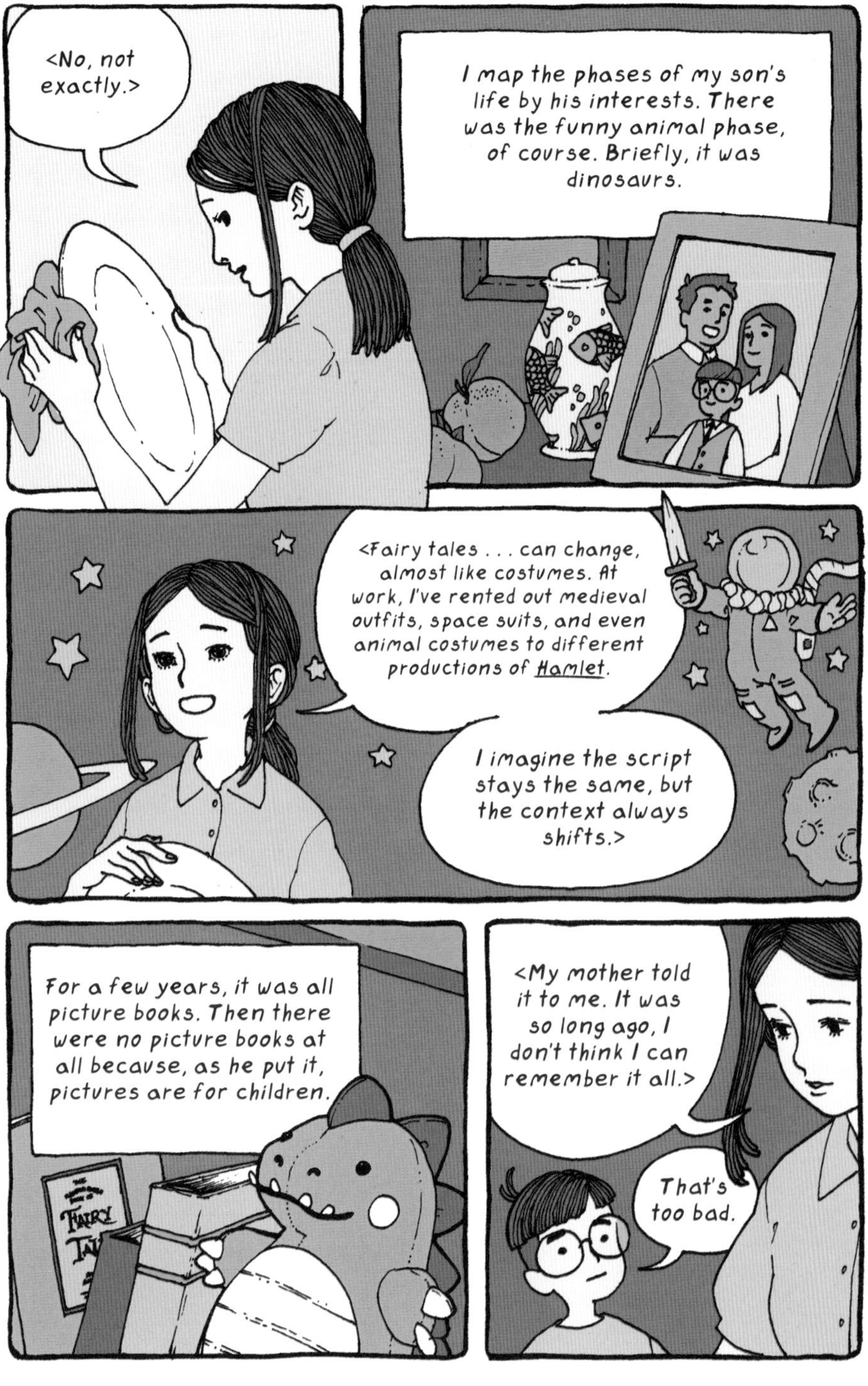
<No, not exactly.>
I map the phases of my son's life by his interests. There was the funny animal phase, of course. Briefly, it was dinosaurs.
<Fairy tales . . . can change, almost like costumes. At work, I've rented out medieval outfits, space suits, and even animal costumes to different productions of Hamlet.
I imagine the script stays the same, but the context always shifts.>
For a few years, it was all picture books. Then there were no picture books at all because, as he put it, pictures are for children.
<My mother told it to me. It was so long ago, I don't think I can remember it all.>
That's too bad.

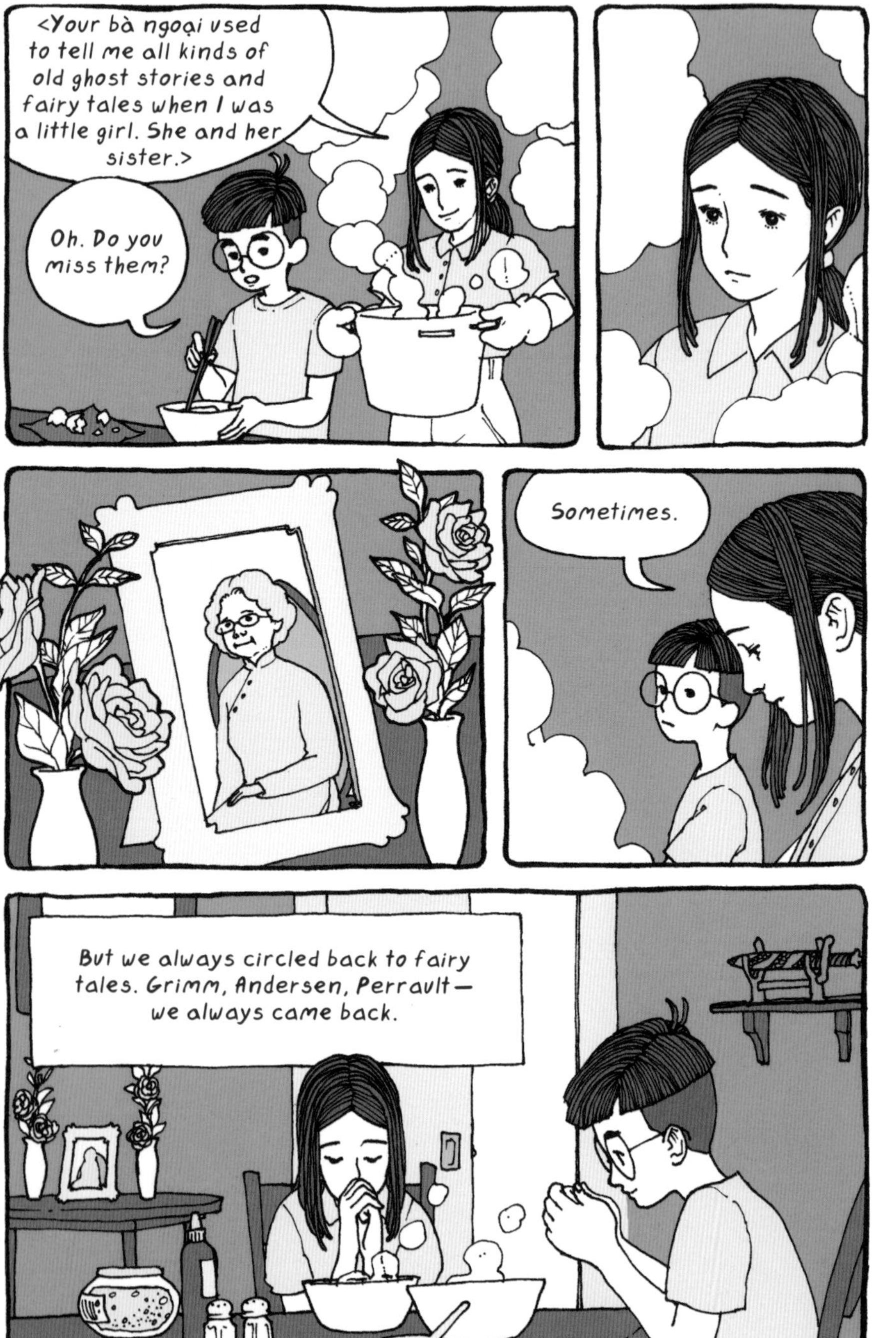
<Your bà ngoại used to tell me all kinds of old ghost stories and fairy tales when I was a little girl. She and her sister.>
Oh. Do you miss them?
Sometimes.
But we always circled back to fairy tales. Grimm, Andersen, Perrault—we always came back.

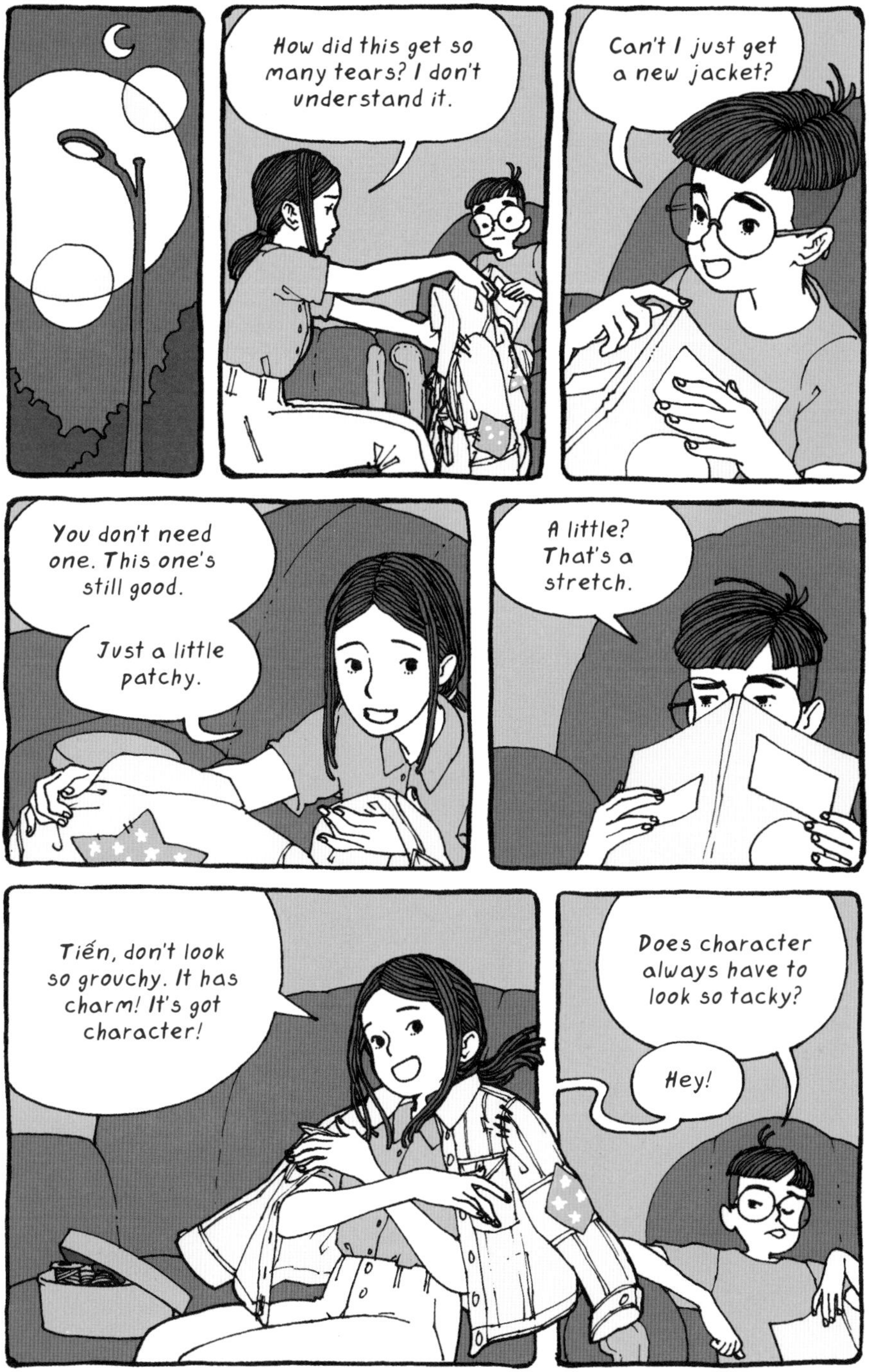
How did this get so many tears? I don't understand it.
Can't I just get a new jacket?
You don't need one. This one's still good.
Just a little patchy.
A little? That's a stretch.
Tiến, don't look so grouchy. It has charm! It's got character!
Does character always have to look so tacky?
Hey!

Why don't you start that story while I start patching?

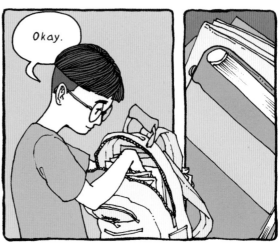

Okay.

. . . a merchant and his wife lived in a little house on a hill by the sea.

Once upon a time . . .

While the merchant was away, his wife tended to a peach grove with her sister, Velvet.

Eventually they had a beautiful daughter.

What should we name her?

She will be called Alera.

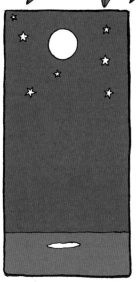

One day, his wife looked out to the sea . . .

. . . stepped into the water . . .

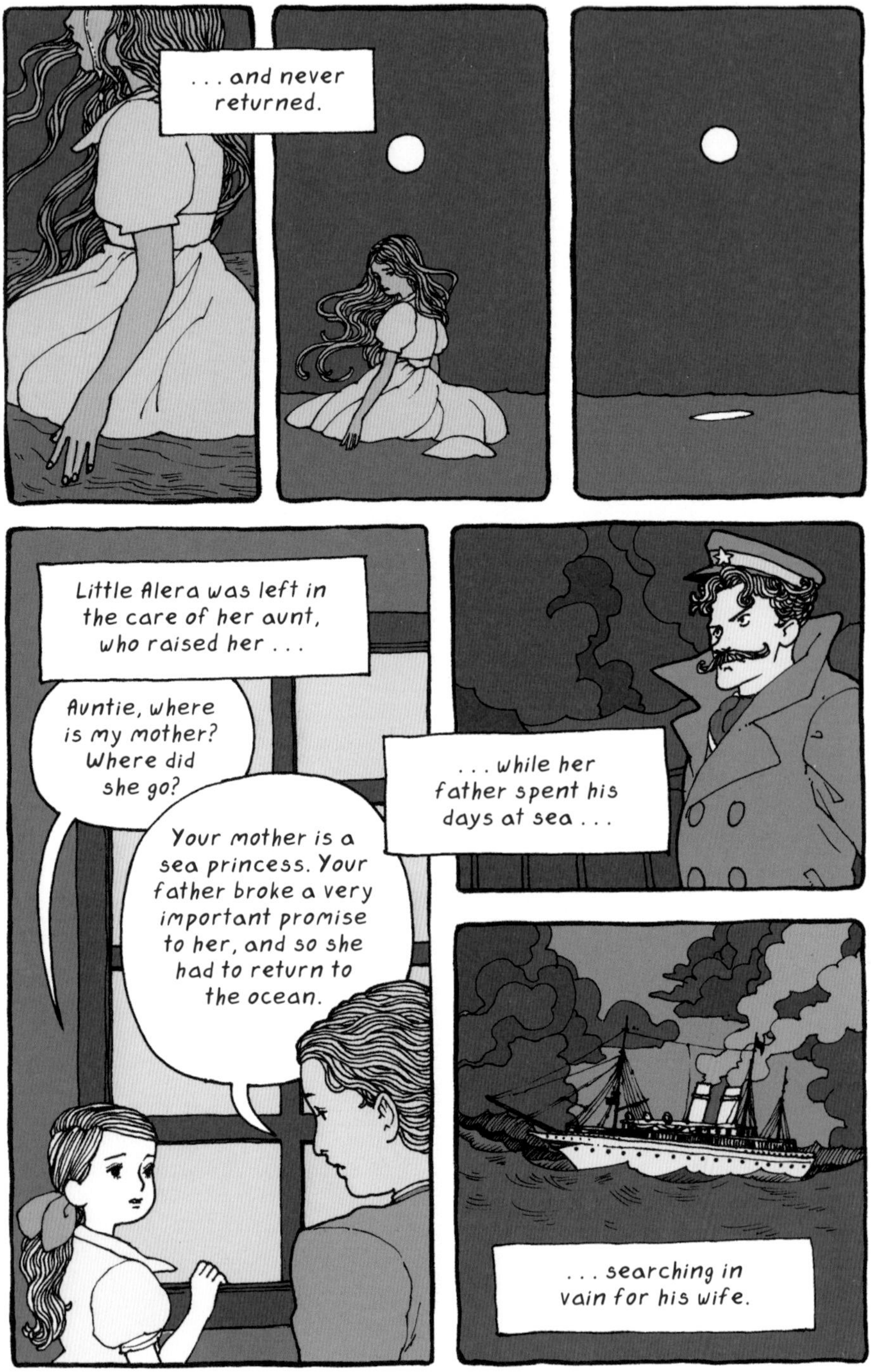
. . . and never returned.
Little Alera was left in the care of her aunt, who raised her . . .
Auntie, where is my mother? Where did she go?
Your mother is a sea princess. Your father broke a very important promise to her, and so she had to return to the ocean.
. . . while her father spent his days at sea . . .
. . . searching in vain for his wife.

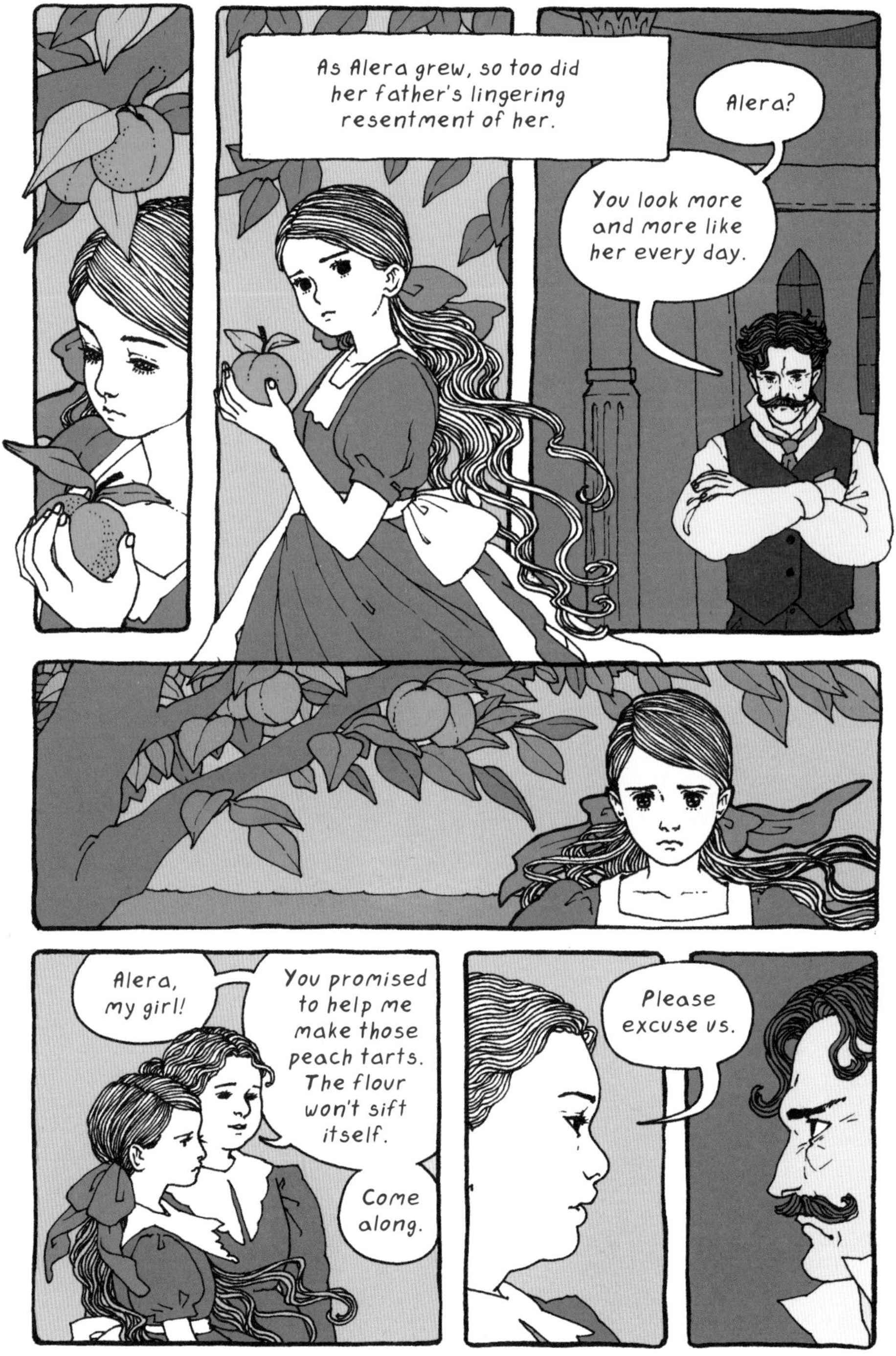
As Alera grew, so too did her father's lingering resentment of her.
Alera?
You look more and more like her every day.
Alera, my girl!
You promised to help me make those peach tarts. The flour won't sift itself.
Come along.
Please excuse us.

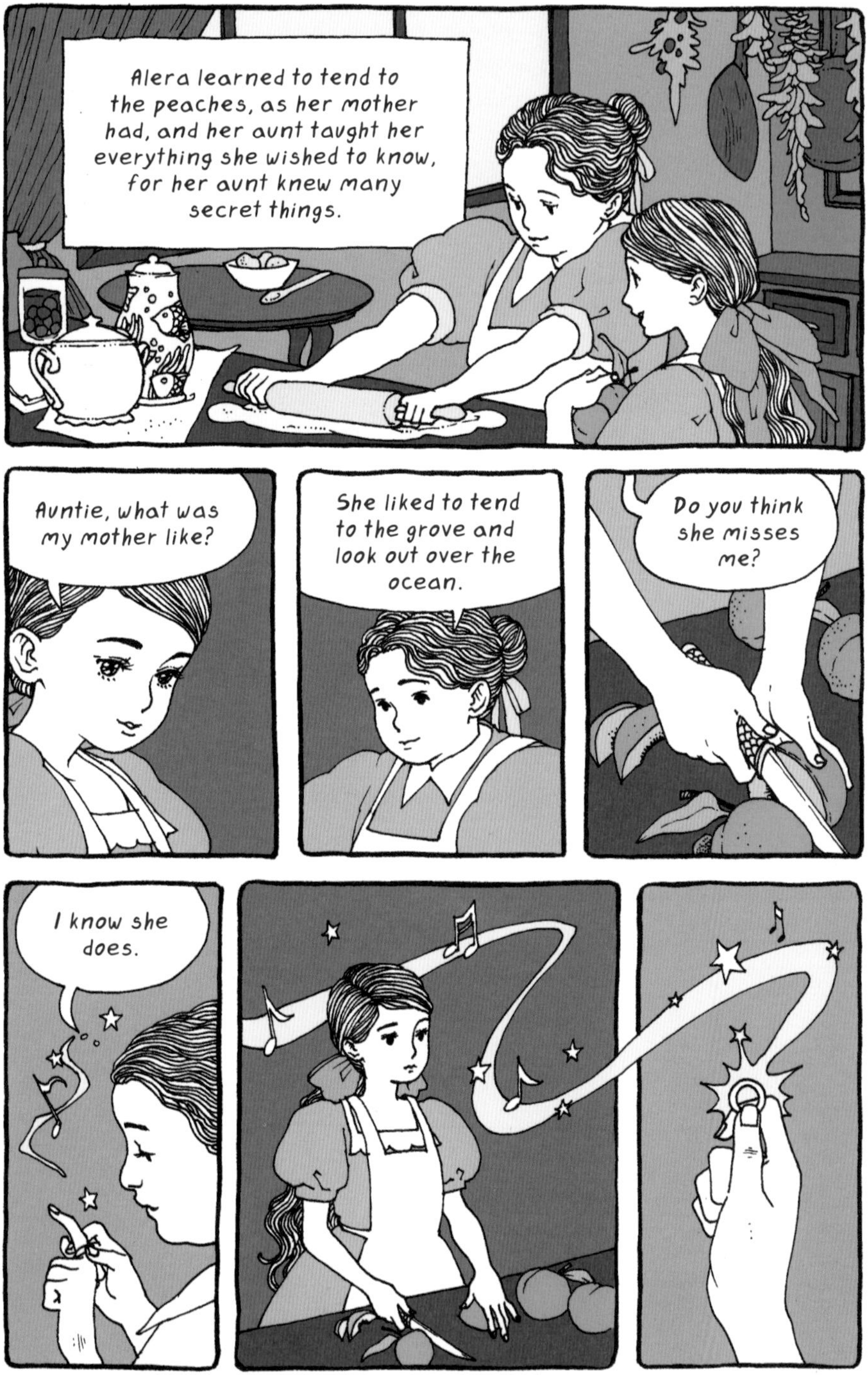
Alera learned to tend to the peaches, as her mother had, and her aunt taught her everything she wished to know, for her aunt knew many secret things.
Auntie, what was my mother like?
She liked to tend to the grove and look out over the ocean.
Do you think she misses me?
I know she does.

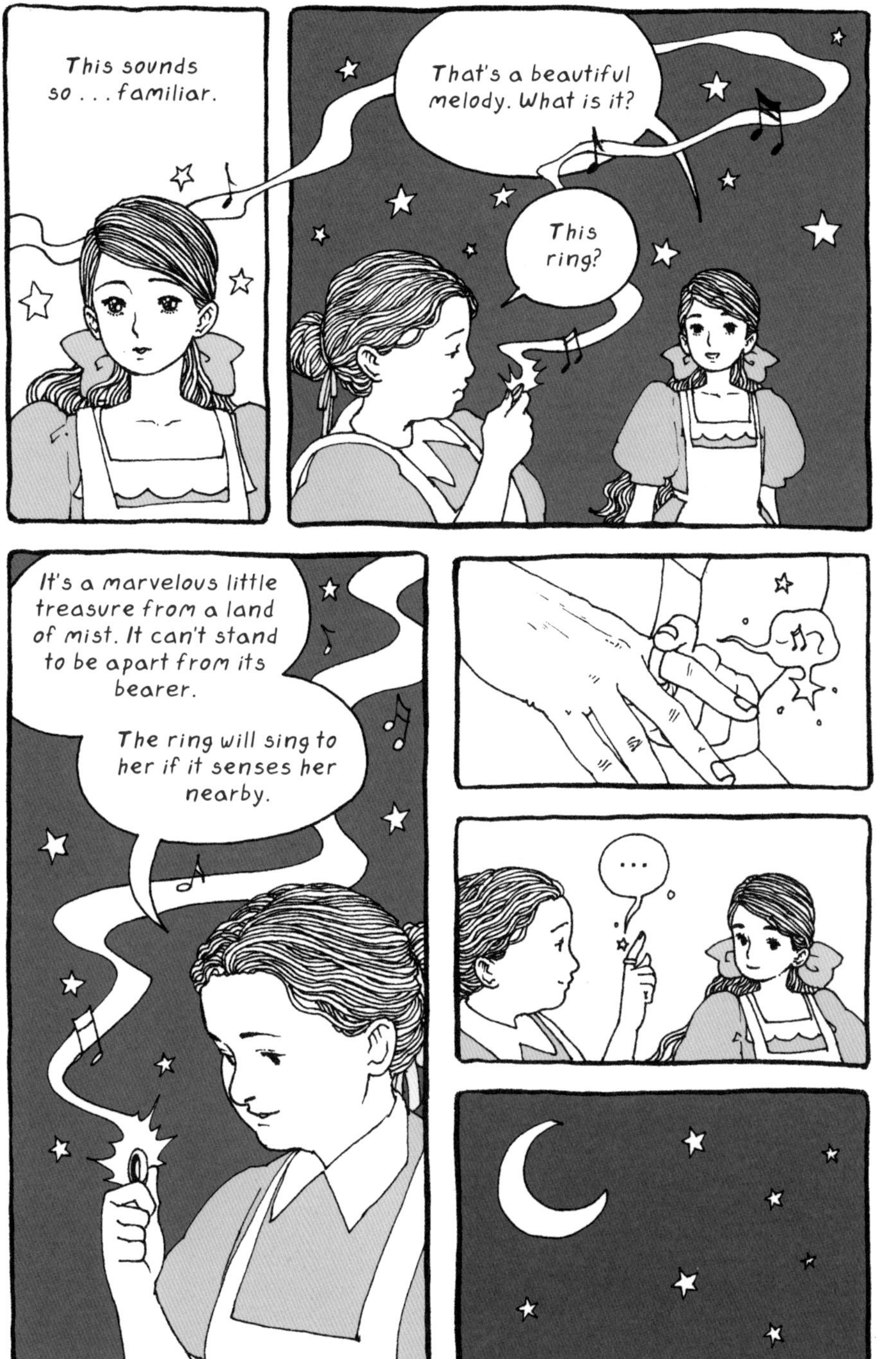
This sounds so . . . familiar.
That's a beautiful melody. What is it?
This ring?
It's a marvelous little treasure from a land of mist. It can't stand to be apart from its bearer.
The ring will sing to her if it senses her nearby.
. . .

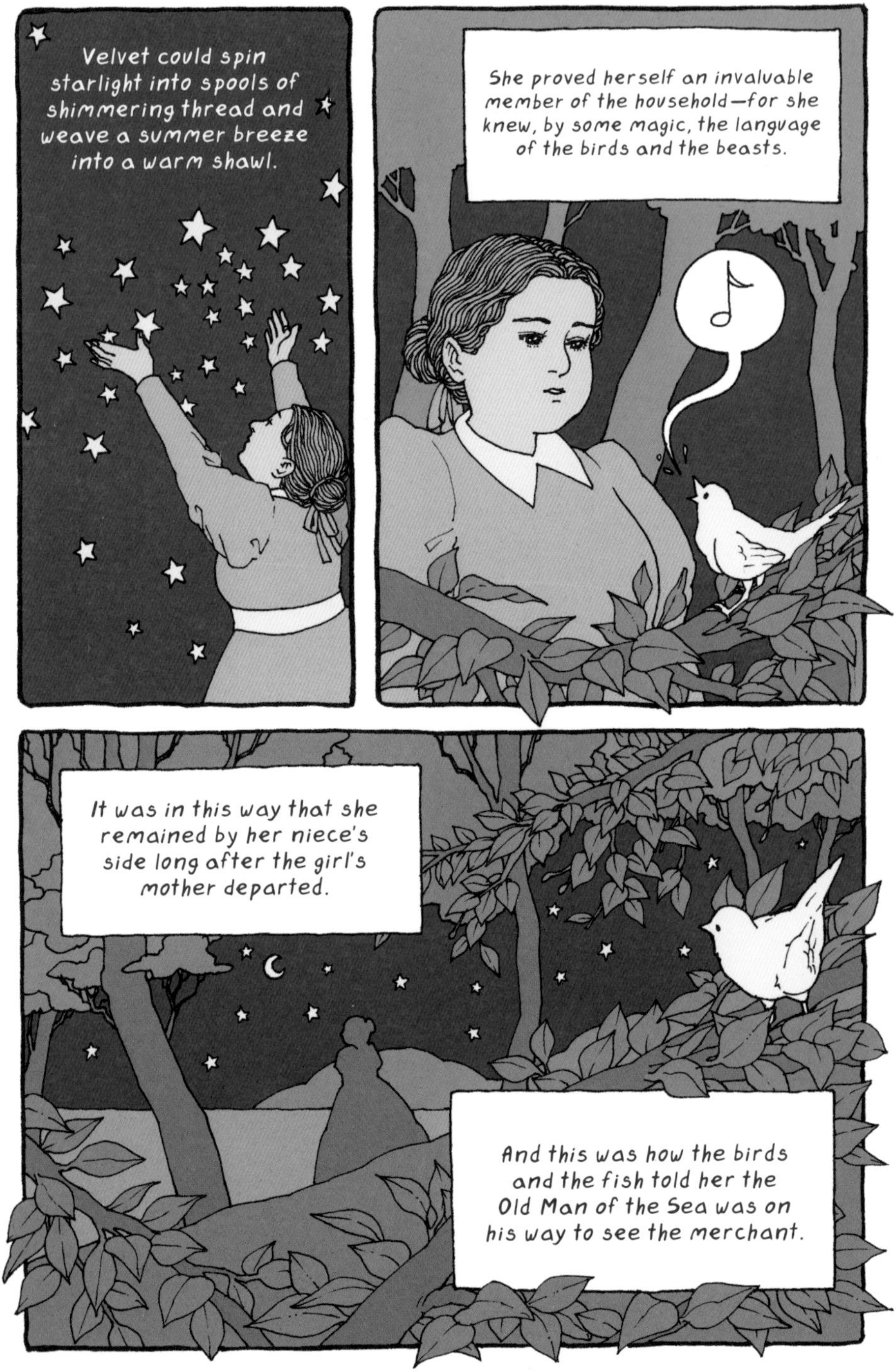
Velvet could spin starlight into spools of shimmering thread and weave a summer breeze into a warm shawl.
She proved herself an invaluable member of the household—for she knew, by some magic, the language of the birds and the beasts.
It was in this way that she remained by her niece's side long after the girl's mother departed.
And this was how the birds and the fish told her the Old Man of the Sea was on his way to see the merchant.

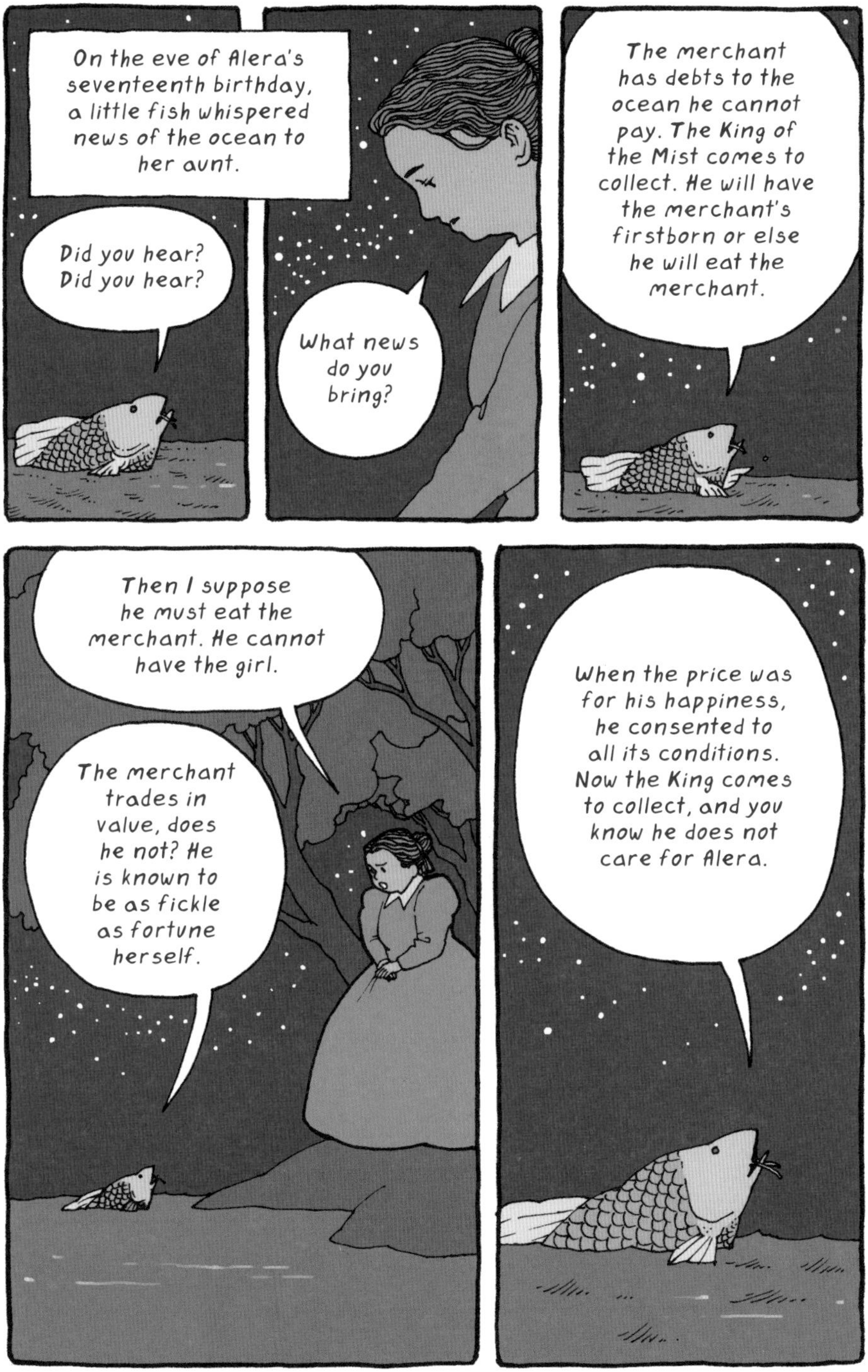
On the eve of Alera's seventeenth birthday, a little fish whispered news of the ocean to her aunt.
Did you hear? Did you hear?
What news do you bring?
The merchant has debts to the ocean he cannot pay. The King of the Mist comes to collect. He will have the merchant's firstborn or else he will eat the merchant.
Then I suppose he must eat the merchant. He cannot have the girl.
The merchant trades in value, does he not? He is known to be as fickle as fortune herself.
When the price was for his happiness, he consented to all its conditions. Now the King comes to collect, and you know he does not care for Alera.

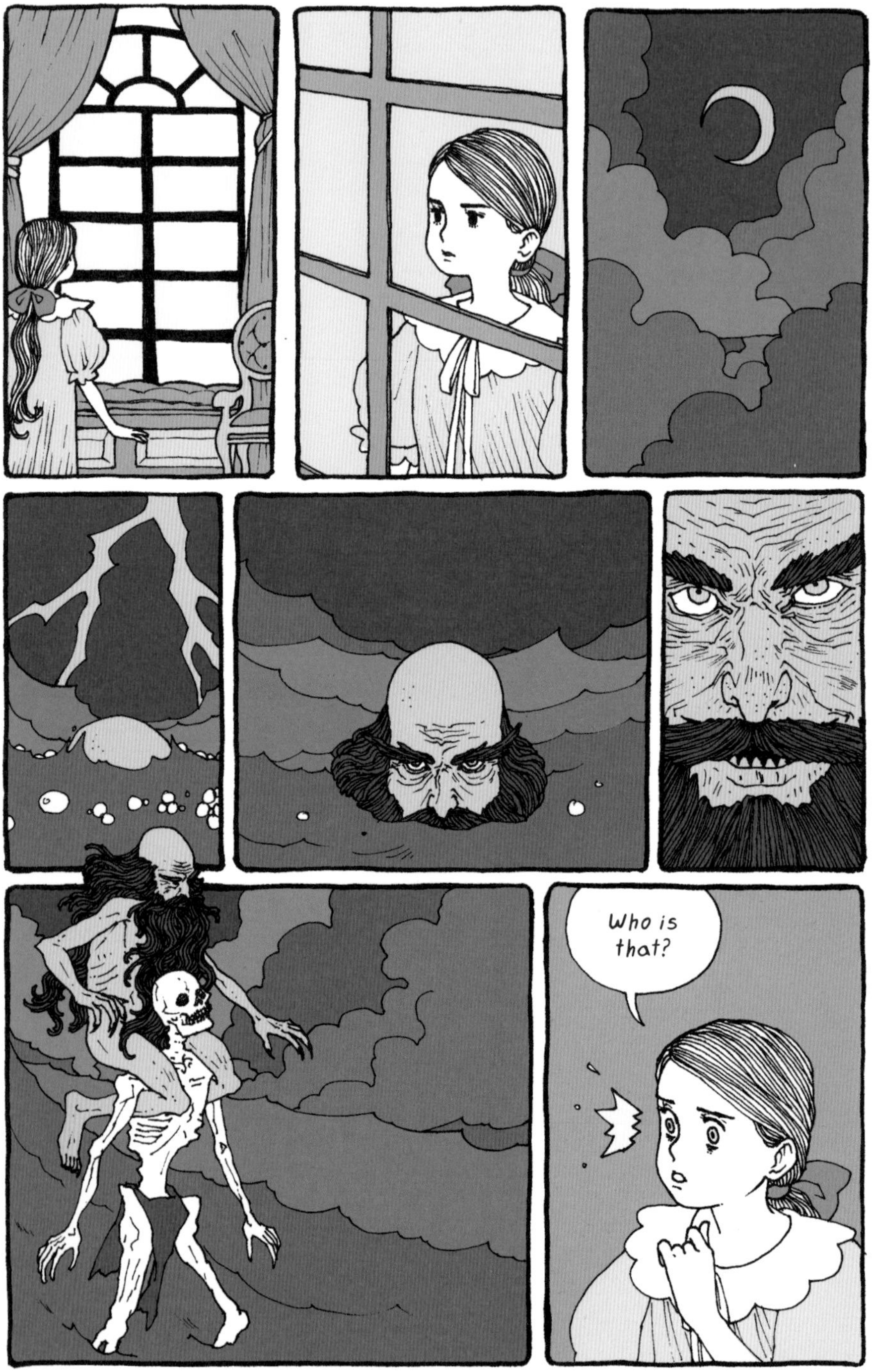
Who is that?

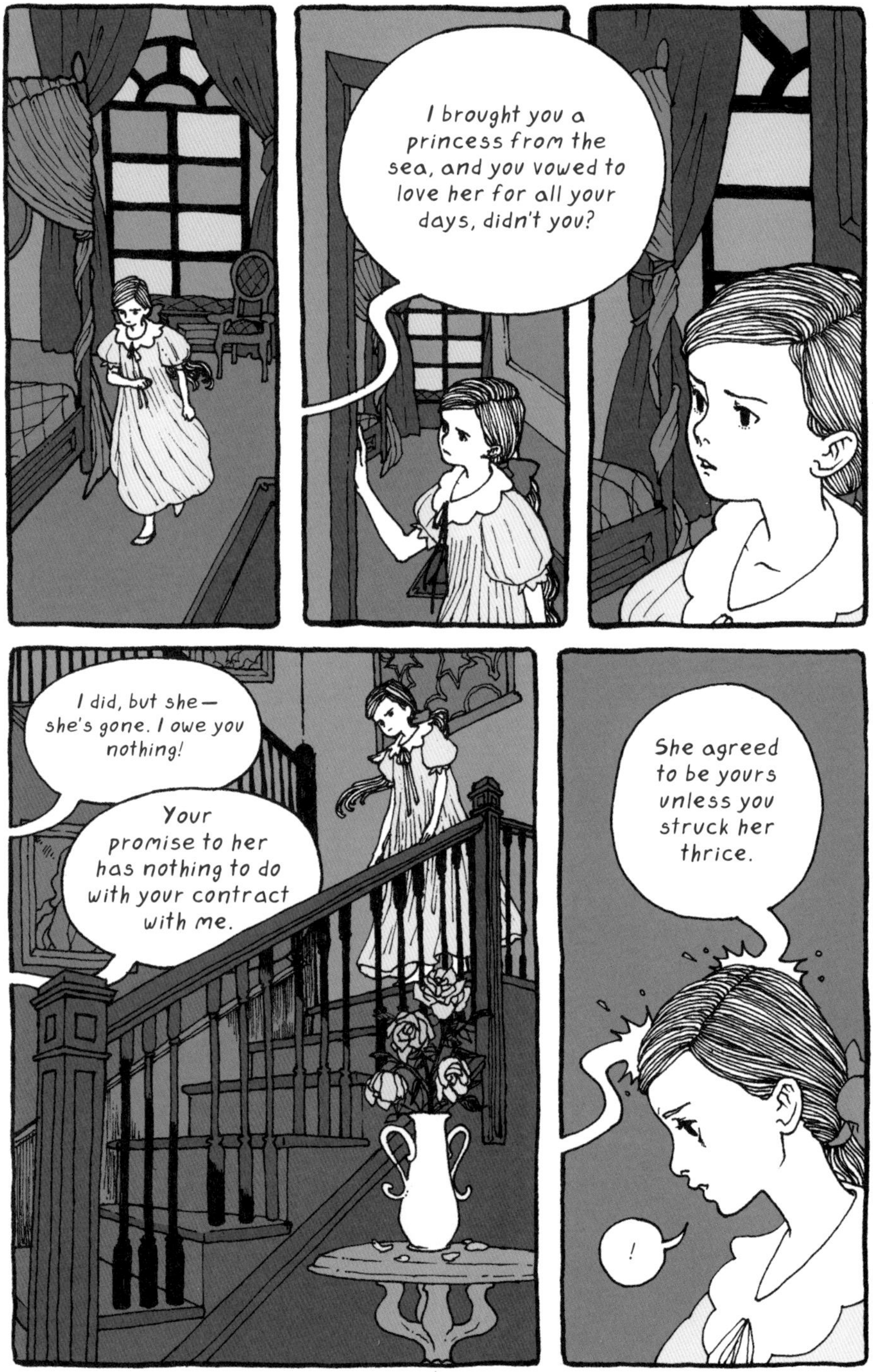
I brought you a princess from the sea, and you vowed to love her for all your days, didn't you?
I did, but she— she's gone. I owe you nothing!
Your promise to her has nothing to do with your contract with me.
She agreed to be yours unless you struck her thrice.
!

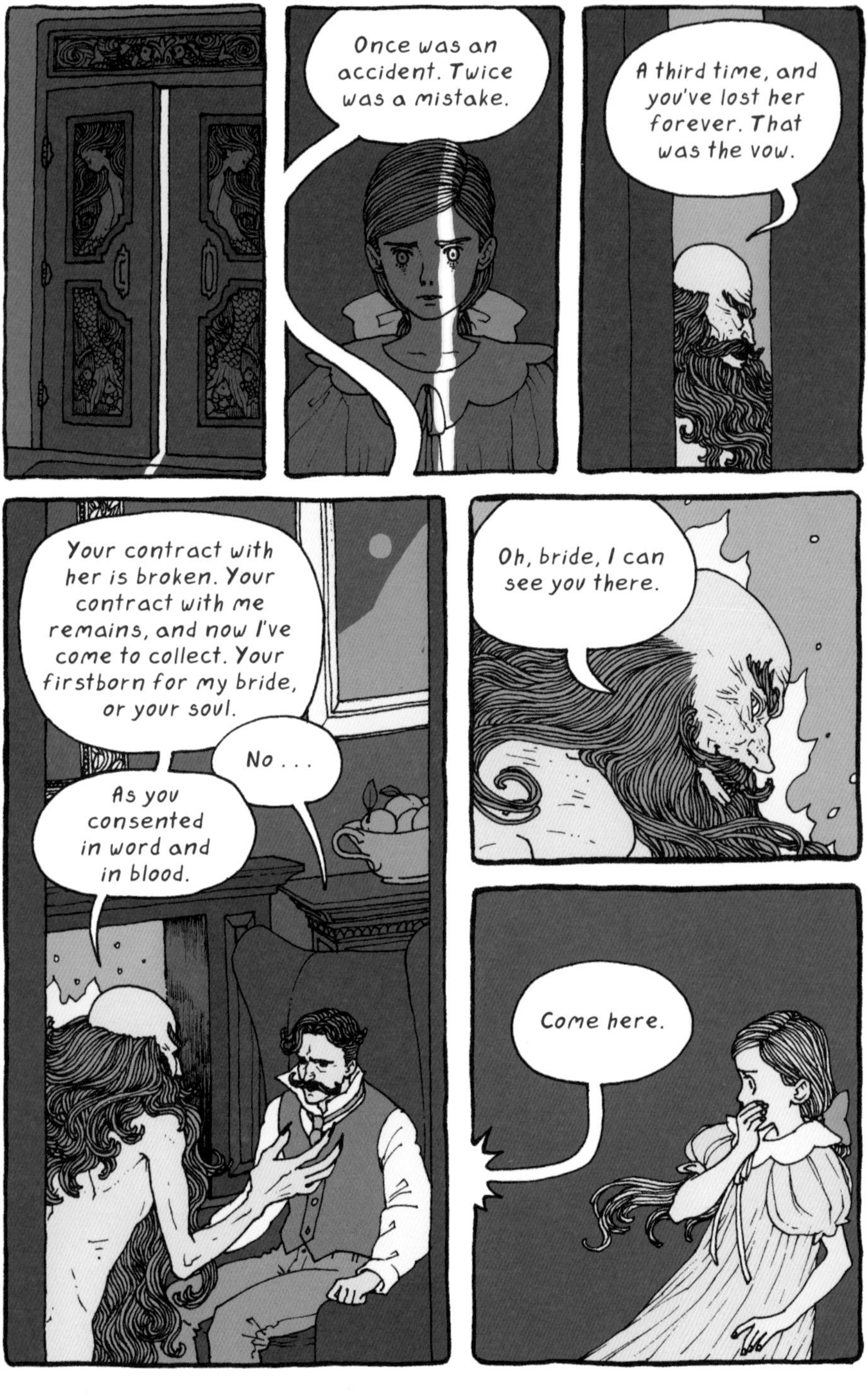
Once was an accident. Twice was a mistake.
A third time, and you've lost her forever. That was the vow.
Your contract with her is broken. Your contract with me remains, and now I've come to collect. Your firstborn for my bride, or your soul.
No . . .
As you consented in word and in blood.
Oh, bride, I can see you there.
Come here.

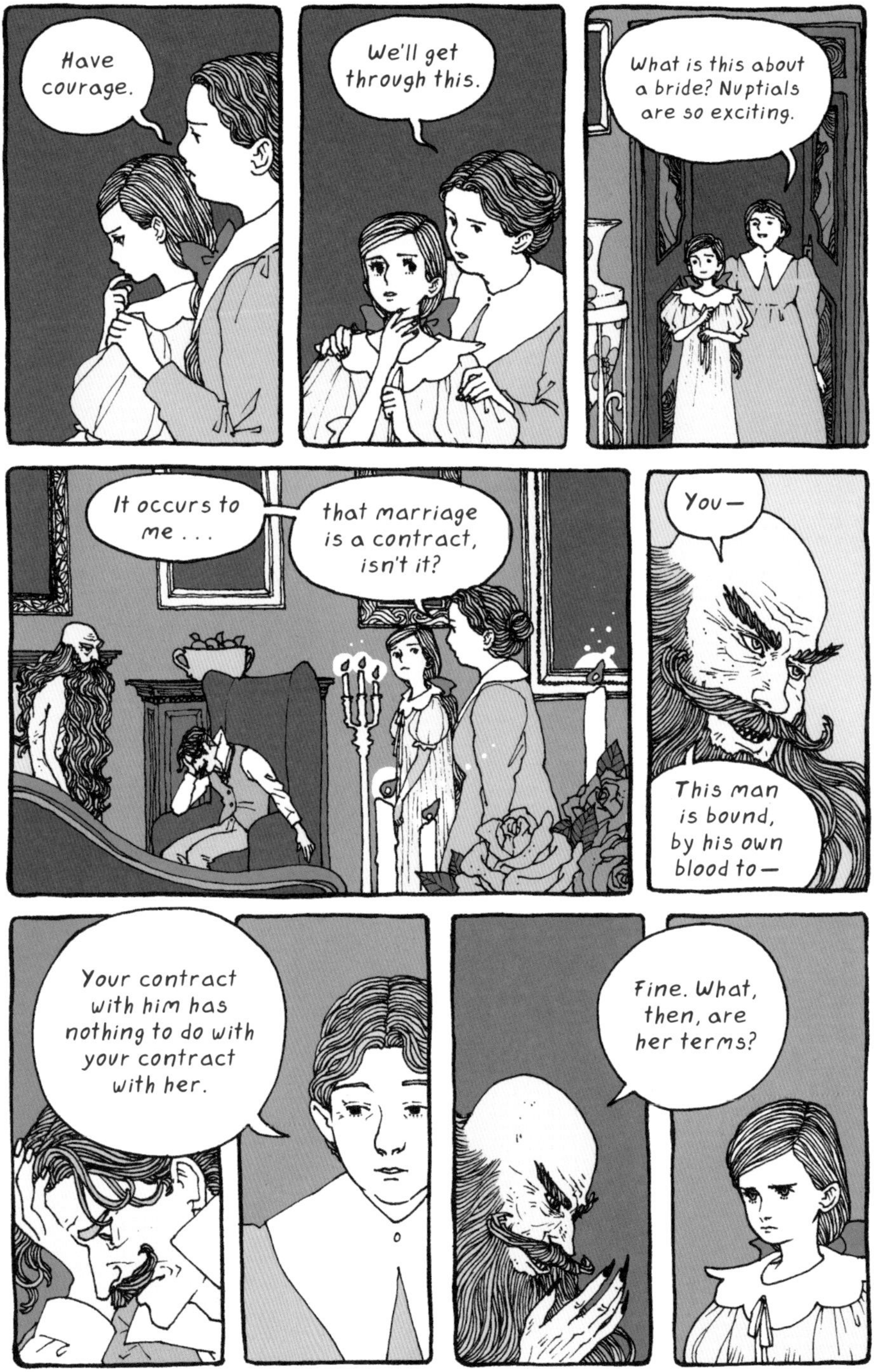
Have courage.
We'll get through this.
What is this about a bride? Nuptials are so exciting.
It occurs to me . . .
that marriage is a contract, isn't it?
You—
This man is bound, by his own blood to—
Your contract with him has nothing to do with your contract with her.
Fine. What, then, are her terms?

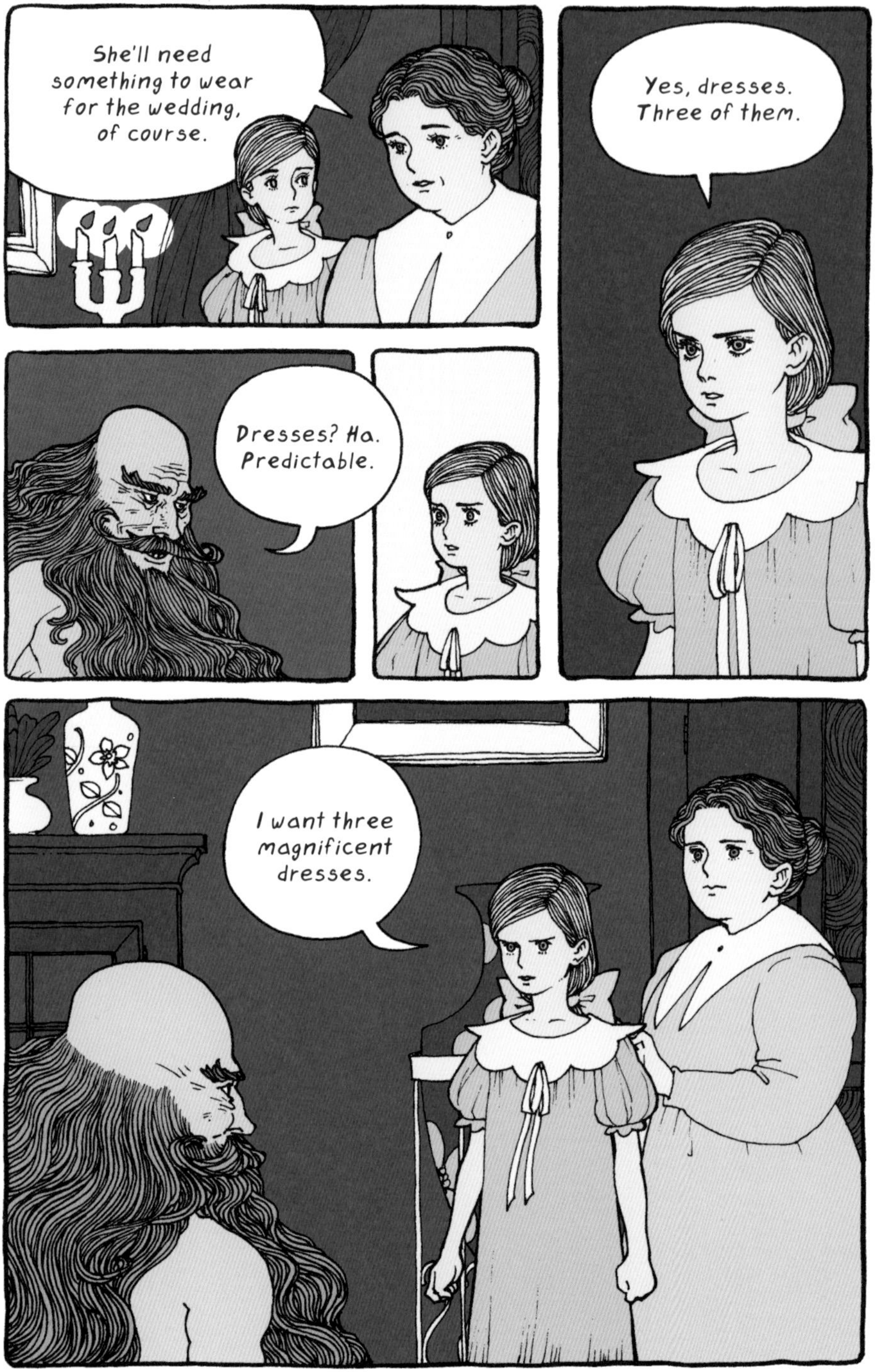
She'll need something to wear for the wedding, of course.
Yes, dresses. Three of them.
Dresses? Ha. Predictable.
I want three magnificent dresses.

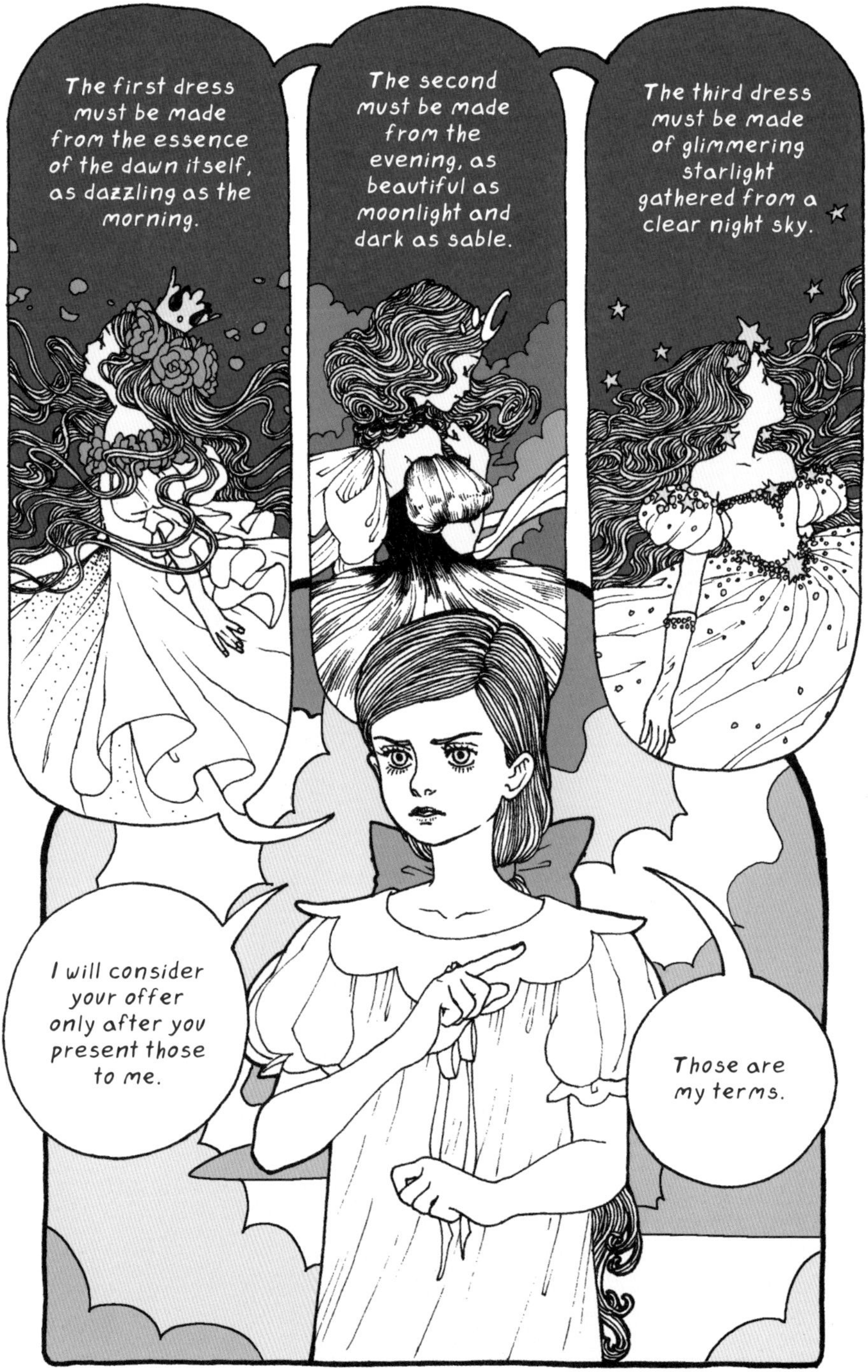

The first dress must be made from the essence of the dawn itself, as dazzling as the morning.
The second must be made from the evening, as beautiful as moonlight and dark as sable.
The third dress must be made of glimmering starlight gathered from a clear night sky.
I will consider your offer only after you present those to me.
Those are my terms.

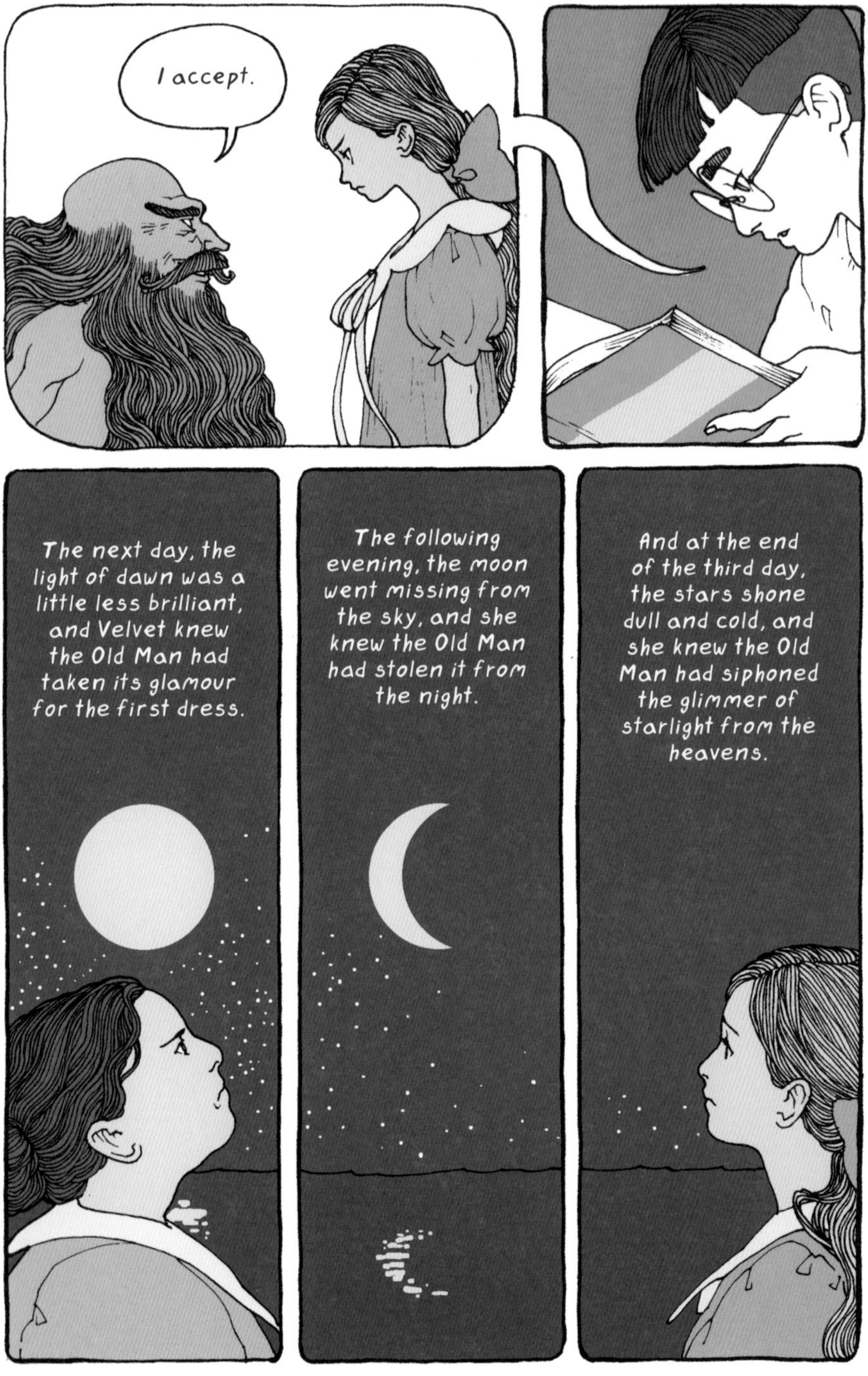
I accept.
The next day, the light of dawn was a little less brilliant, and Velvet knew the Old Man had taken its glamour for the first dress.
The following evening, the moon went missing from the sky, and she knew the Old Man had stolen it from the night.
And at the end of the third day, the stars shone dull and cold, and she knew the Old Man had siphoned the glimmer of starlight from the heavens.

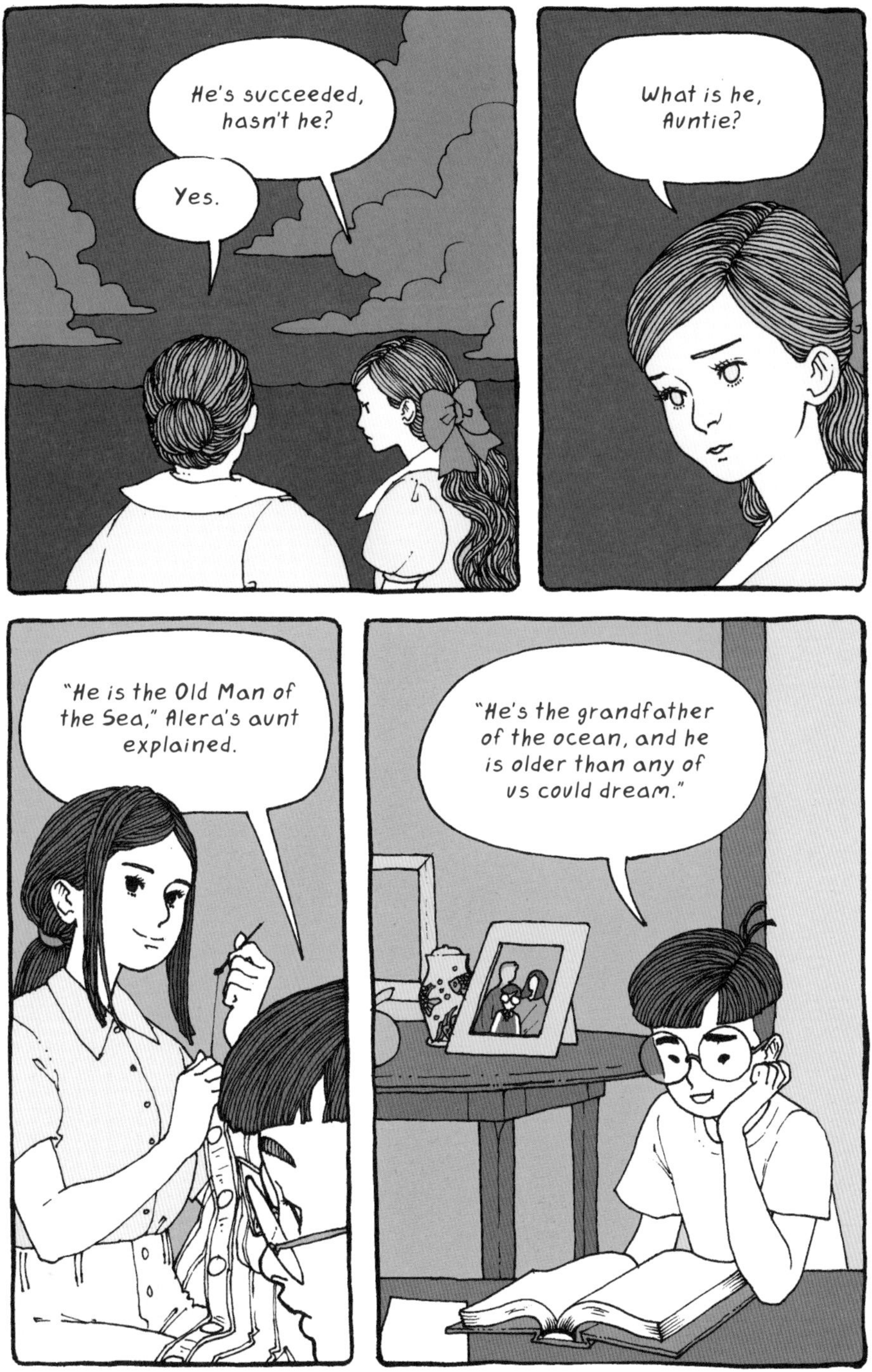
He's succeeded, hasn't he?
Yes.
What is he, Auntie?
"He is the Old Man of the Sea," Alera's aunt explained.
"He's the grandfather of the ocean, and he is older than any of us could dream."

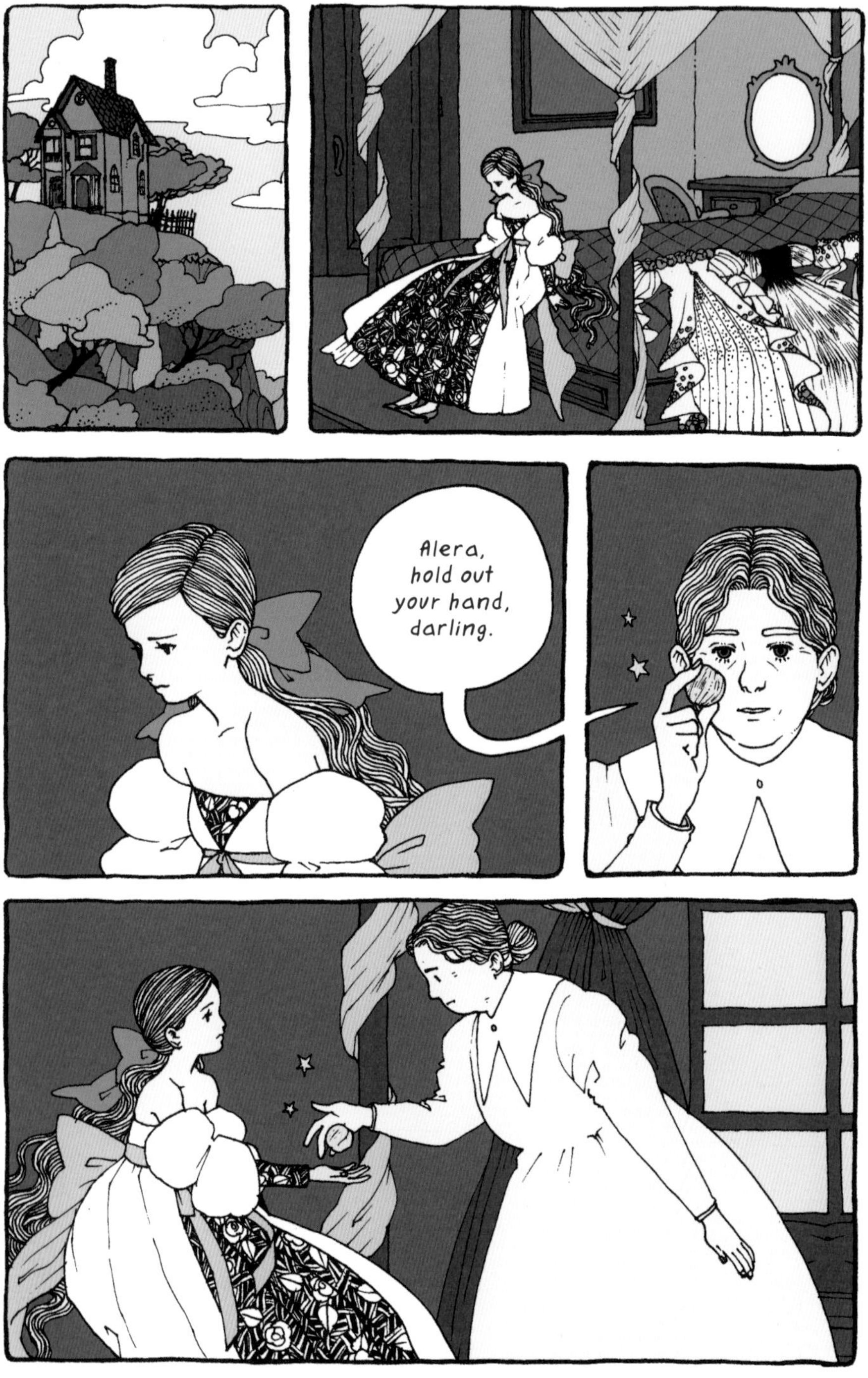
Alera, hold out your hand, darling.

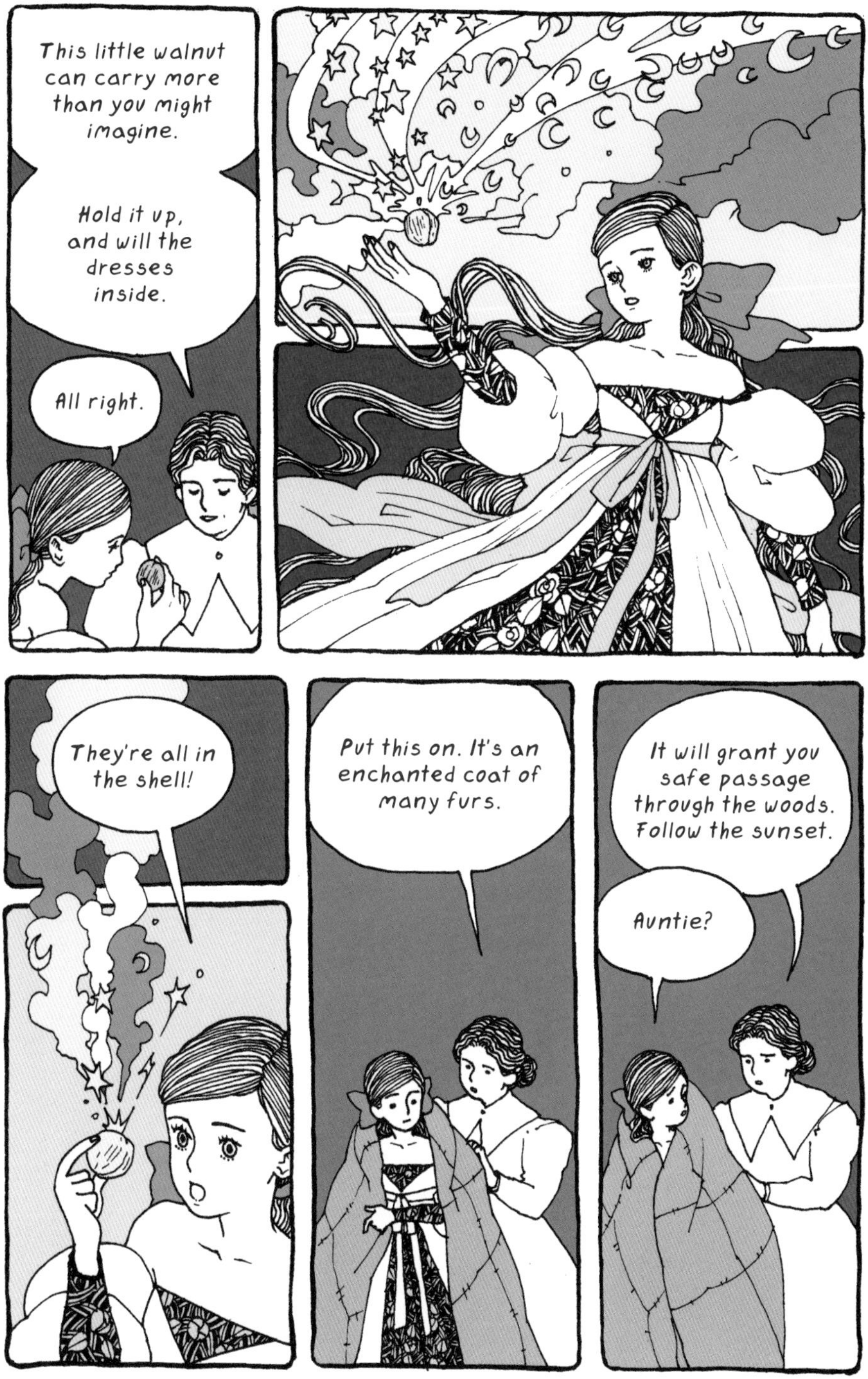
This little walnut can carry more than you might imagine.
Hold it up, and will the dresses inside.
All right.
They're all in the shell!
Put this on. It's an enchanted coat of many furs.
It will grant you safe passage through the woods. Follow the sunset.
Auntie?

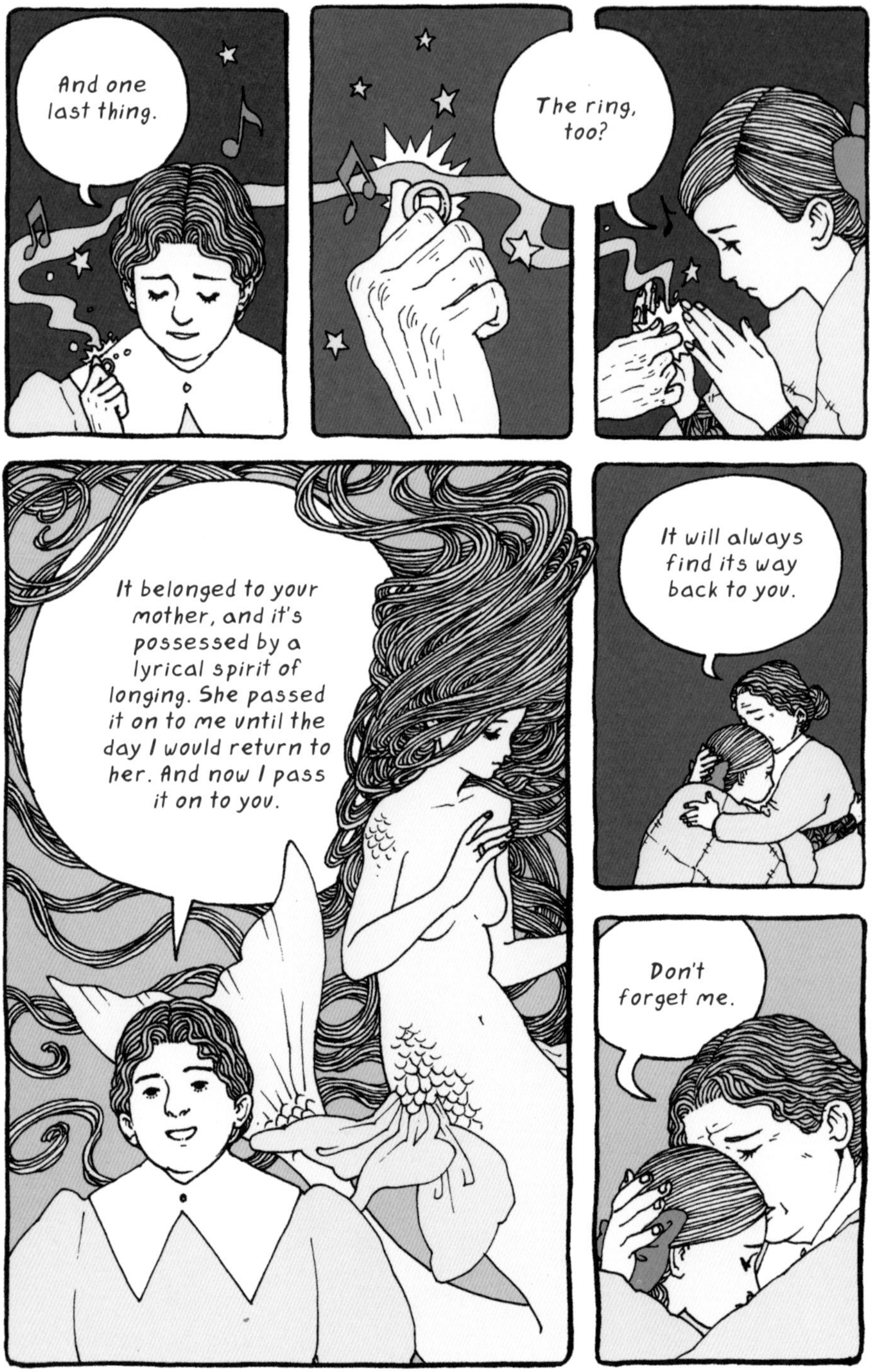
And one last thing.
The ring, too?
It belonged to your mother, and it's possessed by a lyrical spirit of longing. She passed it on to me until the day I would return to her. And now I pass it on to you.
It will always find its way back to you.
Don't forget me.

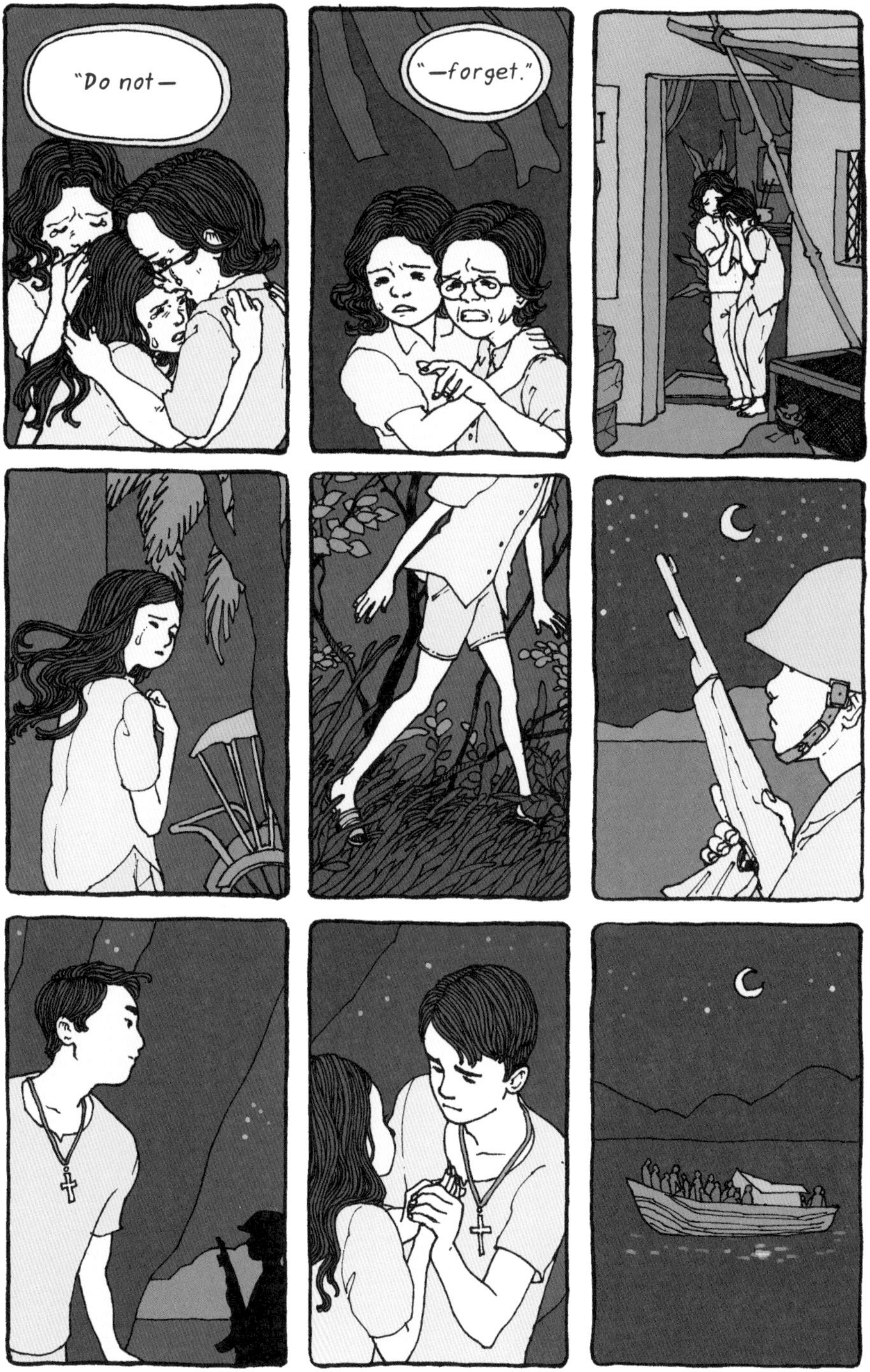
"Do not—
"—forget."

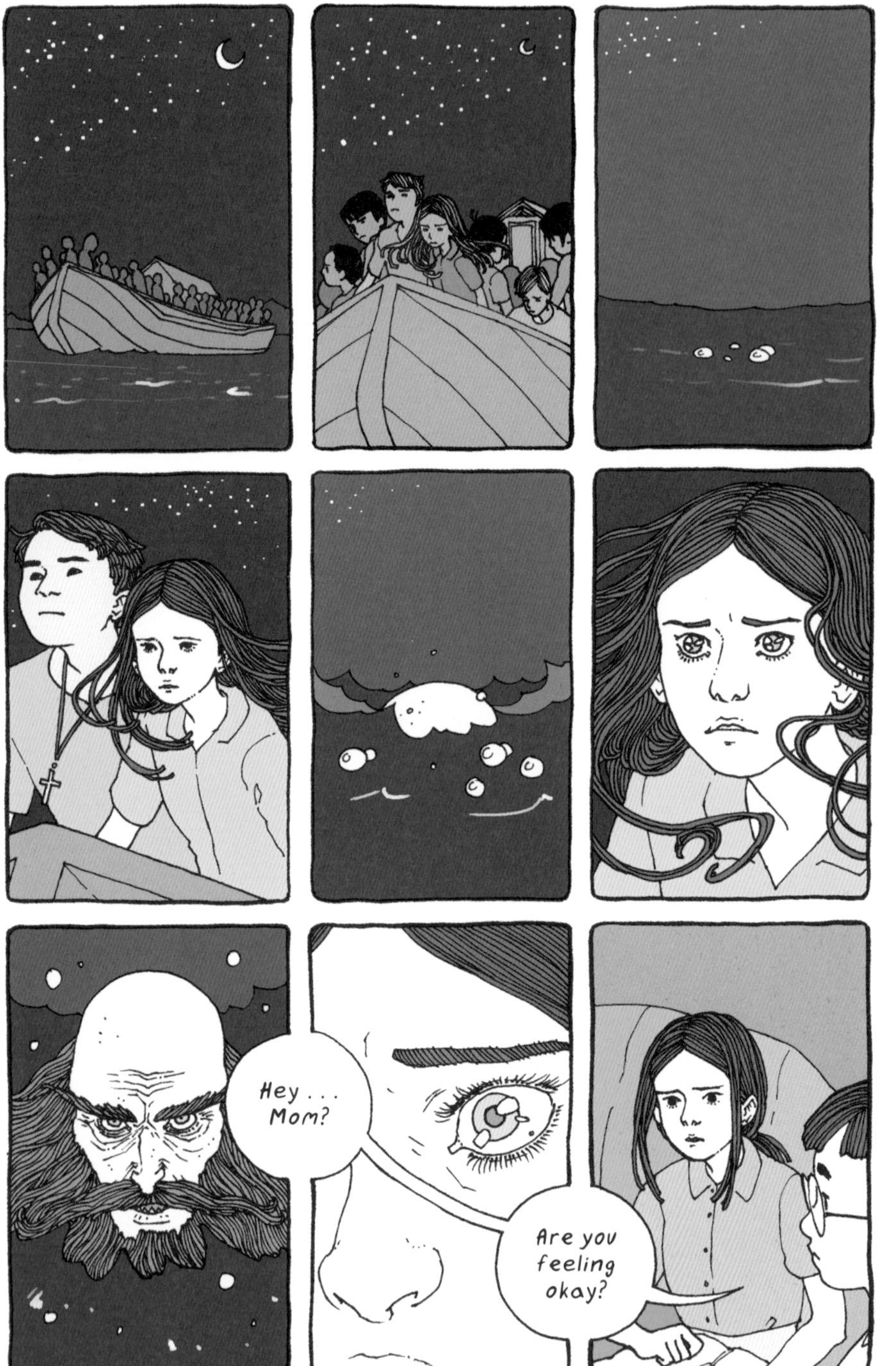
Hey . . .
Mom?
Are you feeling okay?

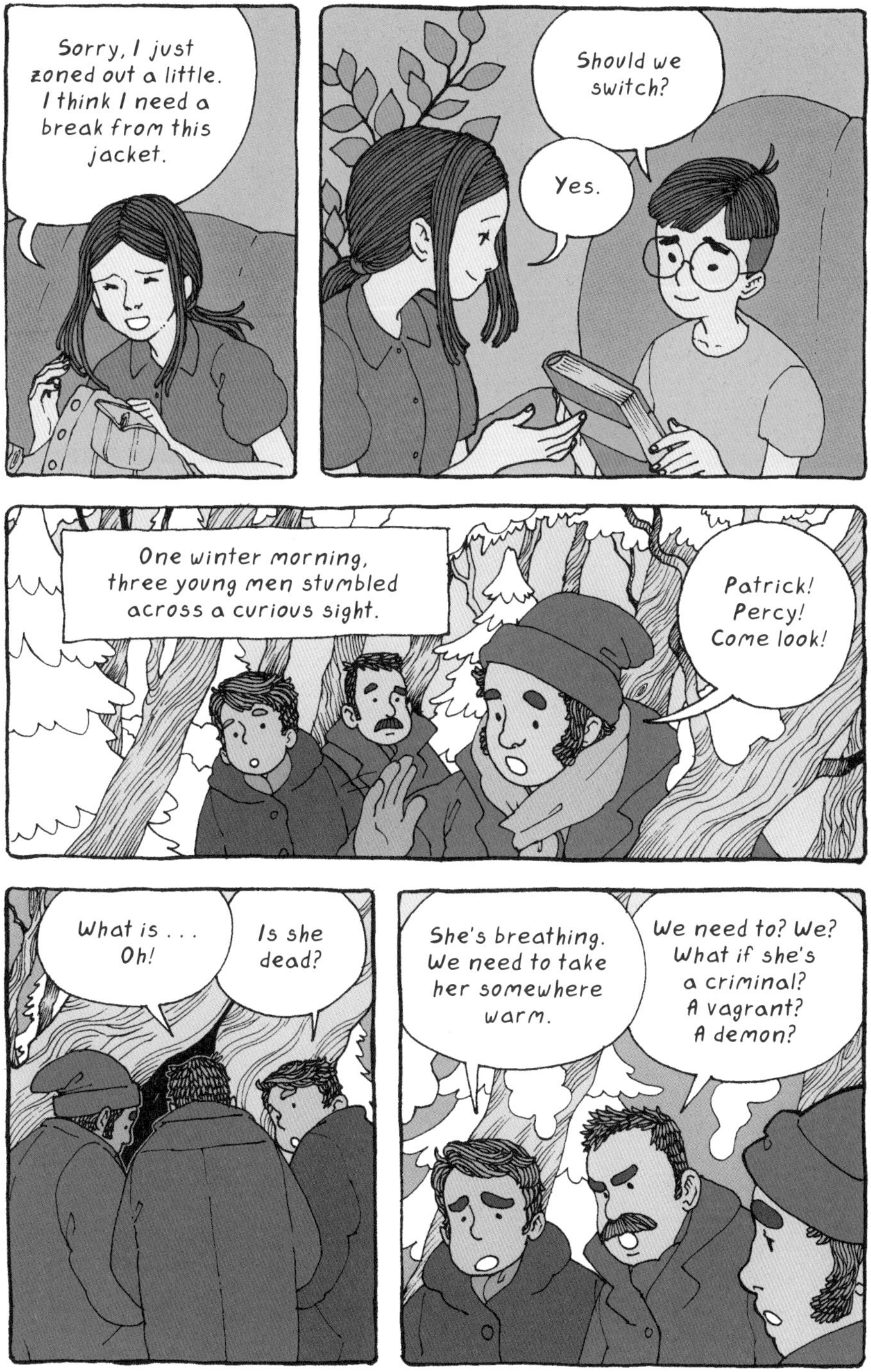
Sorry, I just zoned out a little. I think I need a break from this jacket.
Should we switch?
Yes.
One winter morning, three young men stumbled across a curious sight.
Patrick! Percy! Come look!
What is . . . Oh!
Is she dead?
She's breathing. We need to take her somewhere warm.
We need to? We? What if she's a criminal? A vagrant? A demon?

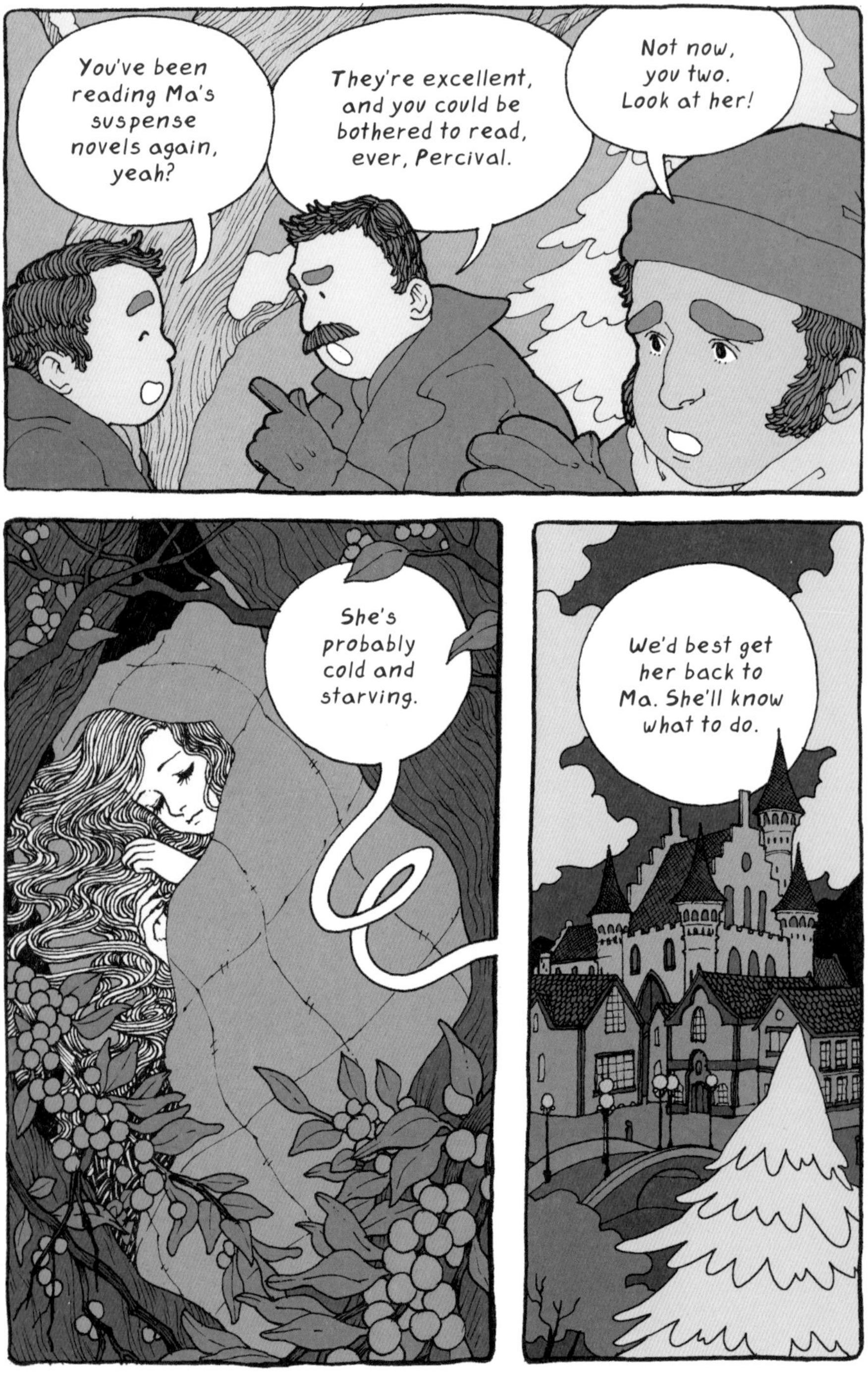
You've been reading Ma's suspense novels again, yeah?
They're excellent, and you could be bothered to read, ever, Percival.
Not now, you two. Look at her!
She's probably cold and starving.
We'd best get her back to Ma. She'll know what to do.

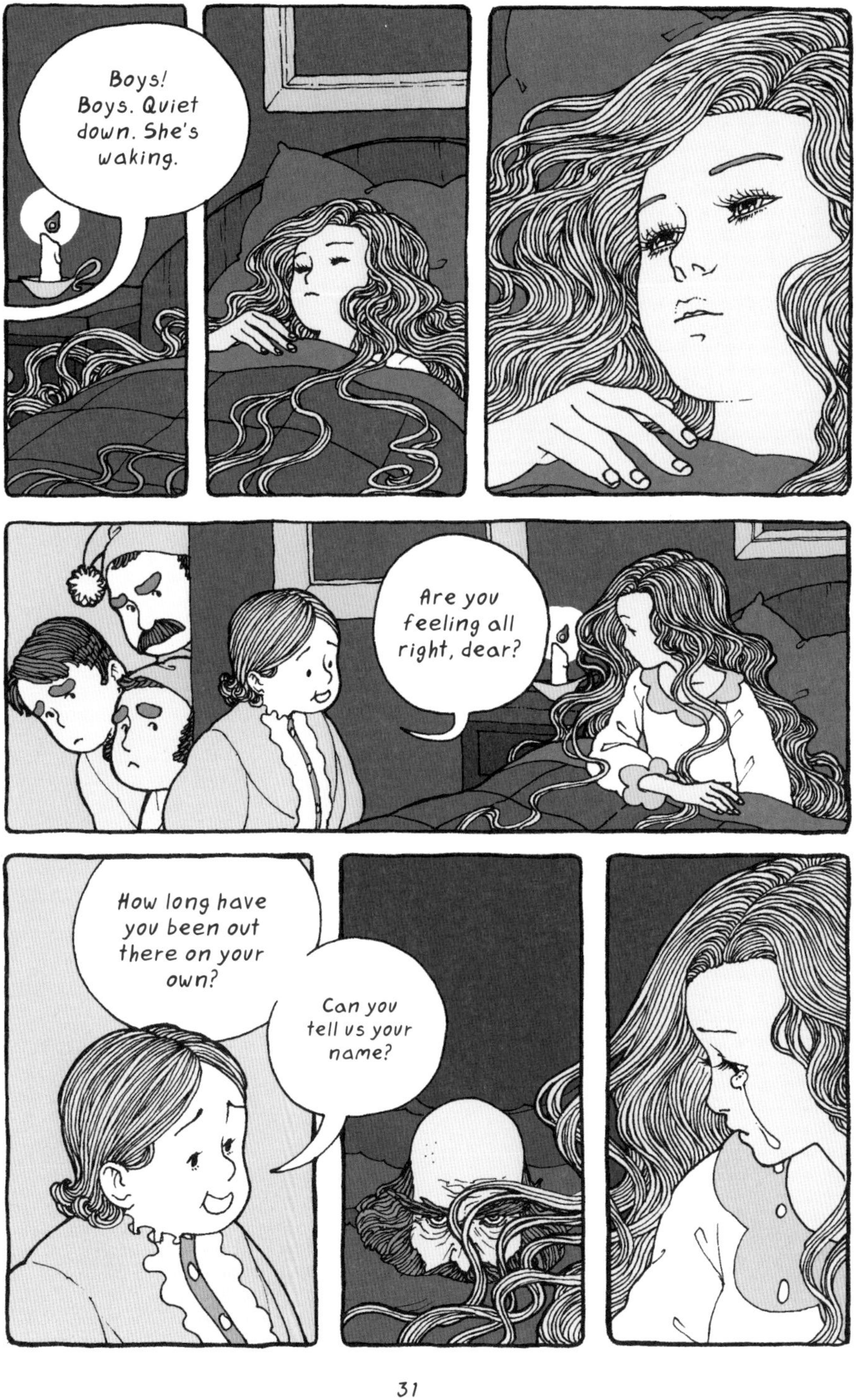
Boys! Boys. Quiet down. She's waking.
Are you feeling all right, dear?
How long have you been out there on your own?
Can you tell us your name?

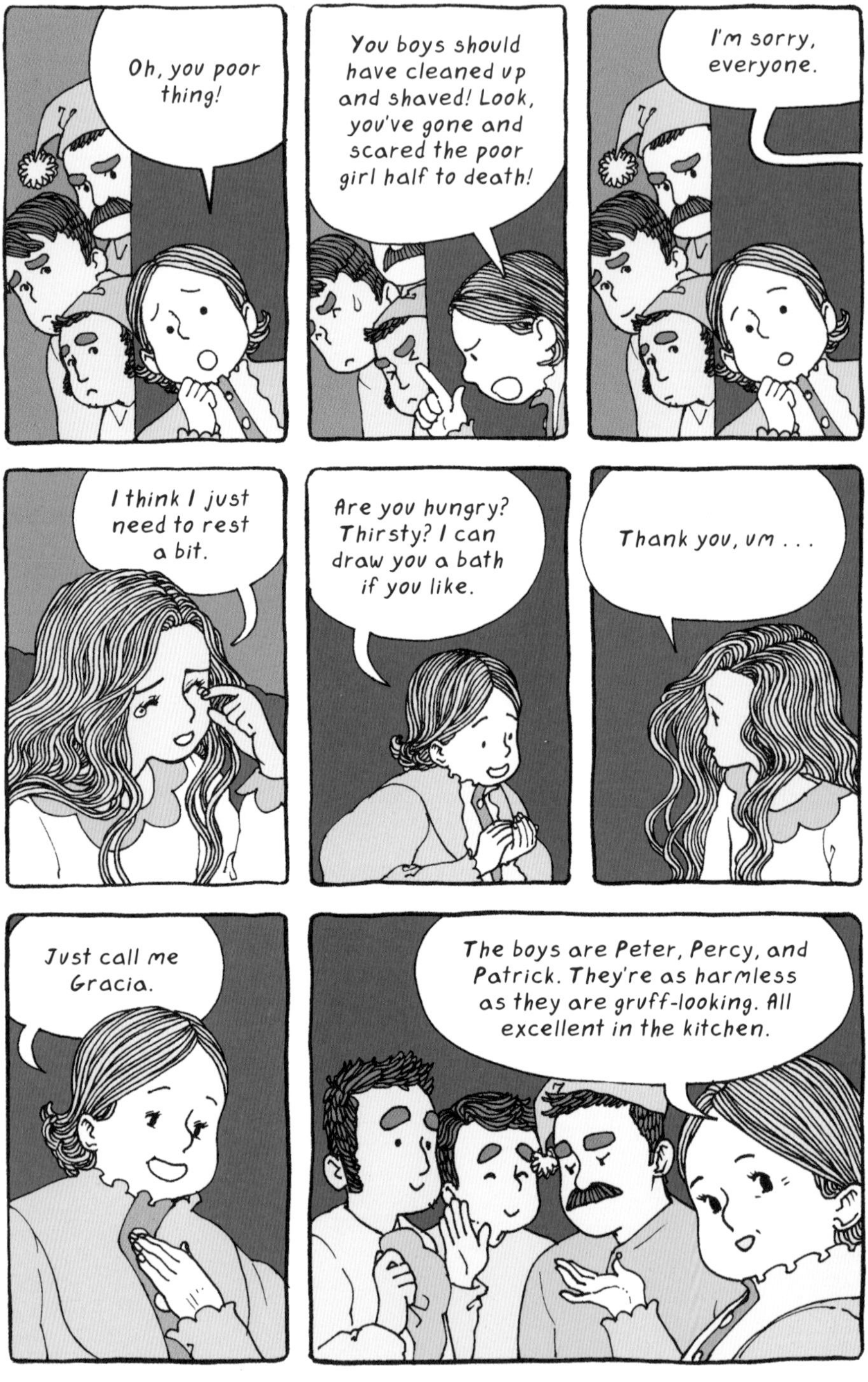
Oh, you poor thing!
You boys should have cleaned up and shaved! Look, you've gone and scared the poor girl half to death!
I'm sorry, everyone.
I think I just need to rest a bit.
Are you hungry? Thirsty? I can draw you a bath if you like.
Thank you, um . . .
Just call me Gracia.
The boys are Peter, Percy, and Patrick. They're as harmless as they are gruff-looking. All excellent in the kitchen.

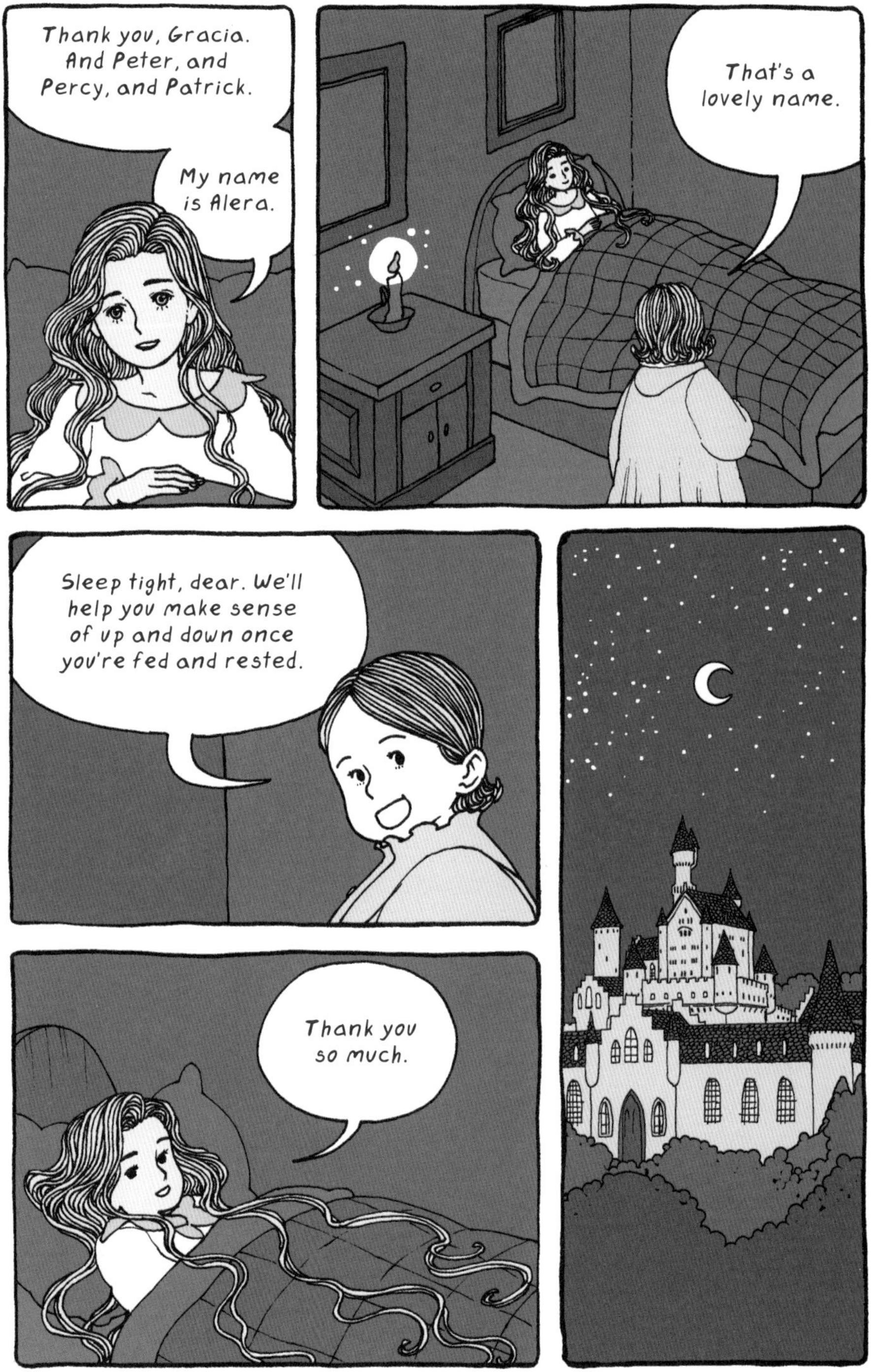
Thank you, Gracia. And Peter, and Percy, and Patrick.
My name is Alera.
That's a lovely name.
Sleep tight, dear. We'll help you make sense of up and down once you're fed and rested.
Thank you so much.

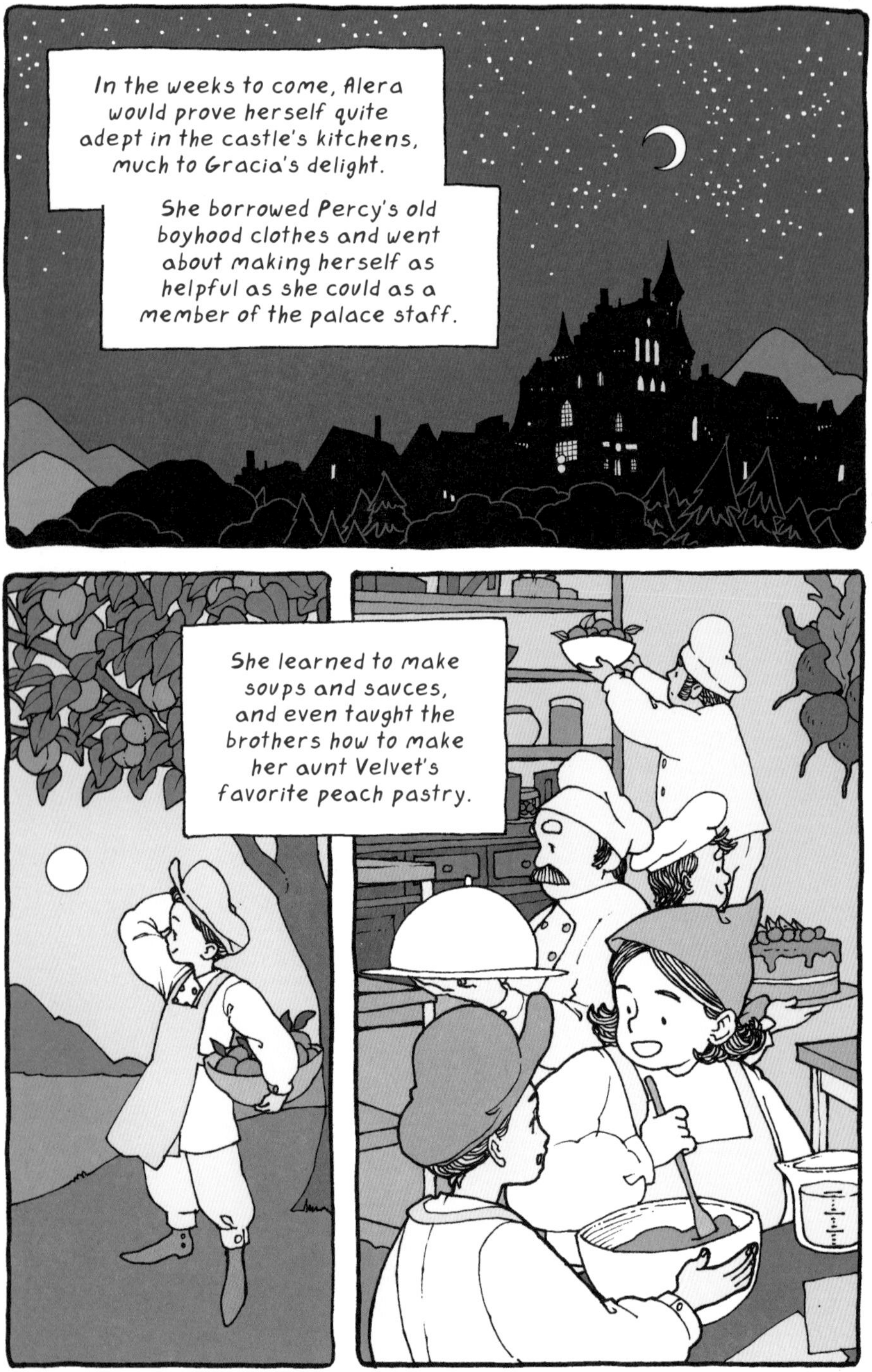
In the weeks to come, Alera would prove herself quite adept in the castle's kitchens, much to Gracia's delight.
She borrowed Percy's old boyhood clothes and went about making herself as helpful as she could as a member of the palace staff.
She learned to make soups and sauces, and even taught the brothers how to make her aunt Velvet's favorite peach pastry.

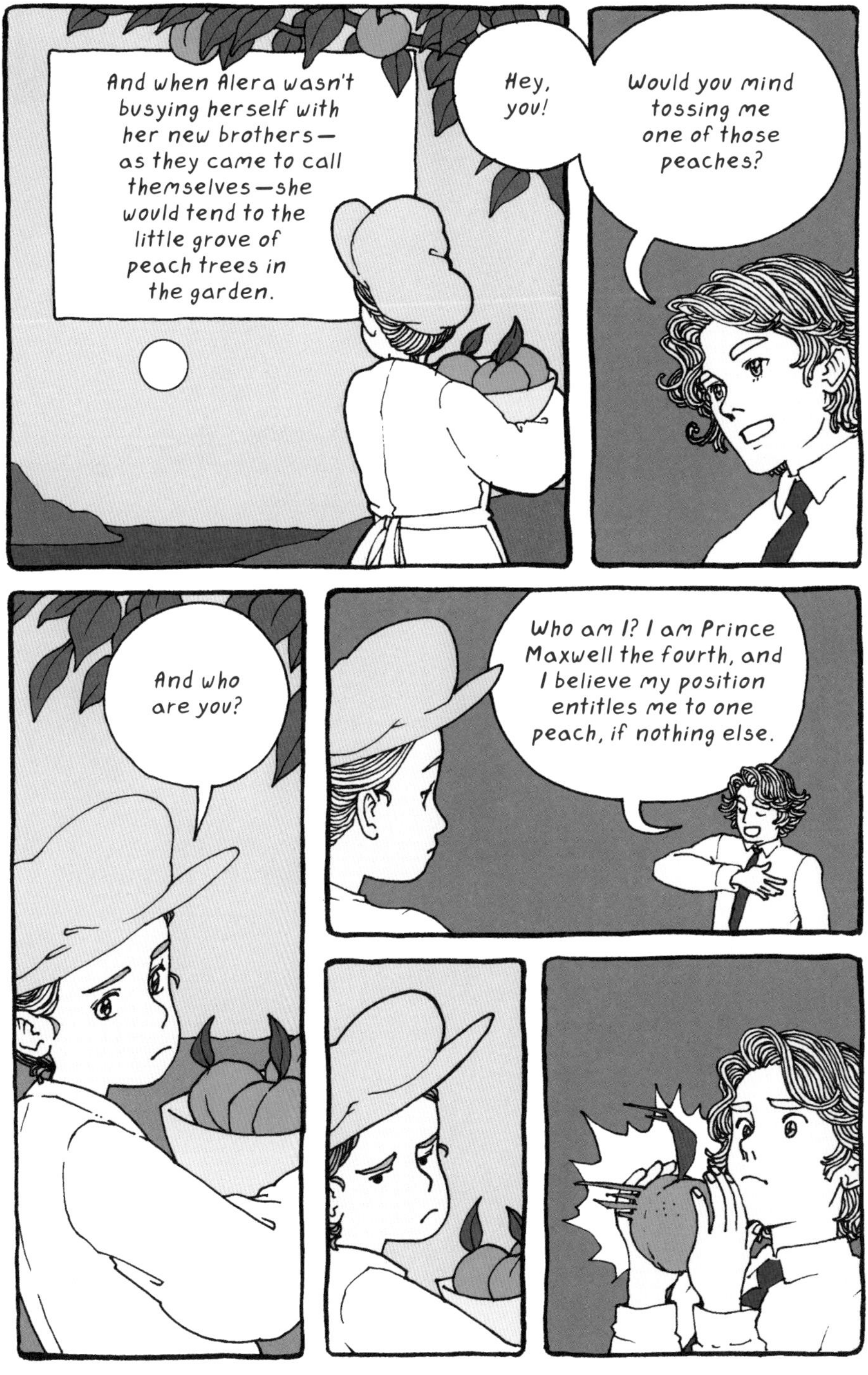
And when Alera wasn't busying herself with her new brothers— as they came to call themselves—she would tend to the little grove of peach trees in the garden.
Hey, you!
Would you mind tossing me one of those peaches?
And who are you?
Who am I? I am Prince Maxwell the fourth, and I believe my position entitles me to one peach, if nothing else.

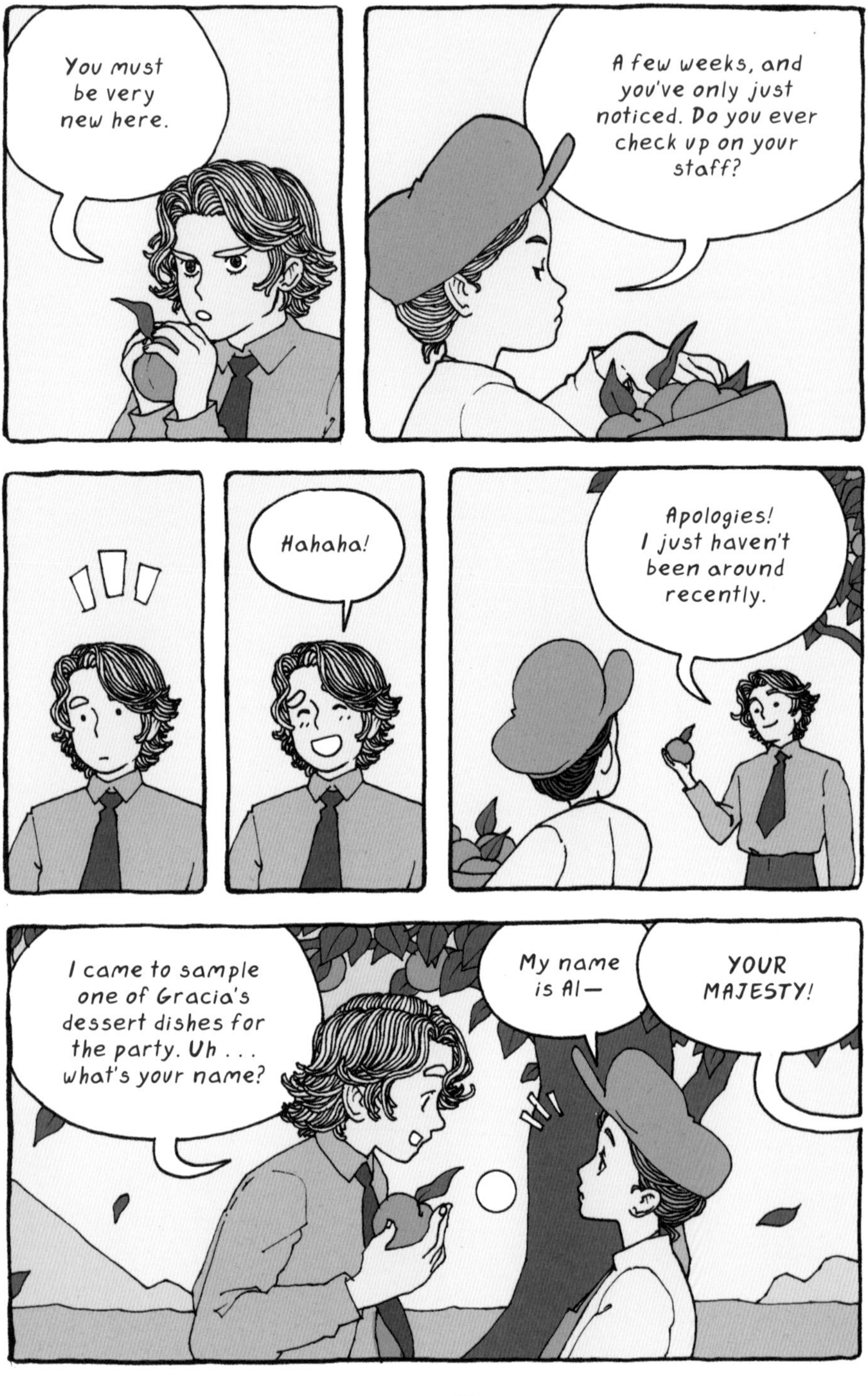
You must be very new here.
A few weeks, and you've only just noticed. Do you ever check up on your staff?
Hahaha!
Apologies! I just haven't been around recently.
I came to sample one of Gracia's dessert dishes for the party. Uh . . . what's your name?
My name is Al—
YOUR MAJESTY!

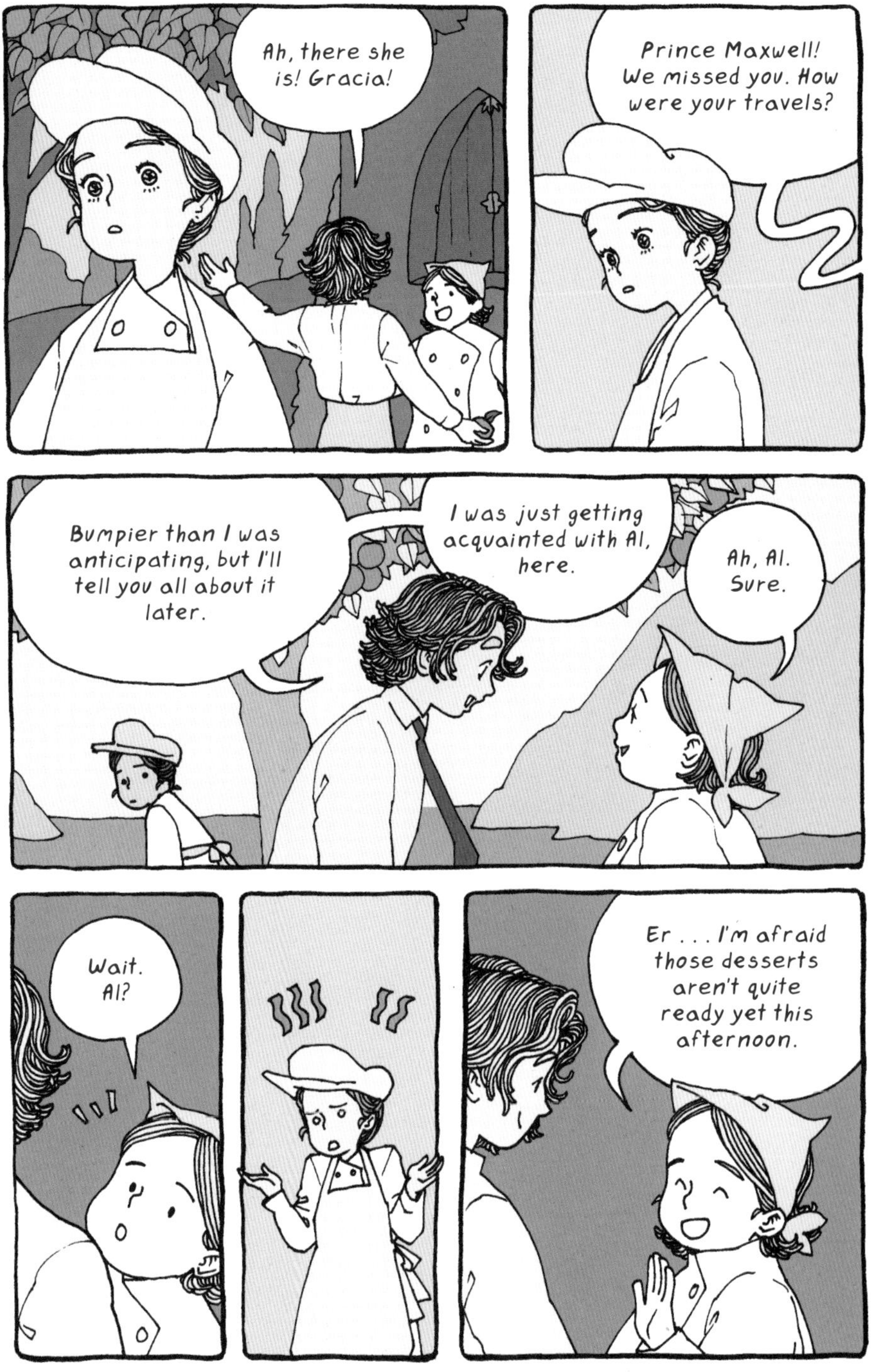
Ah, there she is! Gracia!
Prince Maxwell! We missed you. How were your travels?
Bumpier than I was anticipating, but I'll tell you all about it later.
I was just getting acquainted with Al, here.
Ah, Al. Sure.
Wait. Al?
Er . . . I'm afraid those desserts aren't quite ready yet this afternoon.

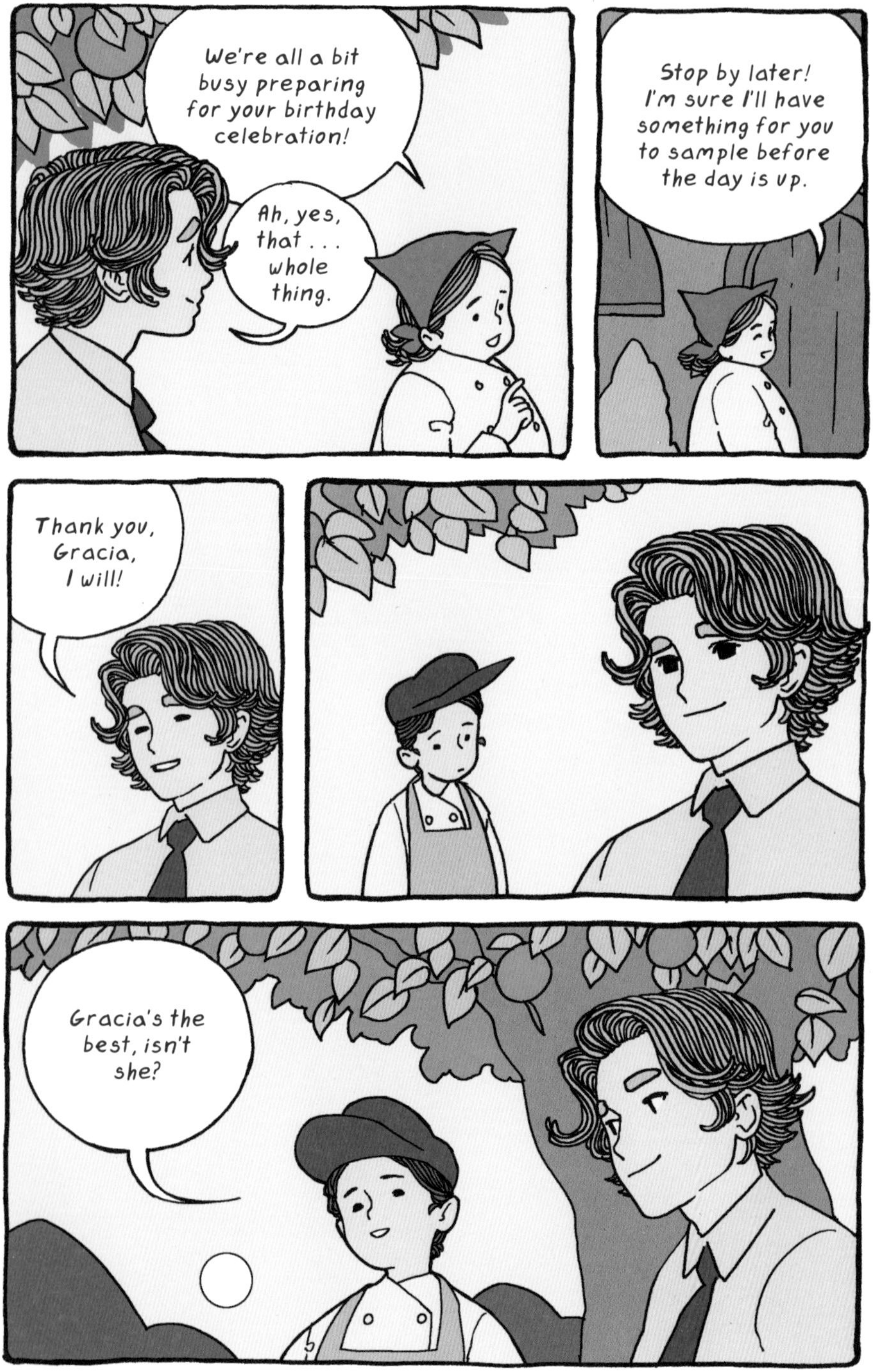
We're all a bit busy preparing for your birthday celebration!
Ah, yes, that . . . whole thing.
Stop by later! I'm sure I'll have something for you to sample before the day is up.
Thank you, Gracia, I will!
Gracia's the best, isn't she?

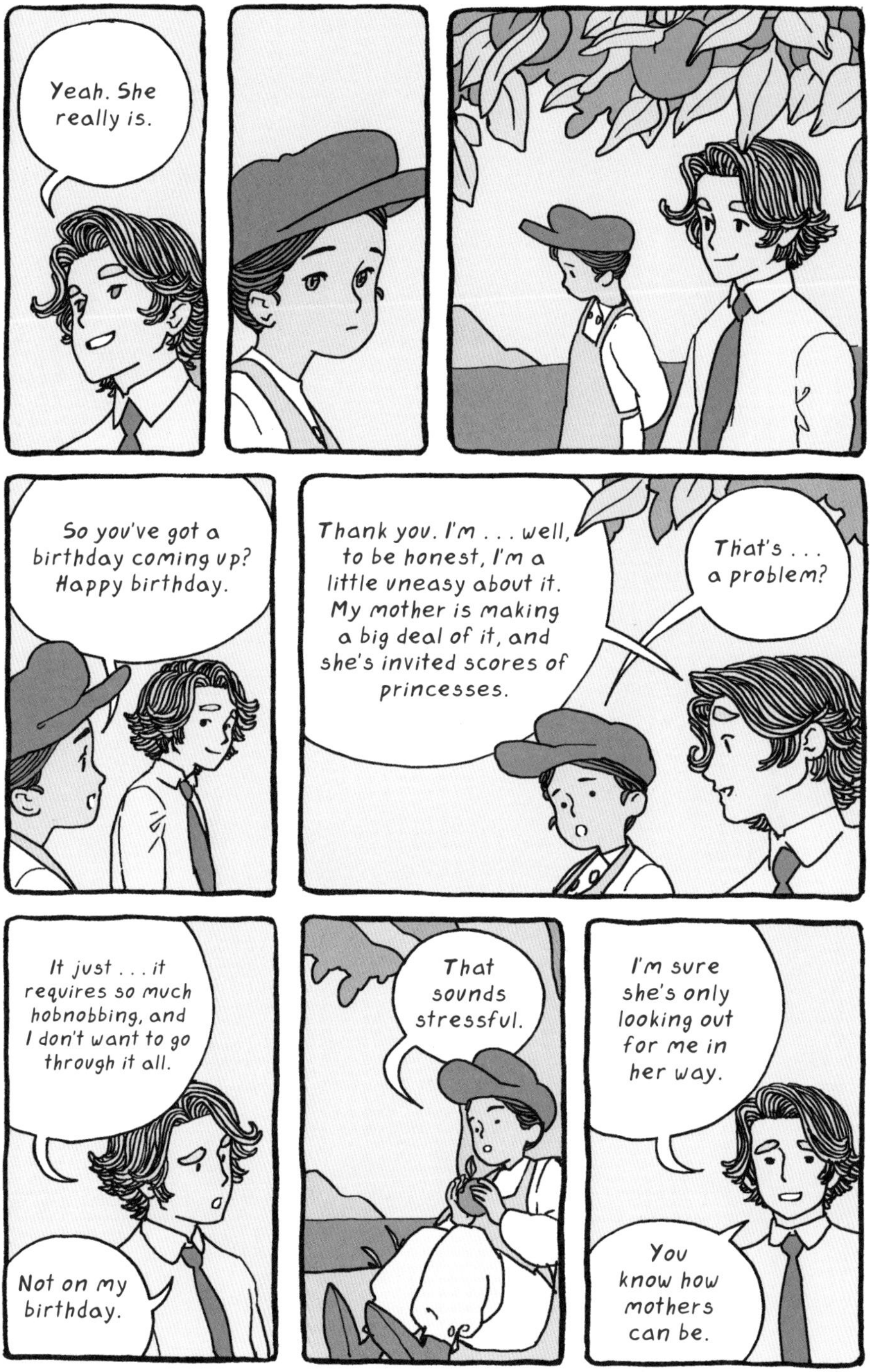
Yeah. She really is.
So you've got a birthday coming up? Happy birthday.
Thank you. I'm . . . well, to be honest, I'm a little uneasy about it. My mother is making a big deal of it, and she's invited scores of princesses.
That's . . . a problem?
It just . . . it requires so much hobnobbing, and I don't want to go through it all.
Not on my birthday.
That sounds stressful.
I'm sure she's only looking out for me in her way.
You know how mothers can be.

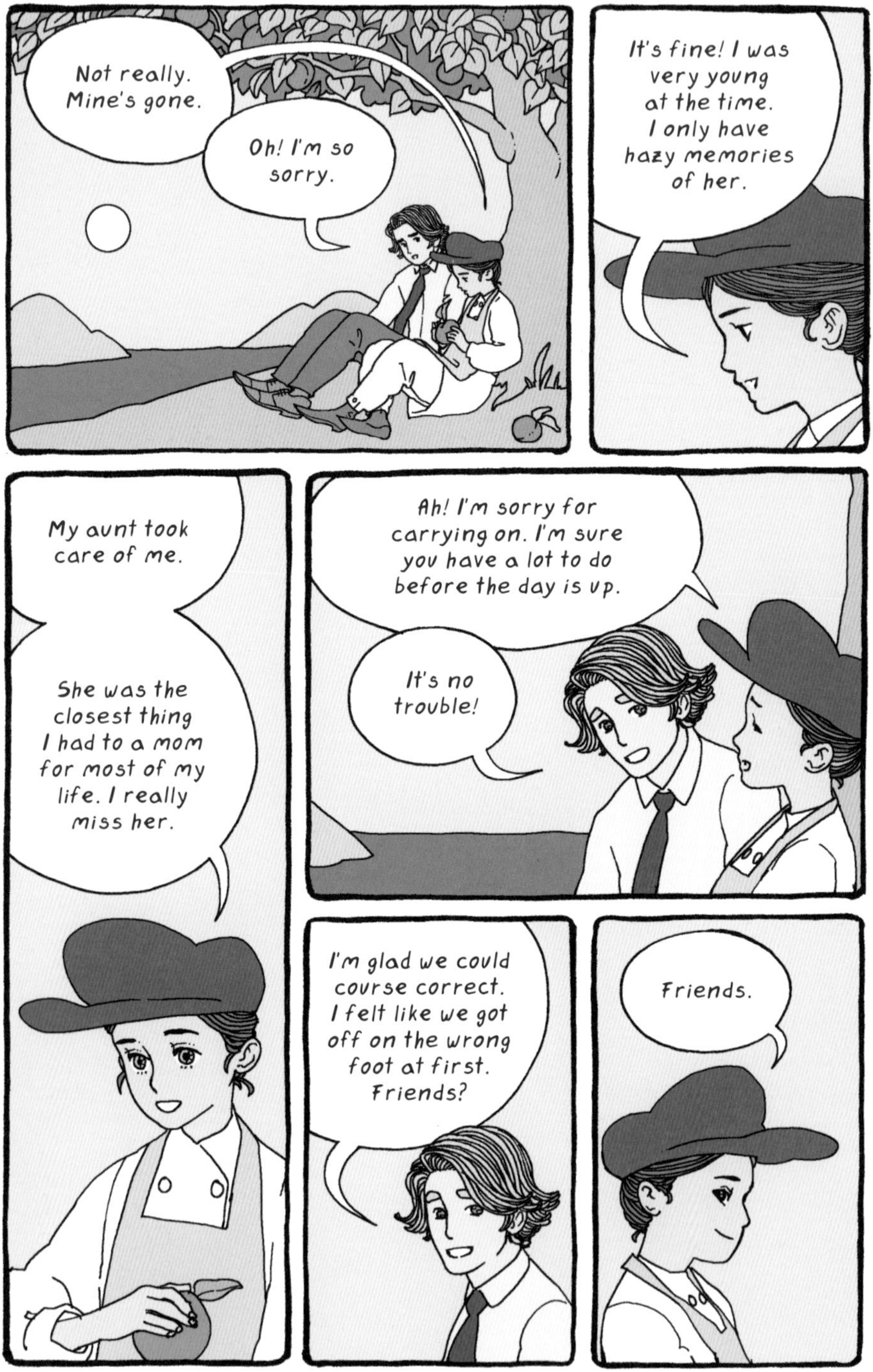
Not really. Mine's gone.
Oh! I'm so sorry.
It's fine! I was very young at the time. I only have hazy memories of her.
My aunt took care of me.
She was the closest thing I had to a mom for most of my life. I really miss her.
Ah! I'm sorry for carrying on. I'm sure you have a lot to do before the day is up.
It's no trouble!
I'm glad we could course correct. I felt like we got off on the wrong foot at first. Friends?
Friends.

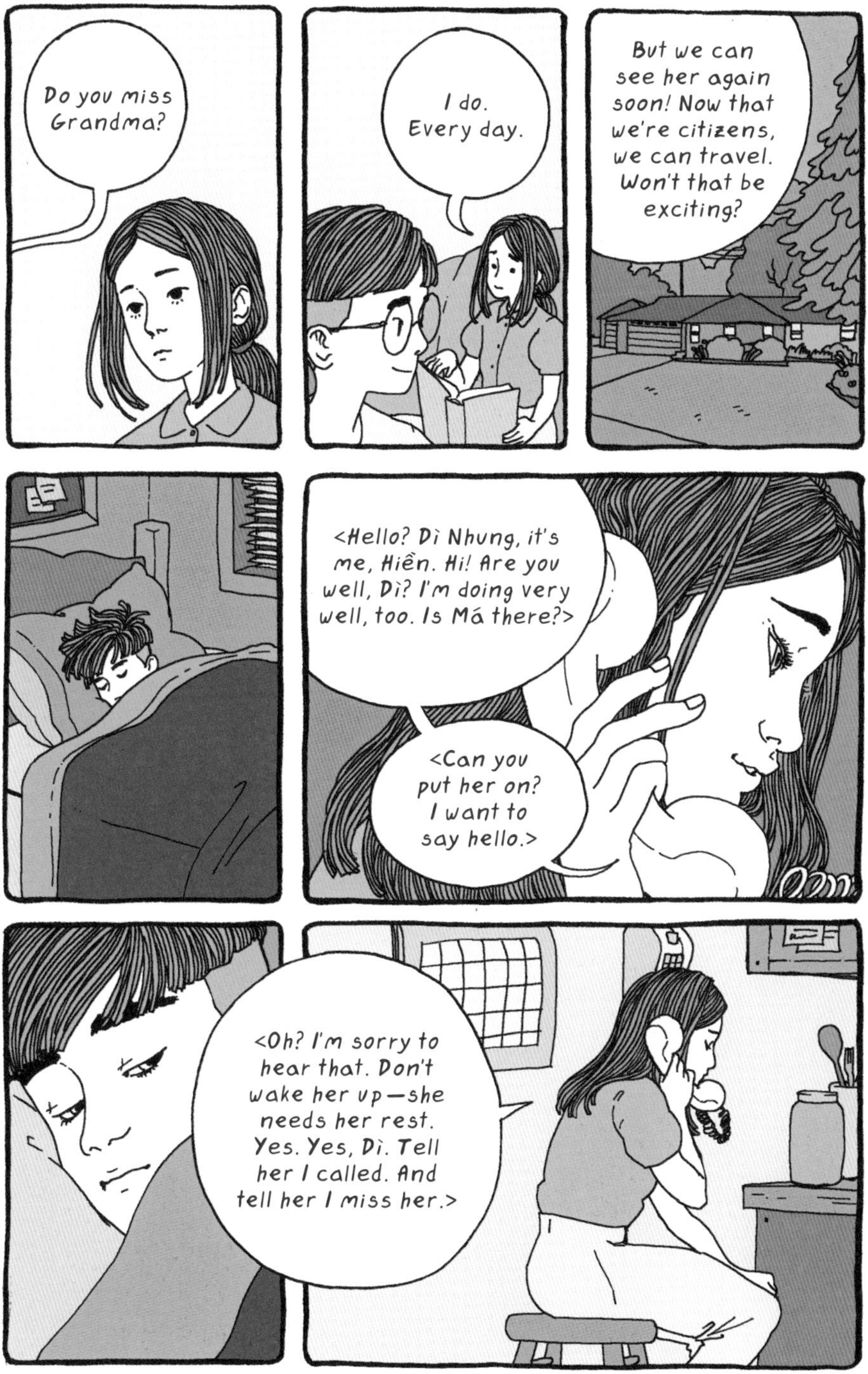
Do you miss Grandma?
I do. Every day.
But we can see her again soon! Now that we're citizens, we can travel. Won't that be exciting?
<Hello? Dì Nhung, it's me, Hiền. Hi! Are you well, Dì? I'm doing very well, too. Is Má there?>
<Can you put her on? I want to say hello.>
<Oh? I'm sorry to hear that. Don't wake her up—she needs her rest. Yes. Yes, Dì. Tell her I called. And tell her I miss her.>

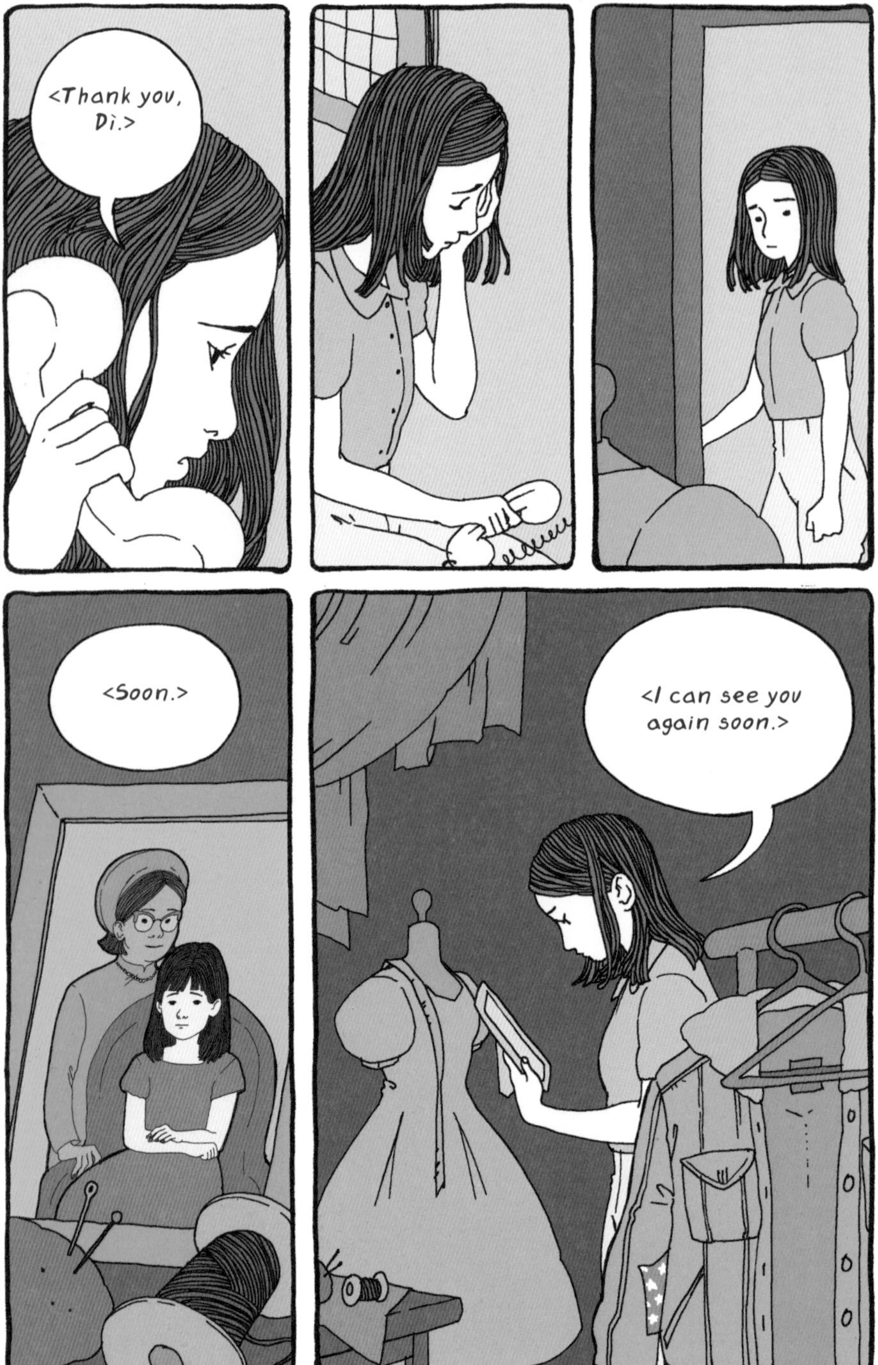
<Thank you, Di.>
<Soon.>
<I can see you again soon.>

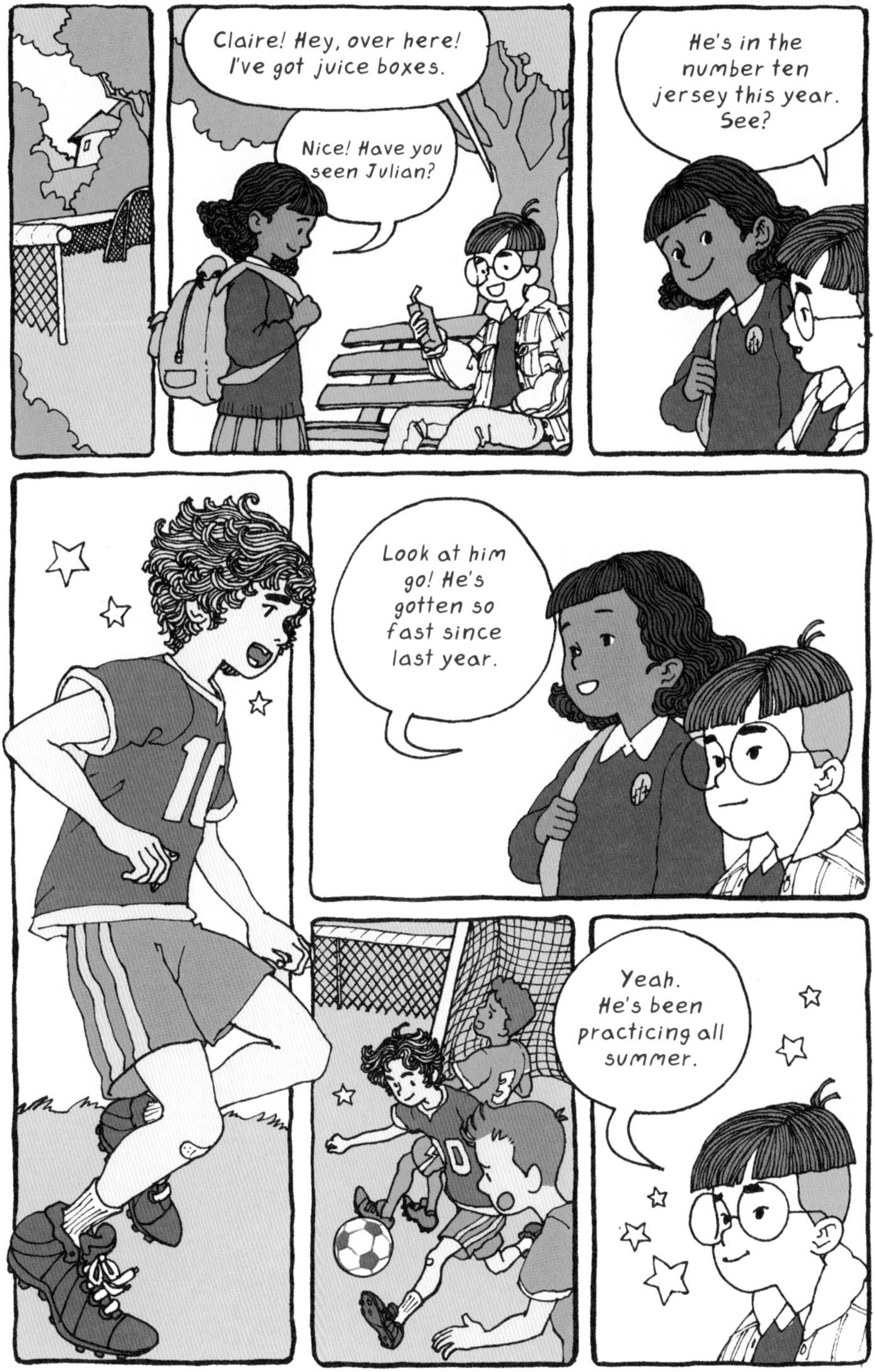
Claire! Hey, over here! I've got juice boxes.
Nice! Have you seen Julian?
He's in the number ten jersey this year. See?
Look at him go! He's gotten so fast since last year.
Yeah. He's been practicing all summer.

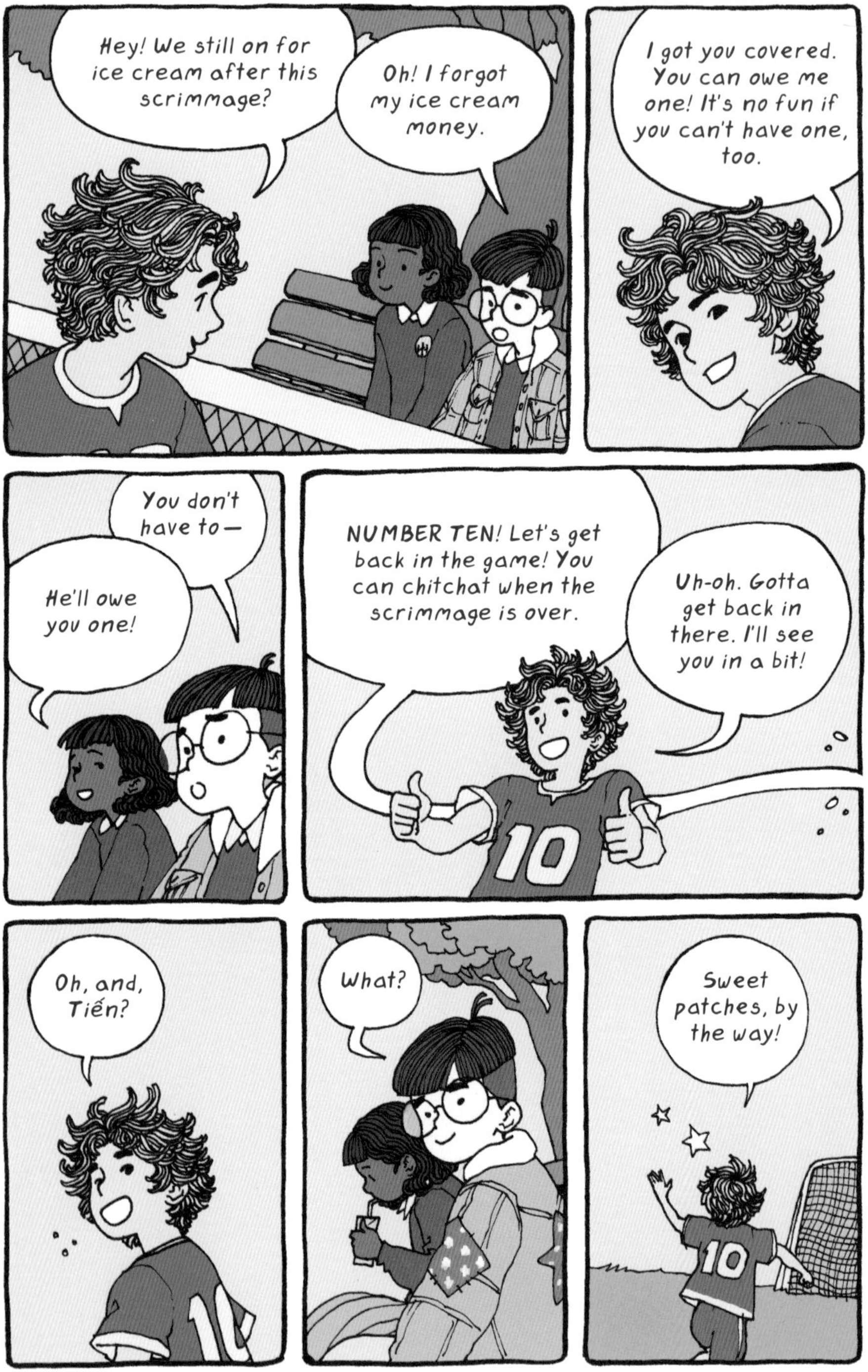
Hey! We still on for ice cream after this scrimmage?
Oh! I forgot my ice cream money.
I got you covered. You can owe me one! It's no fun if you can't have one, too.
You don't have to—
He'll owe you one!
NUMBER TEN! Let's get back in the game! You can chitchat when the scrimmage is over.
Uh-oh. Gotta get back in there. I'll see you in a bit!
10
Oh, and, Tiến?
What?
Sweet patches, by the way!
10

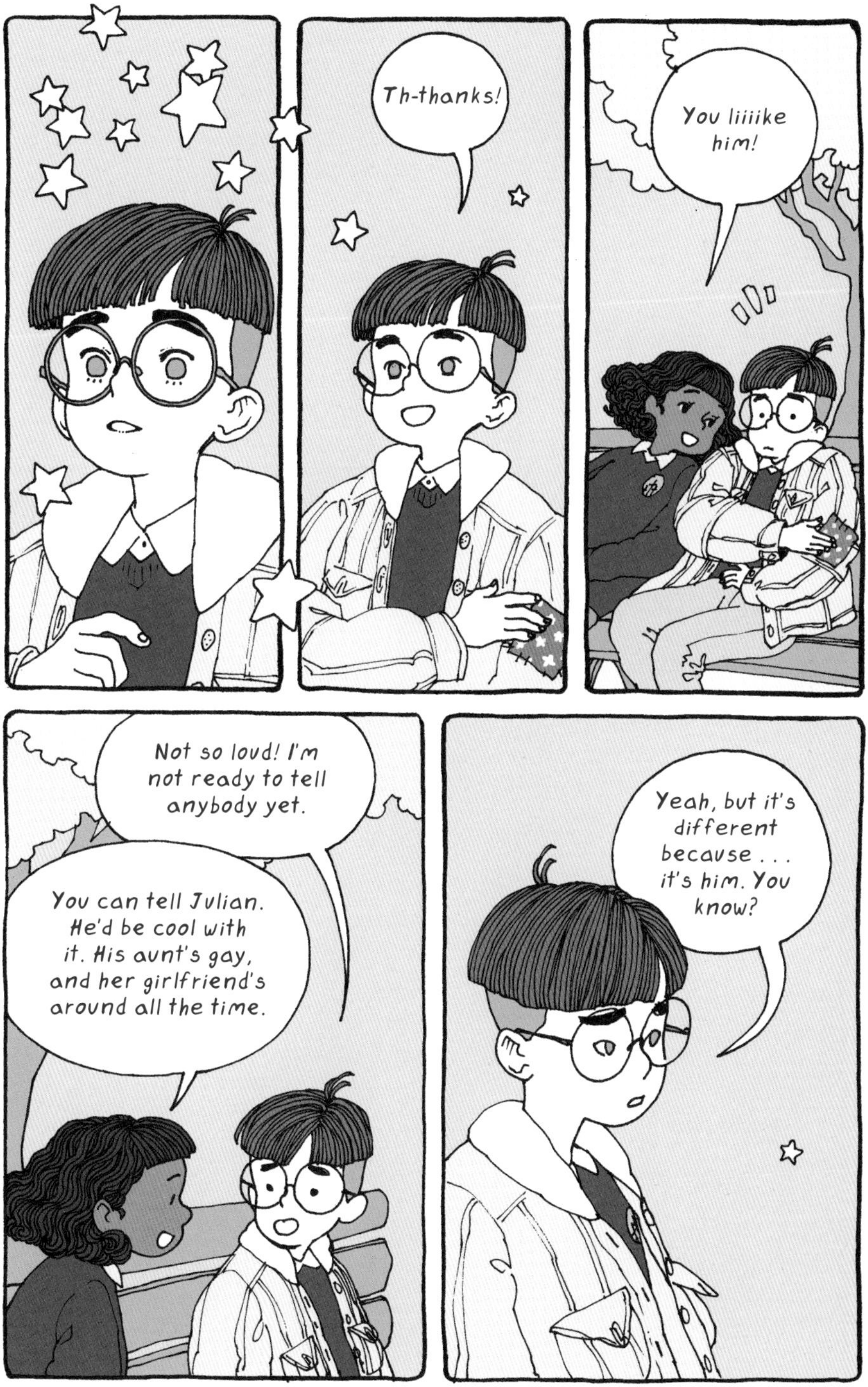
Th-thanks!
You liiiike him!
Not so loud! I'm not ready to tell anybody yet.
You can tell Julian. He'd be cool with it. His aunt's gay, and her girlfriend's around all the time.
Yeah, but it's different because . . . it's him. You know?

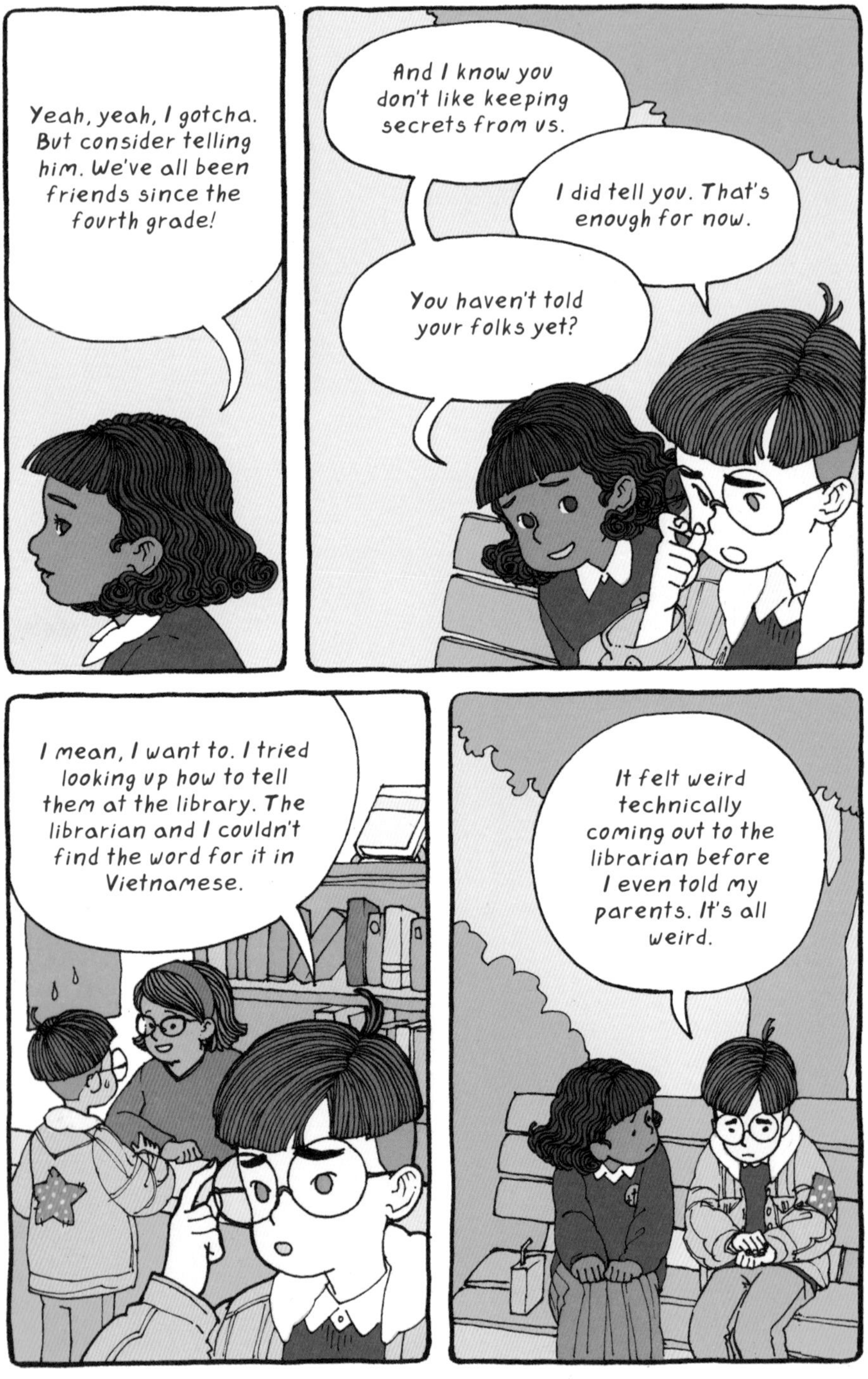
Yeah, yeah, I gotcha. But consider telling him. We've all been friends since the fourth grade!
And I know you don't like keeping secrets from us.
I did tell you. That's enough for now.
You haven't told your folks yet?
I mean, I want to. I tried looking up how to tell them at the library. The librarian and I couldn't find the word for it in Vietnamese.
It felt weird technically coming out to the librarian before I even told my parents. It's all weird.

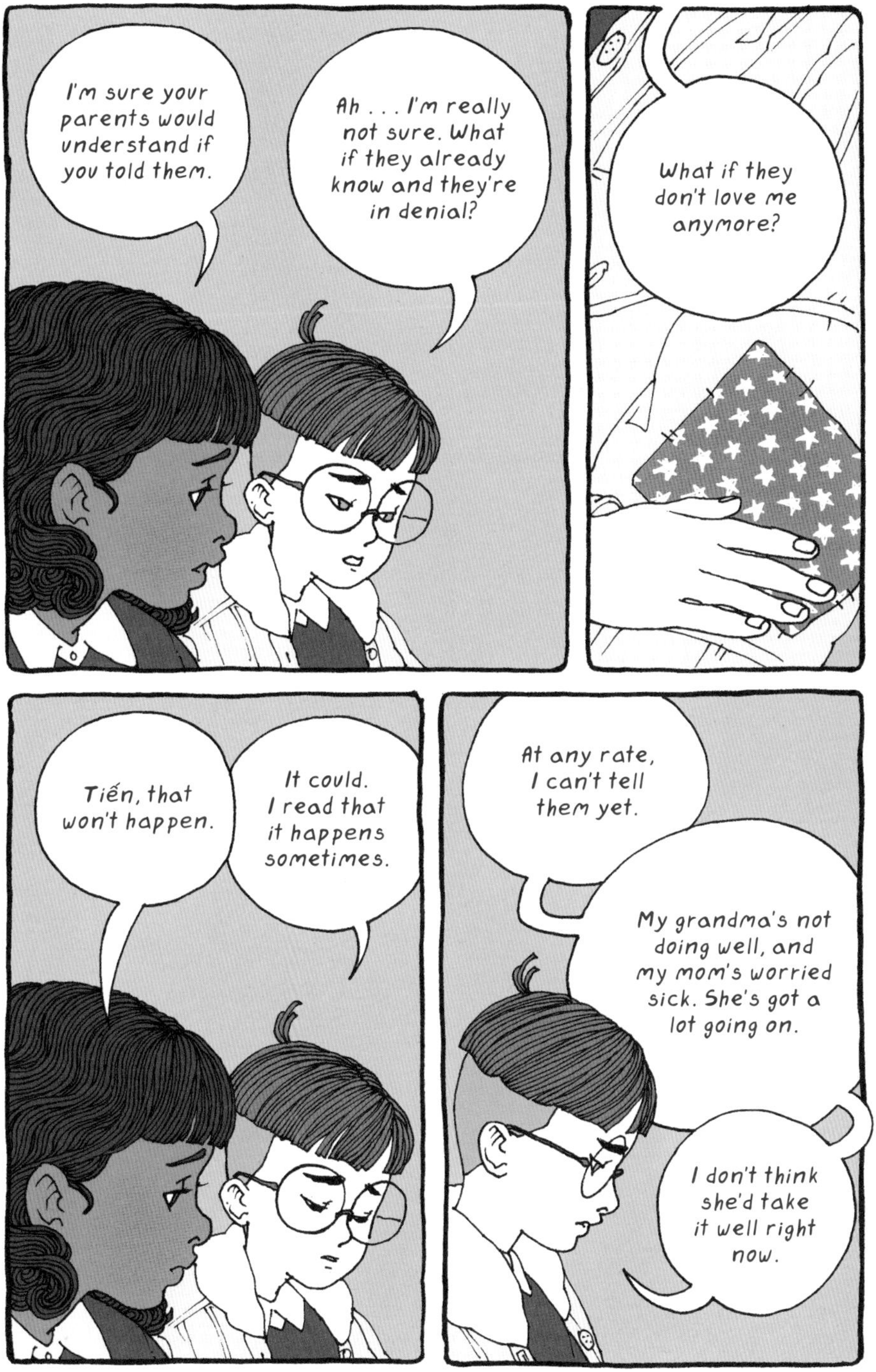
I'm sure your parents would understand if you told them.
Ah . . . I'm really not sure. What if they already know and they're in denial?
What if they don't love me anymore?
Tiến, that won't happen.
It could. I read that it happens sometimes.
At any rate, I can't tell them yet.
My grandma's not doing well, and my mom's worried sick. She's got a lot going on.
I don't think she'd take it well right now.

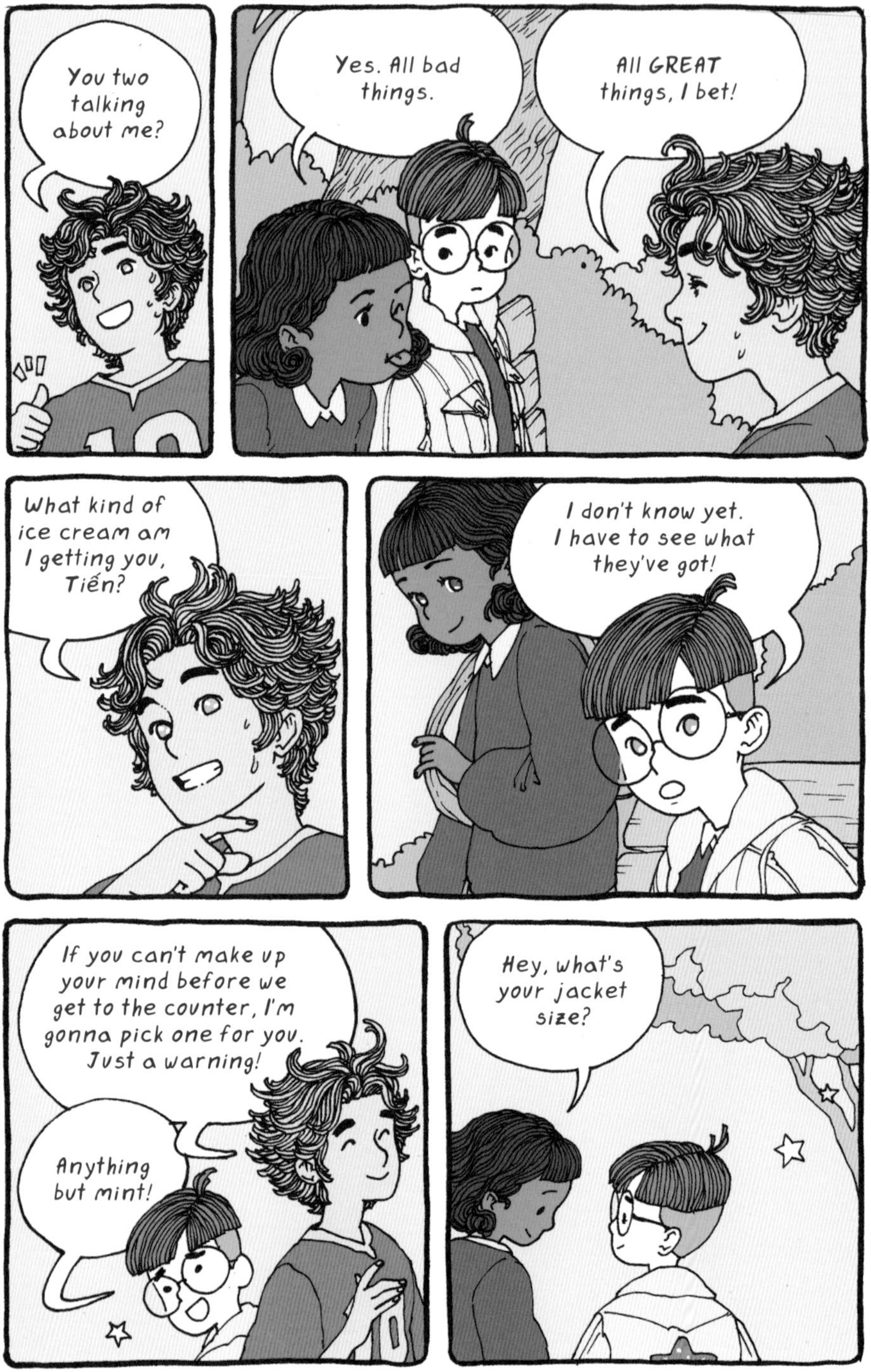
You two talking about me?
Yes. All bad things.
All GREAT things, I bet!
What kind of ice cream am I getting you, Tiến?
I don't know yet. I have to see what they've got!
If you can't make up your mind before we get to the counter, I'm gonna pick one for you. Just a warning!
Anything but mint!
Hey, what's your jacket size?

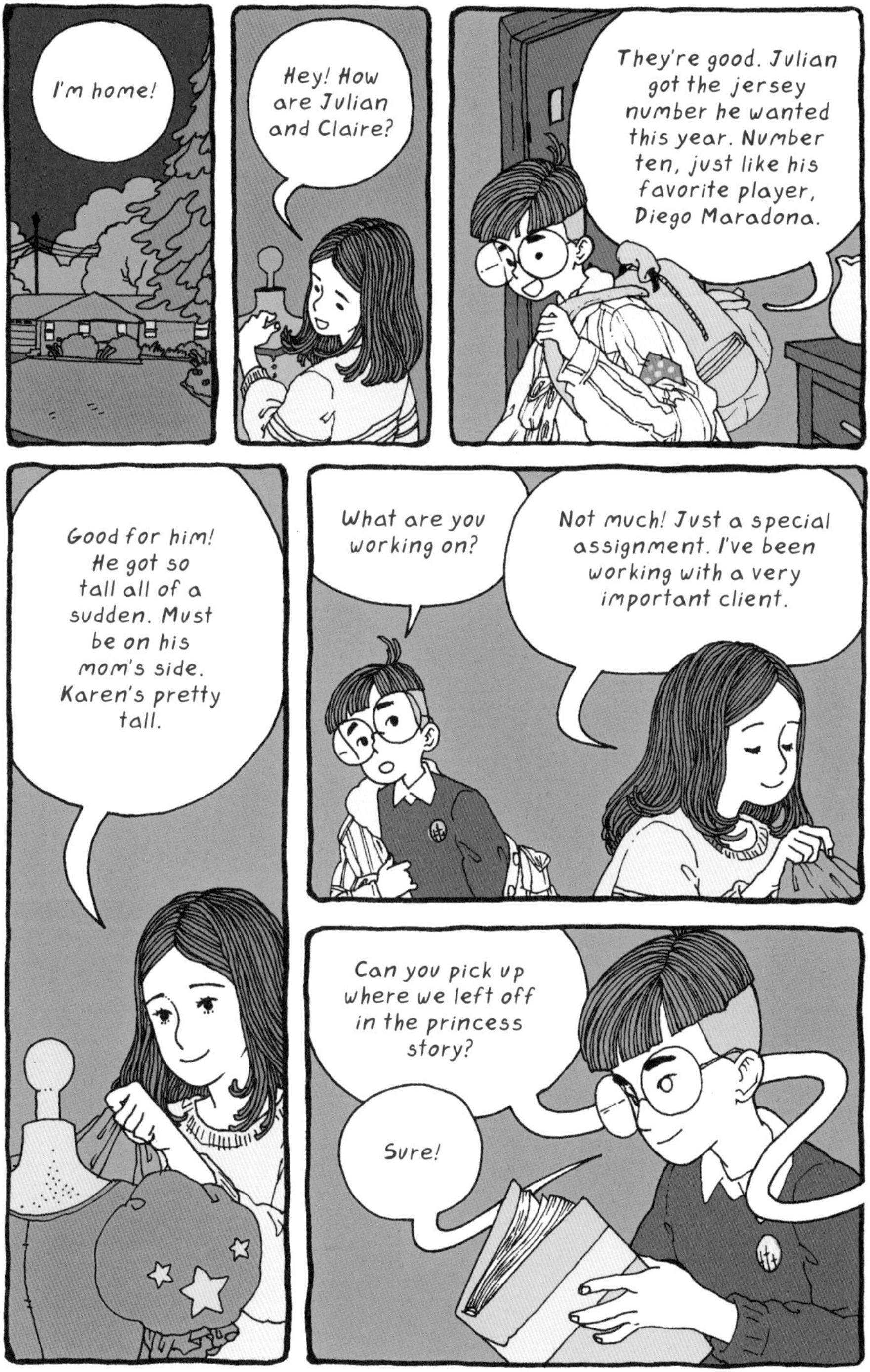
I'm home!
Hey! How are Julian and Claire?
They're good. Julian got the jersey number he wanted this year. Number ten, just like his favorite player, Diego Maradona.
Good for him! He got so tall all of a sudden. Must be on his mom's side. Karen's pretty tall.
What are you working on?
Not much! Just a special assignment. I've been working with a very important client.
Can you pick up where we left off in the princess story?
Sure!

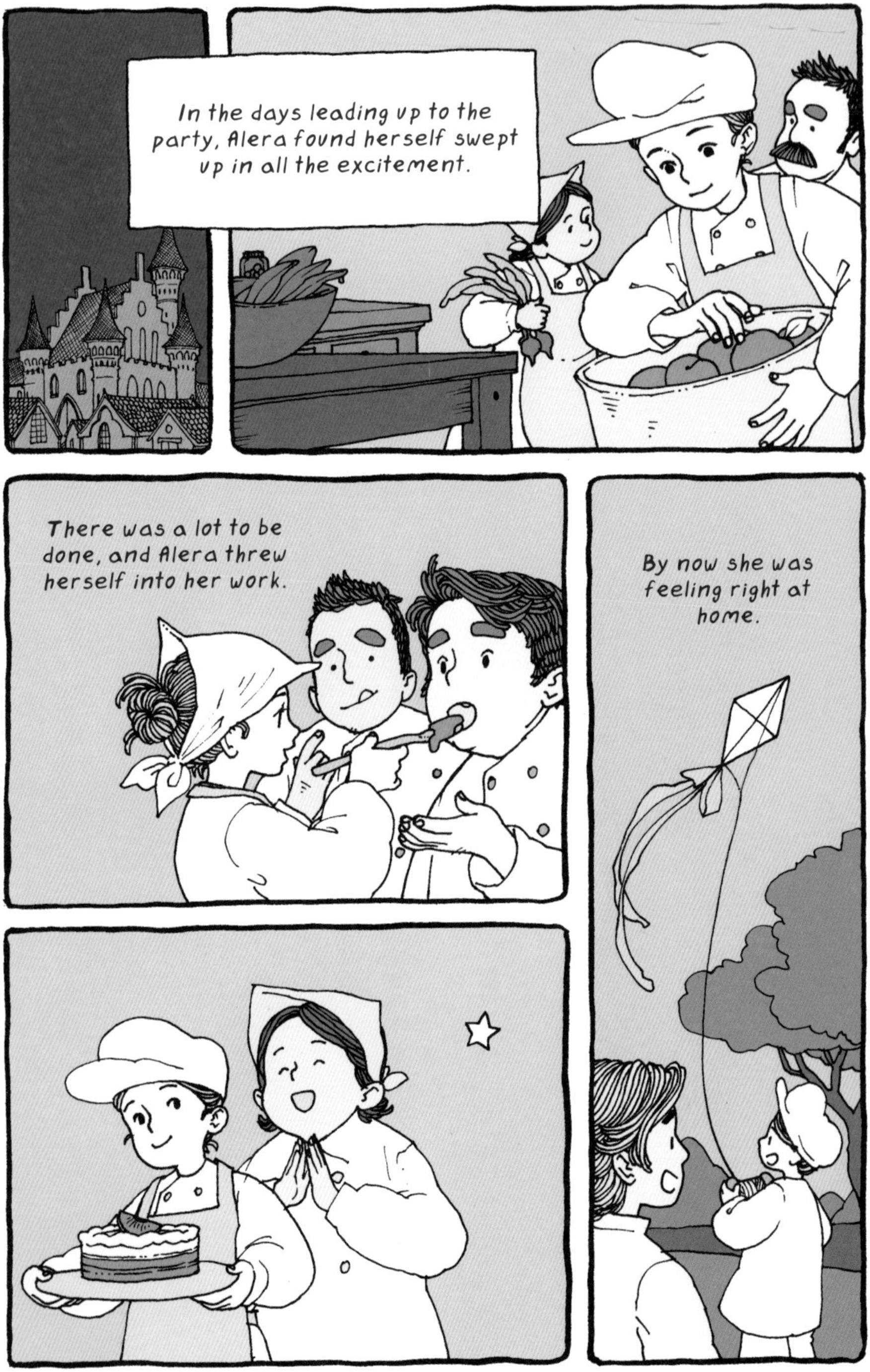
In the days leading up to the party, Alera found herself swept up in all the excitement.
There was a lot to be done, and Alera threw herself into her work.
By now she was feeling right at home.

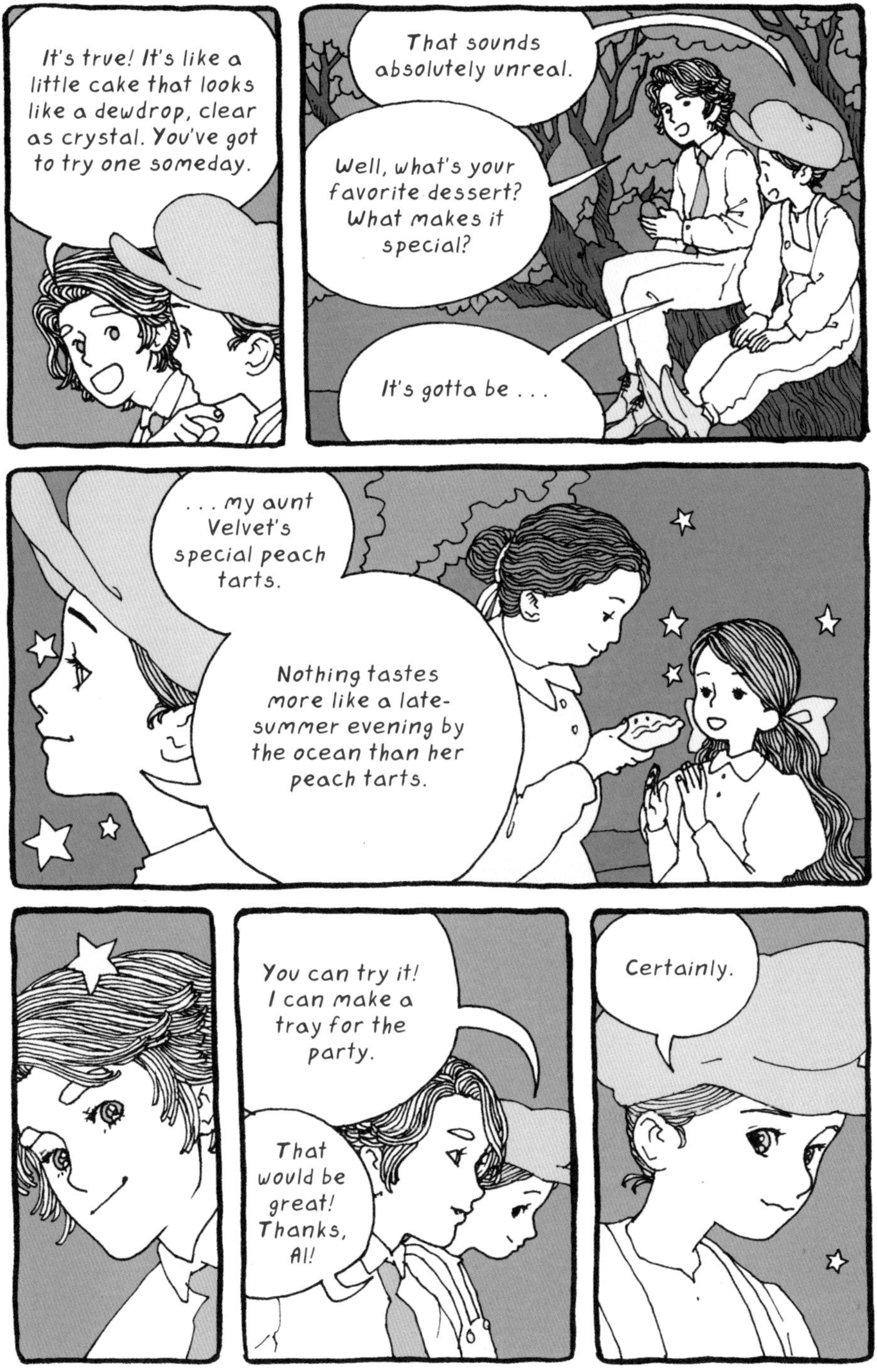
It's true! It's like a little cake that looks like a dewdrop, clear as crystal. You've got to try one someday.
That sounds absolutely unreal.
Well, what's your favorite dessert? What makes it special?
It's gotta be . . .
. . . my aunt Velvet's special peach tarts.
Nothing tastes more like a late-summer evening by the ocean than her peach tarts.
You can try it! I can make a tray for the party.
That would be great! Thanks, Al!
Certainly.

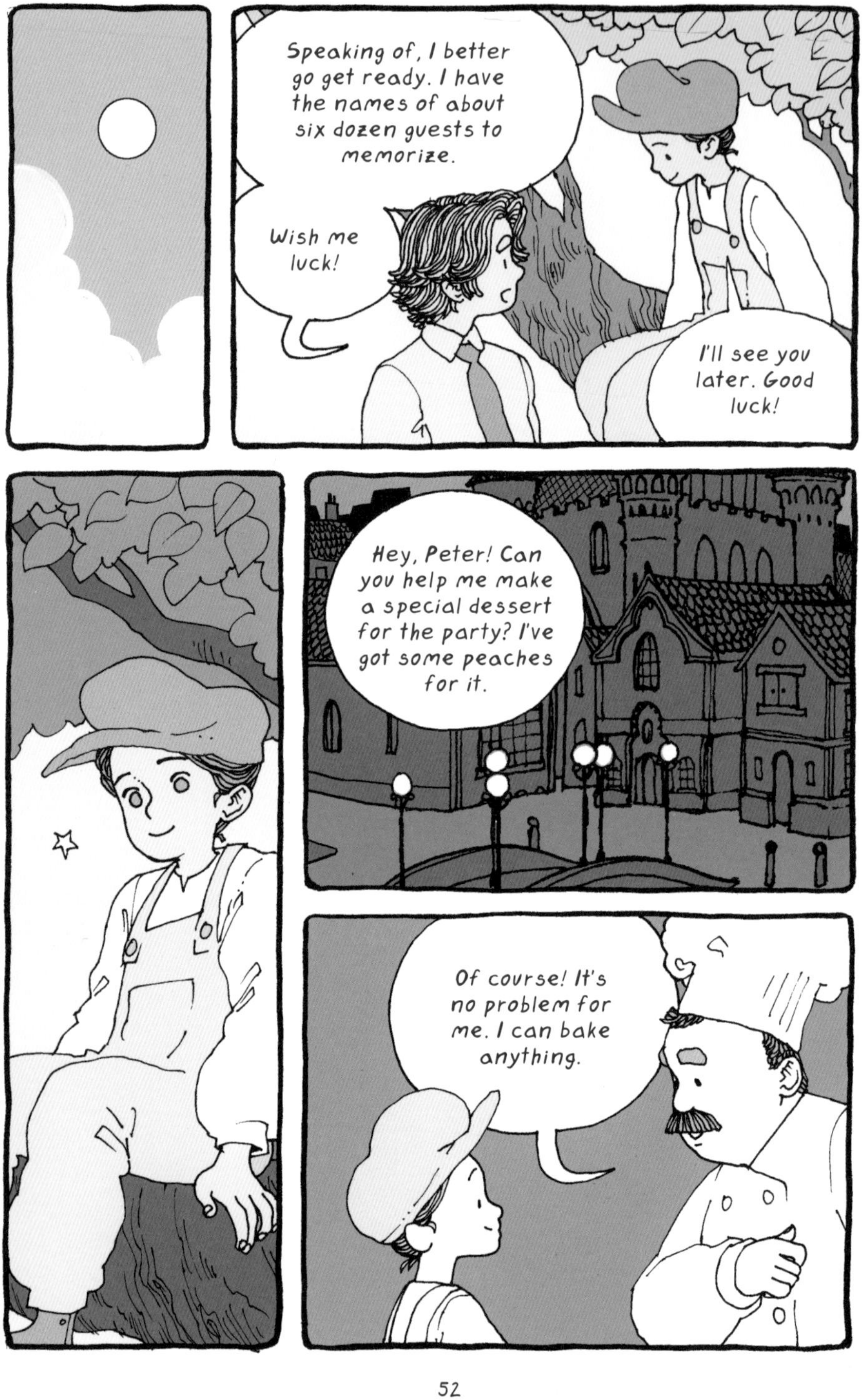
Speaking of, I better go get ready. I have the names of about six dozen guests to memorize.
Wish me luck!
I'll see you later. Good luck!
Hey, Peter! Can you help me make a special dessert for the party? I've got some peaches for it.
Of course! It's no problem for me. I can bake anything.

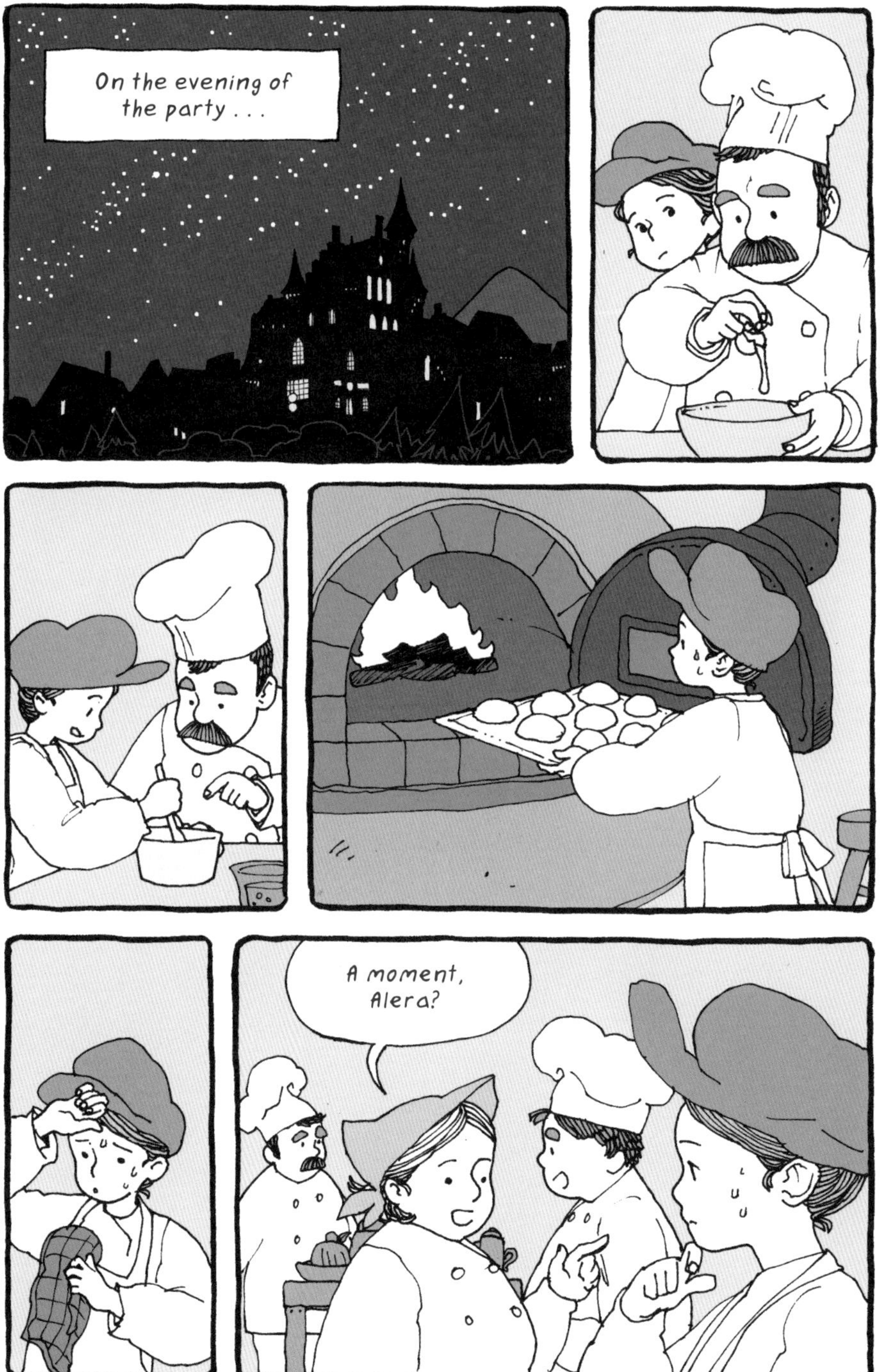
On the evening of the party . . .
A moment, Alera?

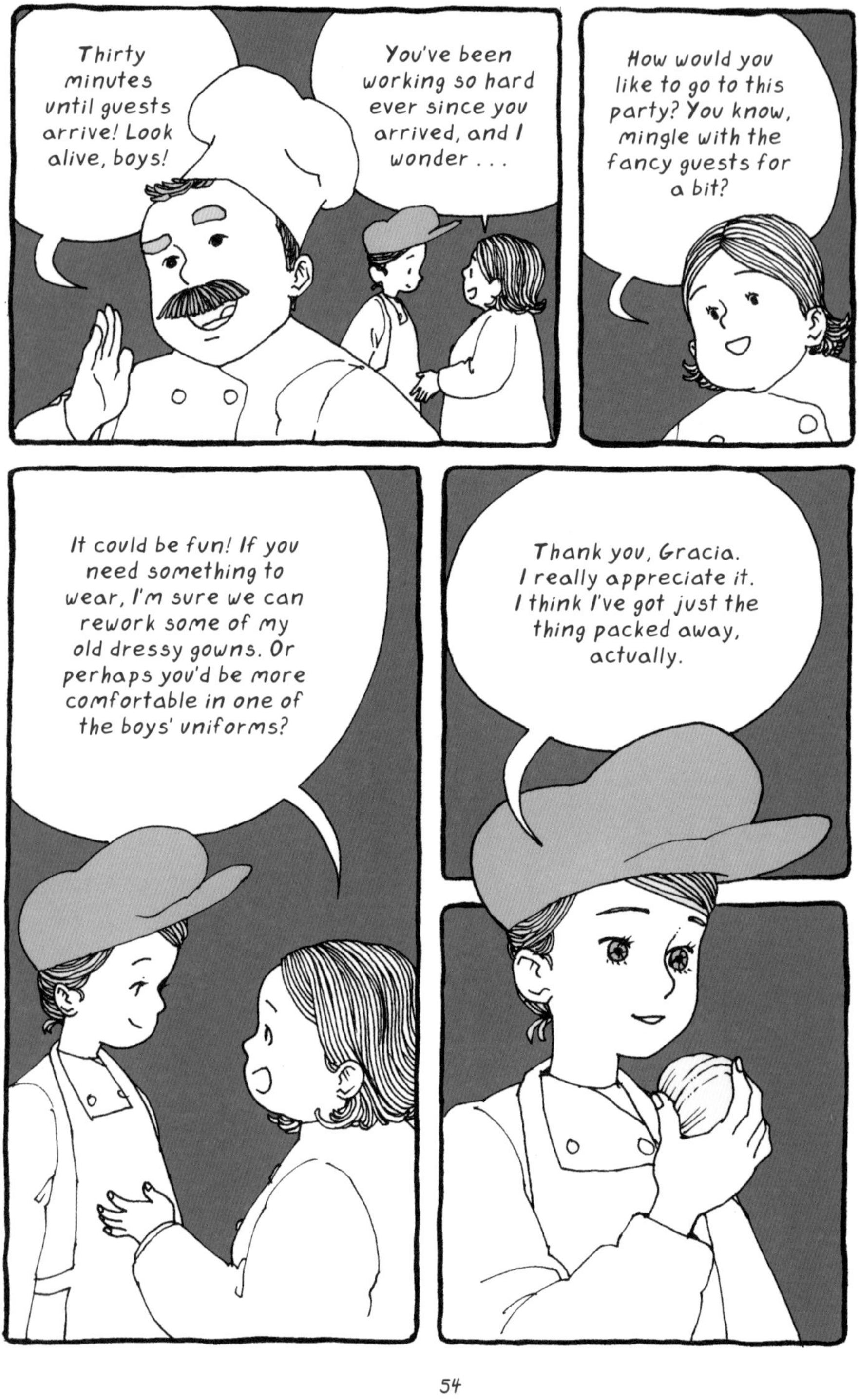
Thirty minutes until guests arrive! Look alive, boys!
You've been working so hard ever since you arrived, and I wonder . . .
How would you like to go to this party? You know, mingle with the fancy guests for a bit?
It could be fun! If you need something to wear, I'm sure we can rework some of my old dressy gowns. Or perhaps you'd be more comfortable in one of the boys' uniforms?
Thank you, Gracia. I really appreciate it. I think I've got just the thing packed away, actually.

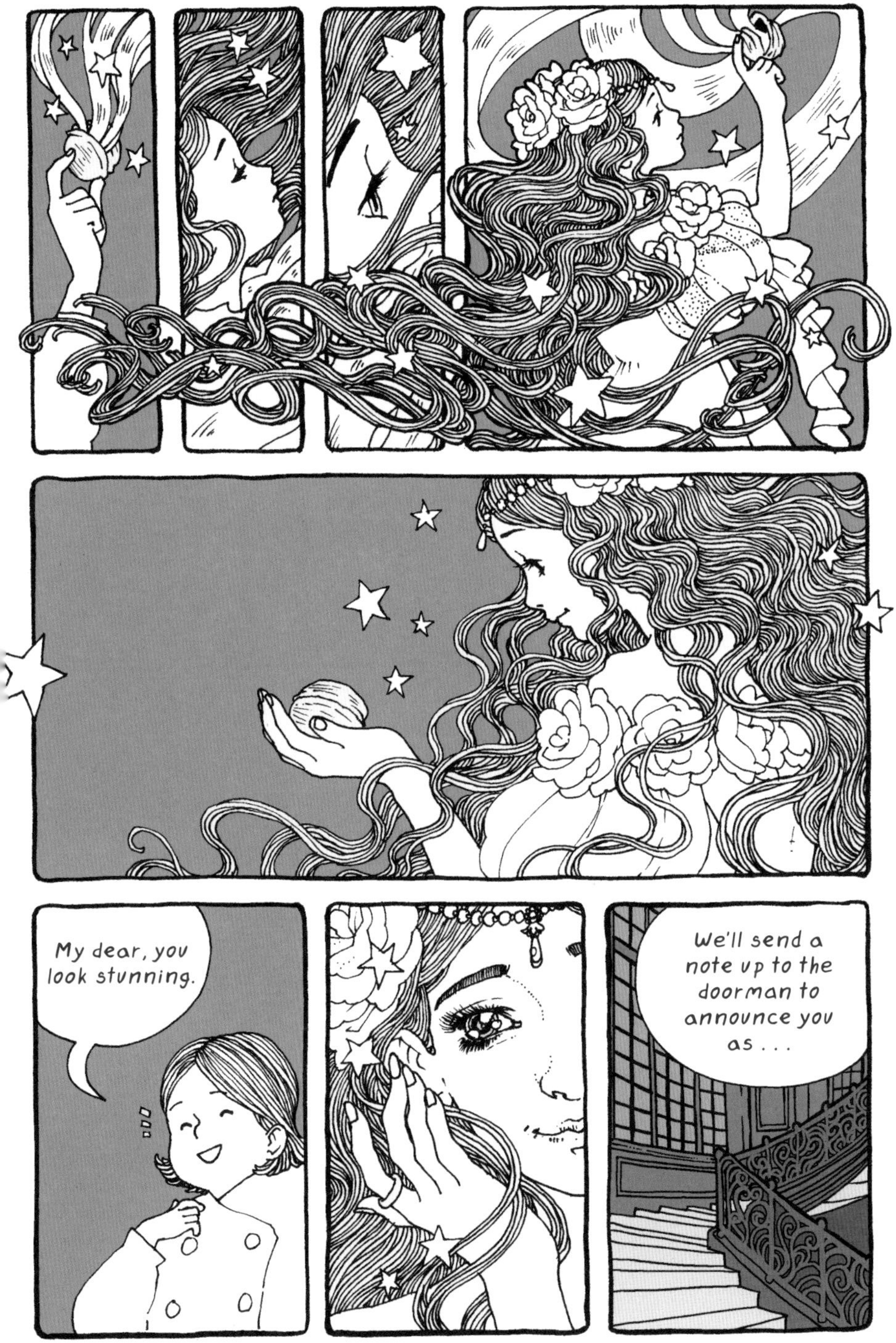
My dear, you look stunning.
We'll send a note up to the doorman to announce you as . . .

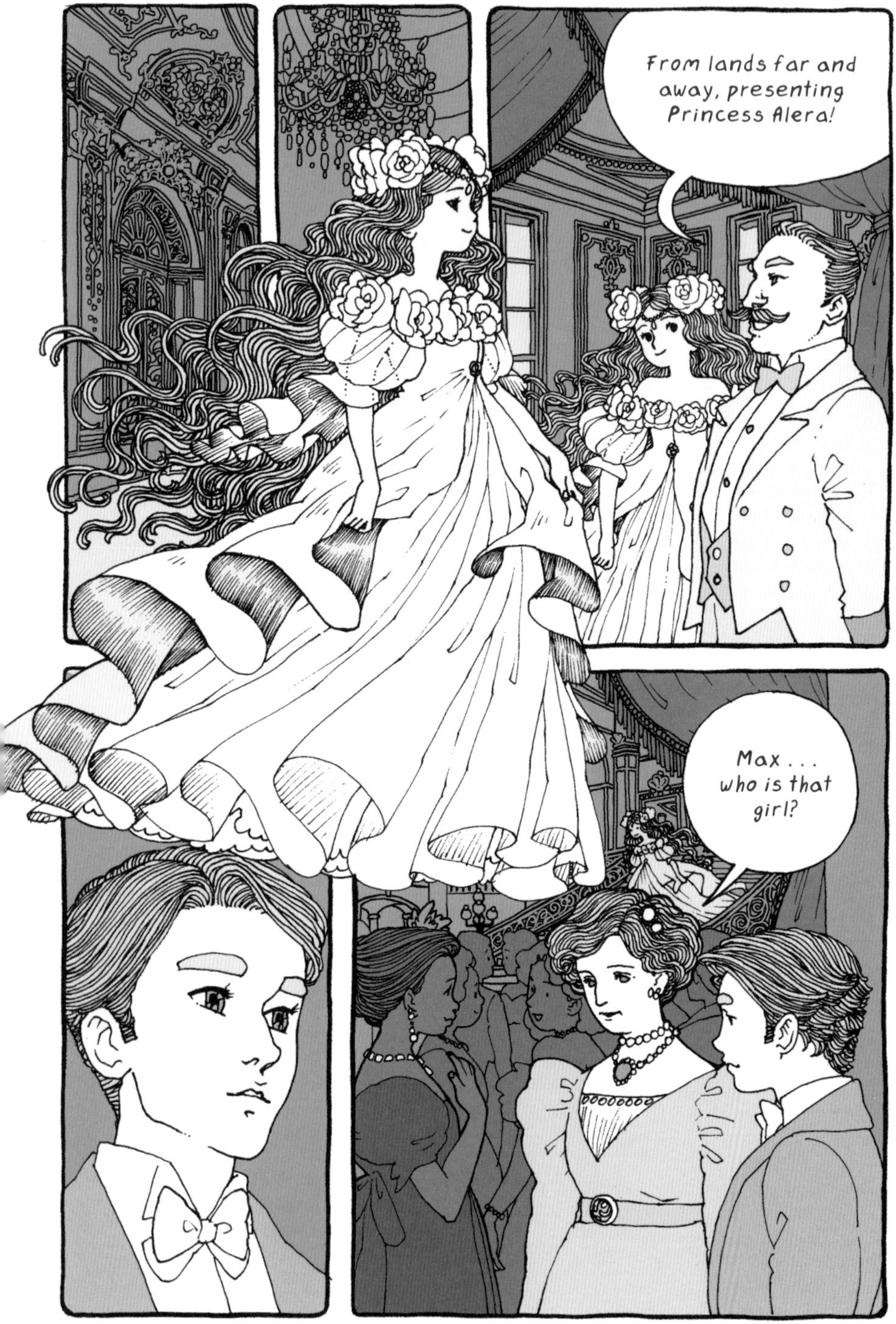
From lands far and away, presenting Princess Alera!
Max . . . who is that girl?

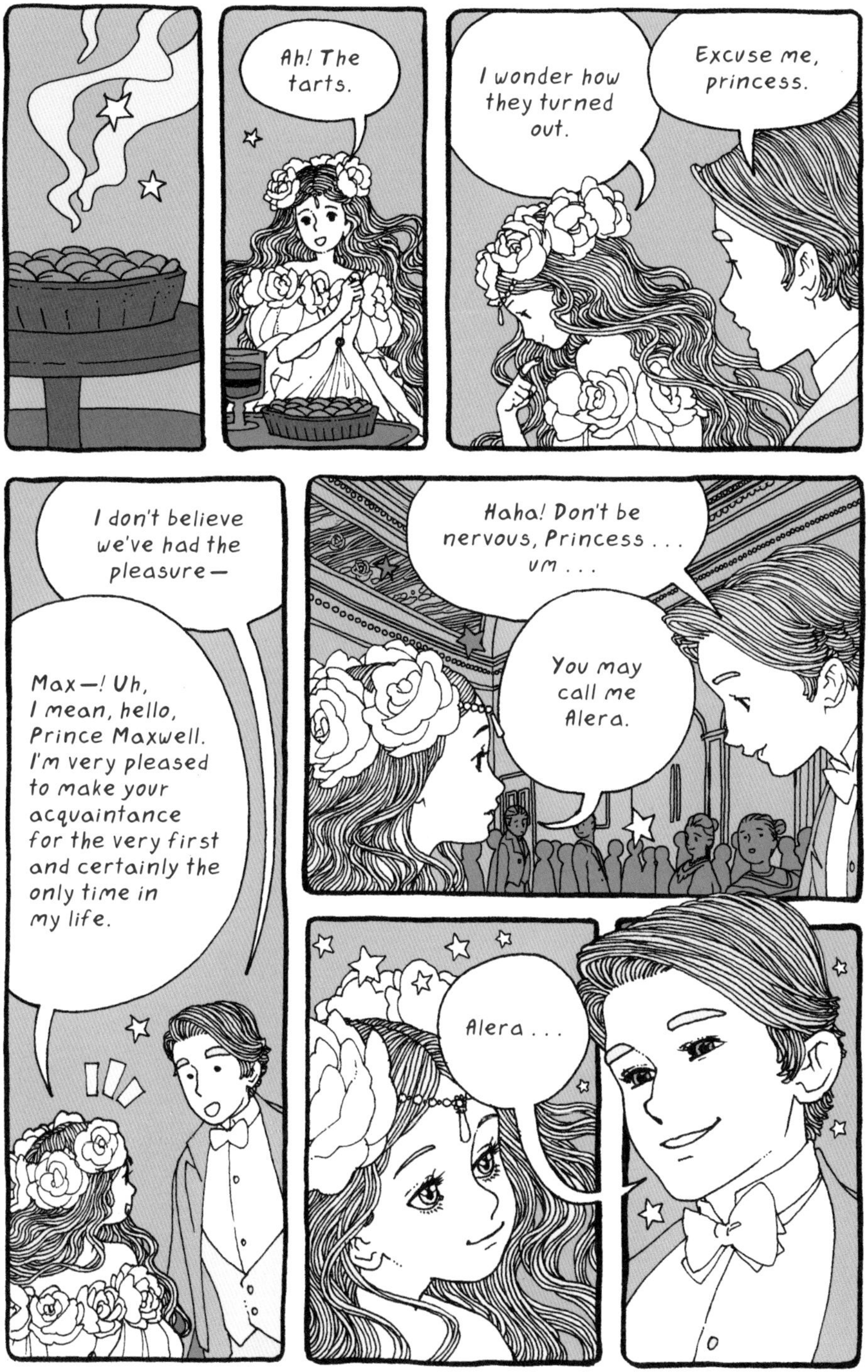
Ah! The tarts.
I wonder how they turned out.
Excuse me, princess.
I don't believe we've had the pleasure—
Max—! Uh, I mean, hello, Prince Maxwell. I'm very pleased to make your acquaintance for the very first and certainly the only time in my life.
Haha! Don't be nervous, Princess . . . um . . .
You may call me Alera.
Alera . . .

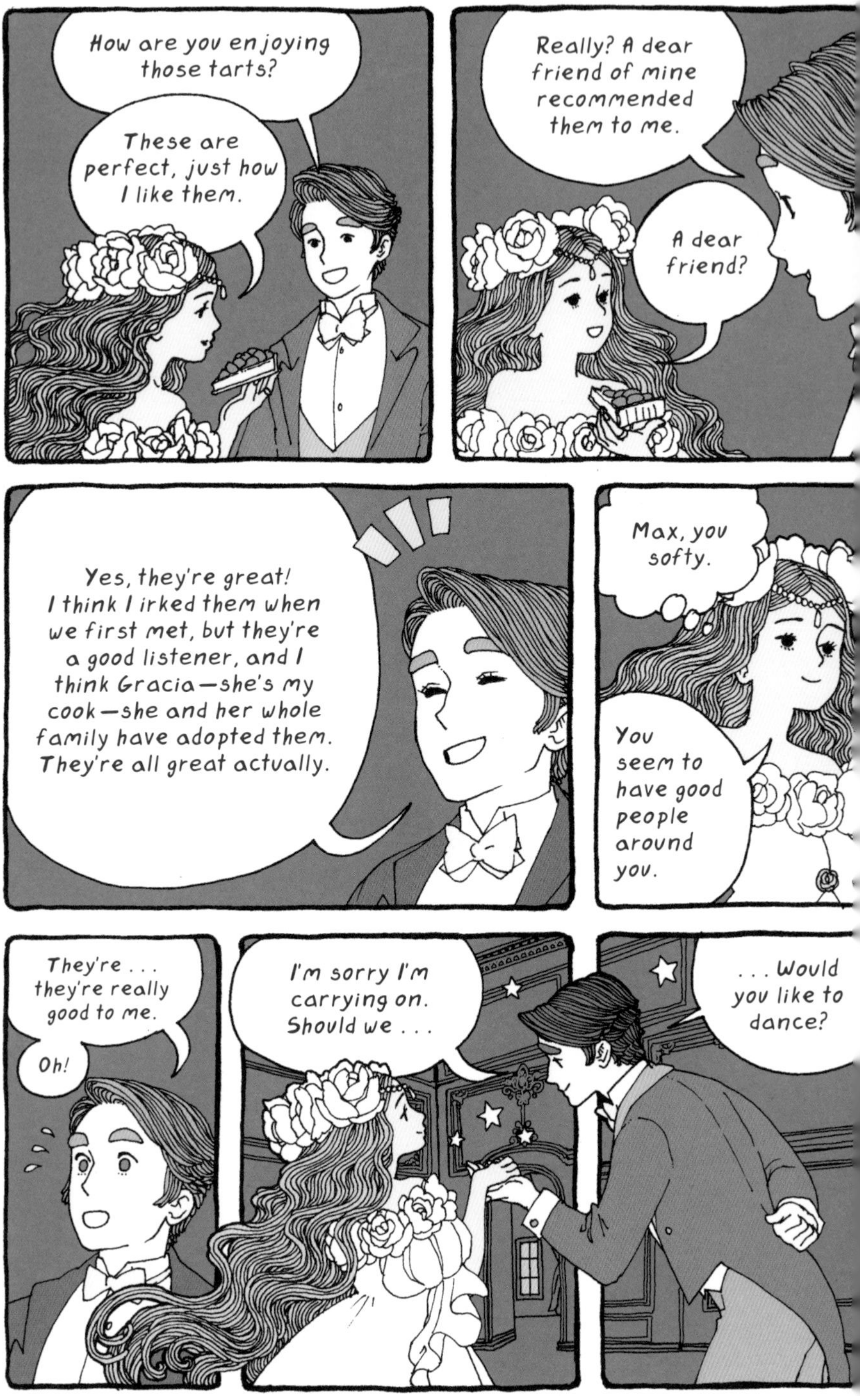
How are you enjoying those tarts?
These are perfect, just how I like them.
Really? A dear friend of mine recommended them to me.
A dear friend?
Yes, they're great! I think I irked them when we first met, but they're a good listener, and I think Gracia—she's my cook—she and her whole family have adopted them. They're all great actually.
Max, you softy.
You seem to have good people around you.
They're . . . they're really good to me.
Oh!
I'm sorry I'm carrying on. Should we . . .
. . . Would you like to dance?

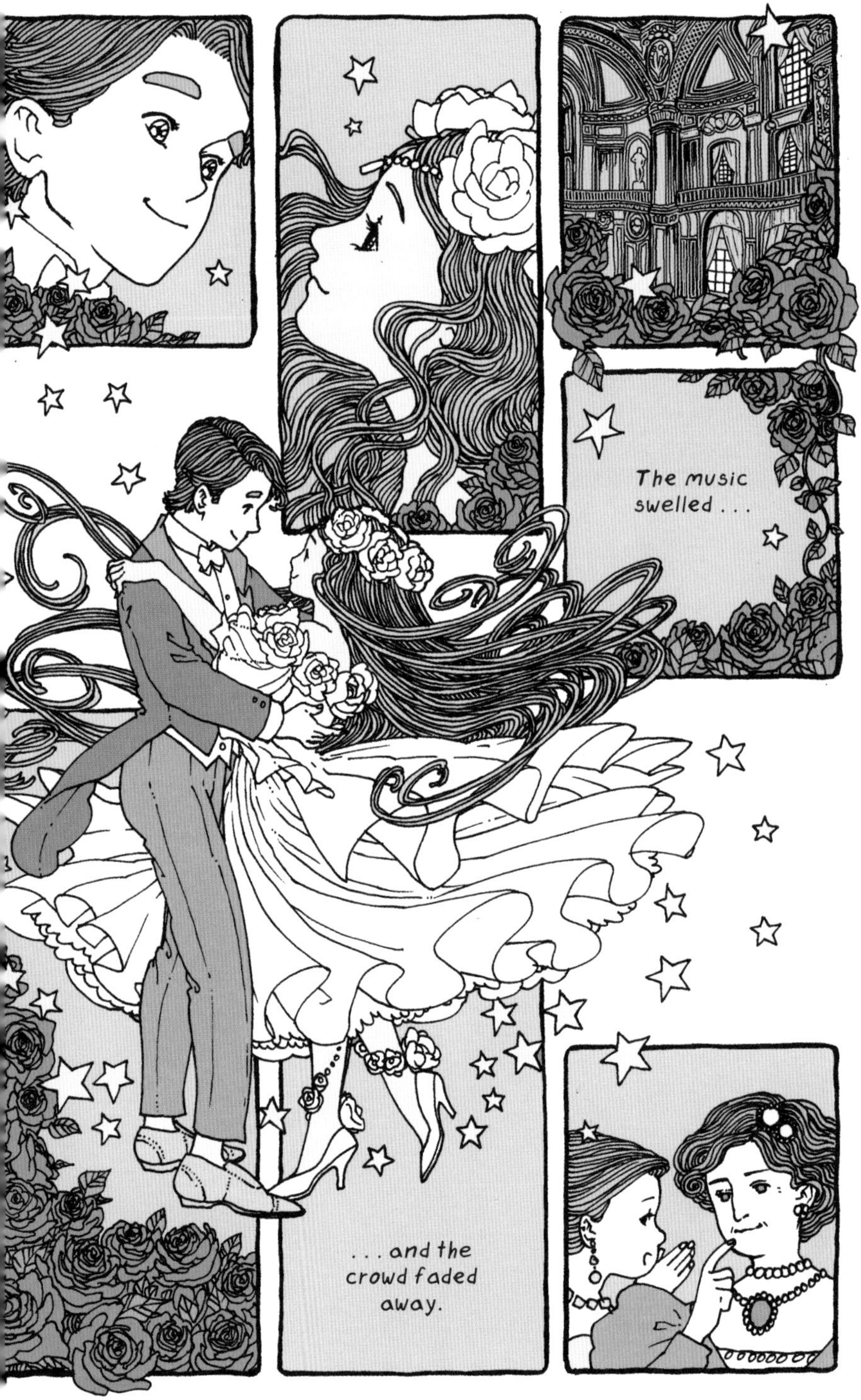
The music swelled . . .
. . . and the crowd faded away.

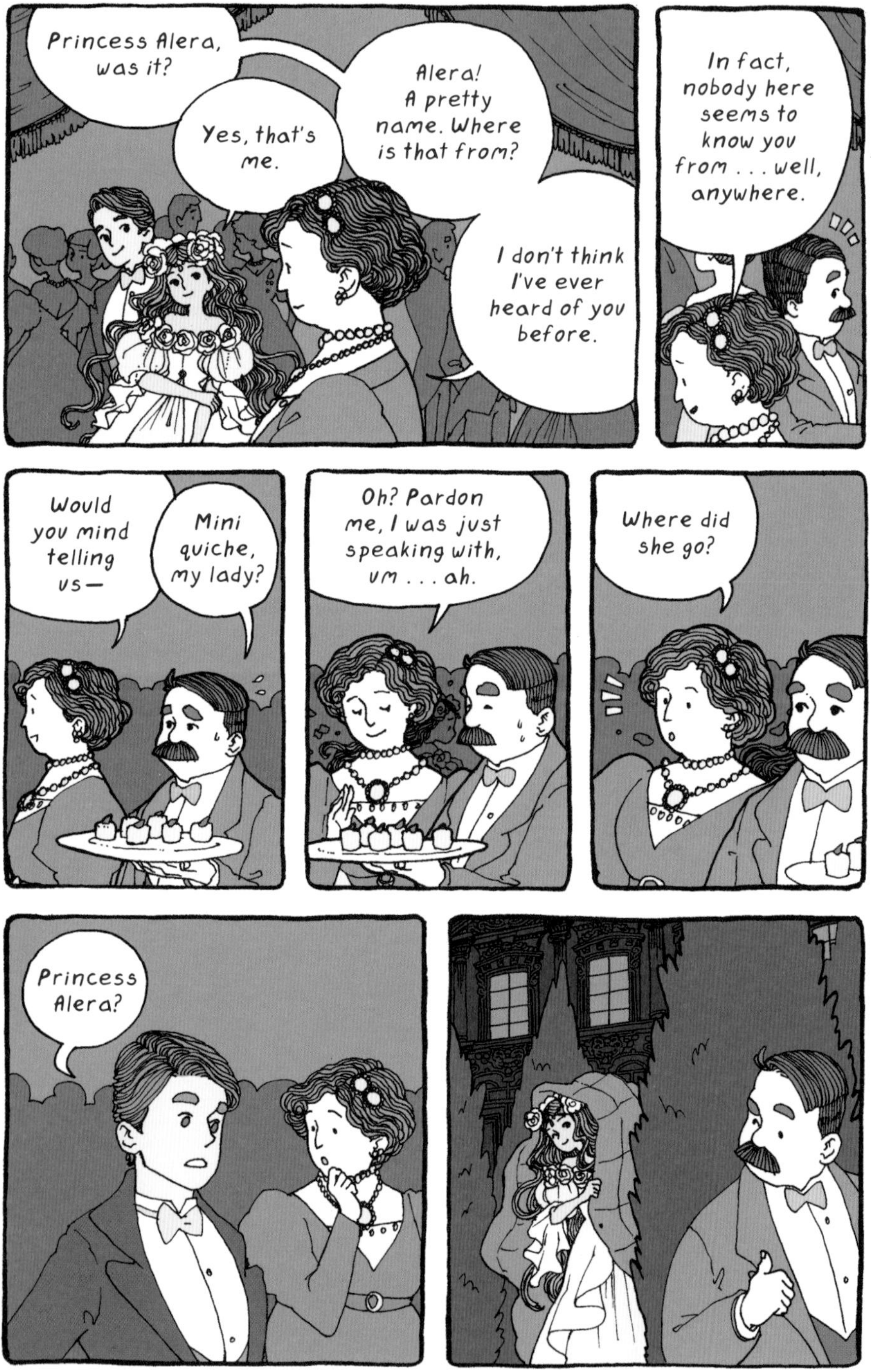
Princess Alera, was it?
Yes, that's me.
Alera! A pretty name. Where is that from?
I don't think I've ever heard of you before.
In fact, nobody here seems to know you from . . . well, anywhere.
Would you mind telling us—
Mini quiche, my lady?
Oh? Pardon me, I was just speaking with, um . . . ah.
Where did she go?
Princess Alera?

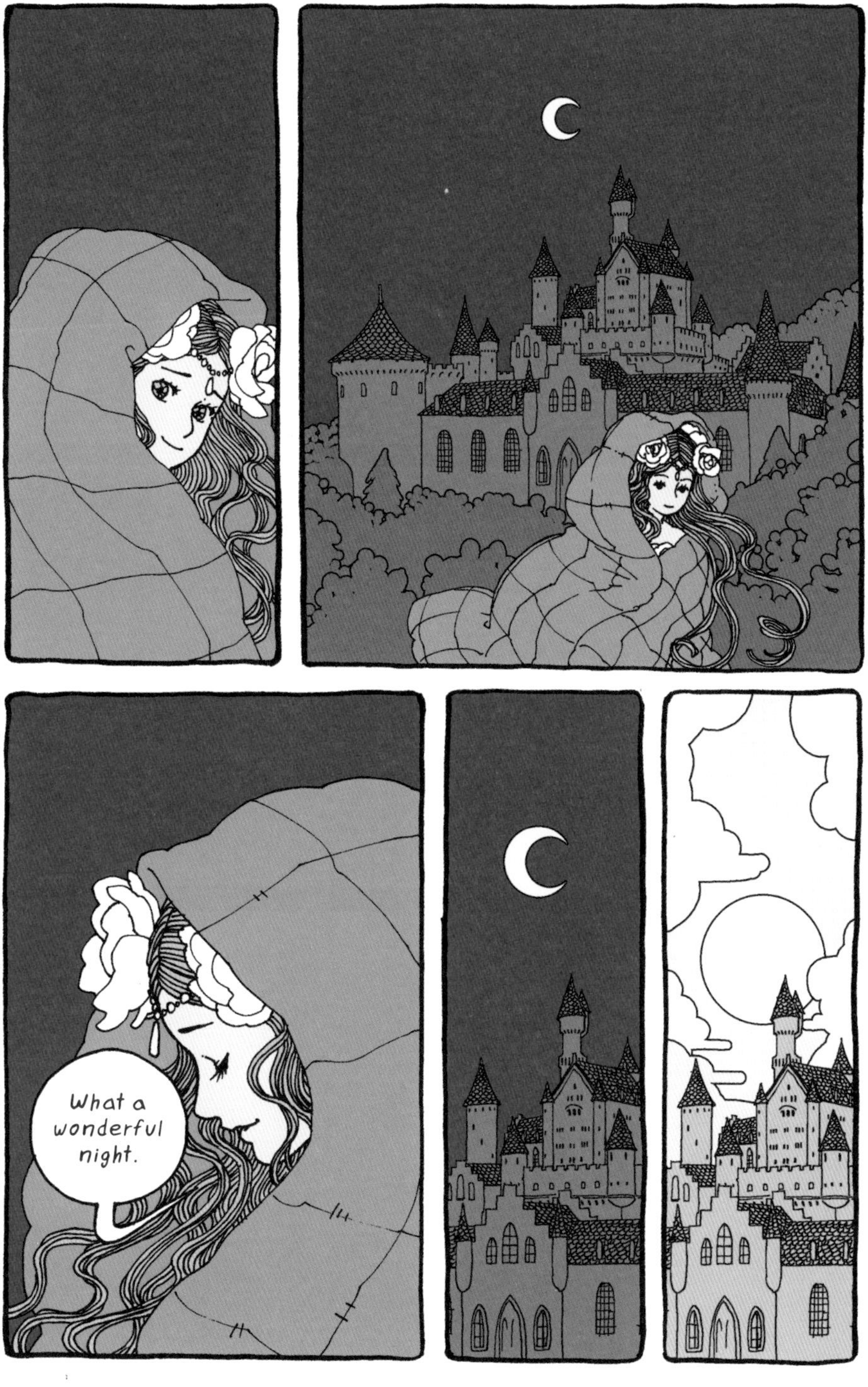
What a wonderful night.

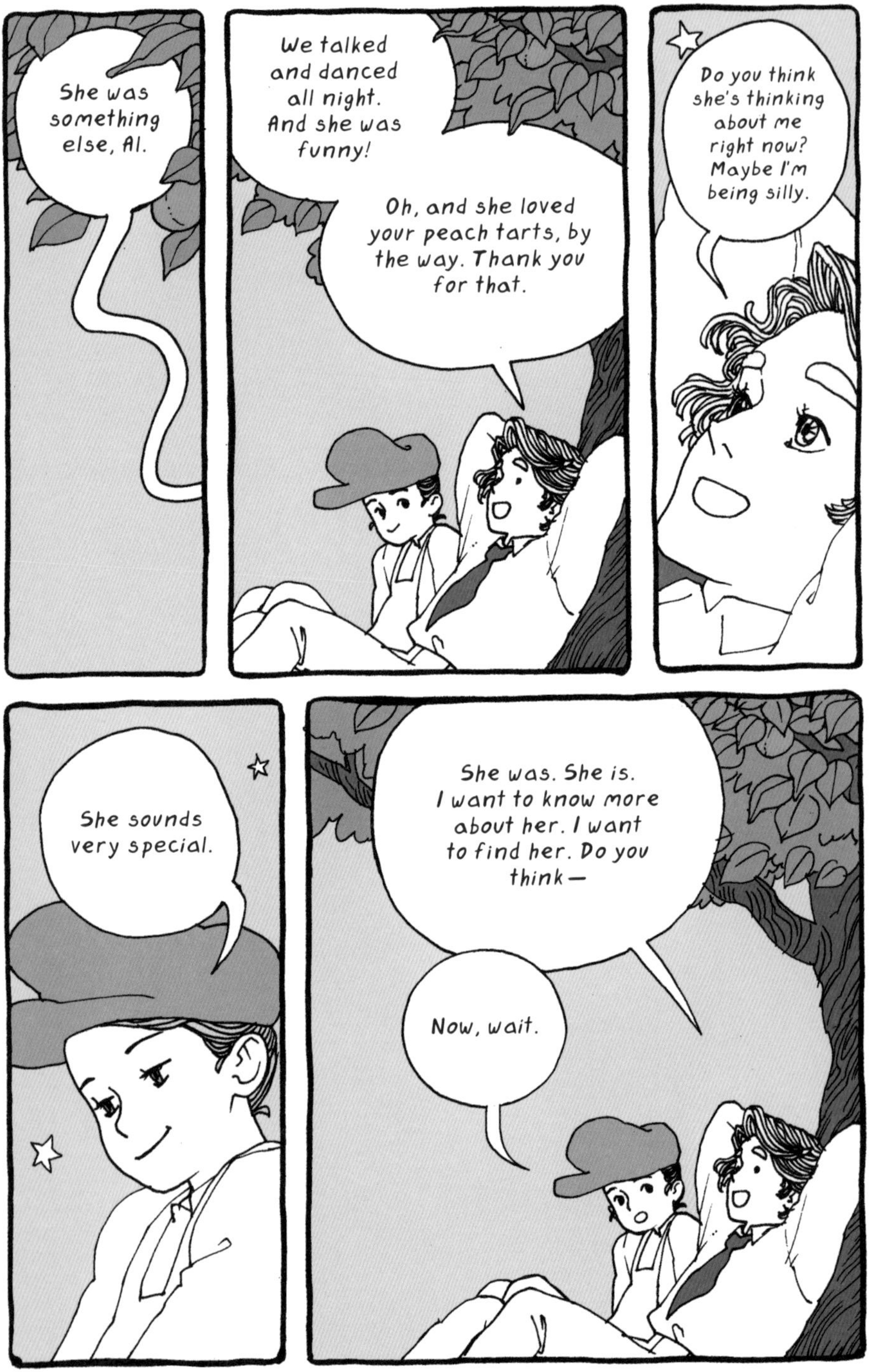
She was something else, Al.
We talked and danced all night. And she was funny!
Oh, and she loved your peach tarts, by the way. Thank you for that.
Do you think she's thinking about me right now? Maybe I'm being silly.
She sounds very special.
She was. She is. I want to know more about her. I want to find her. Do you think—
Now, wait.

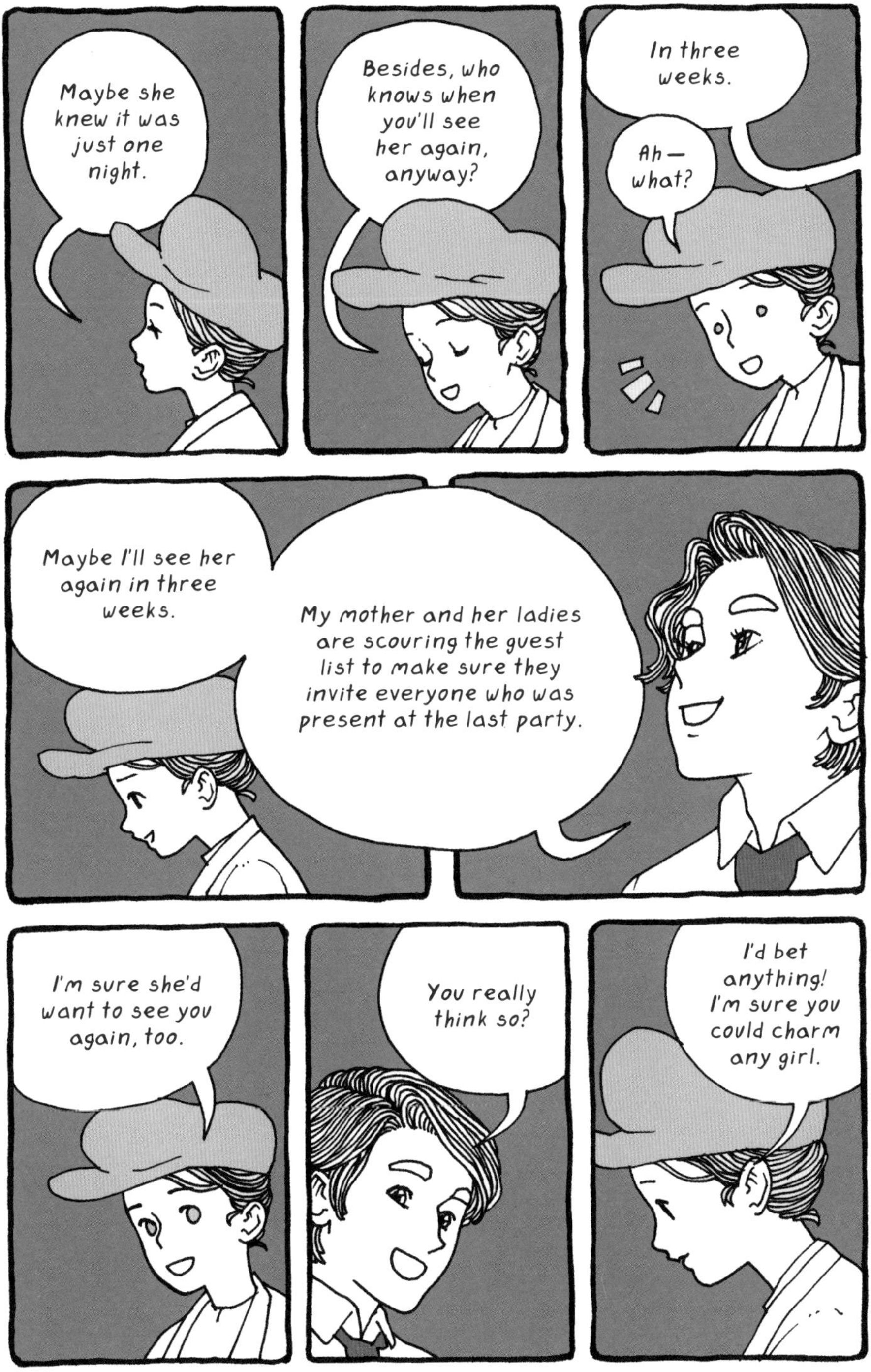

Maybe she knew it was just one night.
Besides, who knows when you'll see her again, anyway?
In three weeks.
Ah— what?
Maybe I'll see her again in three weeks.
My mother and her ladies are scouring the guest list to make sure they invite everyone who was present at the last party.
I'm sure she'd want to see you again, too.
You really think so?
I'd bet anything! I'm sure you could charm any girl.

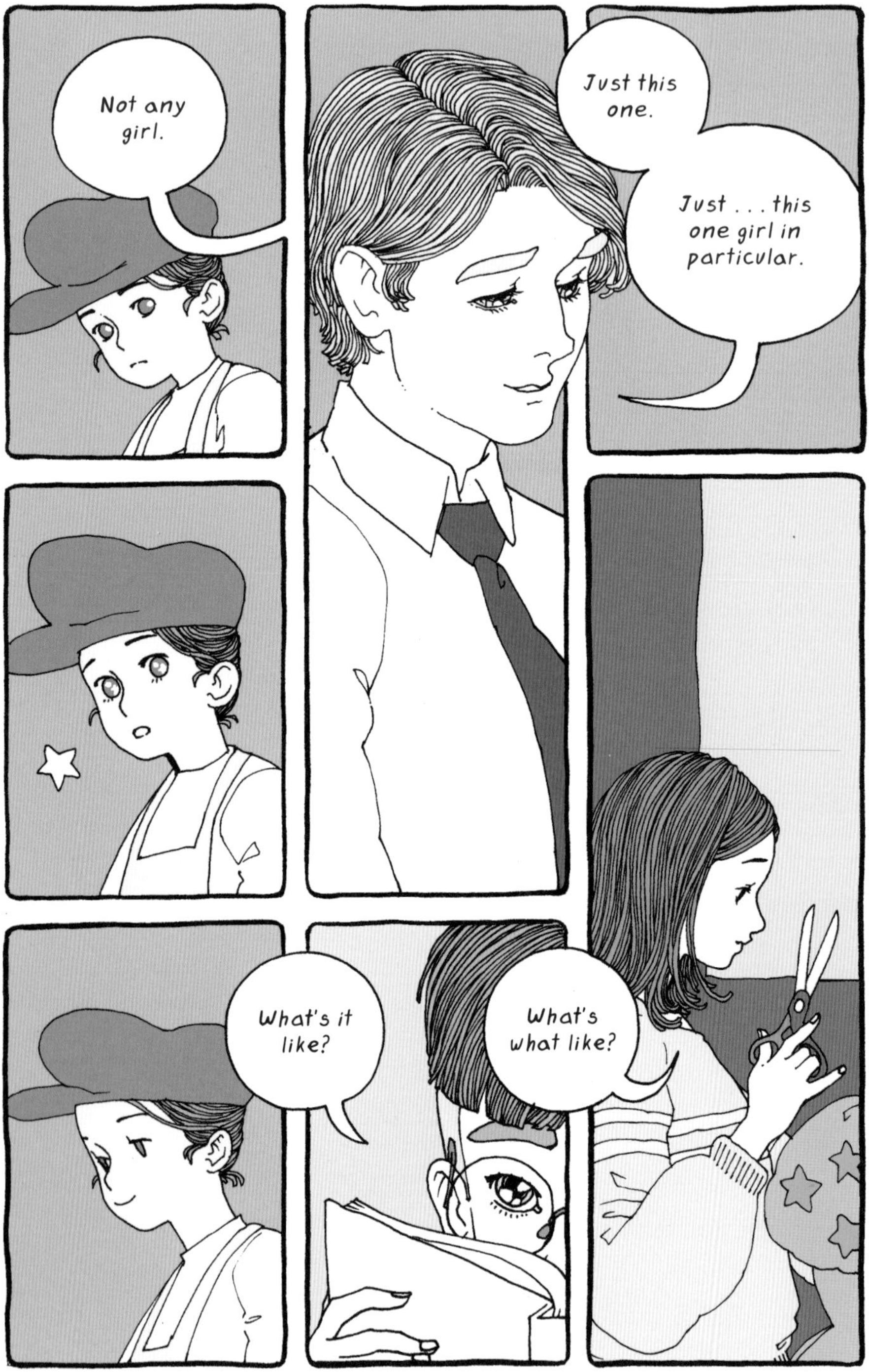
Not any girl.
Just this one.
Just . . . this one girl in particular.
What's it like?
What's what like?

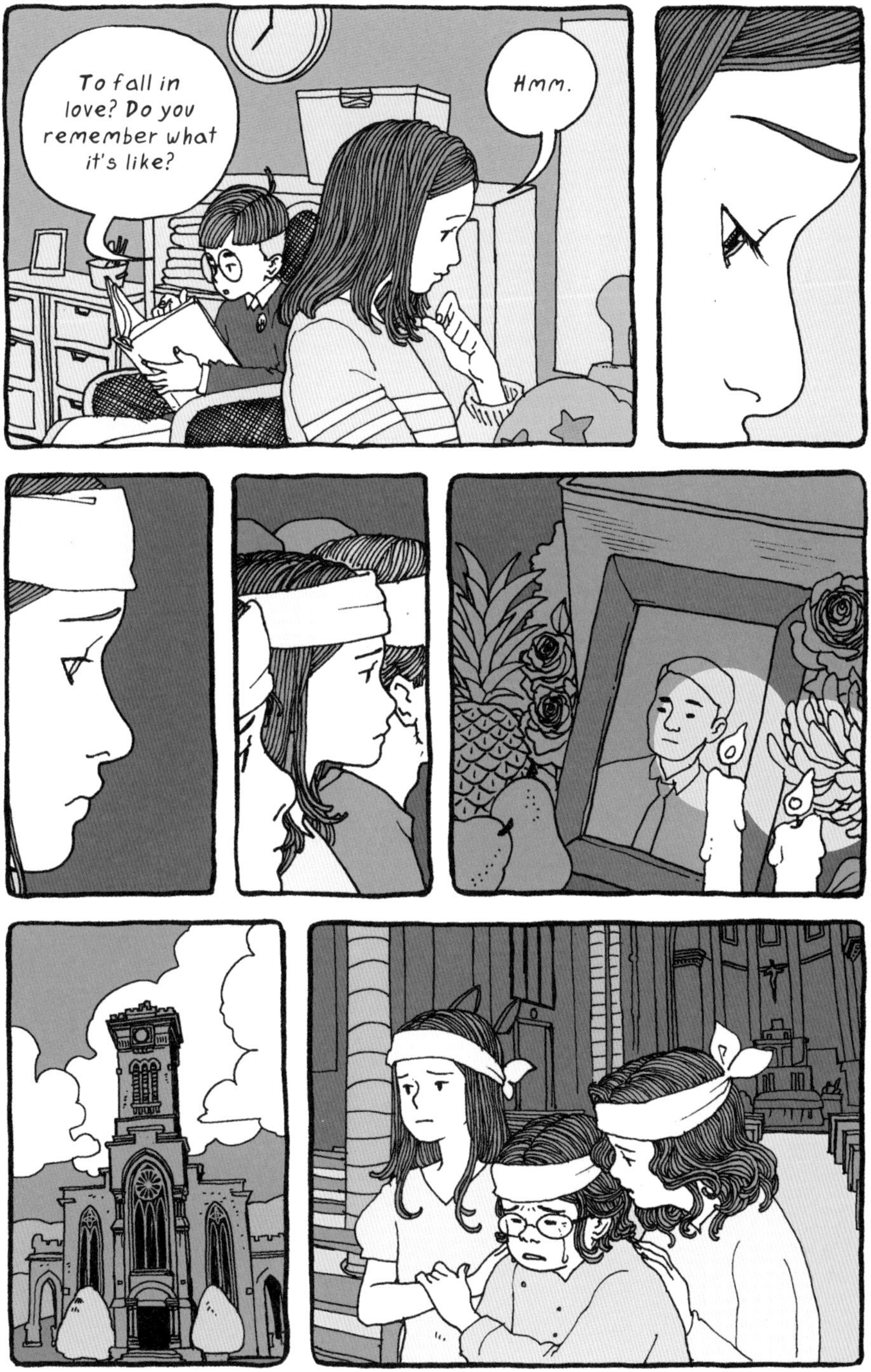
To fall in love? Do you remember what it's like?
Hmm.

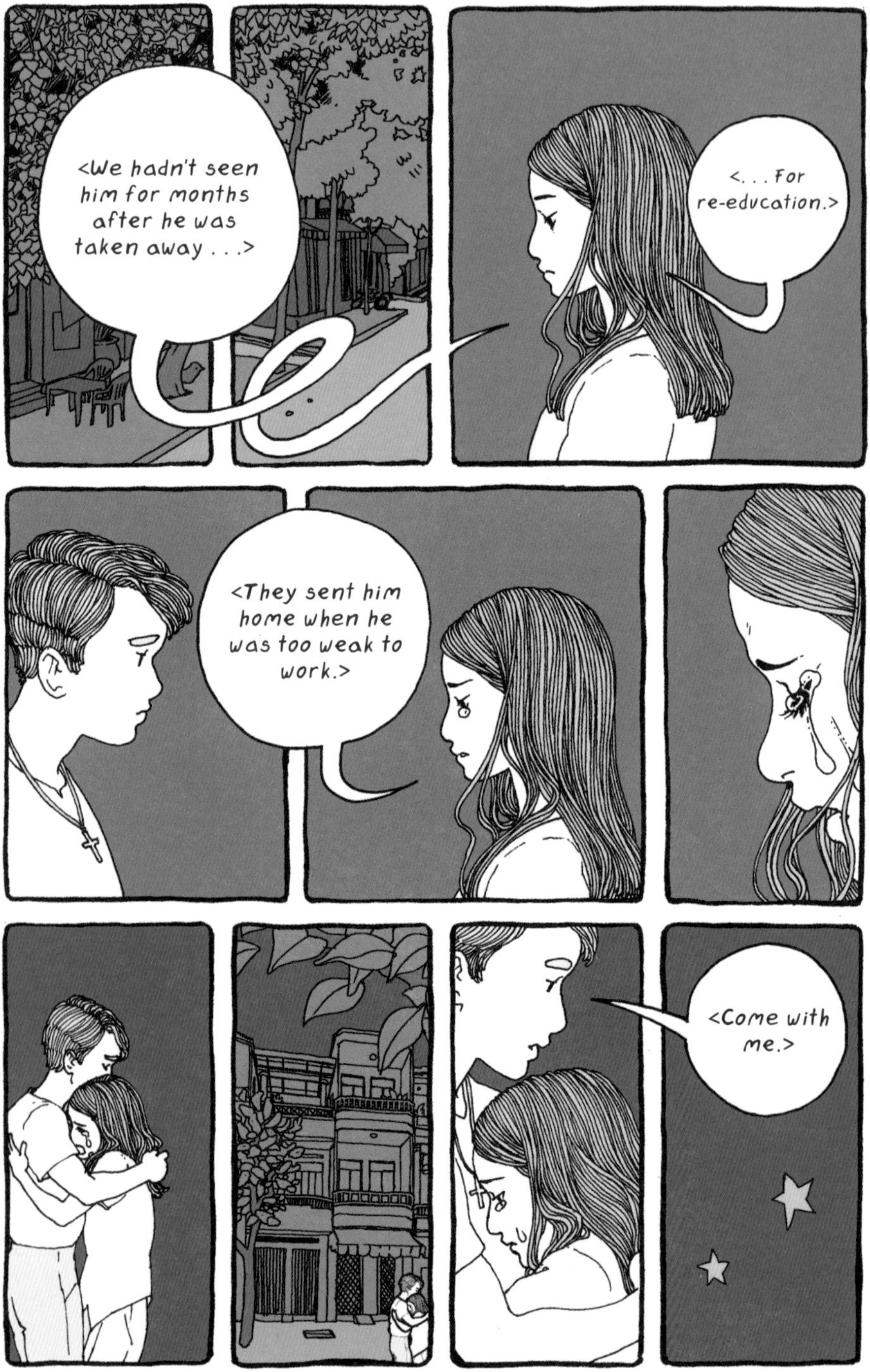
<We hadn't seen him for months after he was taken away . . .>
<. . . For re-education.>
<They sent him home when he was too weak to work.>
<Come with me.>

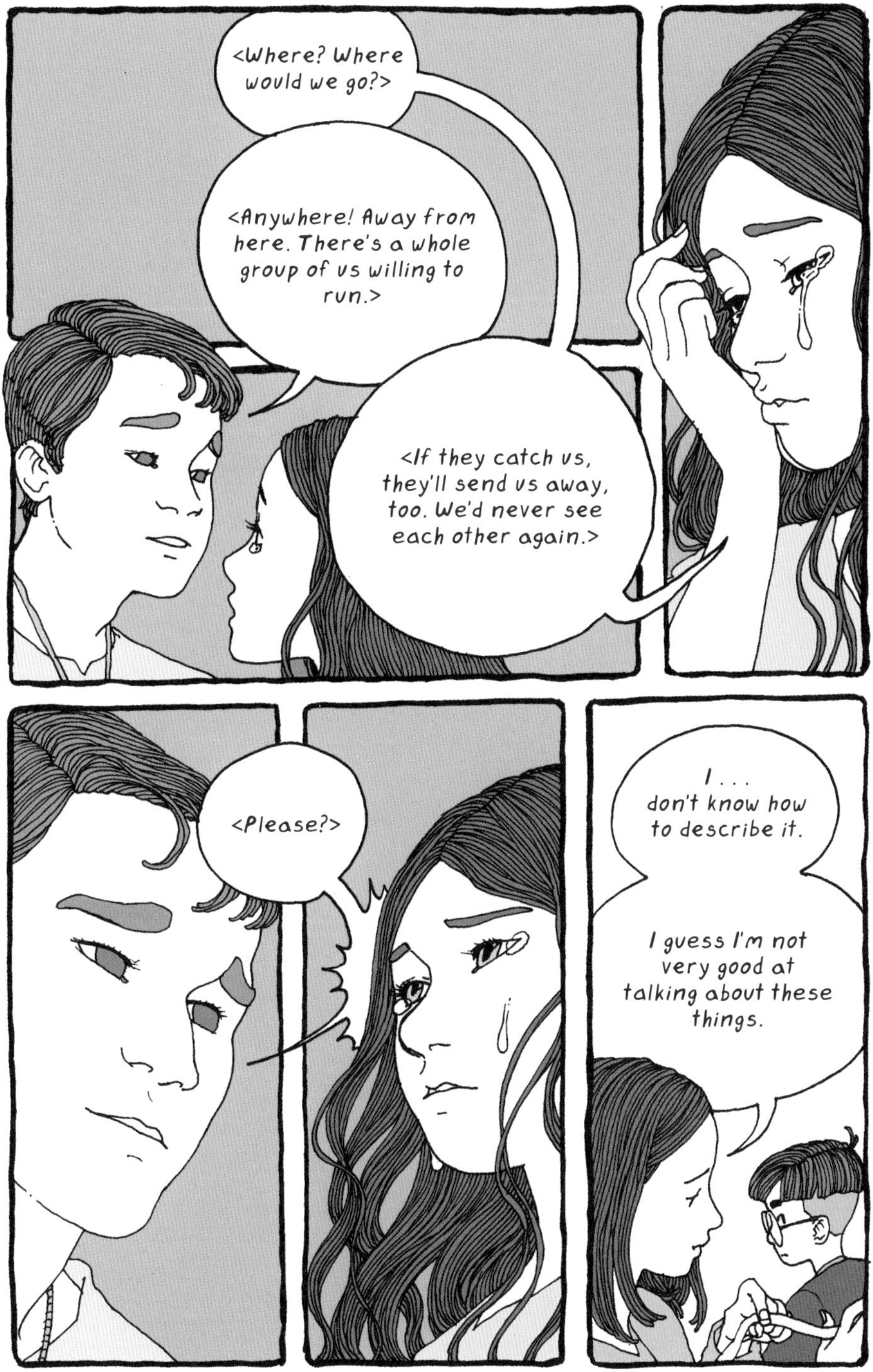
<Where? Where would we go?>
<Anywhere! Away from here. There's a whole group of us willing to run.>
<If they catch us, they'll send us away, too. We'd never see each other again.>
<Please?>
I . . . don't know how to describe it.
I guess I'm not very good at talking about these things.

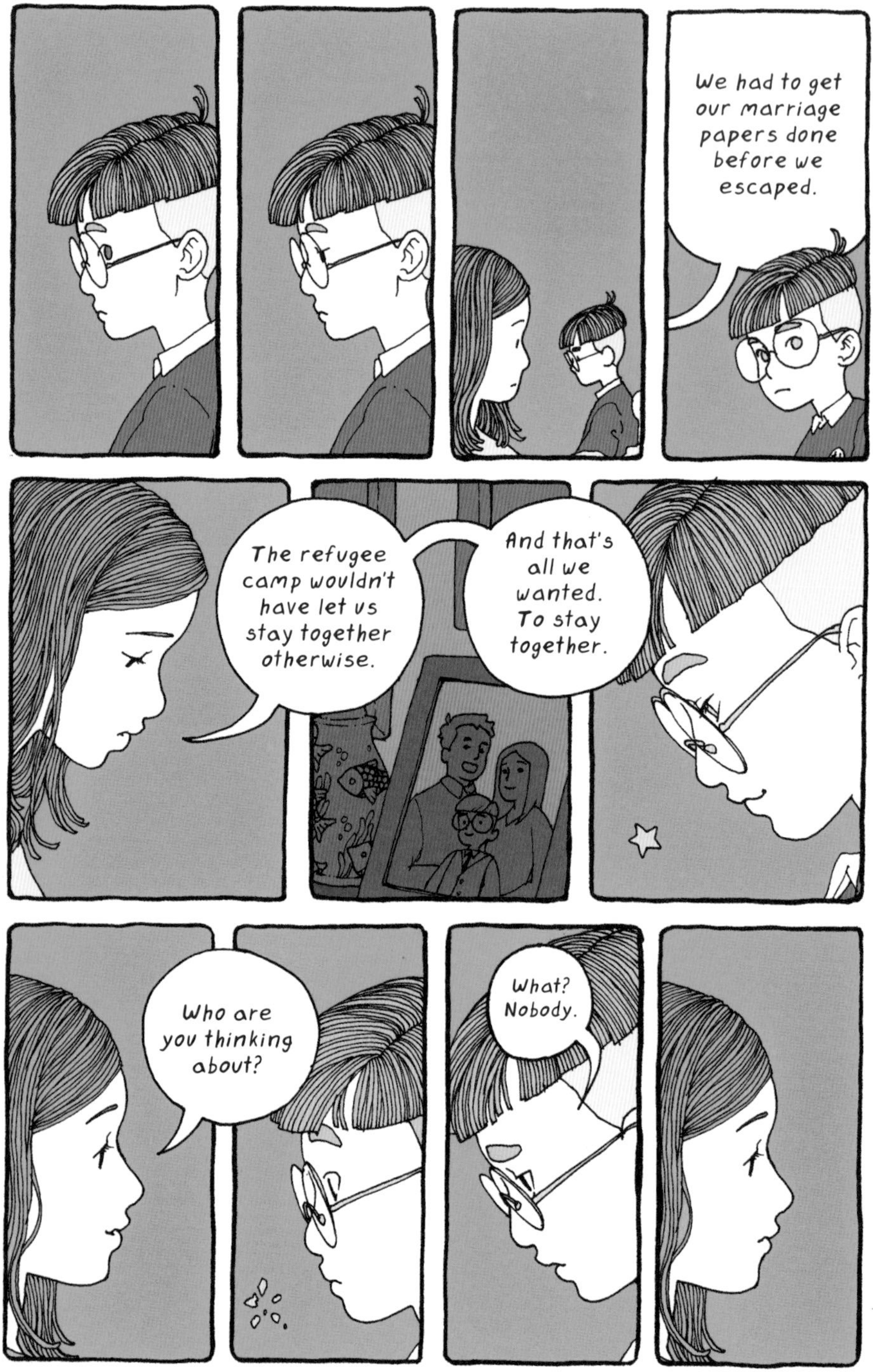
We had to get our marriage papers done before we escaped.
The refugee camp wouldn't have let us stay together otherwise.
And that's all we wanted. To stay together.
Who are you thinking about?
What? Nobody.

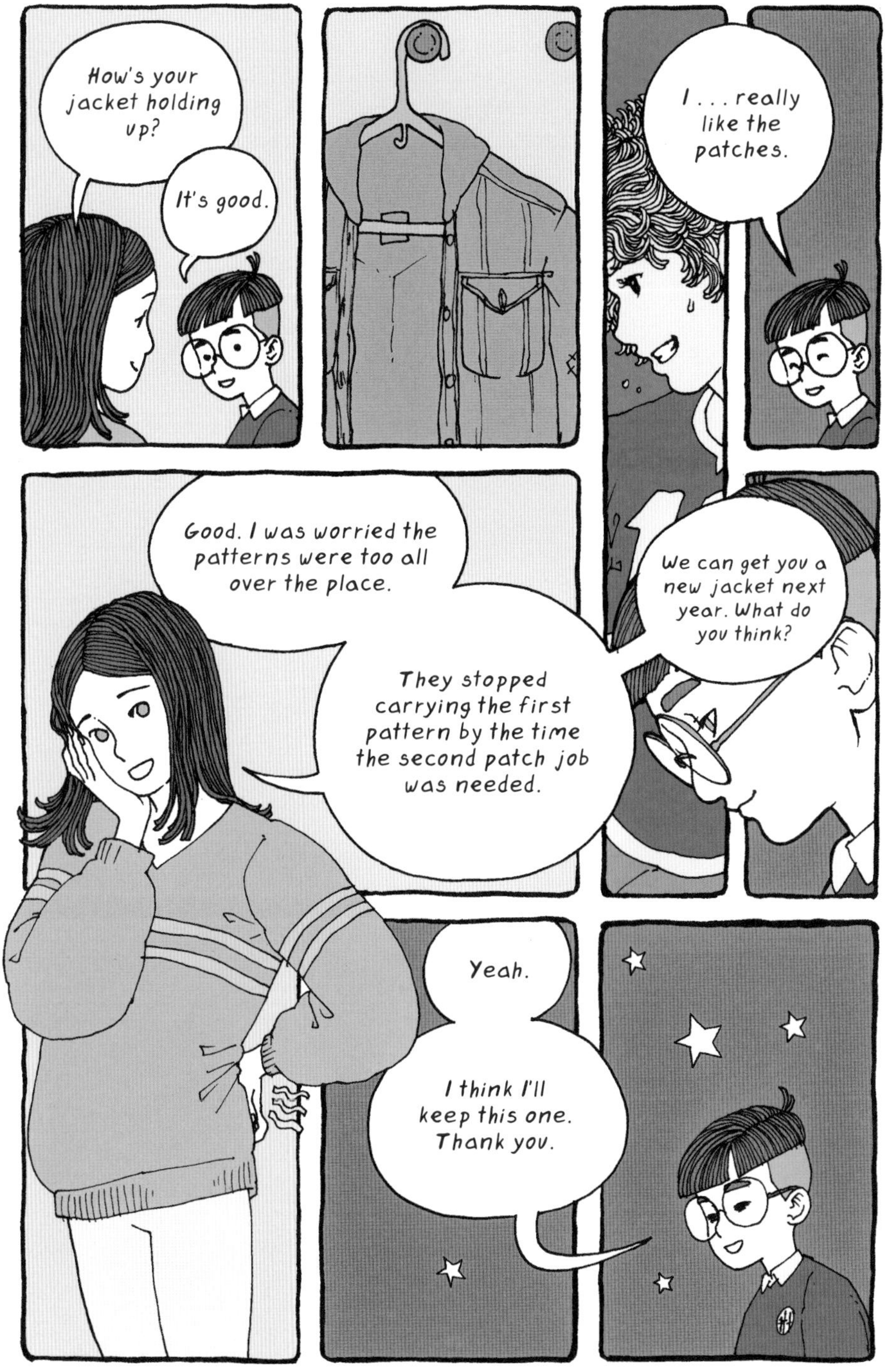

How's your jacket holding up?
It's good.
I . . . really like the patches.
Good. I was worried the patterns were too all over the place.
They stopped carrying the first pattern by the time the second patch job was needed.
We can get you a new jacket next year. What do you think?
Yeah.
I think I'll keep this one. Thank you.

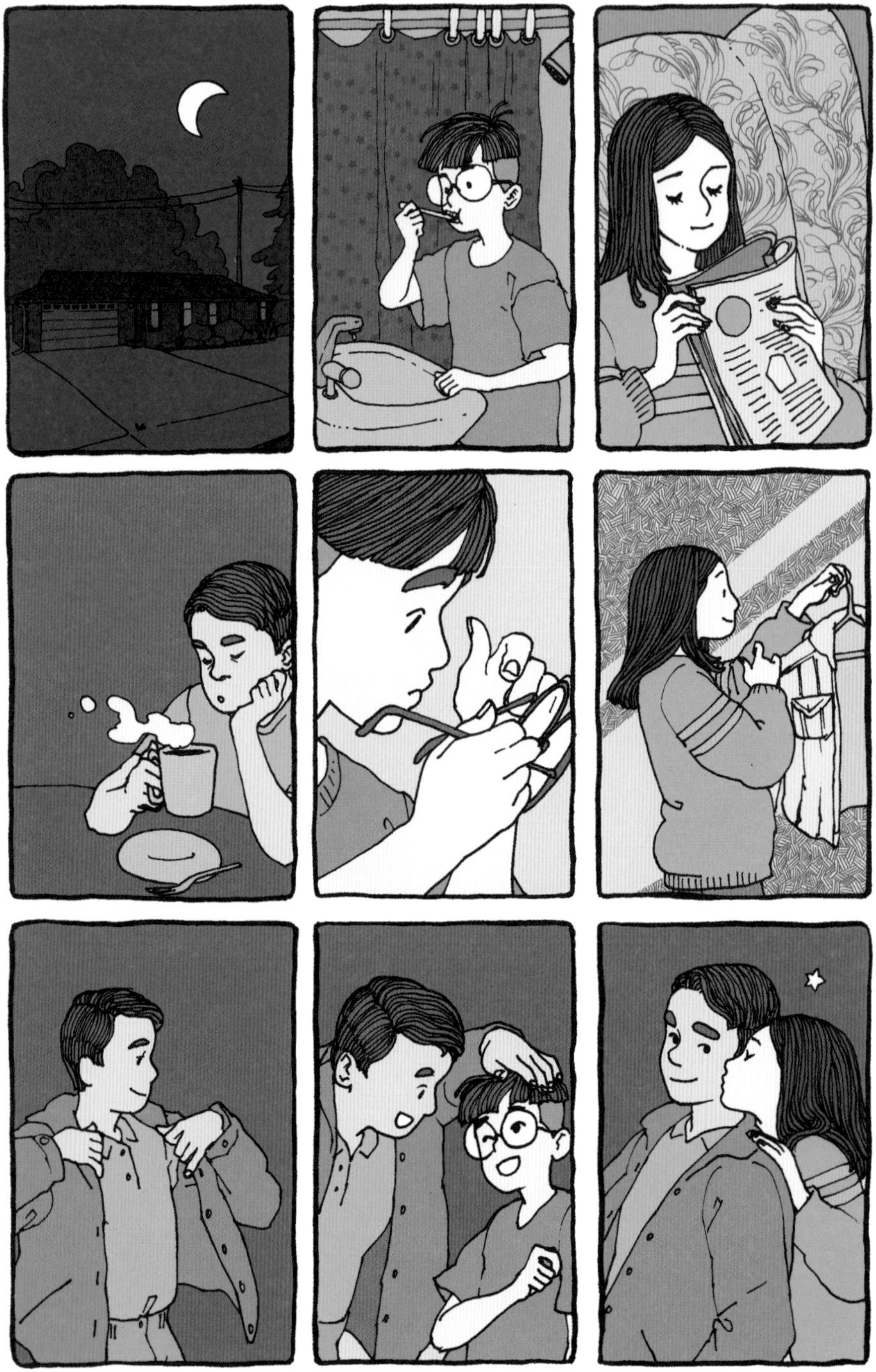

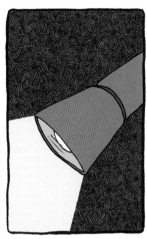

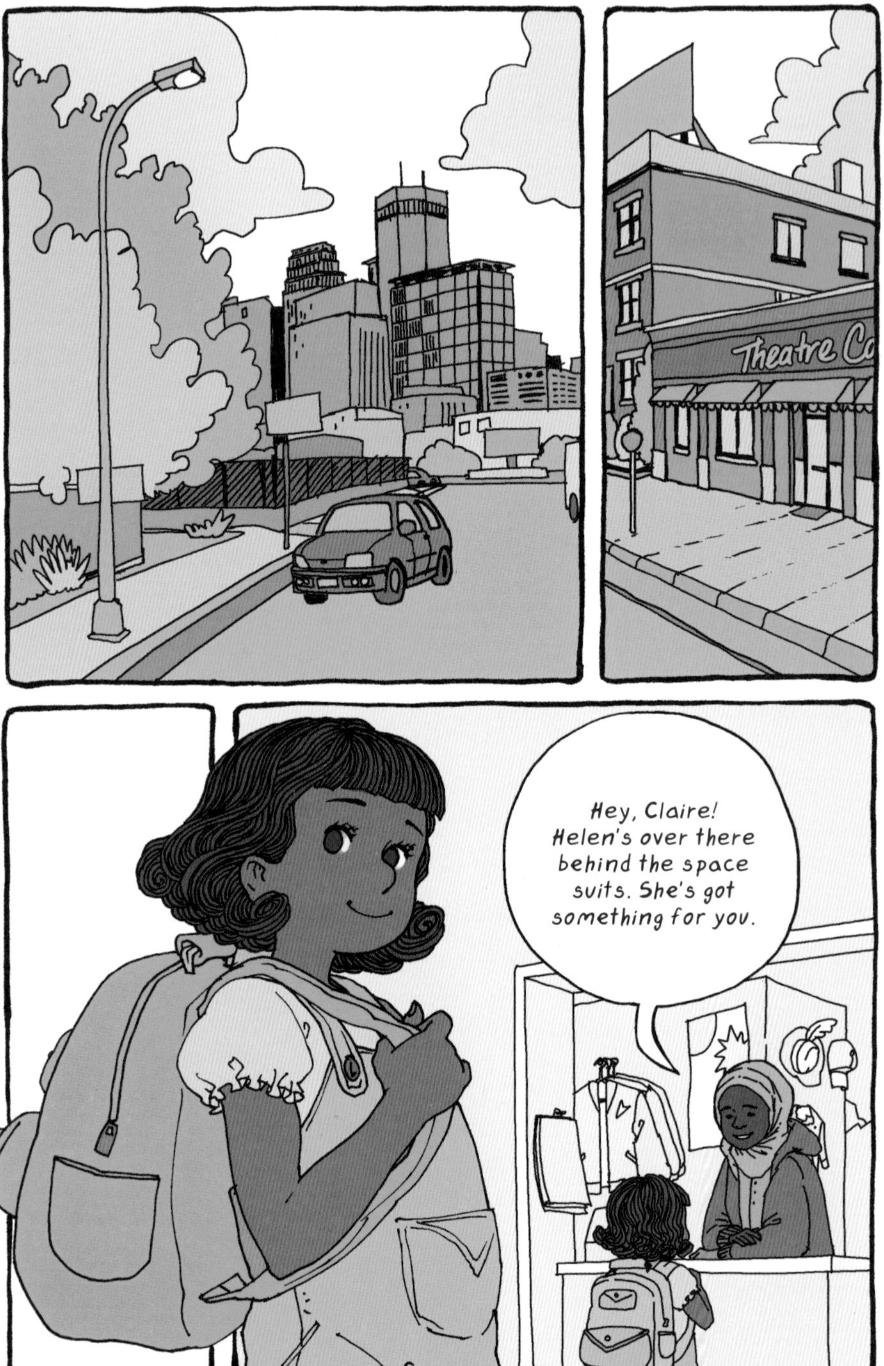
Theatre Co
Hey, Claire! Helen's over there behind the space suits. She's got something for you.

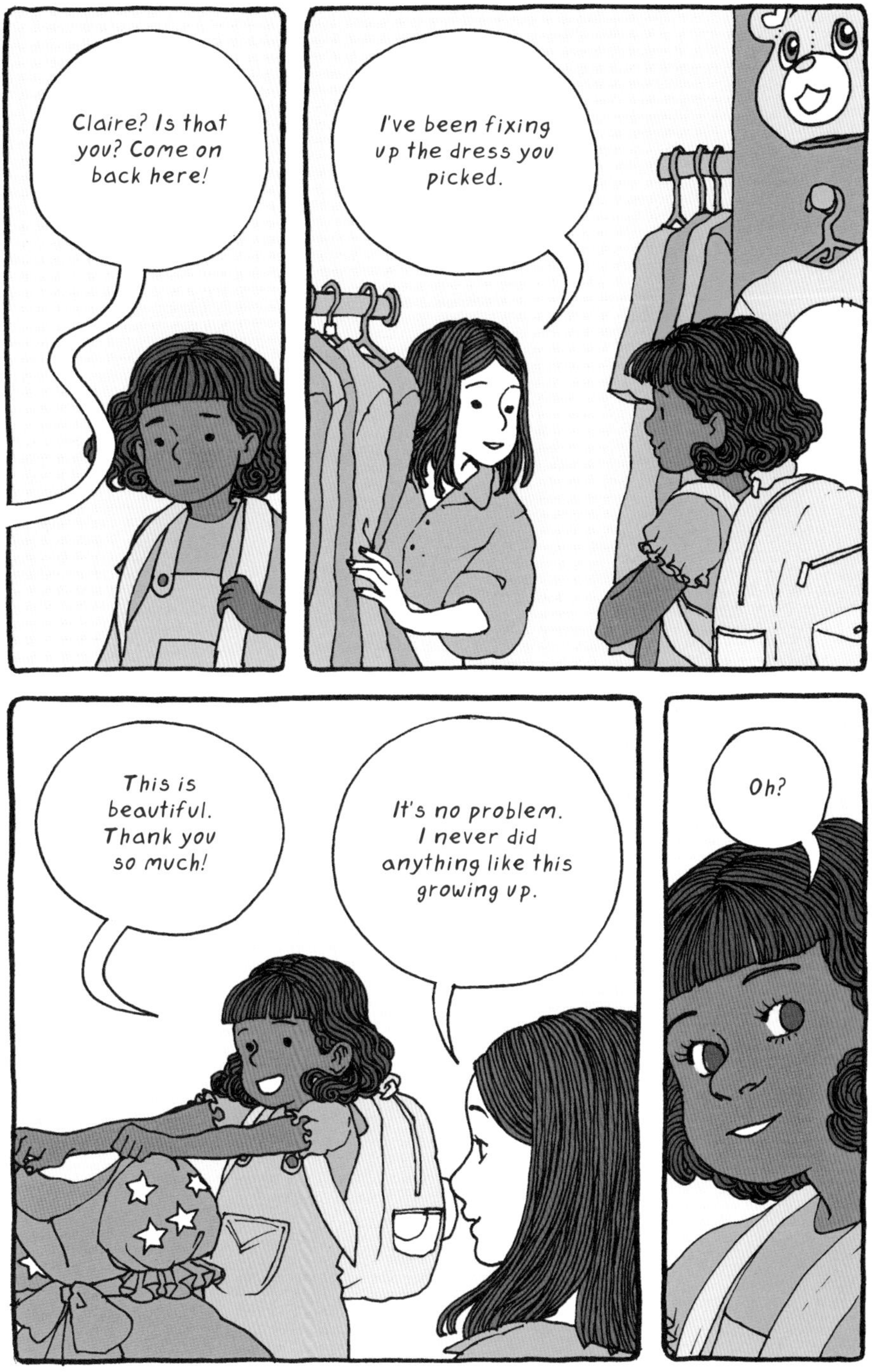
Claire? Is that you? Come on back here!
I've been fixing up the dress you picked.
This is beautiful. Thank you so much!
It's no problem. I never did anything like this growing up.
Oh?

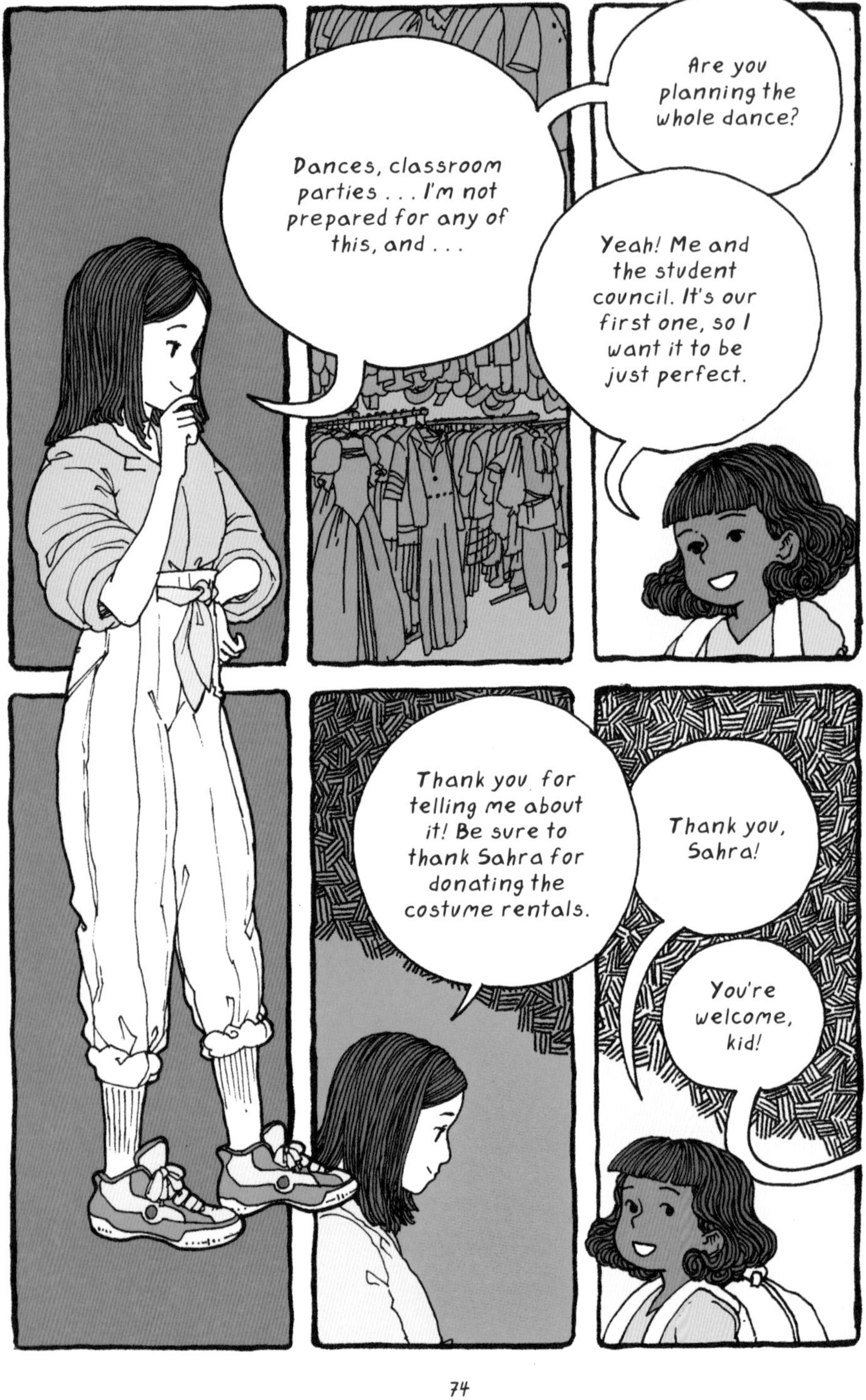
Are you planning the whole dance?
Dances, classroom parties . . . I'm not prepared for any of this, and . . .
Yeah! Me and the student council. It's our first one, so I want it to be just perfect.
Thank you for telling me about it! Be sure to thank Sahra for donating the costume rentals.
Thank you, Sahra!
You're welcome, kid!

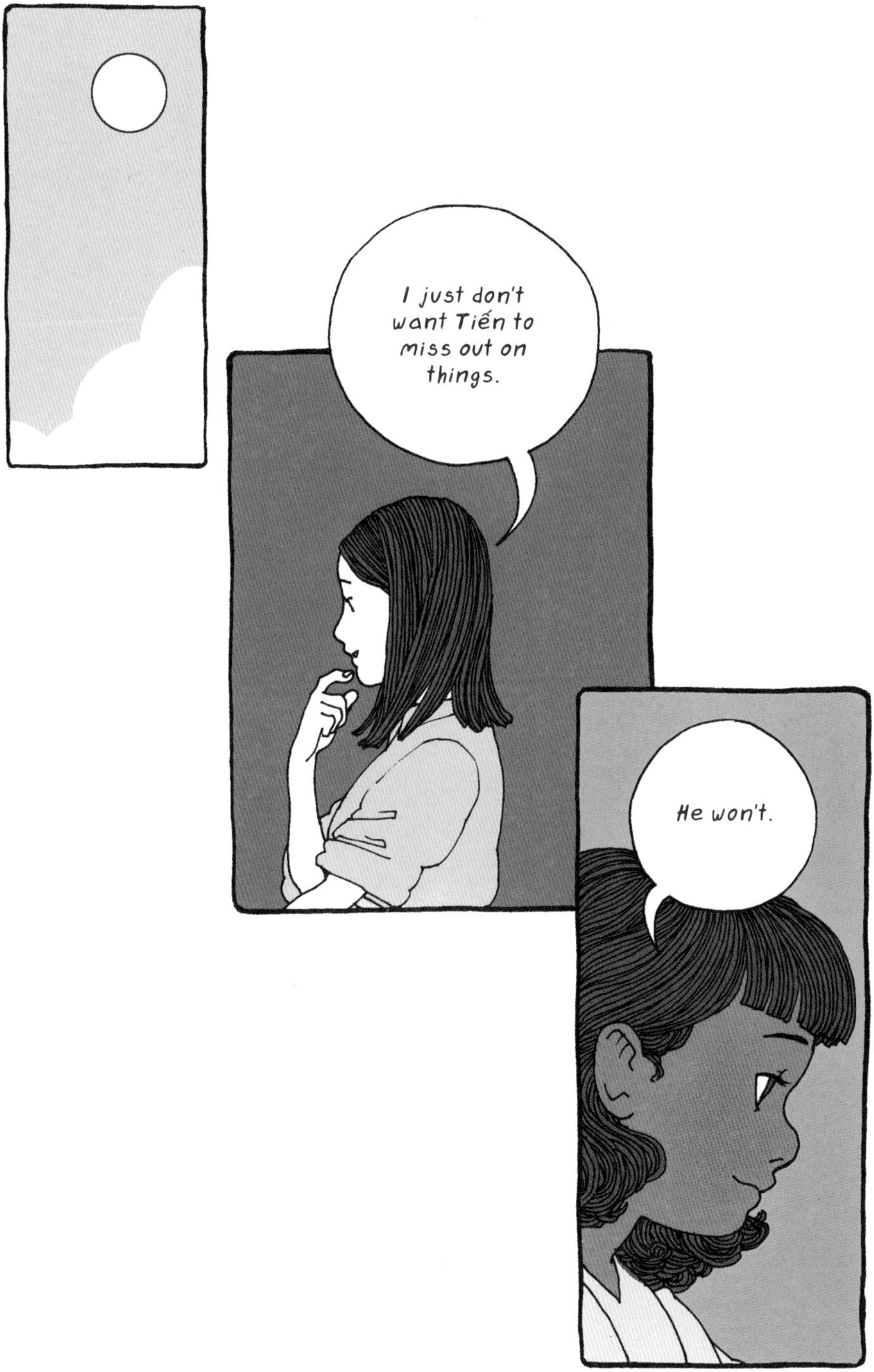
I just don't want Tiến to miss out on things.
He won't.

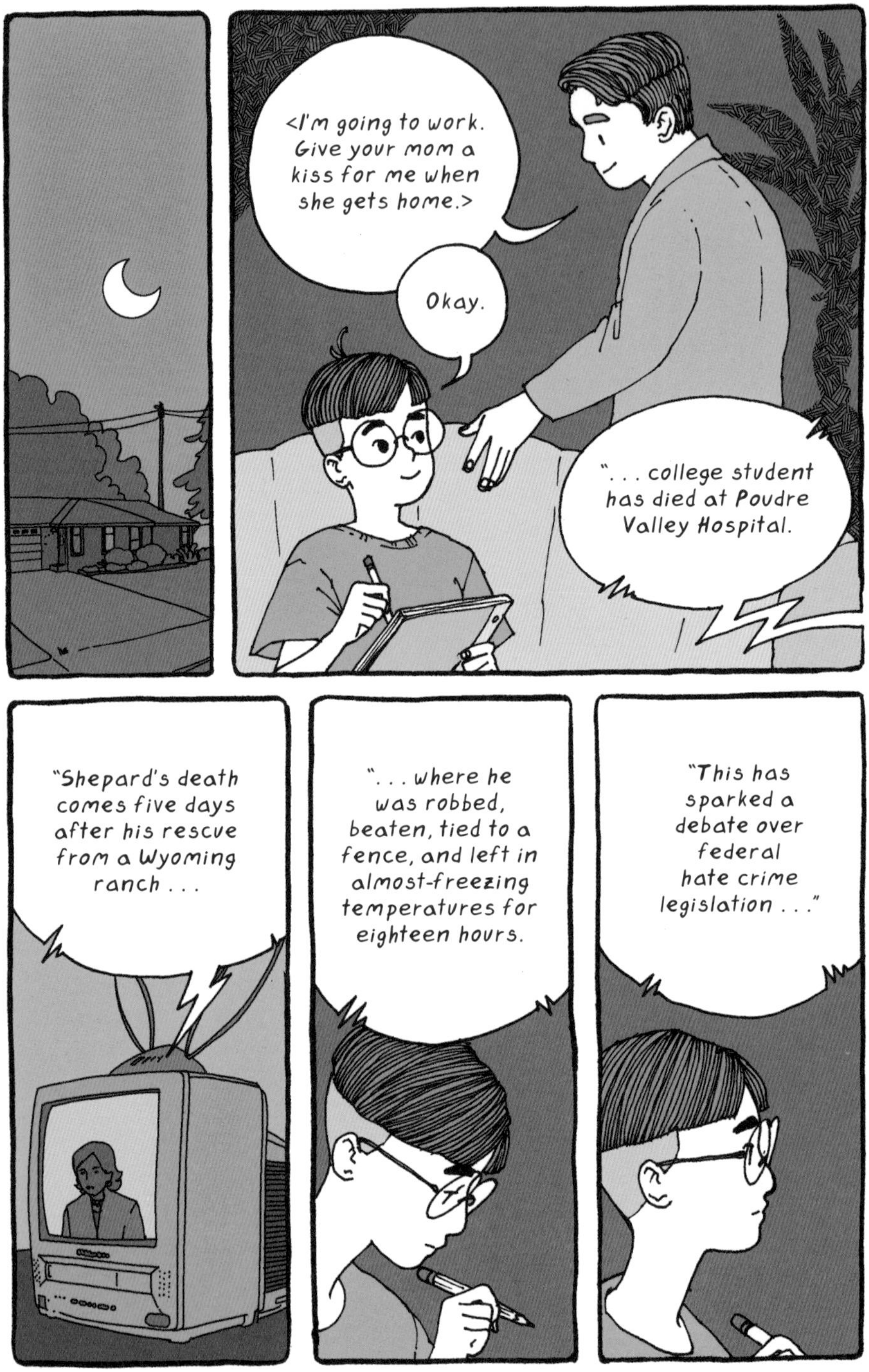
<I'm going to work. Give your mom a kiss for me when she gets home.>
Okay.
". . . college student has died at Poudre Valley Hospital.
"Shepard's death comes five days after his rescue from a Wyoming ranch . . .
". . . where he was robbed, beaten, tied to a fence, and left in almost-freezing temperatures for eighteen hours.
"This has sparked a debate over federal hate crime legislation . . ."

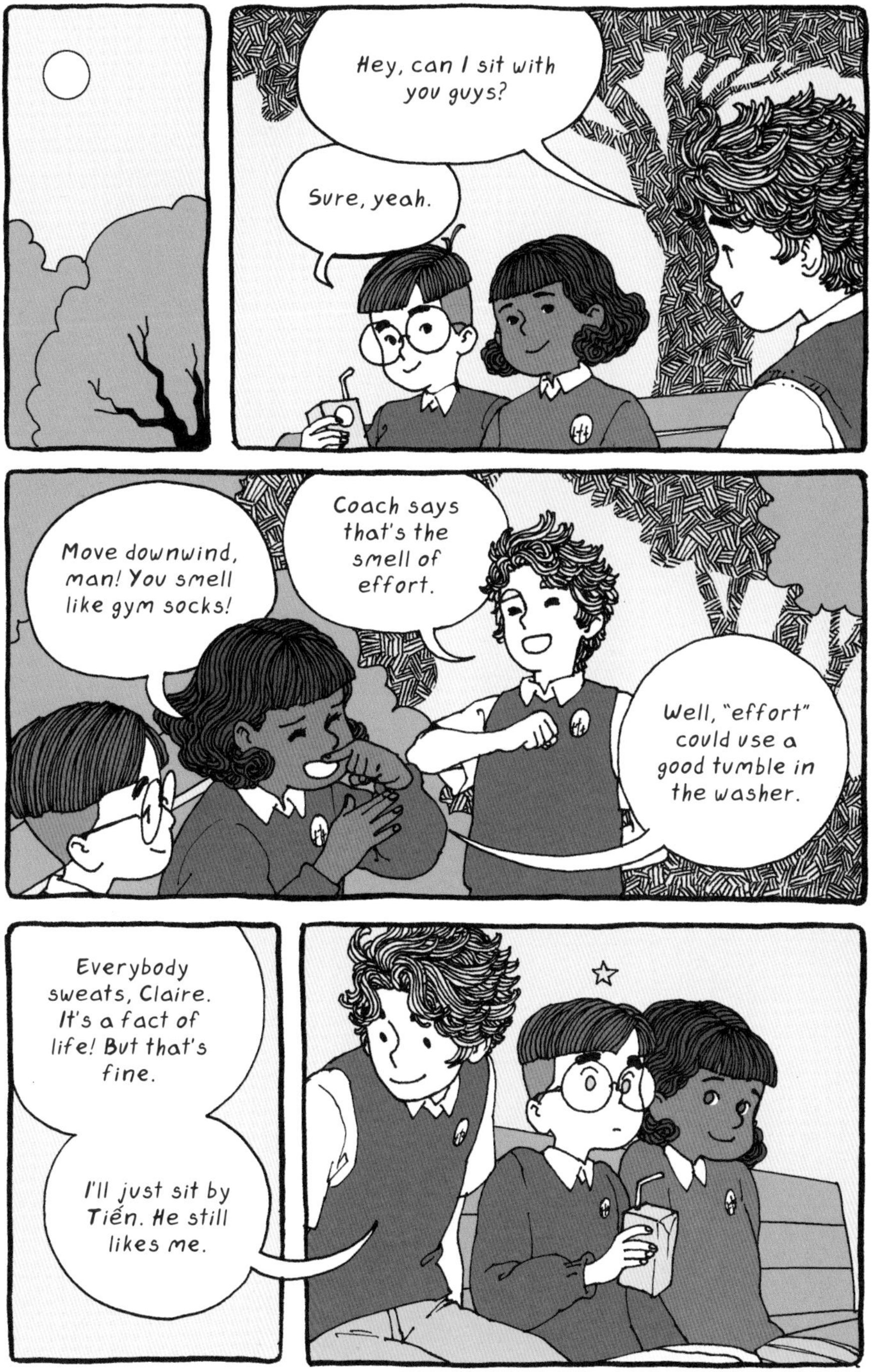

Hey, can I sit with you guys?
Sure, yeah.
Move downwind, man! You smell like gym socks!
Coach says that's the smell of effort.
Well, "effort" could use a good tumble in the washer.
Everybody sweats, Claire. It's a fact of life! But that's fine.
I'll just sit by Tiến. He still likes me.

You coming to my next game?

I'm planning on it.

Is that a yes?

It's a yes.

Awesome. Claire?

Maybe if you go to one of my things.

What thing?

Like . . . the Back to School Dance. Wanna go with me and Tiến?

Yeah, sure. Why not.

Excellent. That was easy.

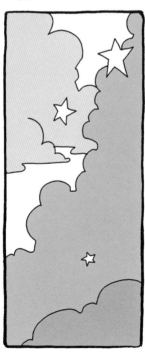

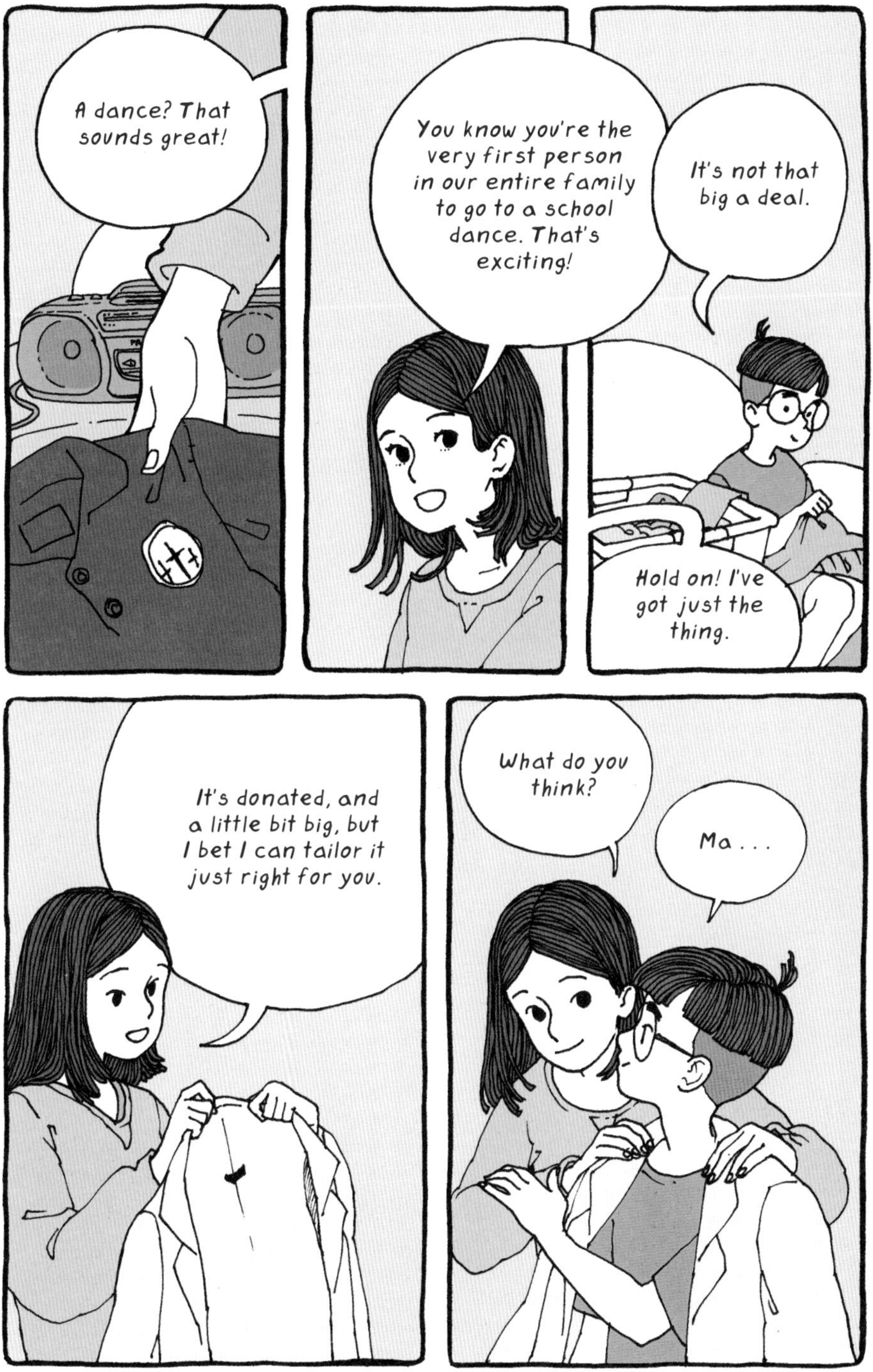
A dance? That sounds great!
You know you're the very first person in our entire family to go to a school dance. That's exciting!
It's not that big a deal.
Hold on! I've got just the thing.
It's donated, and a little bit big, but I bet I can tailor it just right for you.
What do you think?
Ma . . .

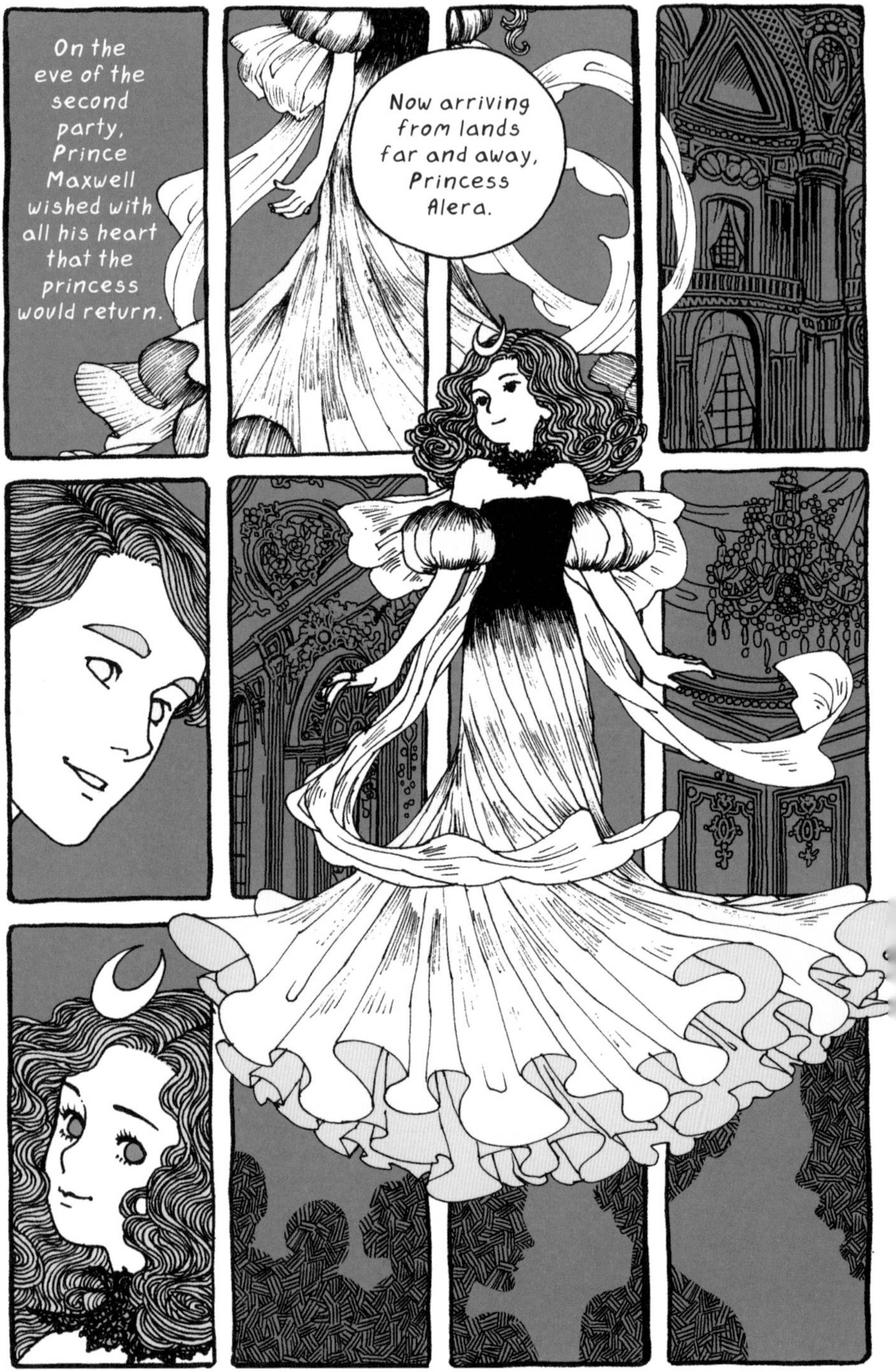
On the eve of the second party, Prince Maxwell wished with all his heart that the princess would return.
Now arriving from lands far and away, Princess Alera.

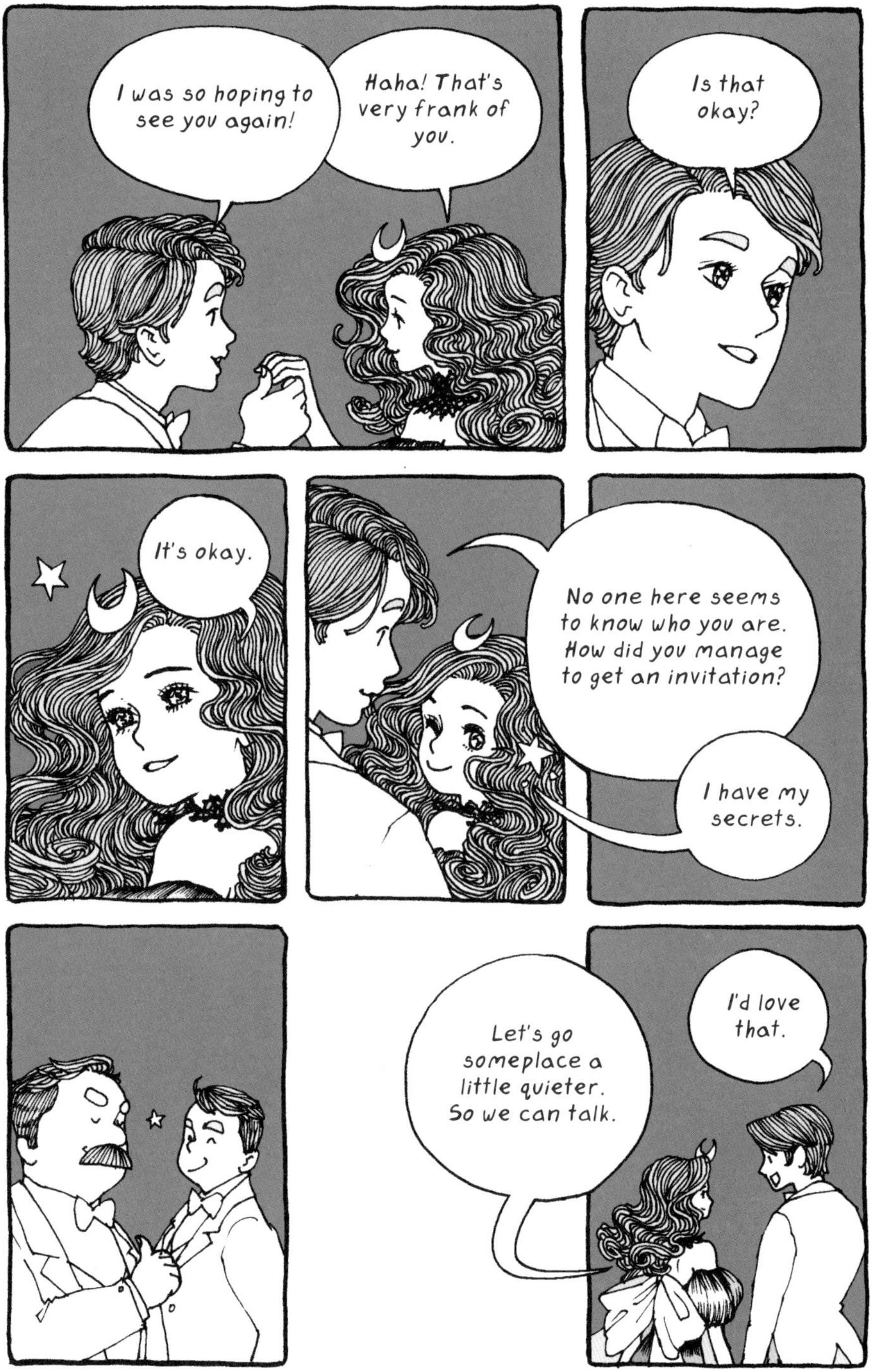
I was so hoping to see you again!
Haha! That's very frank of you.
Is that okay?
It's okay.
No one here seems to know who you are. How did you manage to get an invitation?
I have my secrets.
Let's go someplace a little quieter. So we can talk.
I'd love that.

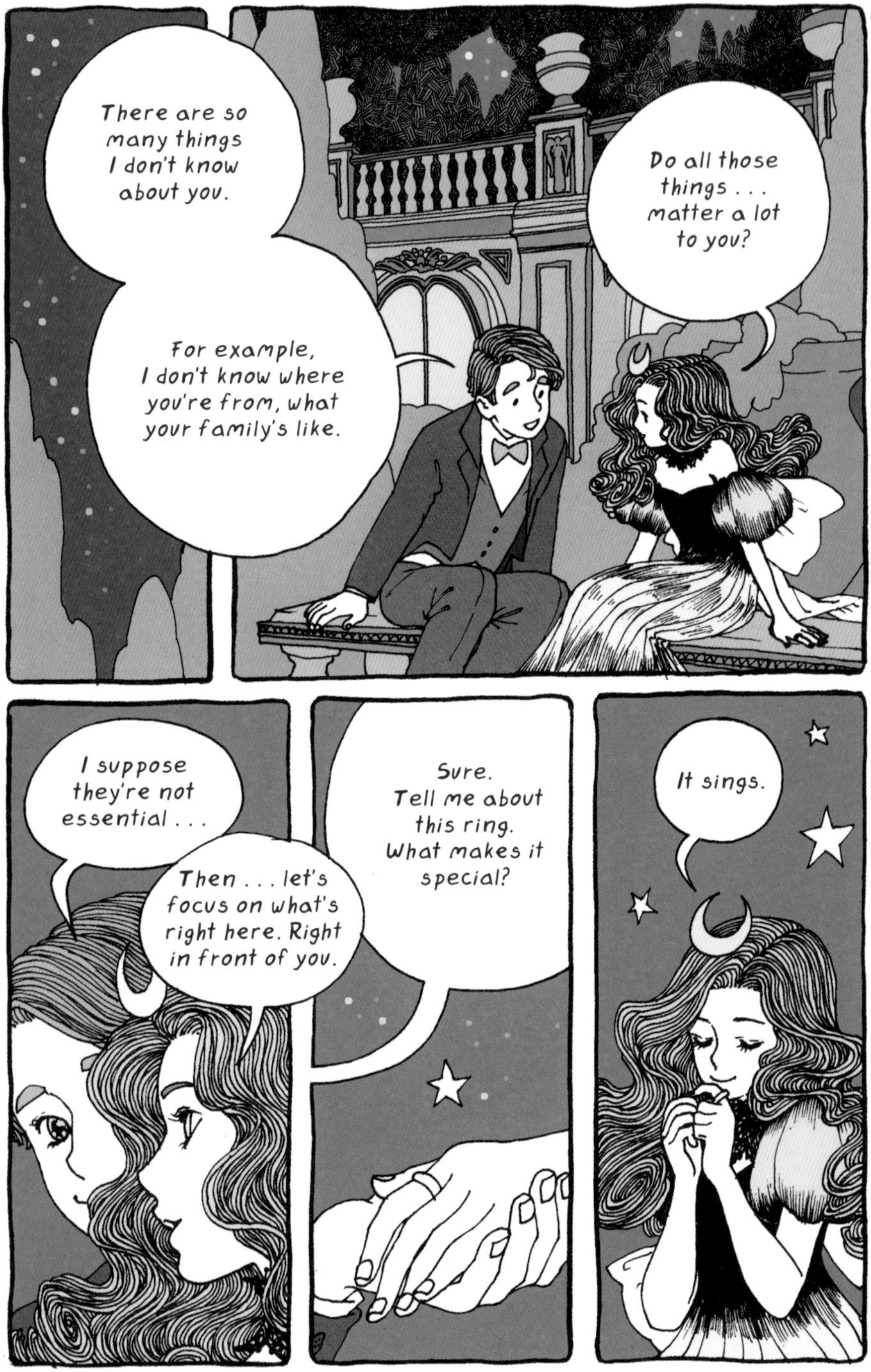
There are so many things I don't know about you.
For example, I don't know where you're from, what your family's like.
Do all those things . . . matter a lot to you?
I suppose they're not essential . . .
Then . . . let's focus on what's right here. Right in front of you.
Sure. Tell me about this ring. What makes it special?
It sings.

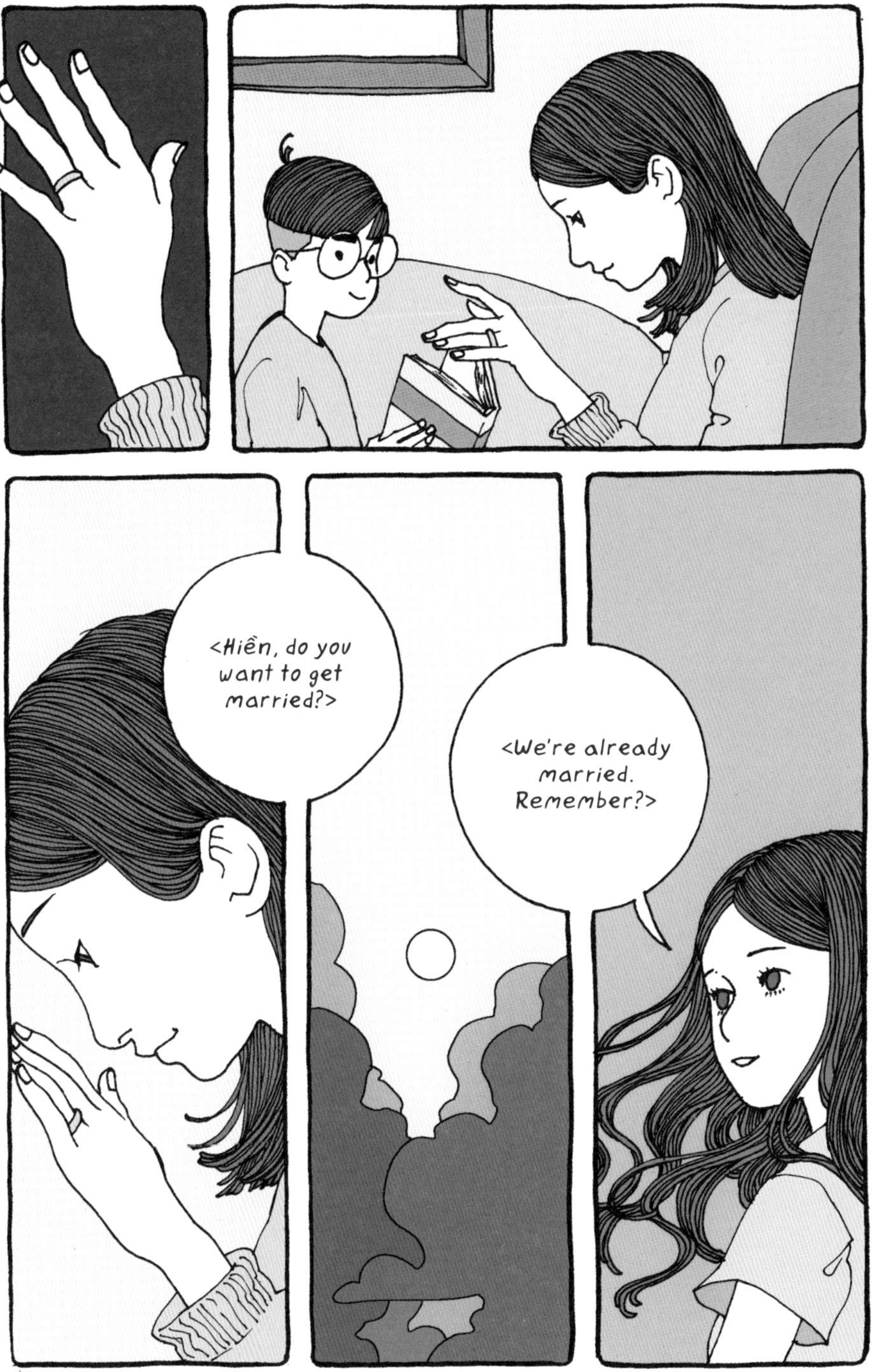
<Hiền, do you want to get married?>
<We're already married. Remember?>

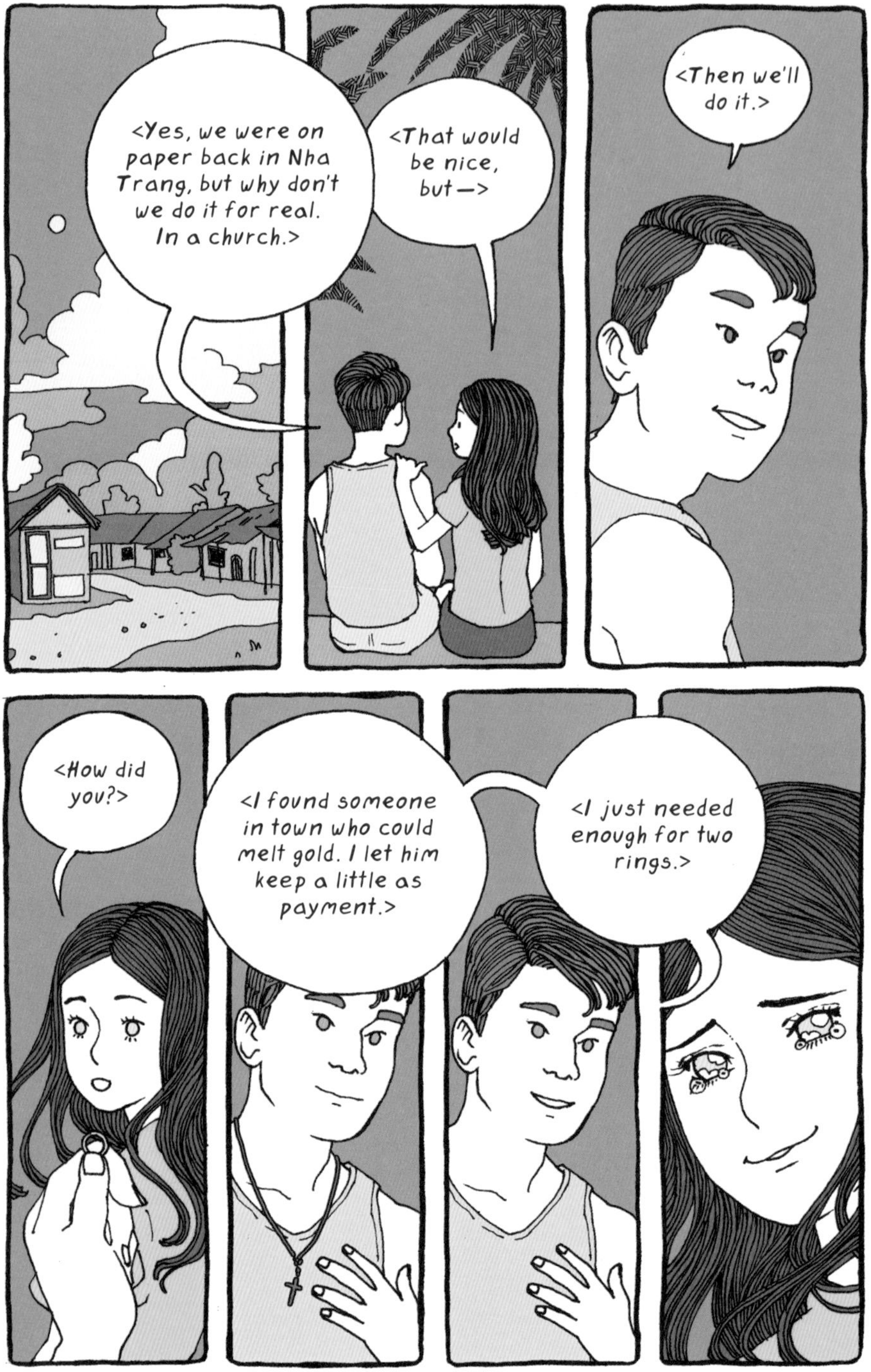
<Yes, we were on paper back in Nha Trang, but why don't we do it for real. In a church.>
<That would be nice, but—>
<Then we'll do it.>
<How did you?>
<I found someone in town who could melt gold. I let him keep a little as payment.>
<I just needed enough for two rings.>

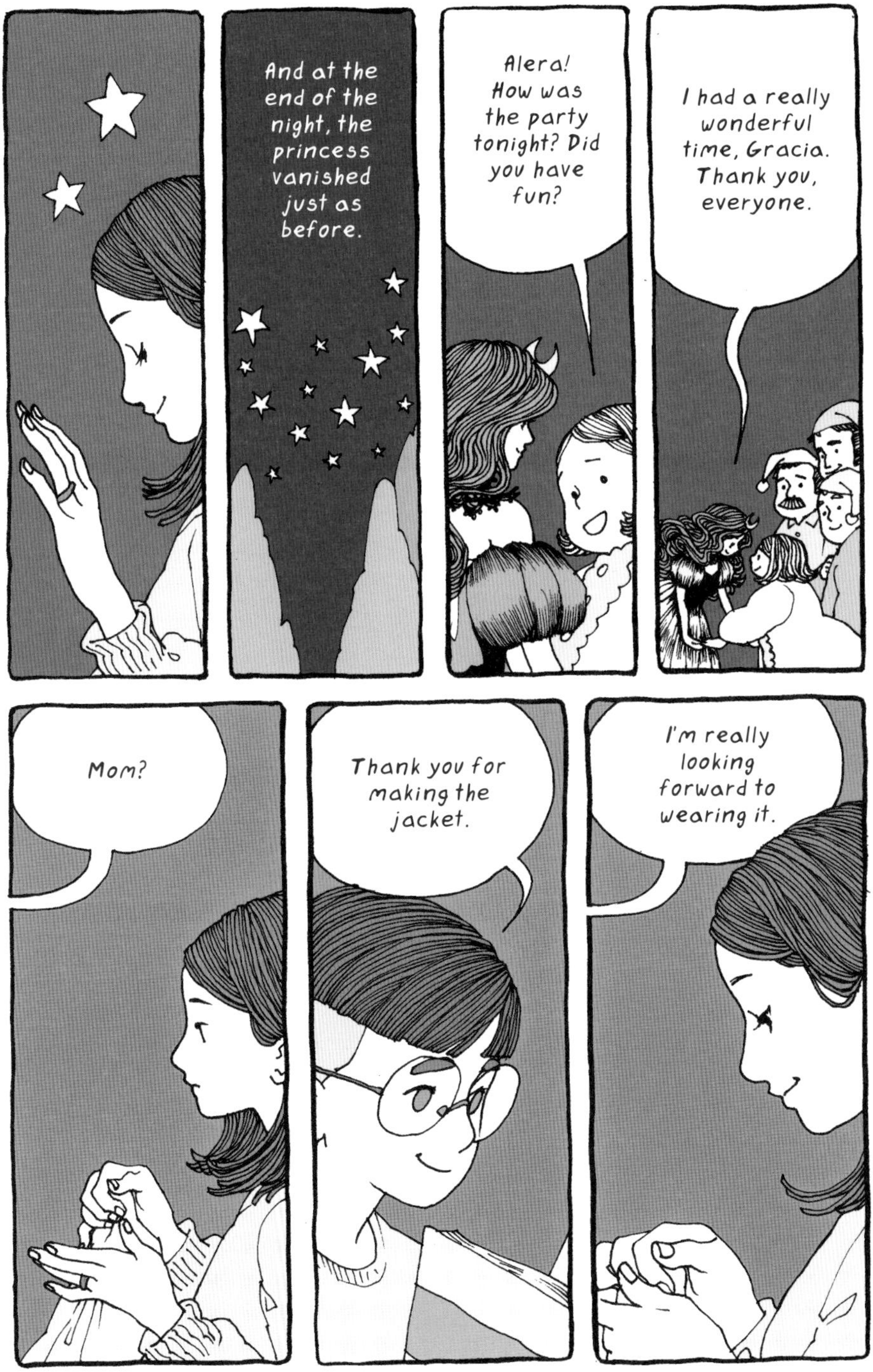
And at the end of the night, the princess vanished just as before.
Alera! How was the party tonight? Did you have fun?
I had a really wonderful time, Gracia. Thank you, everyone.
Mom?
Thank you for making the jacket.
I'm really looking forward to wearing it.

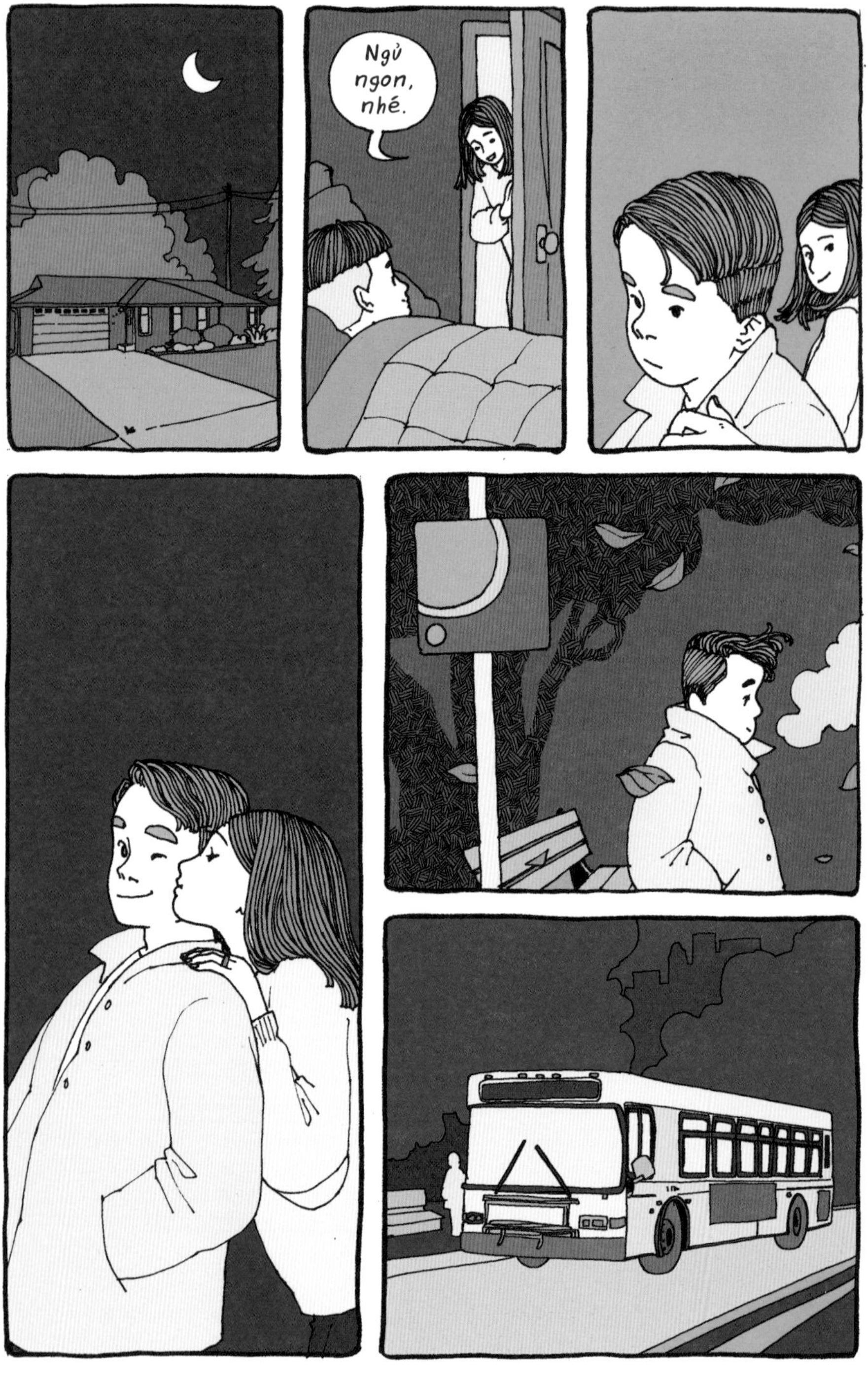
Ngủ ngon, nhé.

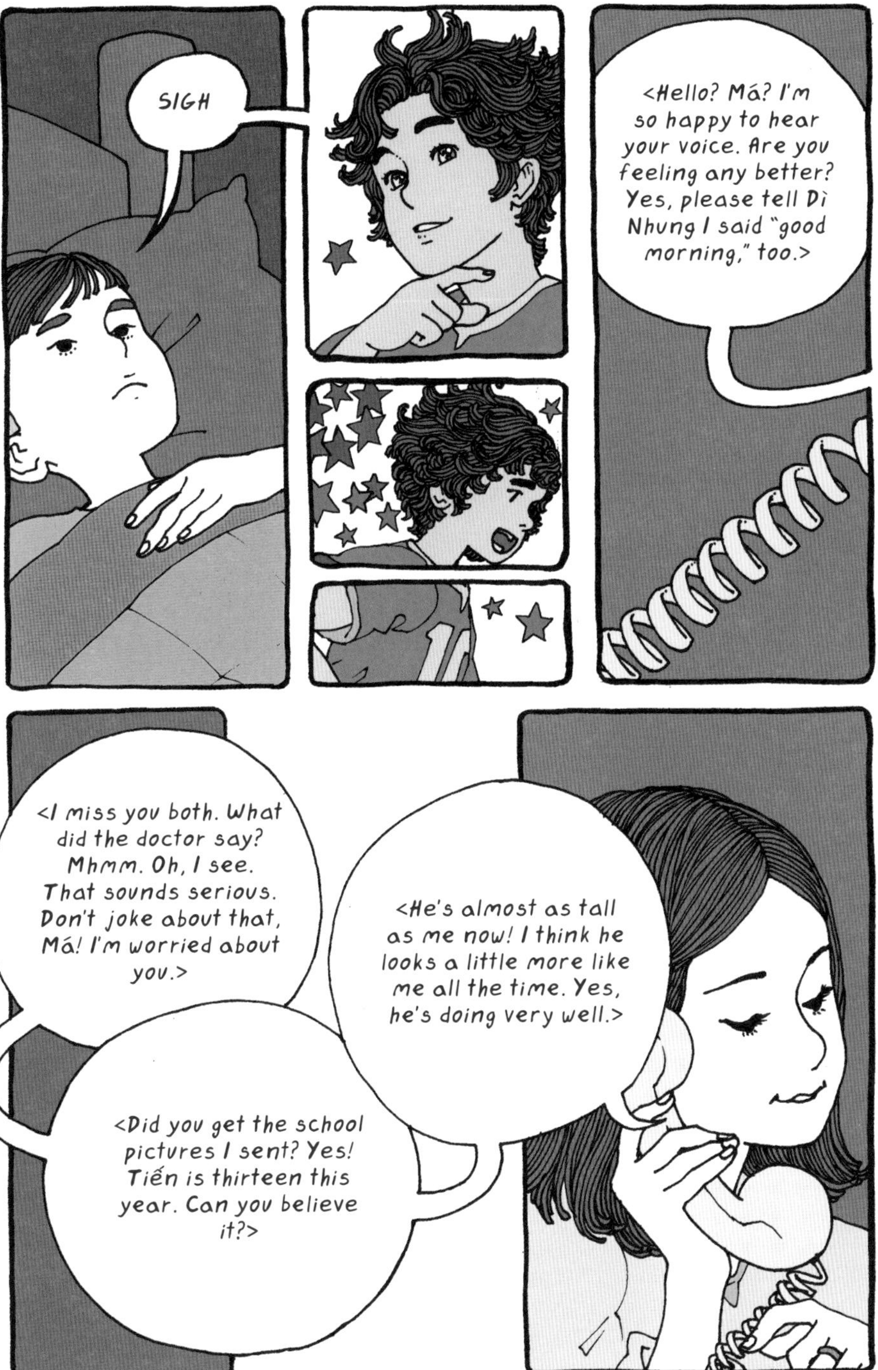
SIGH
<Hello? Má? I'm so happy to hear your voice. Are you feeling any better? Yes, please tell Dì Nhung I said "good morning," too.>
<I miss you both. What did the doctor say? Mhmm. Oh, I see. That sounds serious. Don't joke about that, Má! I'm worried about you.>
<Did you get the school pictures I sent? Yes! Tiến is thirteen this year. Can you believe it?>
<He's almost as tall as me now! I think he looks a little more like me all the time. Yes, he's doing very well.>

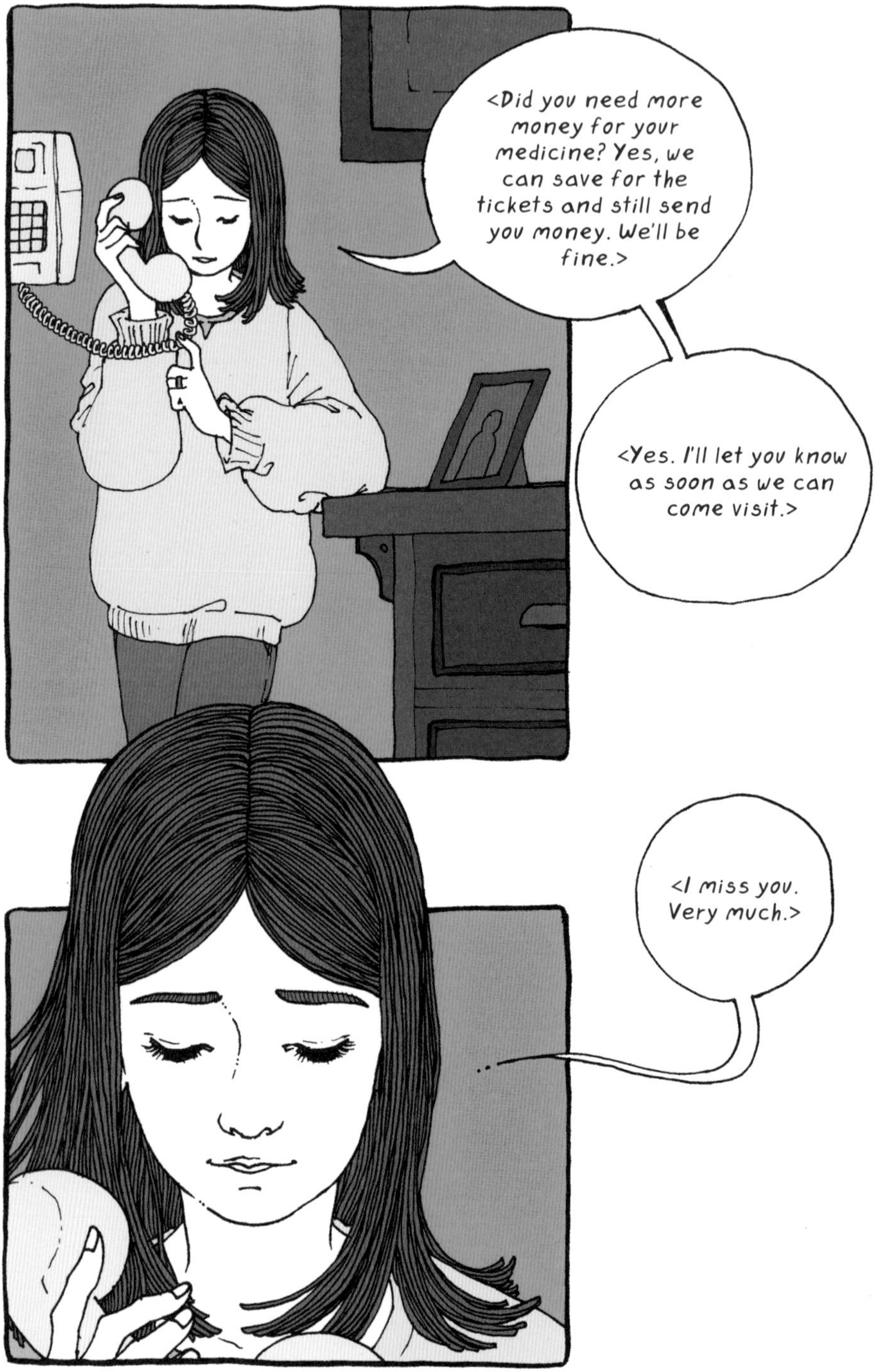
<Did you need more money for your medicine? Yes, we can save for the tickets and still send you money. We'll be fine.>
<Yes. I'll let you know as soon as we can come visit.>
<I miss you. Very much.>

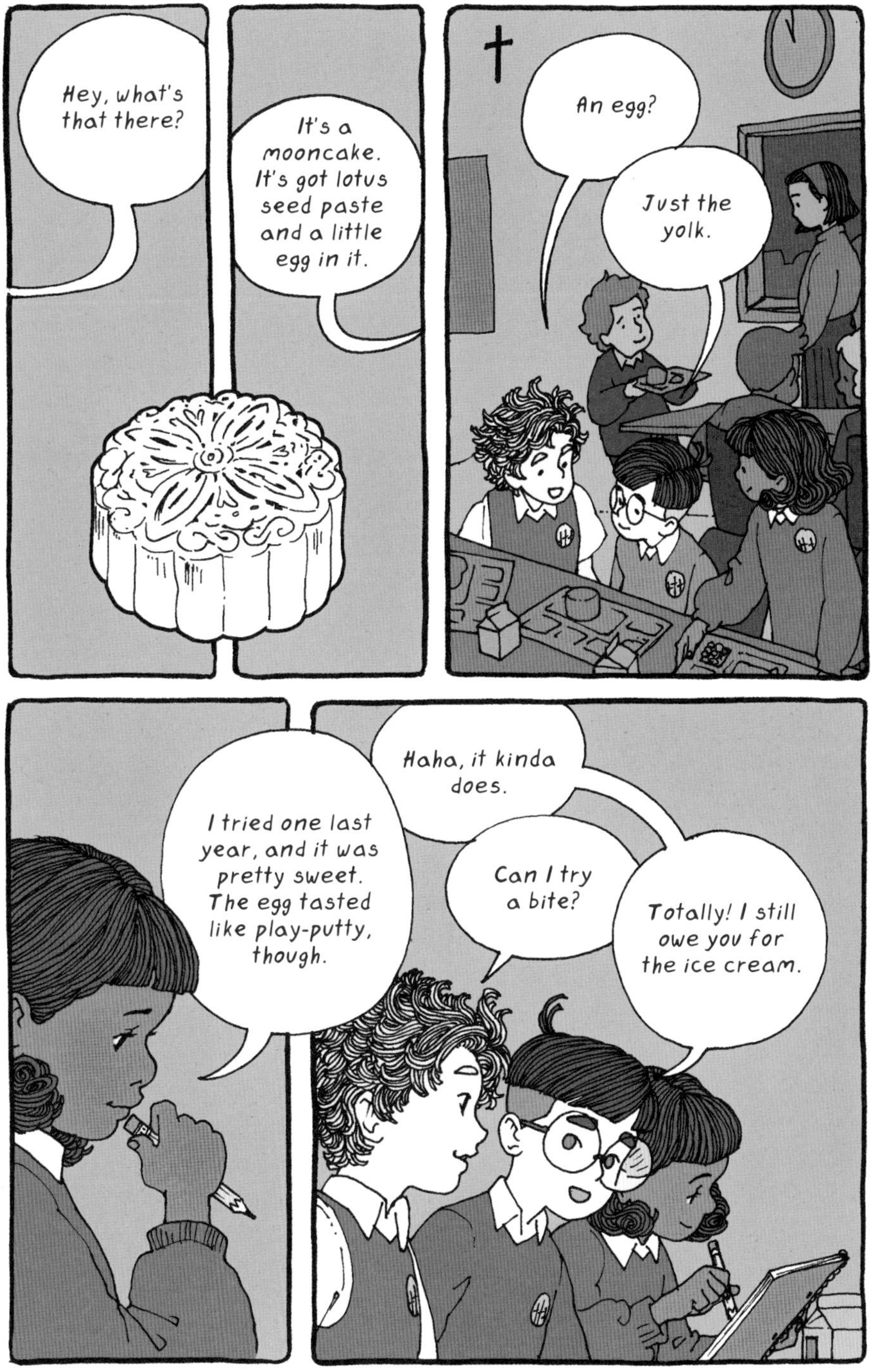
Hey, what's that there?
It's a mooncake. It's got lotus seed paste and a little egg in it.
An egg?
Just the yolk.
I tried one last year, and it was pretty sweet. The egg tasted like play-putty, though.
Haha, it kinda does.
Can I try a bite?
Totally! I still owe you for the ice cream.

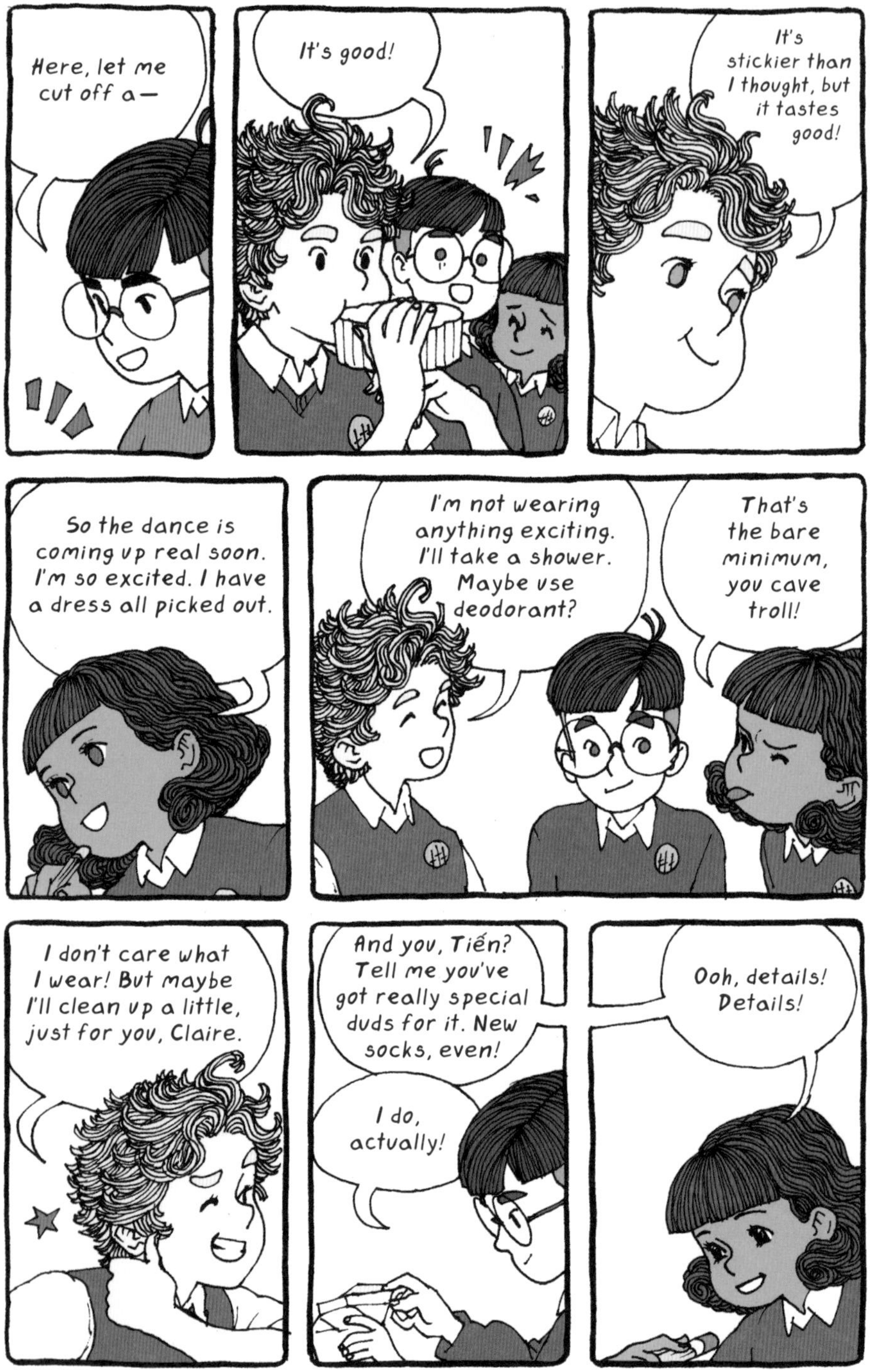
Here, let me cut off a—
It's good!
It's stickier than I thought, but it tastes good!
So the dance is coming up real soon. I'm so excited. I have a dress all picked out.
I'm not wearing anything exciting. I'll take a shower. Maybe use deodorant?
That's the bare minimum, you cave troll!
I don't care what I wear! But maybe I'll clean up a little, just for you, Claire.
And you, Tiến? Tell me you've got really special duds for it. New socks, even!
I do, actually!
Ooh, details! Details!

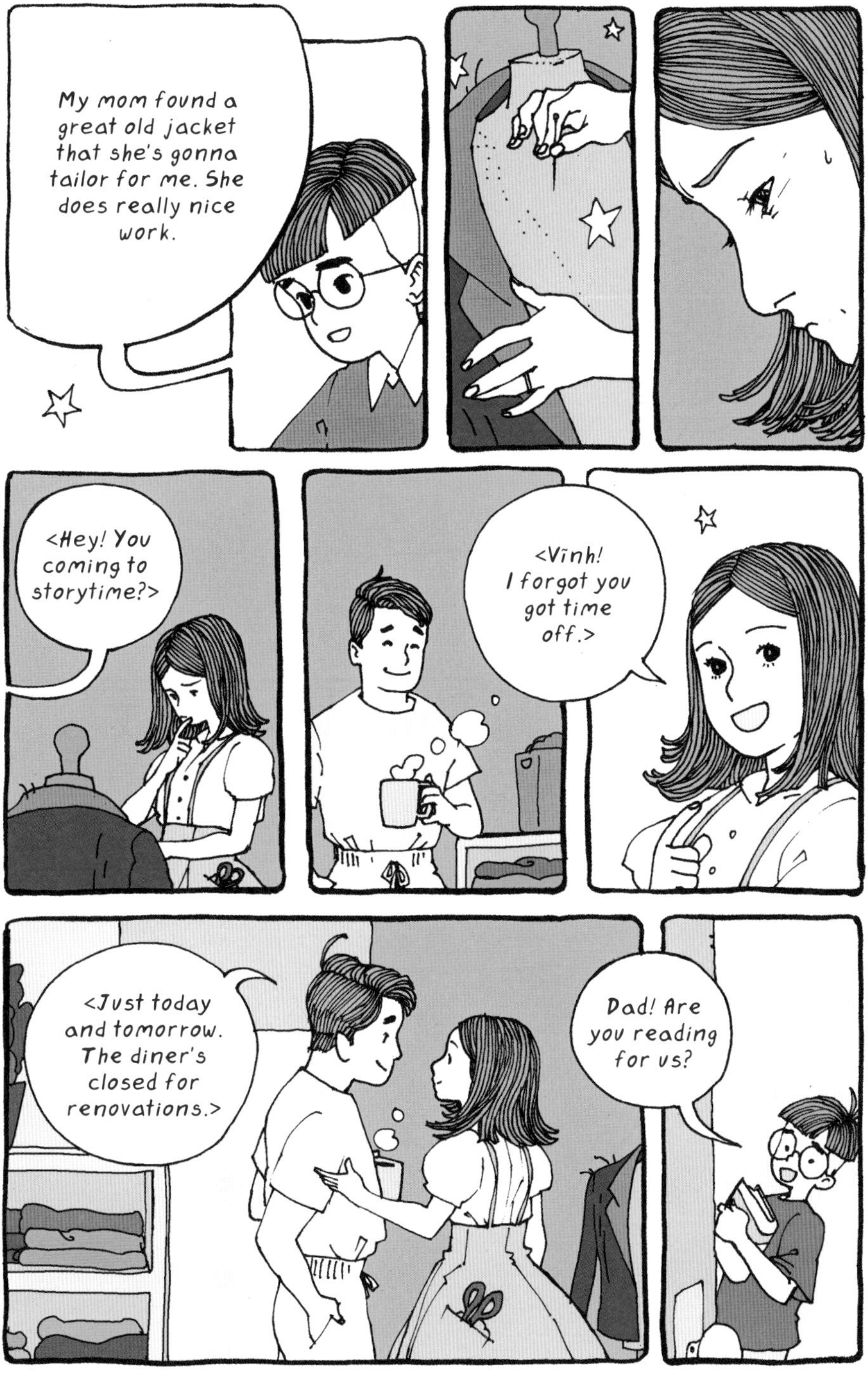
My mom found a great old jacket that she's gonna tailor for me. She does really nice work.
<Hey! You coming to storytime?>
<Vĩnh! I forgot you got time off.>
<Just today and tomorrow. The diner's closed for renovations.>
Dad! Are you reading for us?

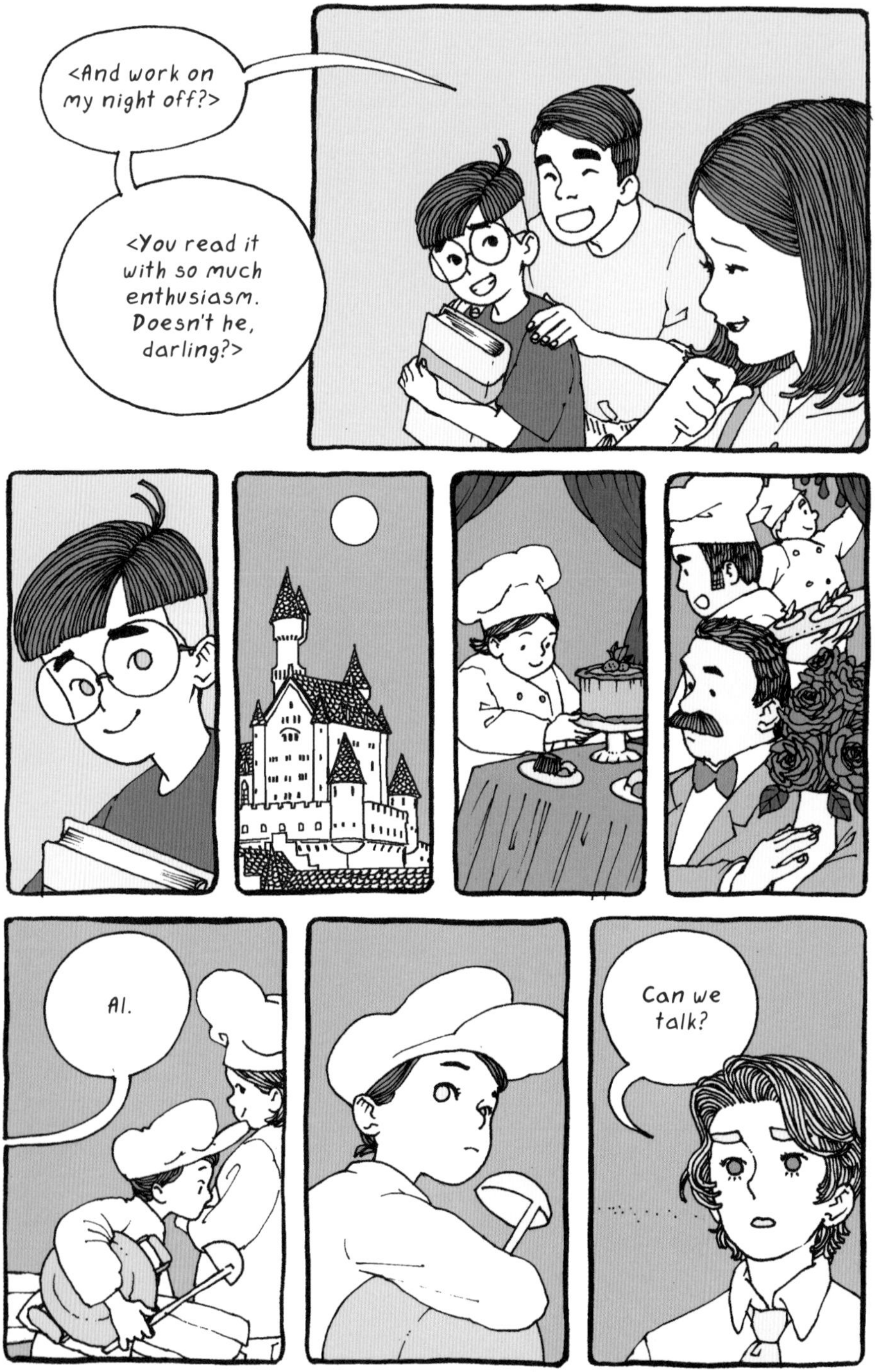
<And work on my night off?>
<You read it with so much enthusiasm. Doesn't he, darling?>
Al.
Can we talk?

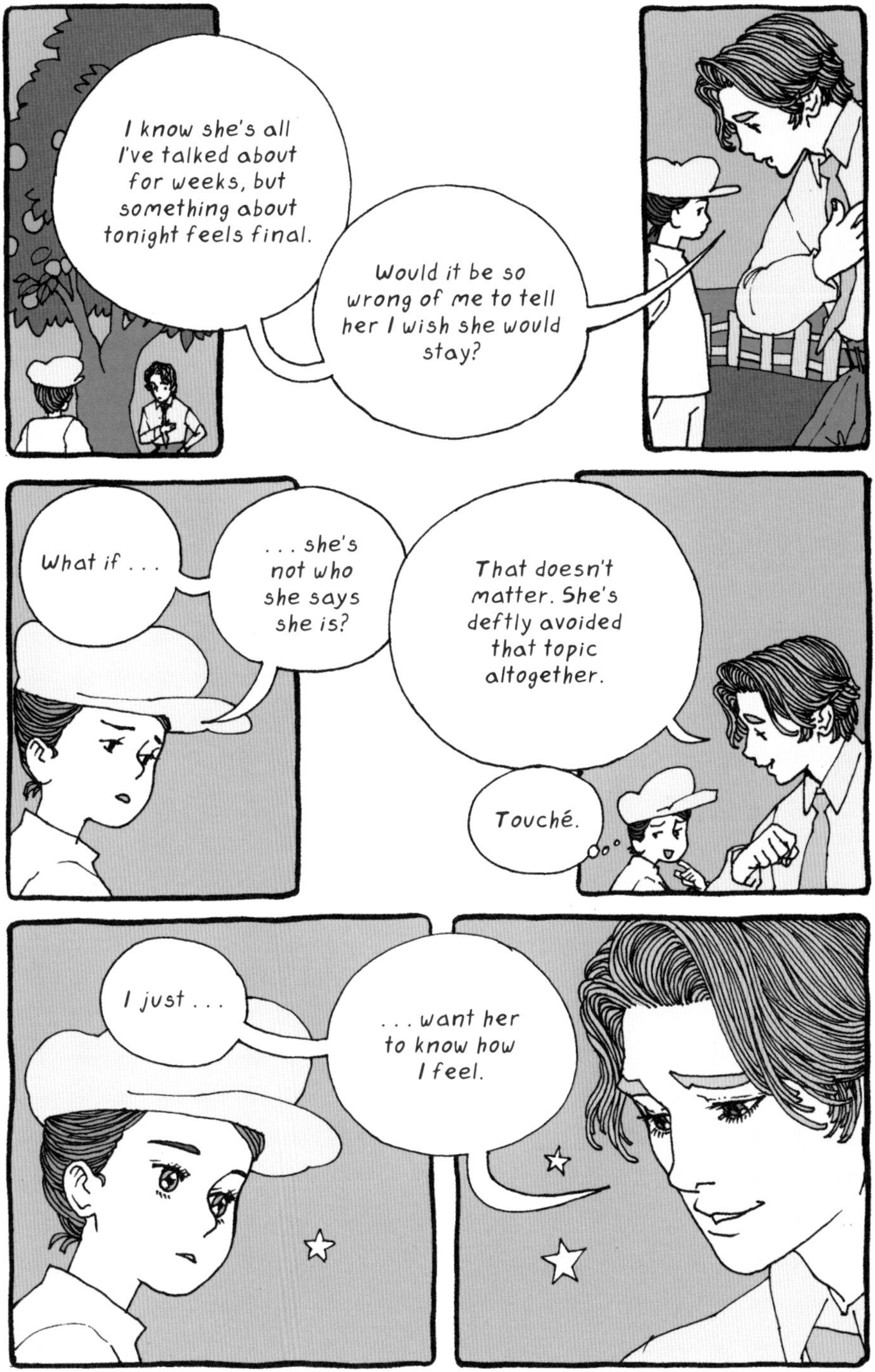
I know she's all I've talked about for weeks, but something about tonight feels final.
Would it be so wrong of me to tell her I wish she would stay?
What if . . .
. . . she's not who she says she is?
That doesn't matter. She's deftly avoided that topic altogether.
Touché.
I just . . .
. . . want her to know how I feel.

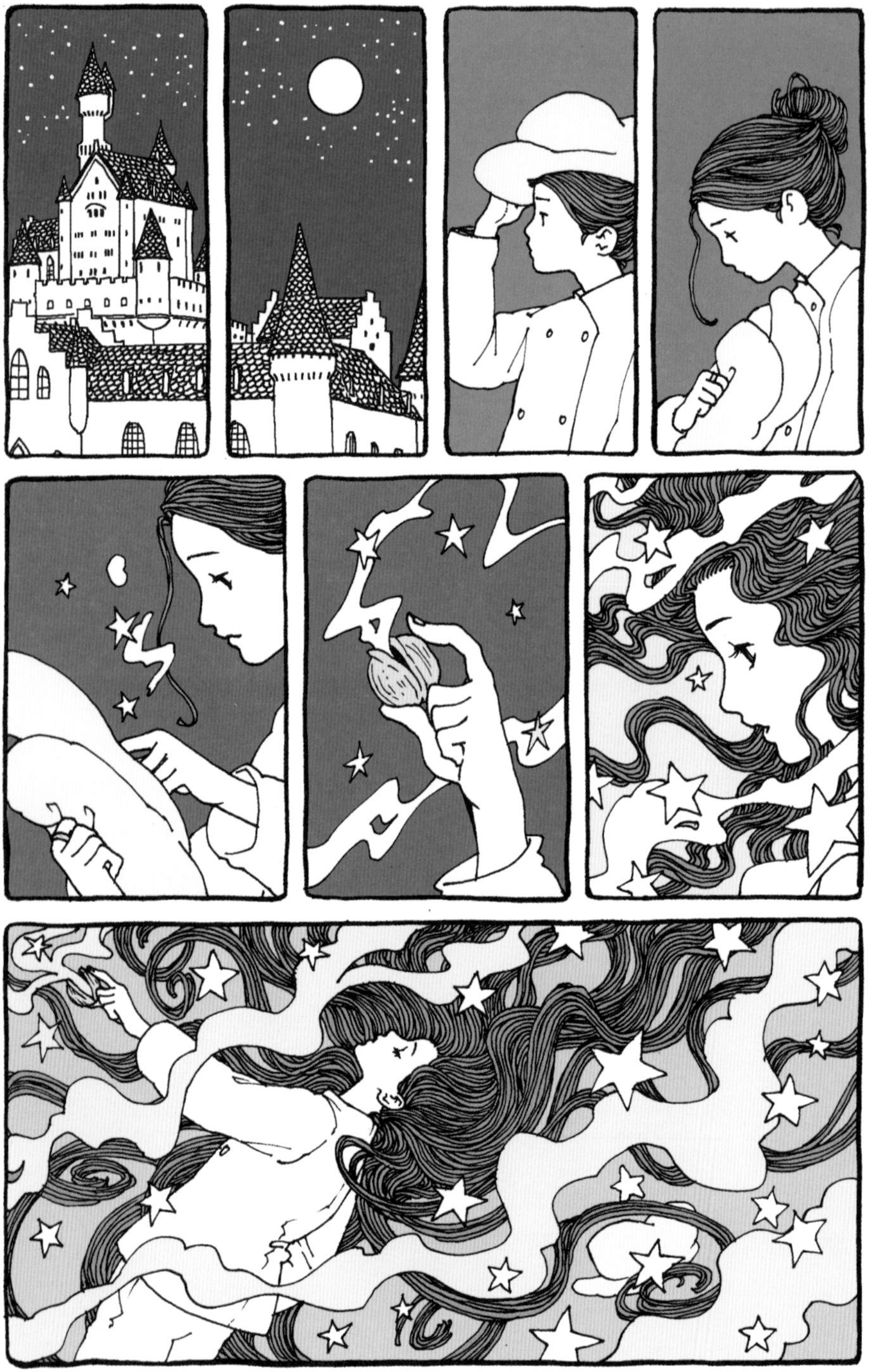

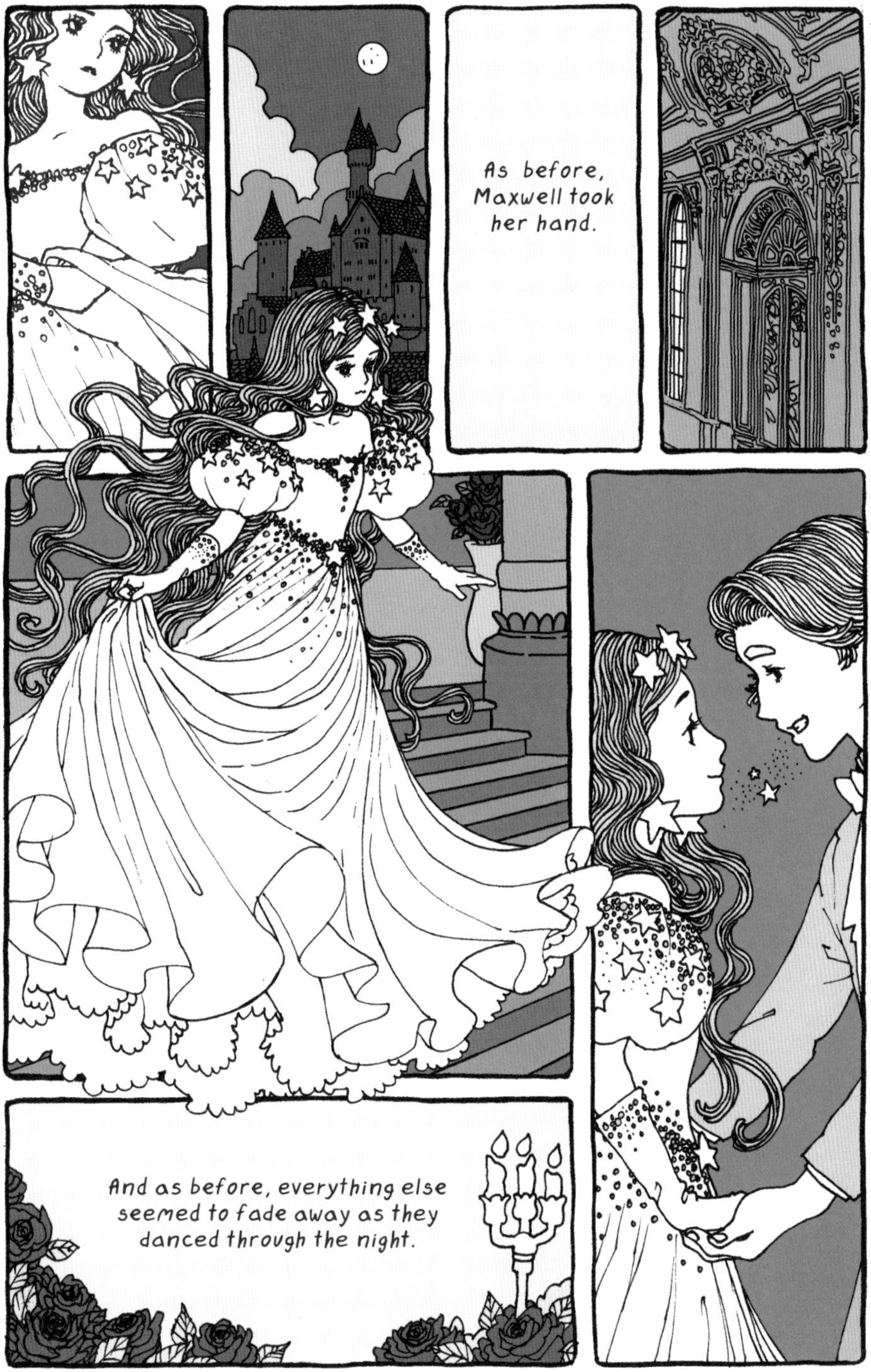
As before, Maxwell took her hand.
And as before, everything else seemed to fade away as they danced through the night.

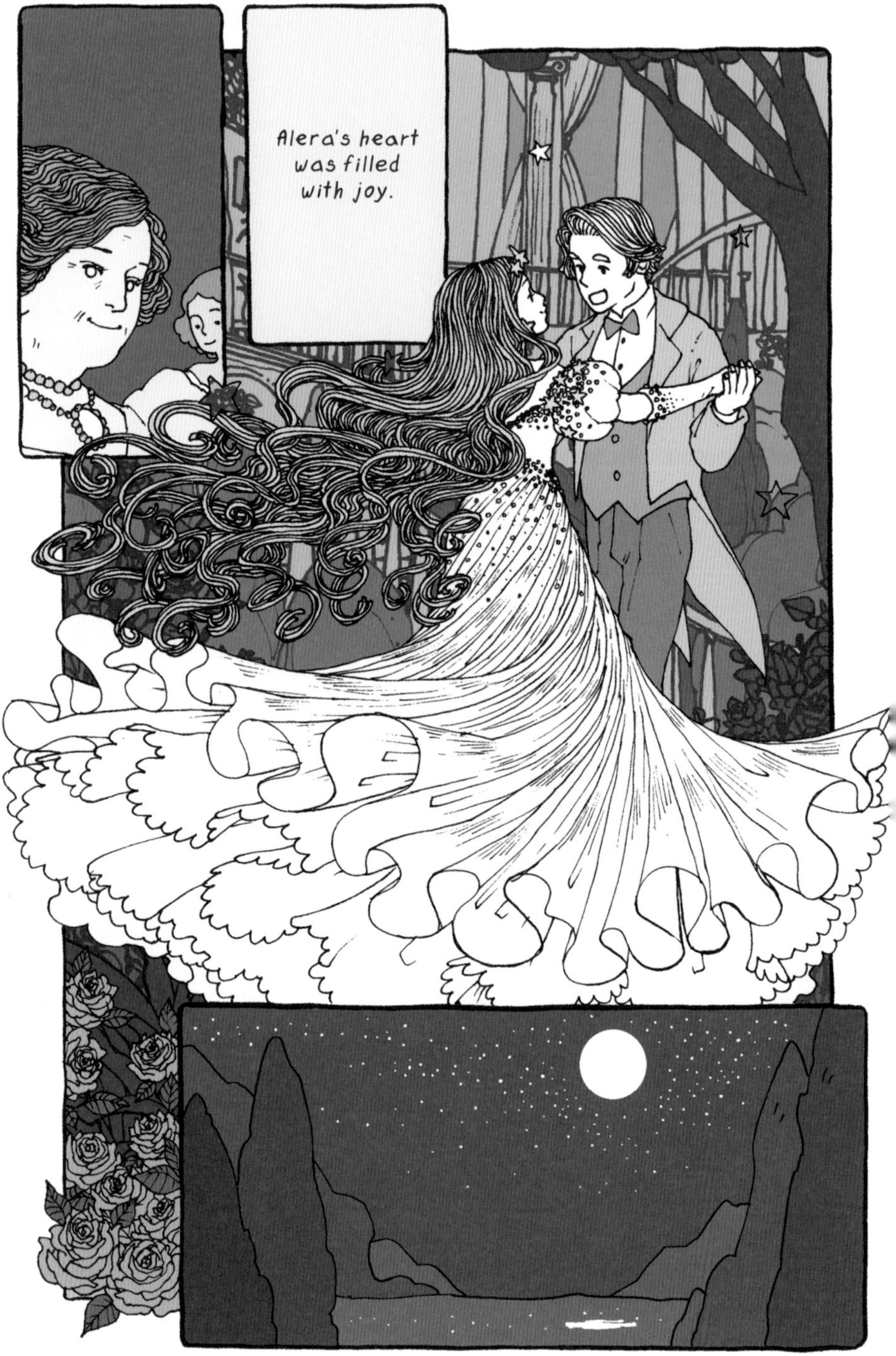
Alera's heart was filled with joy.

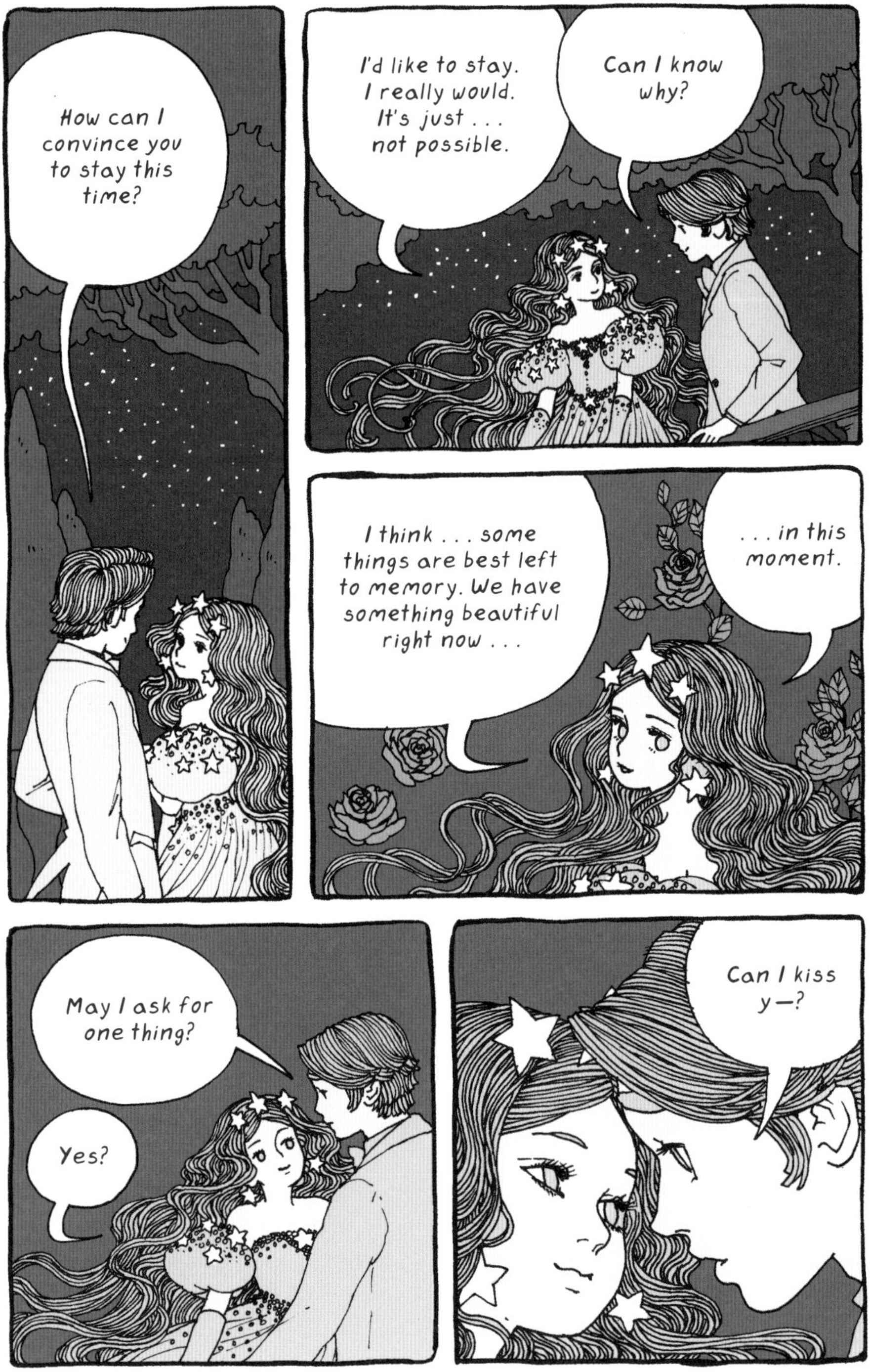
How can I convince you to stay this time?
I'd like to stay. I really would. It's just . . . not possible.
Can I know why?
I think . . . some things are best left to memory. We have something beautiful right now . . .
. . . in this moment.
May I ask for one thing?
Yes?
Can I kiss y—?

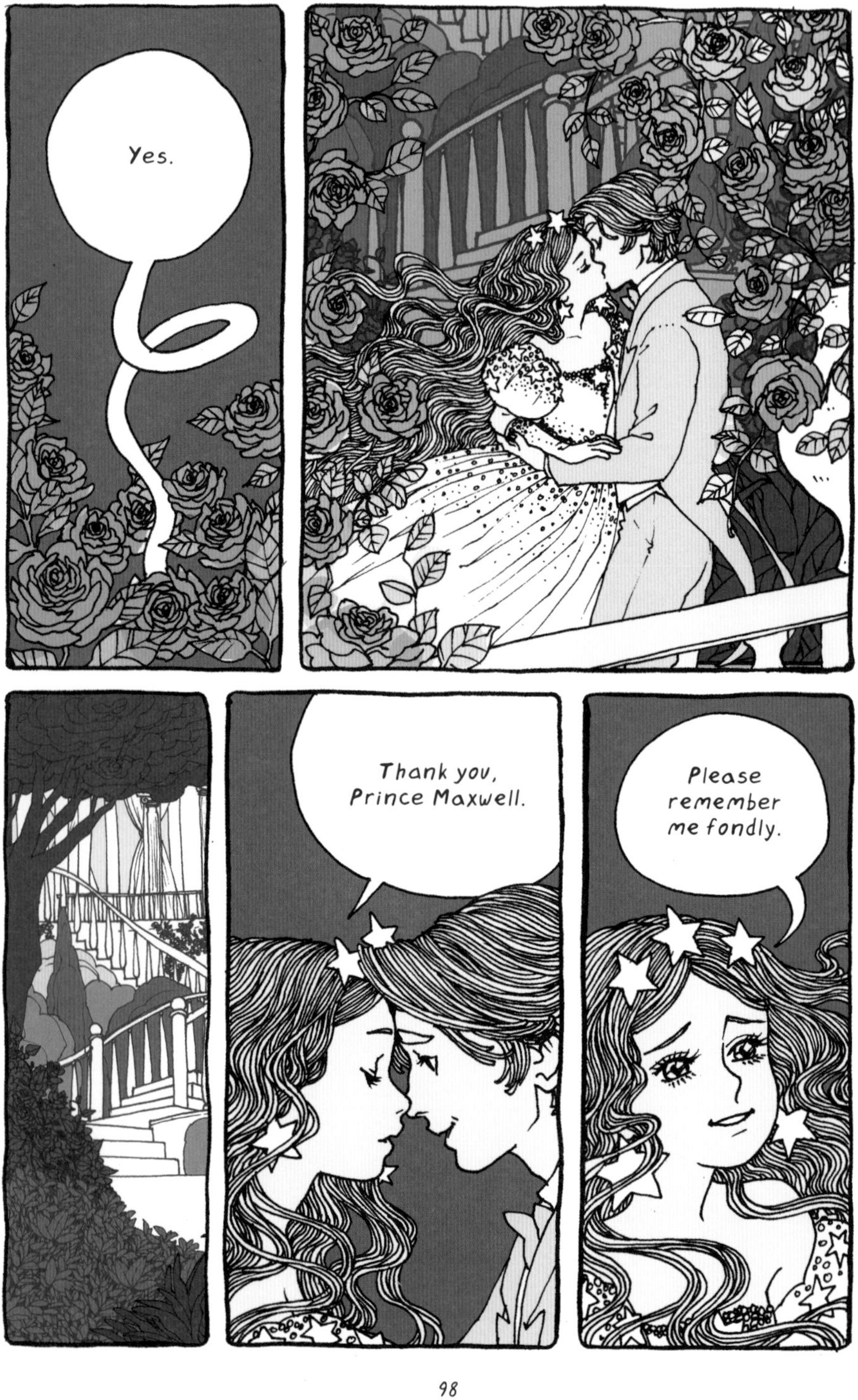
Yes.
Thank you, Prince Maxwell.
Please remember me fondly.

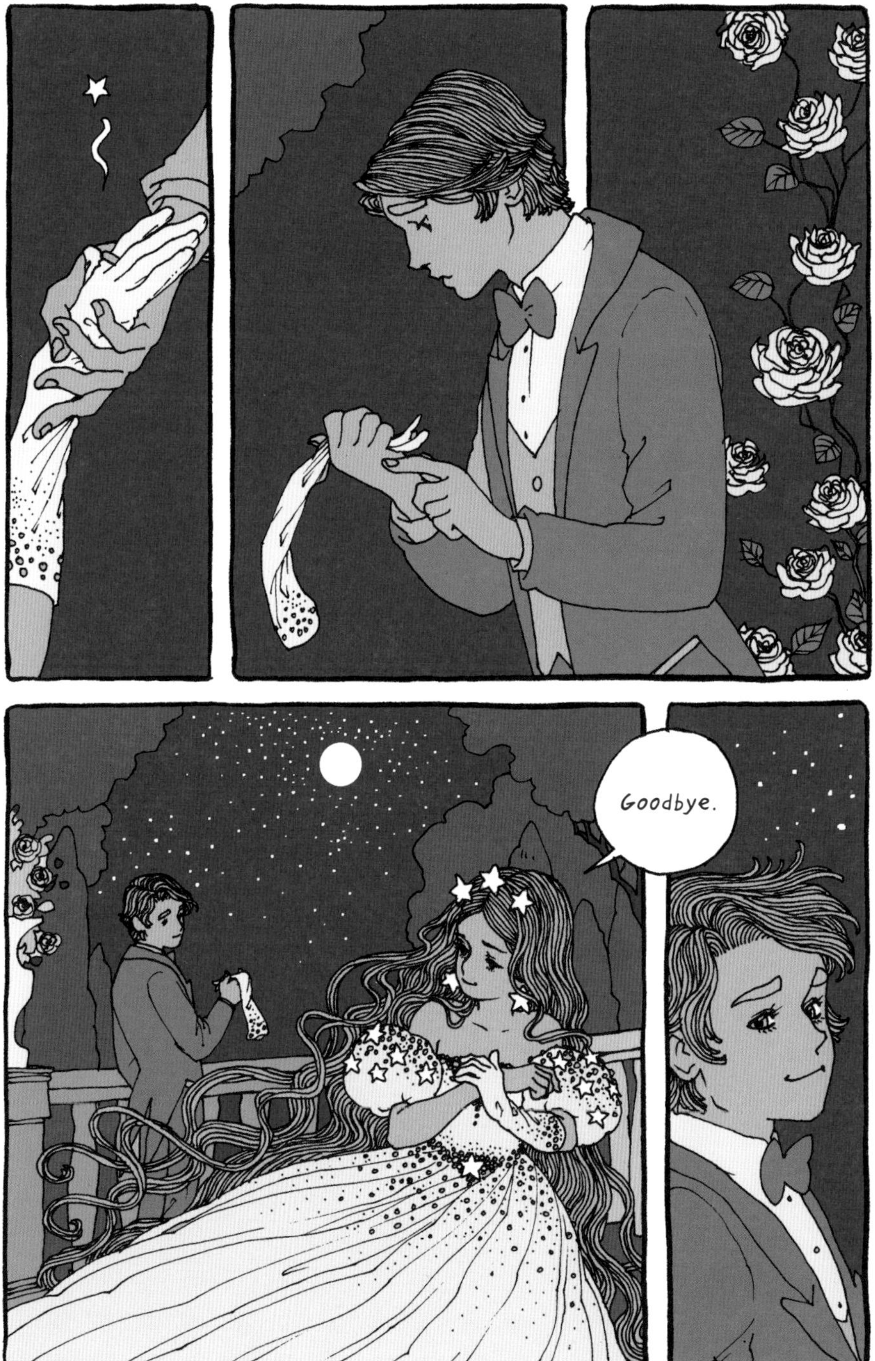
Goodbye.

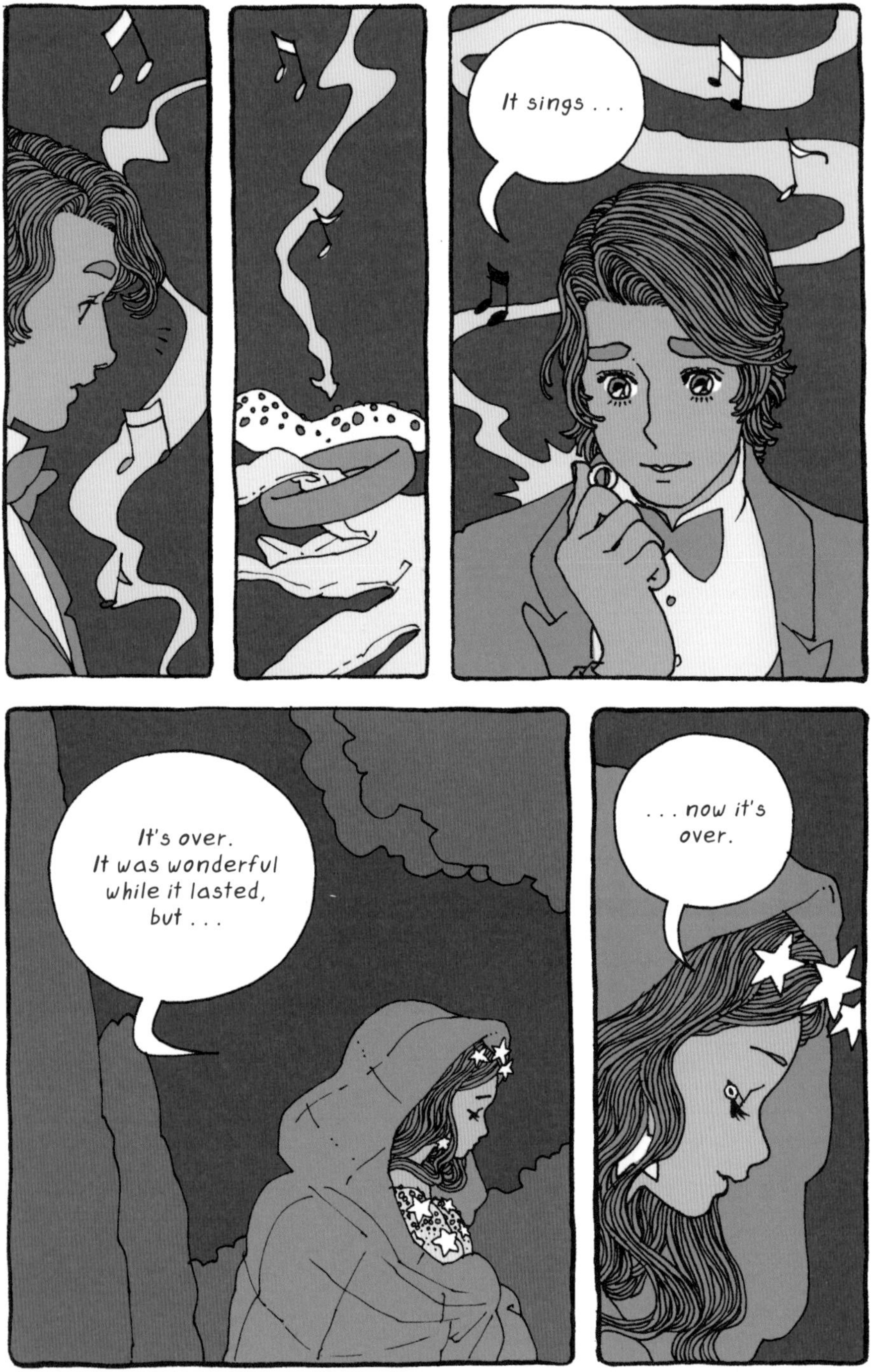

It sings . . .
It's over.
It was wonderful
while it lasted,
but . . .
. . . now it's
over.

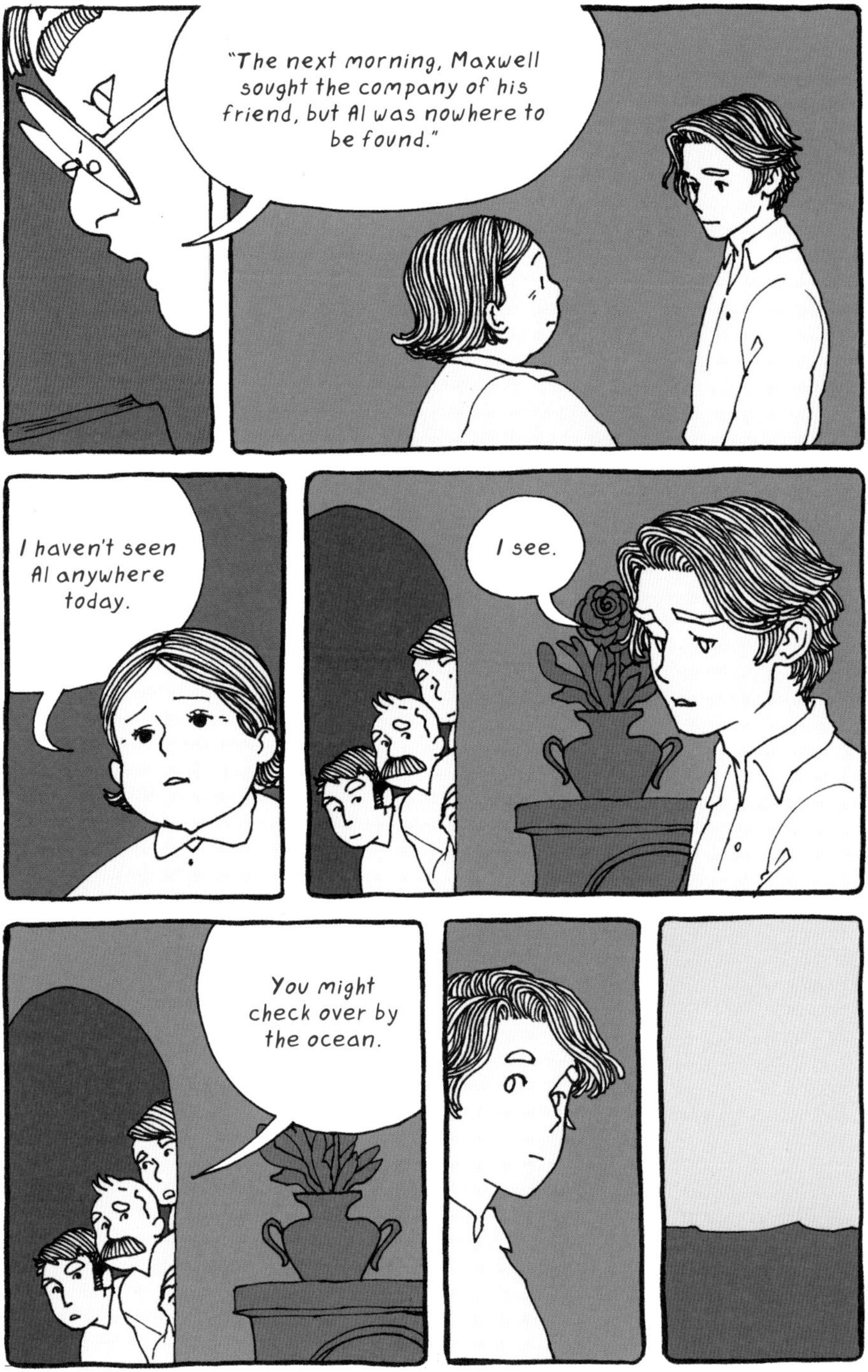
"The next morning, Maxwell sought the company of his friend, but Al was nowhere to be found."
I haven't seen Al anywhere today.
I see.
You might check over by the ocean.

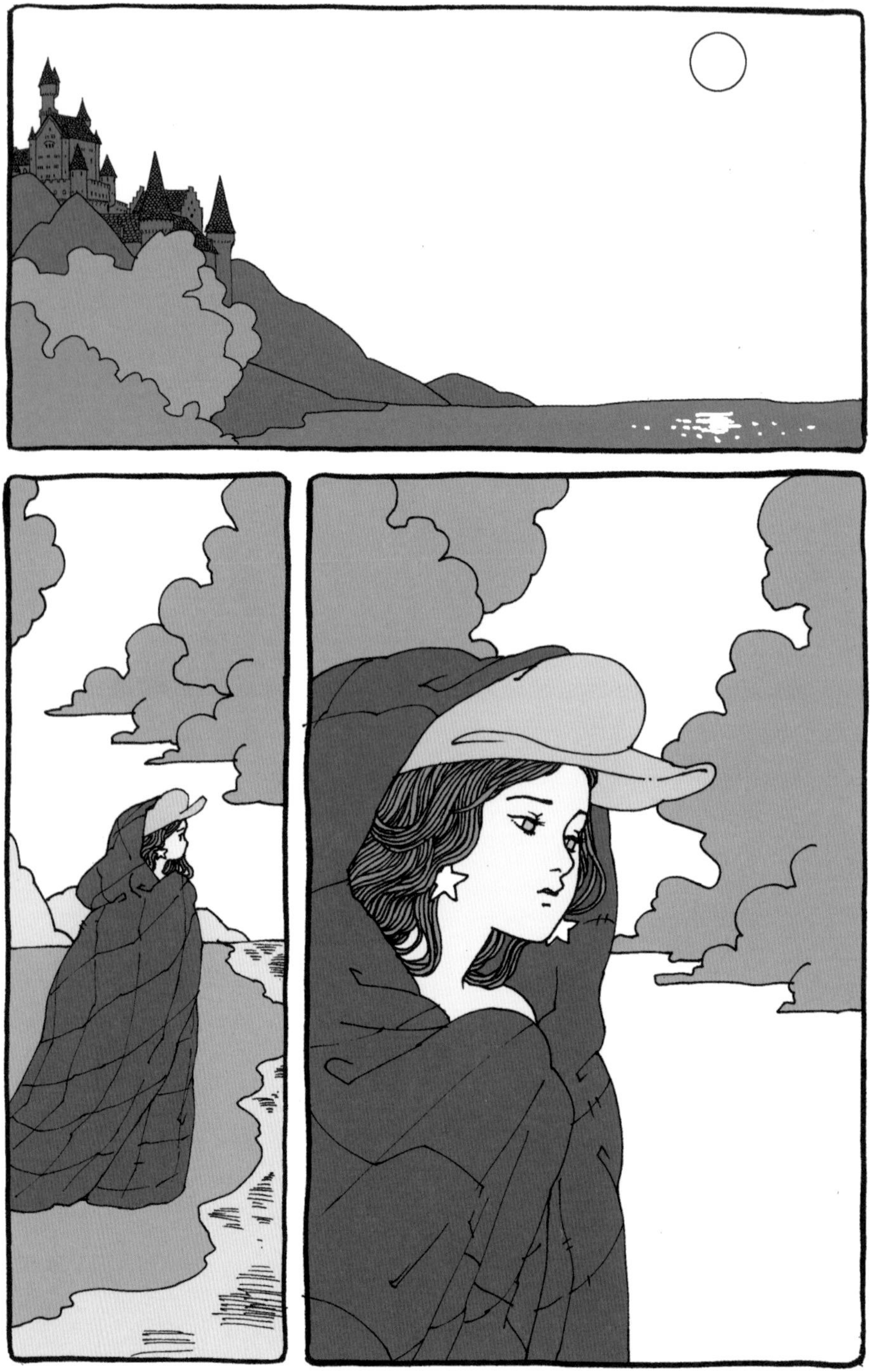

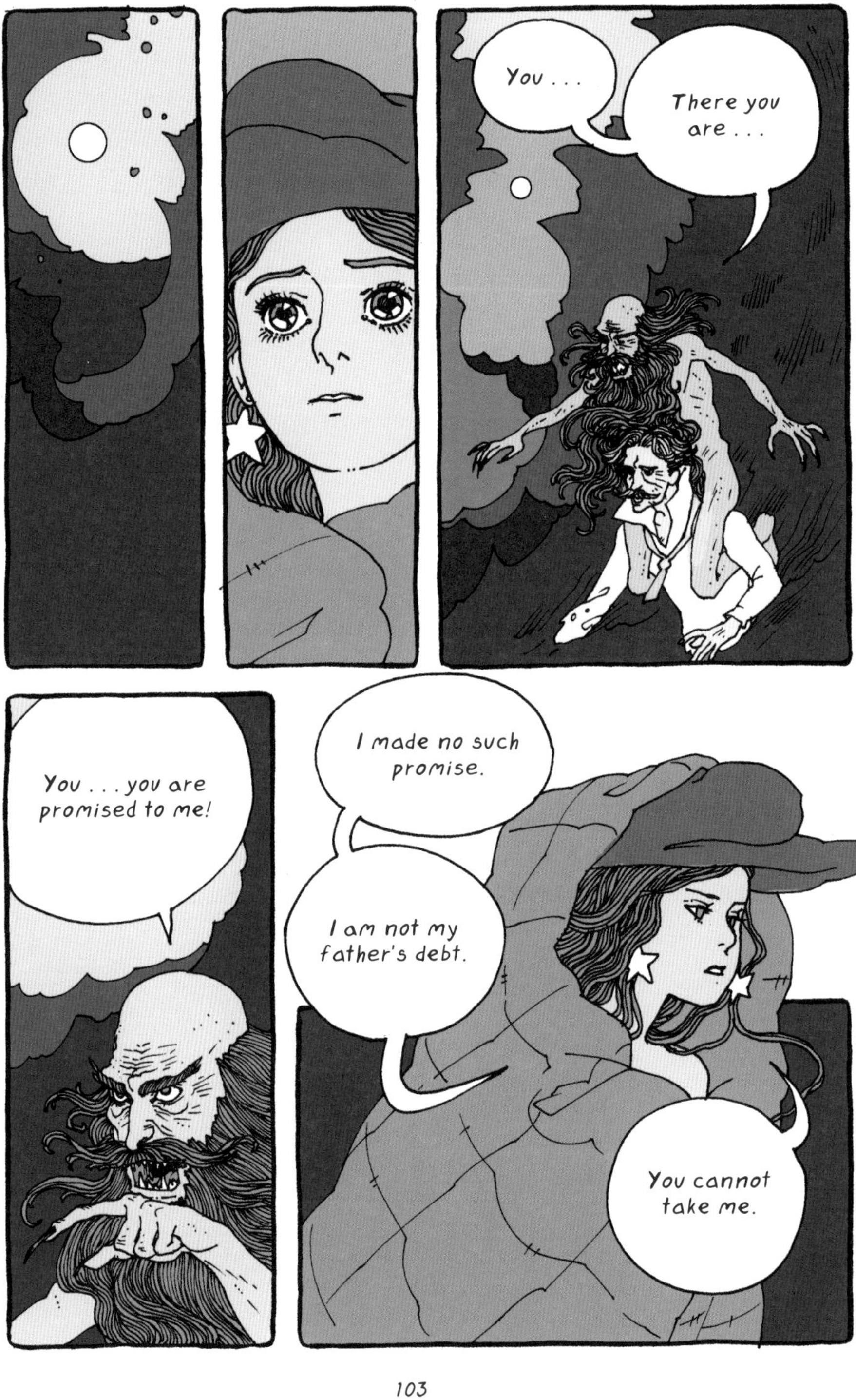
You . . .
There you are . . .
You . . . you are promised to me!
I made no such promise.
I am not my father's debt.
You cannot take me.

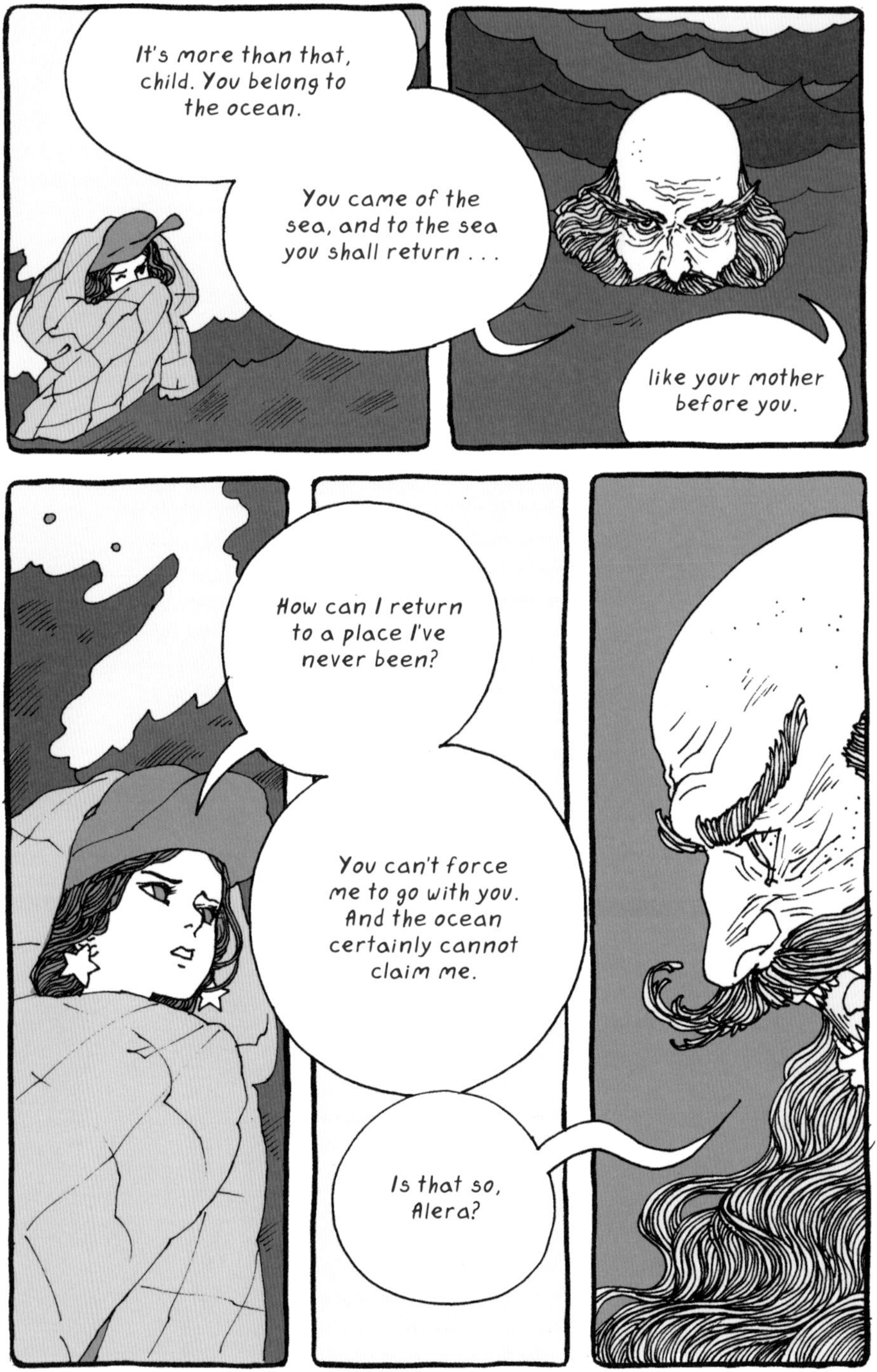
It's more than that, child. You belong to the ocean.
You came of the sea, and to the sea you shall return . . .
like your mother before you.
How can I return to a place I've never been?
You can't force me to go with you. And the ocean certainly cannot claim me.
Is that so, Alera?

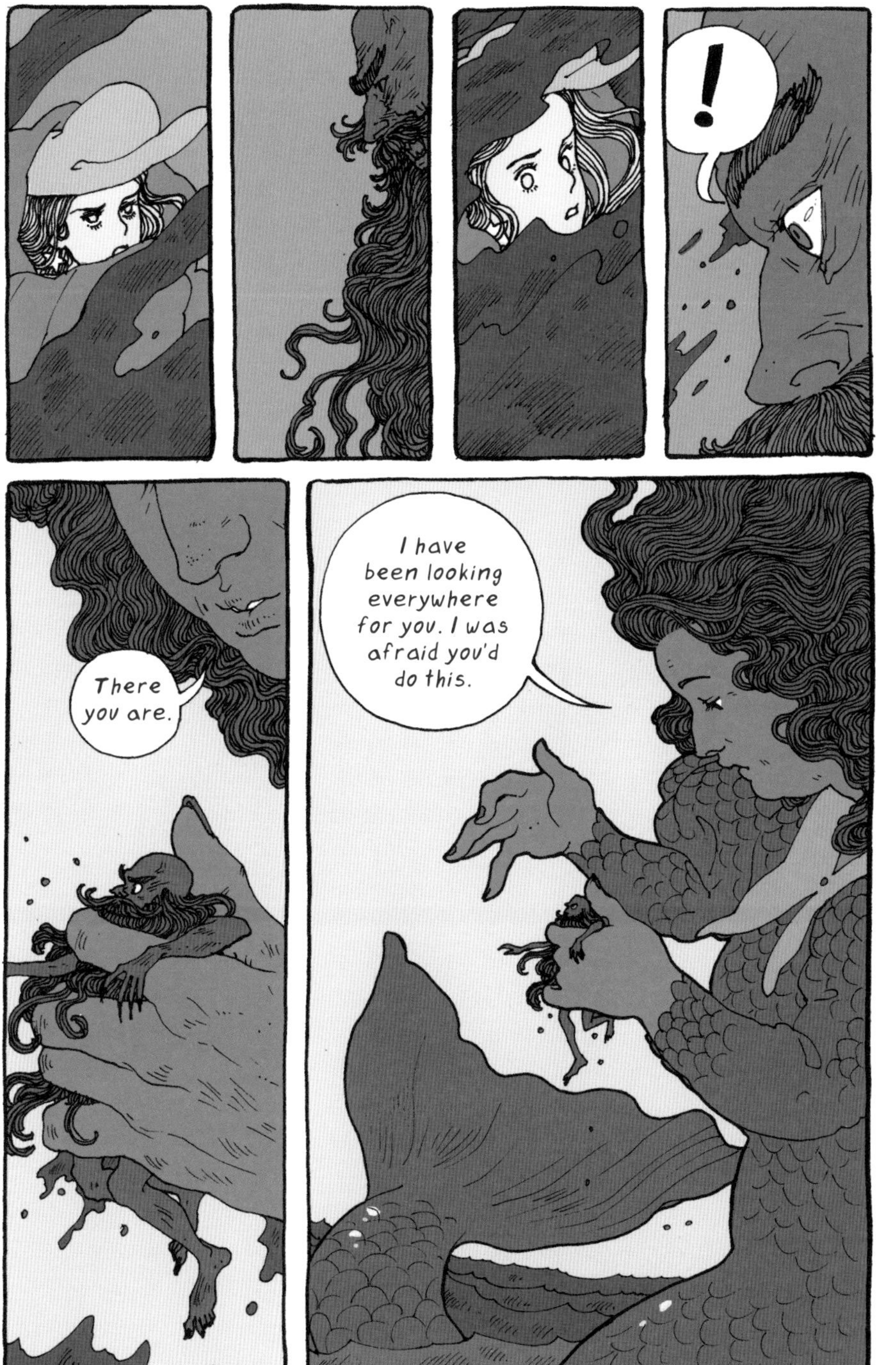
!
There you are.
I have been looking everywhere for you. I was afraid you'd do this.

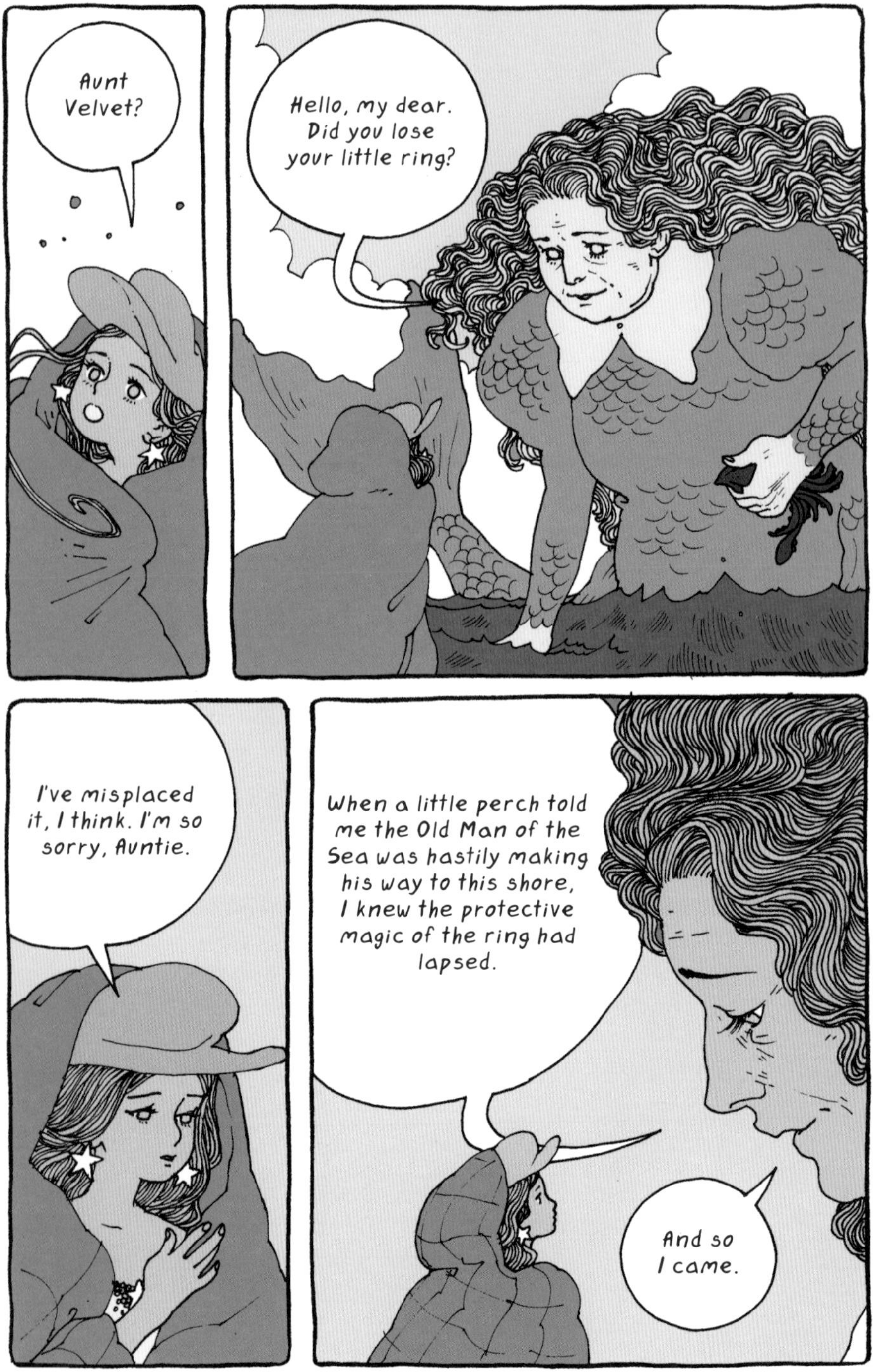
Aunt Velvet?
Hello, my dear. Did you lose your little ring?
I've misplaced it, I think. I'm so sorry, Auntie.
When a little perch told me the Old Man of the Sea was hastily making his way to this shore, I knew the protective magic of the ring had lapsed.
And so I came.

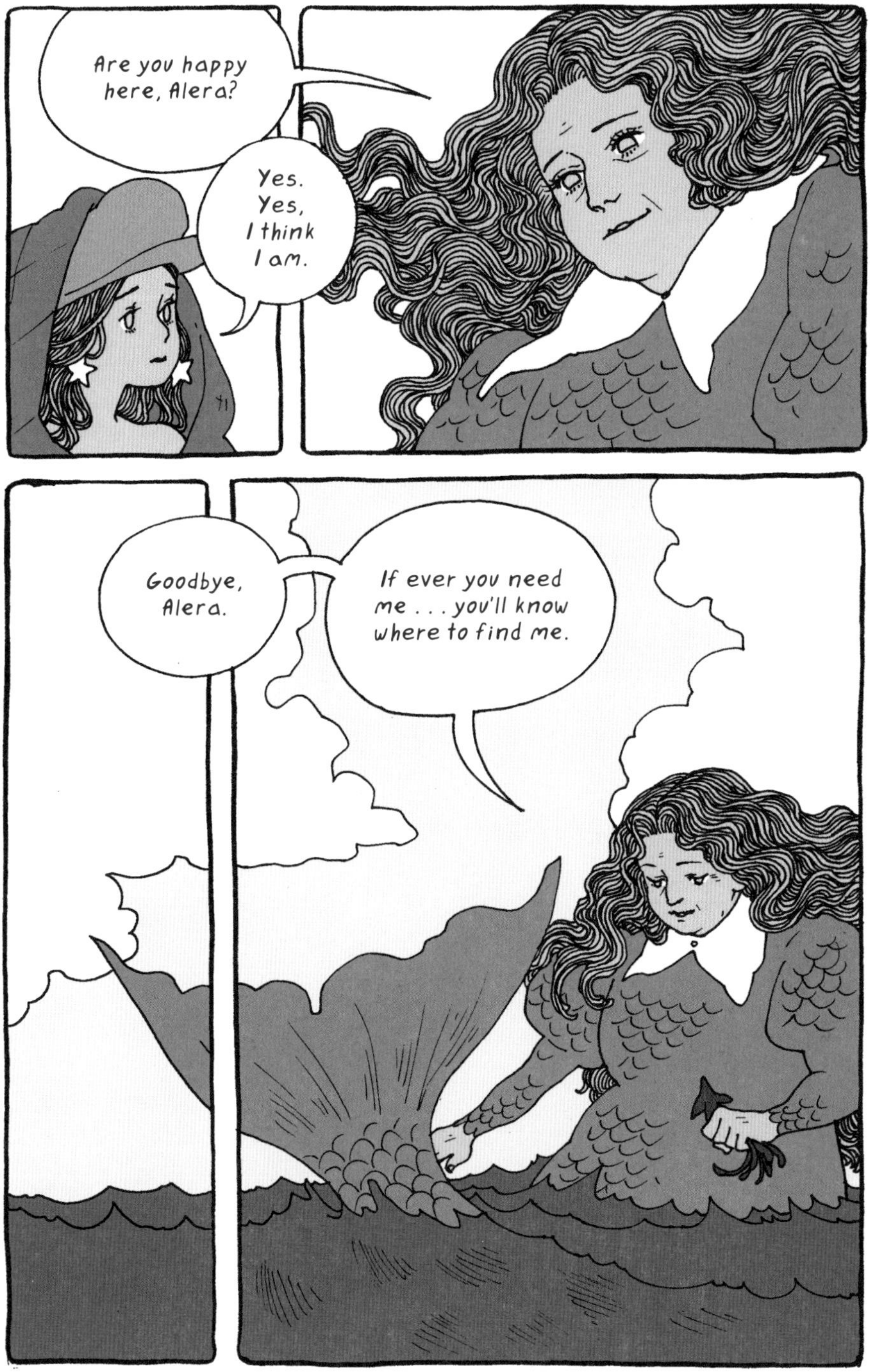

Are you happy here, Alera?
Yes. Yes, I think I am.
Goodbye, Alera.
If ever you need me . . . you'll know where to find me.

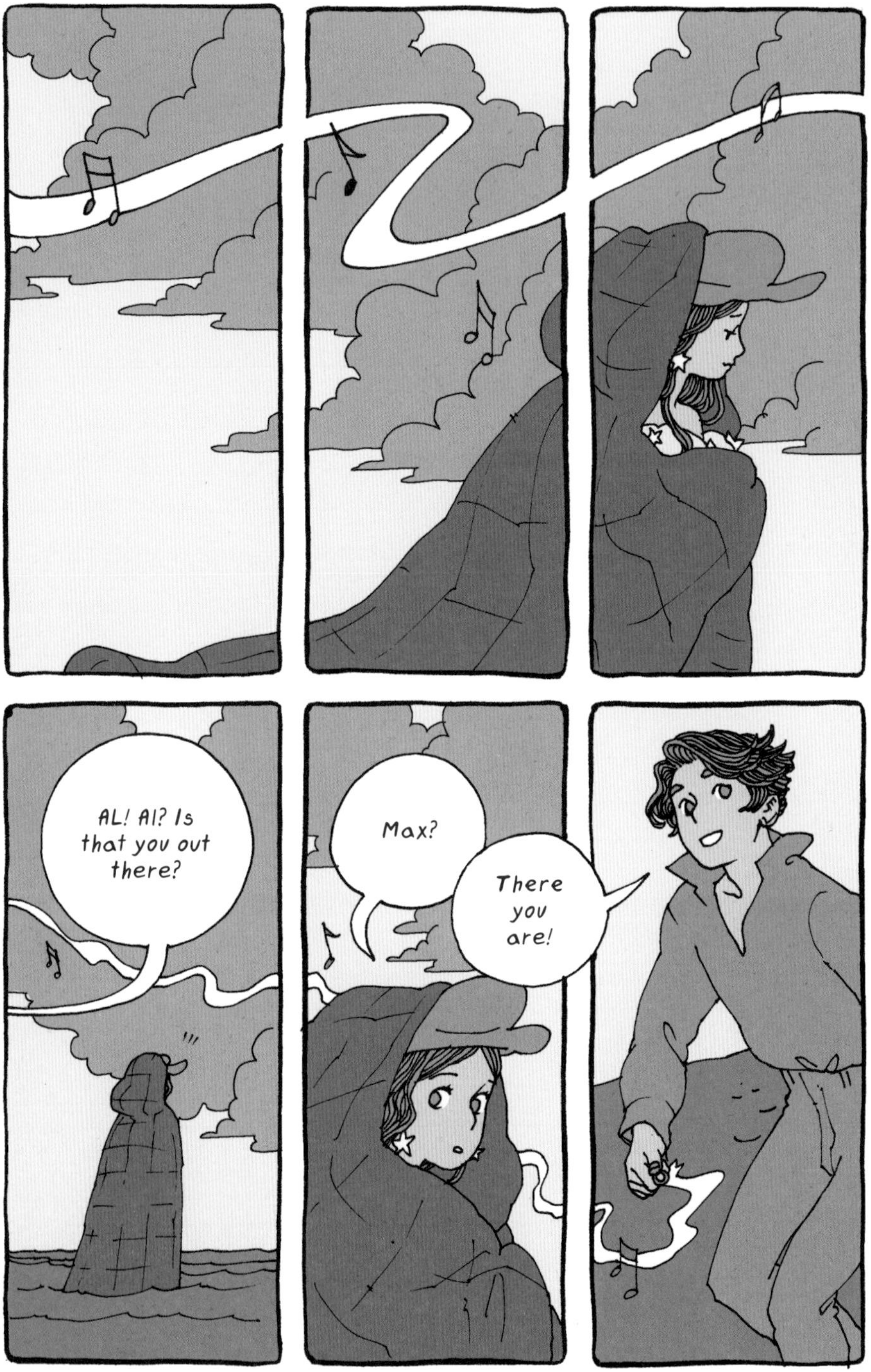
AL! Al? Is that you out there?
Max?
There you are!

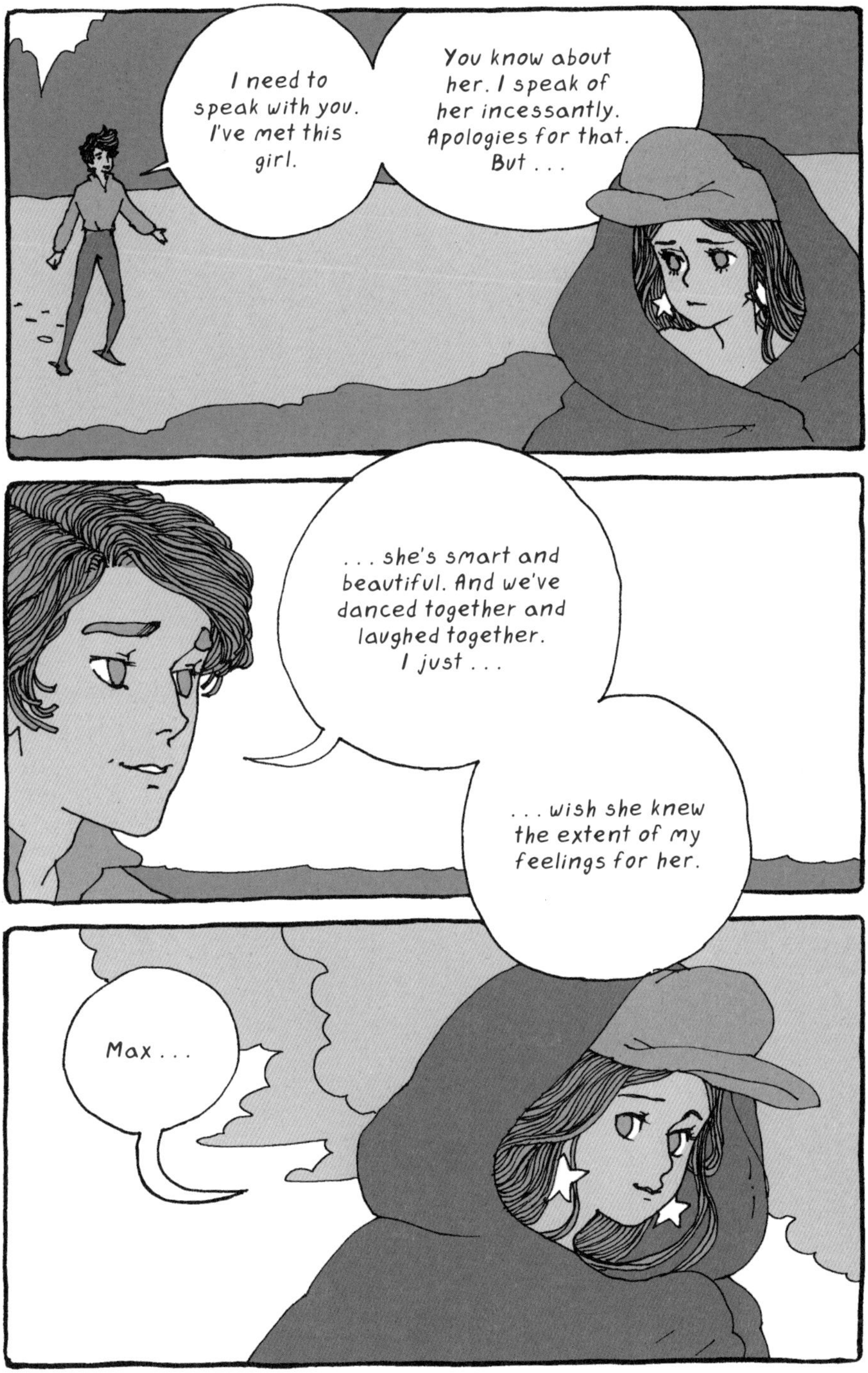
I need to speak with you. I've met this girl.
You know about her. I speak of her incessantly. Apologies for that. But . . .
. . . she's smart and beautiful. And we've danced together and laughed together. I just . . .
. . . wish she knew the extent of my feelings for her.
Max . . .

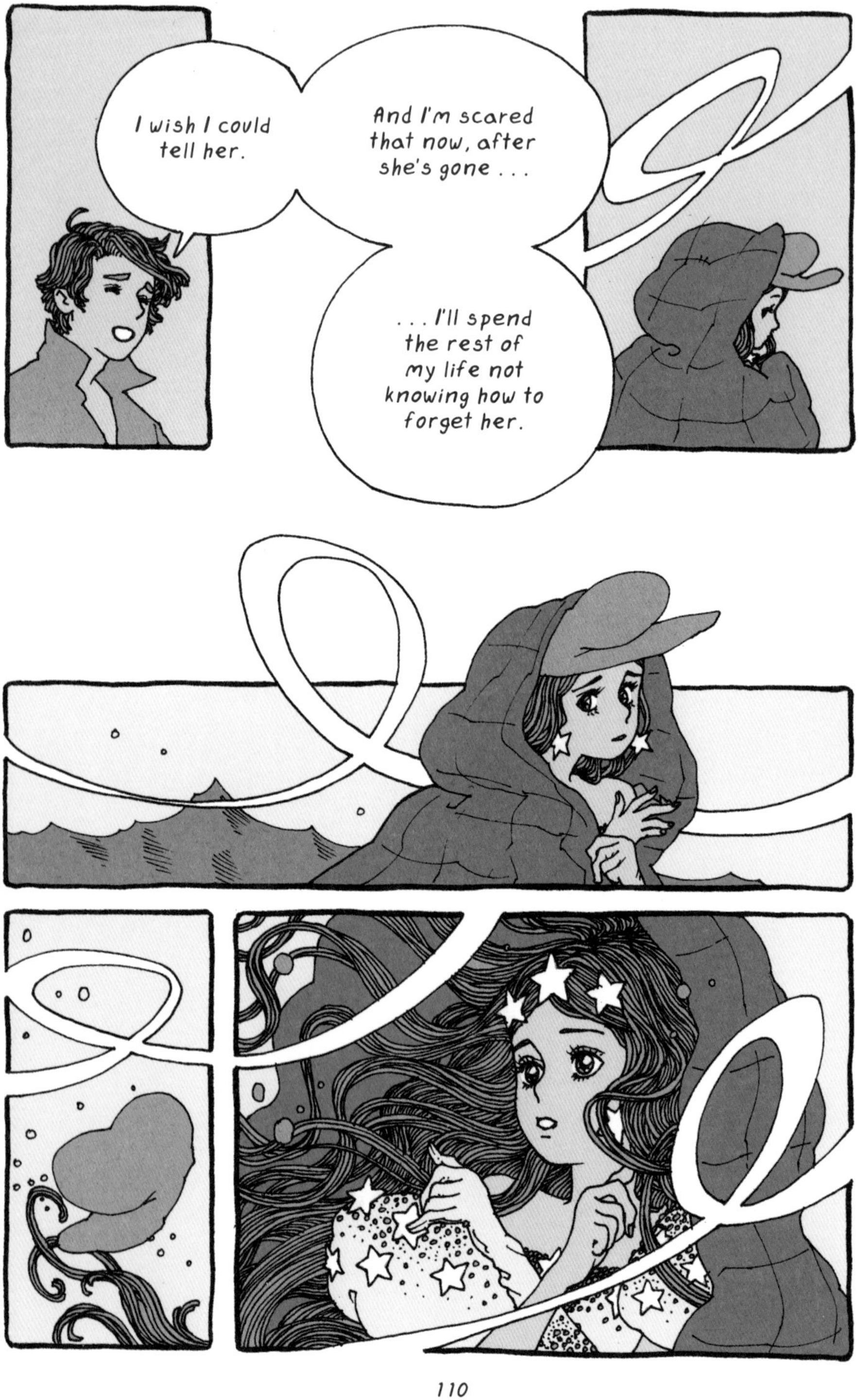
I wish I could tell her.
And I'm scared that now, after she's gone . . .
. . . I'll spend the rest of my life not knowing how to forget her.

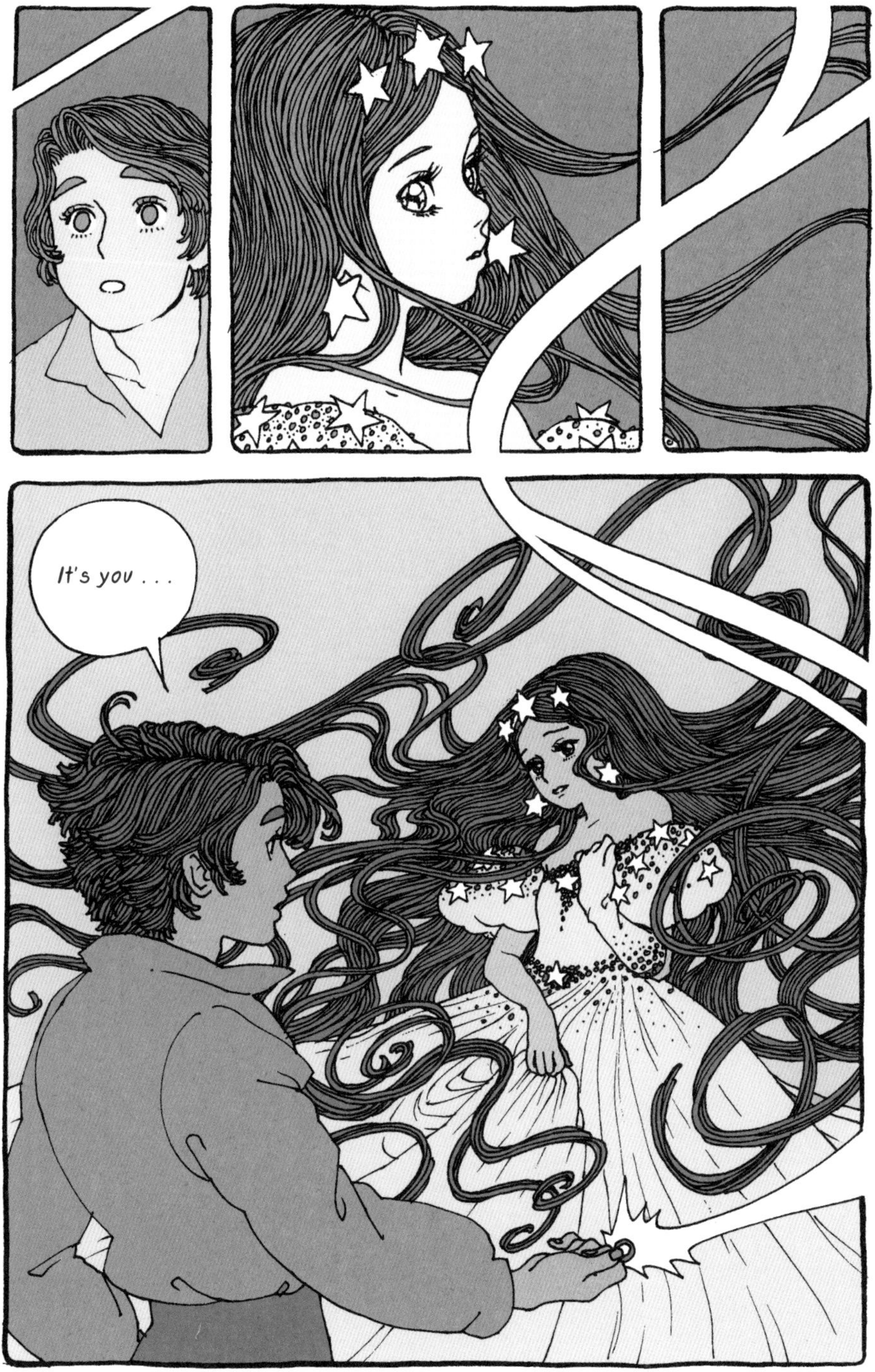
It's you . . .

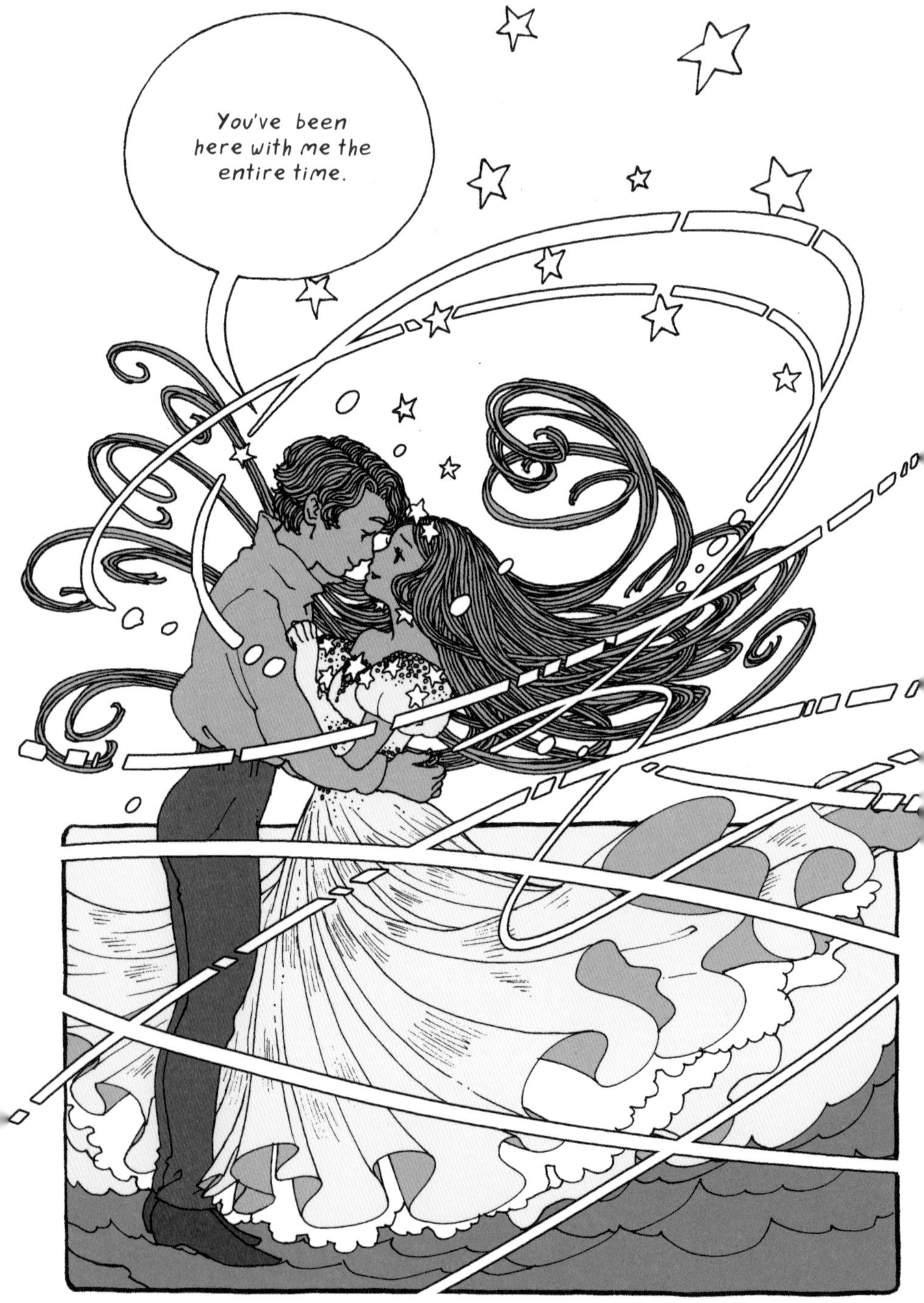
You've been here with me the entire time.

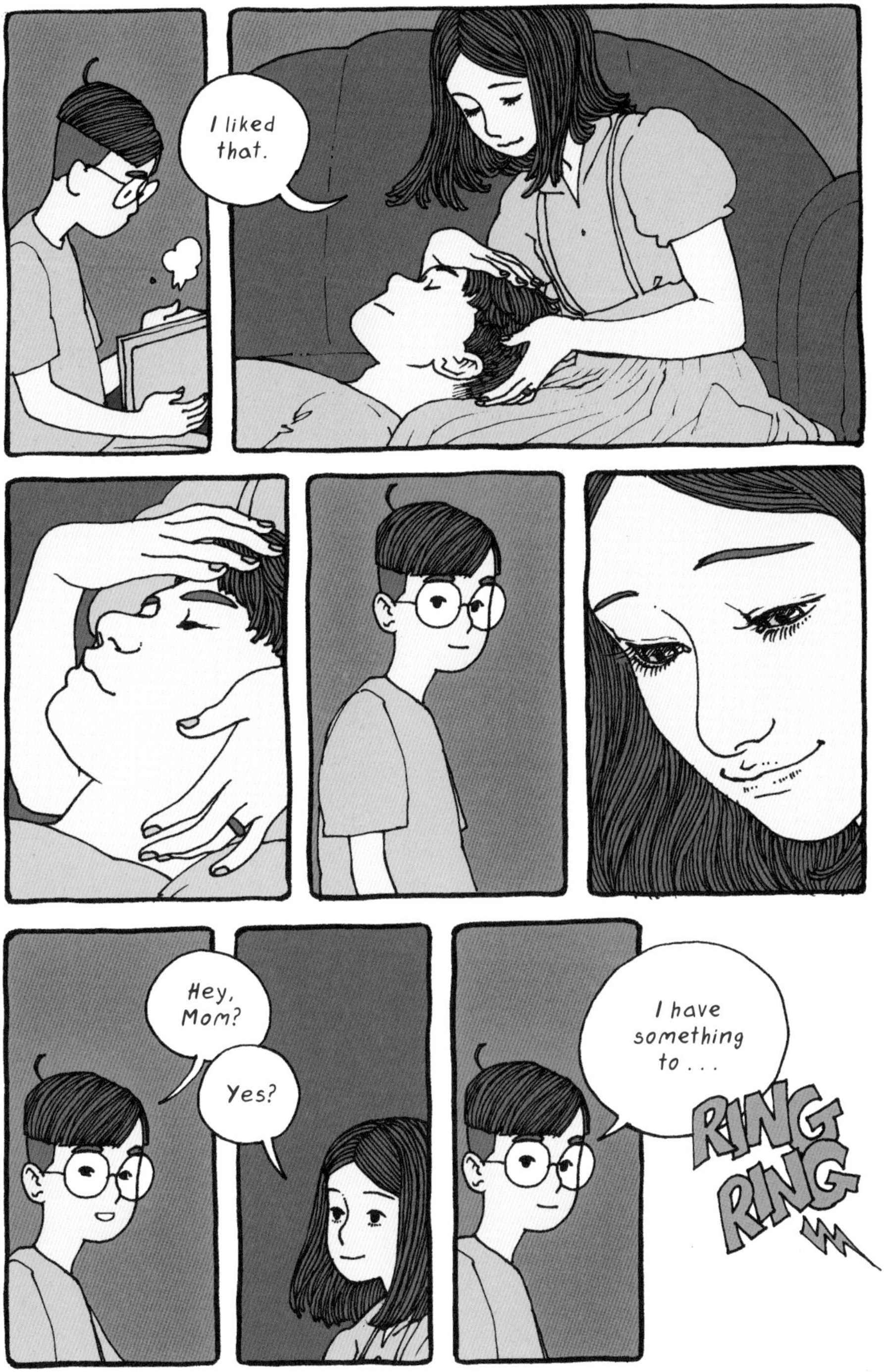
I liked that.
Hey, Mom?
Yes?
I have something to . . .
RING RING

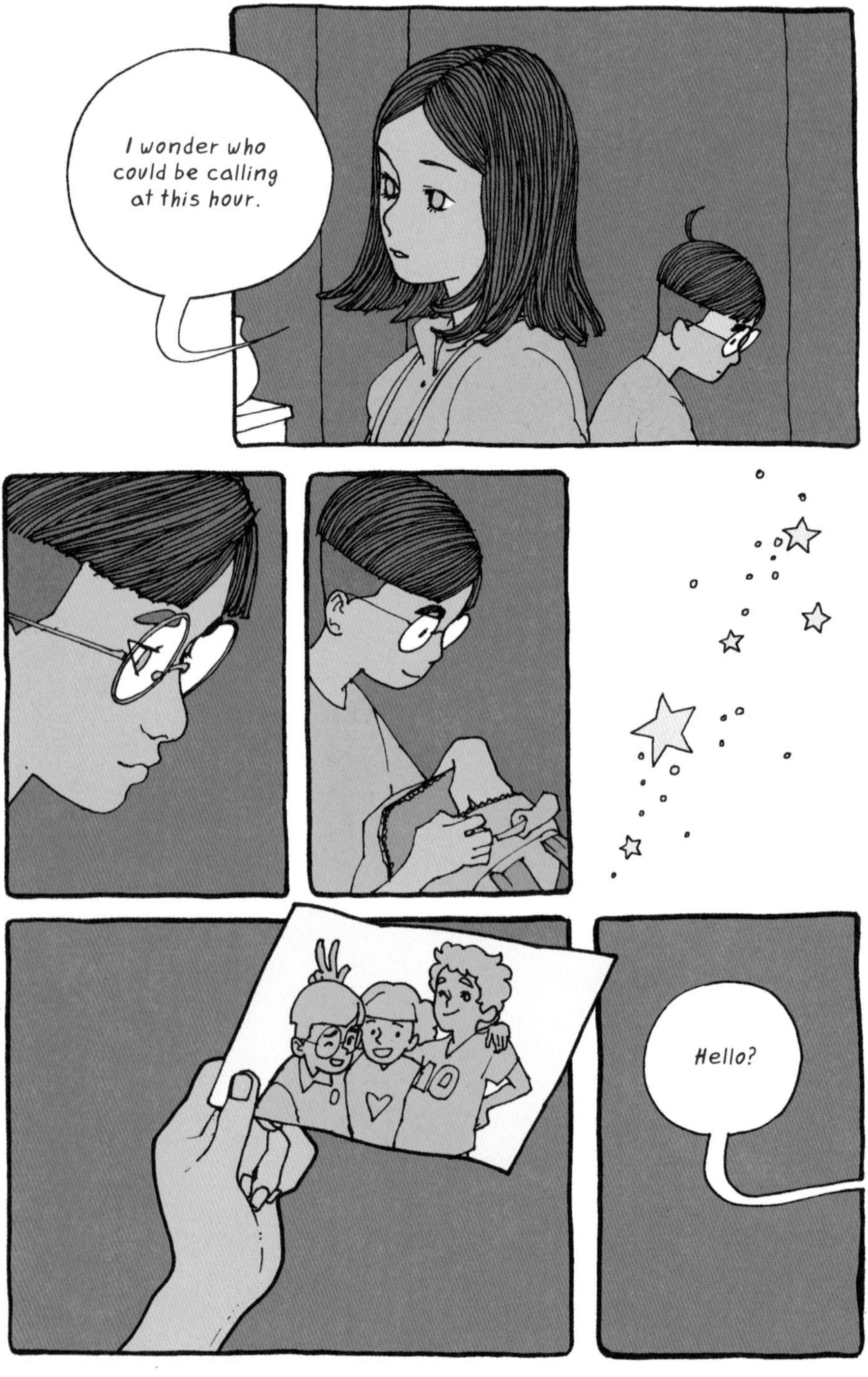
I wonder who could be calling at this hour.
Hello?

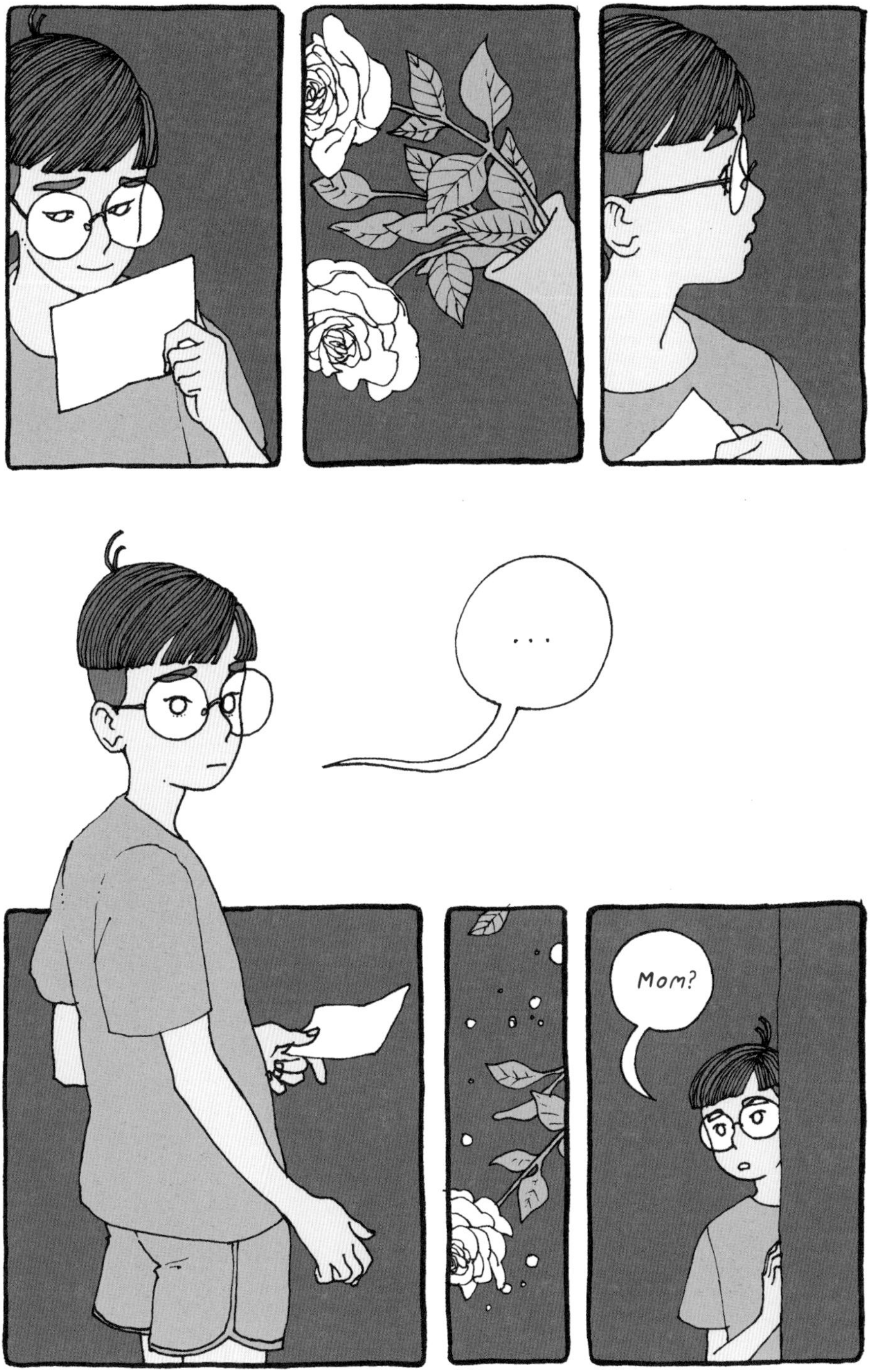
. . .
Mom?

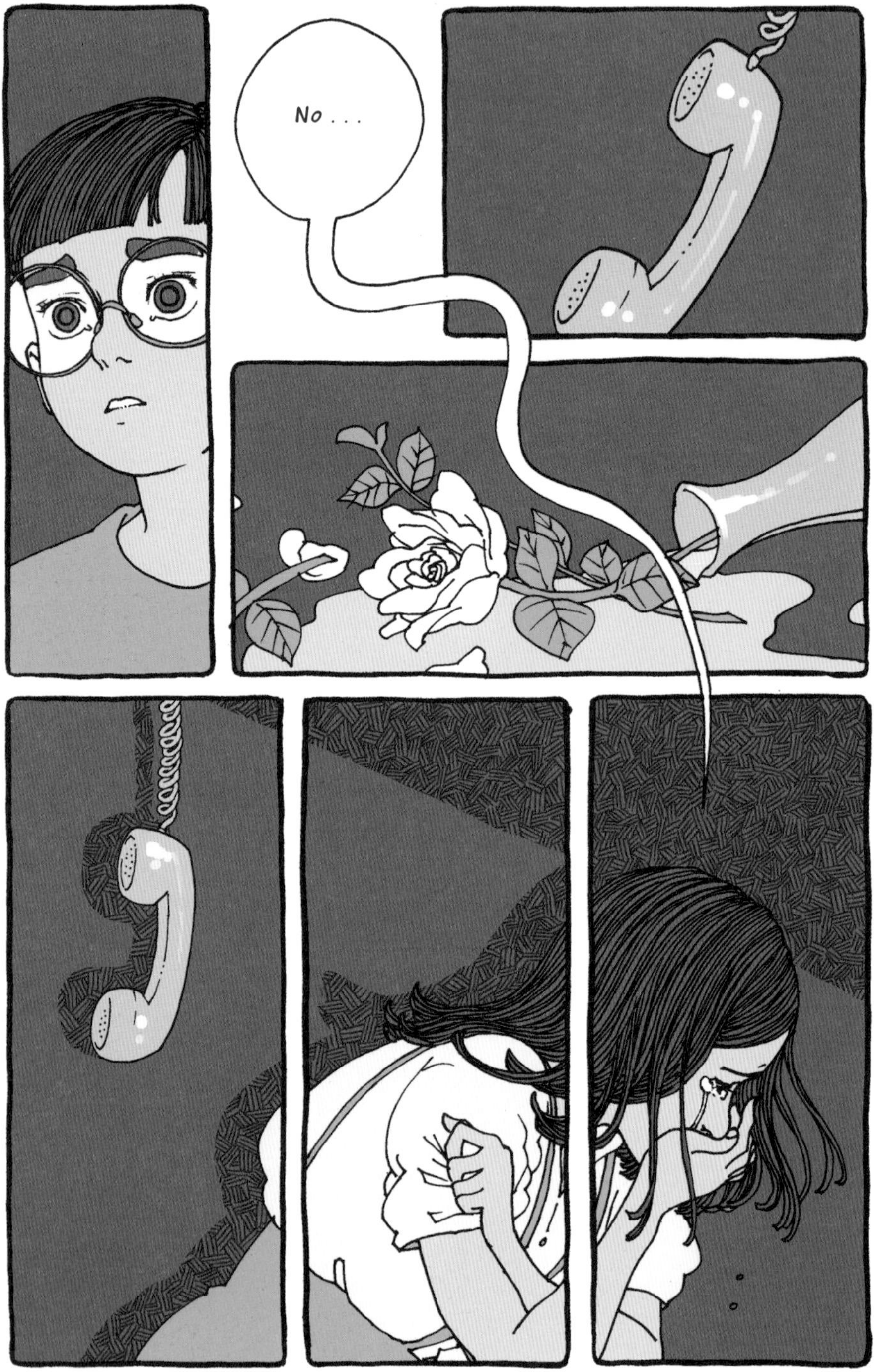
No . . .

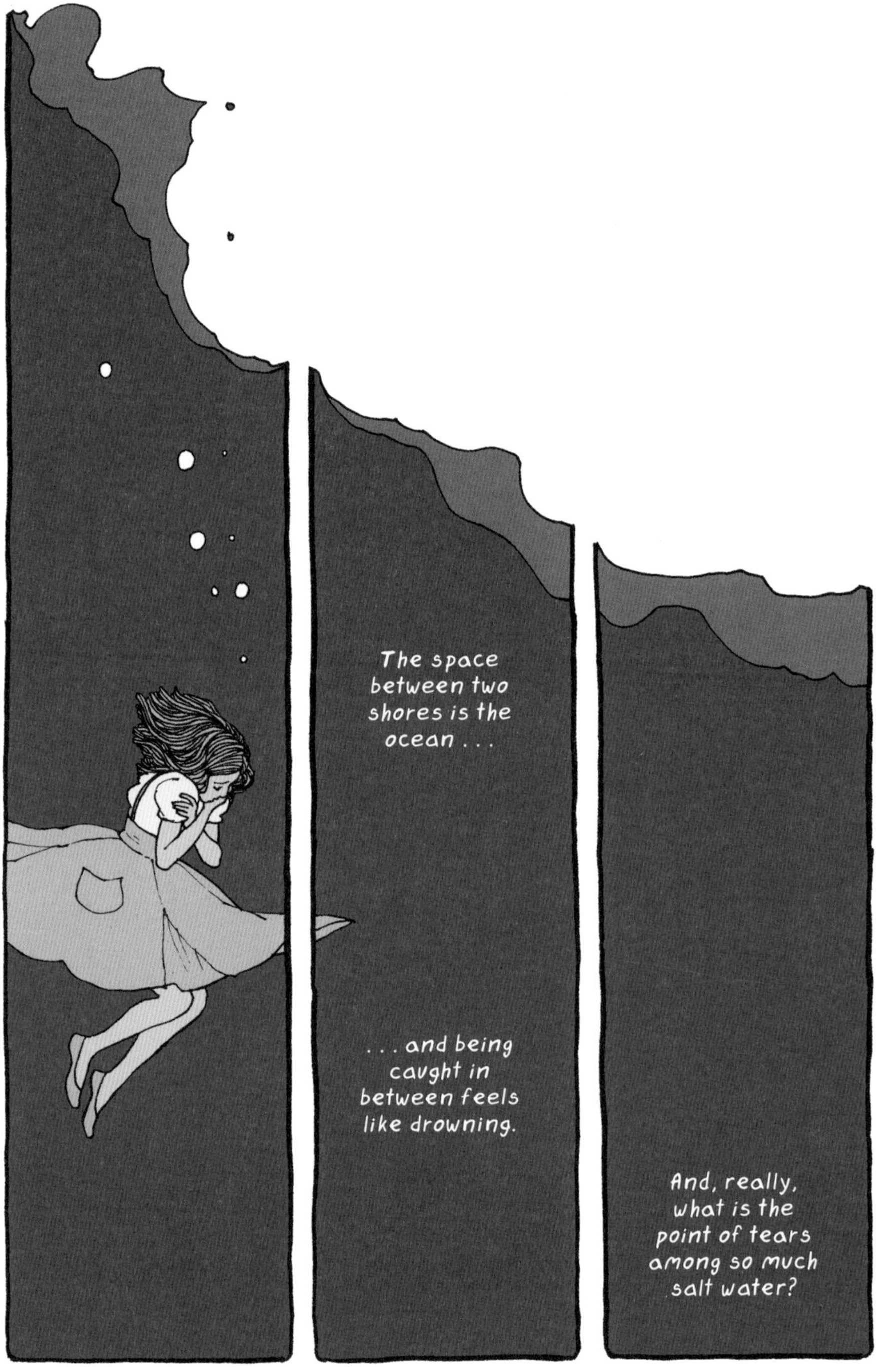
The space between two shores is the ocean . . .
. . . and being caught in between feels like drowning.
And, really, what is the point of tears among so much salt water?

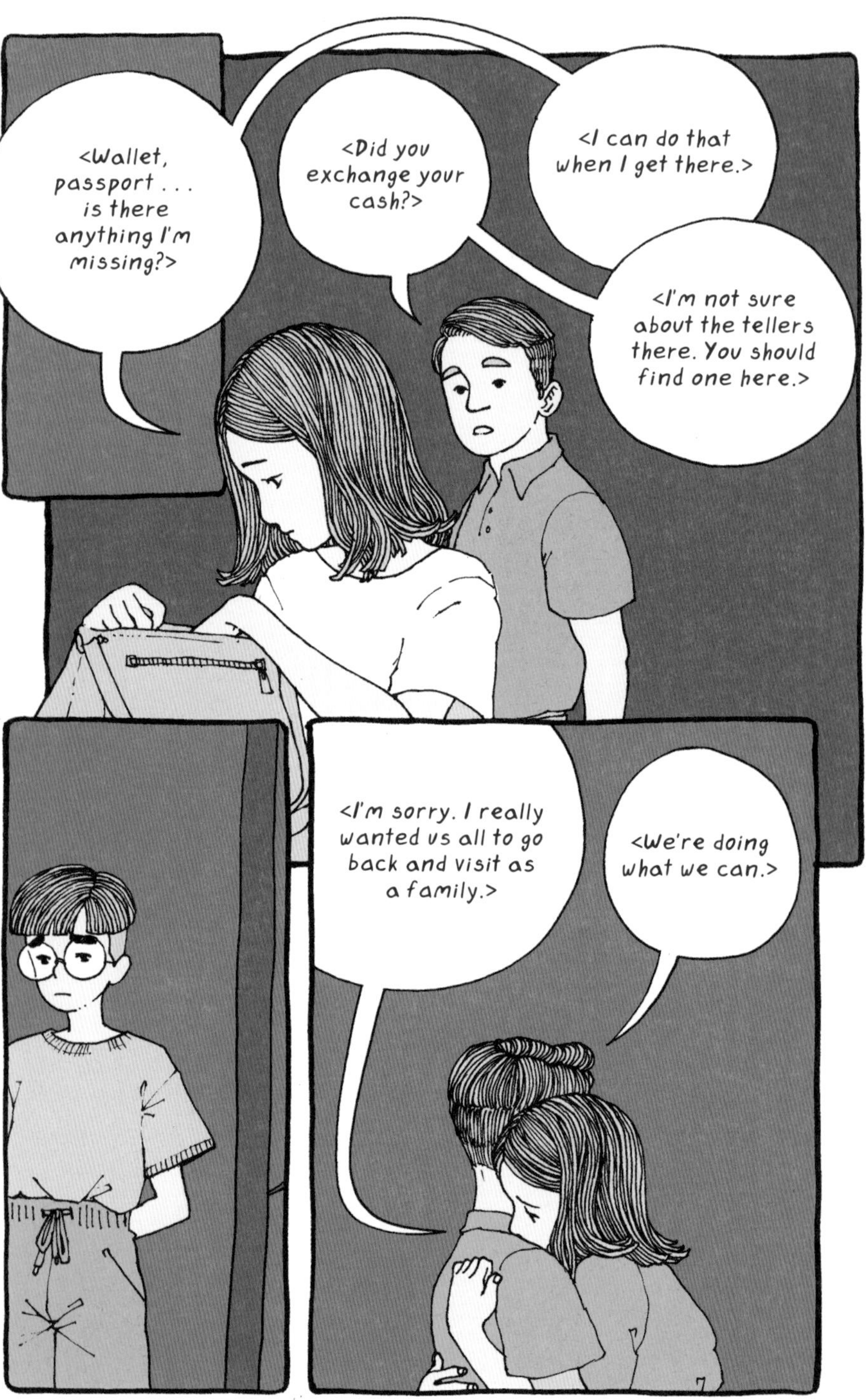
<Wallet, passport . . . is there anything I'm missing?>
<Did you exchange your cash?>
<I can do that when I get there.>
<I'm not sure about the tellers there. You should find one here.>
<I'm sorry. I really wanted us all to go back and visit as a family.>
<We're doing what we can.>

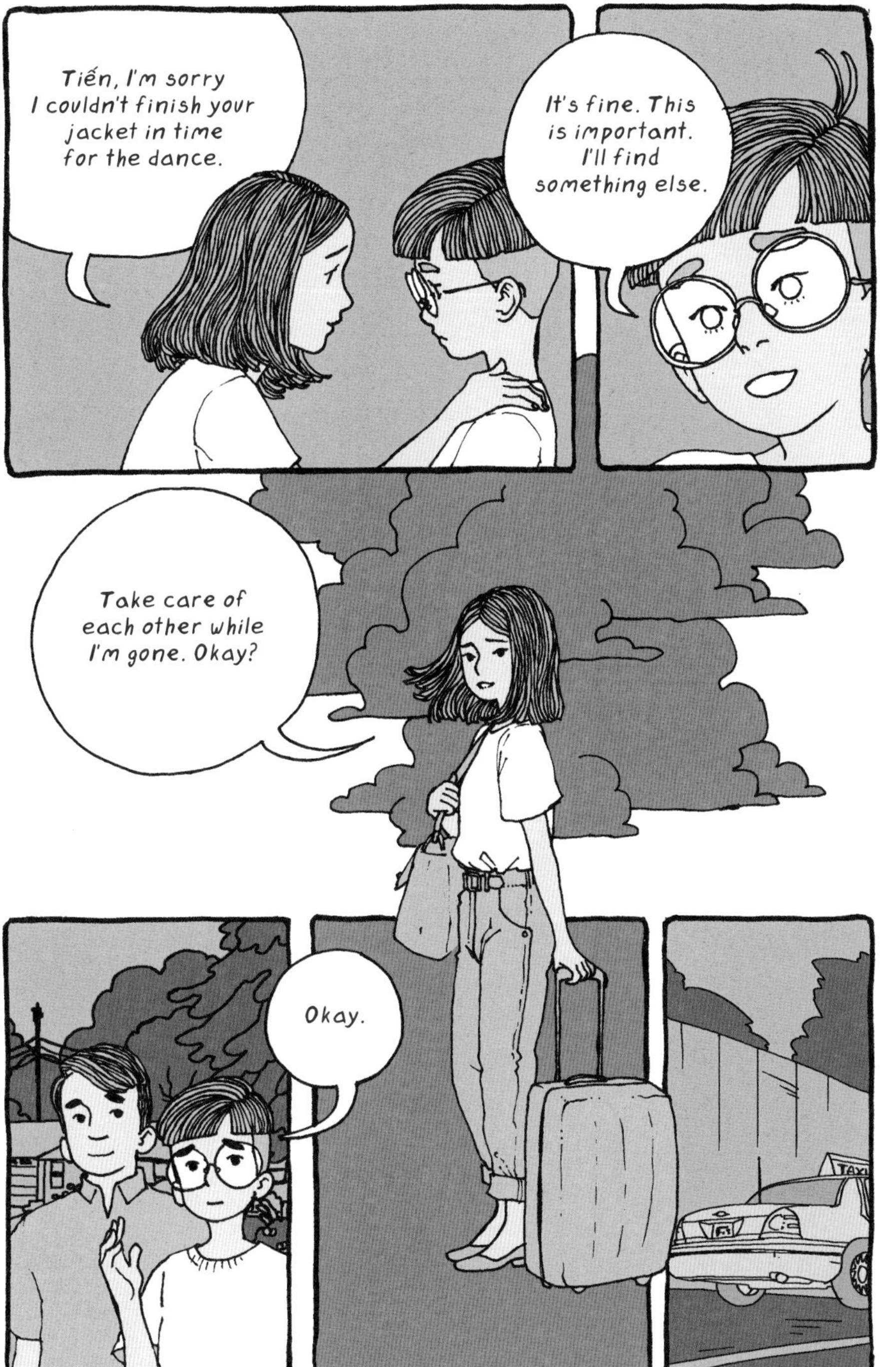
Tiến, I'm sorry I couldn't finish your jacket in time for the dance.
It's fine. This is important. I'll find something else.
Take care of each other while I'm gone. Okay?
Okay.
TAXI

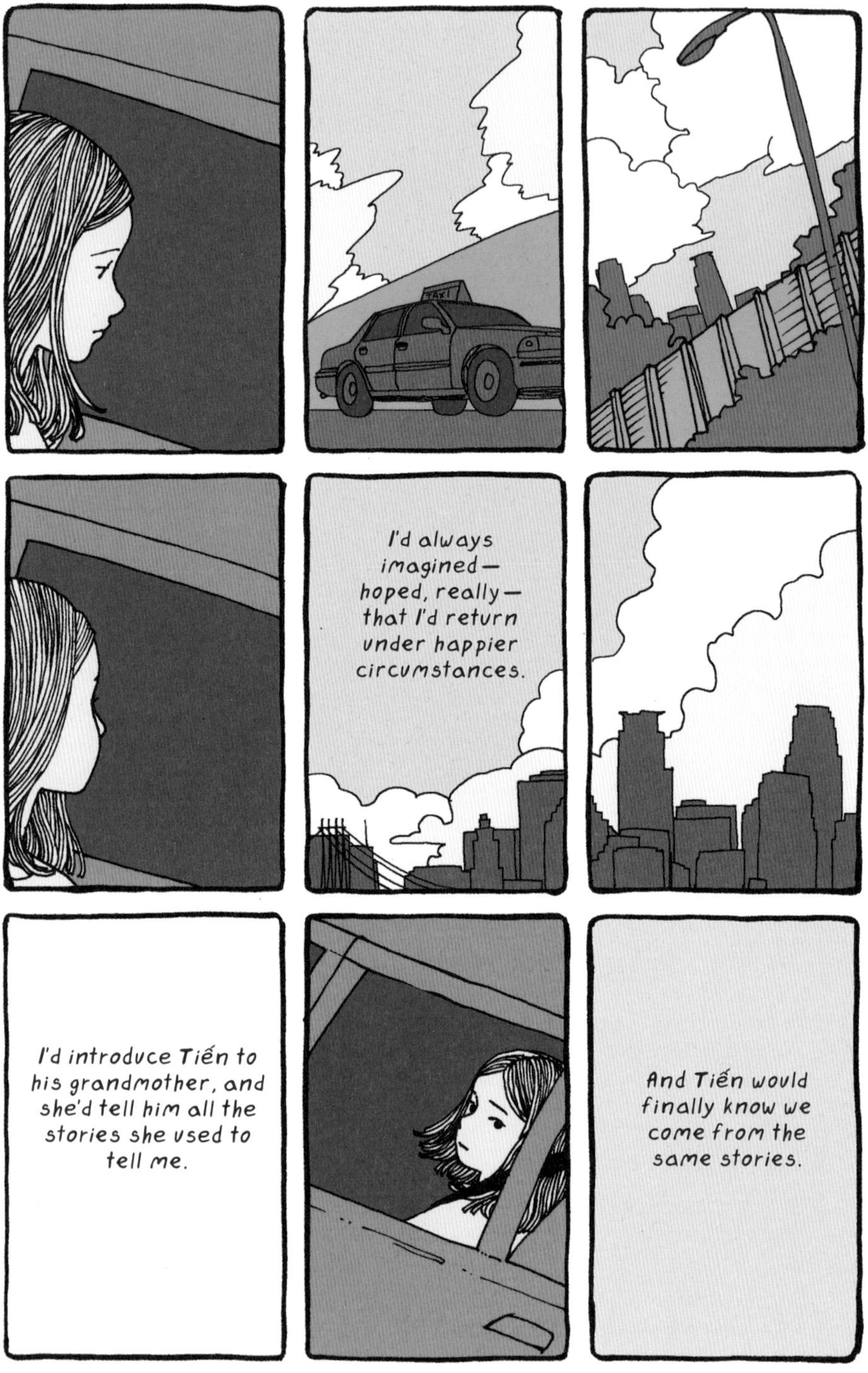
I'd always imagined—hoped, really—that I'd return under happier circumstances.
I'd introduce Tiến to his grandmother, and she'd tell him all the stories she used to tell me.
And Tiến would finally know we come from the same stories.

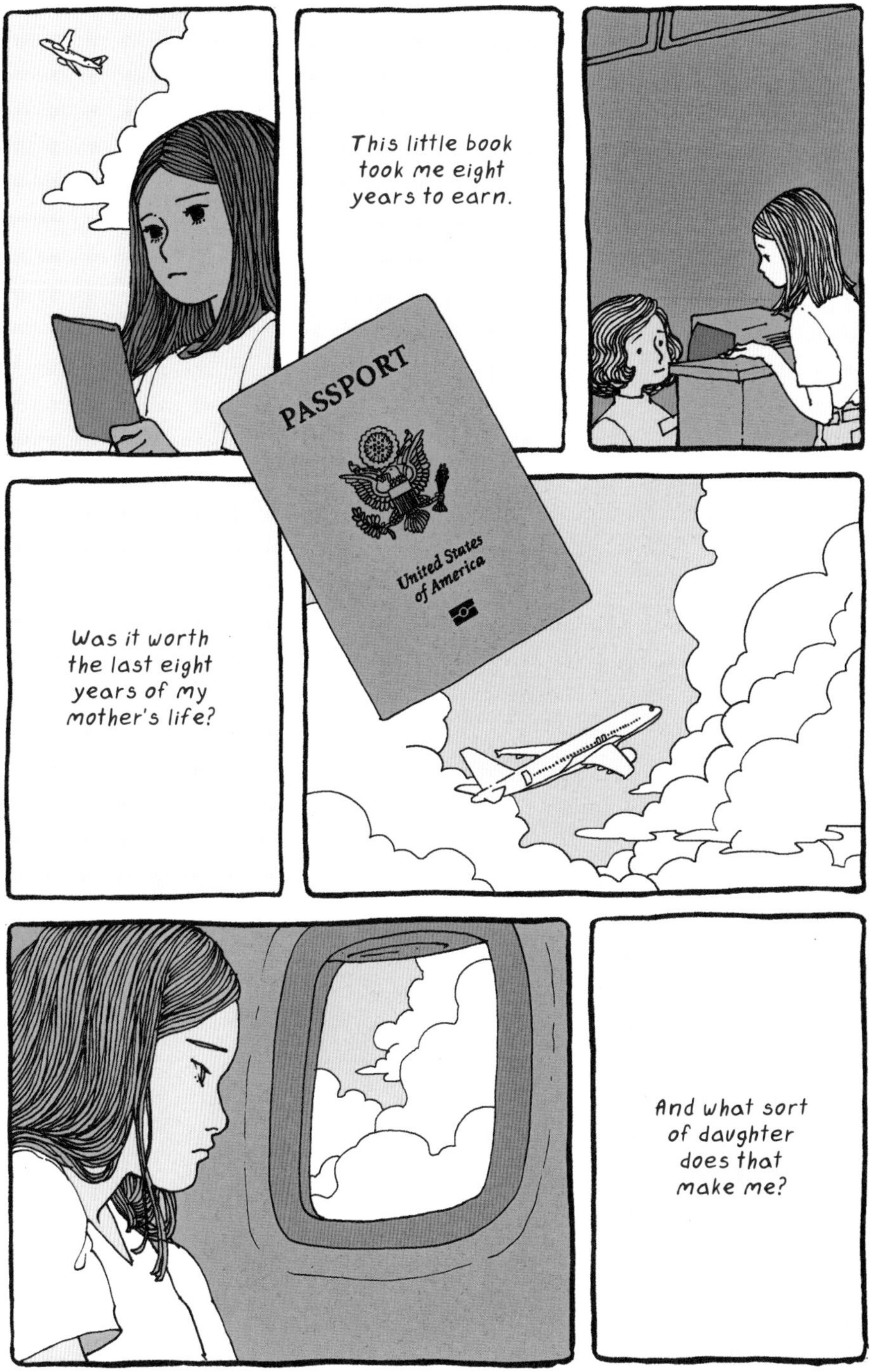
This little book took me eight years to earn.
PASSPORT
United States of America
Was it worth the last eight years of my mother's life?
And what sort of daughter does that make me?

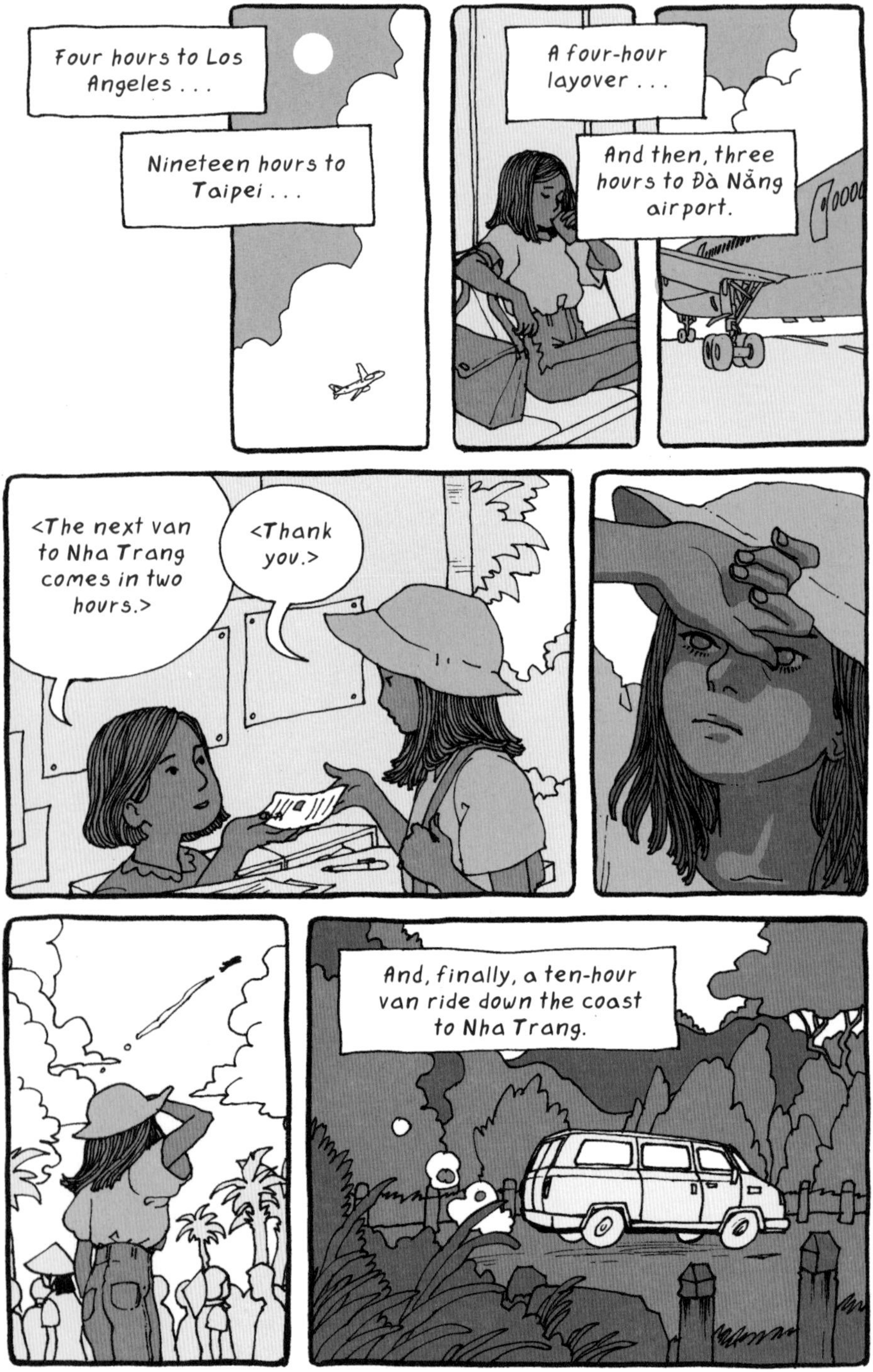
Four hours to Los Angeles . . .
Nineteen hours to Taipei . . .
A four-hour layover . . .
And then, three hours to Đà Nẵng airport.
<The next van to Nha Trang comes in two hours.>
<Thank you.>
And, finally, a ten-hour van ride down the coast to Nha Trang.

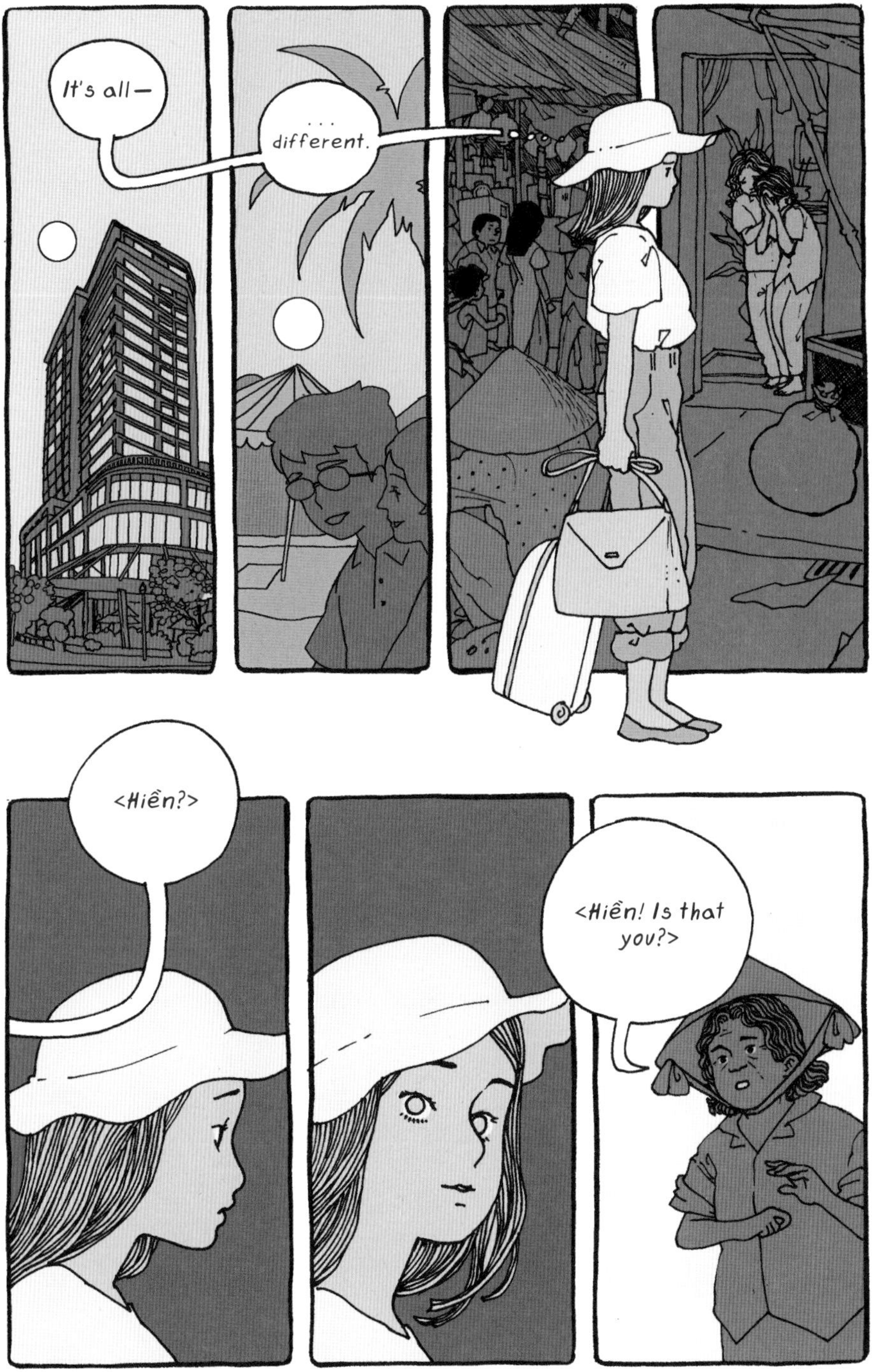
It's all—
. . . different.
<Hiền?>
<Hiền! Is that you?>

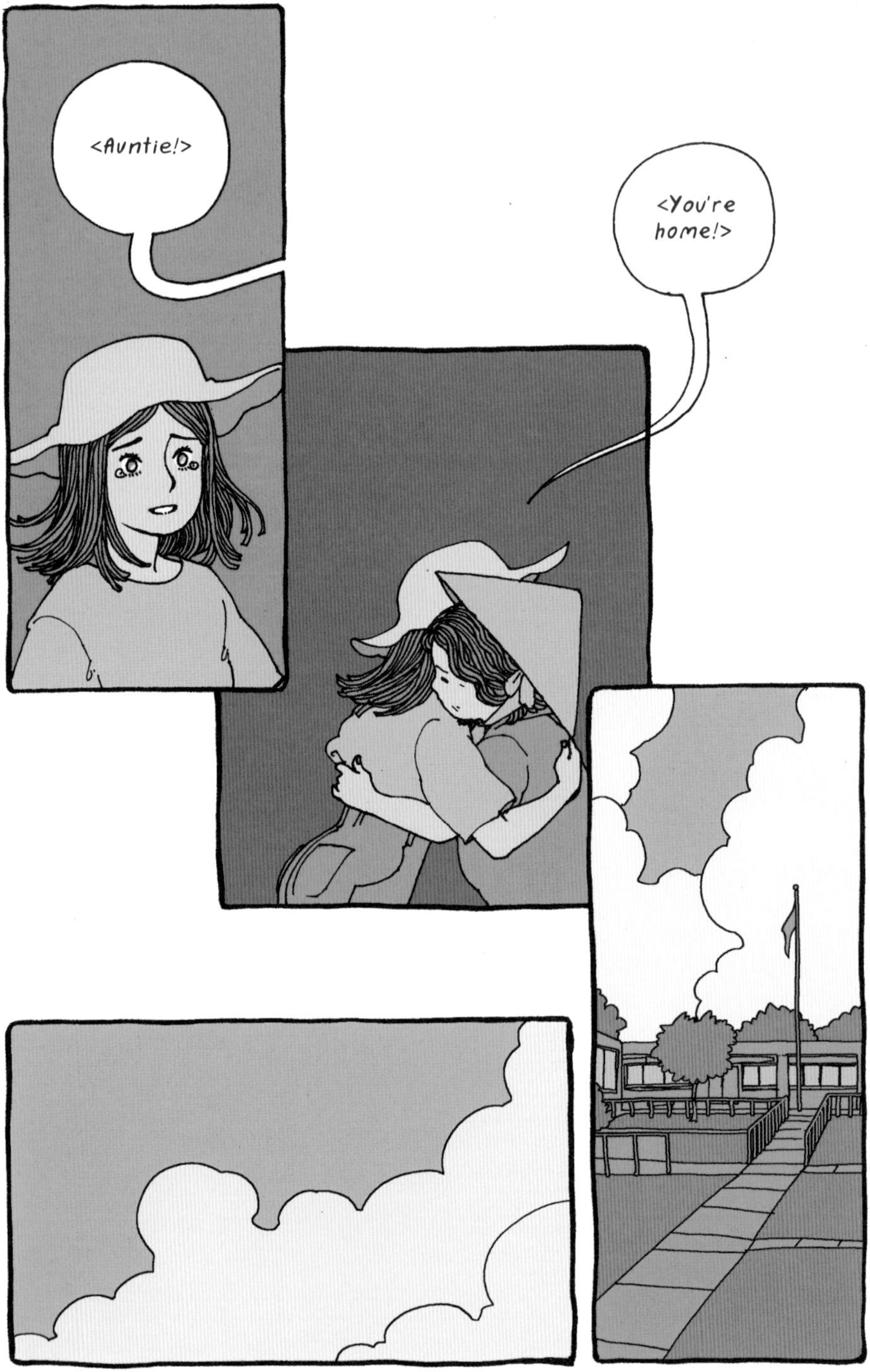
<Auntie!>
<You're home!>

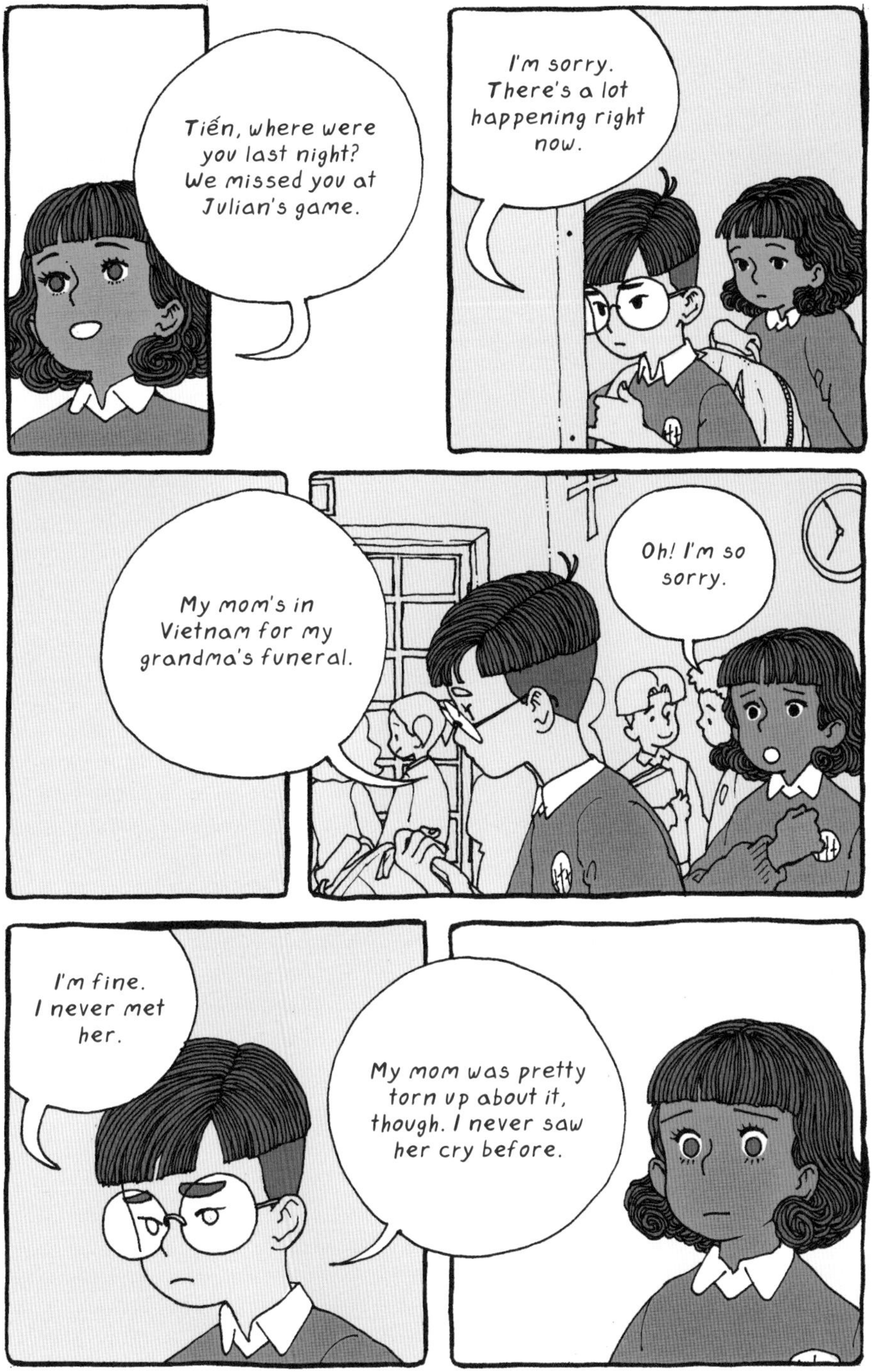

Tiến, where were you last night? We missed you at Julian's game.
I'm sorry. There's a lot happening right now.
My mom's in Vietnam for my grandma's funeral.
Oh! I'm so sorry.
I'm fine. I never met her.
My mom was pretty torn up about it, though. I never saw her cry before.

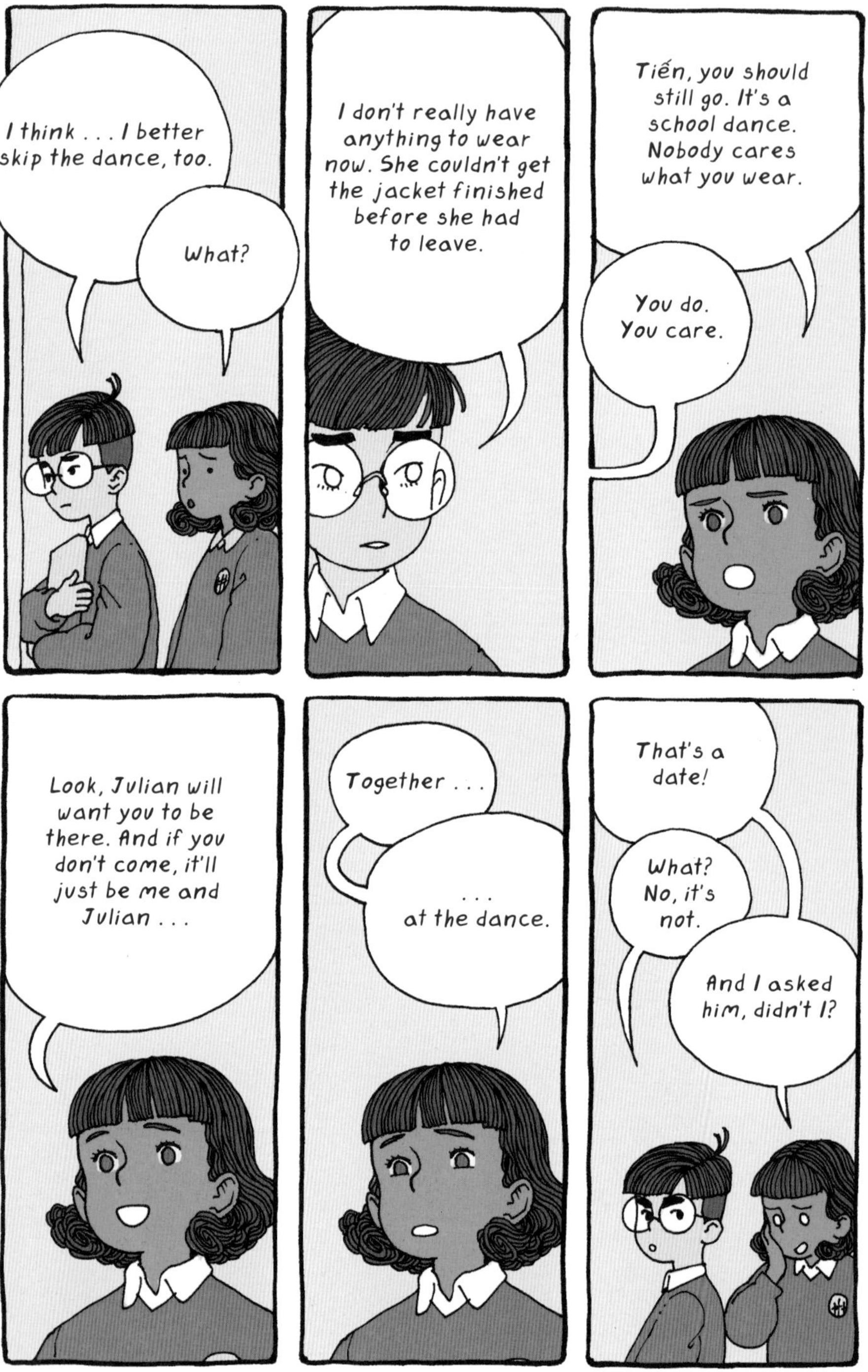
I think . . . I better skip the dance, too.
What?
I don't really have anything to wear now. She couldn't get the jacket finished before she had to leave.
Tiến, you should still go. It's a school dance. Nobody cares what you wear.
You do. You care.
Look, Julian will want you to be there. And if you don't come, it'll just be me and Julian . . .
Together . . .
. . . at the dance.
That's a date!
What? No, it's not.
And I asked him, didn't I?

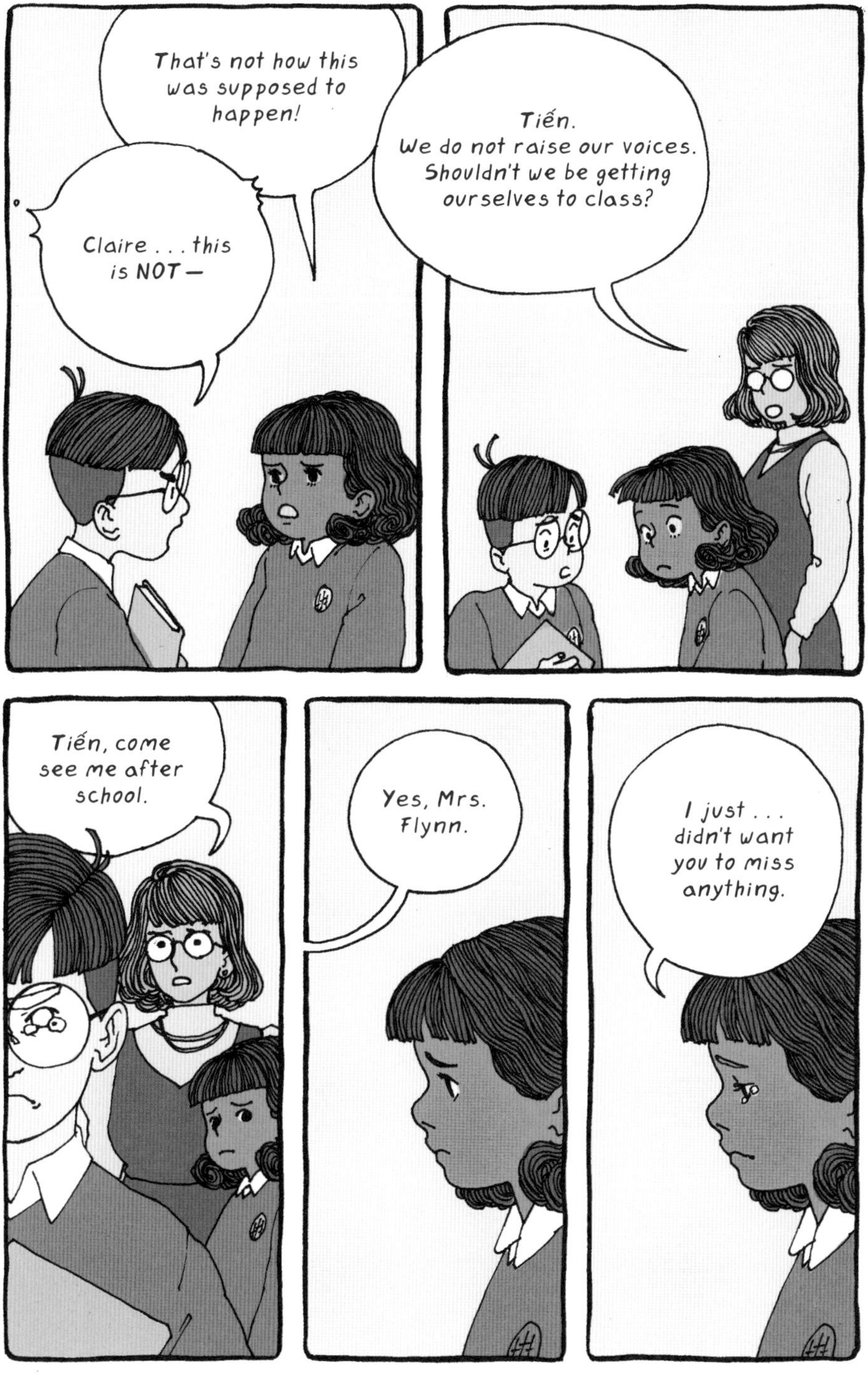
That's not how this was supposed to happen!
Claire . . . this is NOT—
Tiến. We do not raise our voices. Shouldn't we be getting ourselves to class?
Tiến, come see me after school.
Yes, Mrs. Flynn.
I just . . . didn't want you to miss anything.

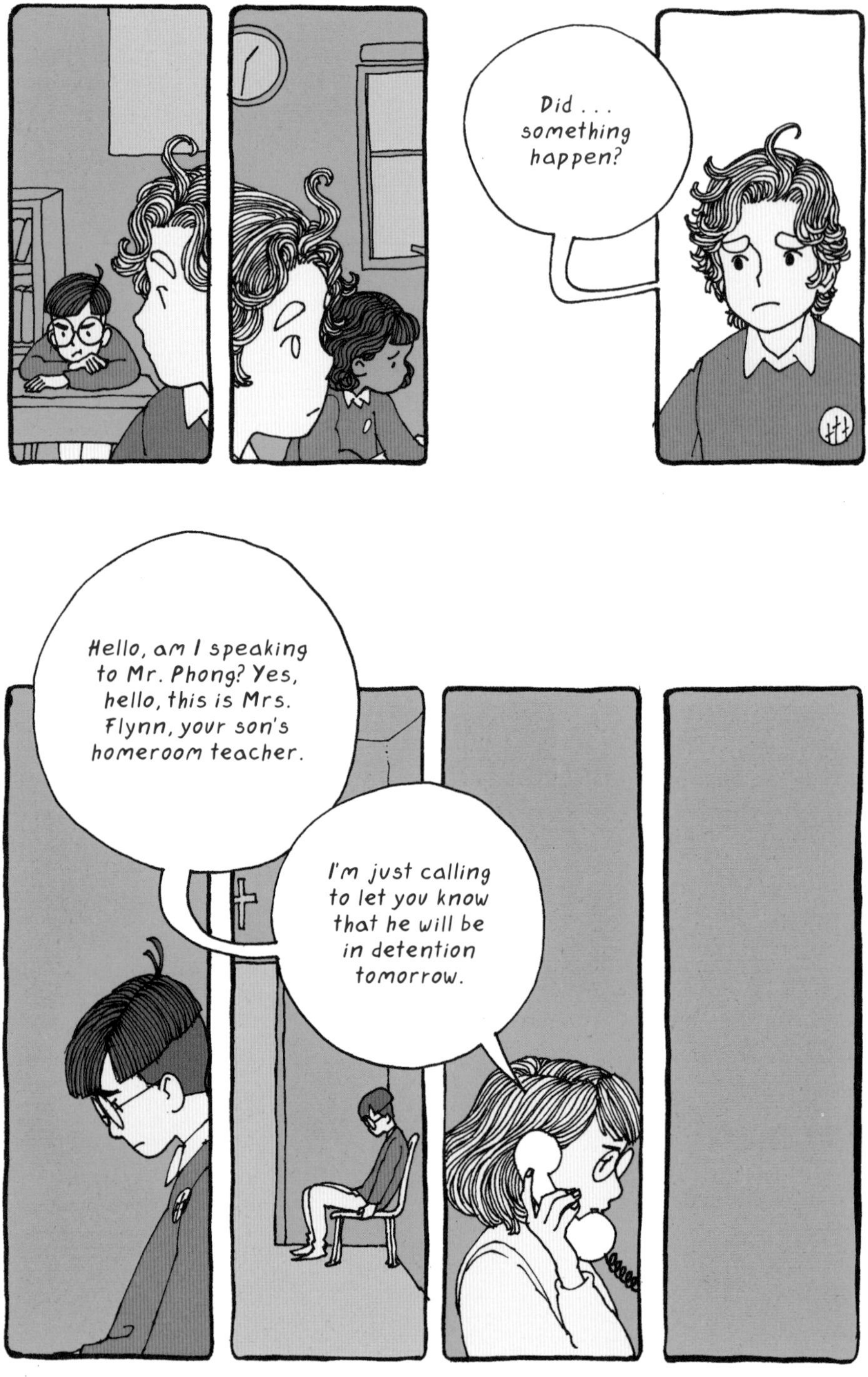
Did . . . something happen?
Hello, am I speaking to Mr. Phong? Yes, hello, this is Mrs. Flynn, your son's homeroom teacher.
I'm just calling to let you know that he will be in detention tomorrow.

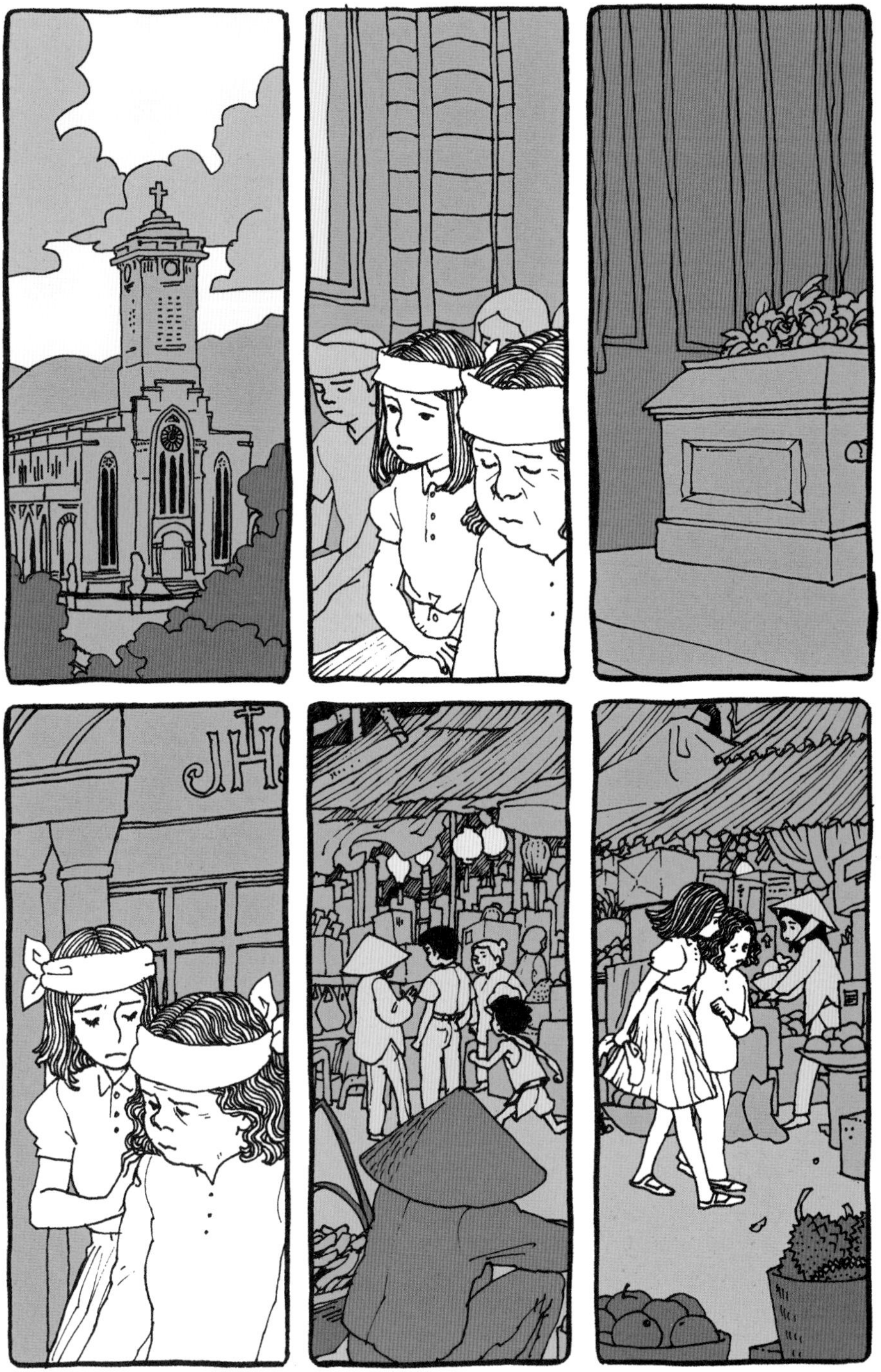

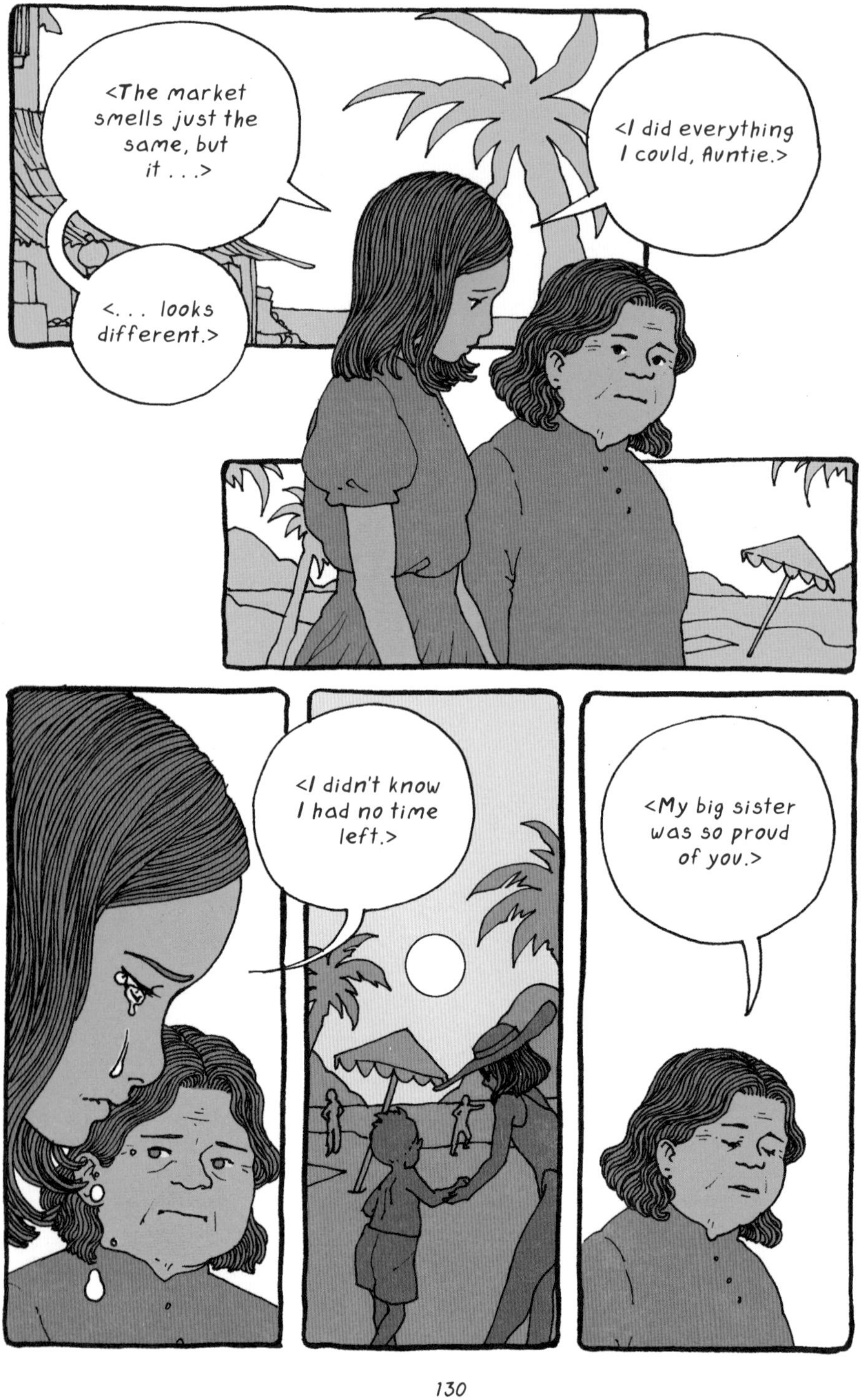
<The market smells just the same, but it . . .>
<. . . looks different.>
<I did everything I could, Auntie.>
<I didn't know I had no time left.>
<My big sister was so proud of you.>

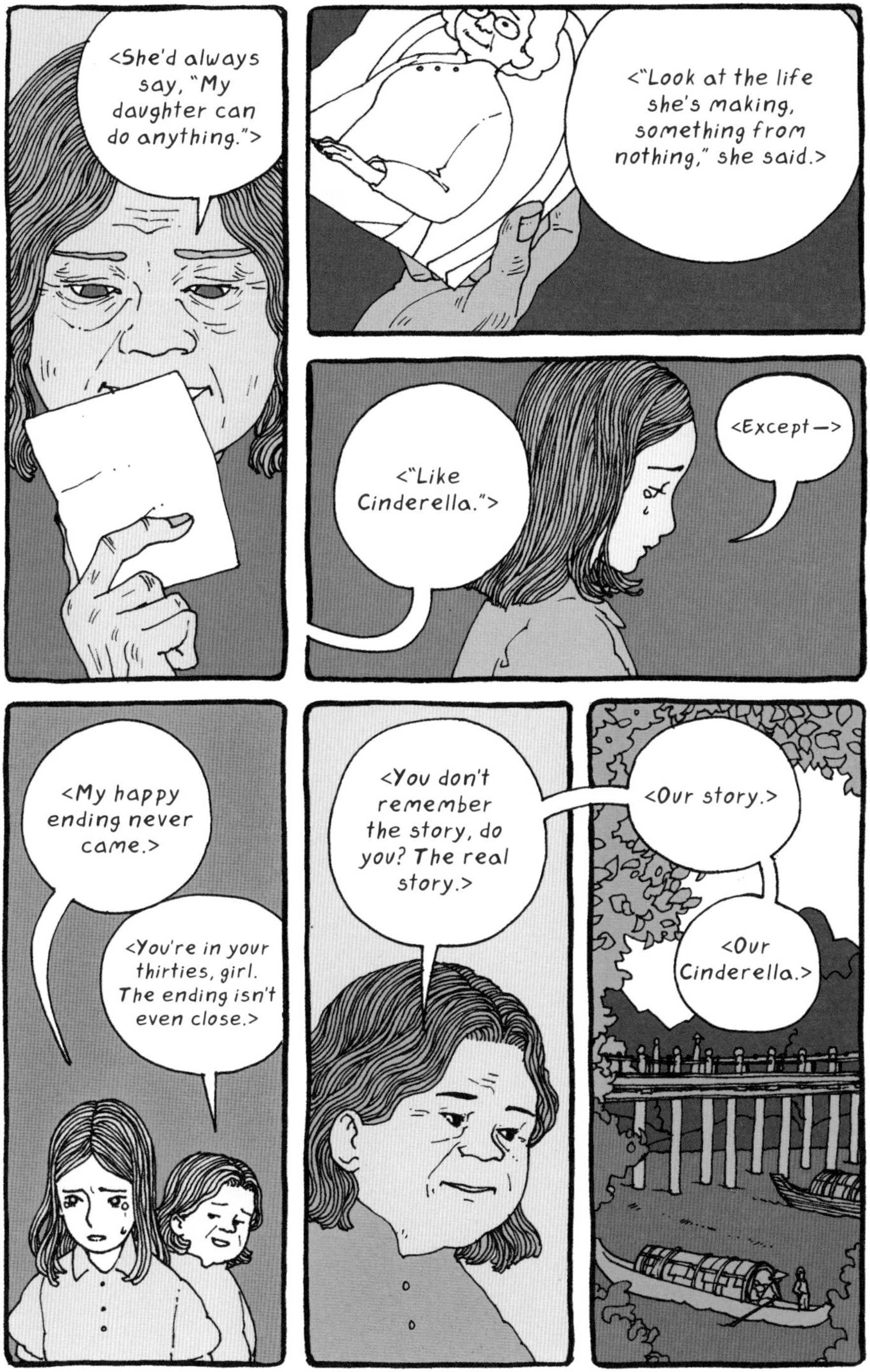
<She'd always say, "My daughter can do anything.">
<"Look at the life she's making, something from nothing," she said.>
<"Like Cinderella.">
<Except—>
<My happy ending never came.>
<You're in your thirties, girl. The ending isn't even close.>
<You don't remember the story, do you? The real story.>
<Our story.>
<Our Cinderella.>

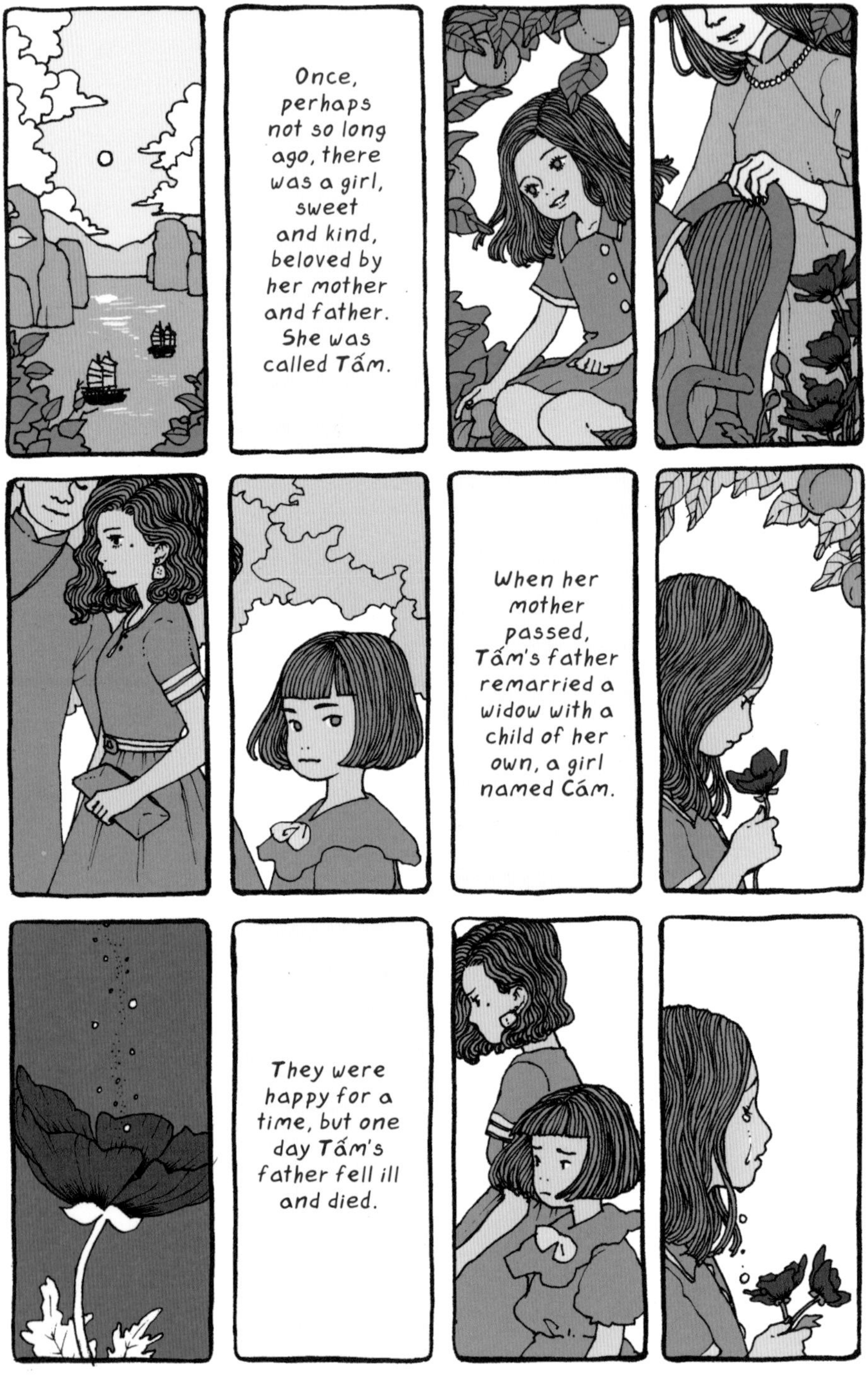
Once, perhaps not so long ago, there was a girl, sweet and kind, beloved by her mother and father. She was called Tấm.
When her mother passed, Tấm's father remarried a widow with a child of her own, a girl named Cám.
They were happy for a time, but one day Tấm's father fell ill and died.

Her stepmother's grief turned to anger, and that anger was directed at Tấm.

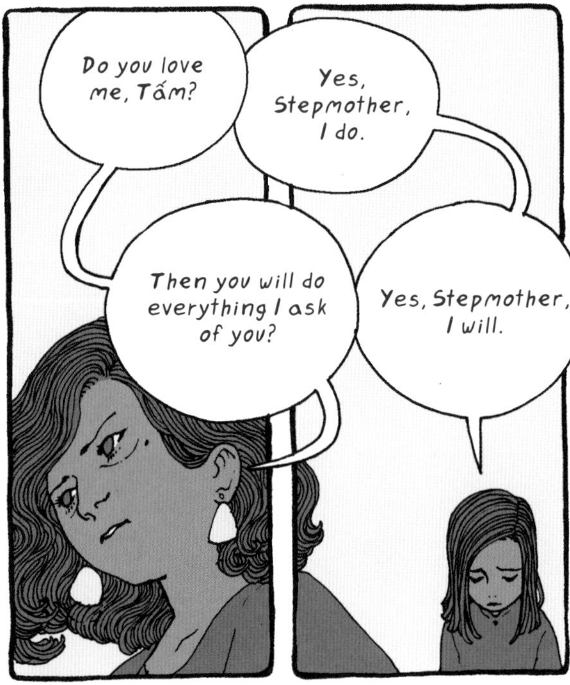
Do you love me, Tấm?
Yes, Stepmother, I do.
Then you will do everything I ask of you?
Yes, Stepmother, I will.

Tấm did her best to comply with all her stepmother's demands. She moved out of the main building and into a little garden in the alley.

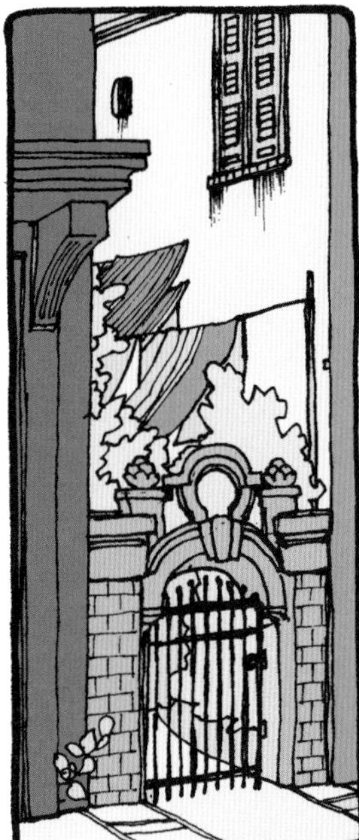

She cooked.

She cleaned.

She took meticulous care of the household.

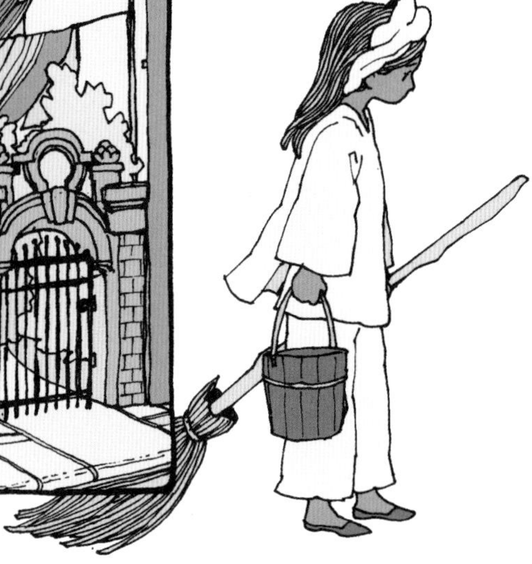

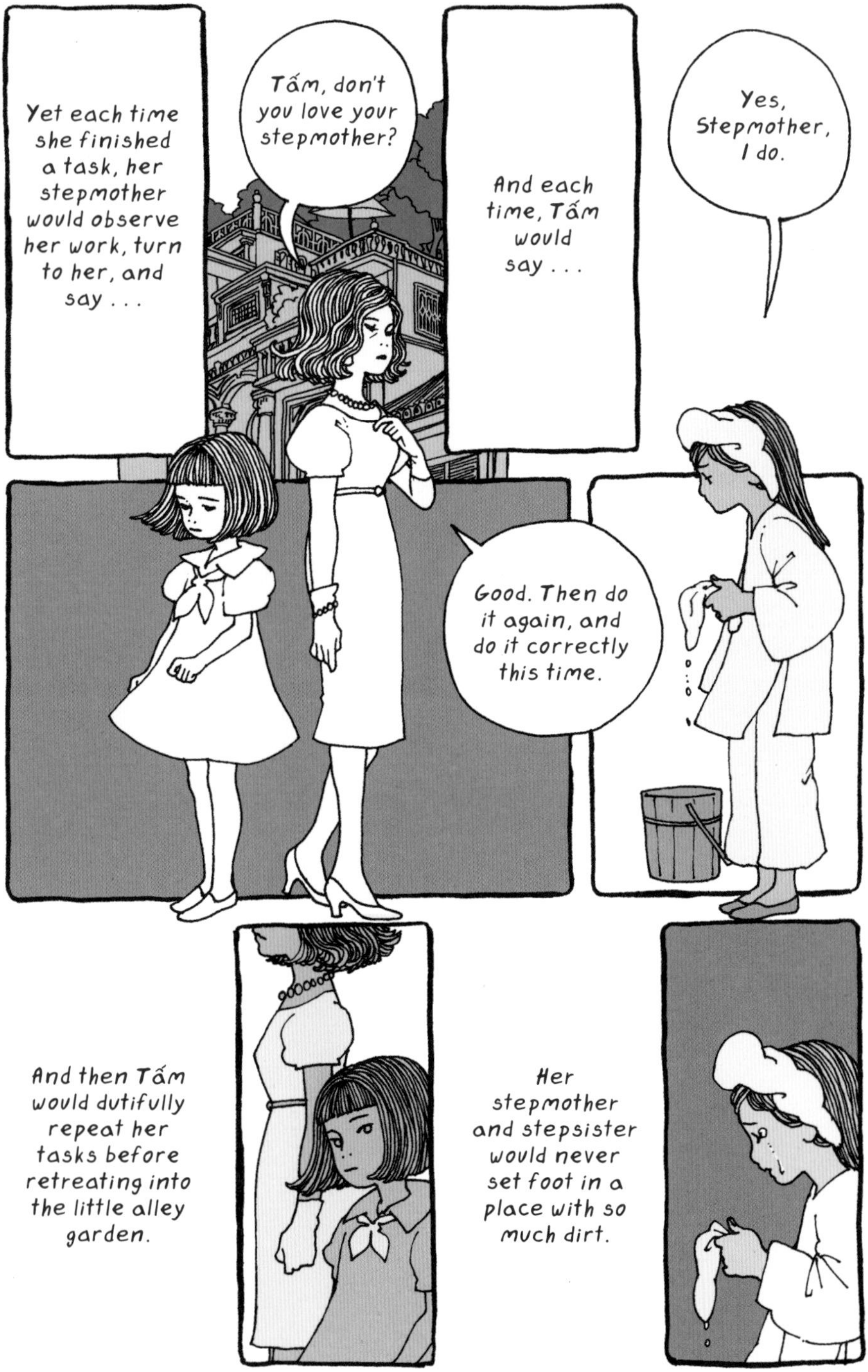
Yet each time she finished a task, her stepmother would observe her work, turn to her, and say . . .
Tấm, don't you love your stepmother?
And each time, Tấm would say . . .
Yes, Stepmother, I do.
Good. Then do it again, and do it correctly this time.
And then Tấm would dutifully repeat her tasks before retreating into the little alley garden.
Her stepmother and stepsister would never set foot in a place with so much dirt.

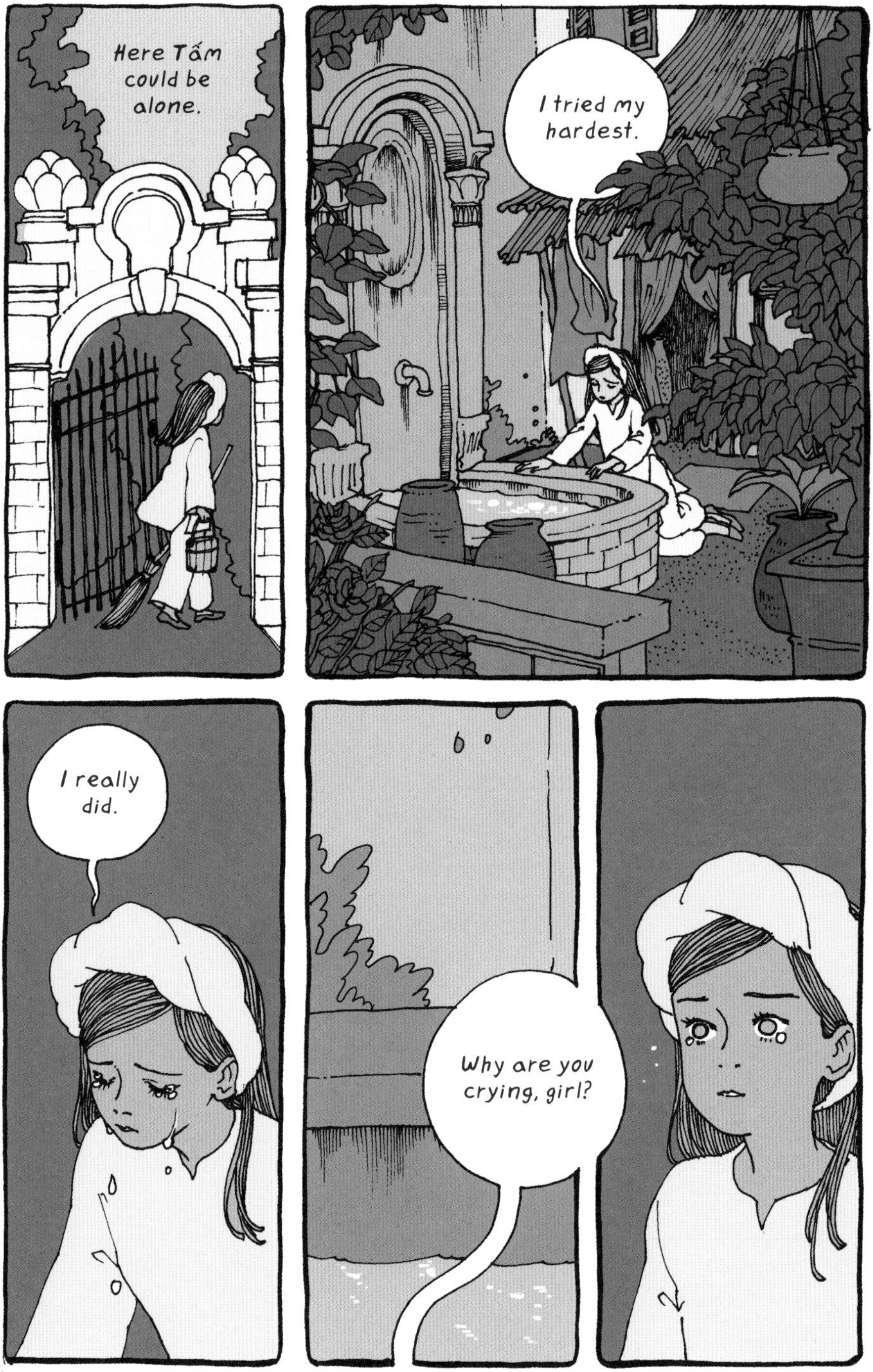
Here Tấm could be alone.
I tried my hardest.
I really did.
Why are you crying, girl?

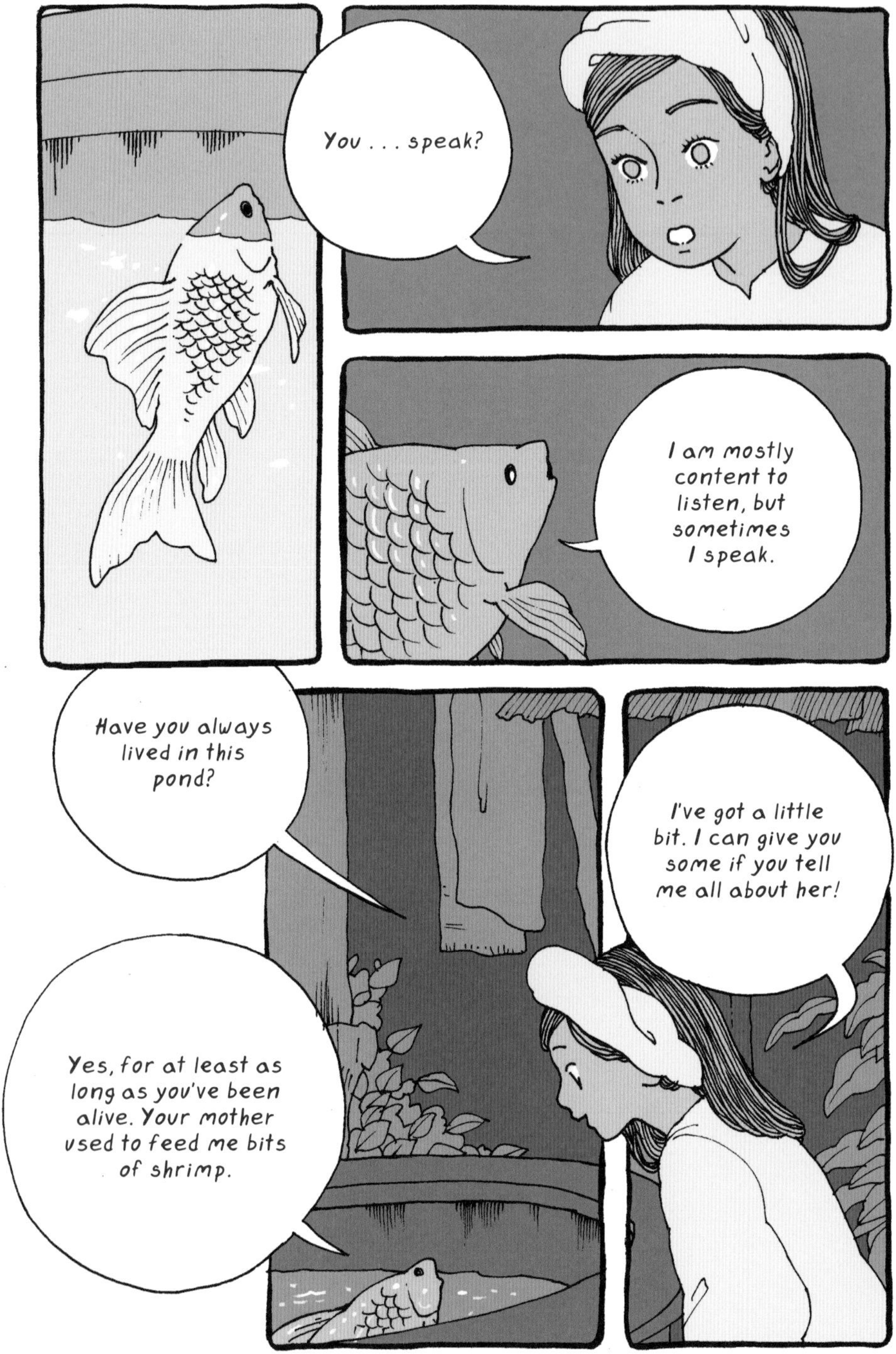
You . . . speak?
I am mostly content to listen, but sometimes I speak.
Have you always lived in this pond?
Yes, for at least as long as you've been alive. Your mother used to feed me bits of shrimp.
I've got a little bit. I can give you some if you tell me all about her!

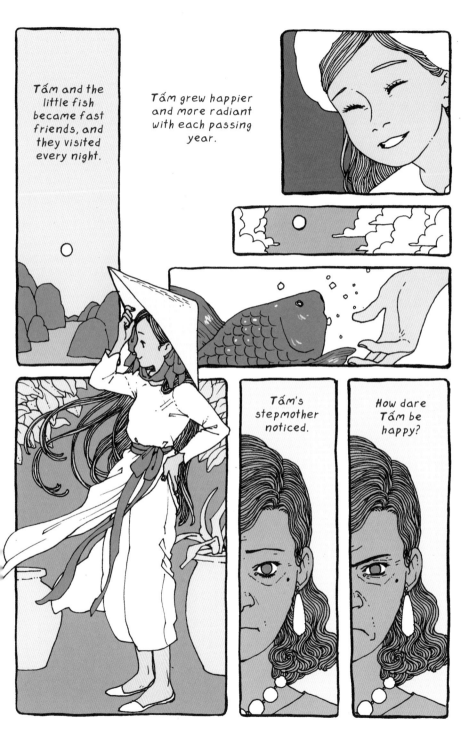

Tấm and the little fish became fast friends, and they visited every night.

Tấm grew happier and more radiant with each passing year.

Tấm's stepmother noticed.

How dare Tấm be happy?

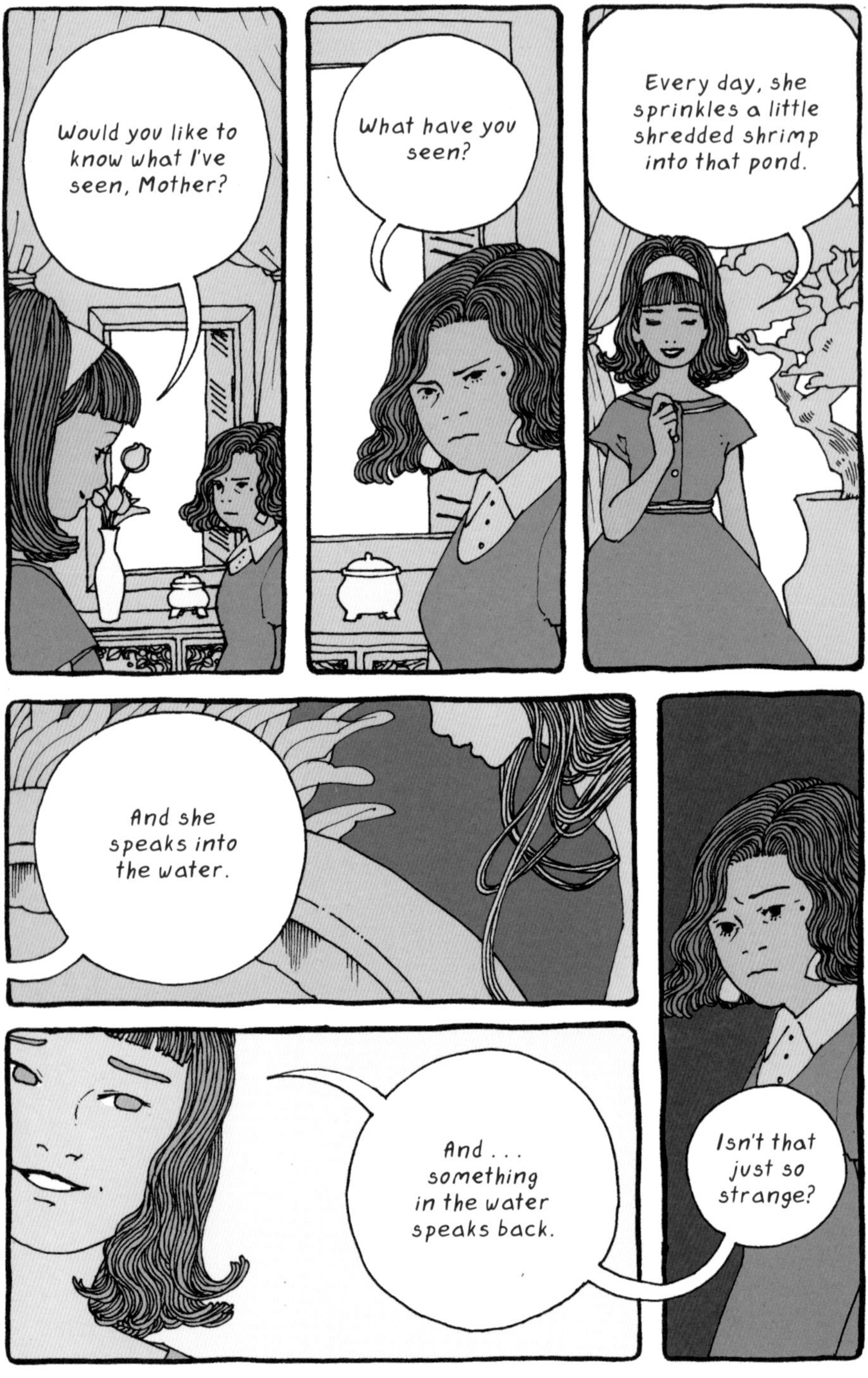
Would you like to know what I've seen, Mother?
What have you seen?
Every day, she sprinkles a little shredded shrimp into that pond.
And she speaks into the water.
And . . . something in the water speaks back.
Isn't that just so strange?

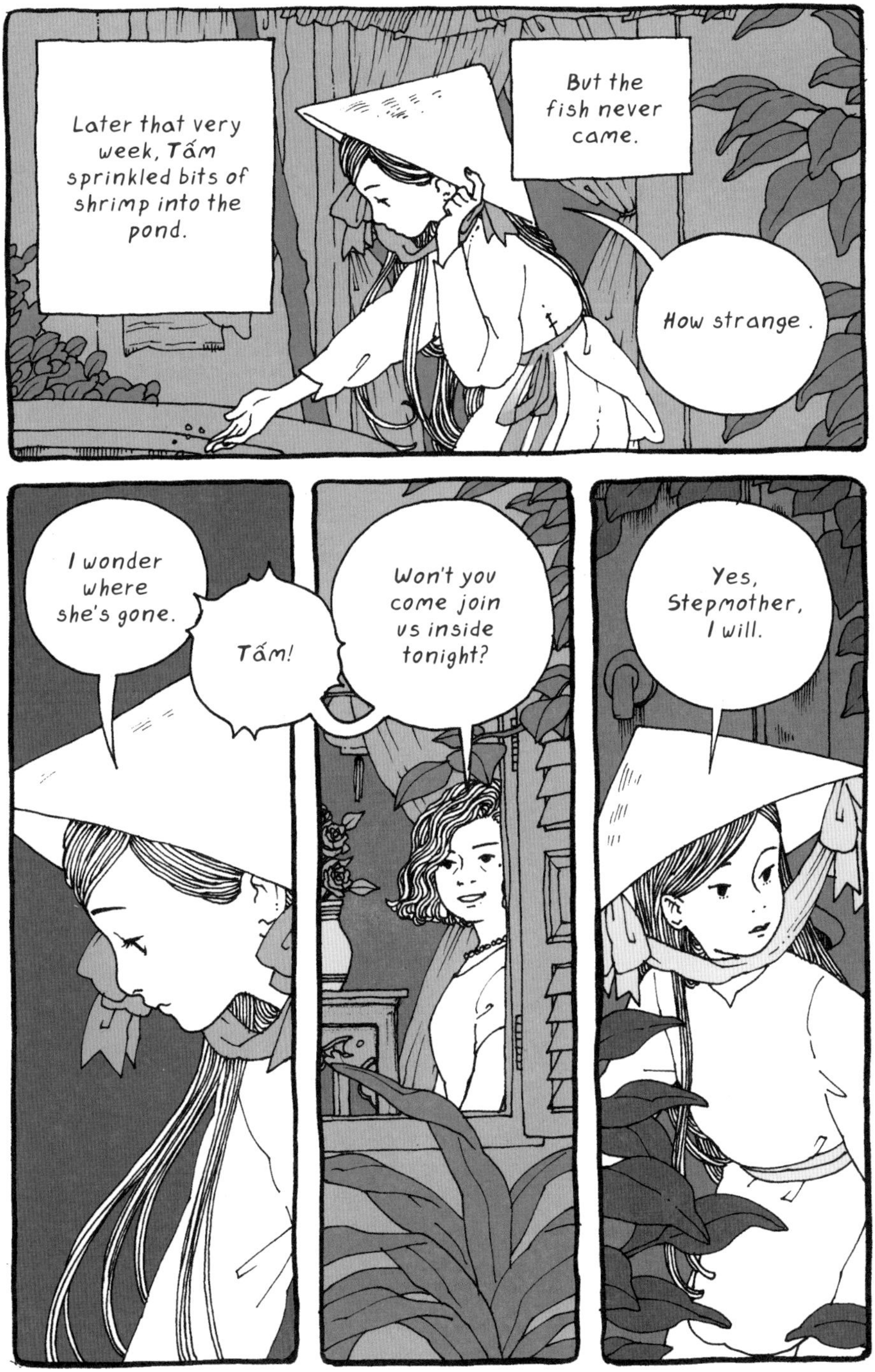

Later that very week, Tấm sprinkled bits of shrimp into the pond.
But the fish never came.
How strange.
I wonder where she's gone.
Tấm!
Won't you come join us inside tonight?
Yes, Stepmother, I will.

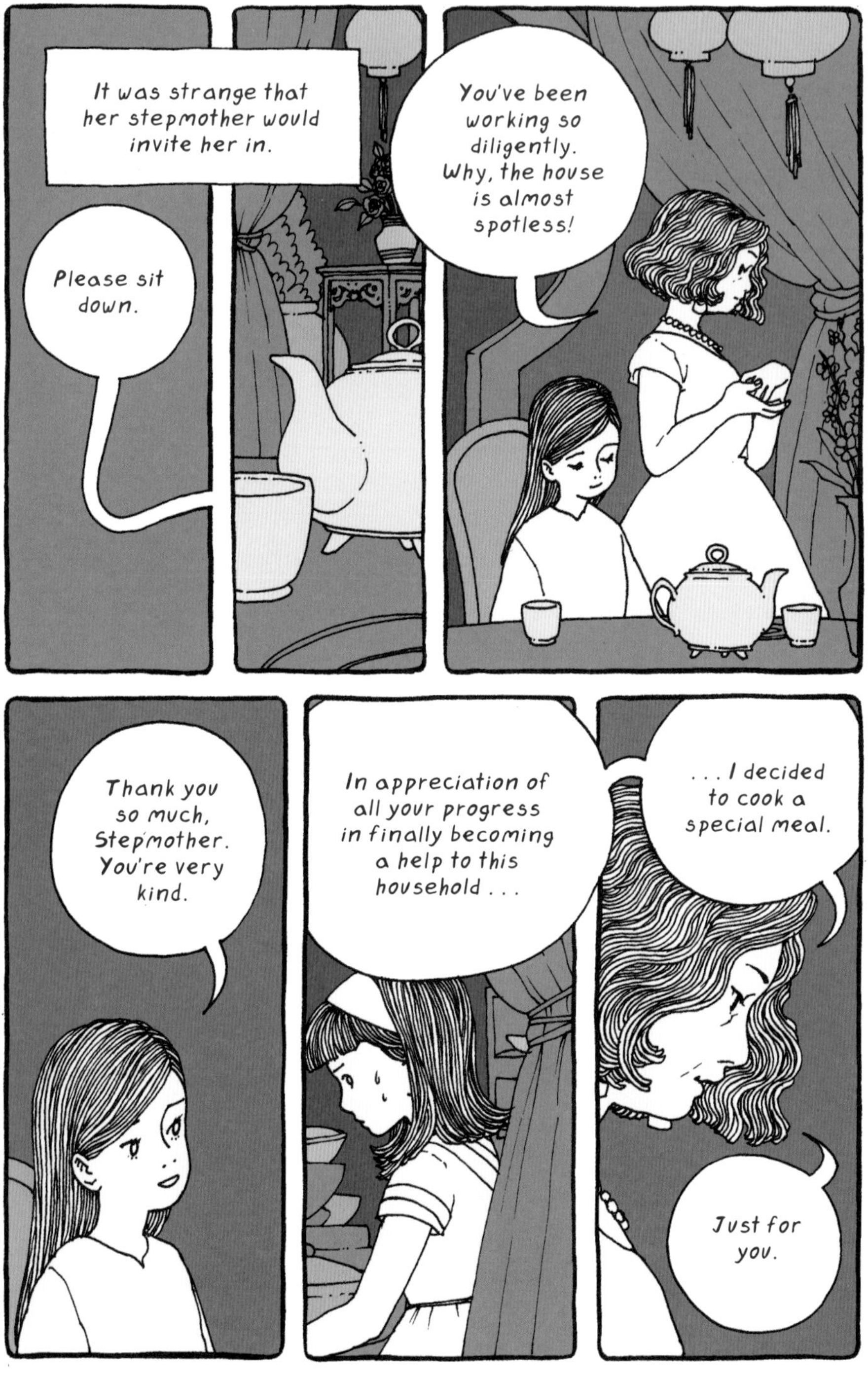
It was strange that her stepmother would invite her in.
Please sit down.
You've been working so diligently. Why, the house is almost spotless!
Thank you so much, Stepmother. You're very kind.
In appreciation of all your progress in finally becoming a help to this household . . .
. . . I decided to cook a special meal.
Just for you.

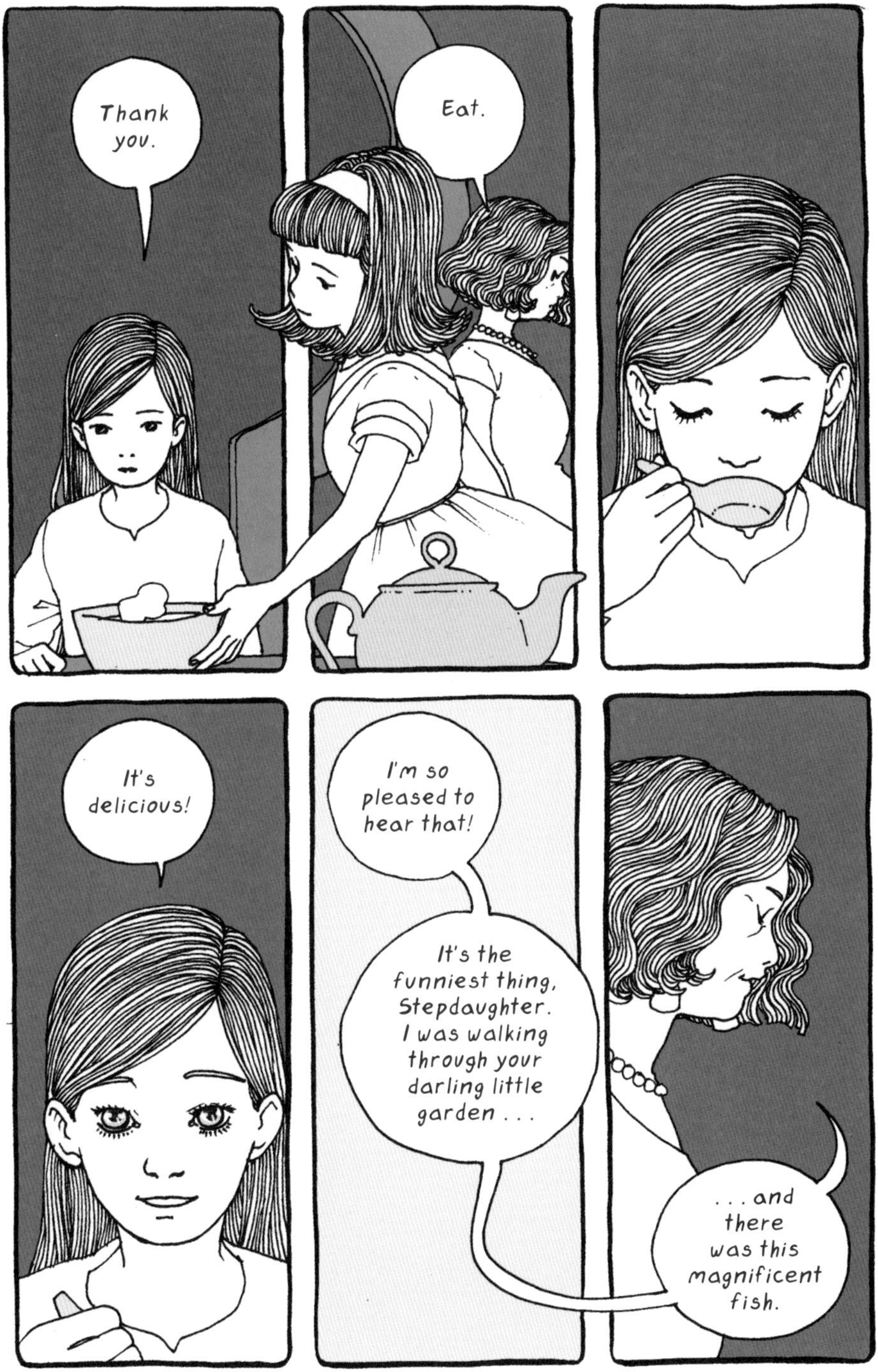
Thank you.
Eat.
It's delicious!
I'm so pleased to hear that!
It's the funniest thing, Stepdaughter. I was walking through your darling little garden . . .
. . . and there was this magnificent fish.

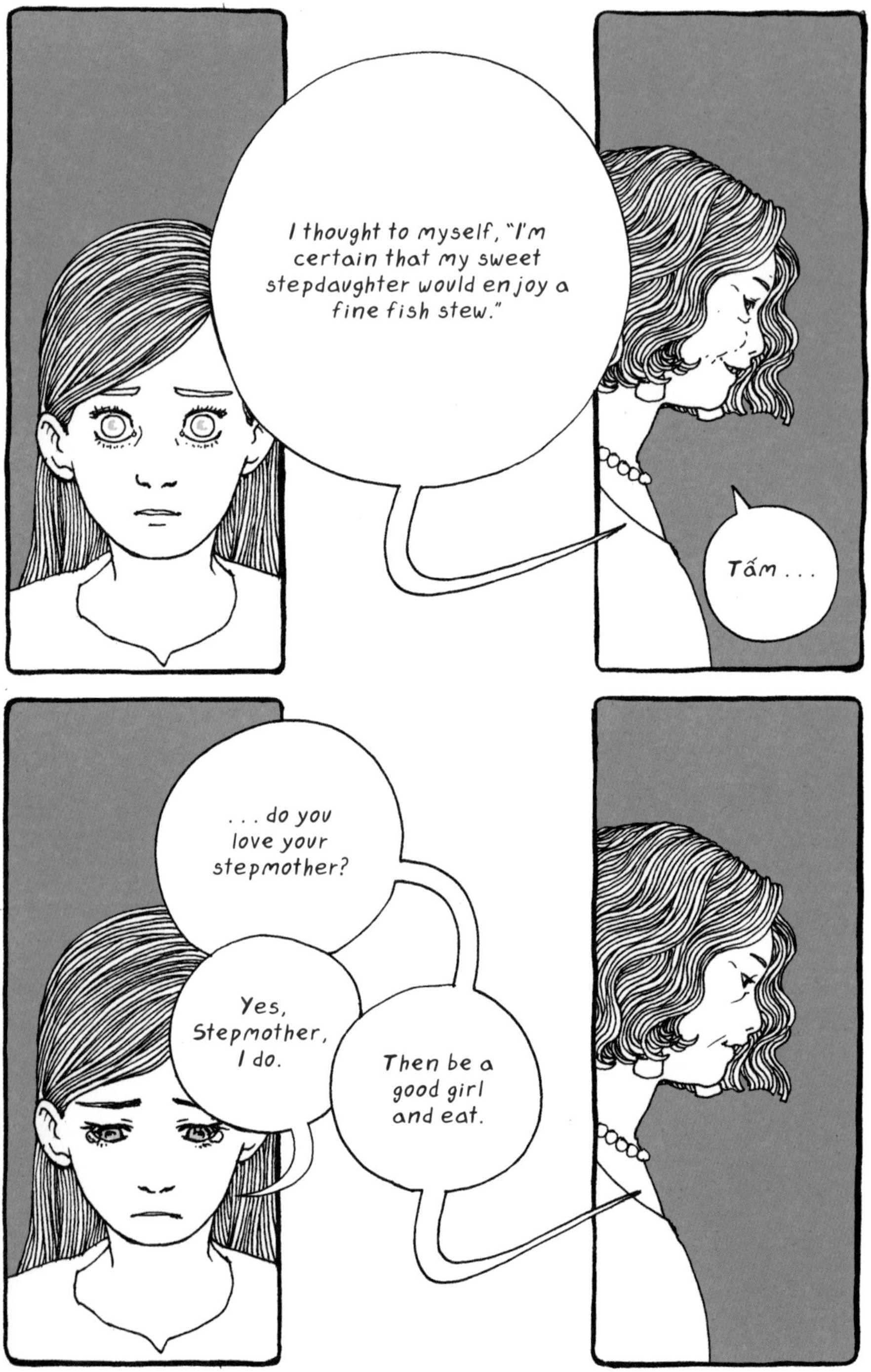
I thought to myself, "I'm certain that my sweet stepdaughter would enjoy a fine fish stew."
Tấm . . .
. . . do you love your stepmother?
Yes, Stepmother, I do.
Then be a good girl and eat.

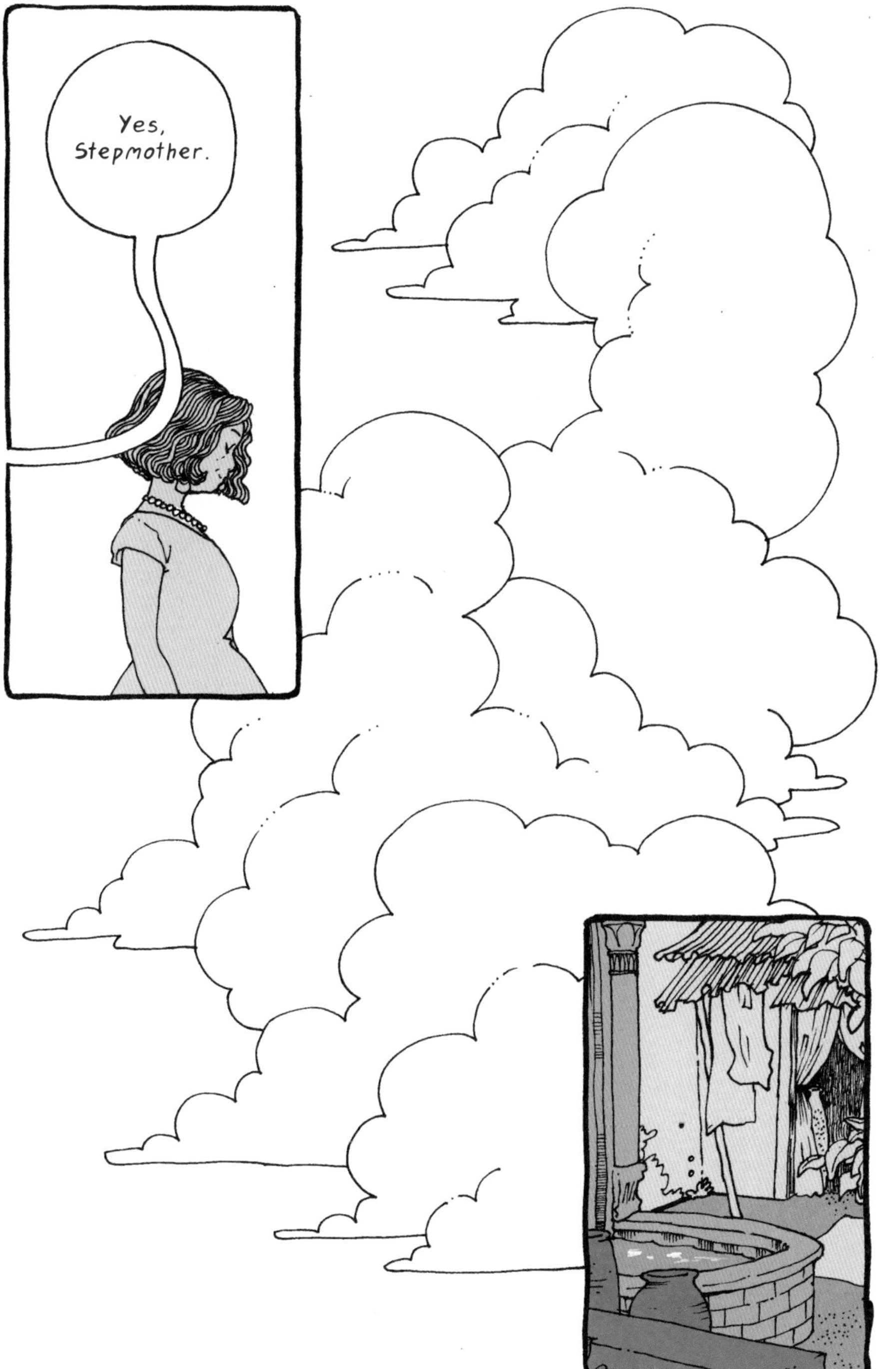
Yes, Stepmother.

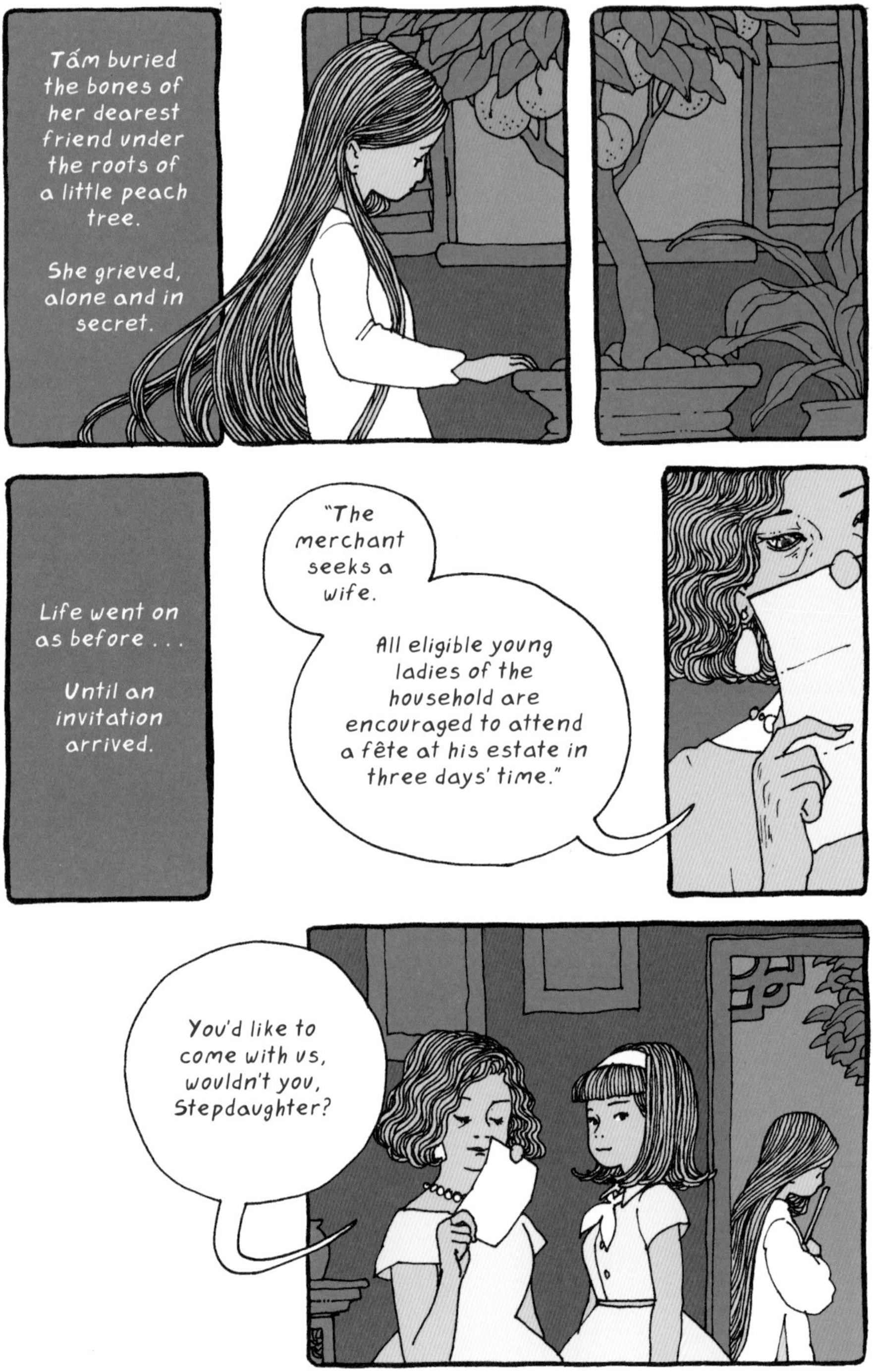
Tấm buried the bones of her dearest friend under the roots of a little peach tree.
She grieved, alone and in secret.
Life went on as before . . .
Until an invitation arrived.
"The merchant seeks a wife.
All eligible young ladies of the household are encouraged to attend a fête at his estate in three days' time."
You'd like to come with us, wouldn't you, Stepdaughter?

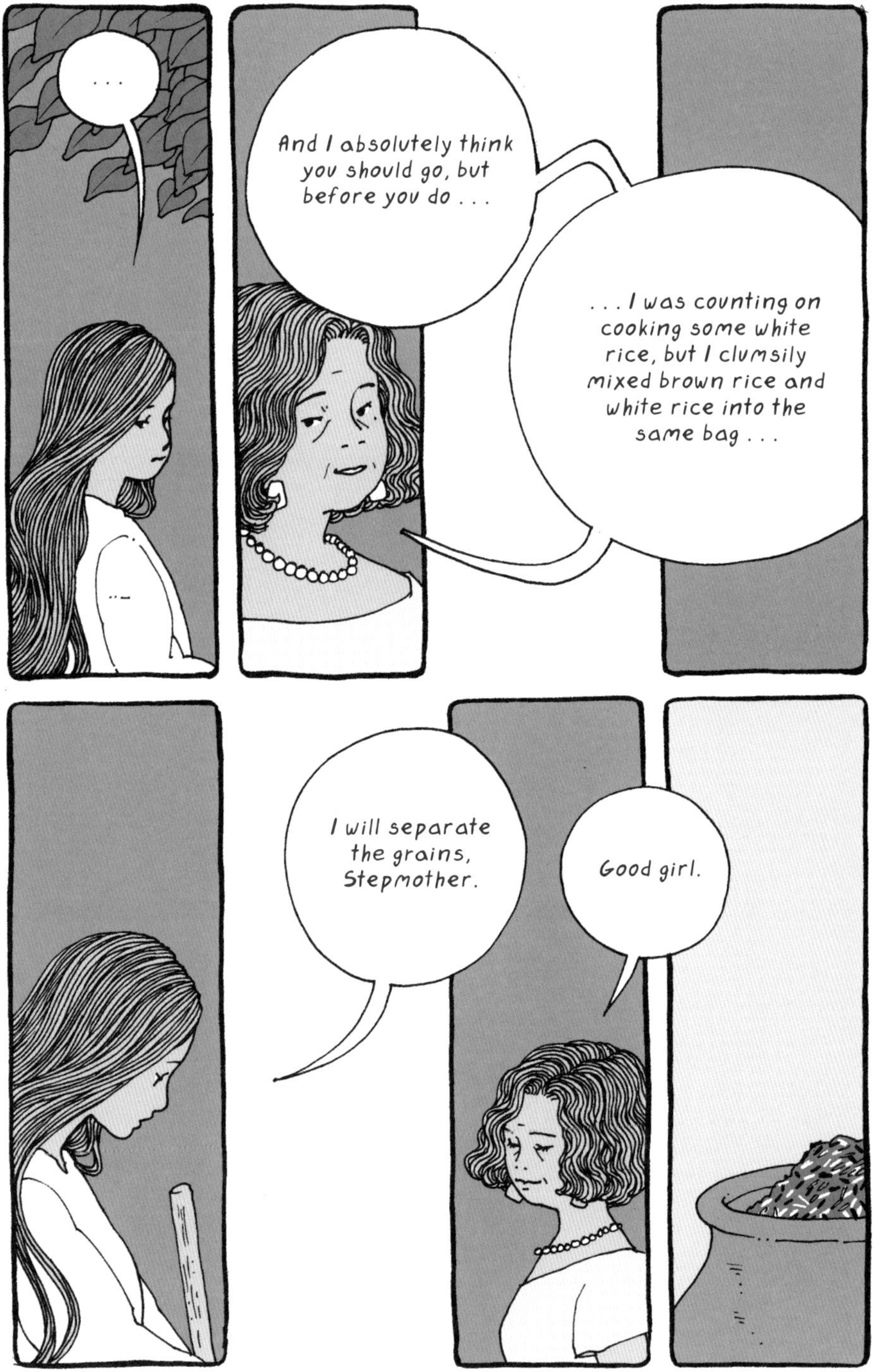
. . .
And I absolutely think you should go, but before you do . . .
. . . I was counting on cooking some white rice, but I clumsily mixed brown rice and white rice into the same bag . . .
I will separate the grains, Stepmother.
Good girl.

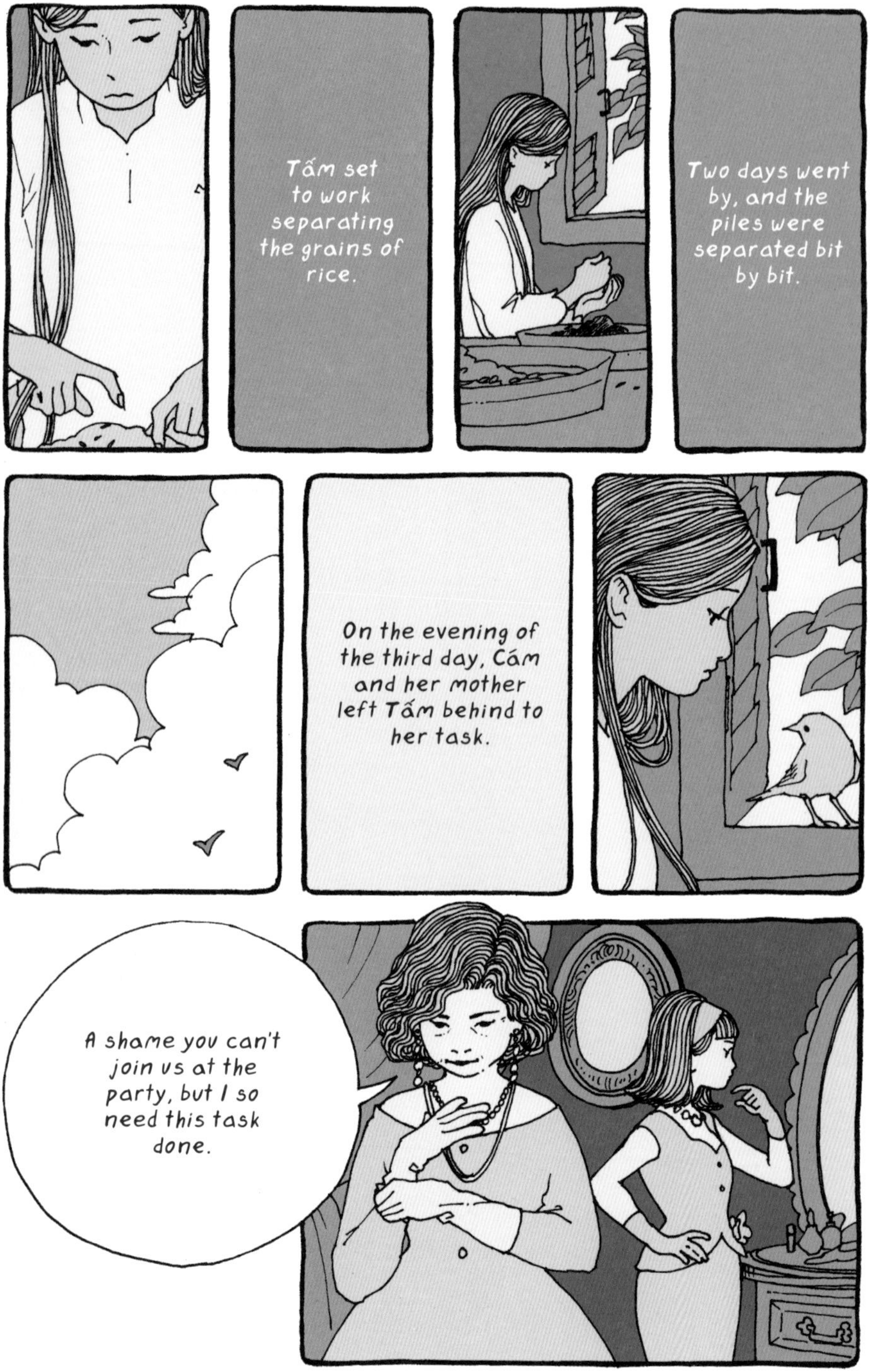
Tấm set to work separating the grains of rice.
Two days went by, and the piles were separated bit by bit.
On the evening of the third day, Cám and her mother left Tấm behind to her task.
A shame you can't join us at the party, but I so need this task done.

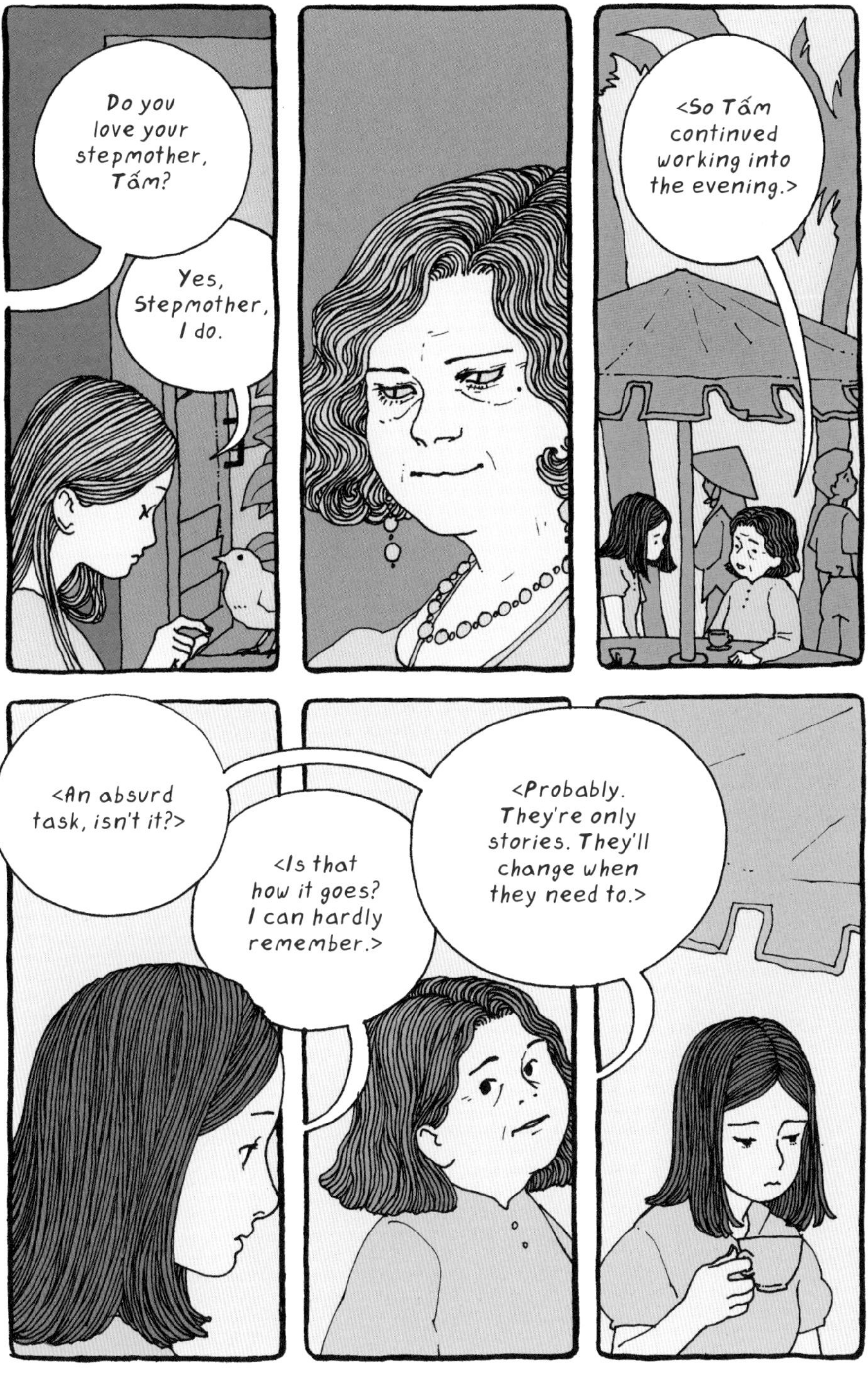
Do you love your stepmother, Tấm?
Yes, Stepmother, I do.
<So Tấm continued working into the evening.>
<An absurd task, isn't it?>
<Is that how it goes? I can hardly remember.>
<Probably. They're only stories. They'll change when they need to.>

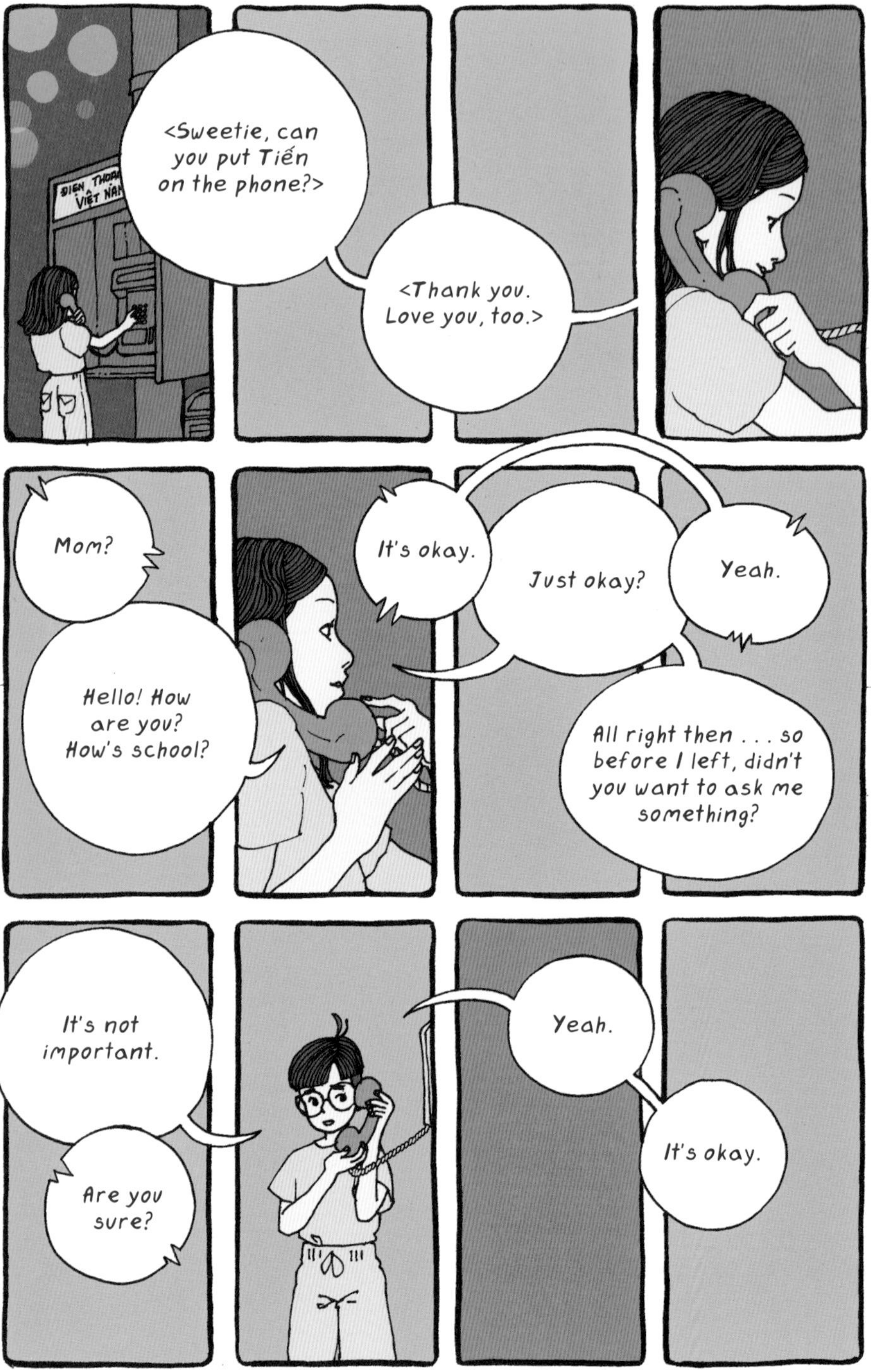
ĐIỆN THOẠI VIỆT NAM
<Sweetie, can you put Tiến on the phone?>
<Thank you. Love you, too.>
Mom?
Hello! How are you? How's school?
It's okay.
Just okay?
Yeah.
All right then . . . so before I left, didn't you want to ask me something?
It's not important.
Are you sure?
Yeah.
It's okay.

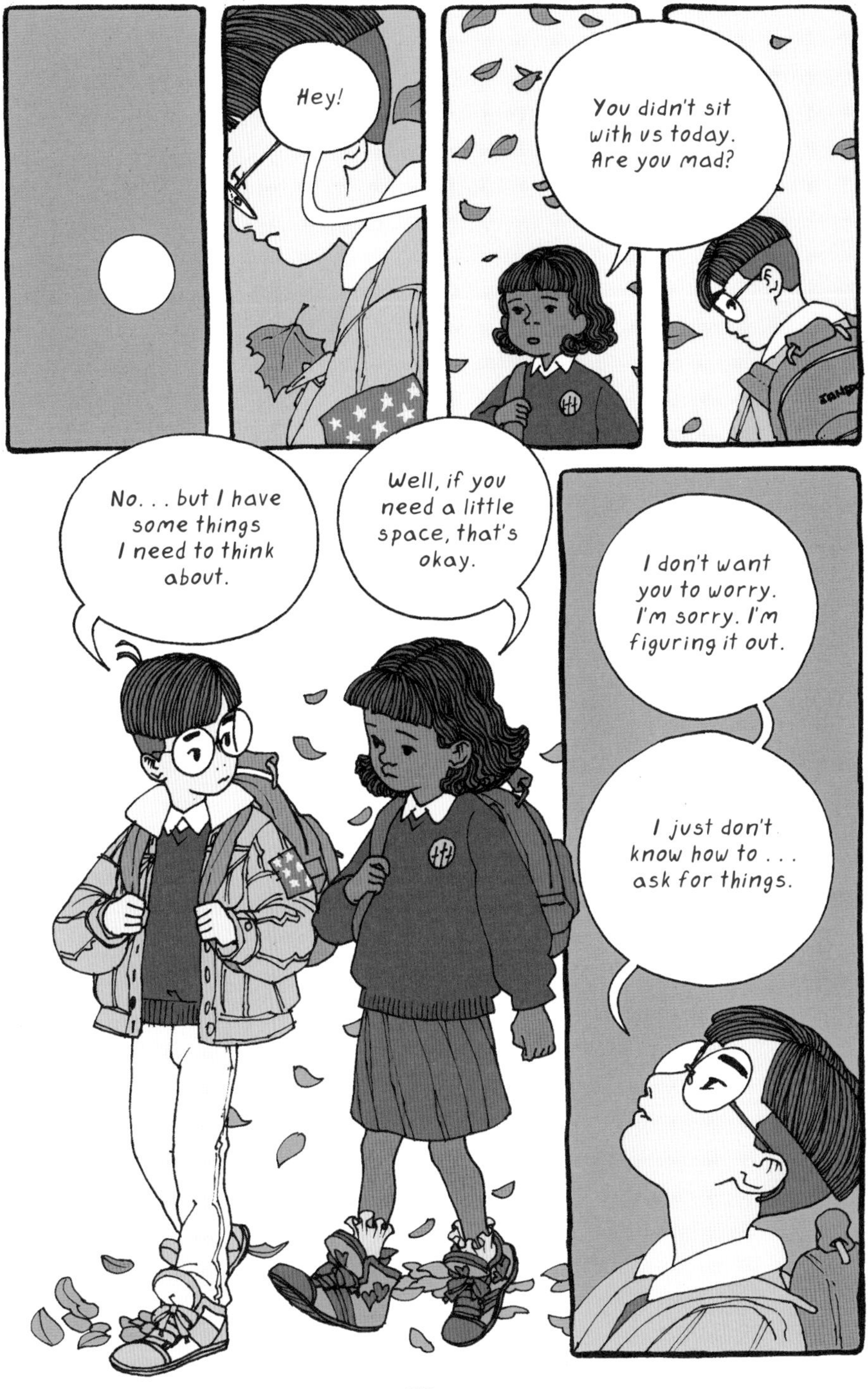
Hey!
You didn't sit with us today. Are you mad?
No. . . but I have some things I need to think about.
Well, if you need a little space, that's okay.
I don't want you to worry. I'm sorry. I'm figuring it out.
I just don't know how to . . . ask for things.

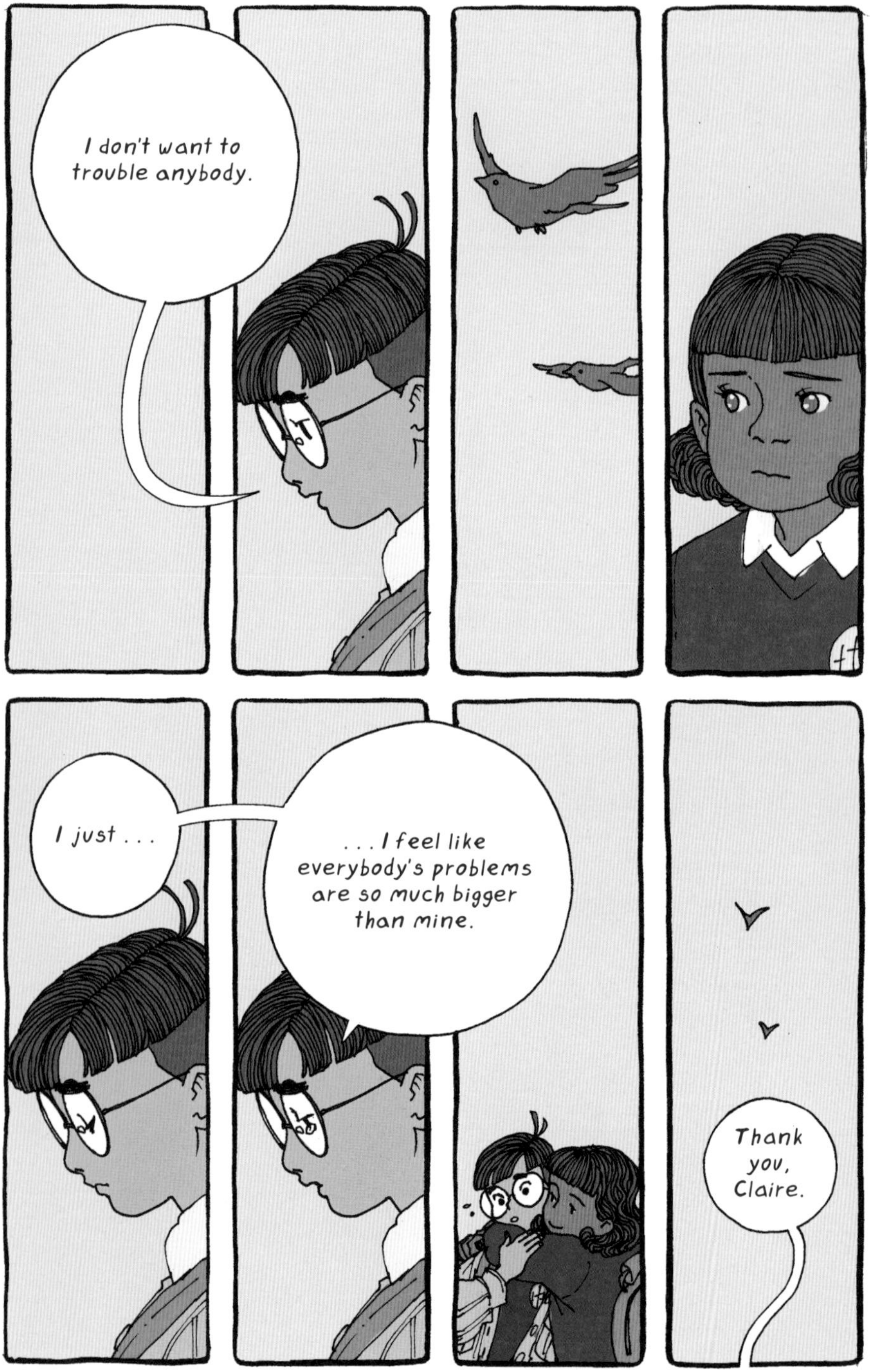
I don't want to trouble anybody.
I just . . .
. . . I feel like everybody's problems are so much bigger than mine.
Thank you, Claire.

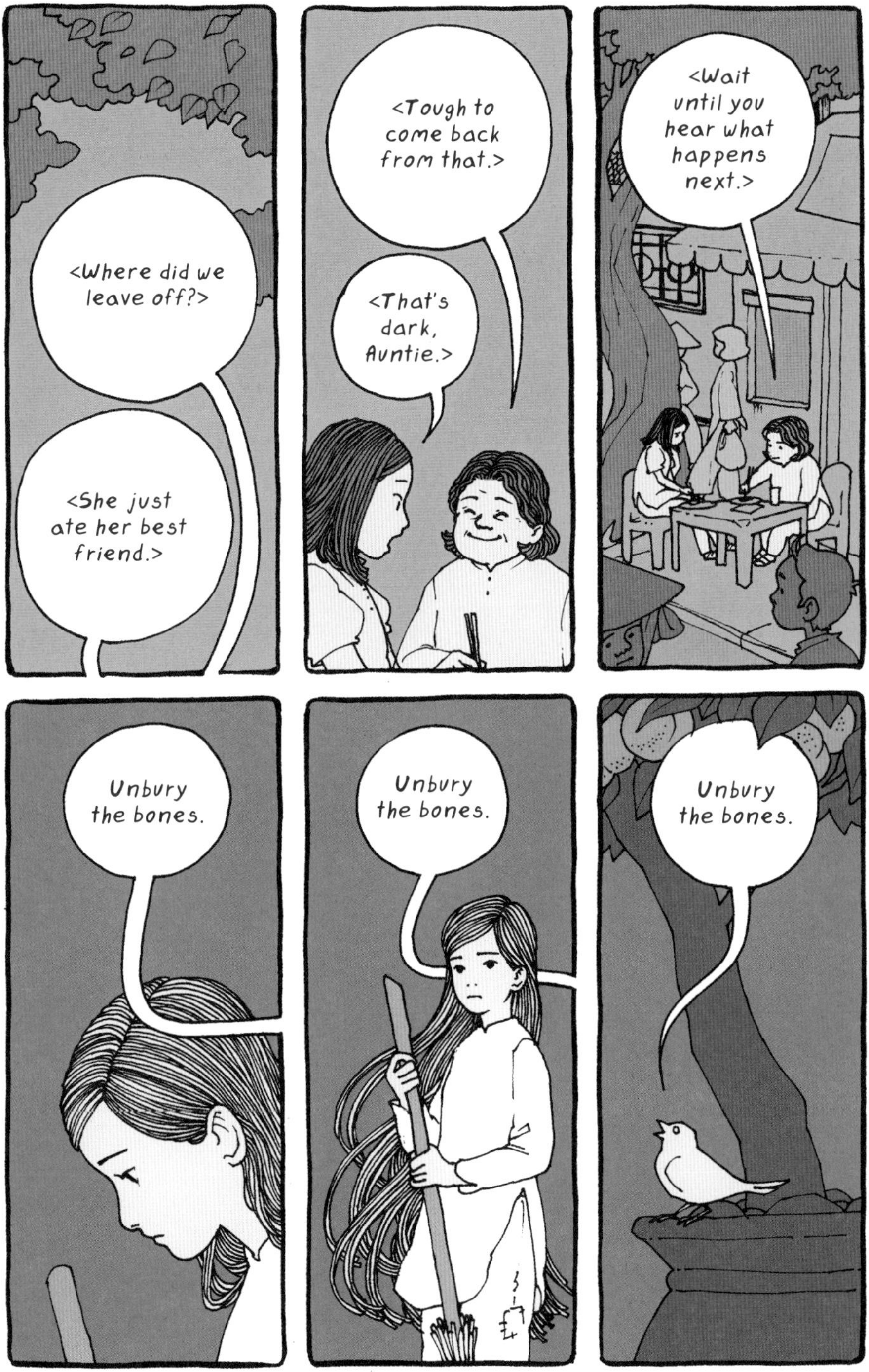
<Where did we leave off?>
<She just ate her best friend.>
<Tough to come back from that.>
<That's dark, Auntie.>
<Wait until you hear what happens next.>
Unbury the bones.
Unbury the bones.
Unbury the bones.

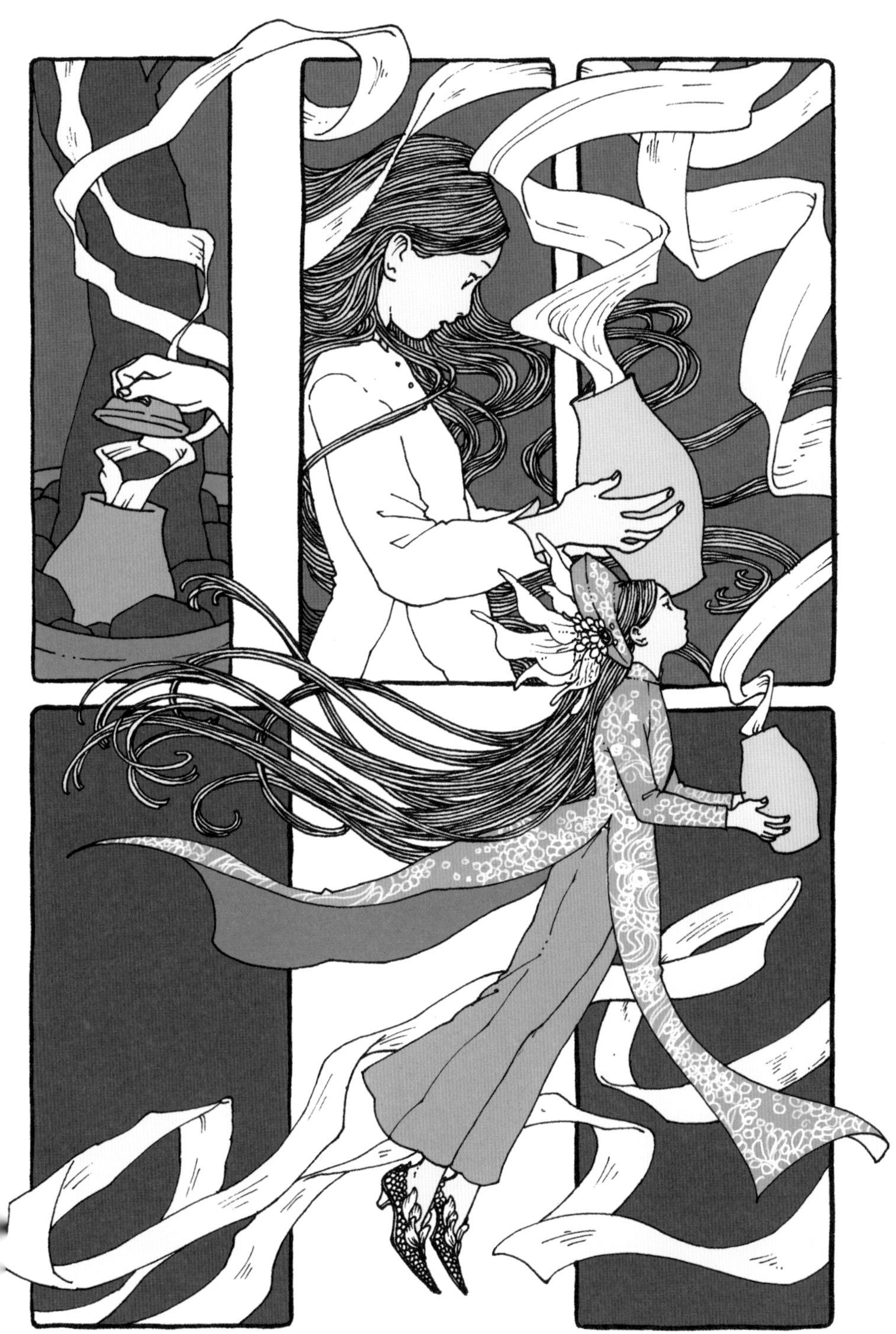

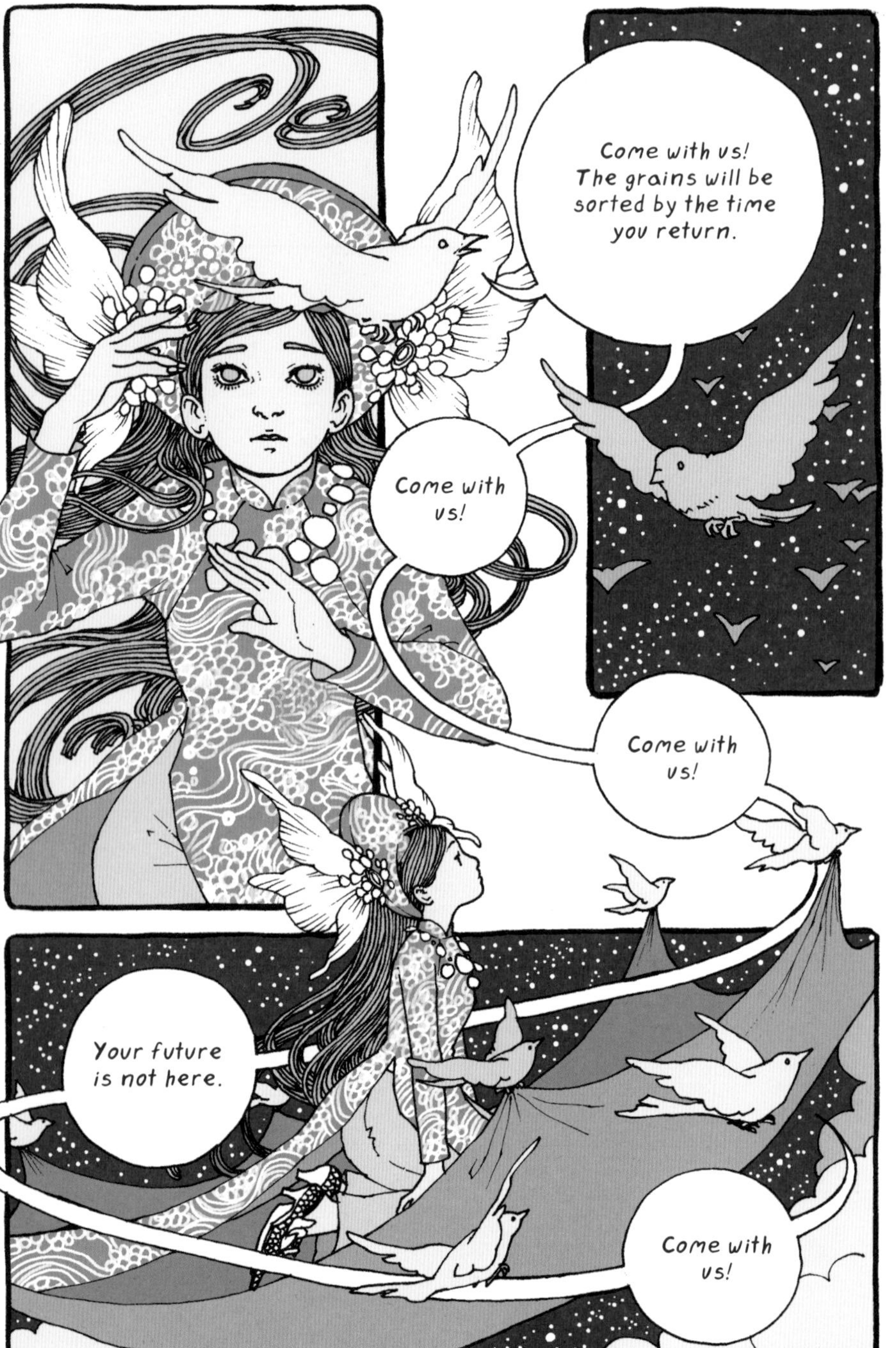
Come with us!
The grains will be sorted by the time you return.
Come with us!
Come with us!
Your future is not here.
Come with us!

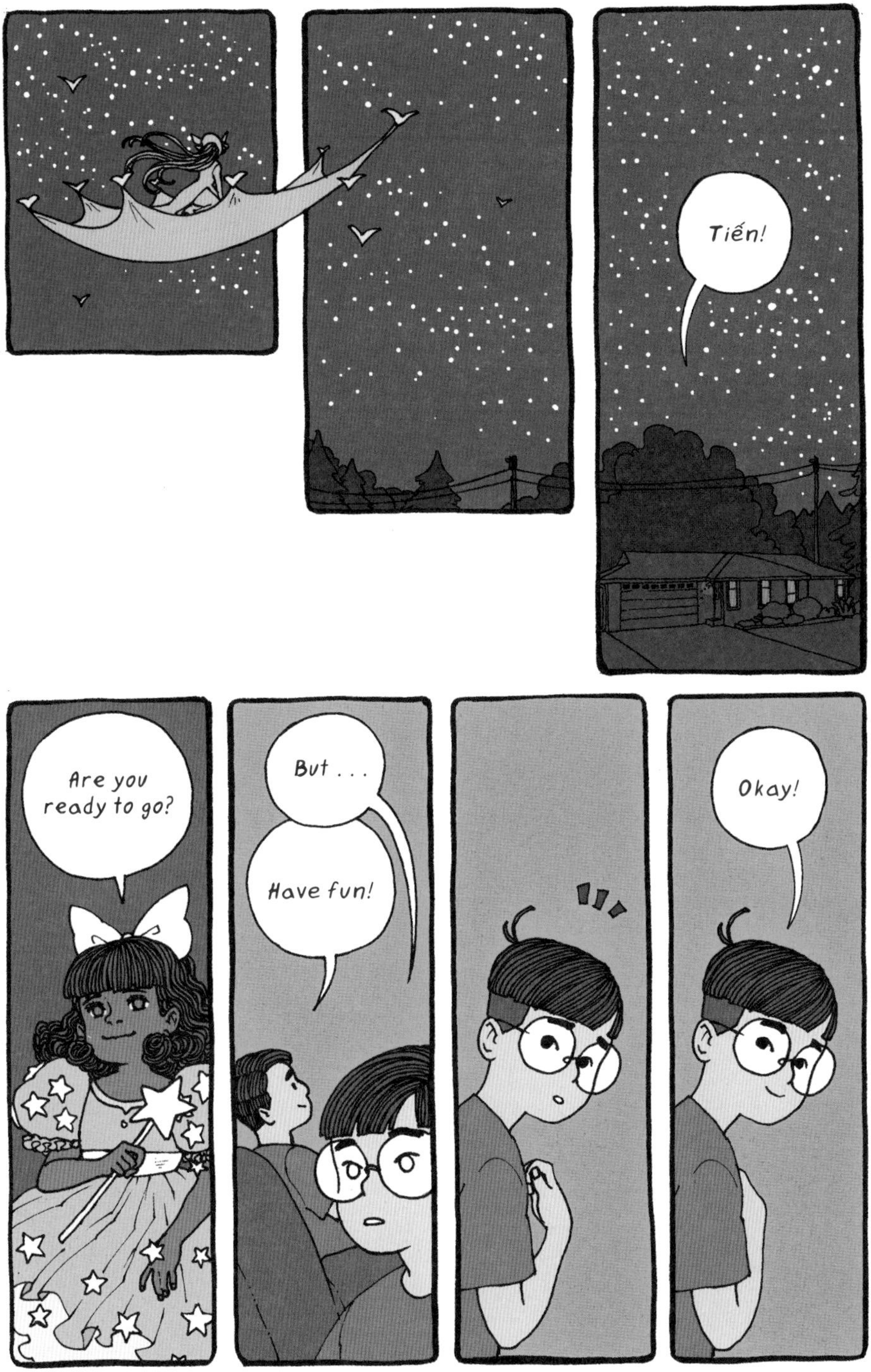
Tiến!
Are you ready to go?
But . . .
Have fun!
Okay!

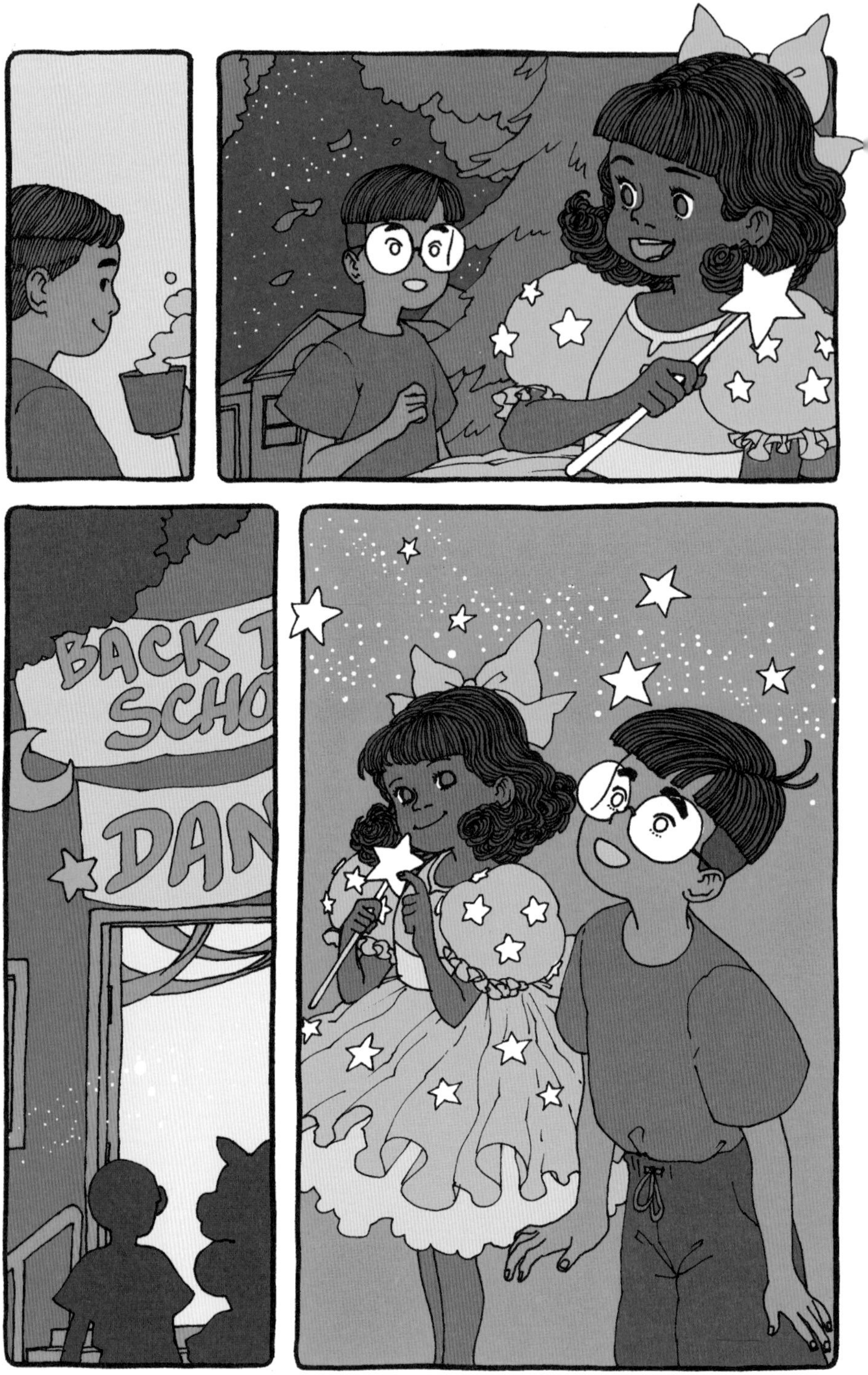
BACK T
SCHO
DAN

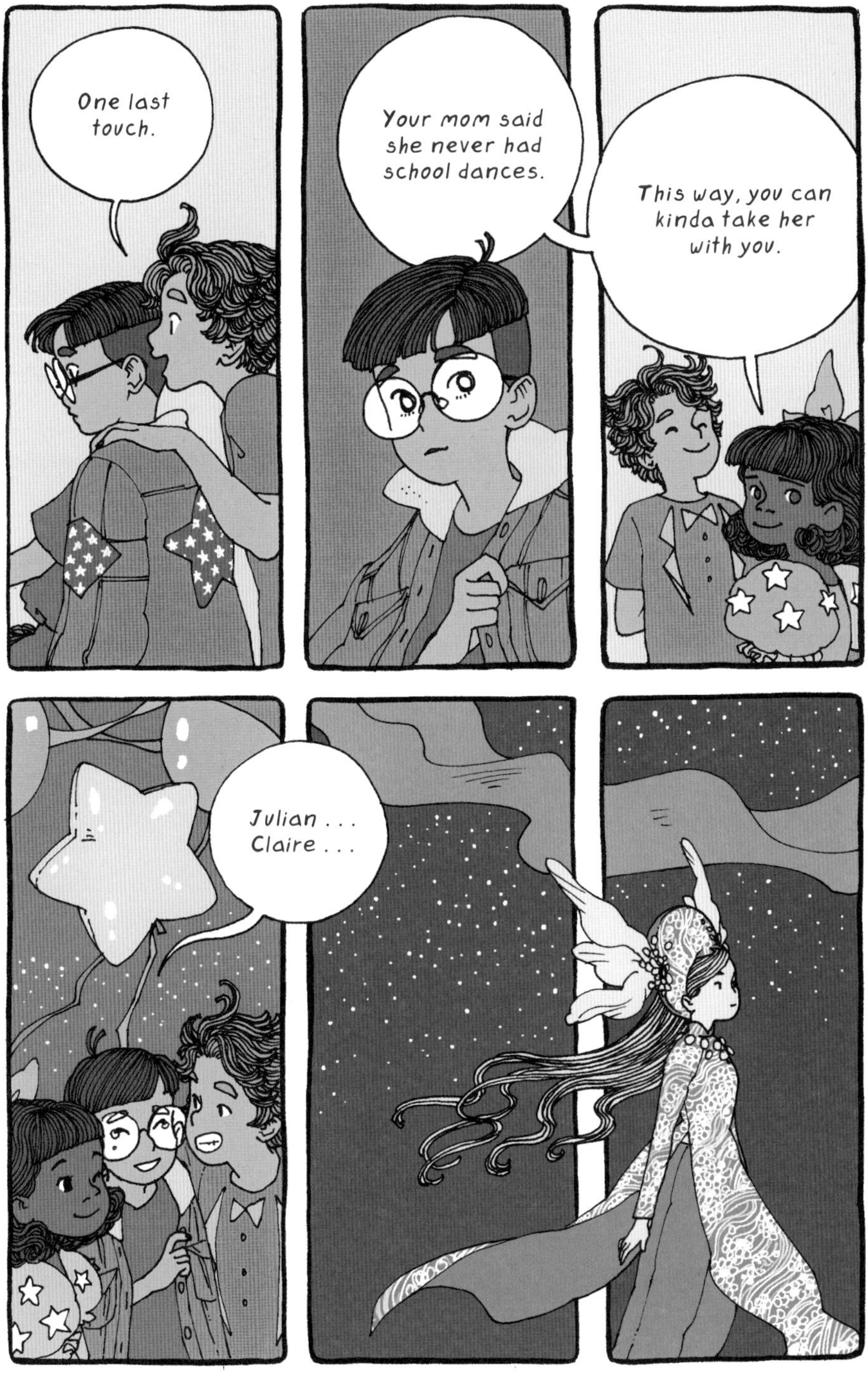
One last touch.
Your mom said she never had school dances.
This way, you can kinda take her with you.
Julian . . . Claire . . .

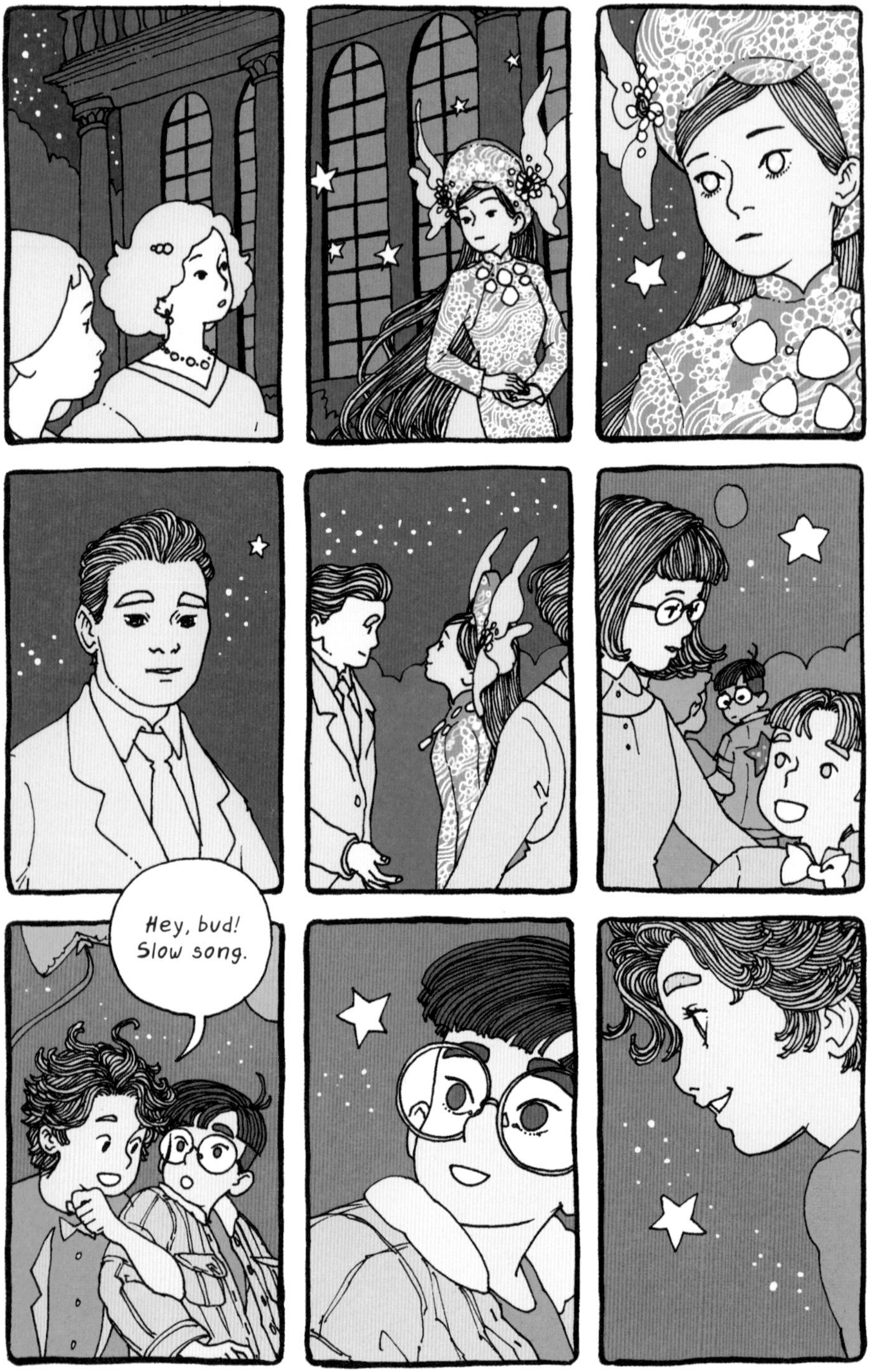
Hey, bud!
Slow song.

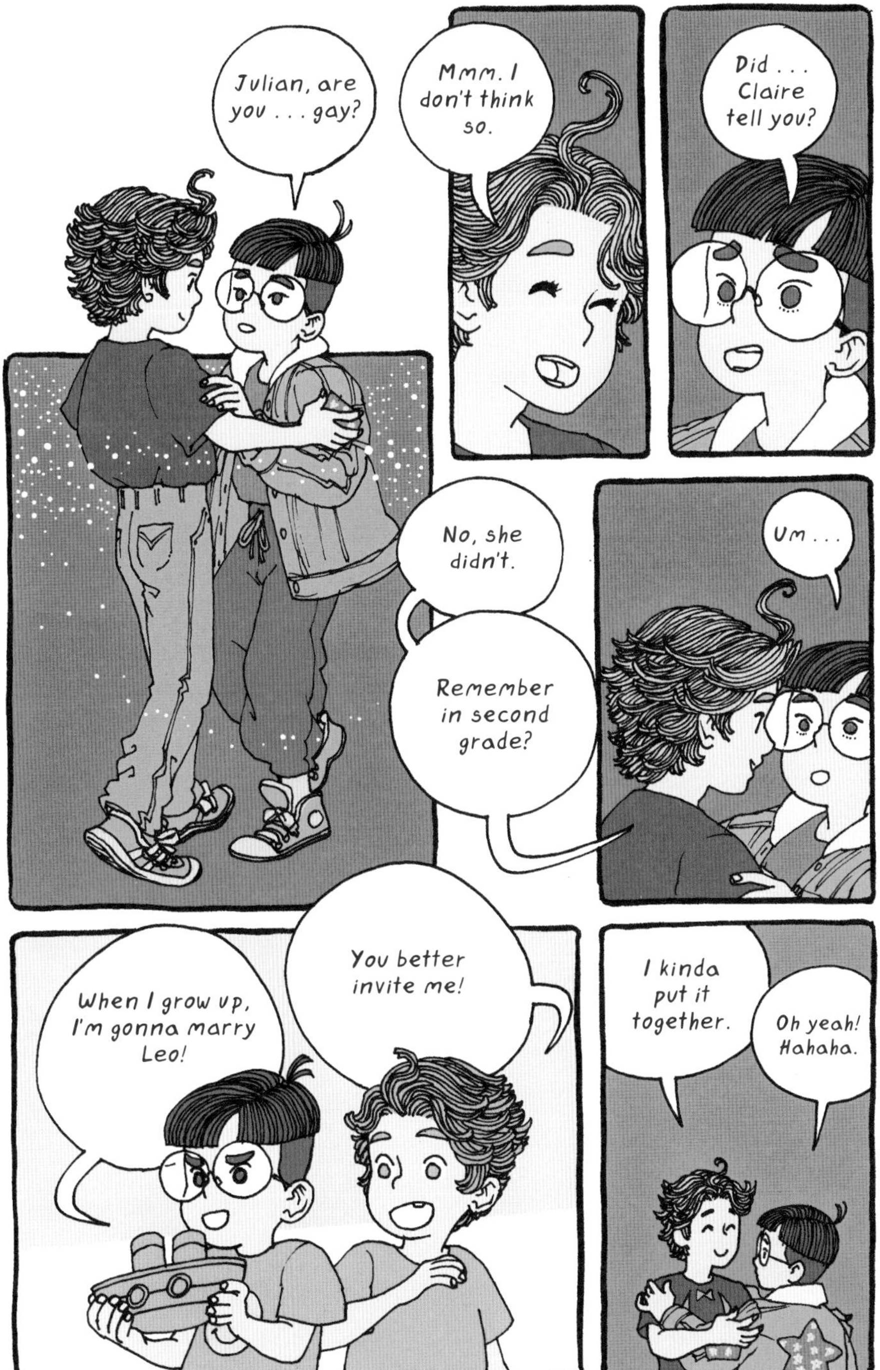
Julian, are you . . . gay?
Mmm. I don't think so.
Did . . . Claire tell you?
No, she didn't.
Remember in second grade?
Um . . .
When I grow up, I'm gonna marry Leo!
You better invite me!
I kinda put it together.
Oh yeah! Hahaha.

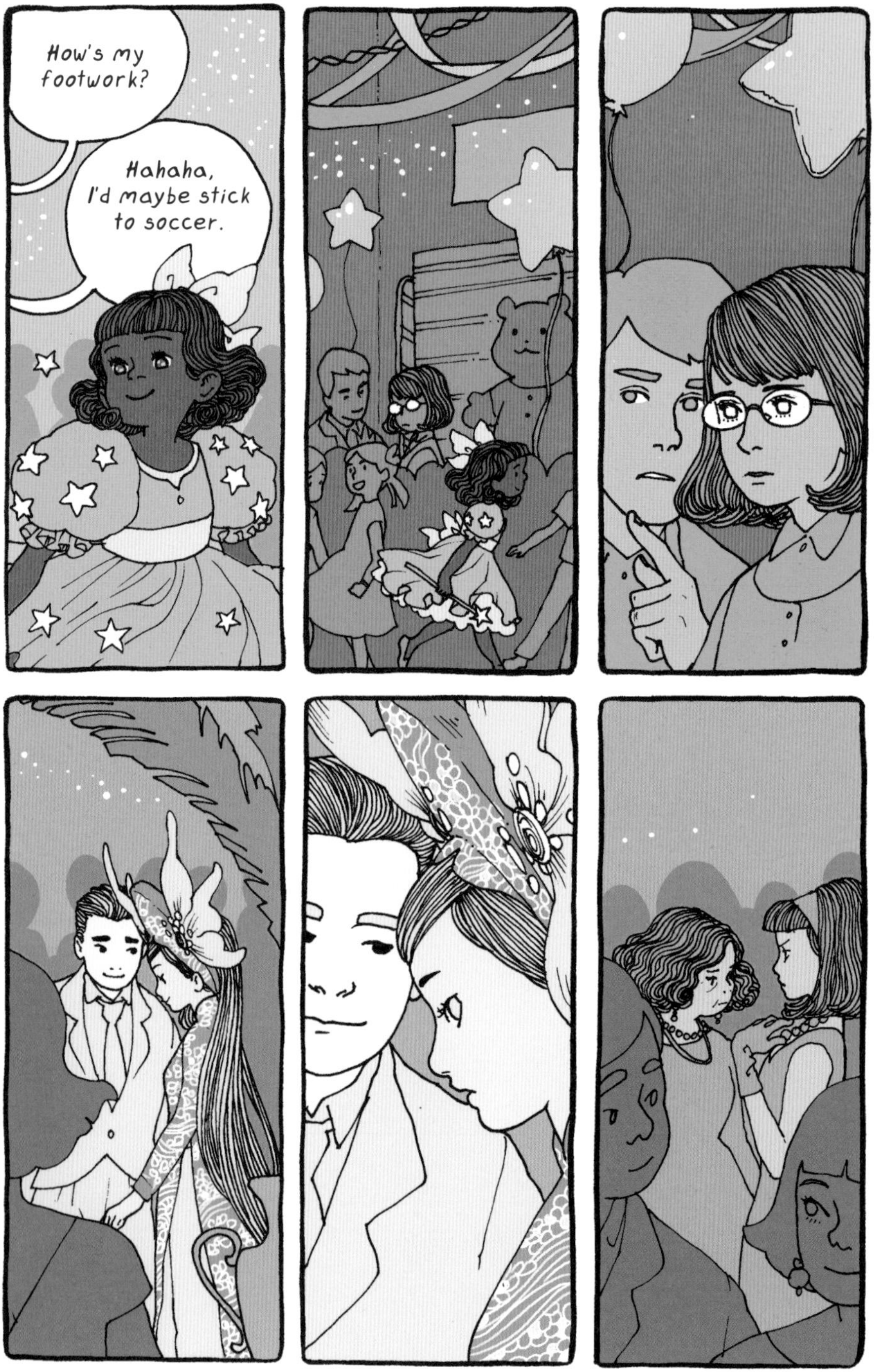
How's my footwork?
Hahaha, I'd maybe stick to soccer.

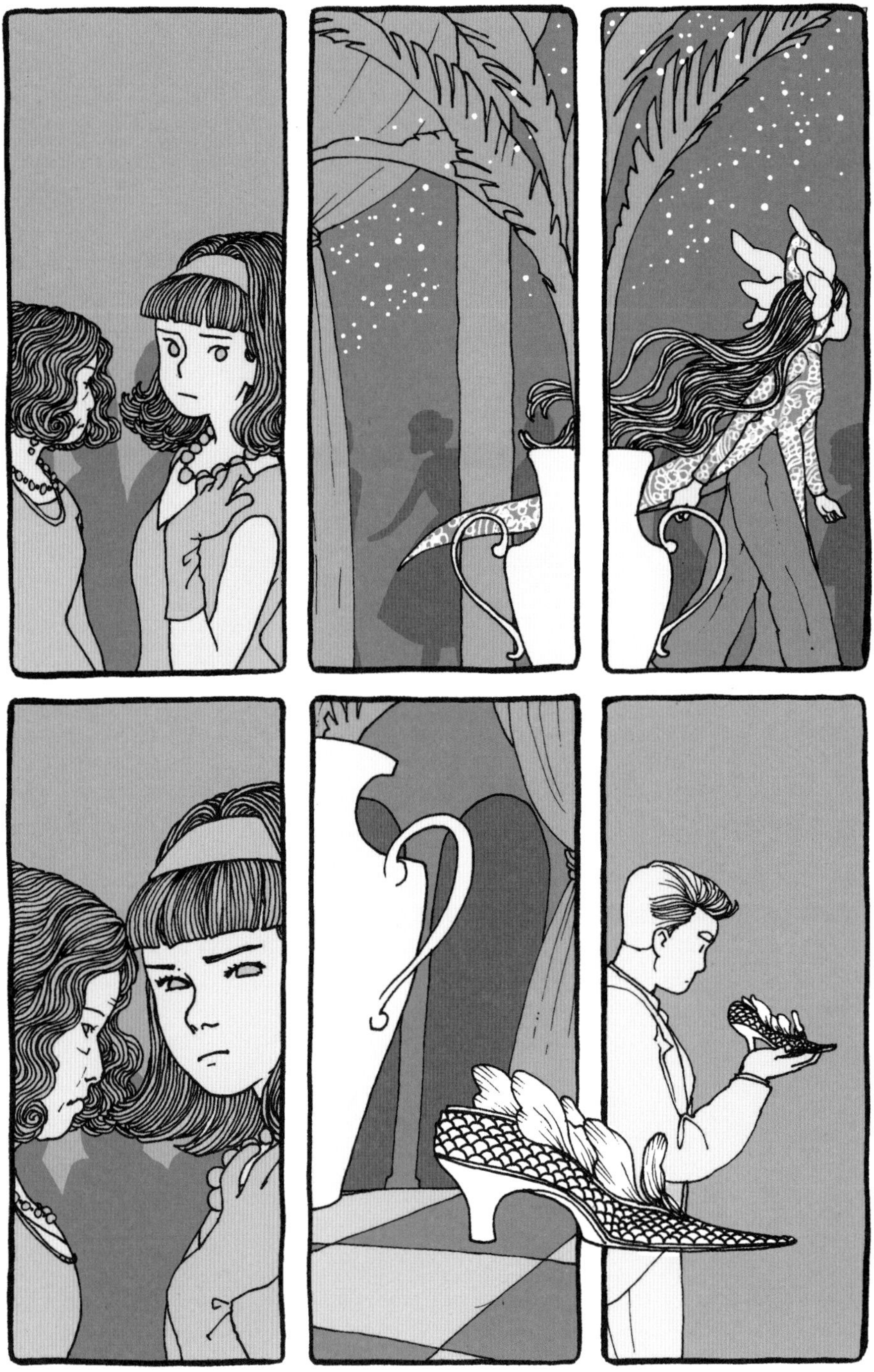

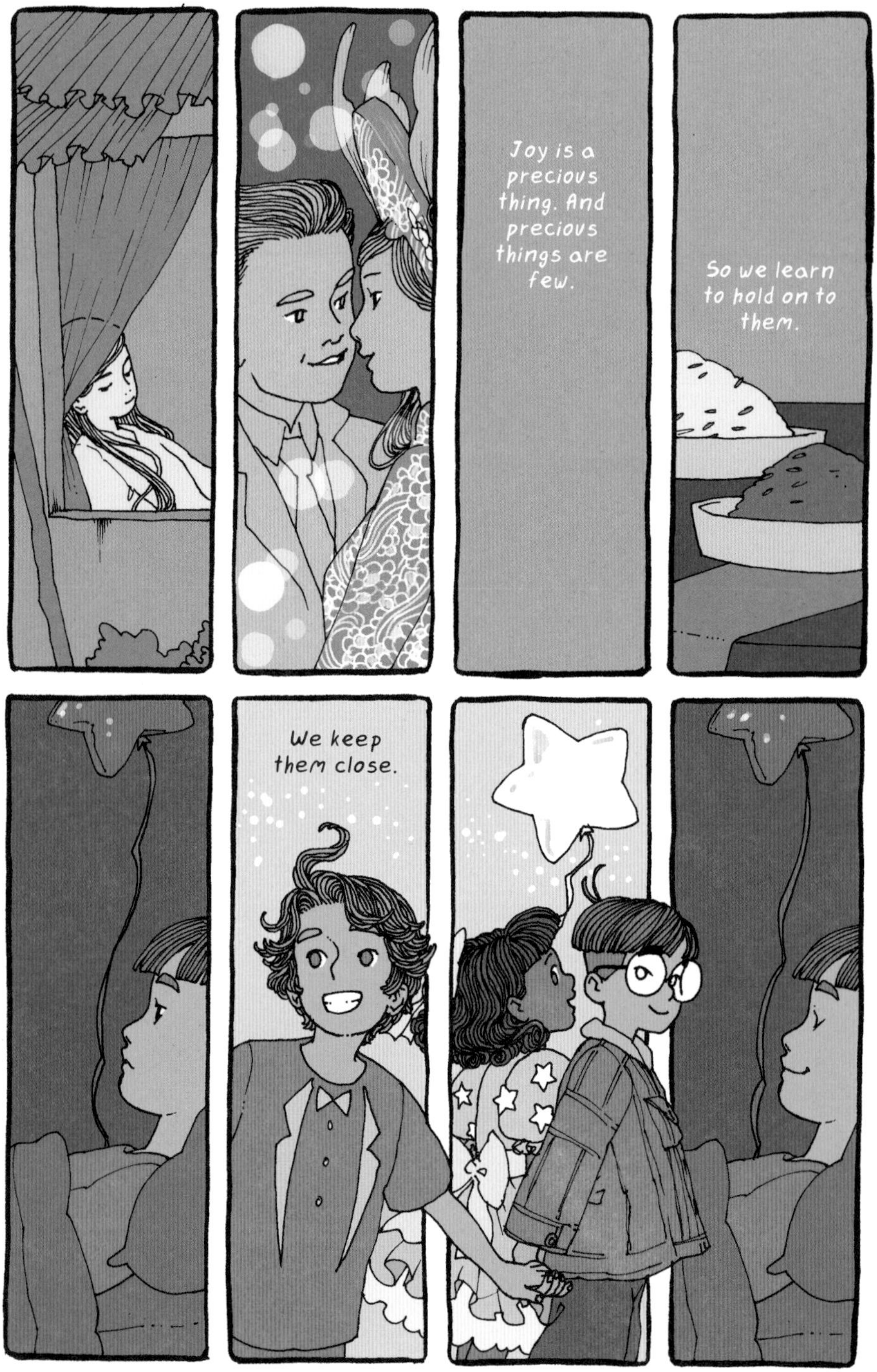
Joy is a precious thing. And precious things are few.
So we learn to hold on to them.
We keep them close.

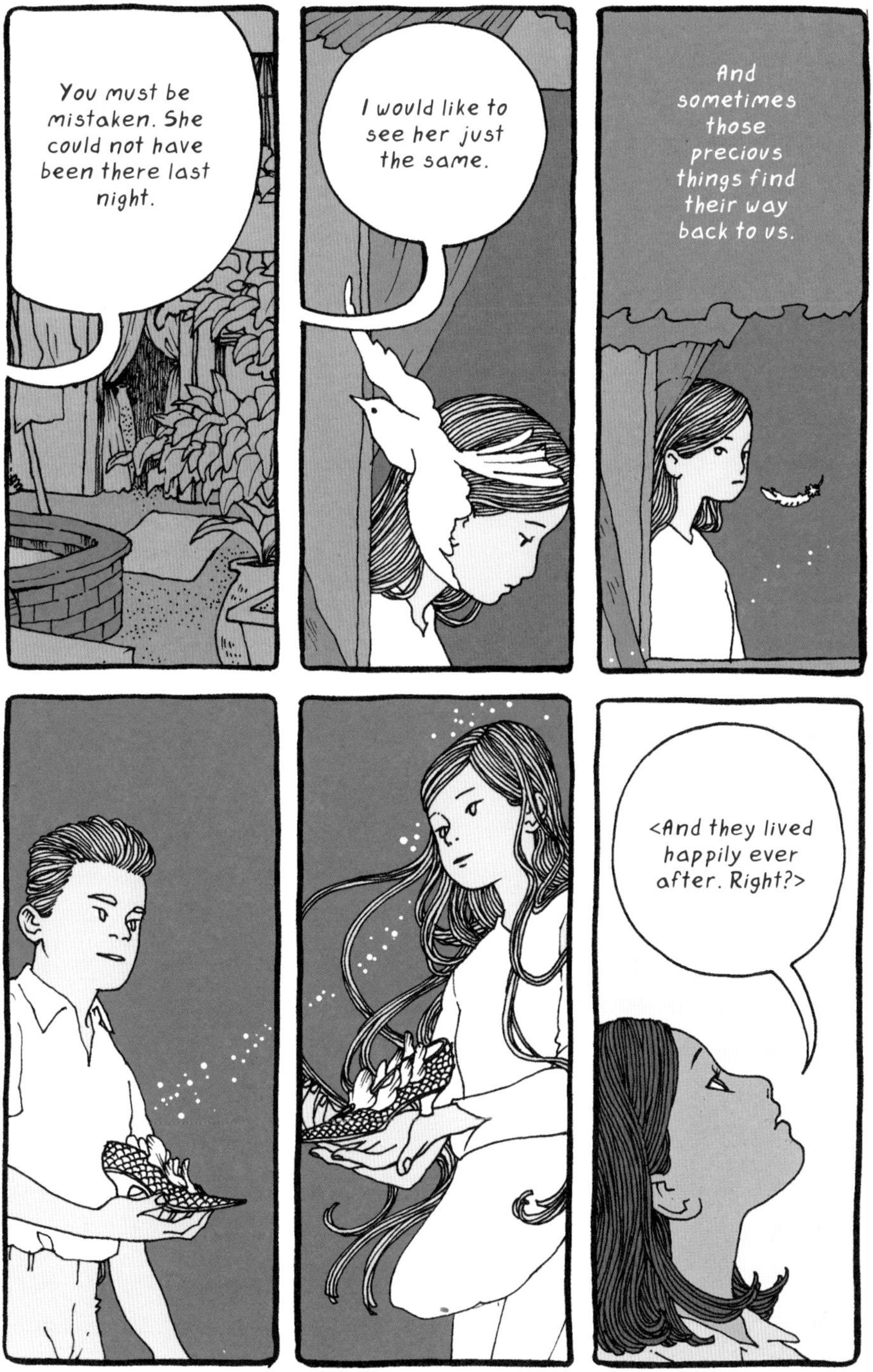
You must be mistaken. She could not have been there last night.
I would like to see her just the same.
And sometimes those precious things find their way back to us.
<And they lived happily ever after. Right?>

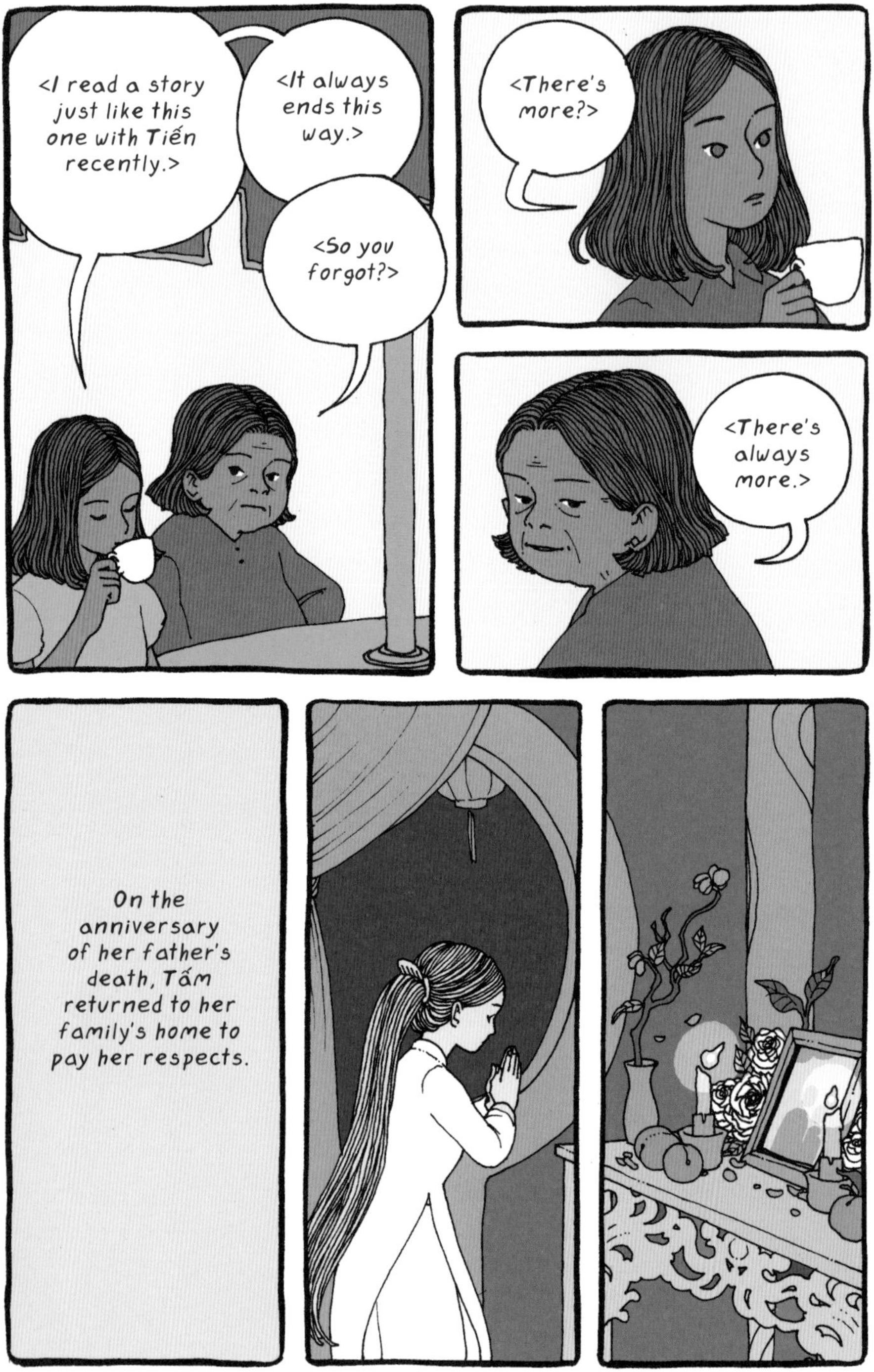
<I read a story just like this one with Tiến recently.>
<It always ends this way.>
<So you forgot?>
<There's more?>
<There's always more.>
On the anniversary of her father's death, Tấm returned to her family's home to pay her respects.

Tám did not notice her stepmother behind her, a golden knife in her grip.

She did not notice her stepmother raise the knife in her fist.

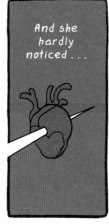

And she hardly noticed . . .

. . . when the golden knife tore through her still-beating heart.

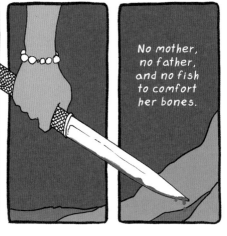

They buried her among the roots of an old camphor tree.

No mother, no father, and no fish to comfort her bones.

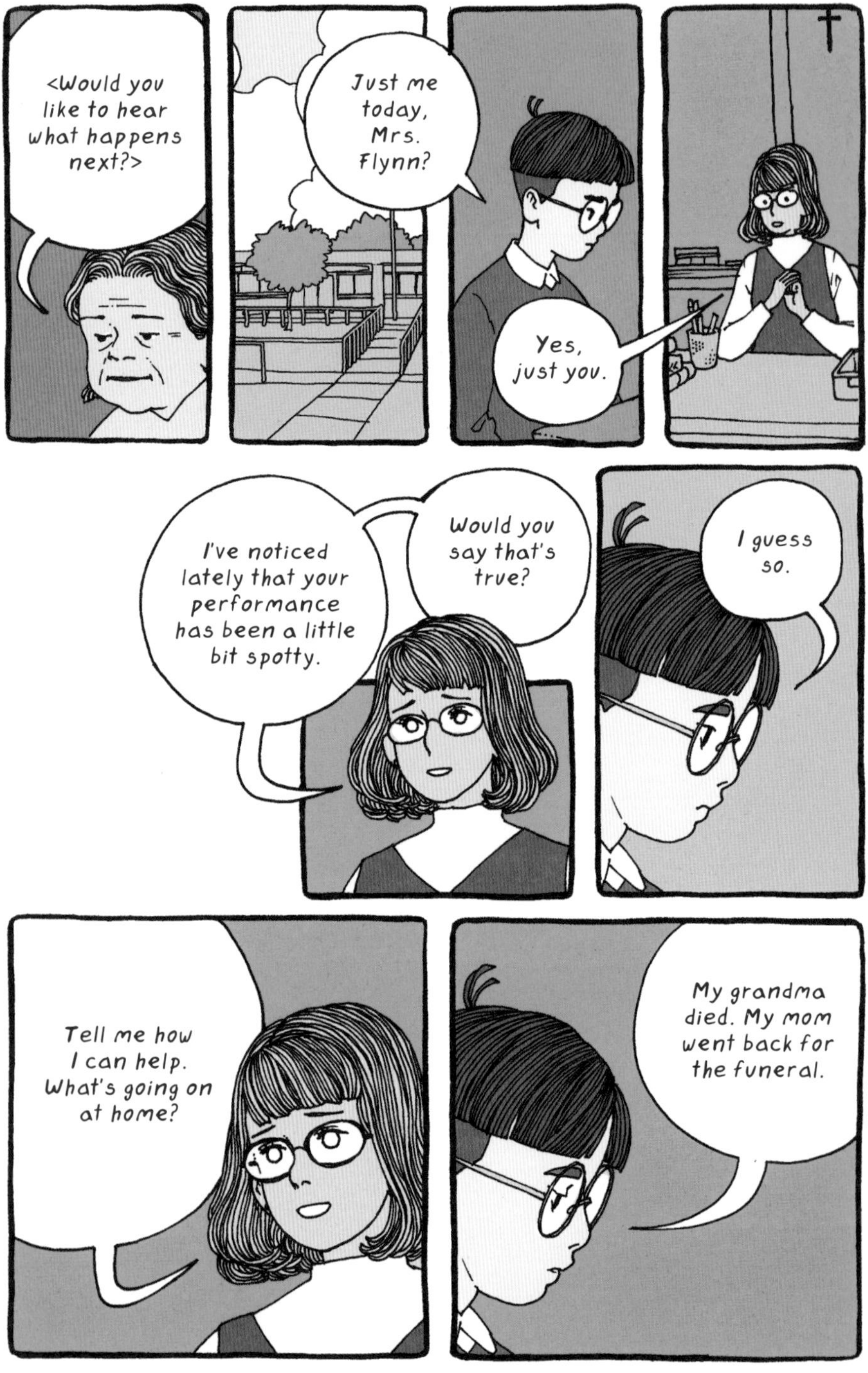
<Would you like to hear what happens next?>
Just me today, Mrs. Flynn?
Yes, just you.
I've noticed lately that your performance has been a little bit spotty.
Would you say that's true?
I guess so.
Tell me how I can help. What's going on at home?
My grandma died. My mom went back for the funeral.

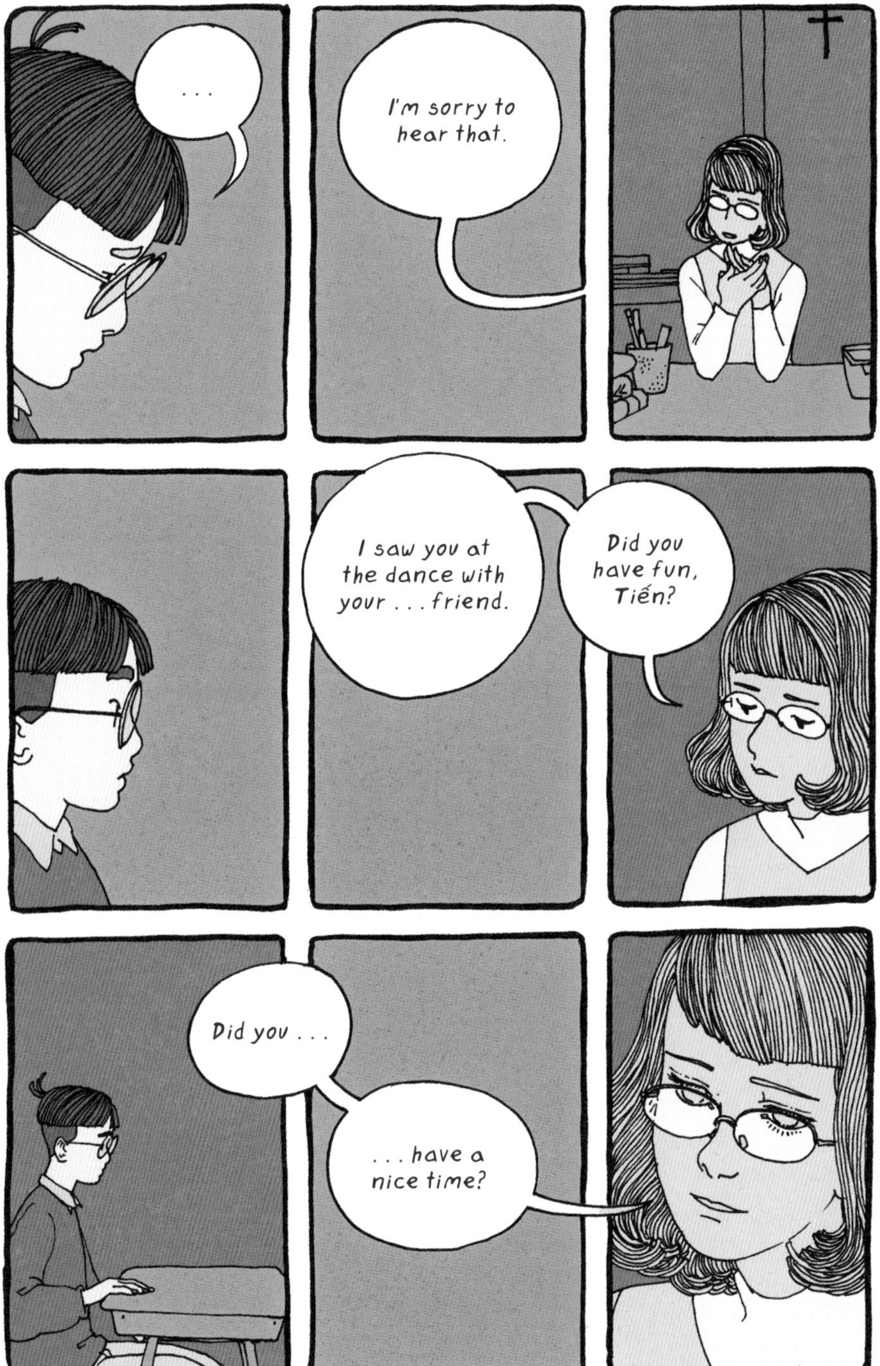
. . .
I'm sorry to hear that.
I saw you at the dance with your . . . friend.
Did you have fun, Tiến?
Did you . . .
. . . have a nice time?

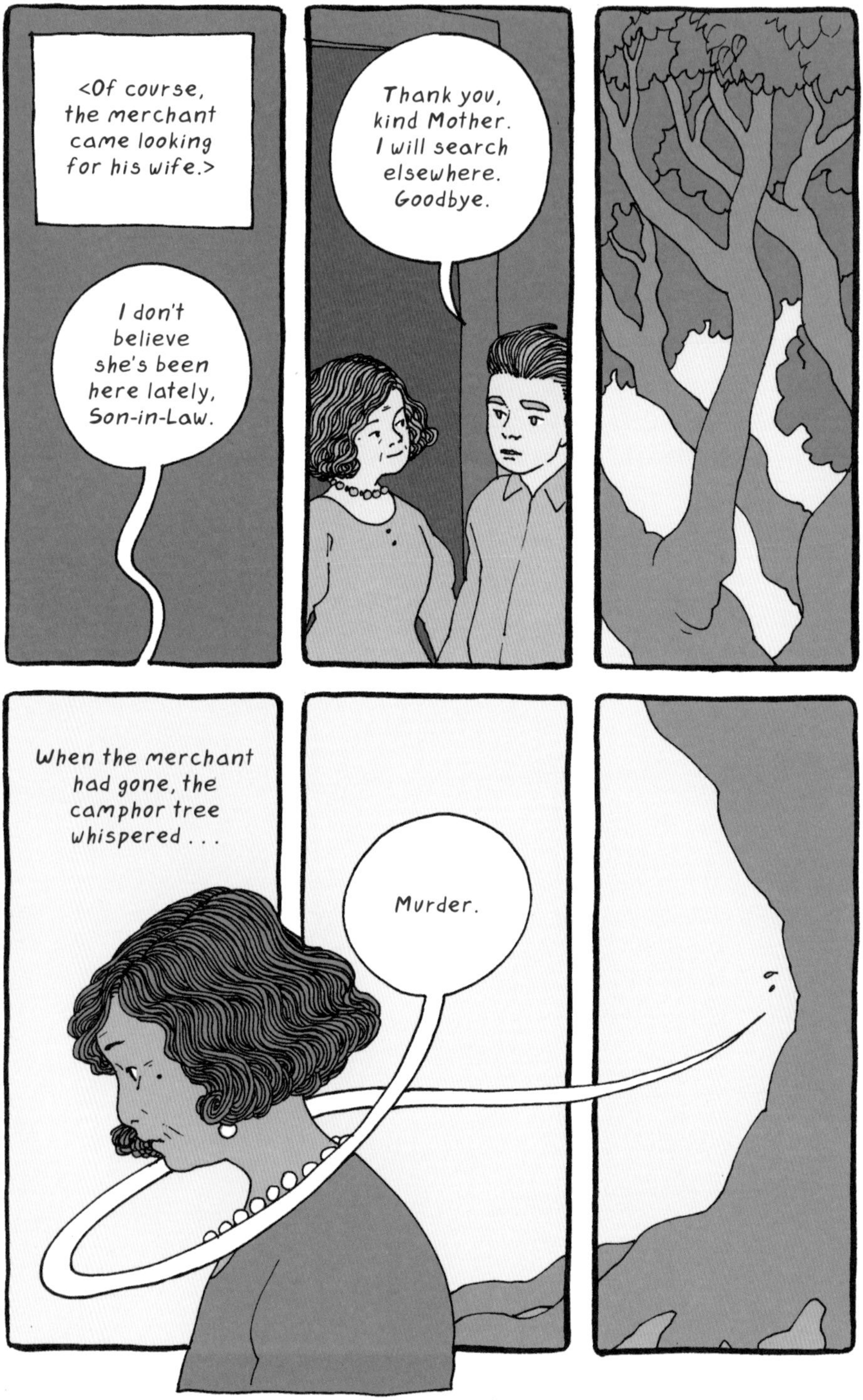
<Of course, the merchant came looking for his wife.>
I don't believe she's been here lately, Son-in-Law.
Thank you, kind Mother. I will search elsewhere. Goodbye.
When the merchant had gone, the camphor tree whispered . . .
Murder.

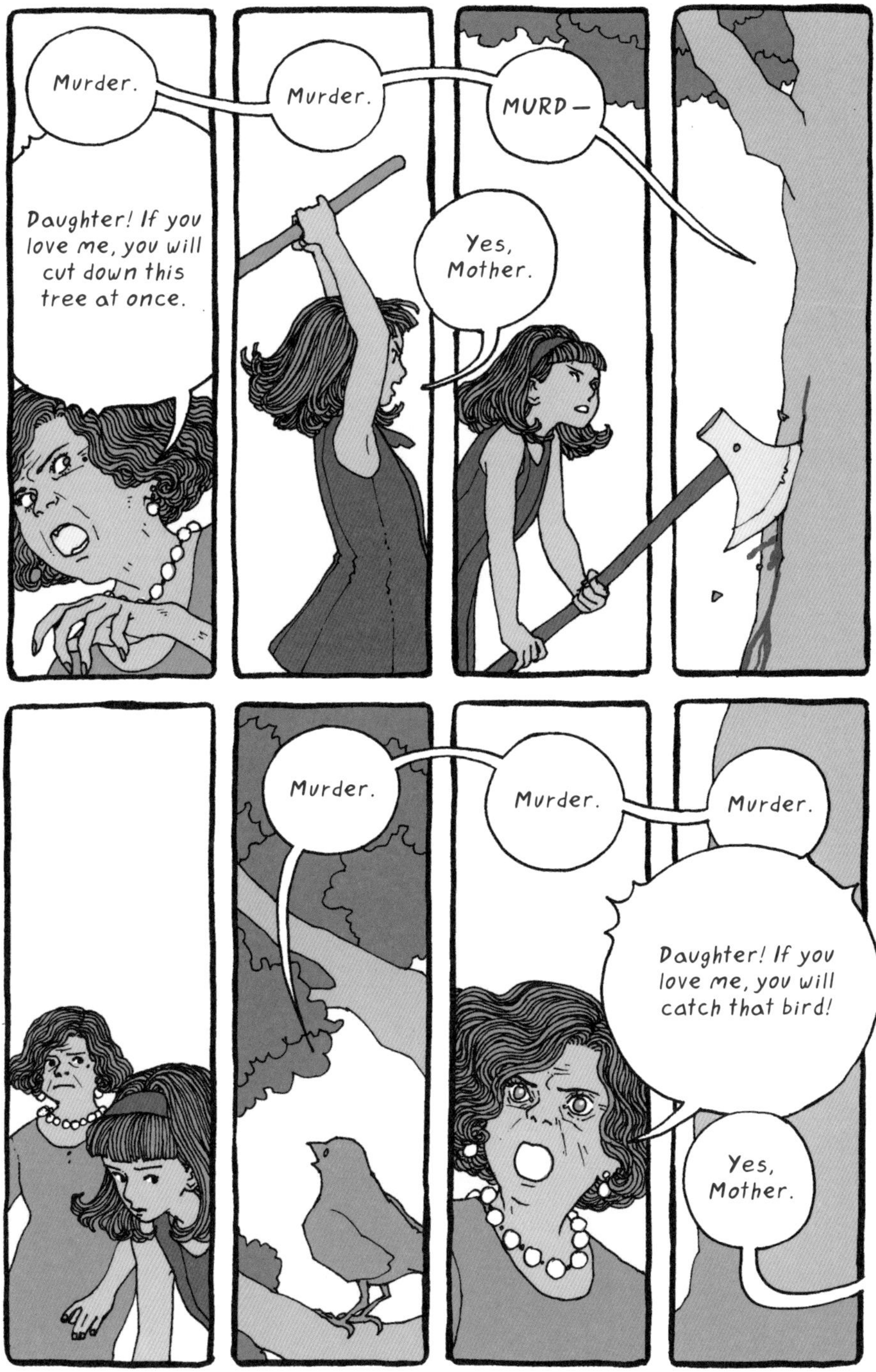
Murder.
Murder.
MURD—
Daughter! If you love me, you will cut down this tree at once.
Yes, Mother.
Murder.
Murder.
Murder.
Daughter! If you love me, you will catch that bird!
Yes, Mother.

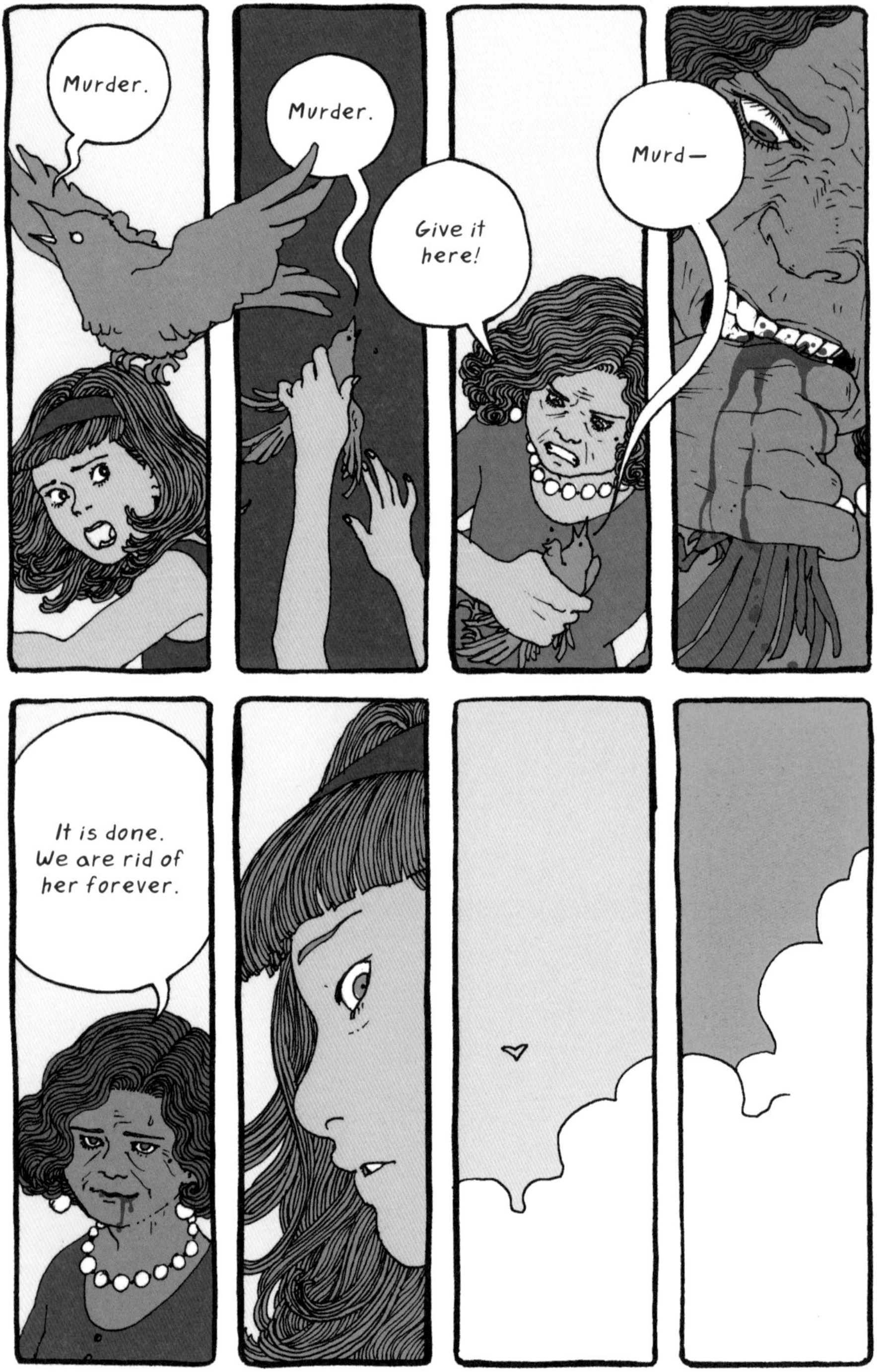

Murder.
Murder.
Give it here!
Murd—
It is done. We are rid of her forever.

Hello, young man. My name is Father Niles.

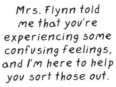

Mrs. Flynn told me that you're experiencing some confusing feelings, and I'm here to help you sort those out.

Tiến?

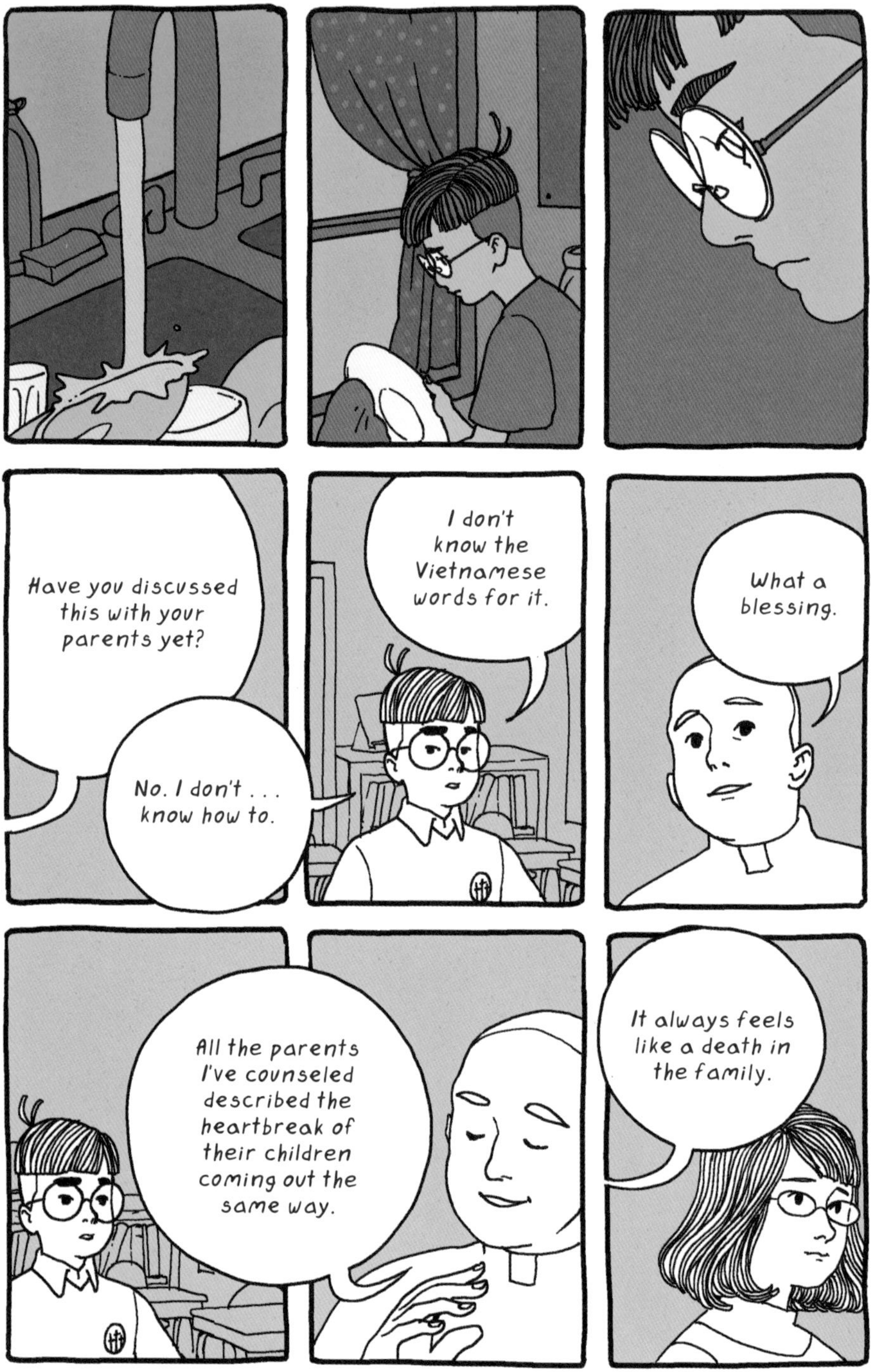
Have you discussed this with your parents yet?
No. I don't . . . know how to.
I don't know the Vietnamese words for it.
What a blessing.
All the parents I've counseled described the heartbreak of their children coming out the same way.
It always feels like a death in the family.

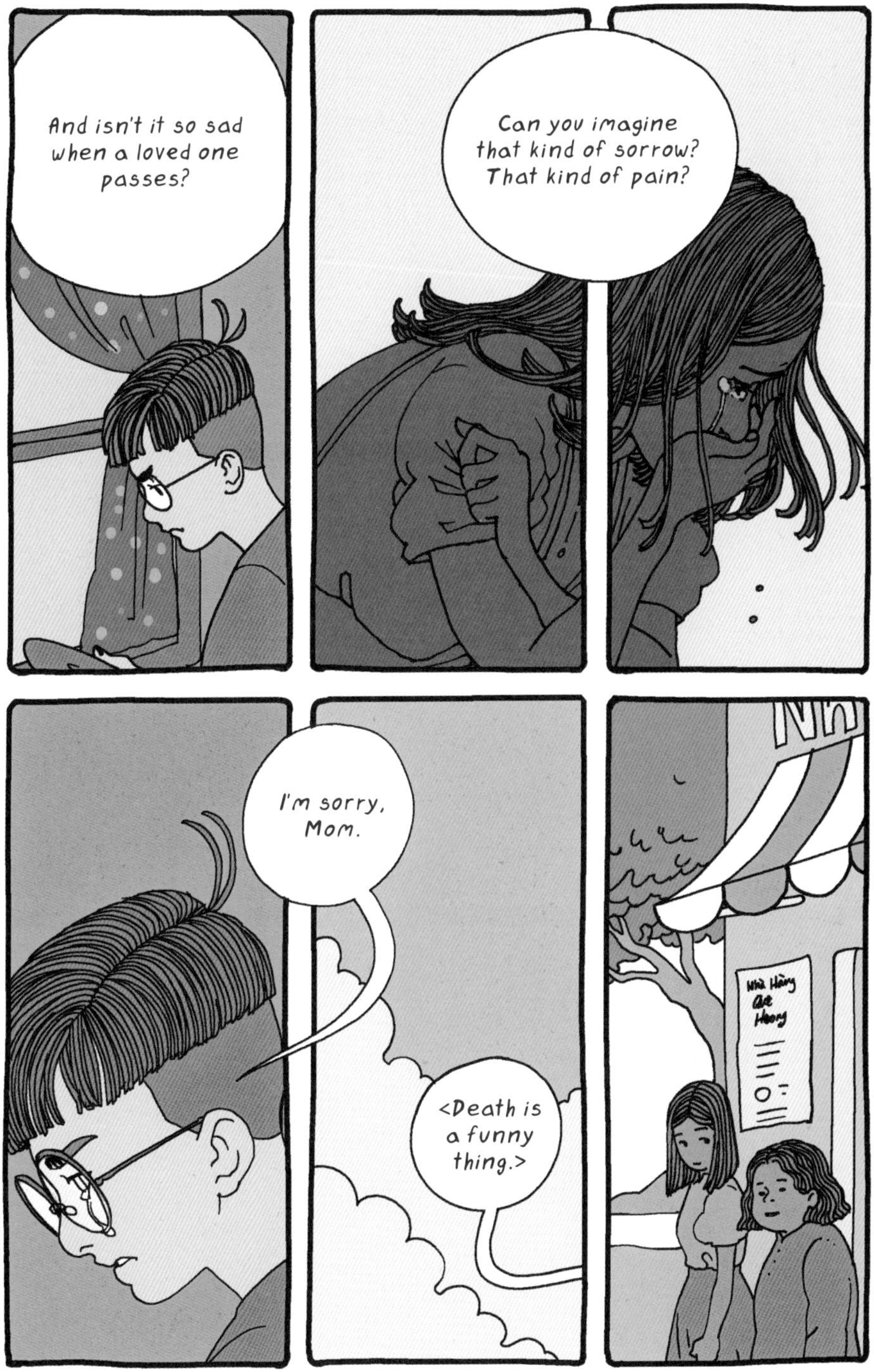
And isn't it so sad when a loved one passes?
Can you imagine that kind of sorrow? That kind of pain?
I'm sorry, Mom.
<Death is a funny thing.>
Nhà Hàng

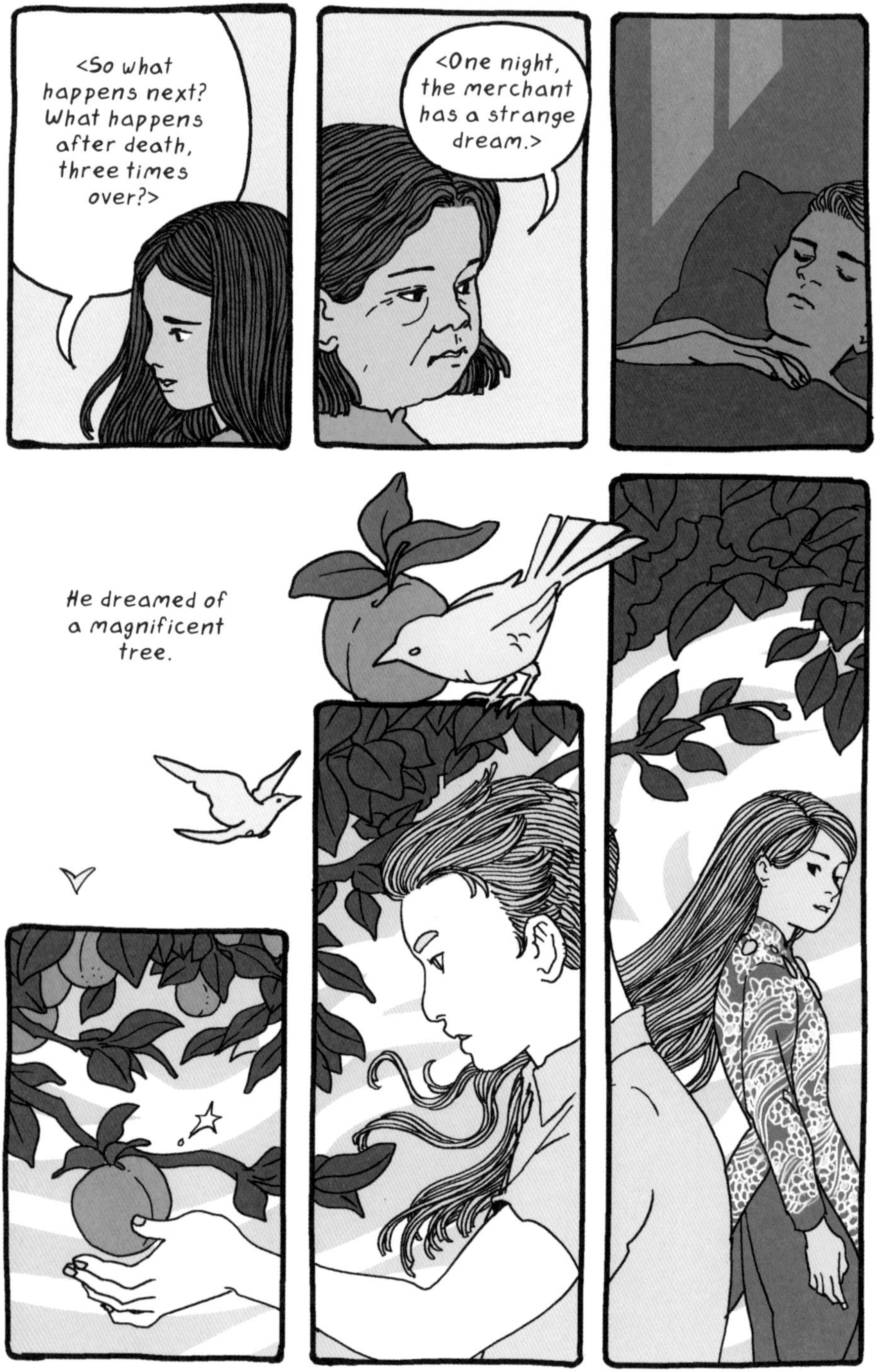
<So what happens next? What happens after death, three times over?>
<One night, the merchant has a strange dream.>
He dreamed of a magnificent tree.

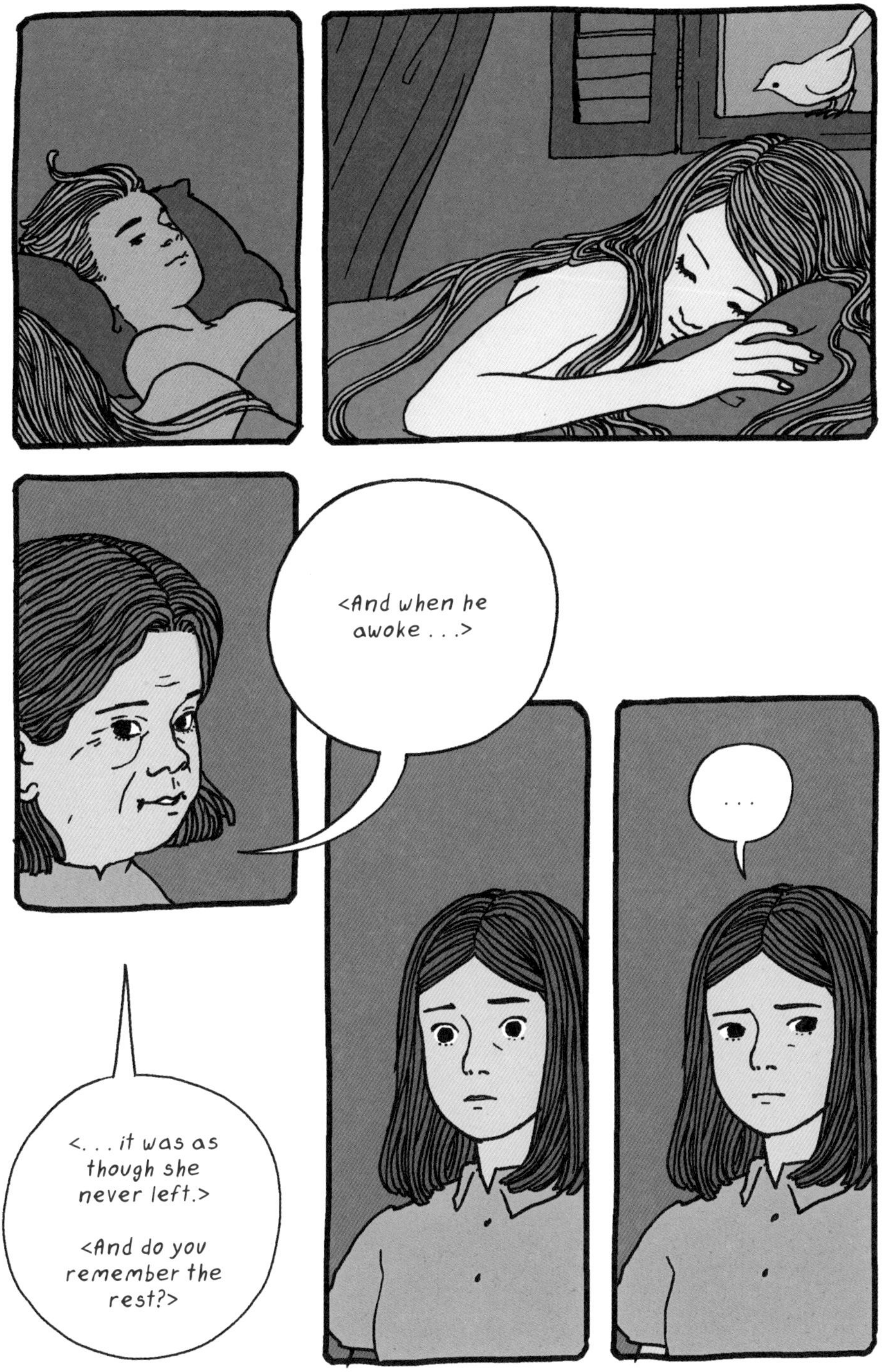
<And when he awoke . . .>
. . .
<. . . it was as though she never left.>
<And do you remember the rest?>

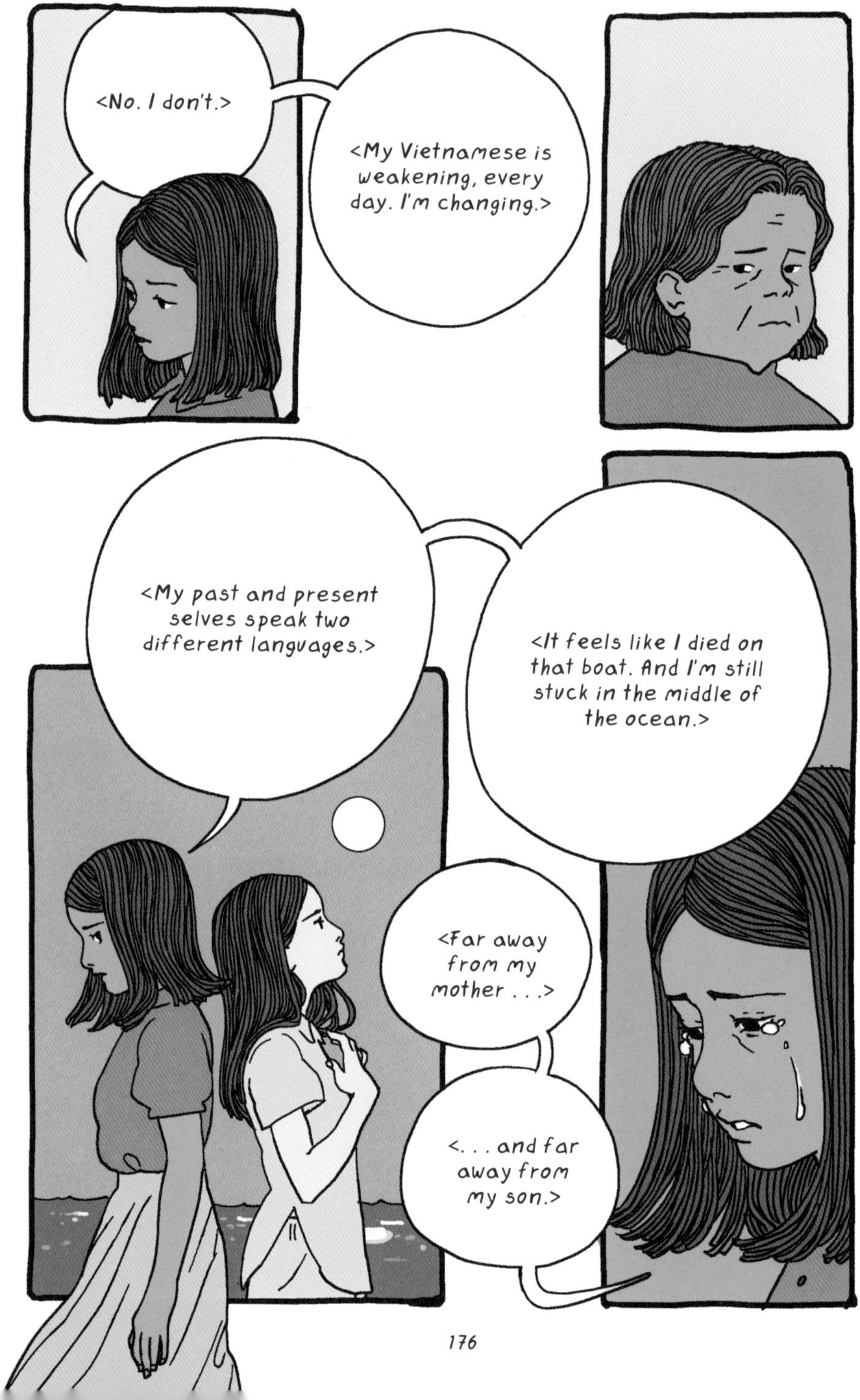
<No. I don't.>
<My Vietnamese is weakening, every day. I'm changing.>
<My past and present selves speak two different languages.>
<It feels like I died on that boat. And I'm still stuck in the middle of the ocean.>
<Far away from my mother . . .>
<. . . and far away from my son.>

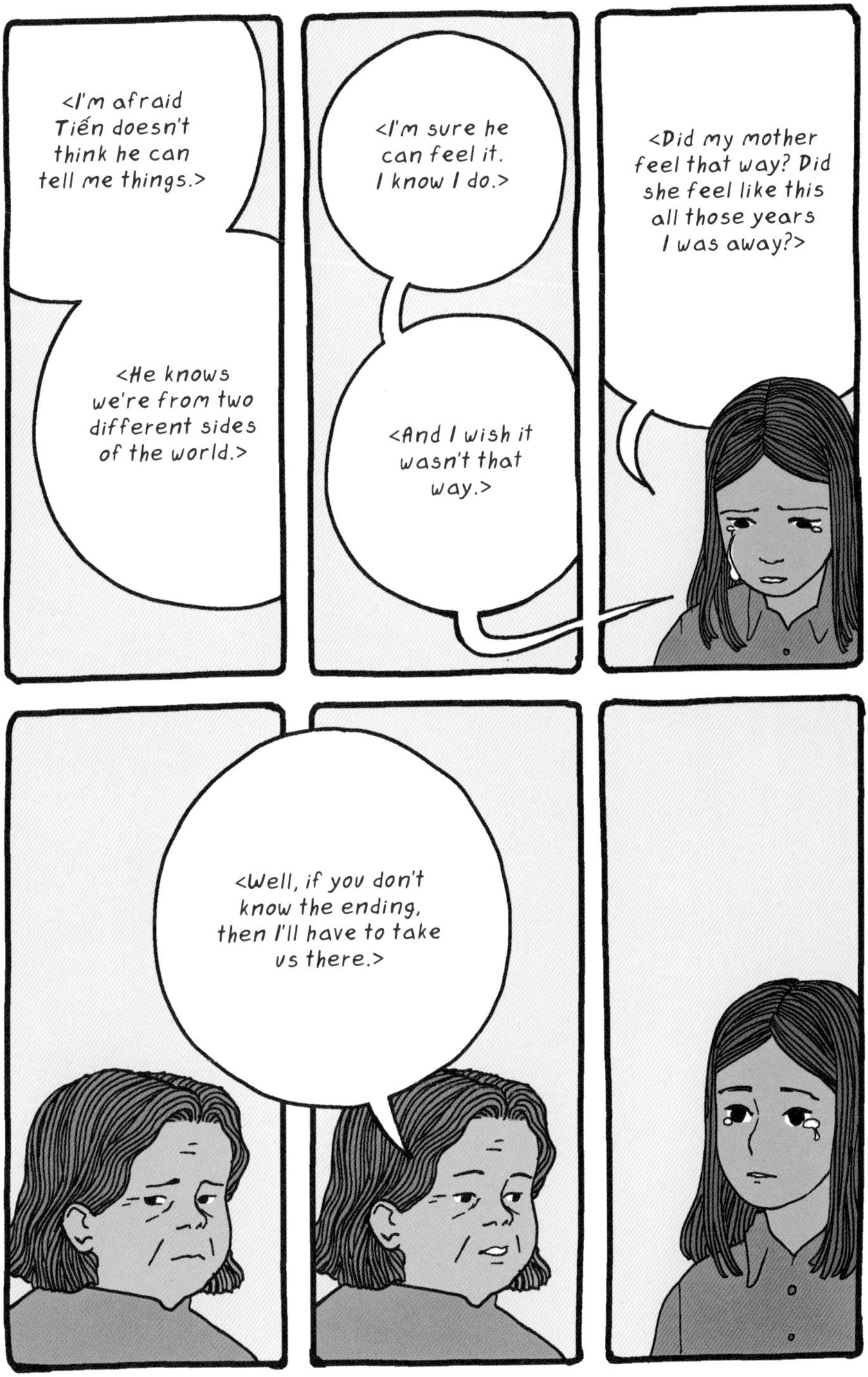
<I'm afraid Tiến doesn't think he can tell me things.>
<He knows we're from two different sides of the world.>
<I'm sure he can feel it. I know I do.>
<And I wish it wasn't that way.>
<Did my mother feel that way? Did she feel like this all those years I was away?>
<Well, if you don't know the ending, then I'll have to take us there.>

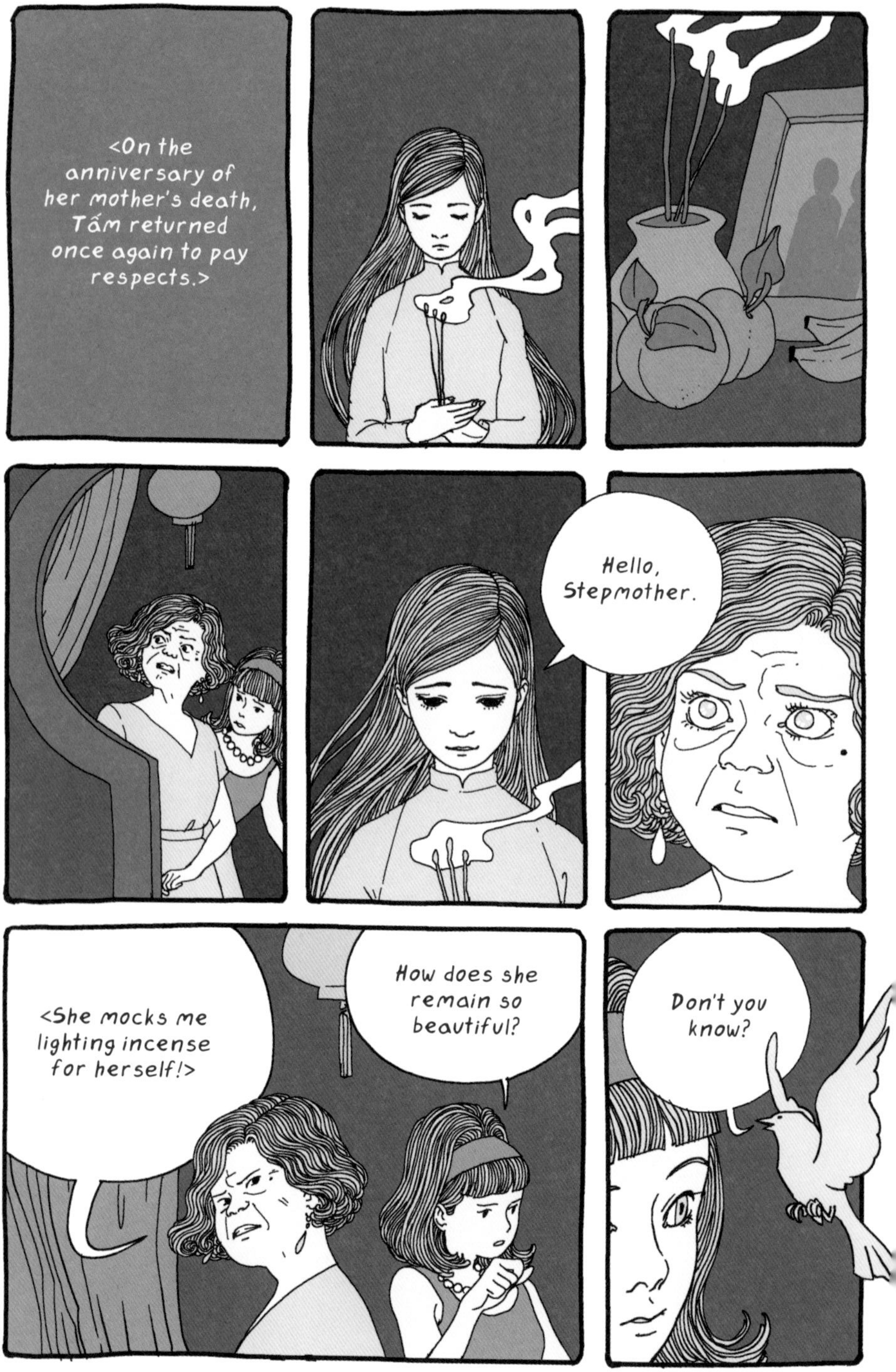
<On the anniversary of her mother's death, Tấm returned once again to pay respects.>
Hello, Stepmother.
<She mocks me lighting incense for herself!>
How does she remain so beautiful?
Don't you know?

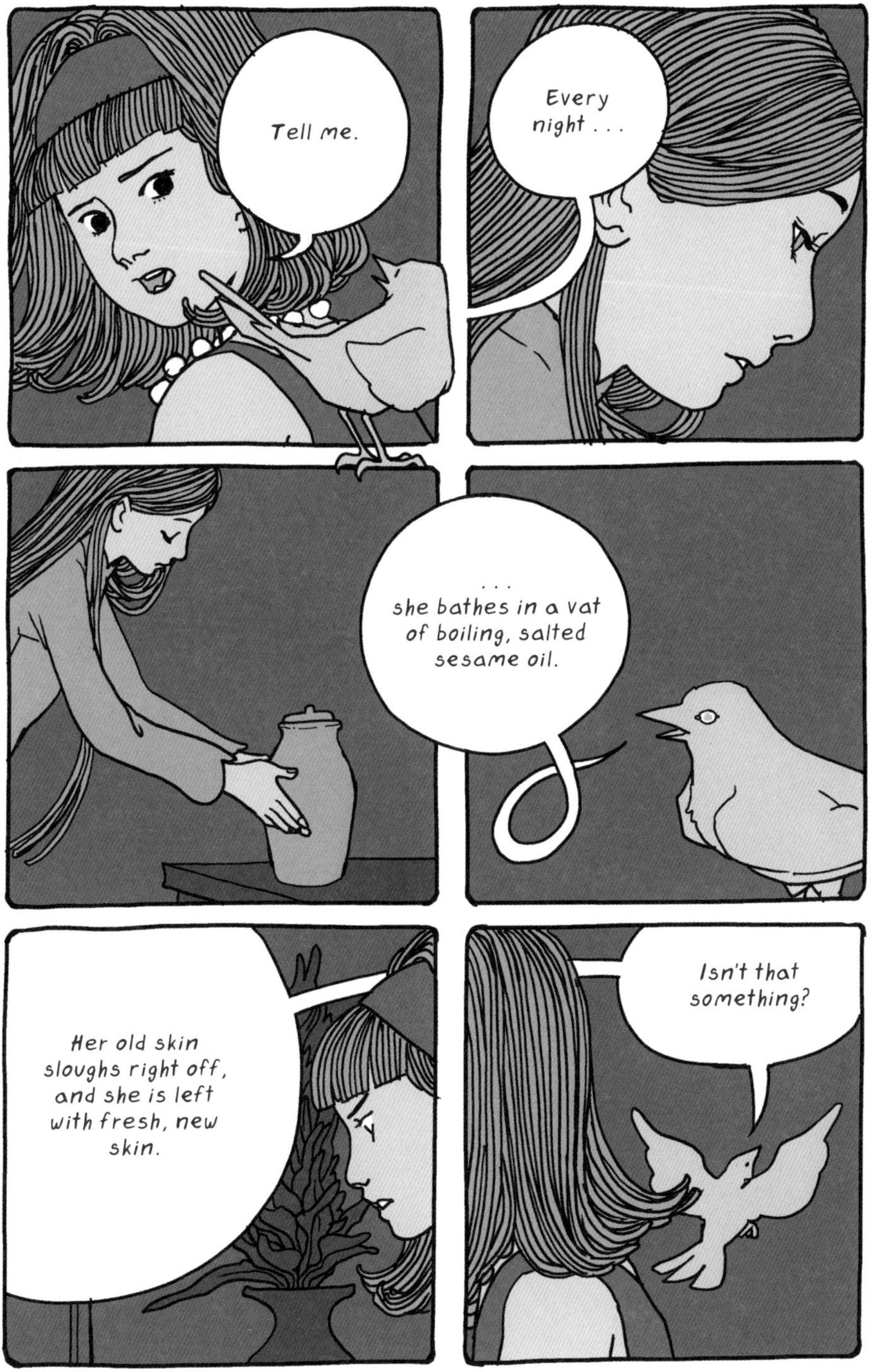
Tell me.
Every night . . .
. . . she bathes in a vat of boiling, salted sesame oil.
Her old skin sloughs right off, and she is left with fresh, new skin.
Isn't that something?

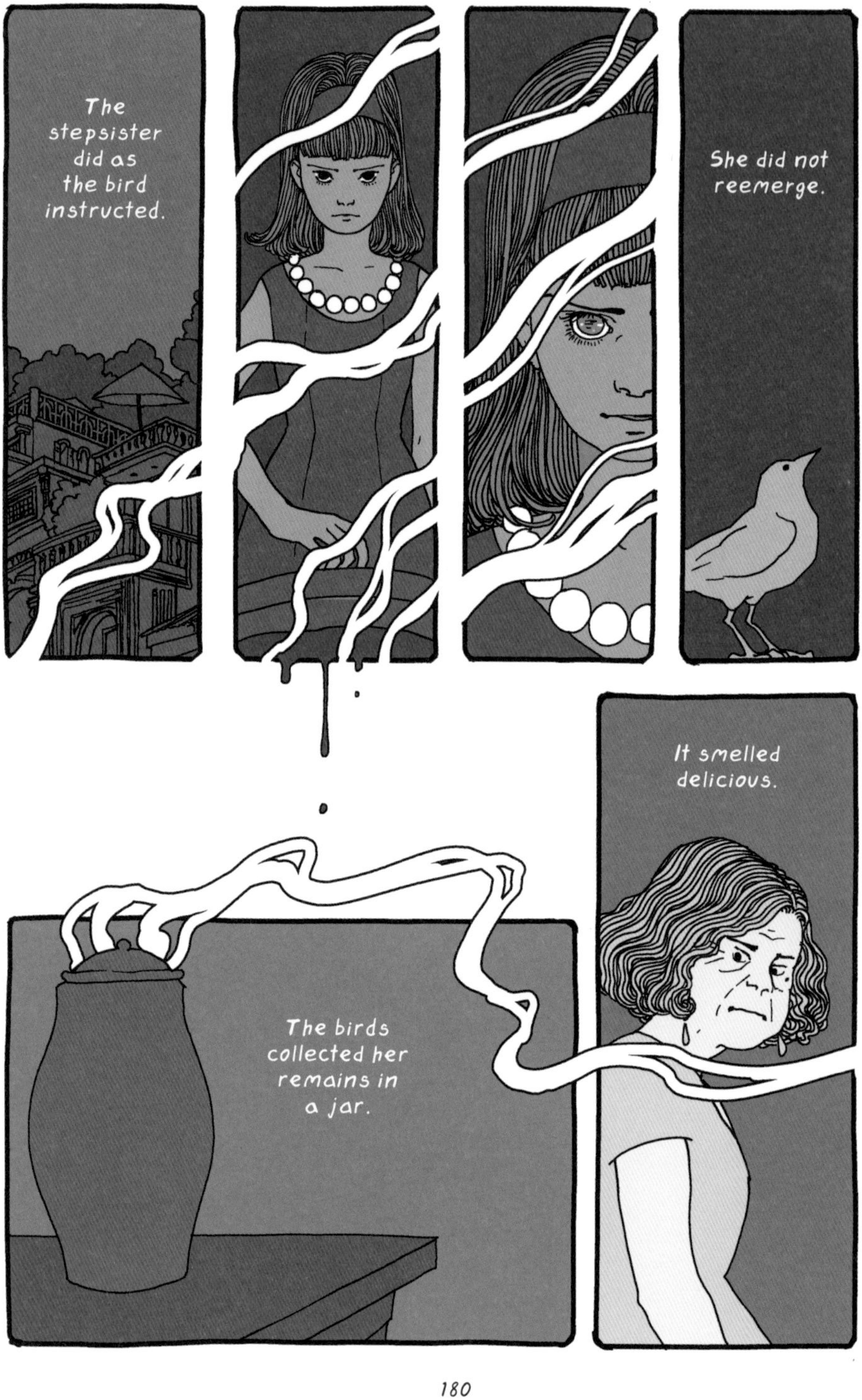
The stepsister did as the bird instructed.
She did not reemerge.
It smelled delicious.
The birds collected her remains in a jar.

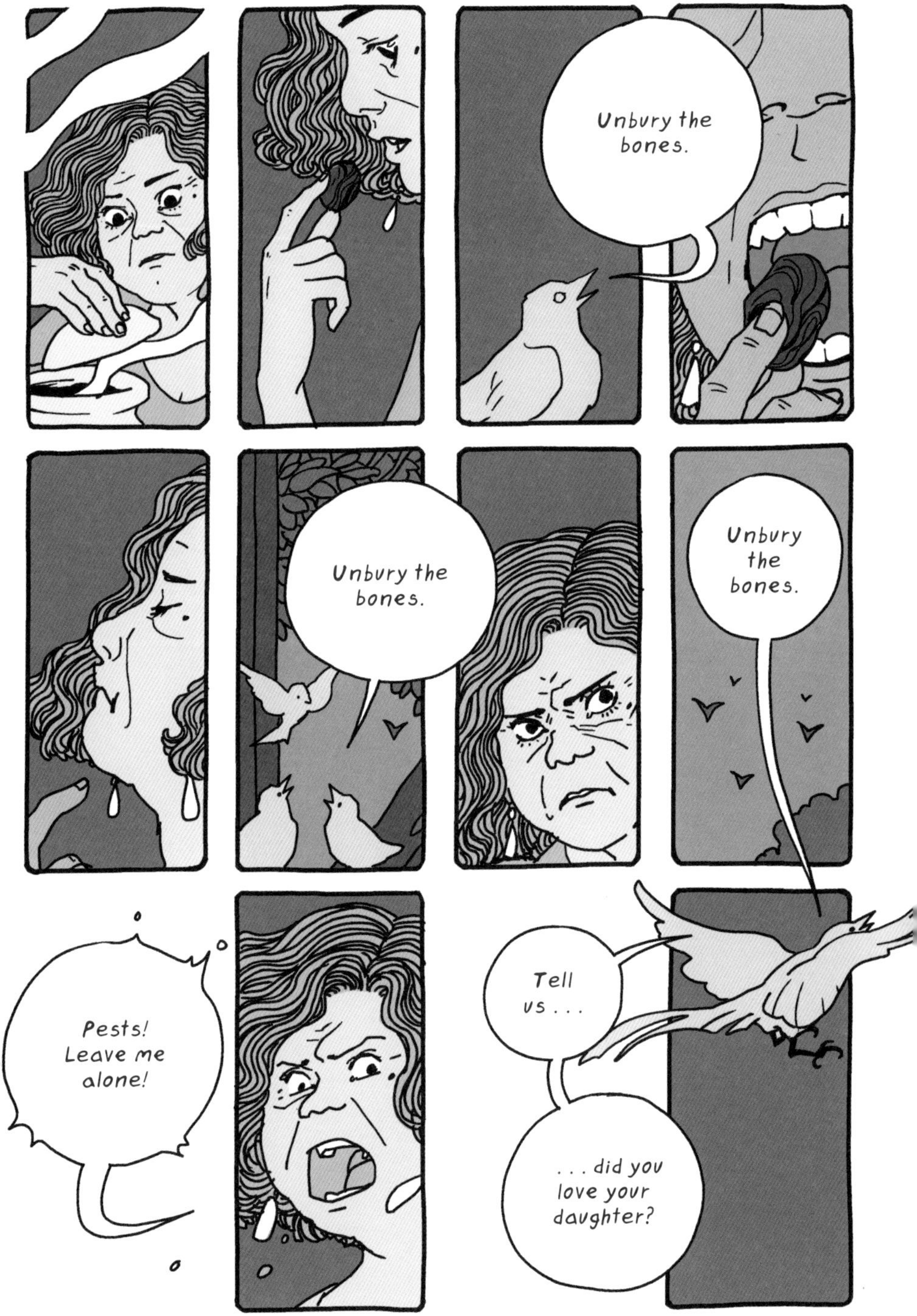
Unbury the bones.
Unbury the bones.
Unbury the bones.
Pests! Leave me alone!
Tell us . . .
. . . did you love your daughter?

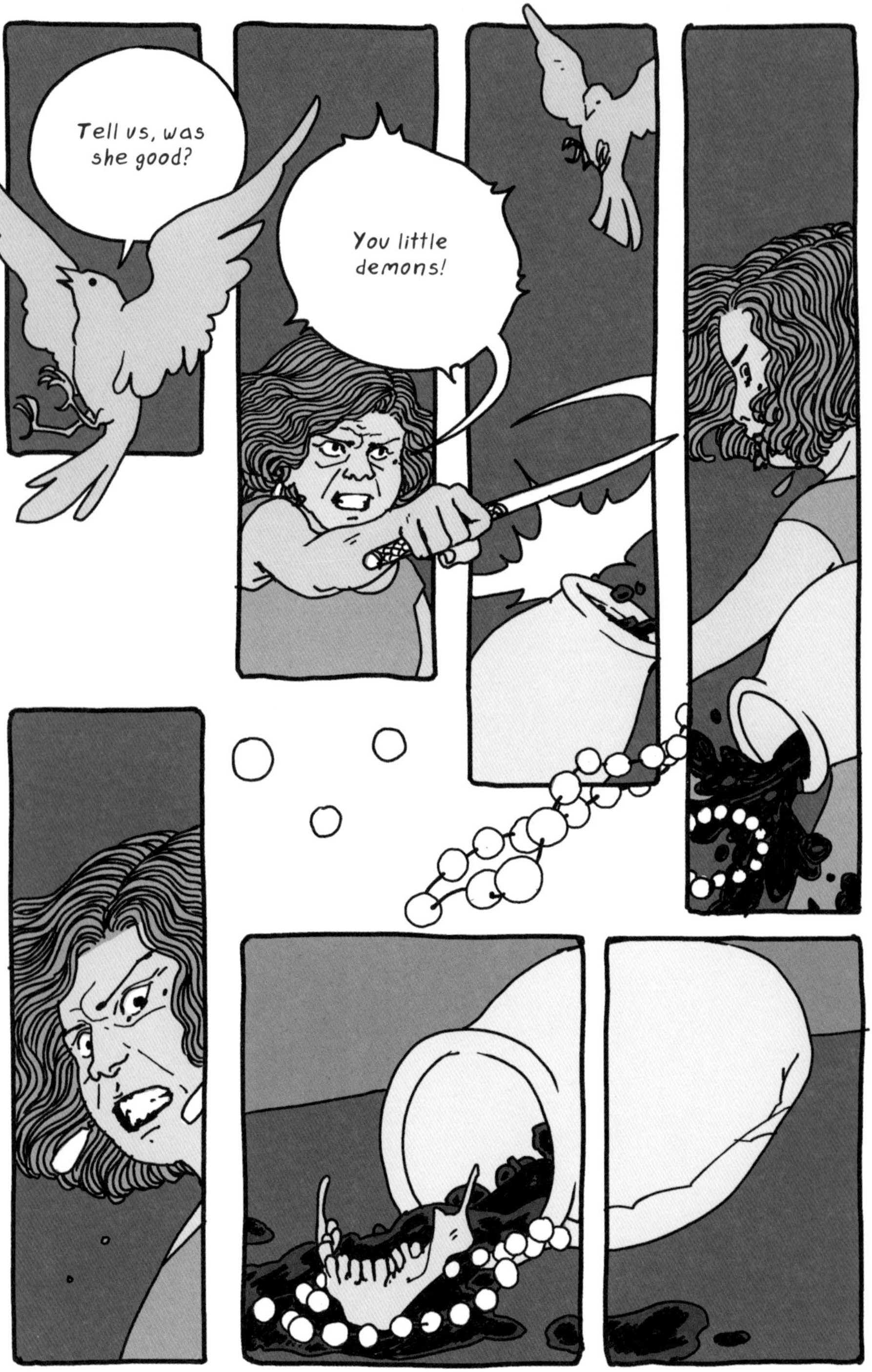
Tell us, was she good?
You little demons!

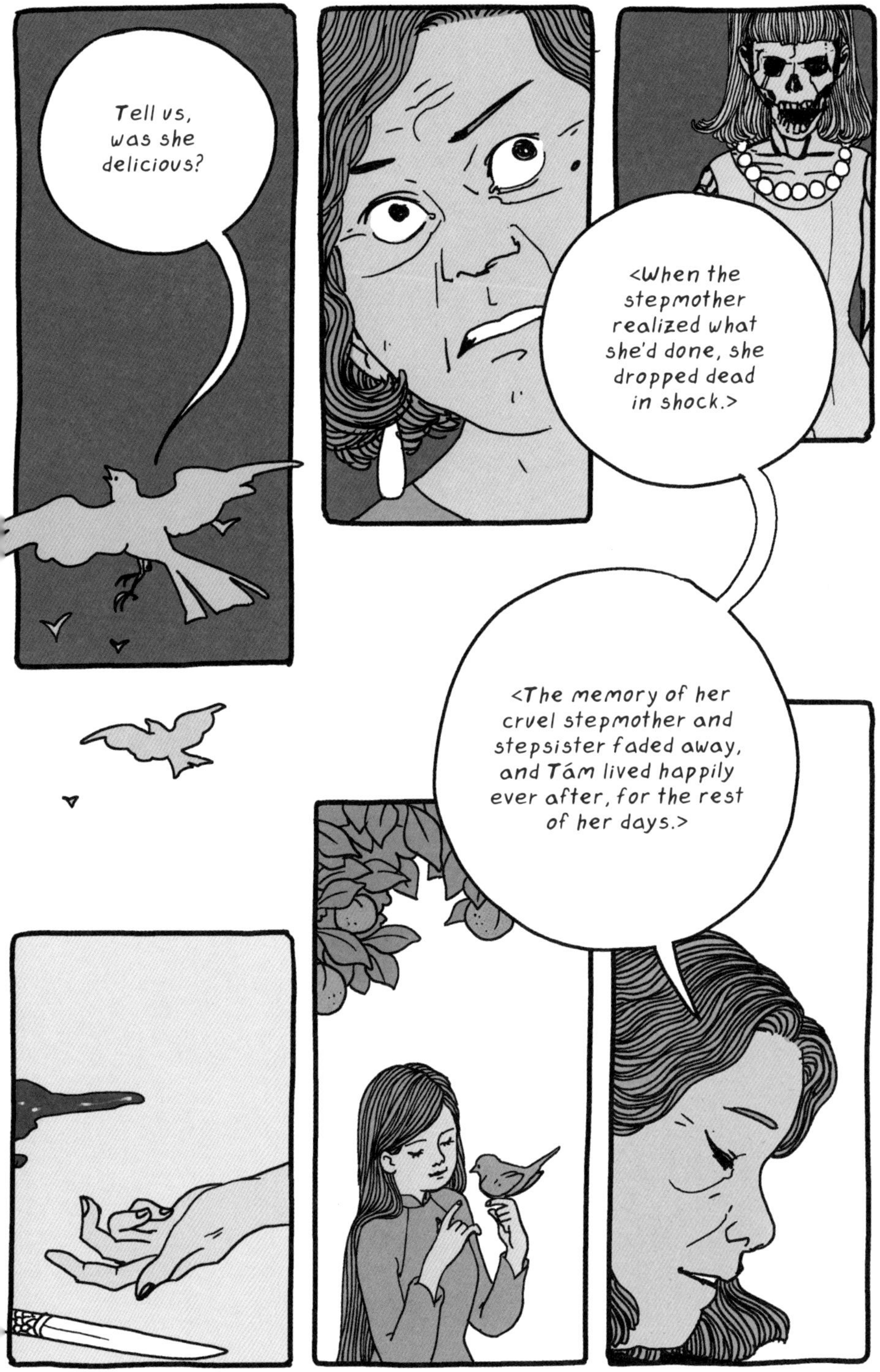
Tell us, was she delicious?
<When the stepmother realized what she'd done, she dropped dead in shock.>
<The memory of her cruel stepmother and stepsister faded away, and Tám lived happily ever after, for the rest of her days.>

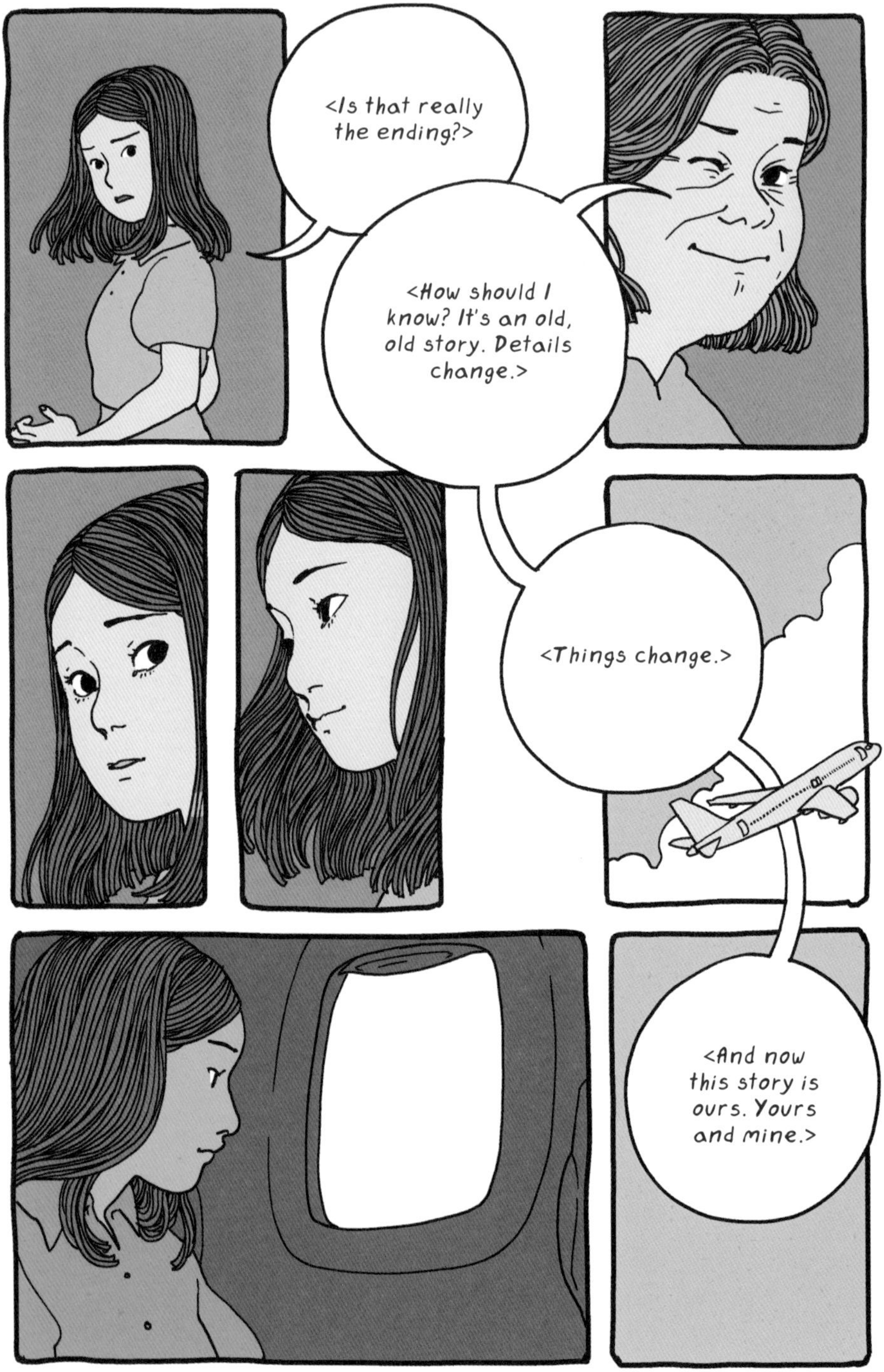
<Is that really the ending?>
<How should I know? It's an old, old story. Details change.>
<Things change.>
<And now this story is ours. Yours and mine.>

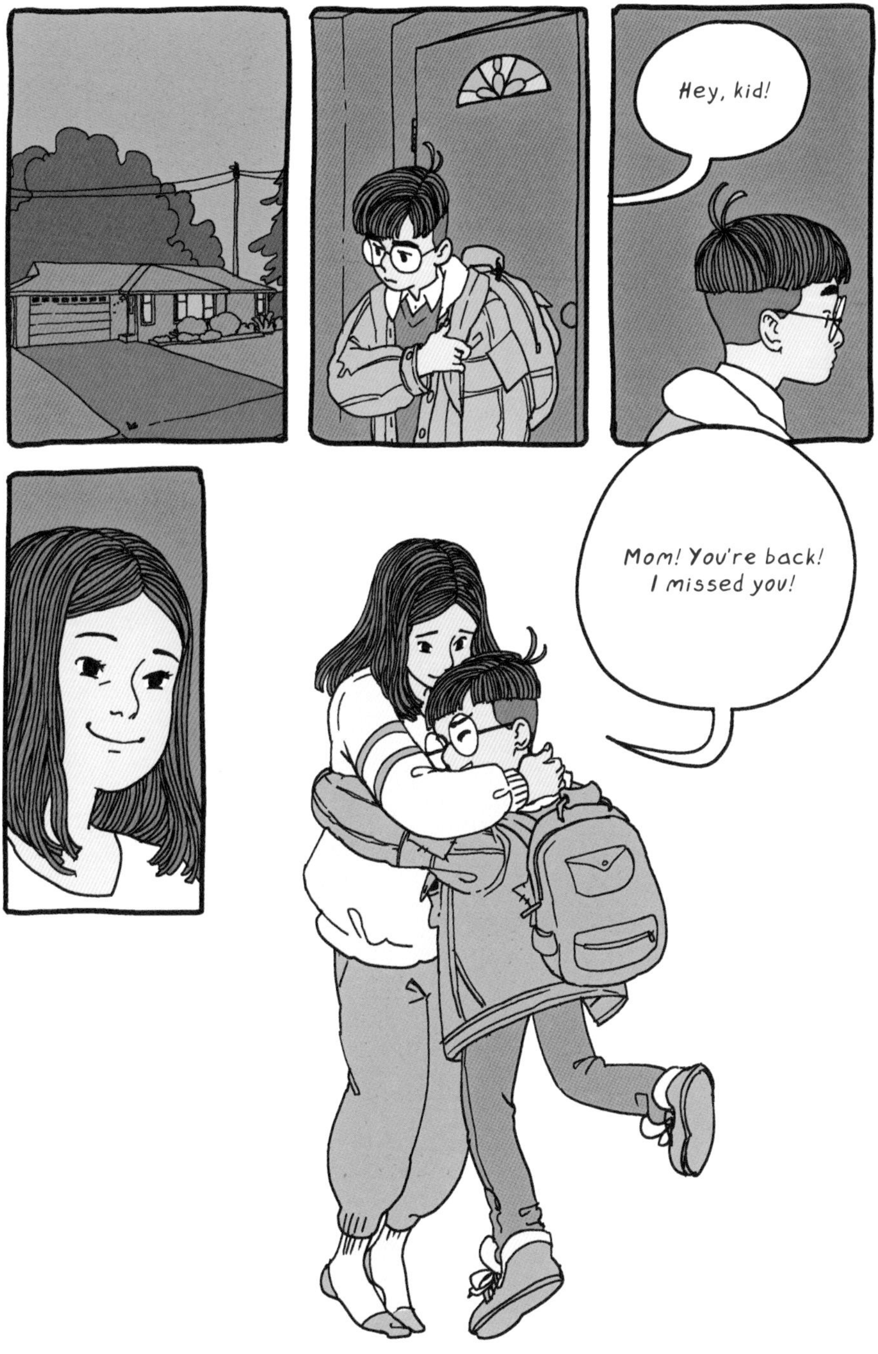
Hey, kid!
Mom! You're back! I missed you!

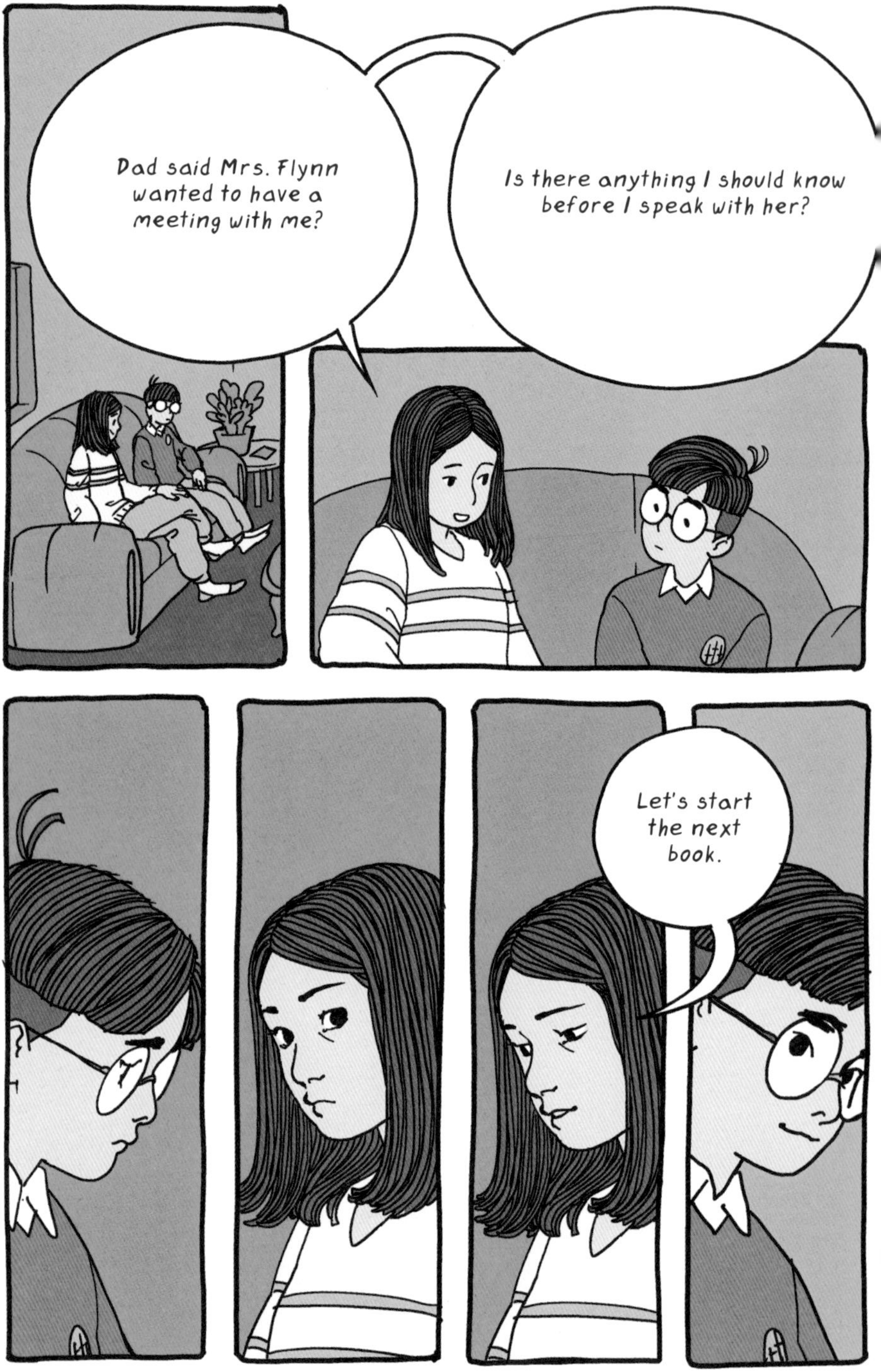
Dad said Mrs. Flynn wanted to have a meeting with me?
Is there anything I should know before I speak with her?
Let's start the next book.

Once upon a time . . .

. . . where the ocean is bluest and where the waters are deepest, there was a rich and vibrant kingdom far beneath the waves.

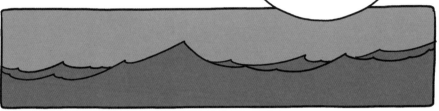

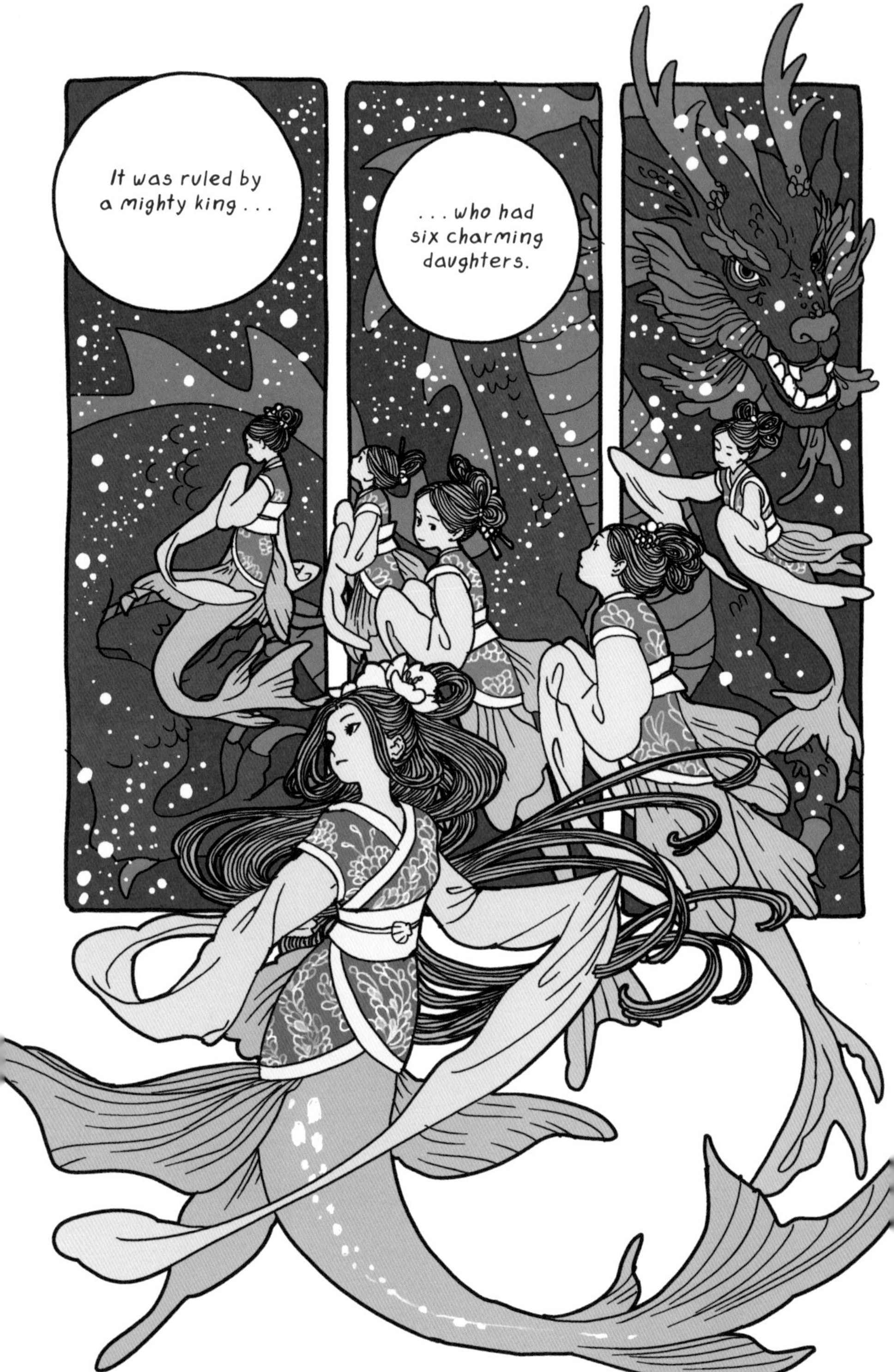
It was ruled by a mighty king . . .
. . . who had six charming daughters.

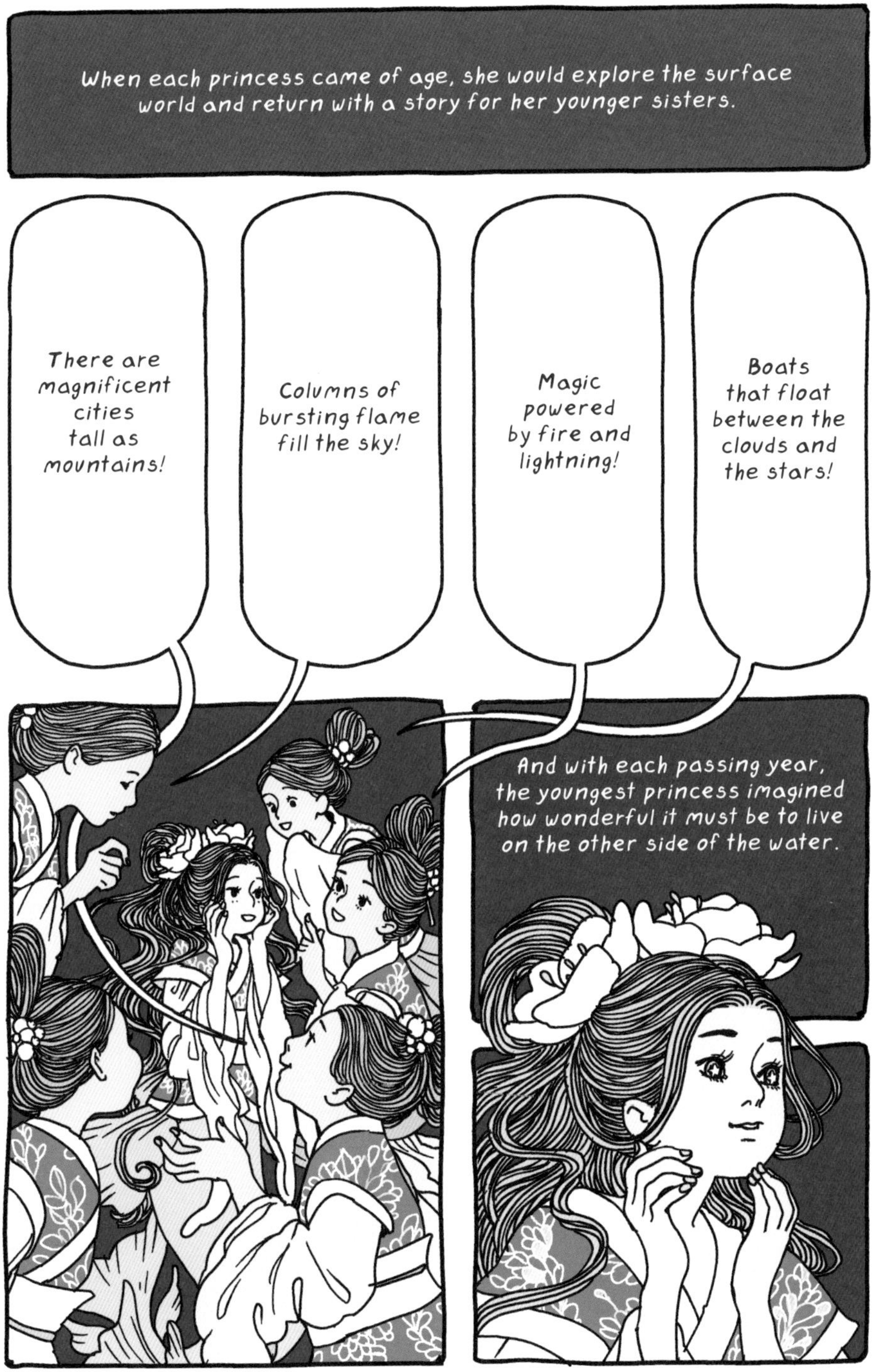
When each princess came of age, she would explore the surface world and return with a story for her younger sisters.
There are magnificent cities tall as mountains!
Columns of bursting flame fill the sky!
Magic powered by fire and lightning!
Boats that float between the clouds and the stars!
And with each passing year, the youngest princess imagined how wonderful it must be to live on the other side of the water.

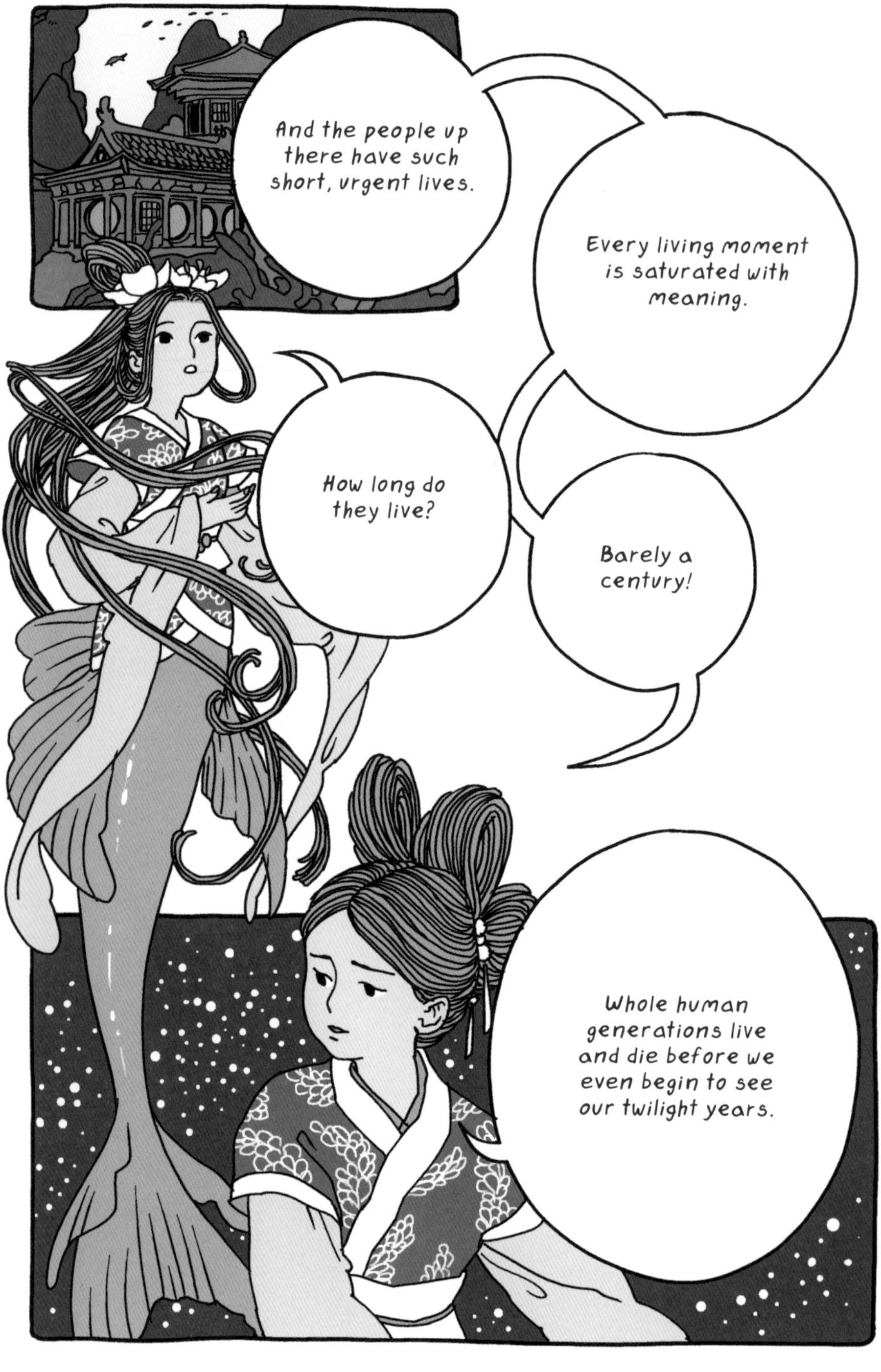
And the people up there have such short, urgent lives.
Every living moment is saturated with meaning.
How long do they live?
Barely a century!
Whole human generations live and die before we even begin to see our twilight years.

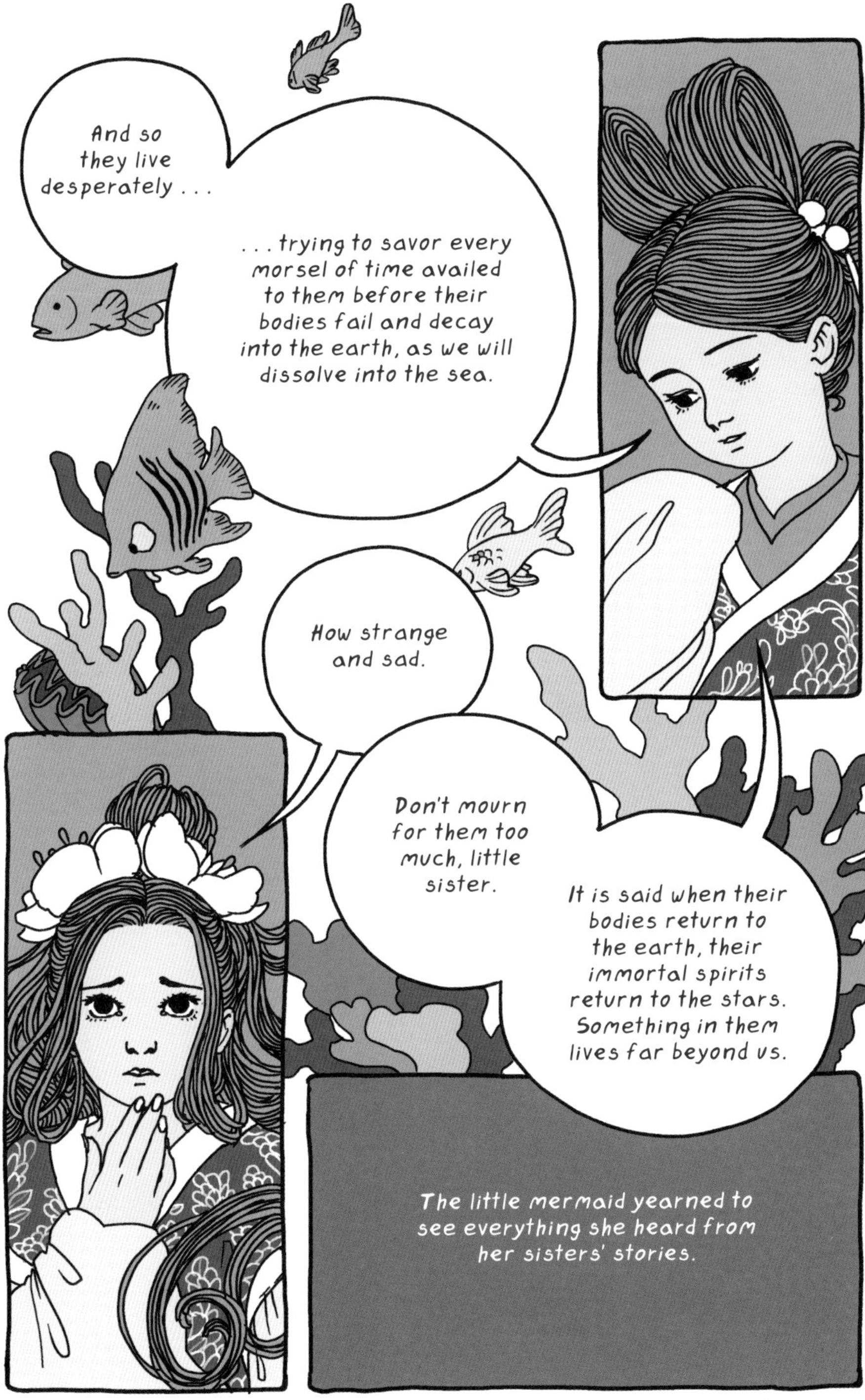
And so they live desperately . . .
. . . trying to savor every morsel of time availed to them before their bodies fail and decay into the earth, as we will dissolve into the sea.
How strange and sad.
Don't mourn for them too much, little sister.
It is said when their bodies return to the earth, their immortal spirits return to the stars. Something in them lives far beyond us.
The little mermaid yearned to see everything she heard from her sisters' stories.

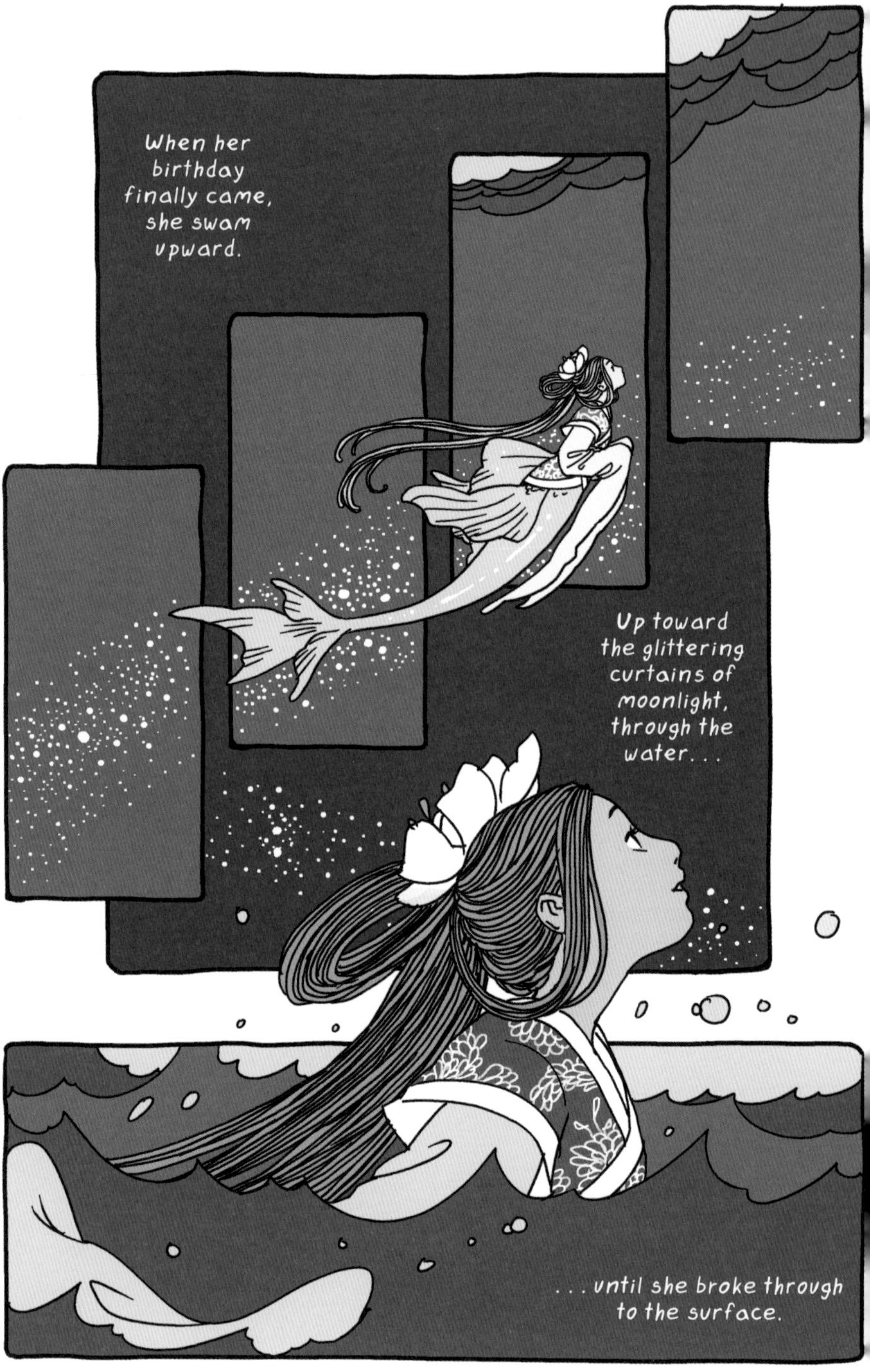
When her birthday finally came, she swam upward.
Up toward the glittering curtains of moonlight, through the water. . .
. . . until she broke through to the surface.

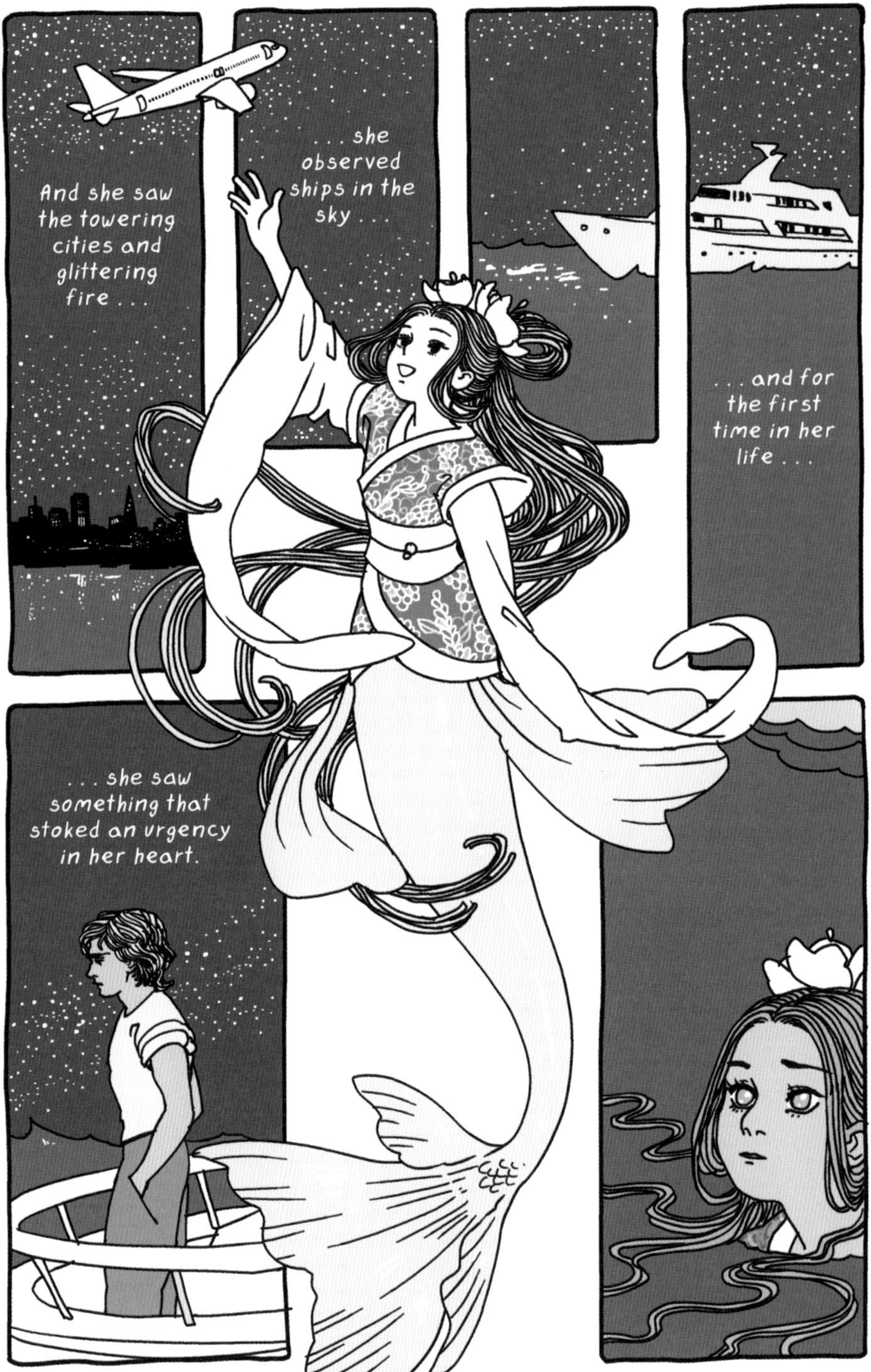
And she saw the towering cities and glittering fire . . .
. . . she observed ships in the sky . . .
. . . and for the first time in her life . . .
. . . she saw something that stoked an urgency in her heart.

She felt the
desperate,
mortal need
to salvage a
precious little
fragment of
time in spite of
the thousands of
years she had
ahead of her.

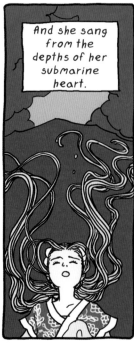

And she sang
from the
depths of her
submarine
heart.

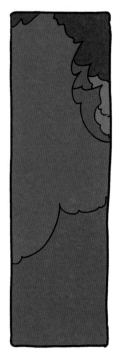

She sang
with a bitter
yearning . . .

. . . that roiled
every current
in the ocean.

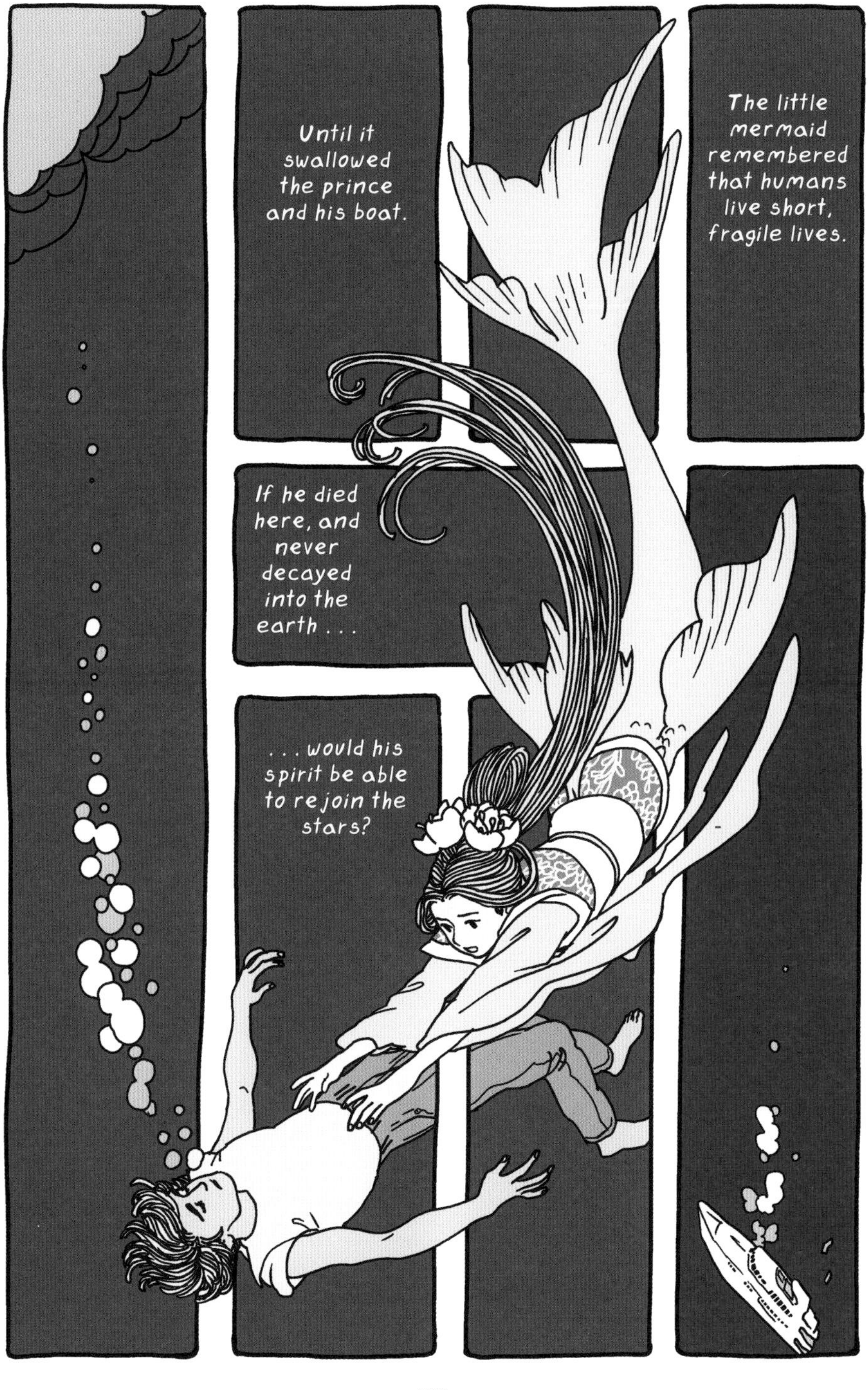
Until it swallowed the prince and his boat.
The little mermaid remembered that humans live short, fragile lives.
If he died here, and never decayed into the earth . . .
. . . would his spirit be able to rejoin the stars?

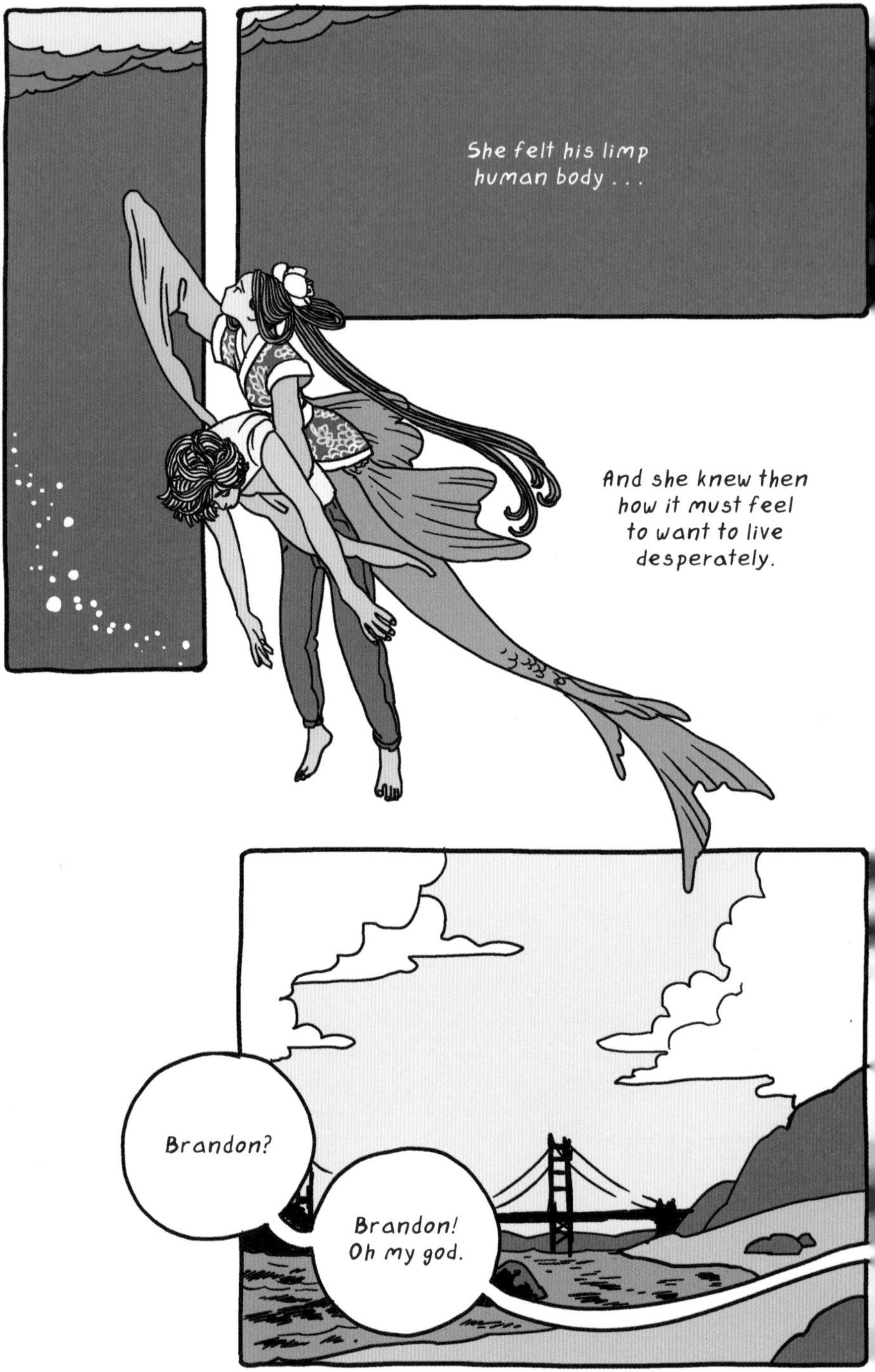
She felt his limp human body . . .
And she knew then how it must feel to want to live desperately.
Brandon?
Brandon! Oh my god.

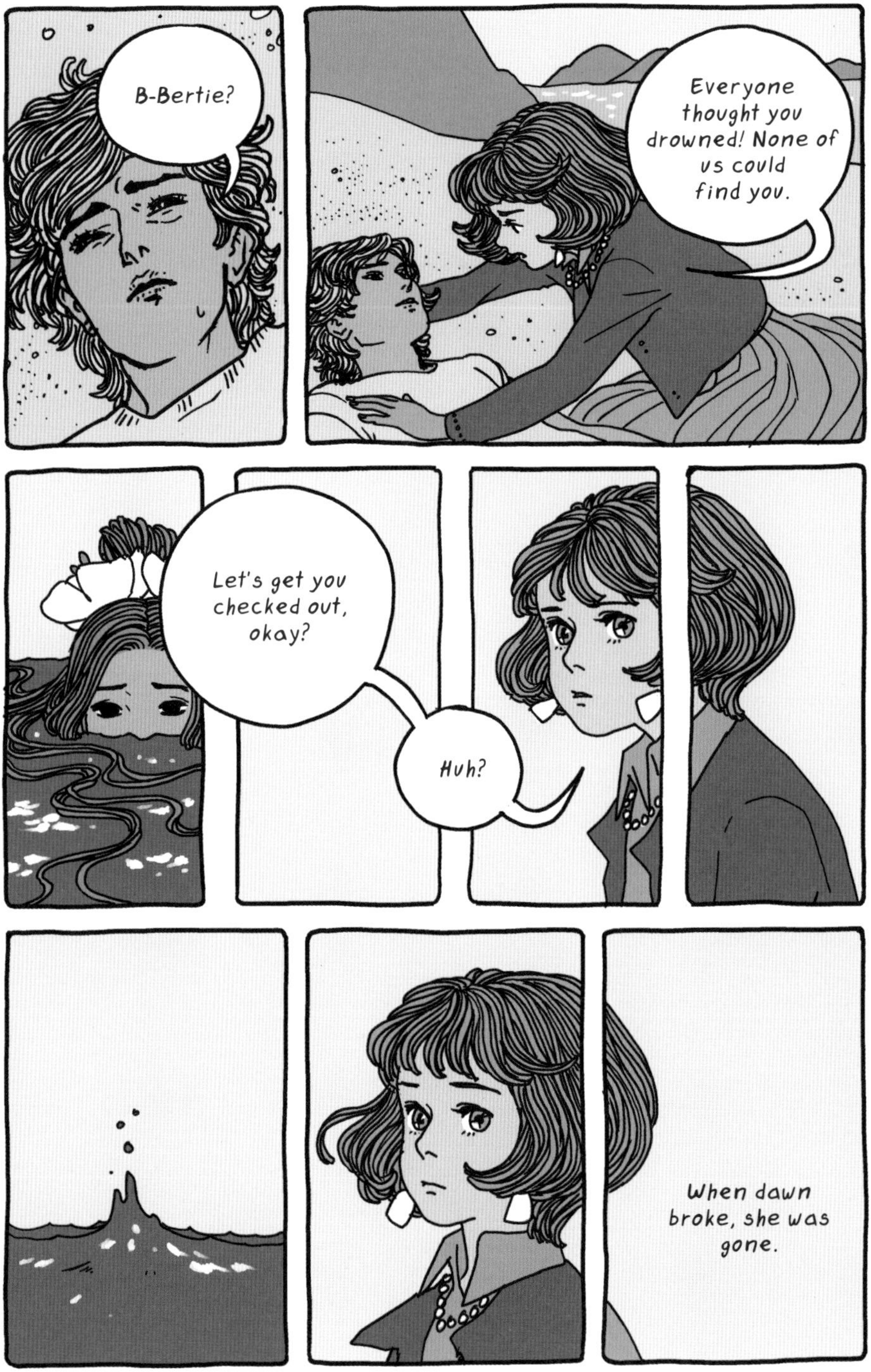
B-Bertie?
Everyone thought you drowned! None of us could find you.
Let's get you checked out, okay?
Huh?
When dawn broke, she was gone.

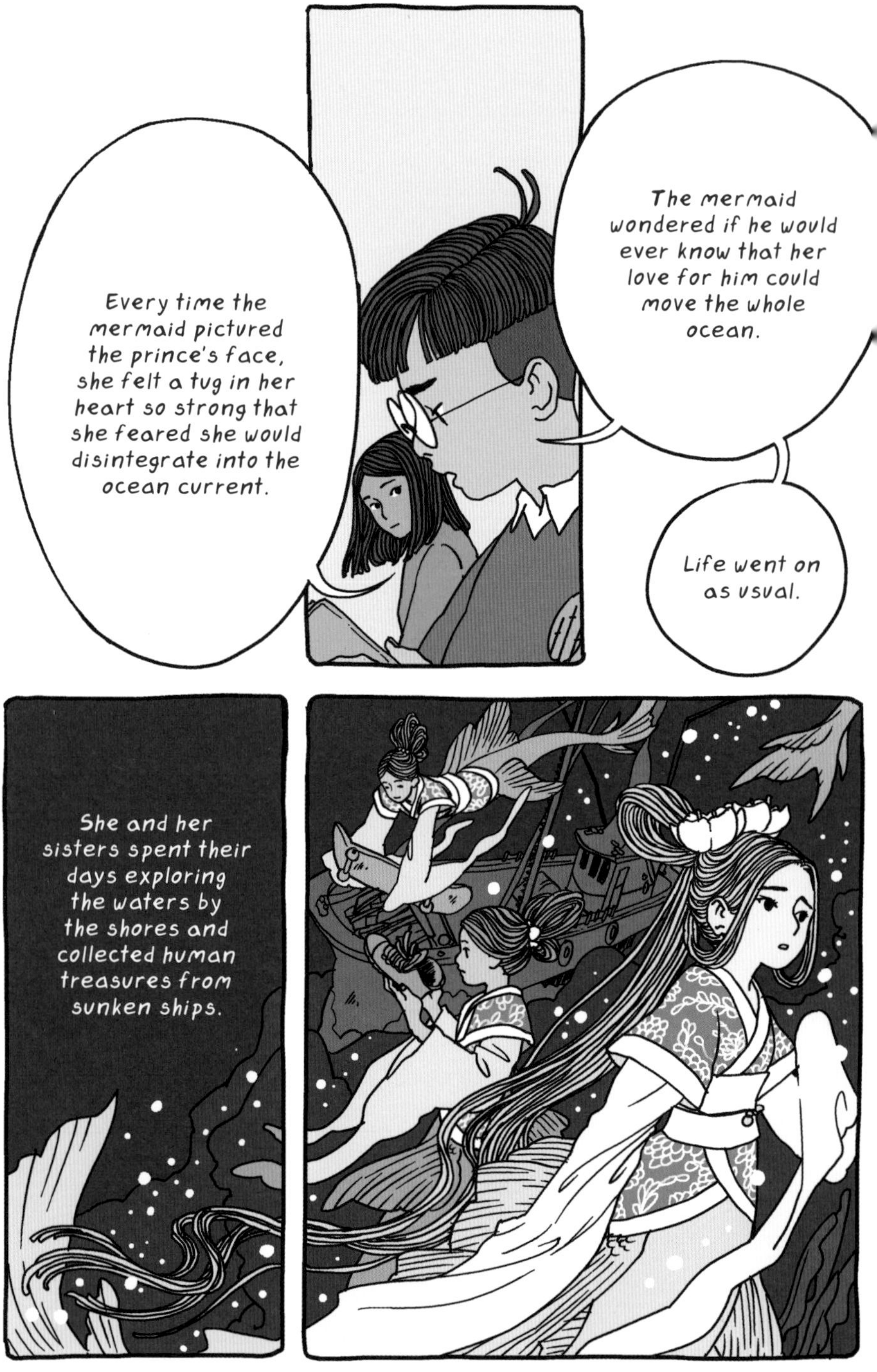
Every time the mermaid pictured the prince's face, she felt a tug in her heart so strong that she feared she would disintegrate into the ocean current.
The mermaid wondered if he would ever know that her love for him could move the whole ocean.
Life went on as usual.
She and her sisters spent their days exploring the waters by the shores and collected human treasures from sunken ships.

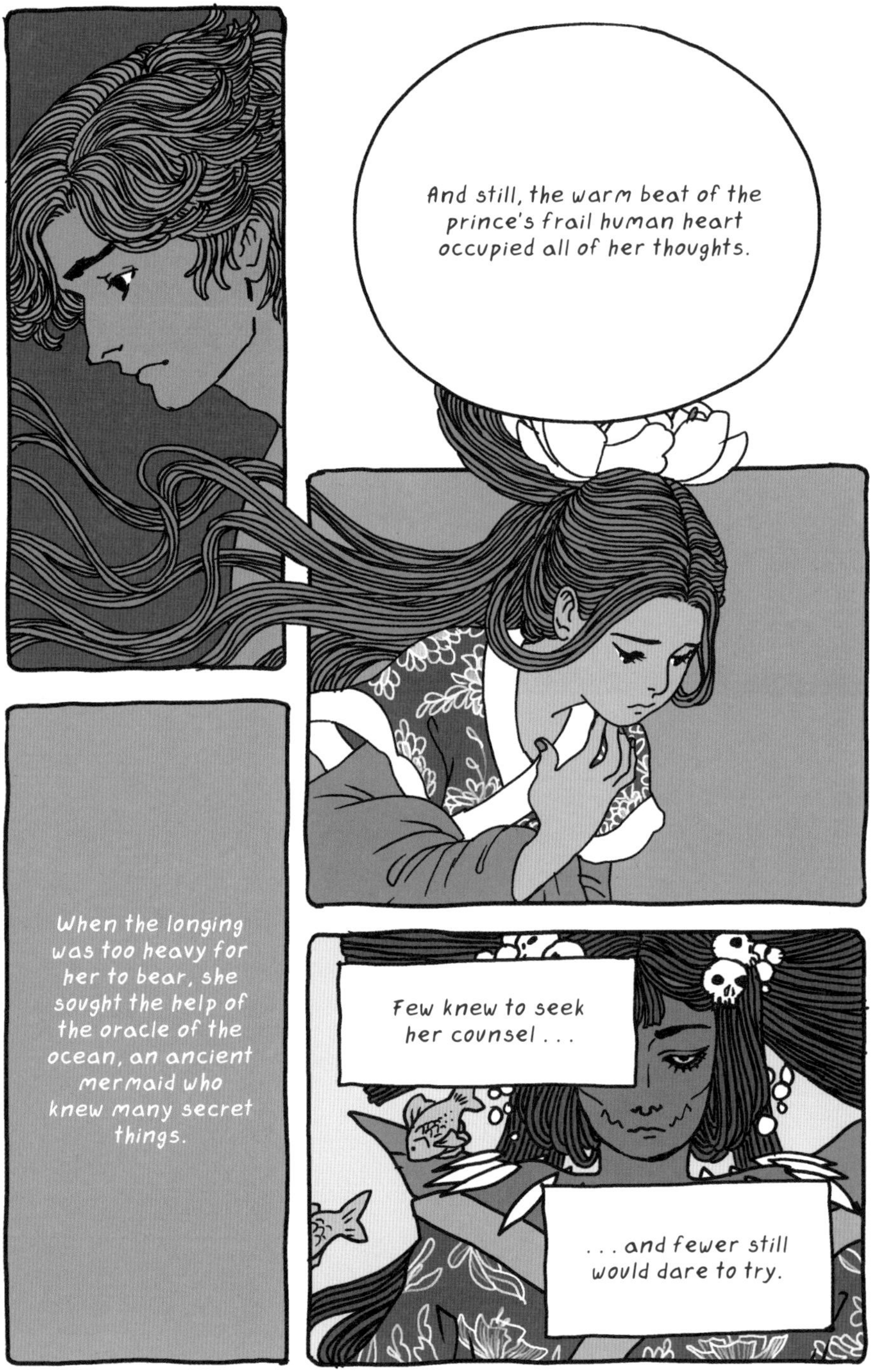
And still, the warm beat of the prince's frail human heart occupied all of her thoughts.
When the longing was too heavy for her to bear, she sought the help of the oracle of the ocean, an ancient mermaid who knew many secret things.
Few knew to seek her counsel . . .
. . . and fewer still would dare to try.

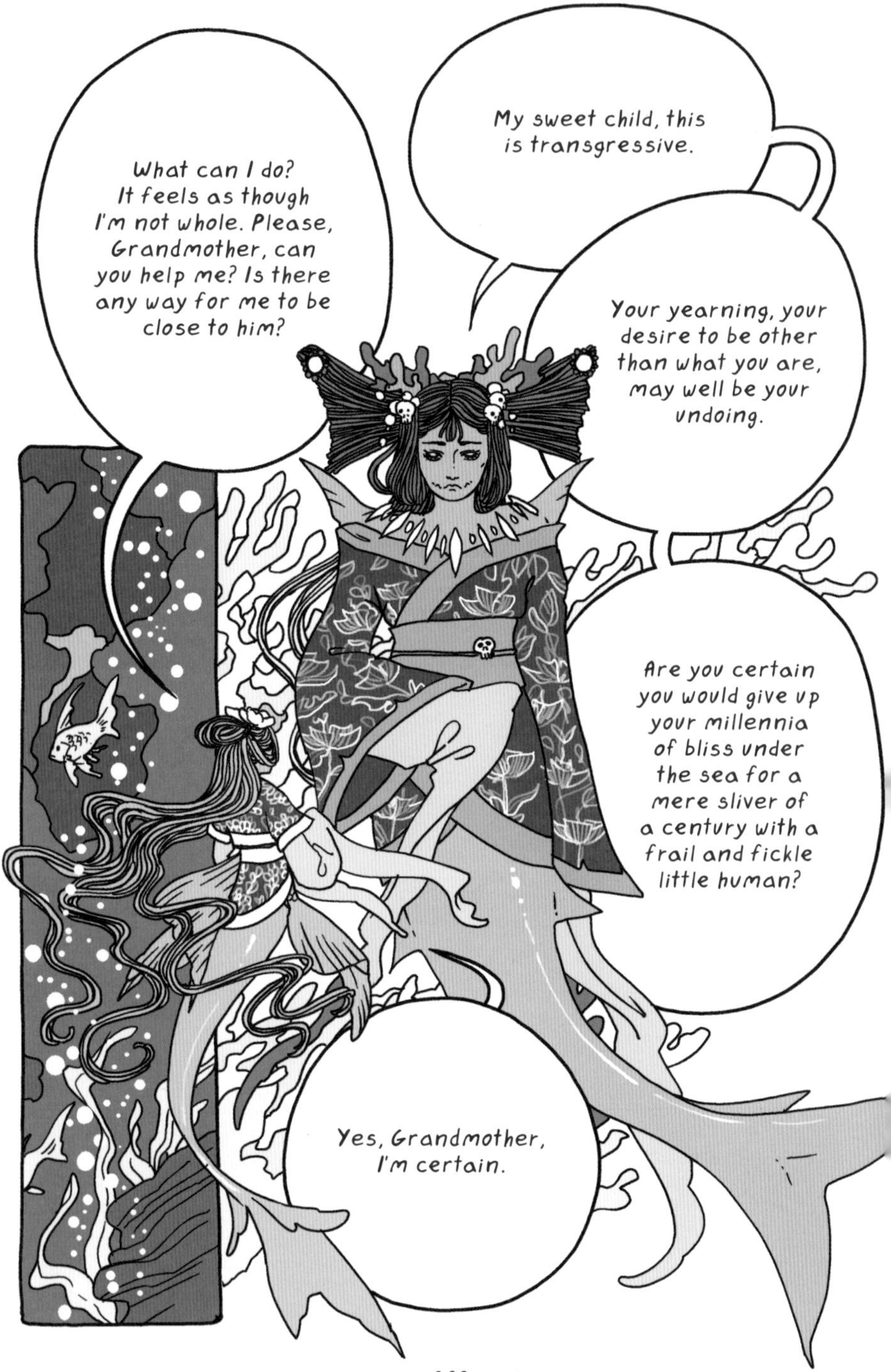
What can I do? It feels as though I'm not whole. Please, Grandmother, can you help me? Is there any way for me to be close to him?
My sweet child, this is transgressive.
Your yearning, your desire to be other than what you are, may well be your undoing.
Are you certain you would give up your millennia of bliss under the sea for a mere sliver of a century with a frail and fickle little human?
Yes, Grandmother, I'm certain.

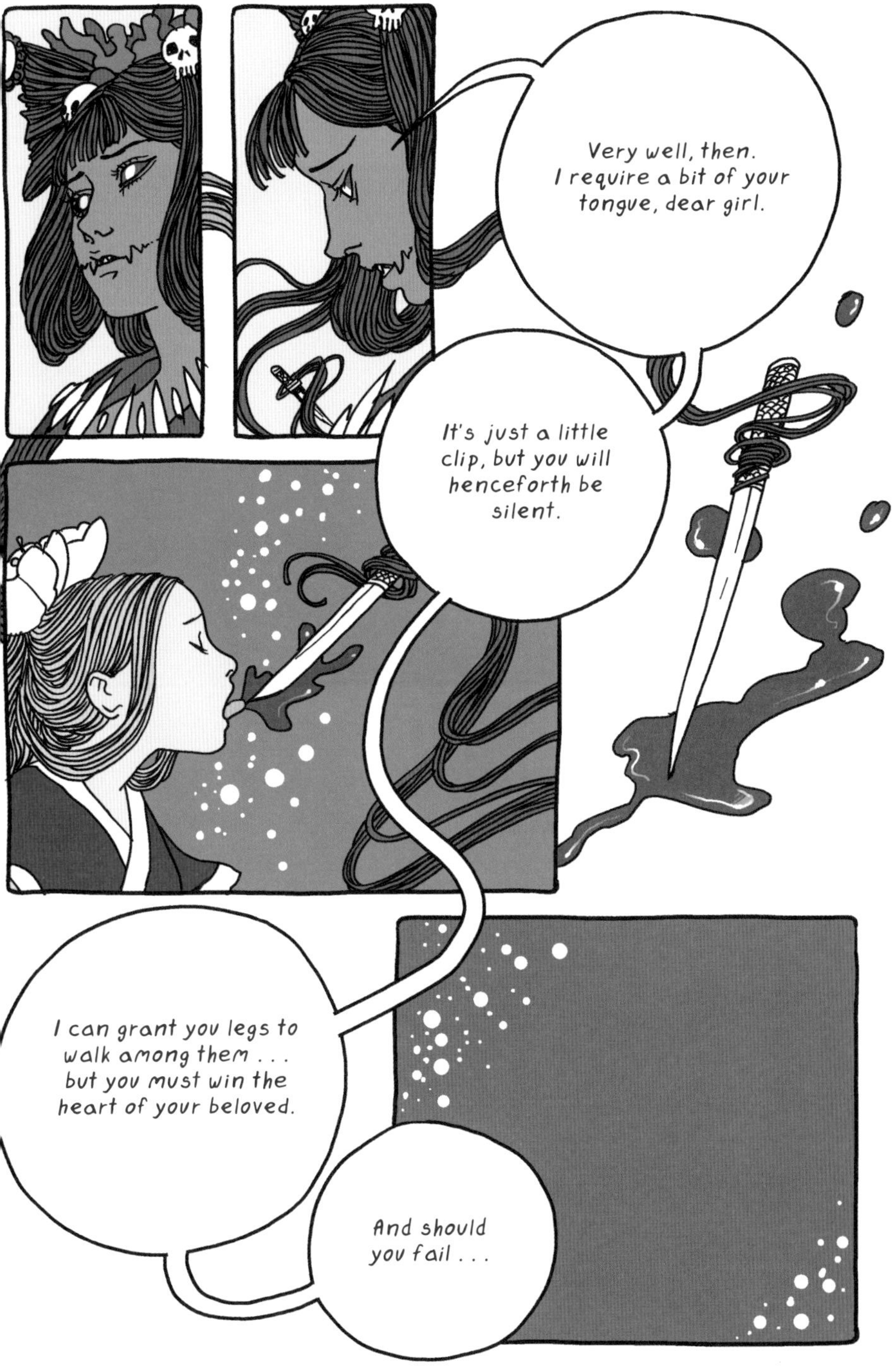
Very well, then. I require a bit of your tongue, dear girl.
It's just a little clip, but you will henceforth be silent.
I can grant you legs to walk among them . . . but you must win the heart of your beloved.
And should you fail . . .

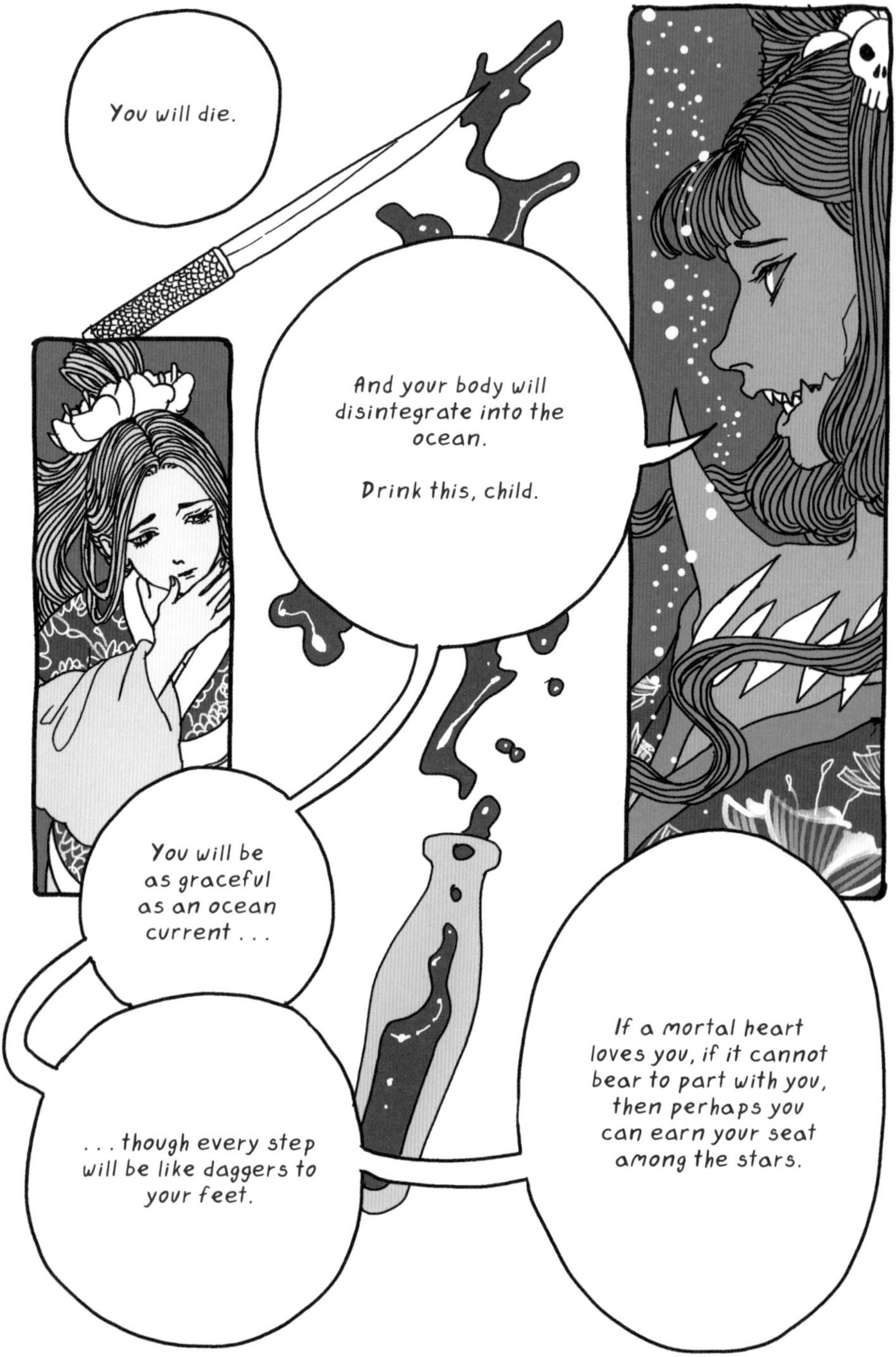
You will die.
And your body will disintegrate into the ocean.
Drink this, child.
You will be as graceful as an ocean current . . .
. . . though every step will be like daggers to your feet.
If a mortal heart loves you, if it cannot bear to part with you, then perhaps you can earn your seat among the stars.

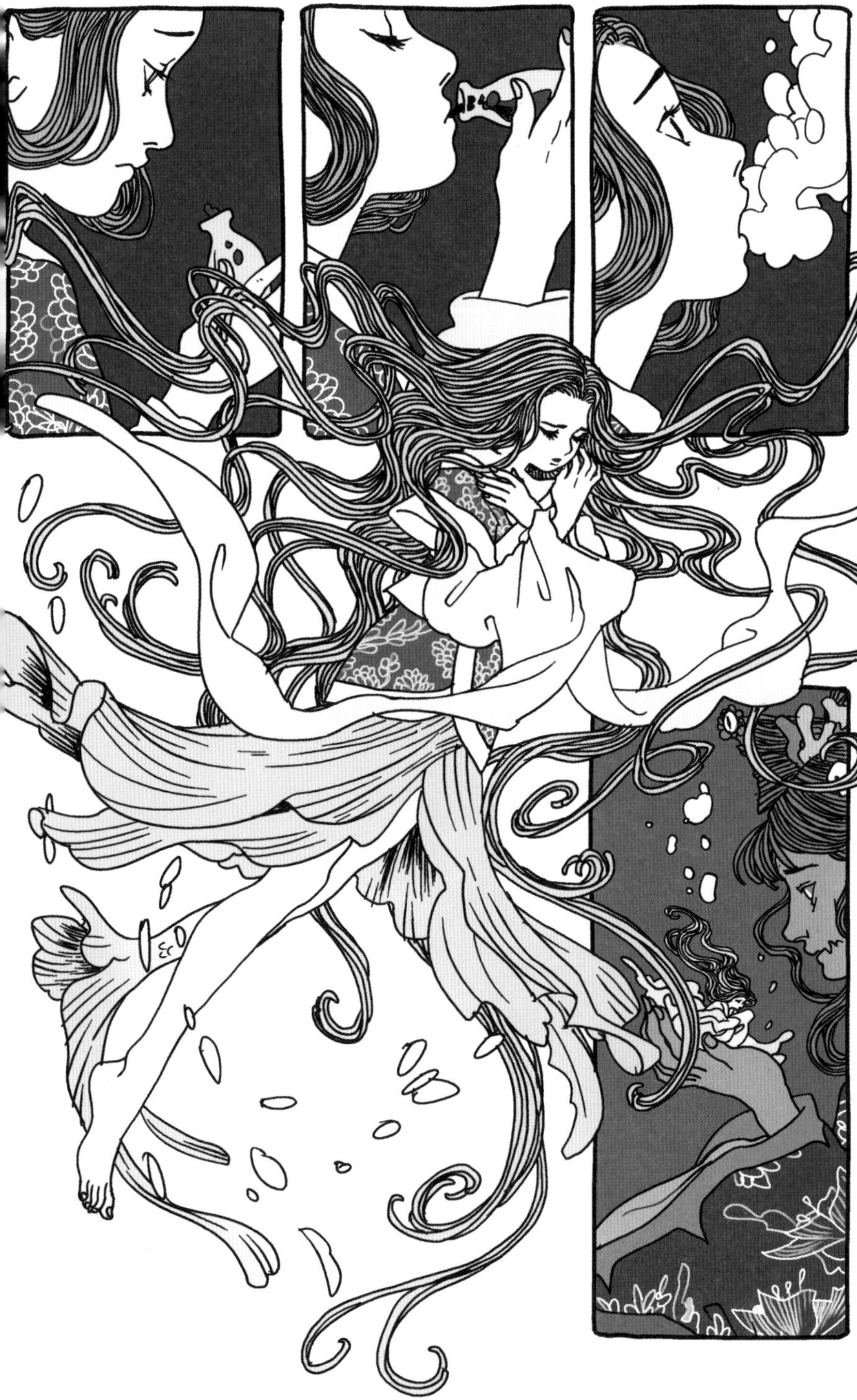

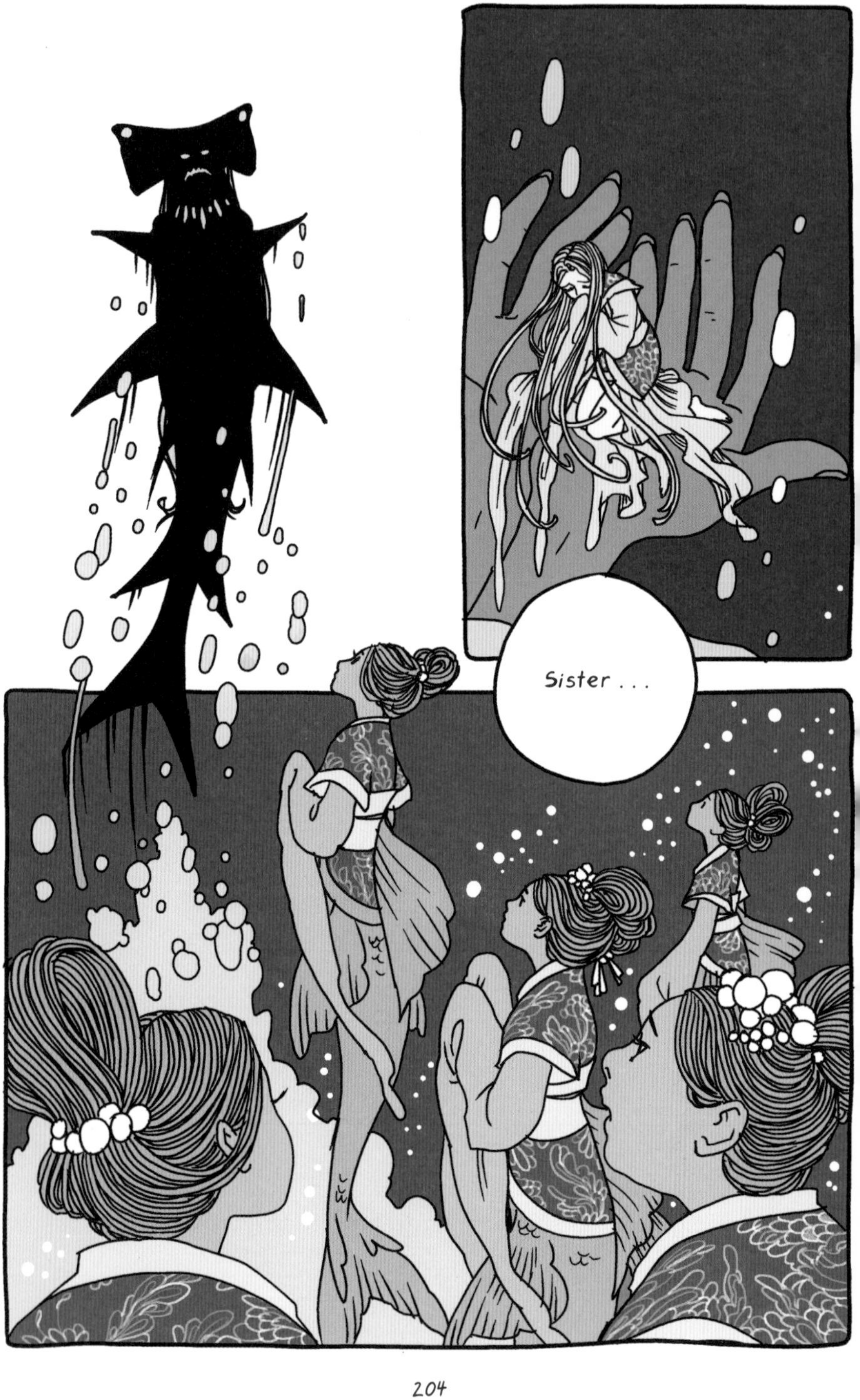
Sister . . .

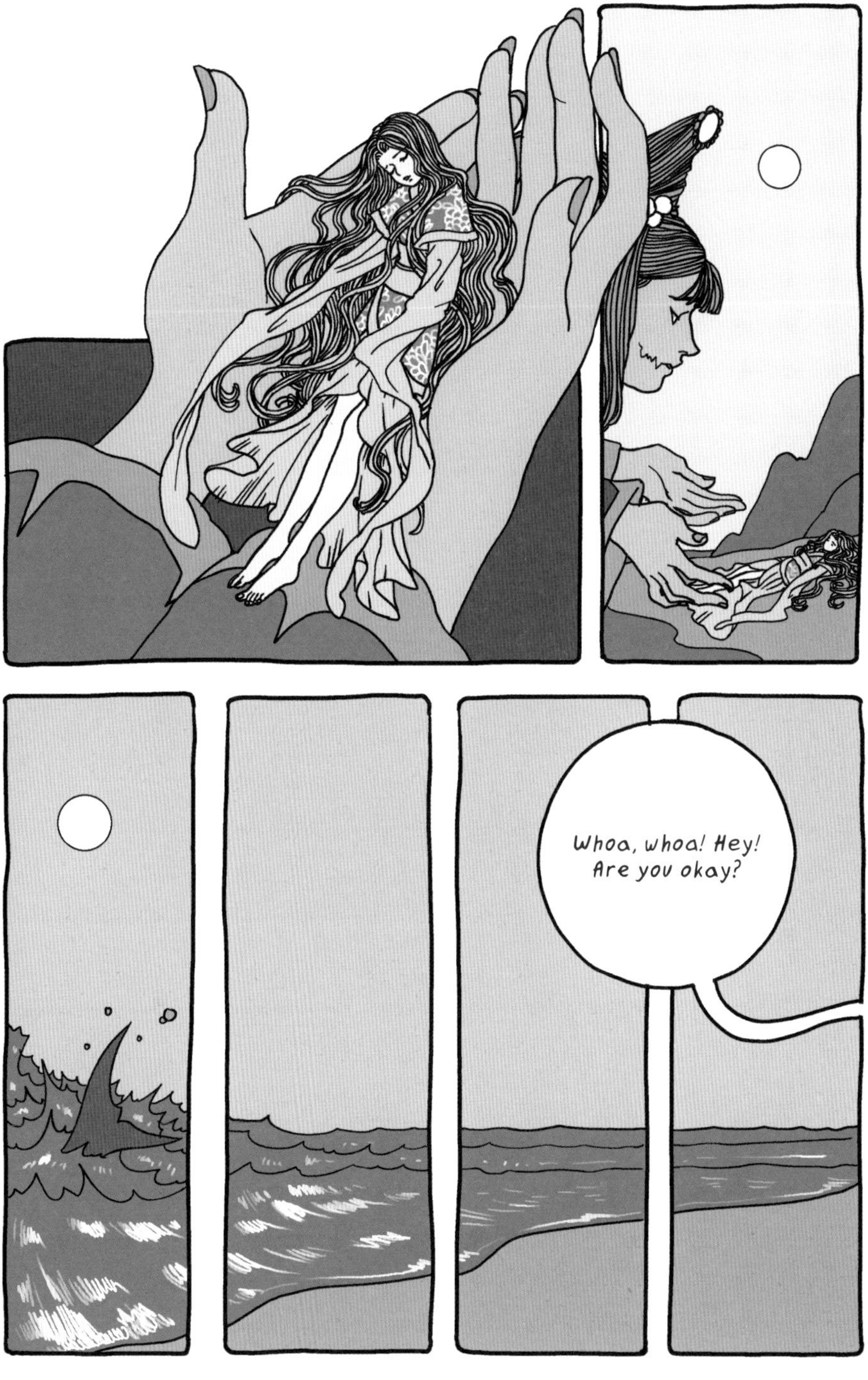
Whoa, whoa! Hey!
Are you okay?

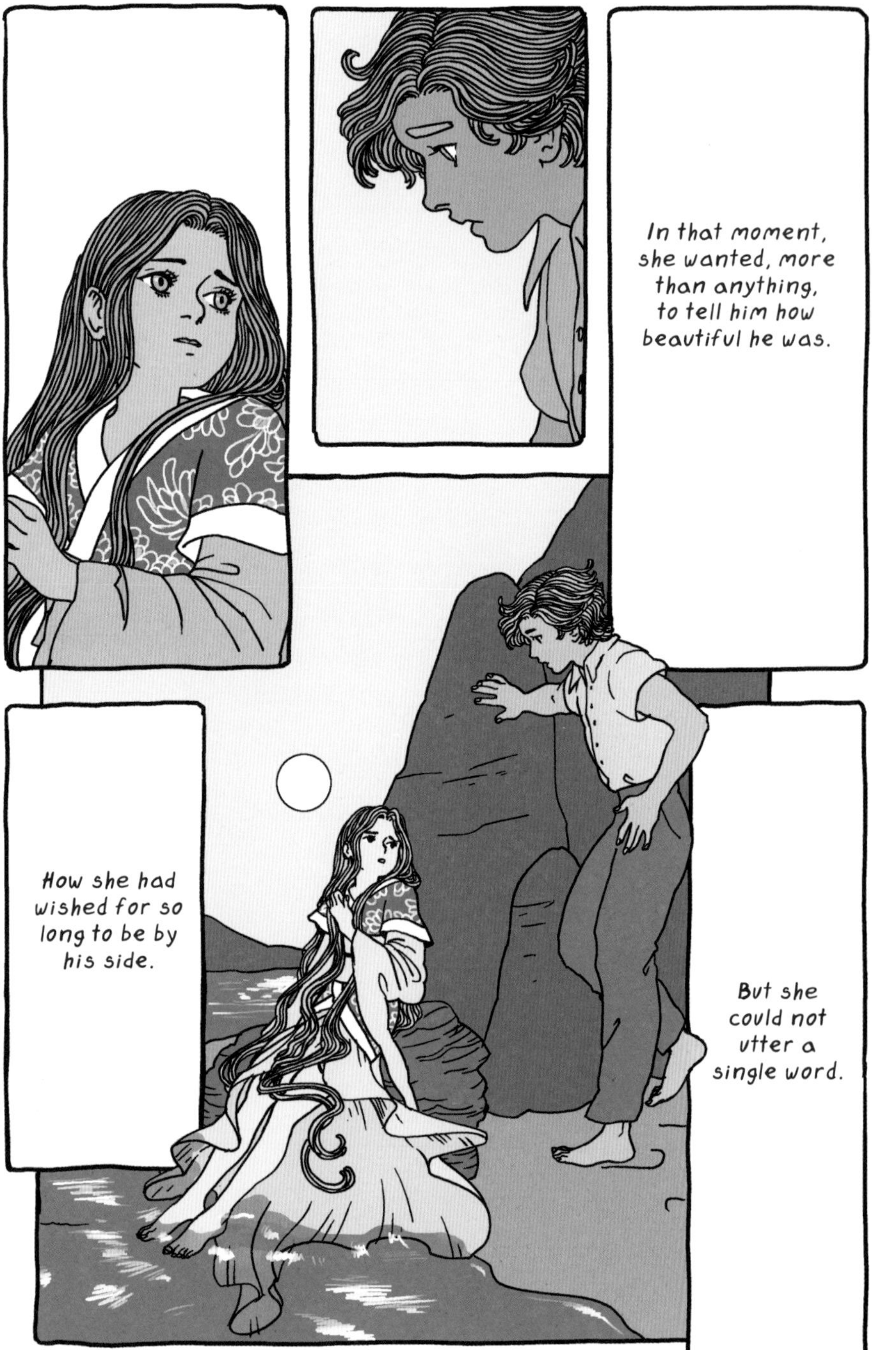

In that moment, she wanted, more than anything, to tell him how beautiful he was.
How she had wished for so long to be by his side.
But she could not utter a single word.

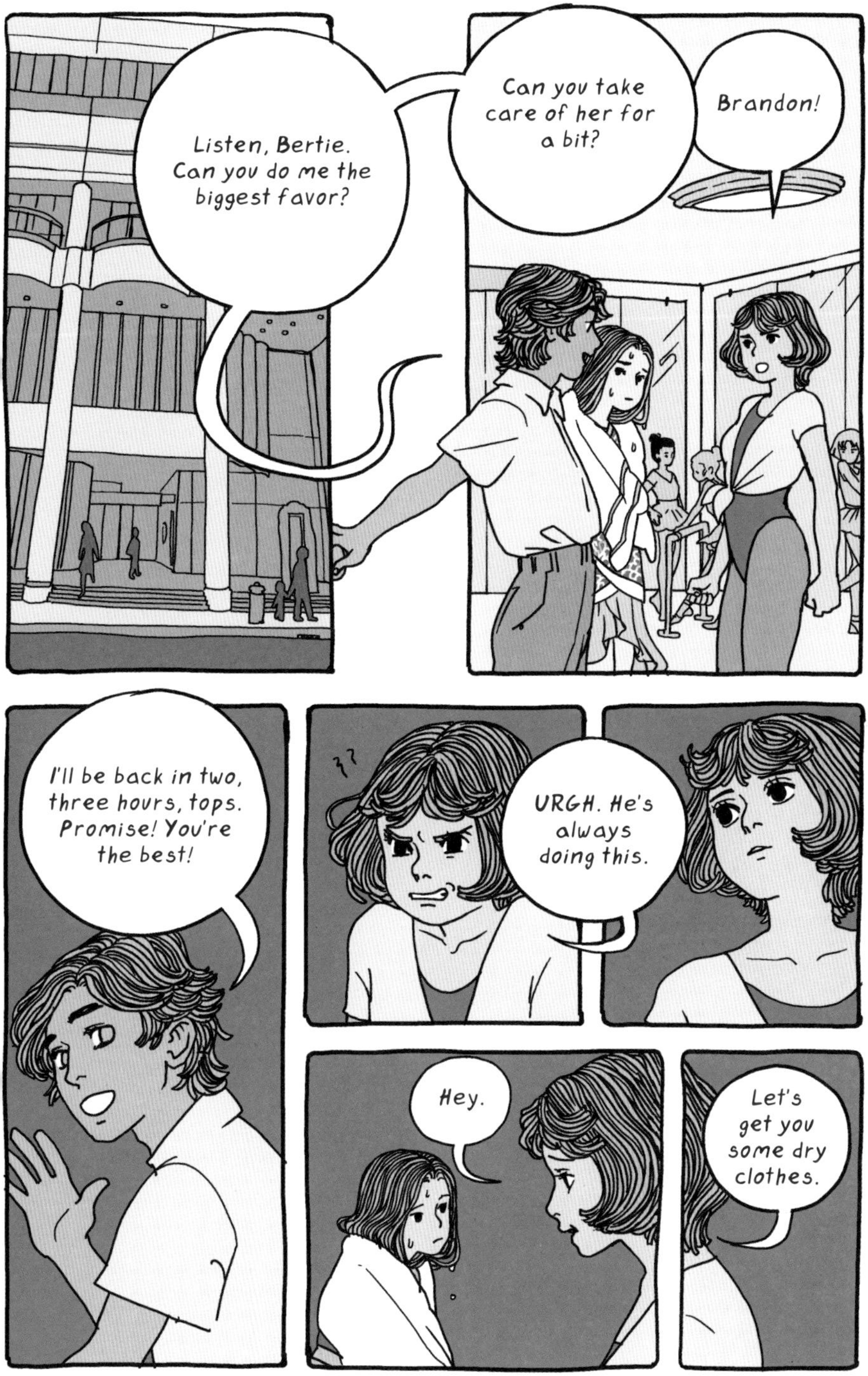
Listen, Bertie. Can you do me the biggest favor?
Can you take care of her for a bit?
Brandon!
I'll be back in two, three hours, tops. Promise! You're the best!
URGH. He's always doing this.
Hey.
Let's get you some dry clothes.

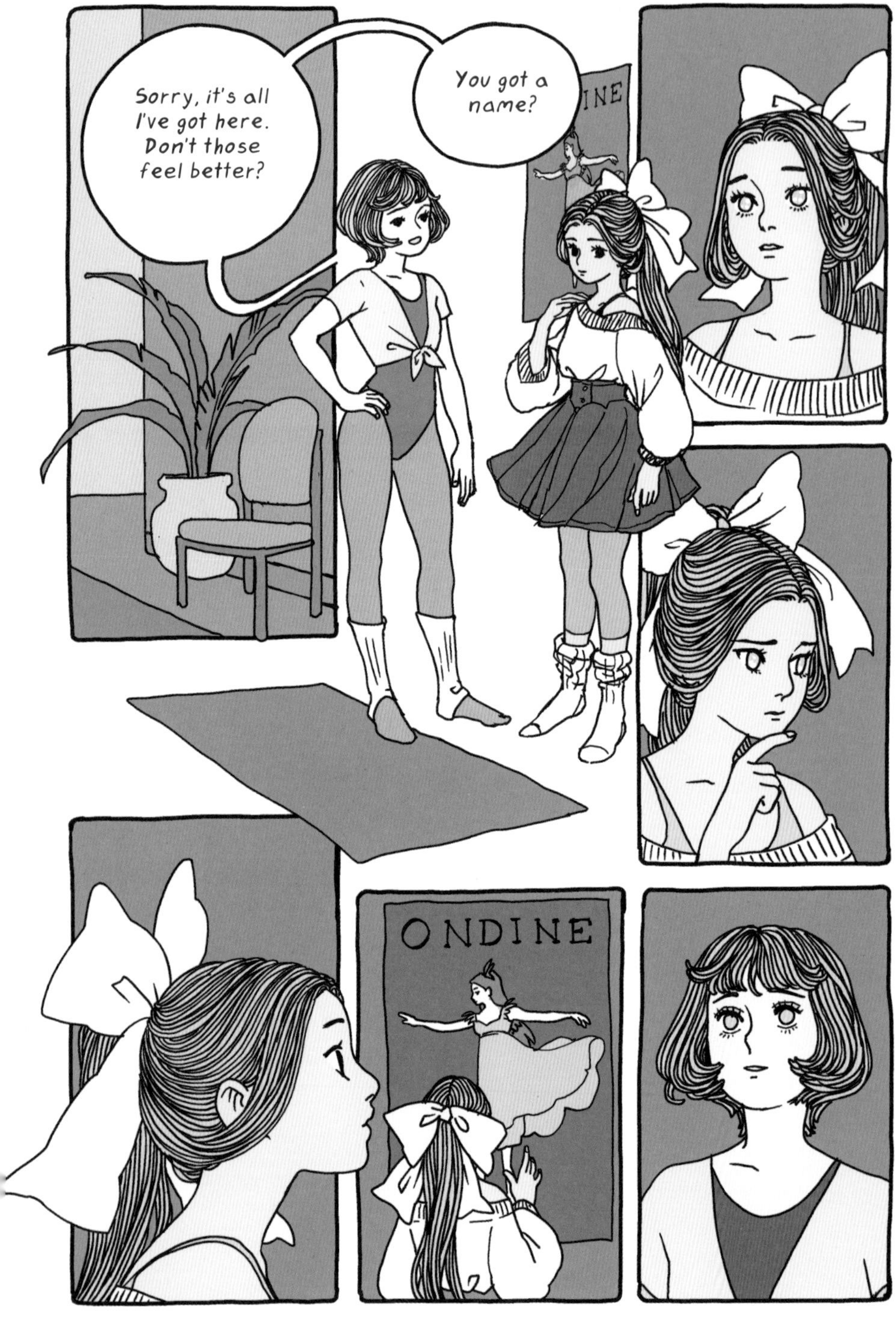
Sorry, it's all I've got here. Don't those feel better?
You got a name?
INE
ONDINE

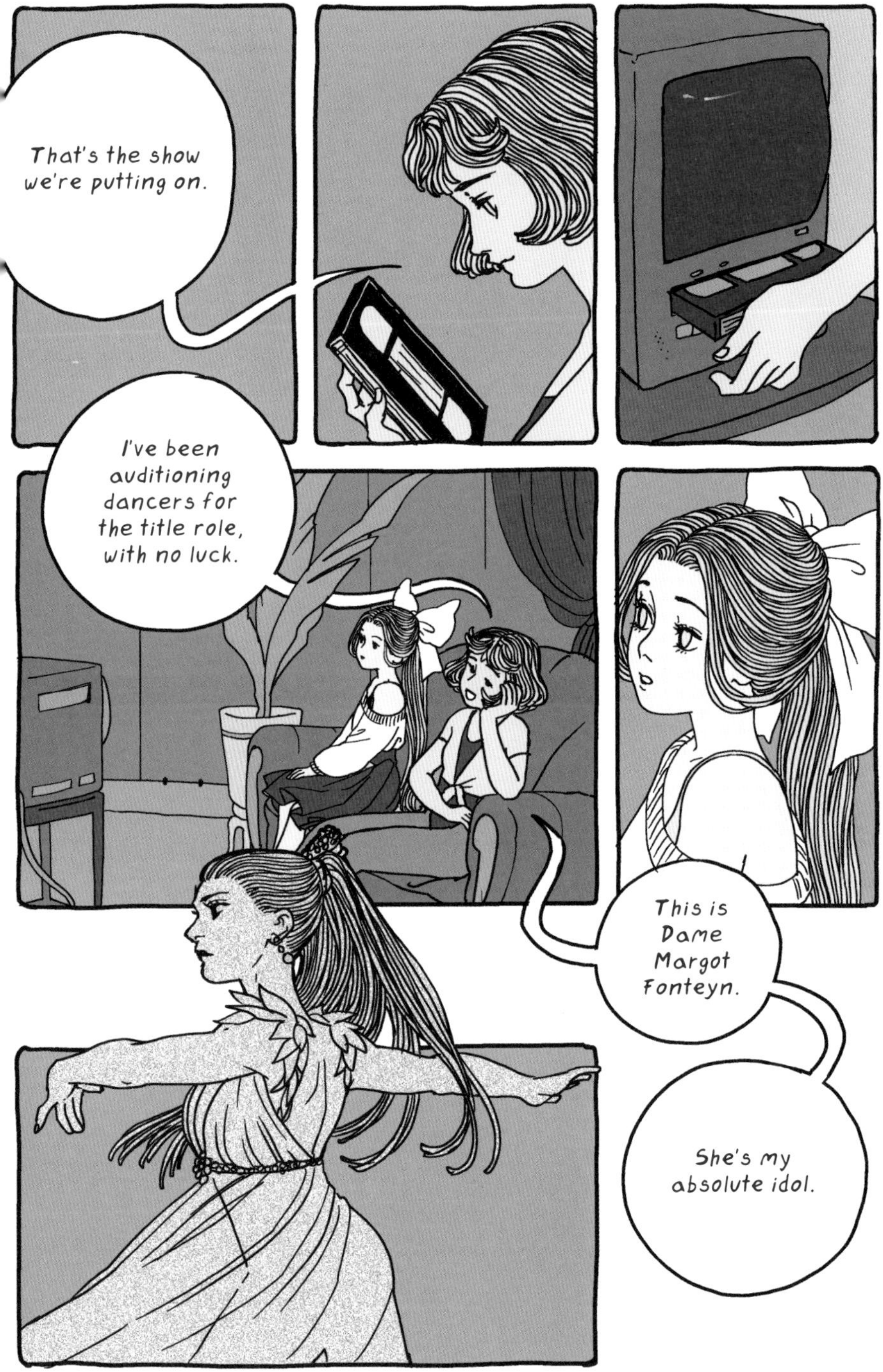
That's the show we're putting on.
I've been auditioning dancers for the title role, with no luck.
This is Dame Margot Fonteyn.
She's my absolute idol.

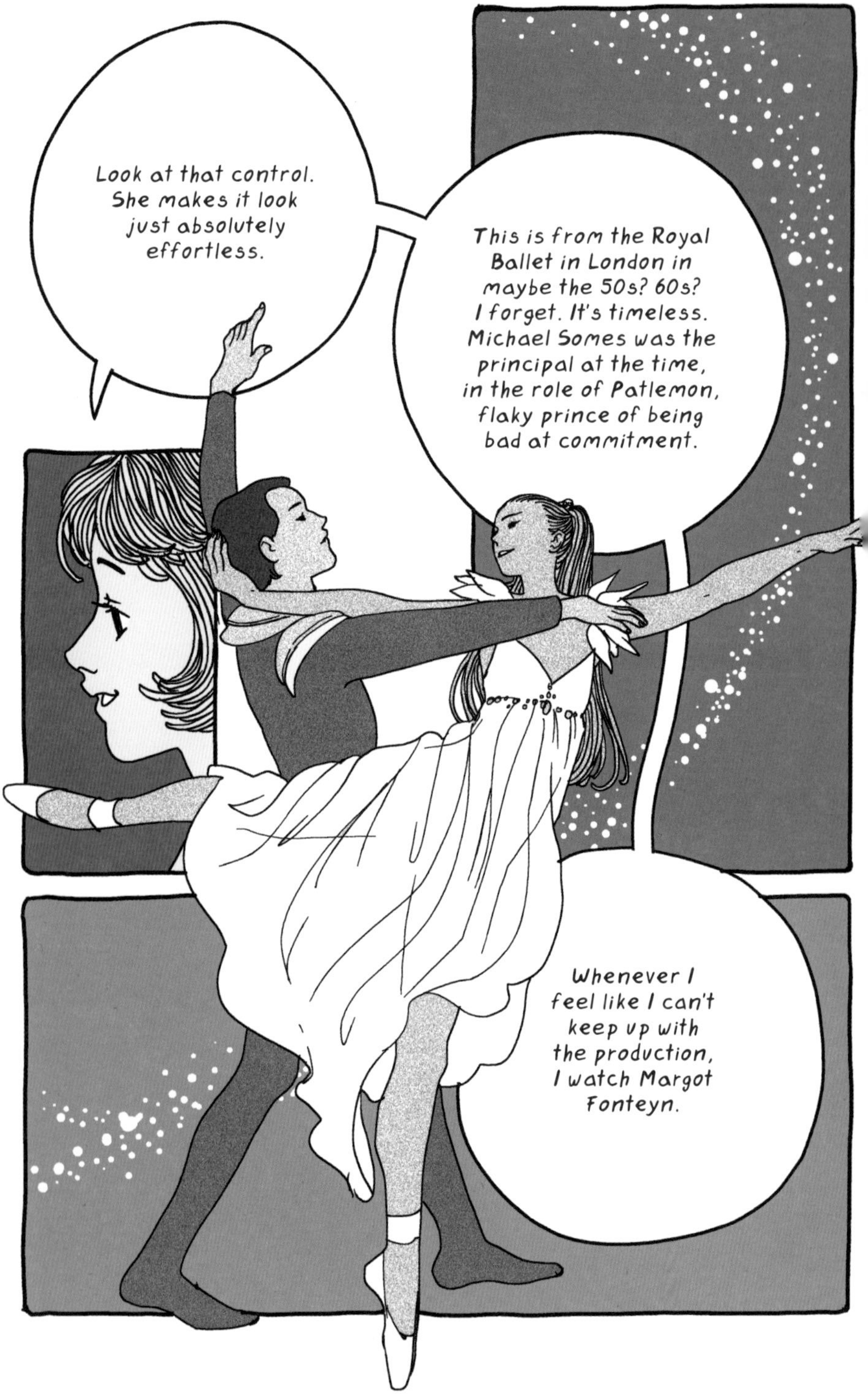
Look at that control. She makes it look just absolutely effortless.
This is from the Royal Ballet in London in maybe the 50s? 60s? I forget. It's timeless. Michael Somes was the principal at the time, in the role of Patlemon, flaky prince of being bad at commitment.
Whenever I feel like I can't keep up with the production, I watch Margot Fonteyn.

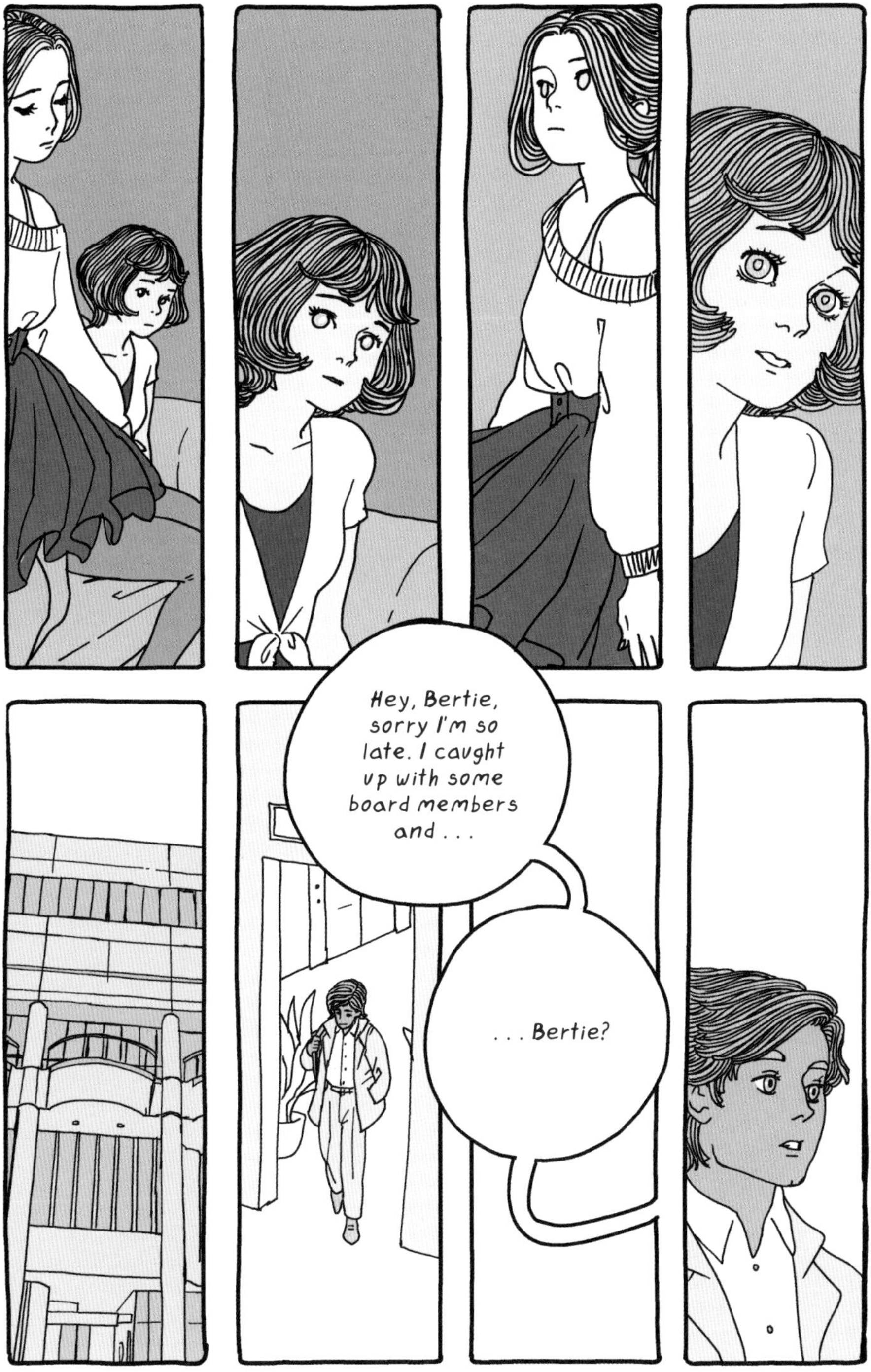
Hey, Bertie, sorry I'm so late. I caught up with some board members and . . .
. . . Bertie?

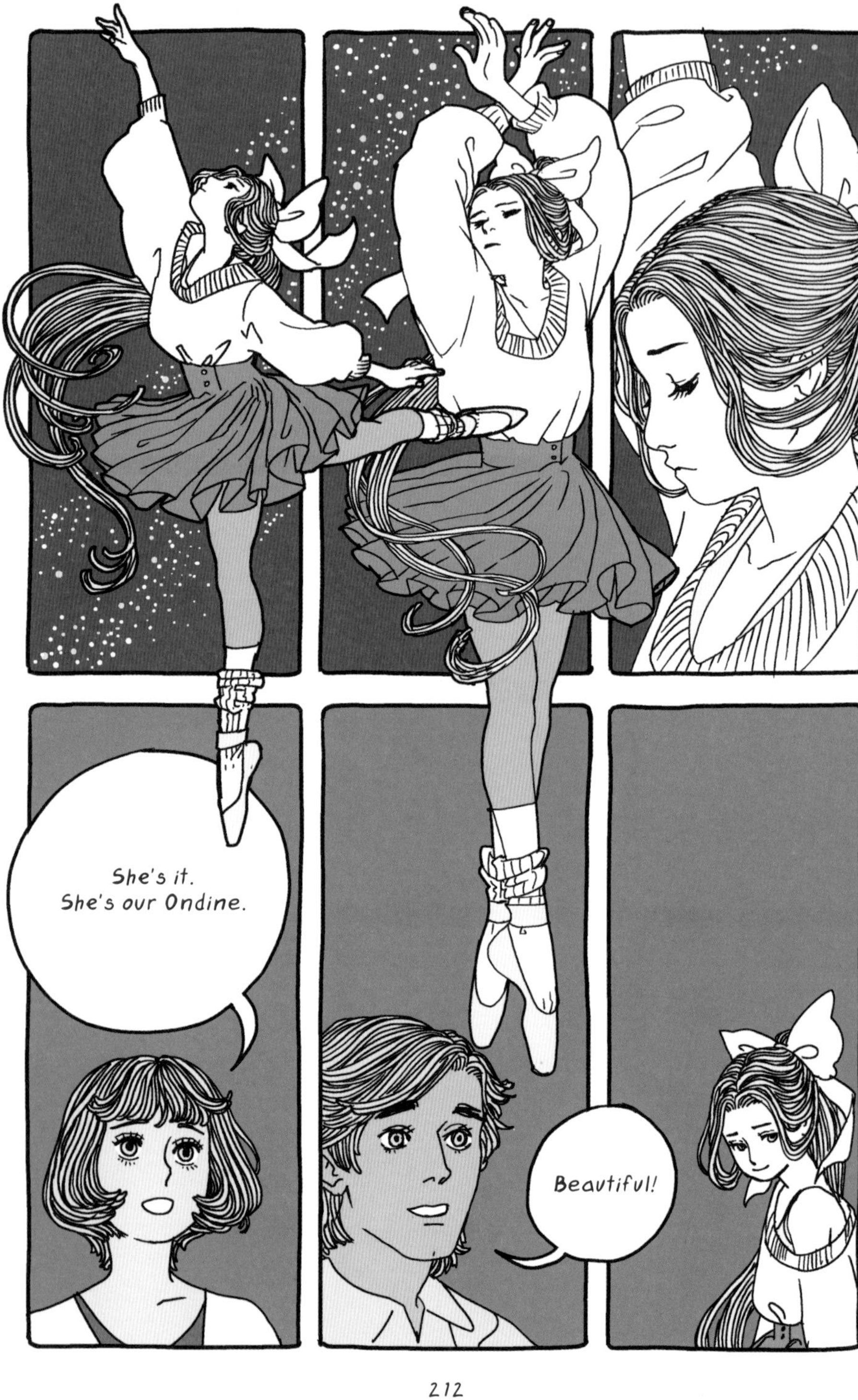
She's it.
She's our Ondine.
Beautiful!

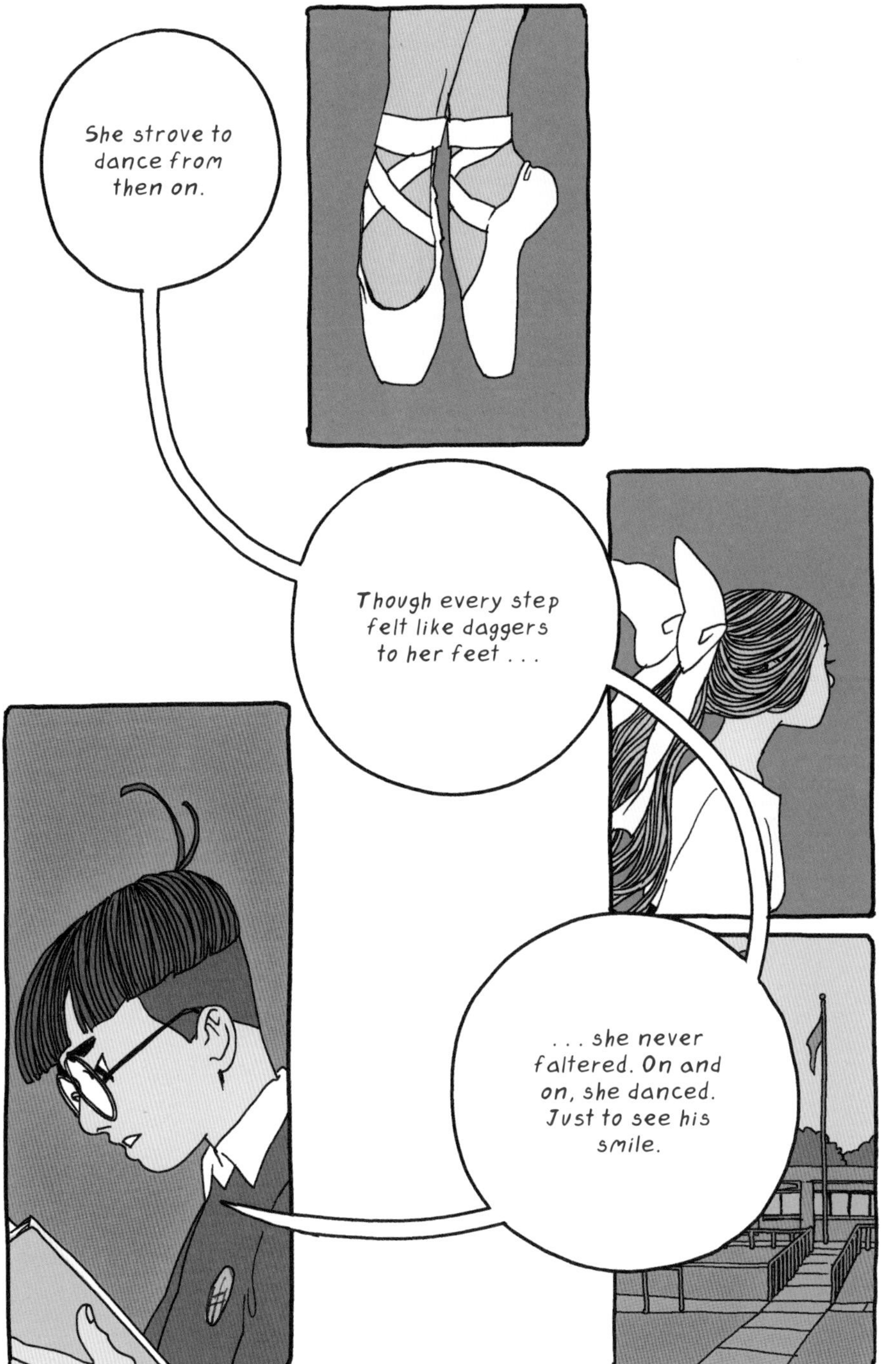
She strove to dance from then on.
Though every step felt like daggers to her feet . . .
. . . she never faltered. On and on, she danced. Just to see his smile.

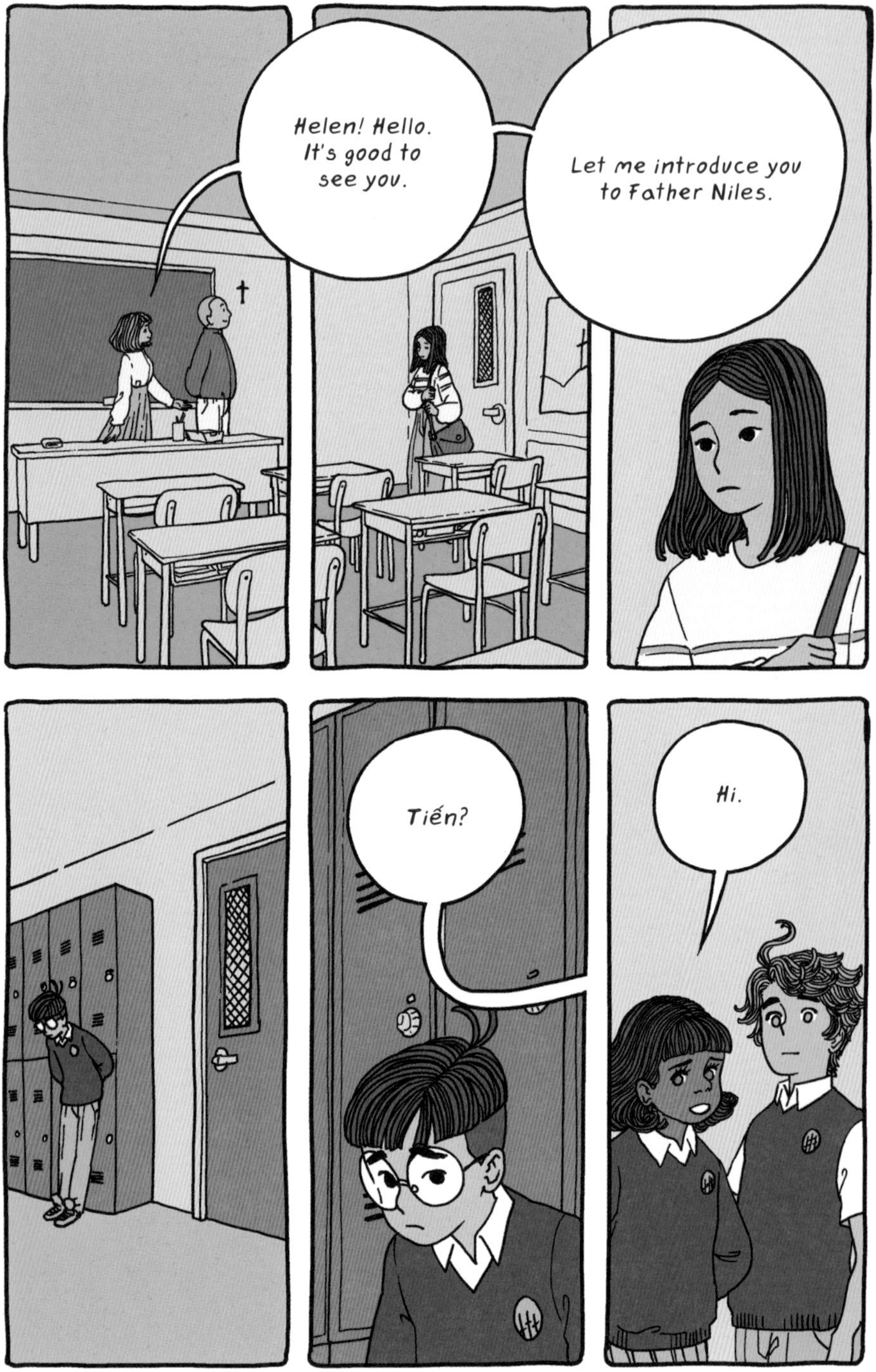
Helen! Hello. It's good to see you.
Let me introduce you to Father Niles.
Tiến?
Hi.

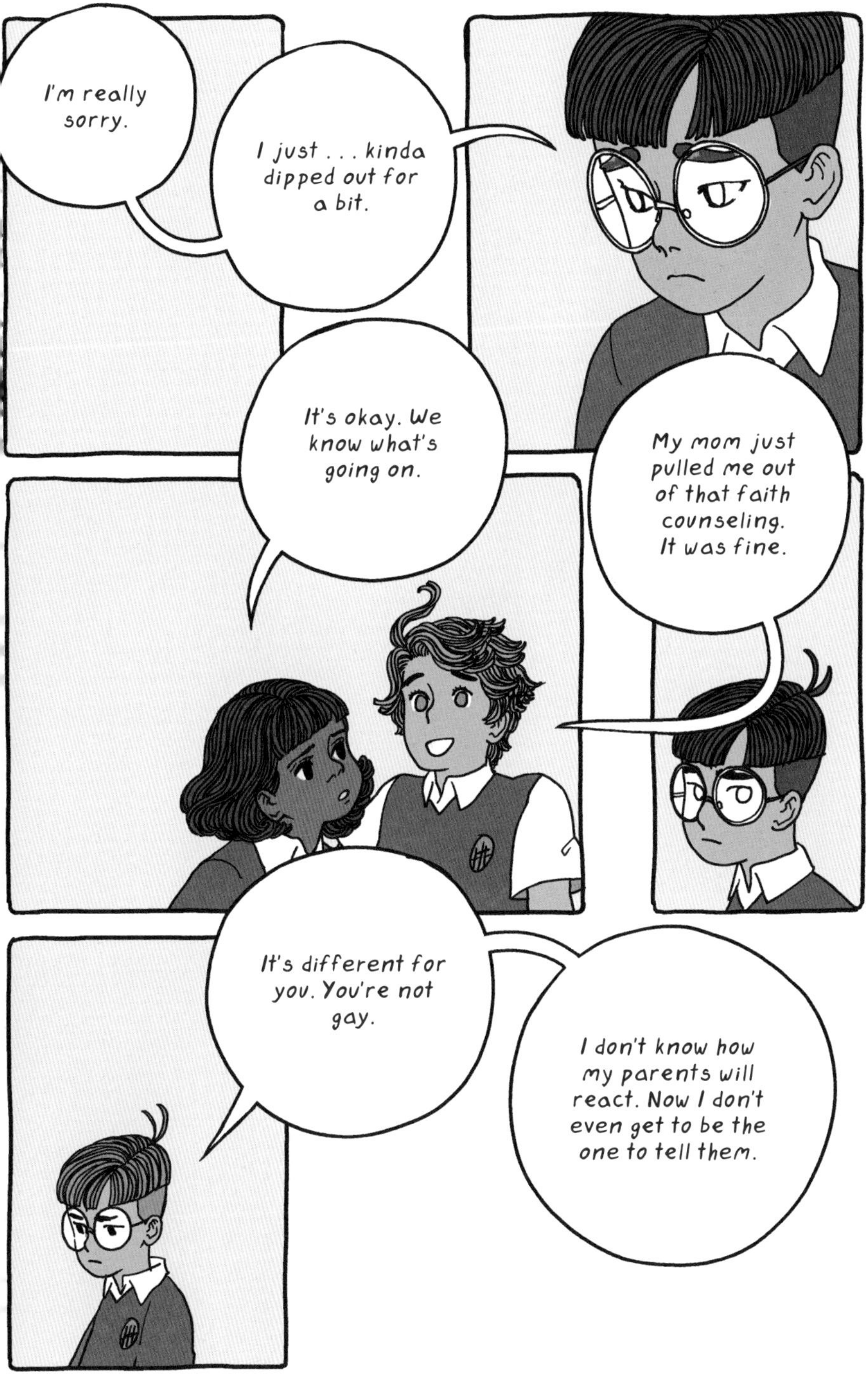
I'm really sorry.
I just . . . kinda dipped out for a bit.
It's okay. We know what's going on.
My mom just pulled me out of that faith counseling. It was fine.
It's different for you. You're not gay.
I don't know how my parents will react. Now I don't even get to be the one to tell them.

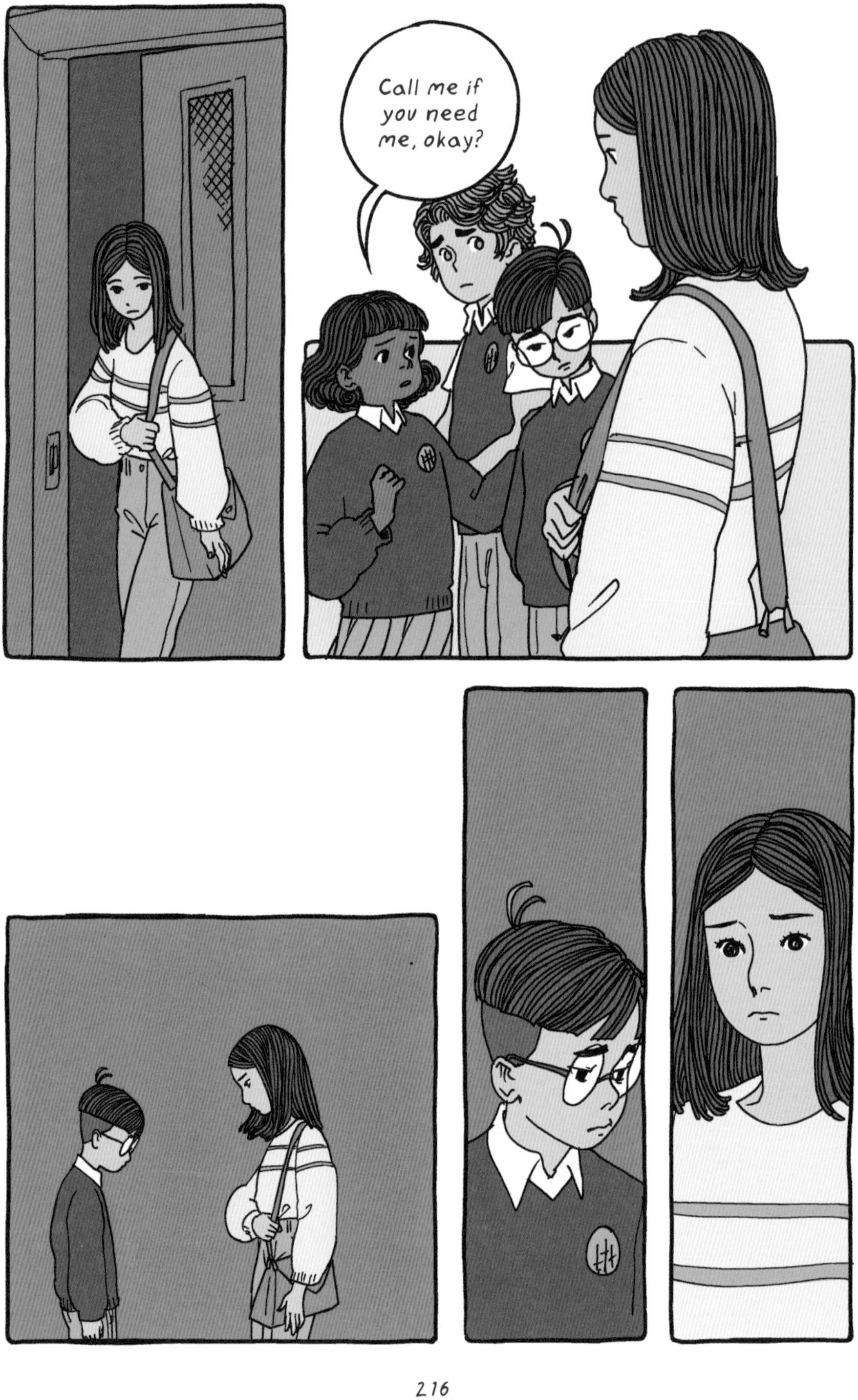
Call me if you need me, okay?

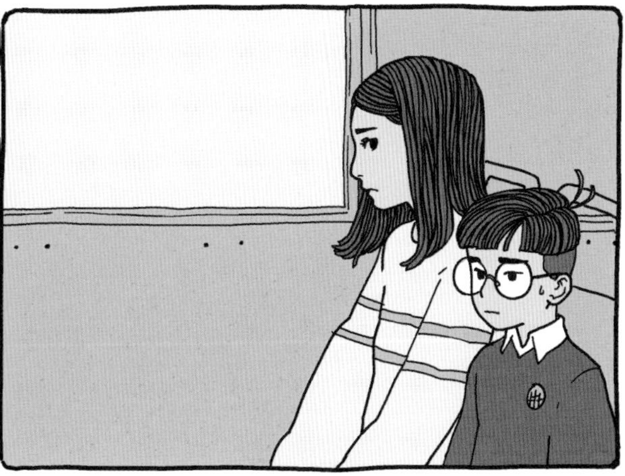

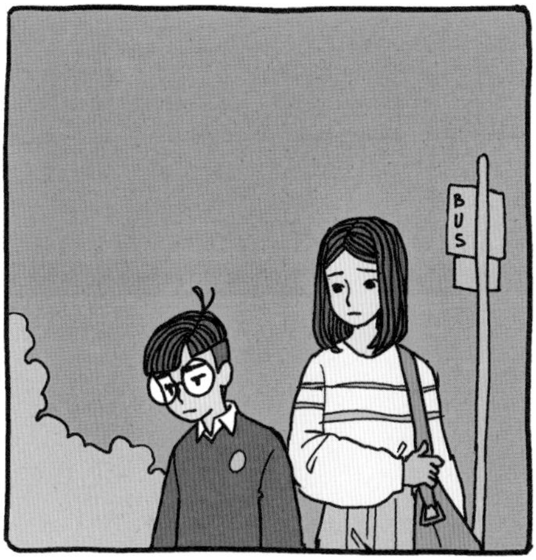
BUS

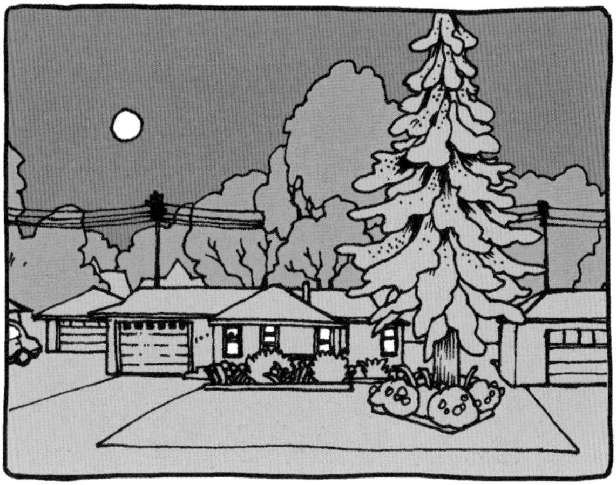

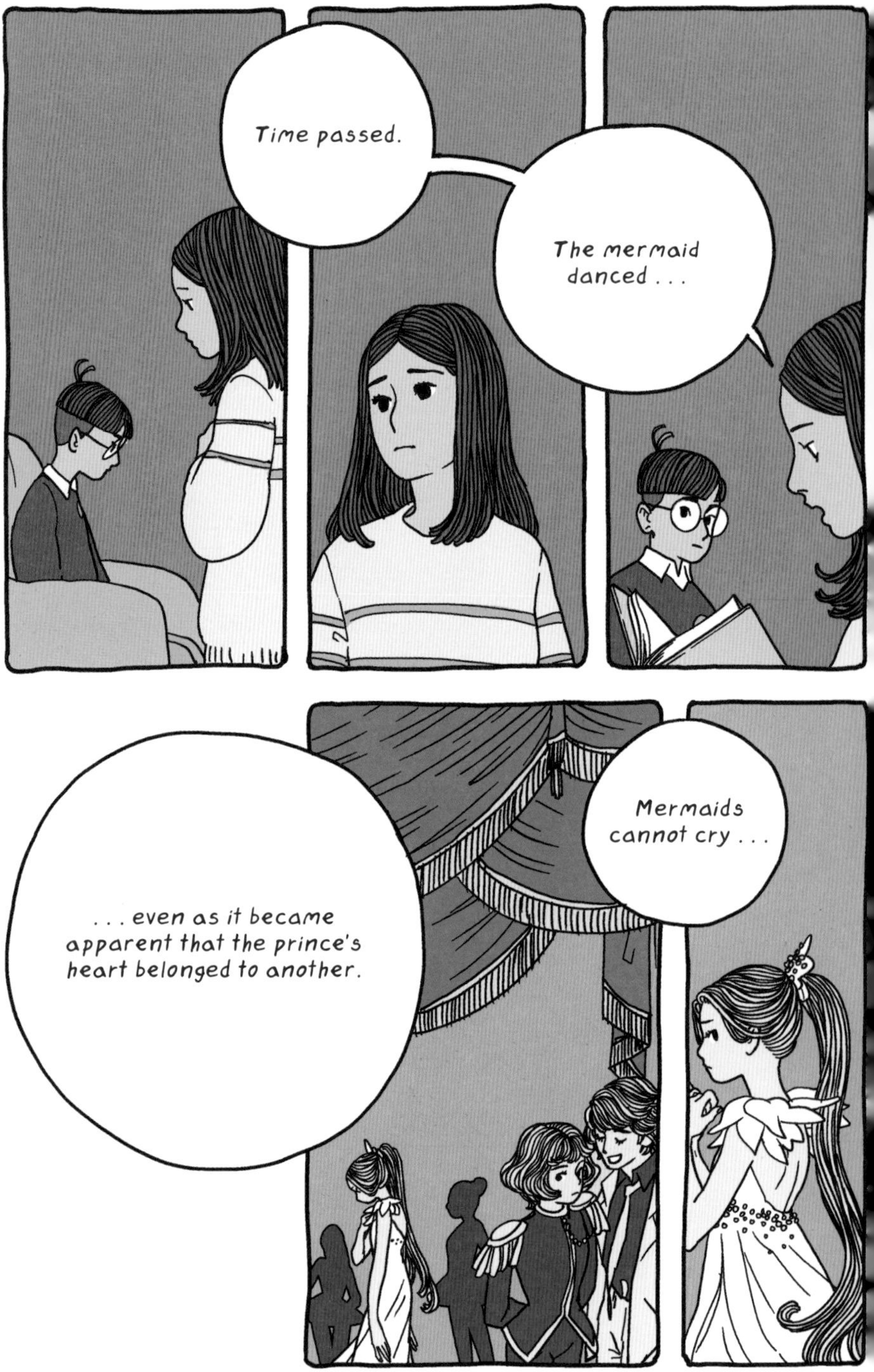
Time passed.
The mermaid danced . . .
Mermaids cannot cry . . .
. . . even as it became apparent that the prince's heart belonged to another.

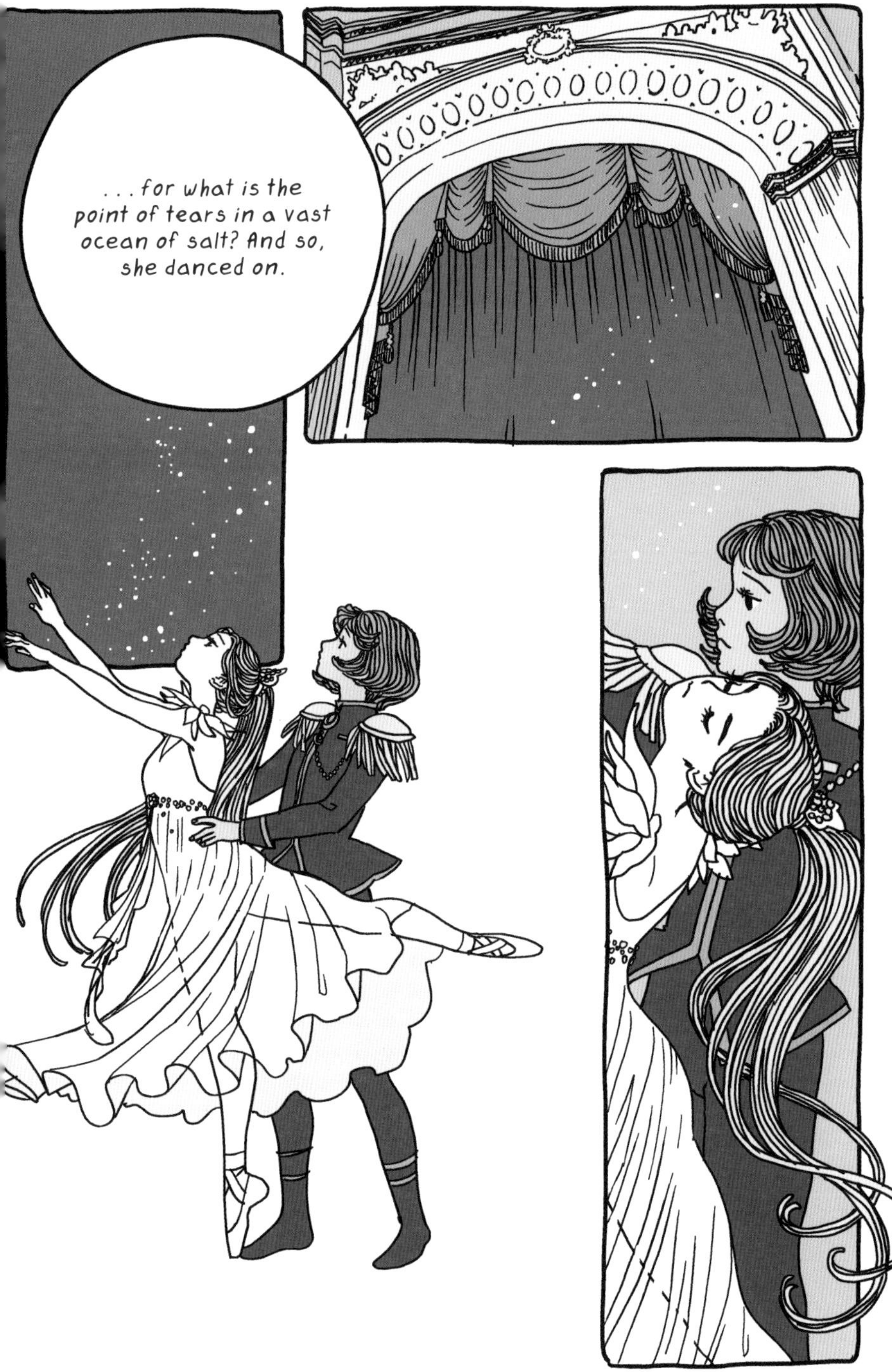
. . . for what is the point of tears in a vast ocean of salt? And so, she danced on.

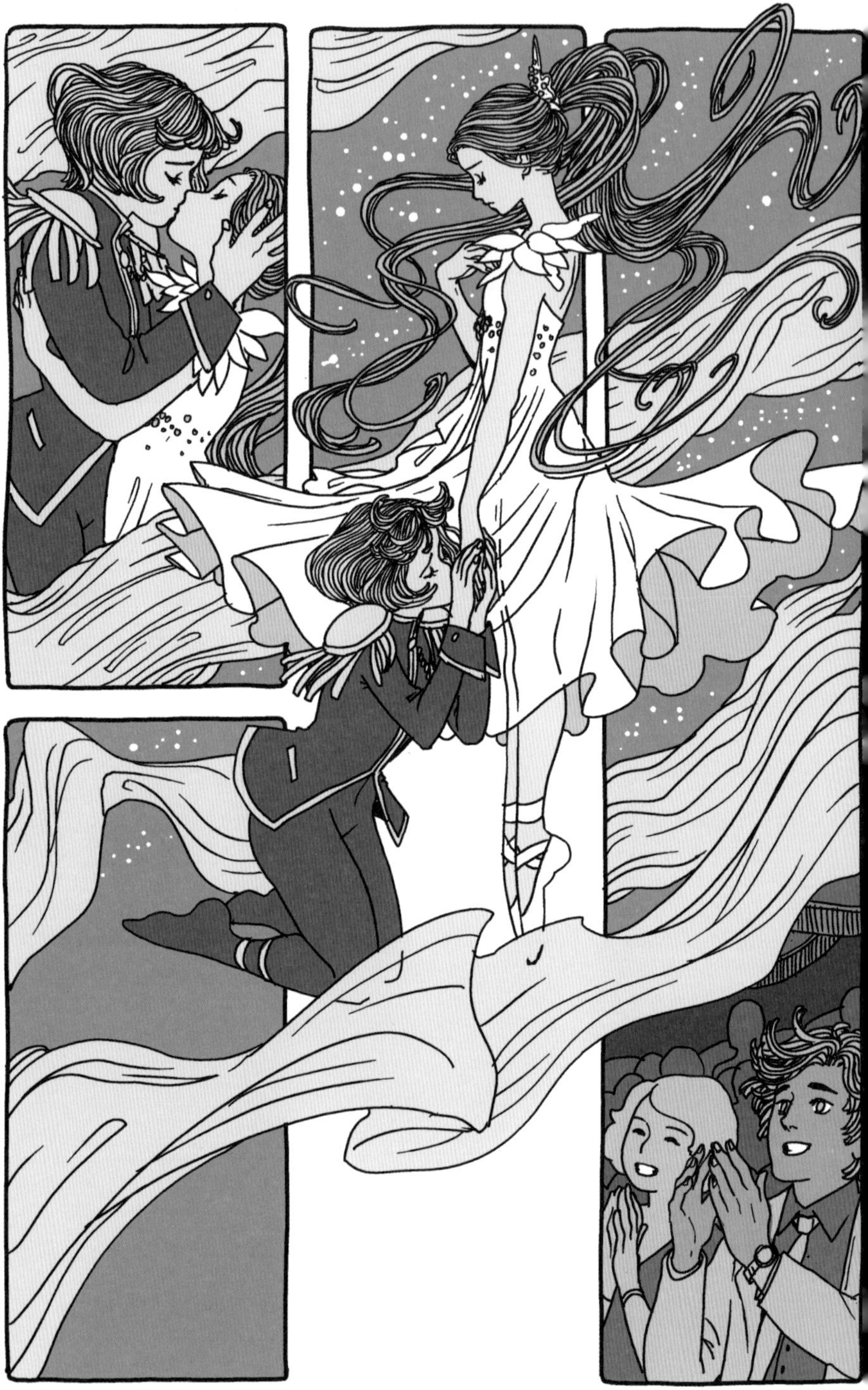

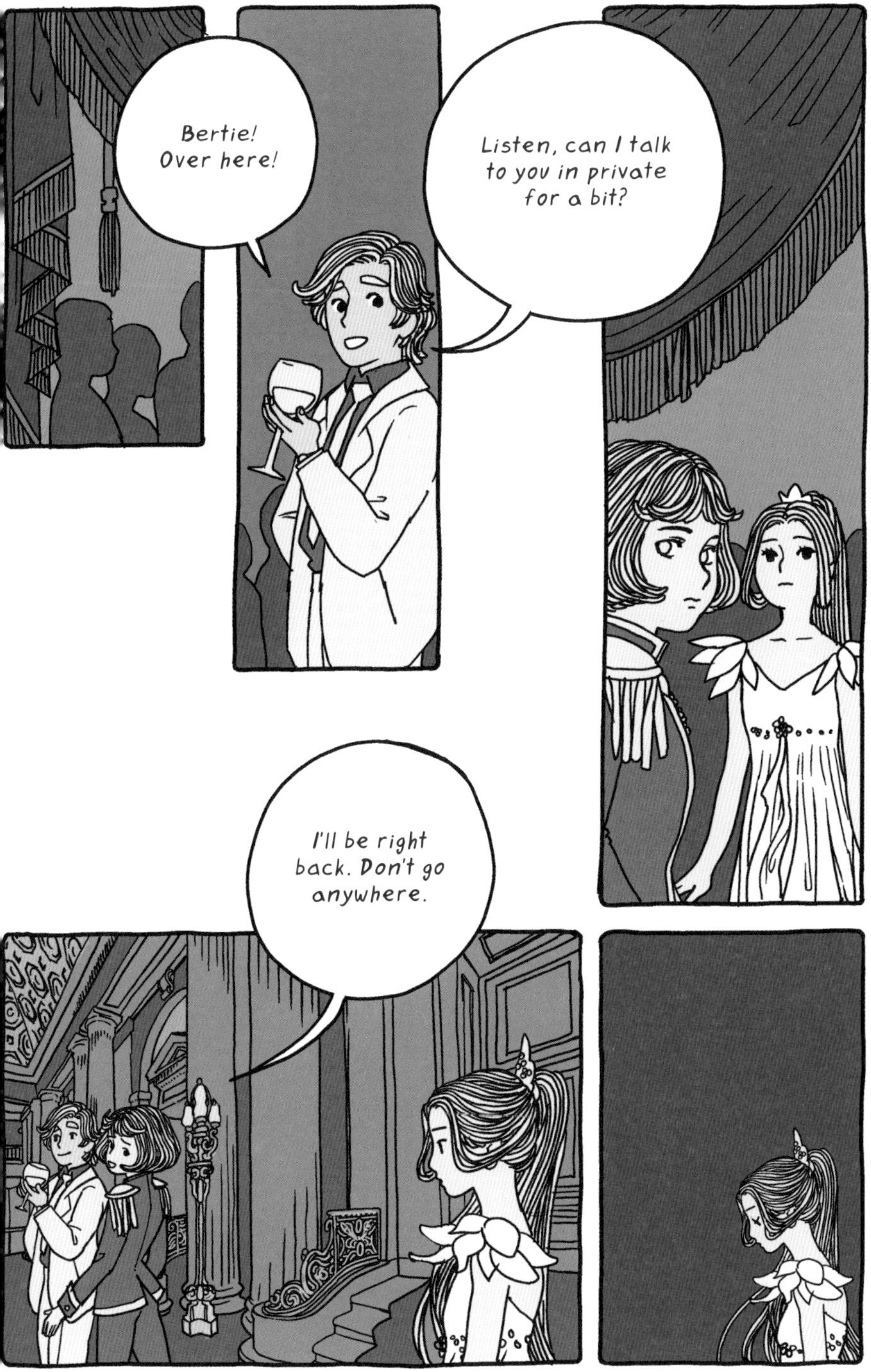
Bertie! Over here!
Listen, can I talk to you in private for a bit?
I'll be right back. **Don't** go anywhere.

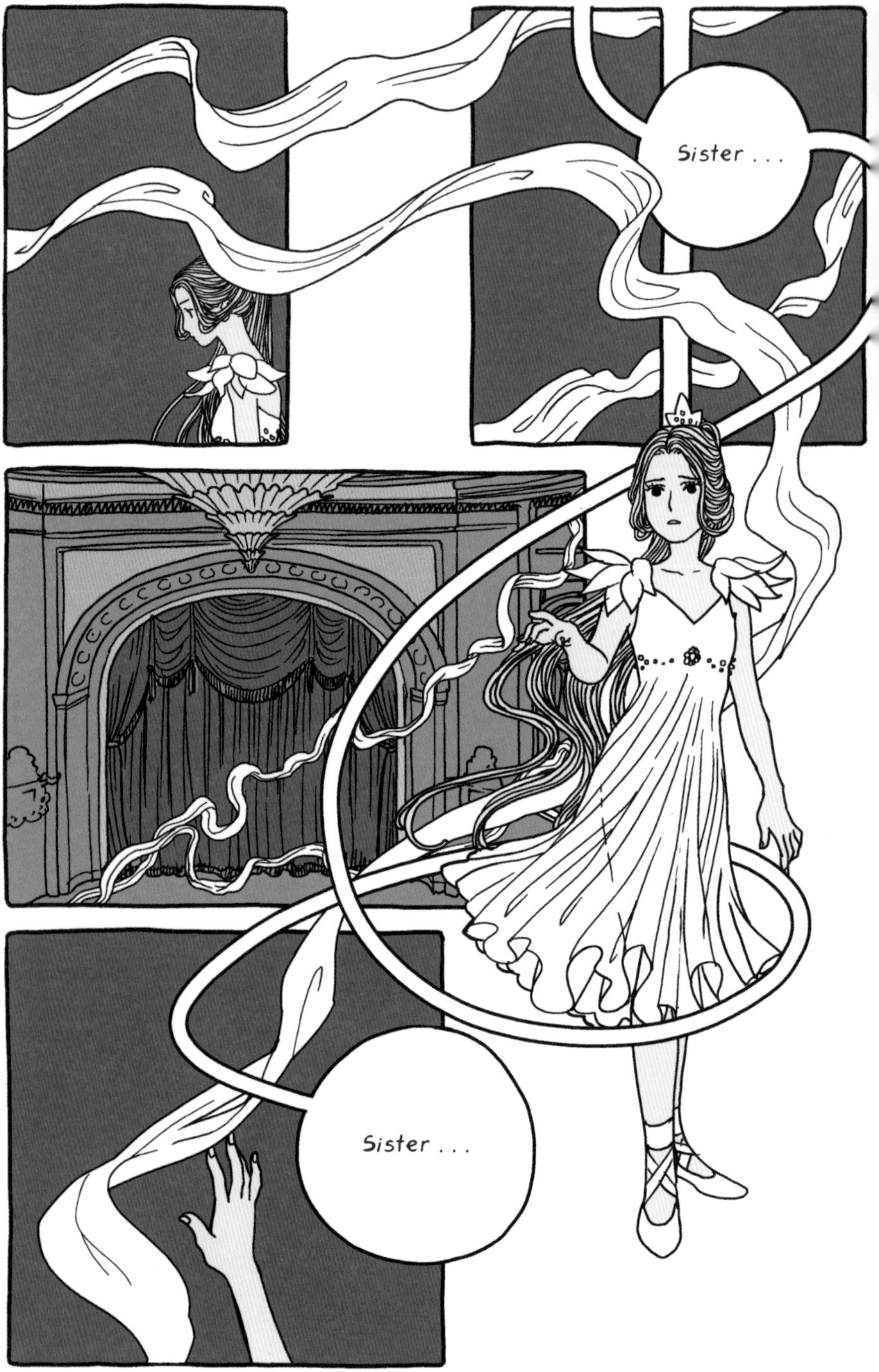
Sister . . .
Sister . . .

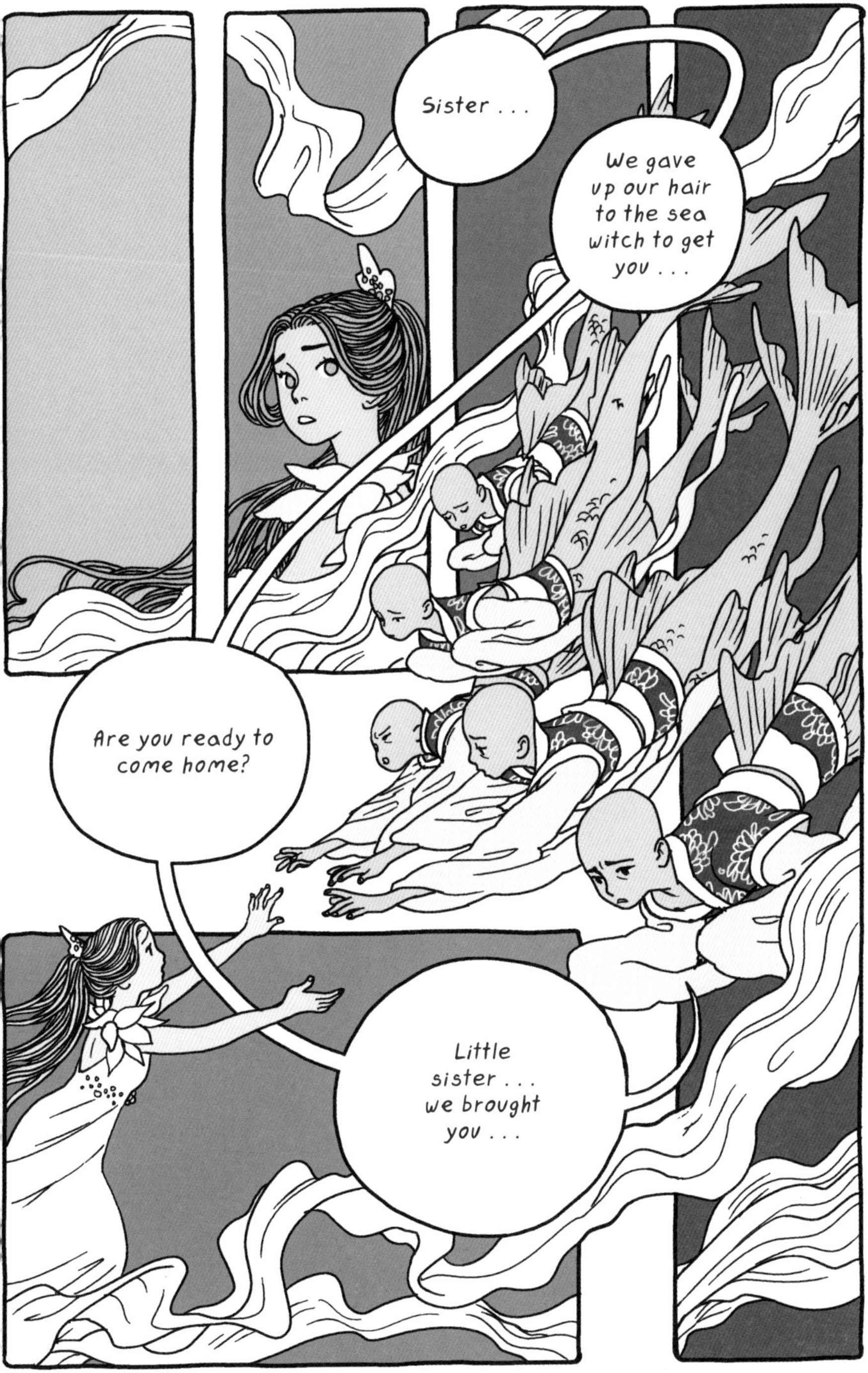
Sister . . .
We gave up our hair to the sea witch to get you . . .
Are you ready to come home?
Little sister . . . we brought you . . .

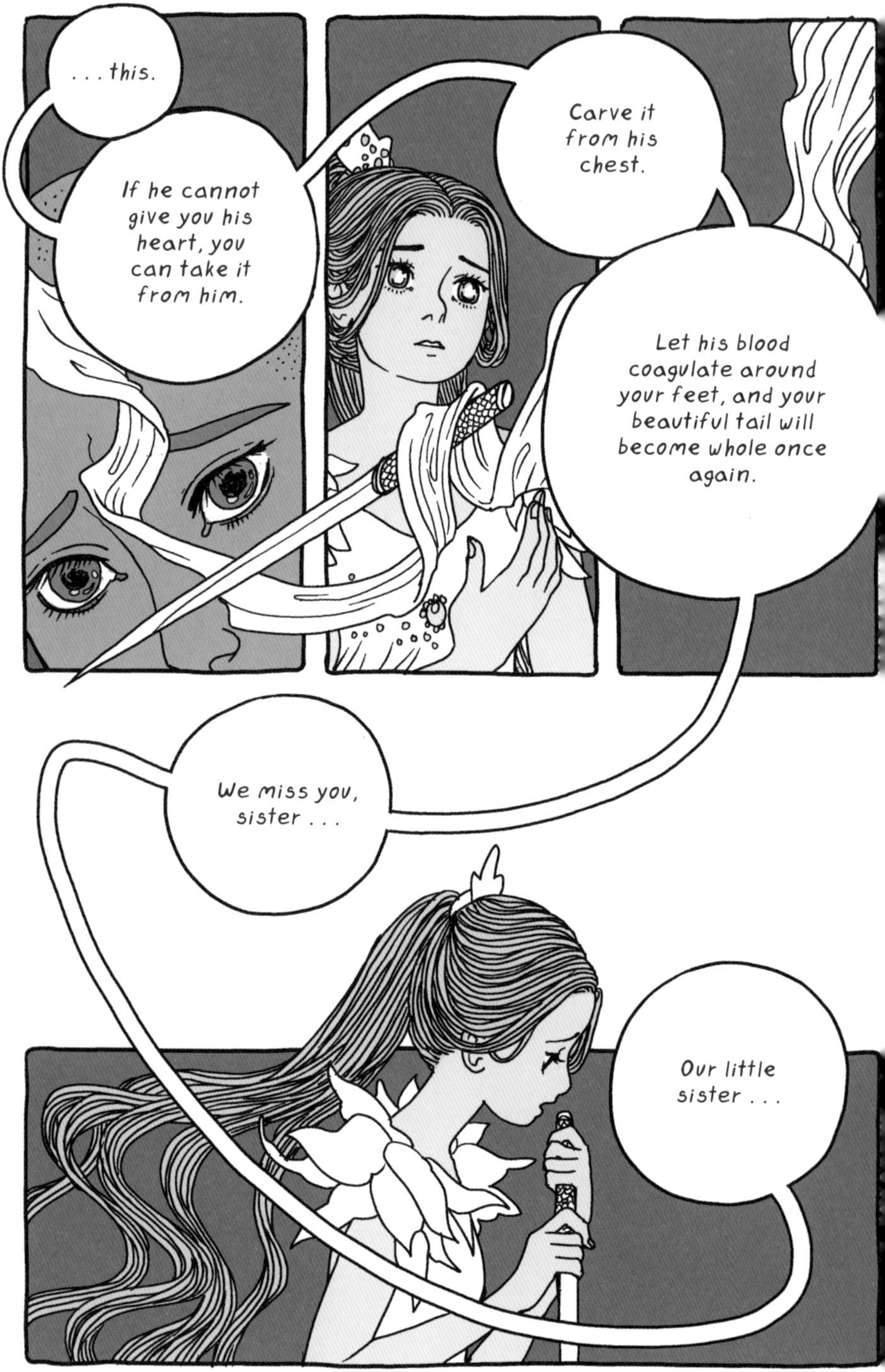
. . . this.
If he cannot give you his heart, you can take it from him.
Carve it from his chest.
Let his blood coagulate around your feet, and your beautiful tail will become whole once again.
We miss you, sister . . .
Our little sister . . .

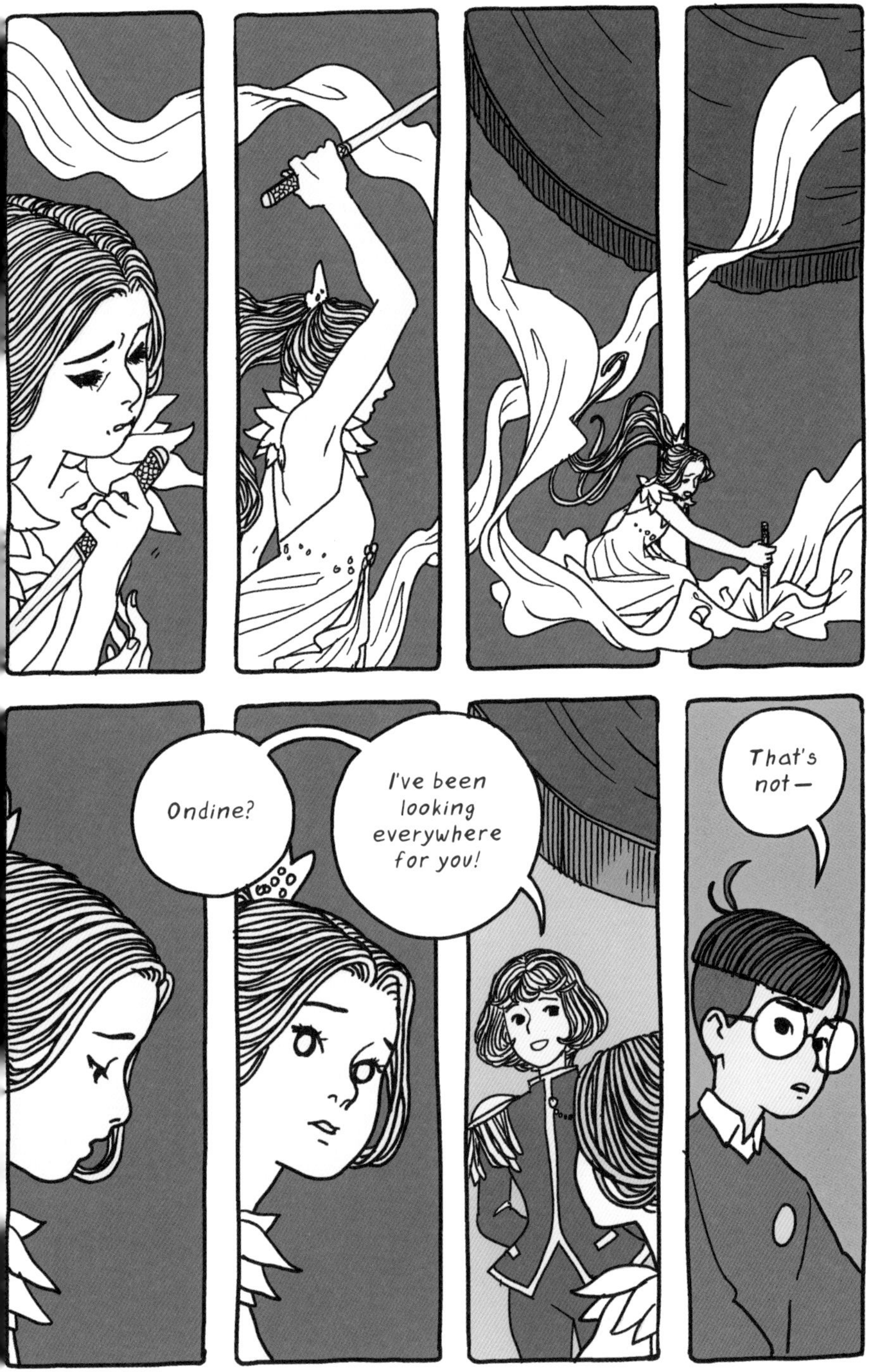
Ondine?
I've been looking everywhere for you!
That's not—

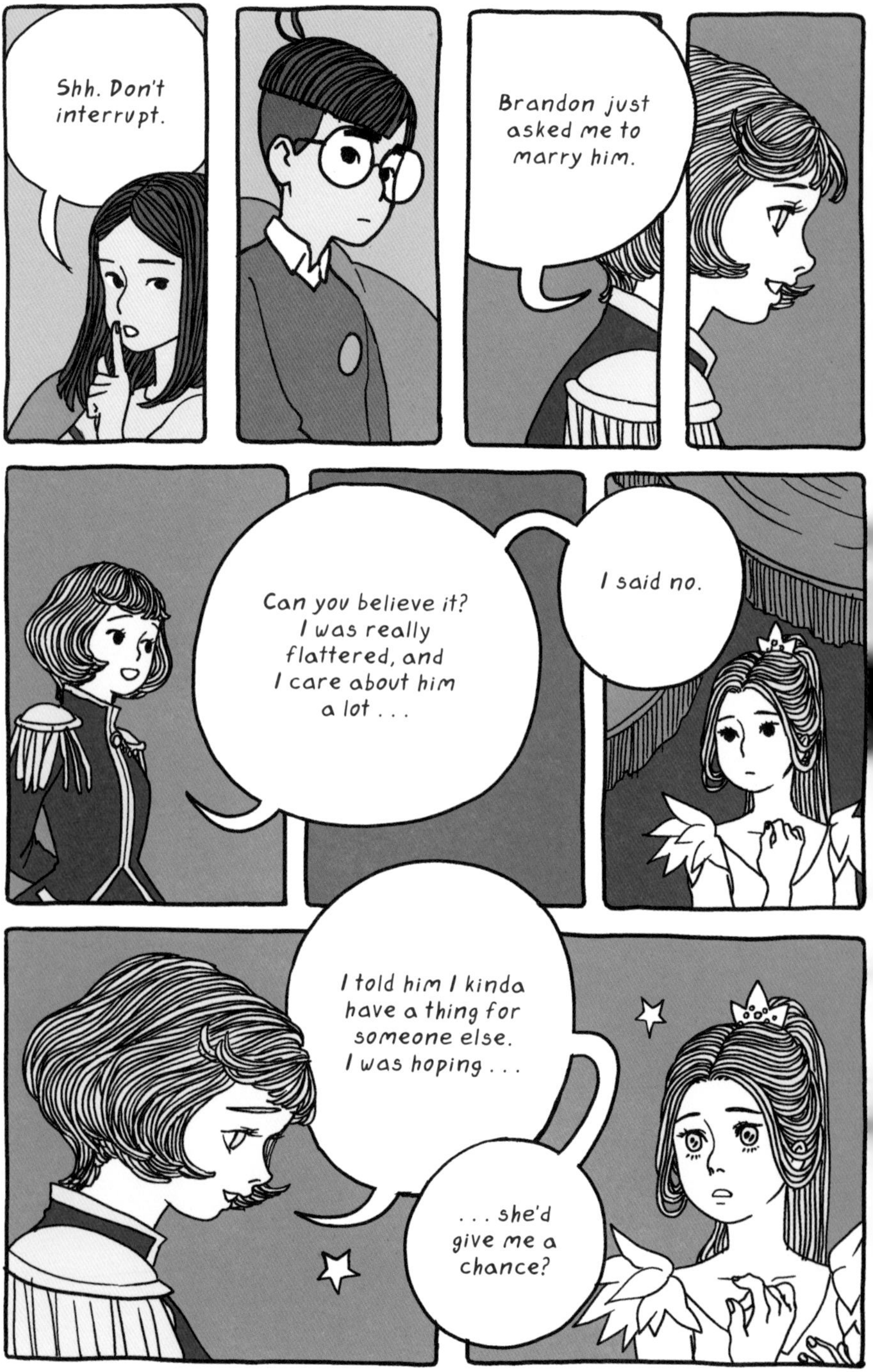
Shh. Don't interrupt.
Brandon just asked me to marry him.
Can you believe it? I was really flattered, and I care about him a lot . . .
I said no.
I told him I kinda have a thing for someone else. I was hoping . . .
. . . she'd give me a chance?

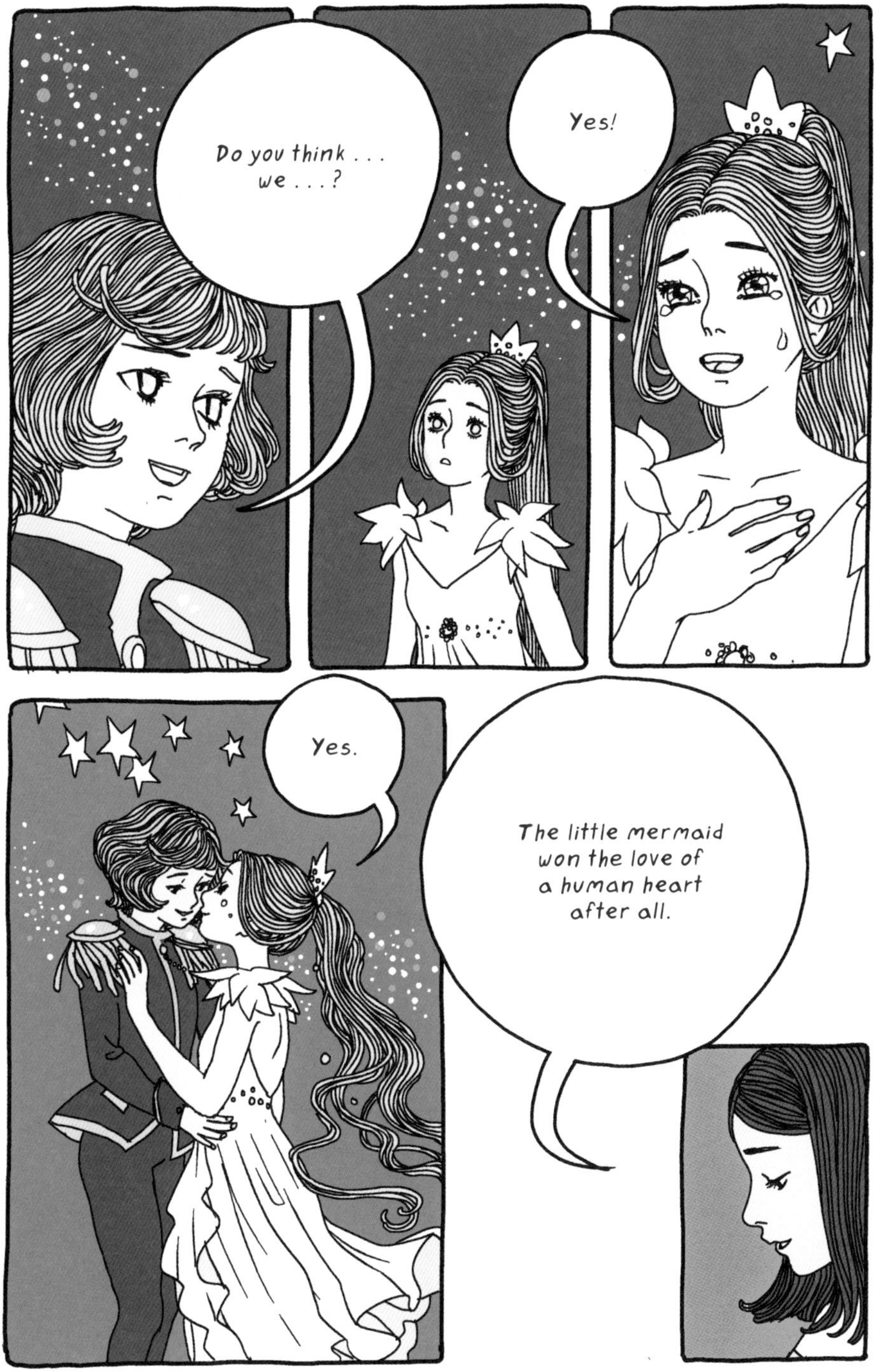
Do you think . . . we . . . ?
Yes!
Yes.
The little mermaid won the love of a human heart after all.

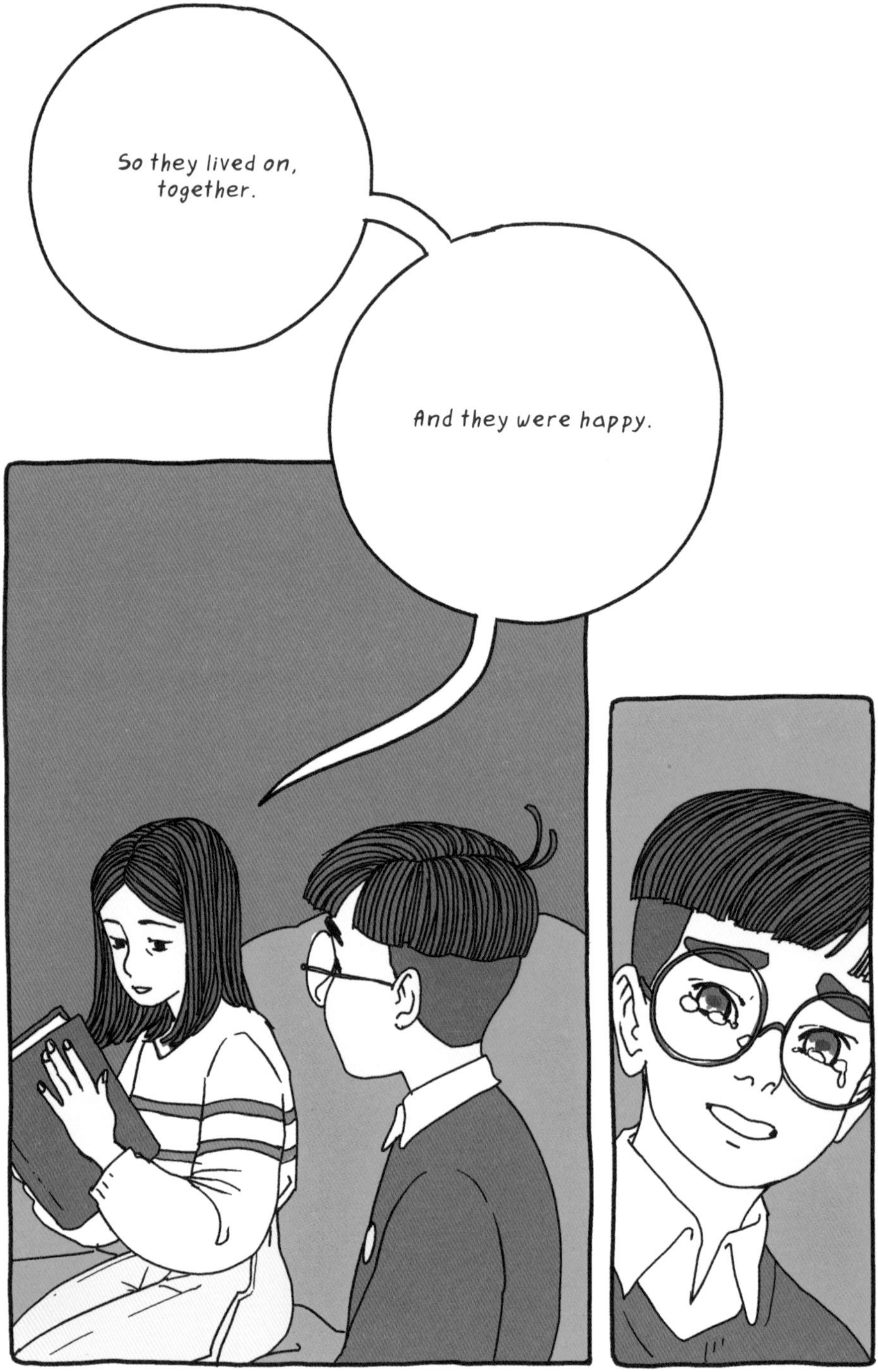
So they lived on, together.
And they were happy.

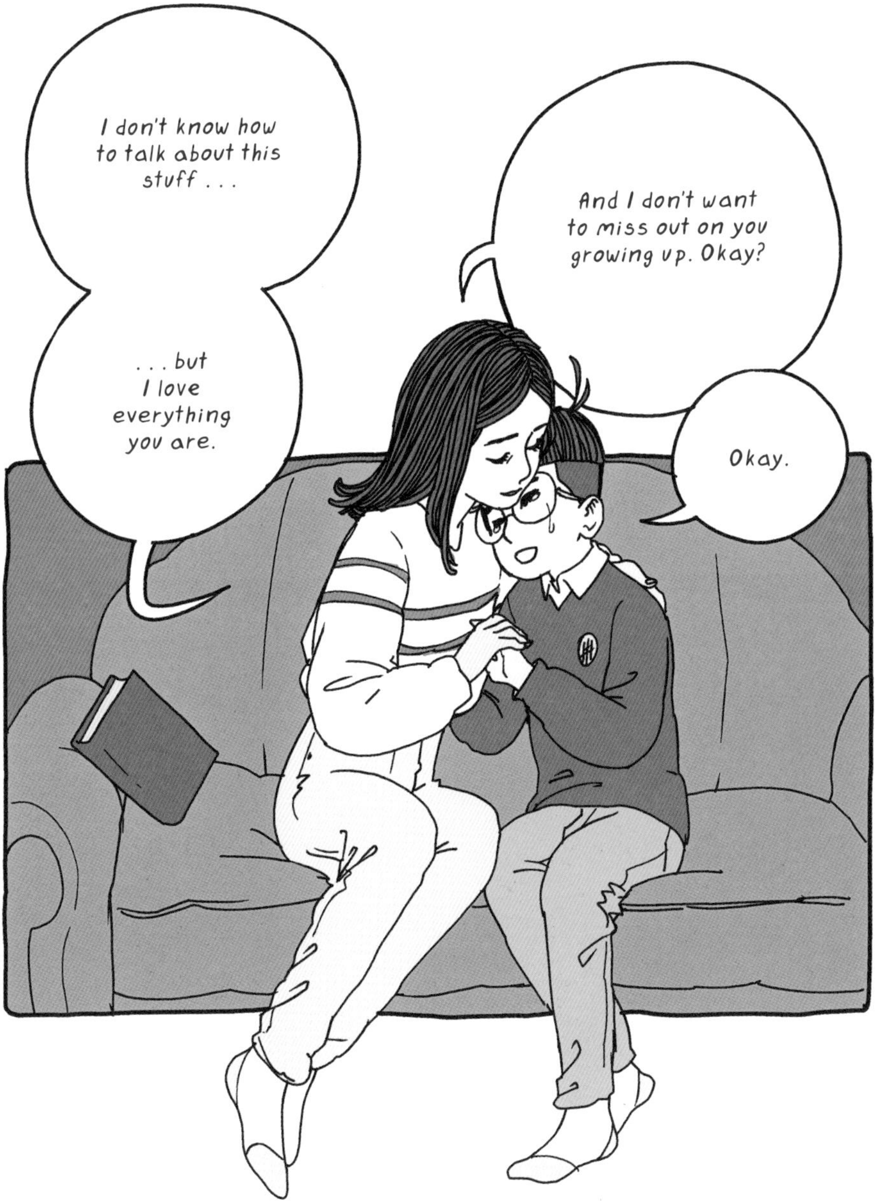
I don't know how to talk about this stuff . . .
. . . but I love everything you are.
And I don't want to miss out on you growing up. Okay?
Okay.

Author's Note

I set out to tell a very small story. One of the odd challenges of writing a story about characters living within any social margins is the gravity of the marginalization itself. It is such a dense thing, seeming to insist that all the pieces of the story should orbit around it. Immigrant stories are like this.

As compassionate readers, we sometimes intellectualize difficult human experiences to keep them at arm's length. There is an appropriate vernacular, a set of vocabulary words in a syllabus, and a common language established for the sake of facilitating dialogue. At our worst, we find the stories of immigration reduced to character tropes employed, for example, by the news for a disaffected viewer. The stories start and end with the arc of an exodus, and we forget that things continue to happen ever after, and that ever after does not happen for everyone all at once. At our best, we want to take a bird's-eye view of the situation in an effort to be as comprehensive as possible.

In this way, immigrants seem to take on the flatness of fairy tale archetypes, as interchangeable pieces in recurring stories of upheaval and diaspora. In both cases, we prefer to look in from the outside. All the quiet yearnings, the ambient heartaches, and the thousand other little indignities of feeling lost in your own tongue are overlooked in our best-intentioned efforts to be broad and comprehensive.

And so I set out to tell a very small story about a boy and his mother figuring out how to express love without the benefit of an appropriate vernacular, a set of vocabulary words in a syllabus, or a common language to facilitate their dialogue. I wanted to explore how stories can serve both as an escape and as an anchor for us in our real lives, and maybe, for at least one story, decenter the gravity of marginalization to tell a story about one of the little pieces that orbit around it.

Acknowledgments

A big thank-you to my partner, J, without whom I would not know whether today was actually a Tuesday. I'd like to emphatically thank my editors, Gina and Whitney, whose infectious enthusiasm makes me excited to turn in every single page. Many thanks to Patrick, our designer, and to Robin, my flatter.

A big thank-you to Kate, my agent, for believing in my work and patiently guiding me through my creative journey. You do marvelous work. To the fine folks in Minneapolis Parks and Recreation, thank you for all you do. I love wandering through Powderhorn on a challenging day.

Trung Le Nguyen,

also known as Trungles, is a comic book artist and illustrator working out of Minnesota. He received his BA from Hamline University, majoring in studio art with a concentration in oil painting and minoring in art history. He is particularly fond of fairy tales, kids' cartoons, and rom-coms of all stripes.
The Magic Fish is his debut graphic novel.

Between Words and Pictures

When I was very young, I learned how to read in English and Vietnamese side by side. Since my parents were new immigrants, we developed a weekly tradition of selecting a few books from the library and reading the stories to each other. This way we could ask each other questions and piece together parts of the stories that one or the other of us might have missed. As my parents and I became more comfortable with both languages, we spoke a combination of the two at home—a hybrid, or mixed language.

I especially loved illustrated fairy tales because, every once in a while, my parents would read me a story and then tell me that they grew up with one very much like it. I fell in love with the idea that a story could have places of origin and its own lineage, not entirely unlike a person. A fairy tale could move from one region to another, and it would change clothes. It could adopt the customs and beliefs of its new home, and it would still retain much of its core. The notion that a story could adjust to suit a new home was such a hopeful one for an immigrant kid who grew up knowing that he and his parents didn't come from the same places.

As I got older, we continued to borrow illustrated books and fairy tales, but I also started picking up comic books and loved them to bits. The way the stories unfolded felt so natural and dynamic. They reminded me of the way my parents and I would sprinkle English words within our spoken Vietnamese to help bridge the sentiments of two different languages. They never felt like separate, incompatible parts.

People tend to think about comic books as two separate parts—the words and the pictures. In illustrated books, the images support the text, but the text can exist entirely without the pictures. Comic books are just the opposite. Here, the images are the text. Comic books speak a hybrid language between orthography and iconography, written text and pictures. It takes a certain level of proficiency in both languages to get by, but it's a whole and complete reading experience altogether.

As I was making this book, I considered that each character has a different visual vocabulary informed by their personal life experiences. Tiến is a kid growing up in the 1990s in the American Midwest, like me. Tiến's mother, Helen, grew up in post-war Vietnam. Helen's aunt holds on to images of a pre-war, post-colonial Vietnam. The way each character envisions their stories is based on the things they might have seen and known, and I did my best to express this in the clothing and the settings around each of their respective fairy tales.

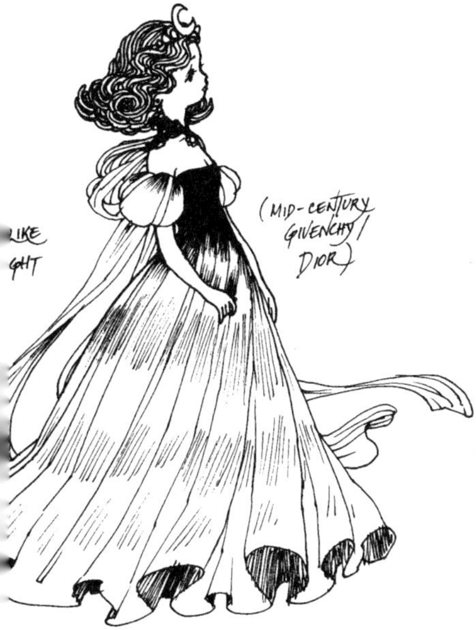
LIKE
(MID-CENTURY GIVENCHY/ DIOR)

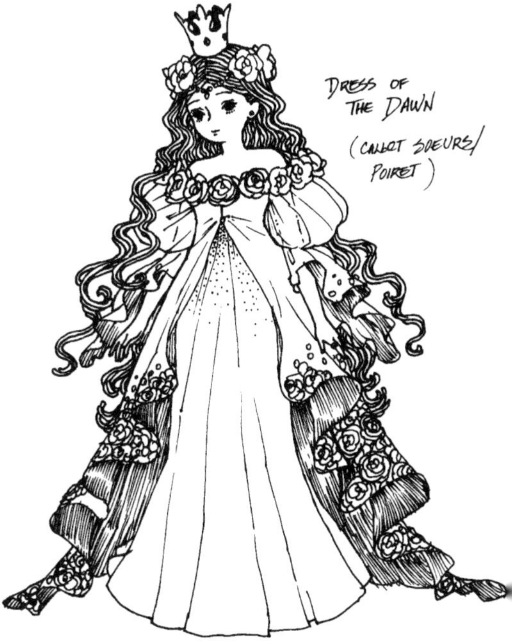
DRESS OF THE DAWN
(CALLOT SOEURS/ POIRET)

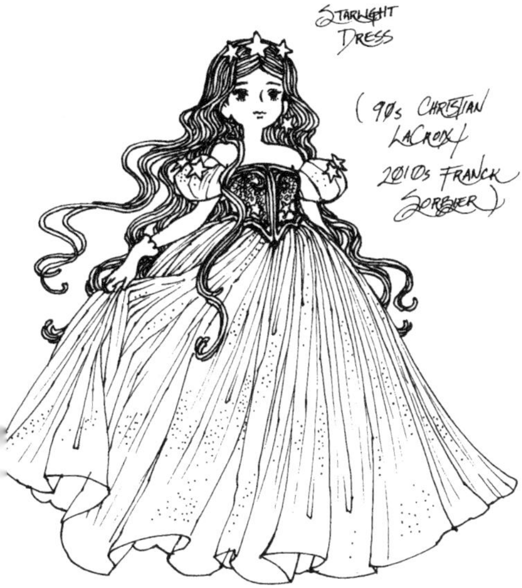
STARLIGHT DRESS
(90s CHRISTIAN LACROIX/ 2010s FRANCK SORBIER)

To contrast Tiến's experience with Helen's, I picked two relatives of the Cinderella fairy tale, the German "Allerleirauh" and the Vietnamese "Tấm Cám." The first fairy tale we encounter is a very loose adaptation of "Allerleirauh," read through the imagination of Tiến. He would be familiar with the stories and images popularized by the toys and cartoons in the mid-to-late 1990s, and his imagination probably hews closely to Western sensibilities about princess stories. The visual vocabulary he brings into the story is cobbled together from decontextualized European visual tropes associated with fairy tales, so many of the details are highly anachronistic, like the dresses worn by Alera, the first story's central character.

The aesthetics of the three dresses fall closely in line with various points in the western history of couture, loosely inspired by different designers over the past century. The Sunlight dress is based on Callot Soeurs pieces from the 1910s. The Moonlight dress is inspired by mid-century Givenchy dresses, like the iconic white dress Audrey Hepburn wore in the 1954 film *Sabrina*. The Starlight dress reflects more contemporary takes on princess dresses that exist in the popular imagination, more or less untethered from their historical roots.

The fairy tale segment of "Tấm Cám" is set in 1950s Vietnam to suit the visual imagination of Helen's aunt. The buildings and apartments are reminiscent of a French colonial style. Some of the characters are dressed in French-style clothing, which would have been popular at the time. The stepmother and stepsister wear fashionable pre-Mod-era French clothing, and Tấm's magically gifted dress is an áo dài.

The áo dài is considered the Vietnamese national dress, but Vietnam is a country that is colored by the forces of its colonizers. It was occupied by China for about a thousand years, punctuated by some brief periods of independence. Then there was nearly a century of French colonial occupation from the mid-nineteenth century through the middle of the twentieth century. All of these transitions affected Vietnamese culture in irreversible ways, and some of it is reflected in the áo dài.

The áo dài might be largely influenced by Chinese clothing from the Ming and Qing dynasties. In the eighteenth century, the áo dài was unisex court clothing, and the garment was much looser. The tightly fitted style of the áo dài first emerged at a Paris fashion show in 1921. It is credited as an innovation of an artist named Nguyễn Cát Tường. Today, the áo dài retains this general design, and I really consider it to be the result of an aesthetic hybrid language.

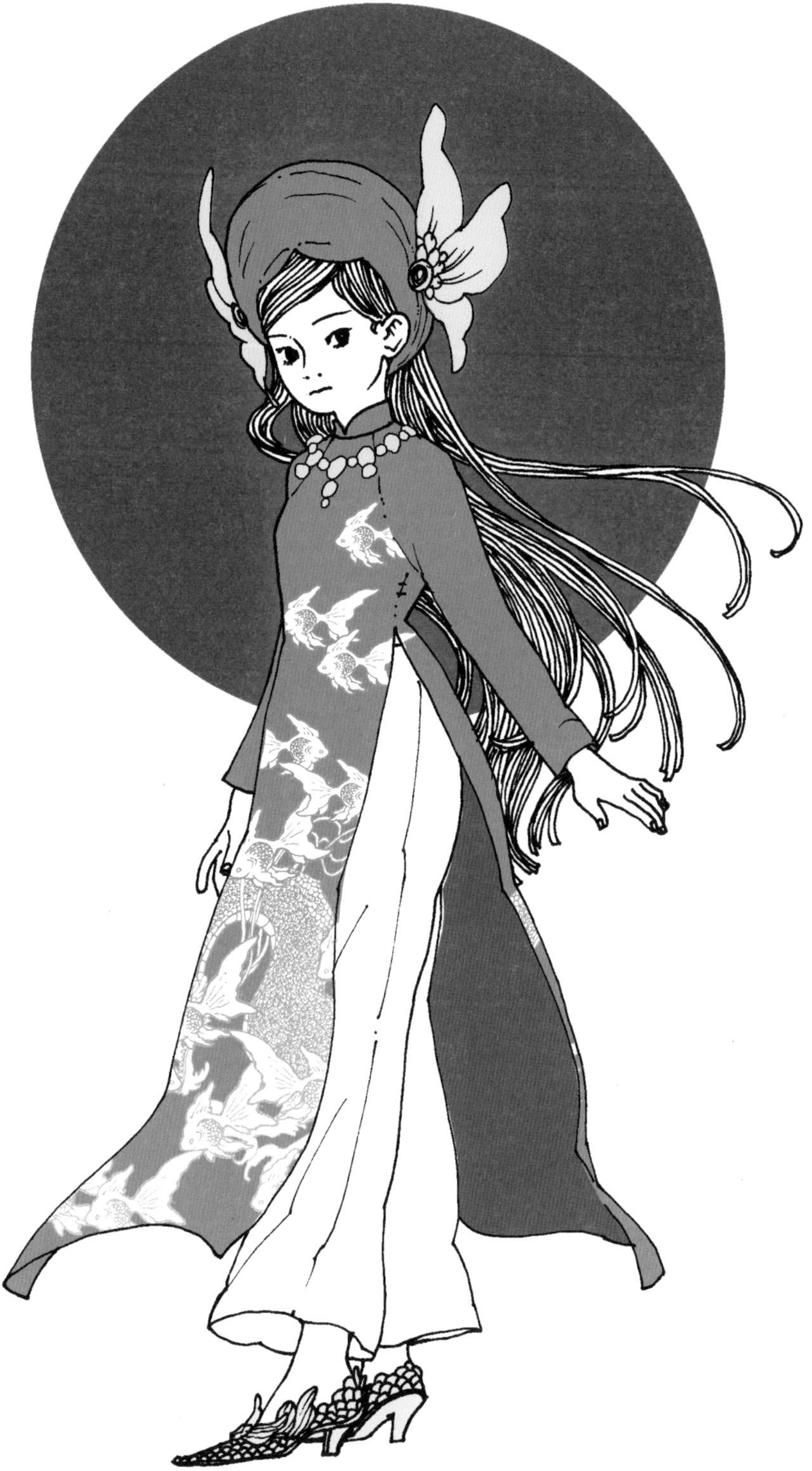

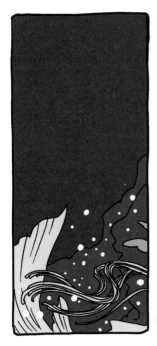

The last fairy tale is a reworking of Hans Christian Andersen's "The Little Mermaid," and it is told out of Helen's visual imagination. She is a Vietnamese woman who was born toward the end of the Vietnam War and grew up in its aftermath. I decided to make the mermaids' underwater home resemble a Hong Kong wuxia film because I remember my parents showing me some of those movies they had seen from the 1980s dubbed in Vietnamese. The underwater kingdom is specifically influenced by the Tsui Hark film *A Chinese Ghost Story*. The above-water world is based on San Francisco in the 1980s, and the theater in which the mermaid performs is based on the War Memorial Opera House in San Francisco.

The mermaid is a stand-in for Helen's experiences, a woman who wanted to escape to another world and manages to make it there at the cost of her ability to communicate. The mermaid's transition from a world that resembles a Hong Kong wuxia film to 1980s San Francisco mirrors the way Helen envisions her own journey from Vietnam to the United States.

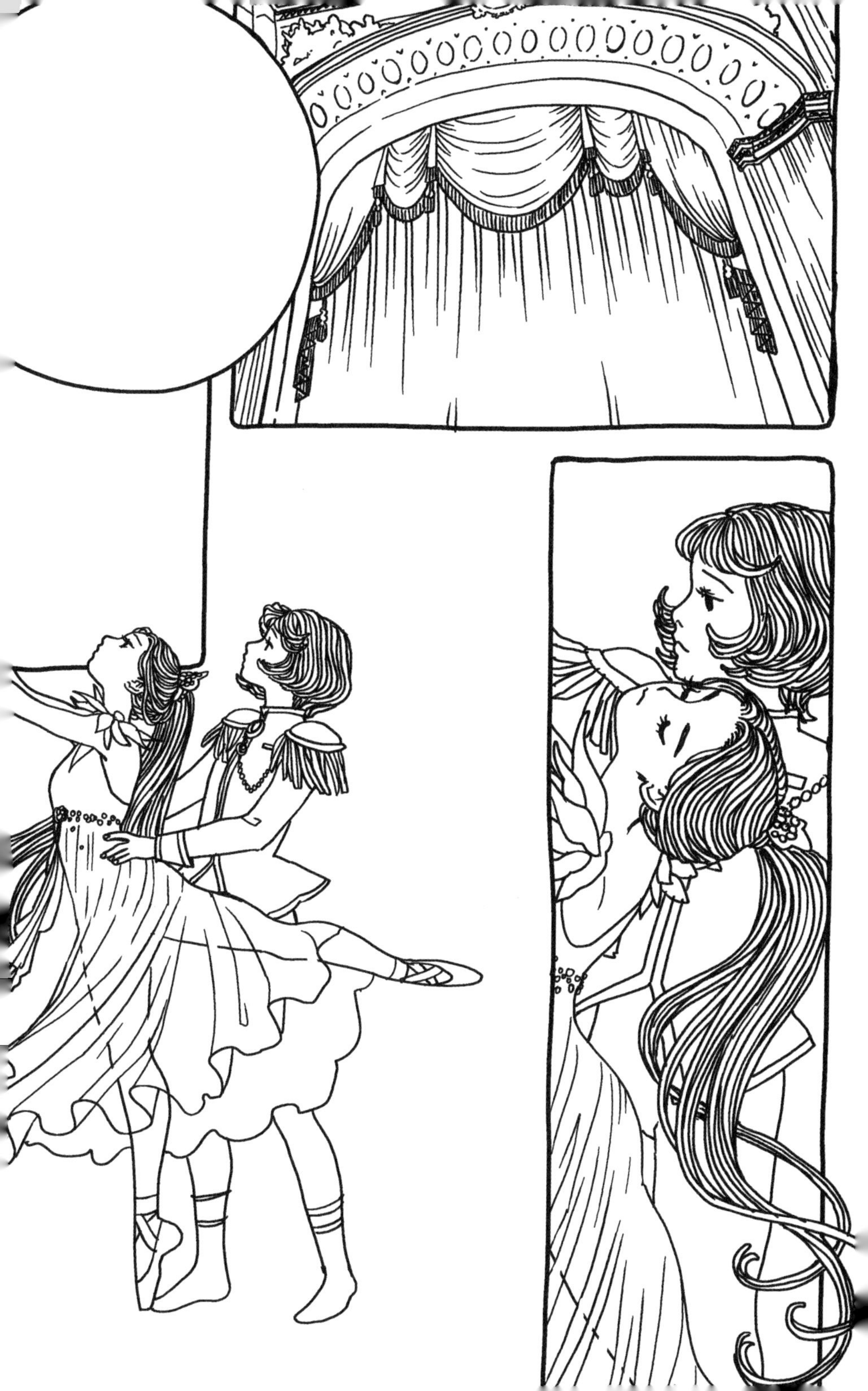

I've always thought of "The Little Mermaid" as a story about immigration. Even though Andersen's version is the most widely recognized, it was hardly the first. Some of the characters and names in this comic have been shifted around as a nod to the 1958 ballet *Ondine,* which was based on an 1811 novella by German Romantic writer Friedrich Heinrich Karl de la Motte Fouqué. The dance segments were referenced from footage of Dame Margot Fonteyn as the water sprite Ondine, a role that was explicitly created for her. The mermaid's ballet dress is modeled after Fonteyn's costume for the ballet.

The common thread between the novel, the ballet, and the children's story is the tragedy of the mermaid. She is a figure who attempts to transition between two worlds, and in most instances she fails and dies. I wanted to show Helen recognizing her son's desire for a different narrative. She might not yet be able to discuss the nuances of queerness at length, but that doesn't stop her from doing her best to find a way to make her love and support known, even if she needs to break from tradition and make do with what she knows.

Natural hybrid languages are informal. The uninitiated might hear two broken languages hastily cobbled together, but the interweaving Vietnamese and English hybrid I speak with my family is incredibly special to me.

It's the sound of people from very different worlds doing their best to come together and make each other feel at home.

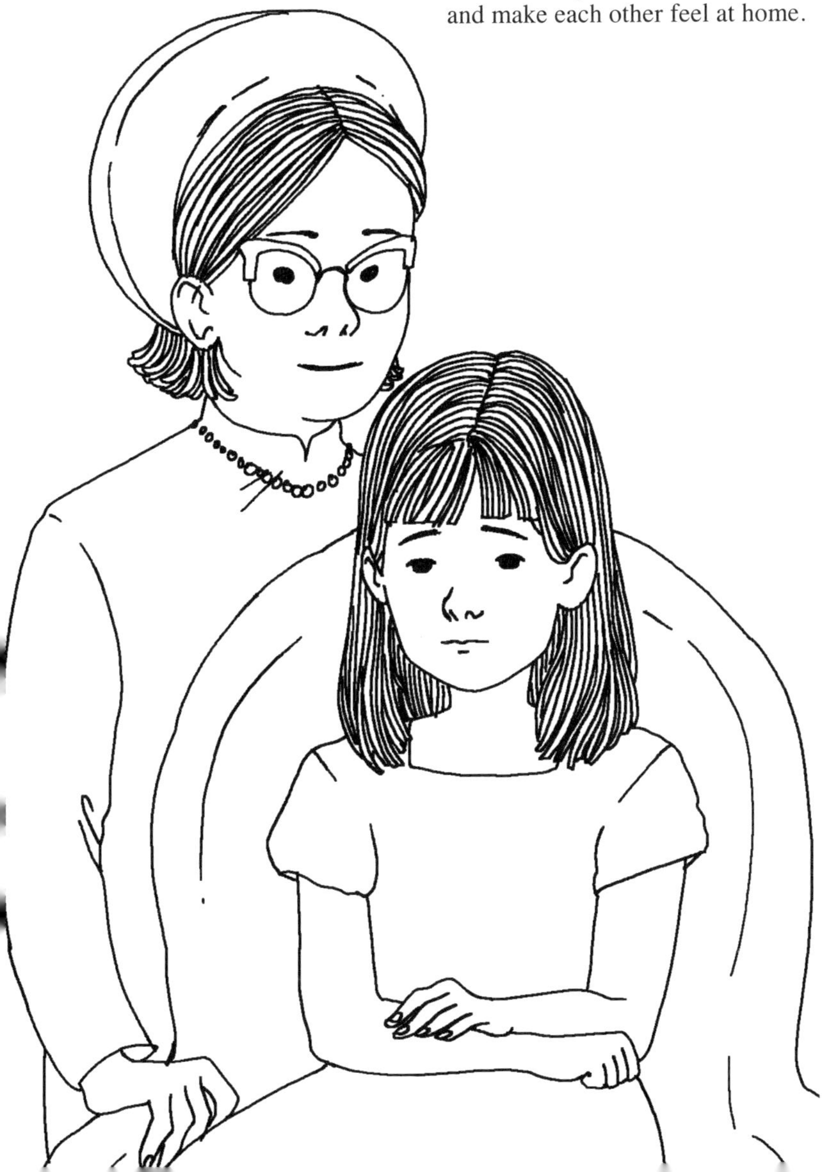

Bonus artwork

Mother and Son Between Stories

Before I started writing the book, I had drawn
a few drafts based on nonnarrative projects
I had previously done. This was the very earliest
conception of one unified story —the girl in the
tattered coat, the girl wearing the fish's dress, and
the little mermaid are all present.

Cover Line Art (opposite page)

This was a fun image to draw! Our designer, Patrick
Crotty, is responsible for the colors on the cover.
I drew several small thumbnail illustrations for
preferred compositions, and this was the one we
selected.

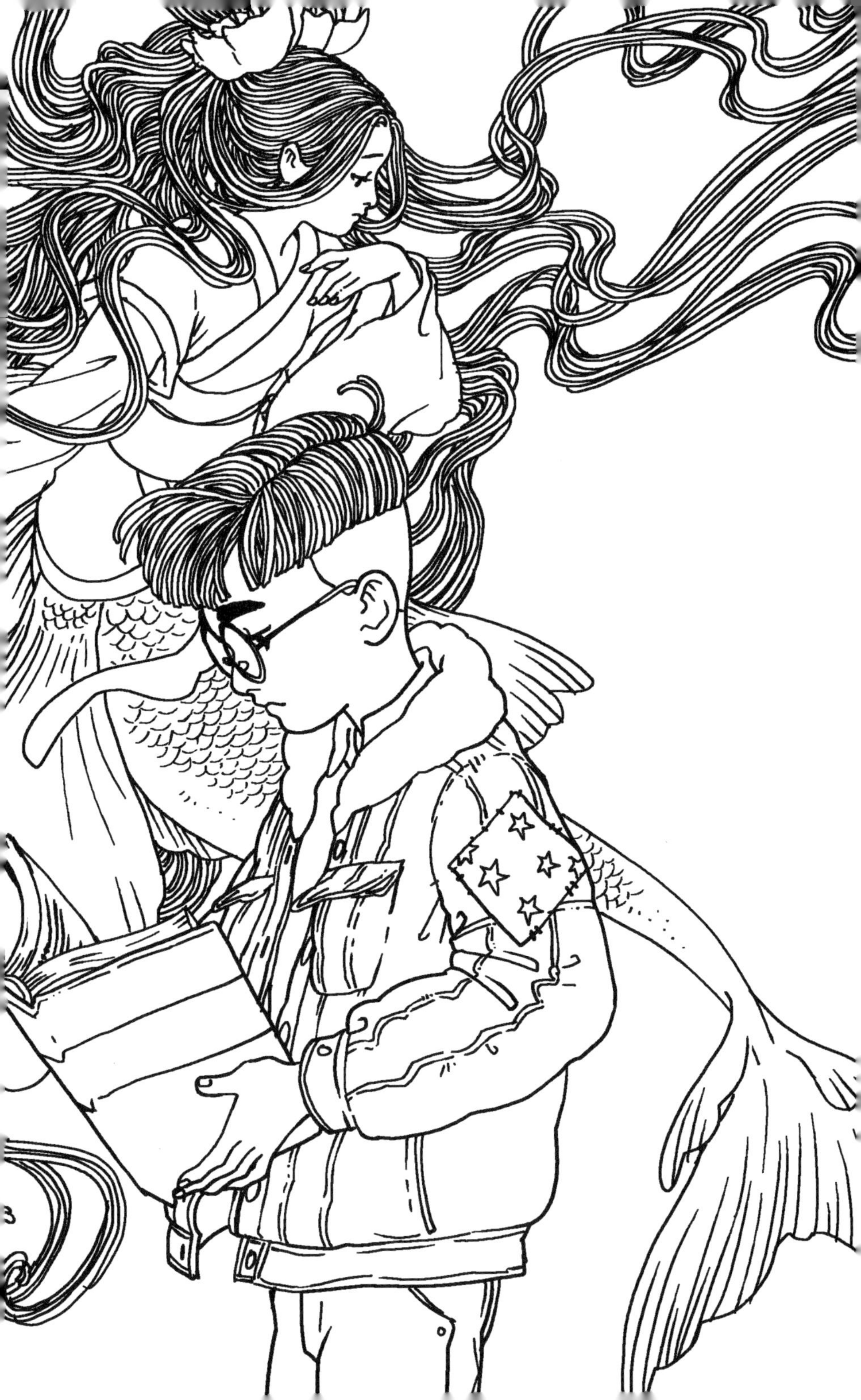

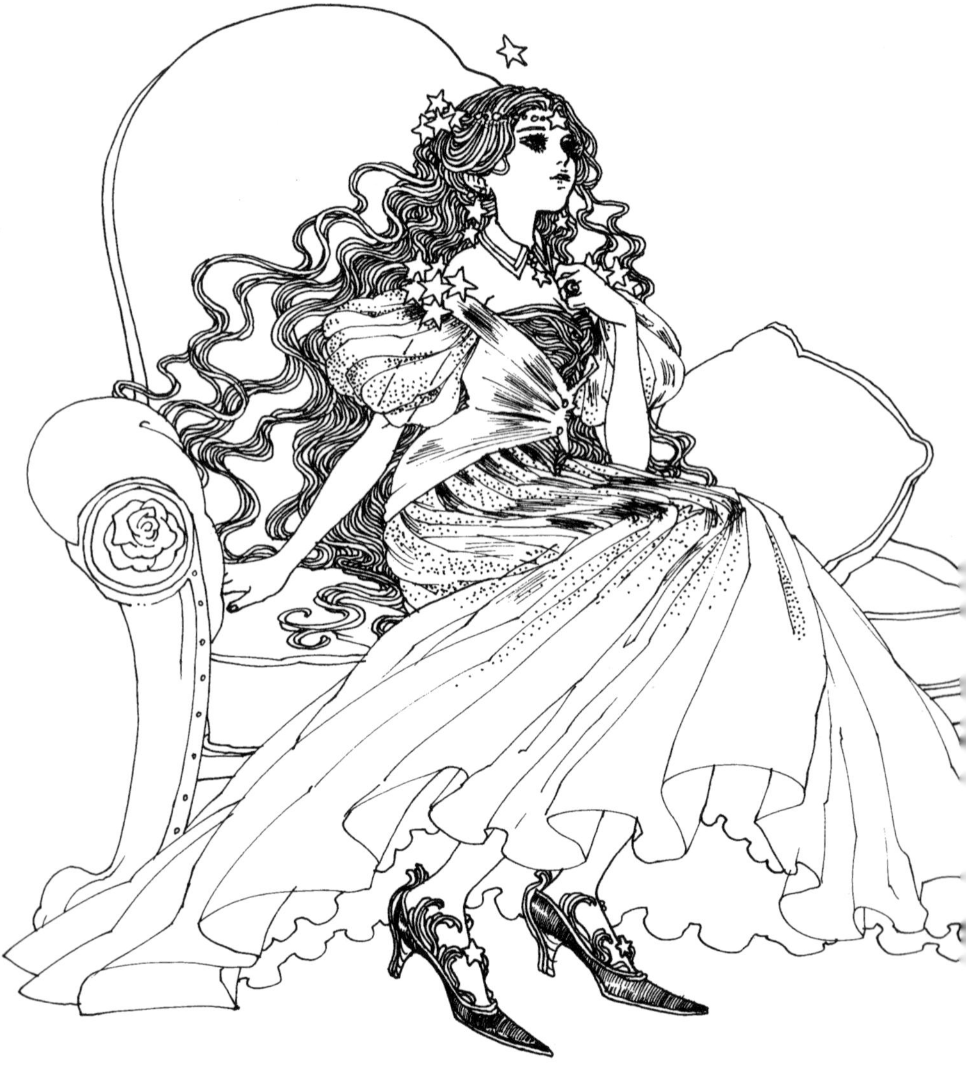

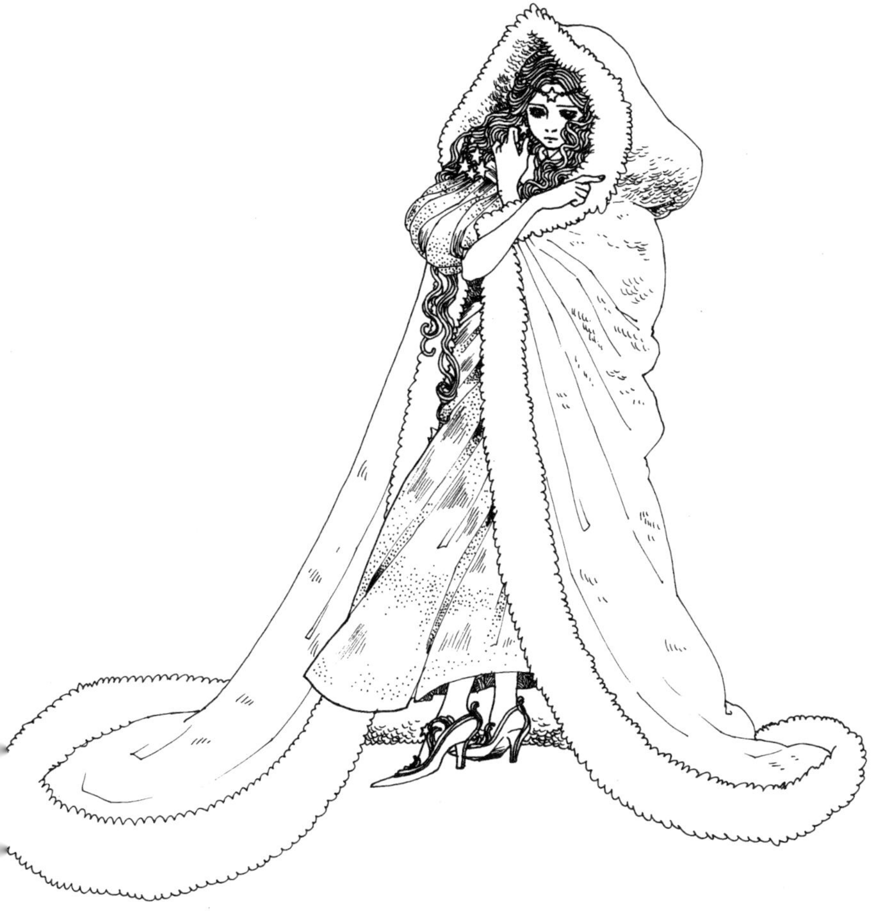

Alera on the Couch and Alera Under the Furs

The first fairy tale Tiến reads is "Tattercoats," and that one required the most preparation in terms of drawing. I had conceived of the book as a black-and-white project, so at this stage I was concerned about making sure I could adequately mix very different textures while working in one line weight. I combined stippling and hatching to give the fabrics the illusion of iridescence. I love putting very nitpicky patterns right next to large areas of empty space. It gives the picture nice visual tension. Ultimately, the limited palette in the book helped carry the different textures, so I could rely on color value on top of textures. It really saved my wrist!

HELEN

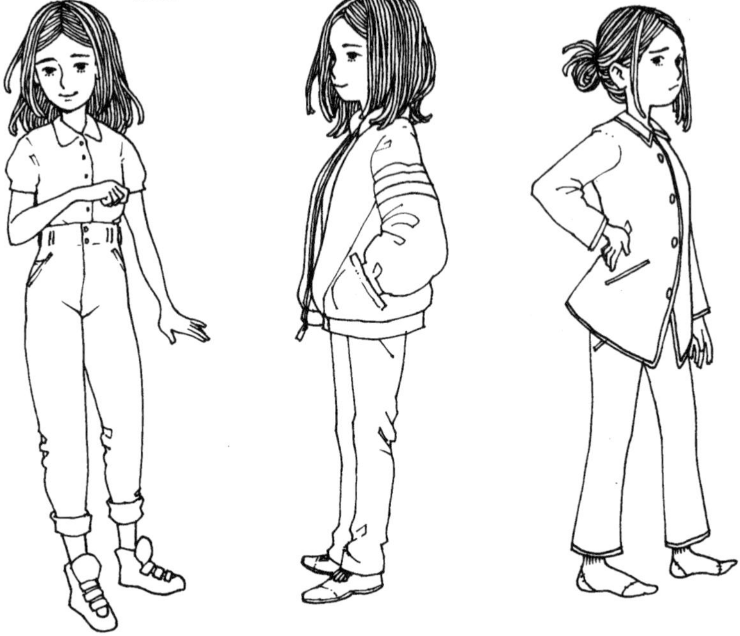

TÂM

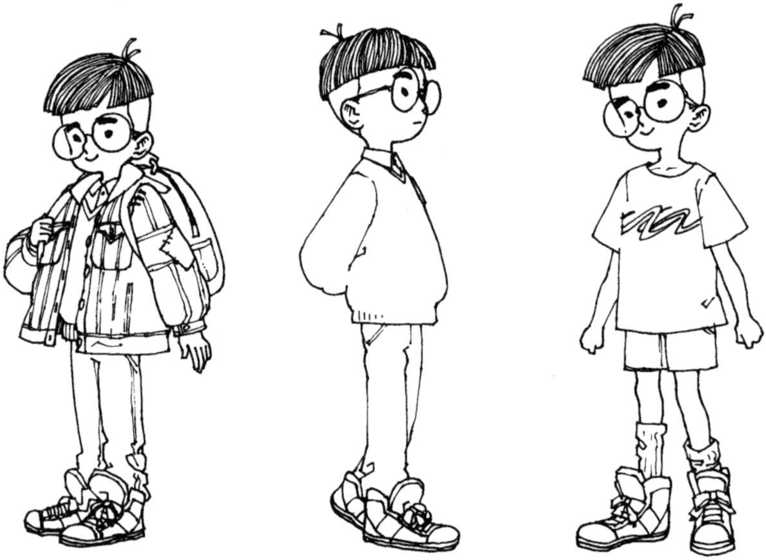

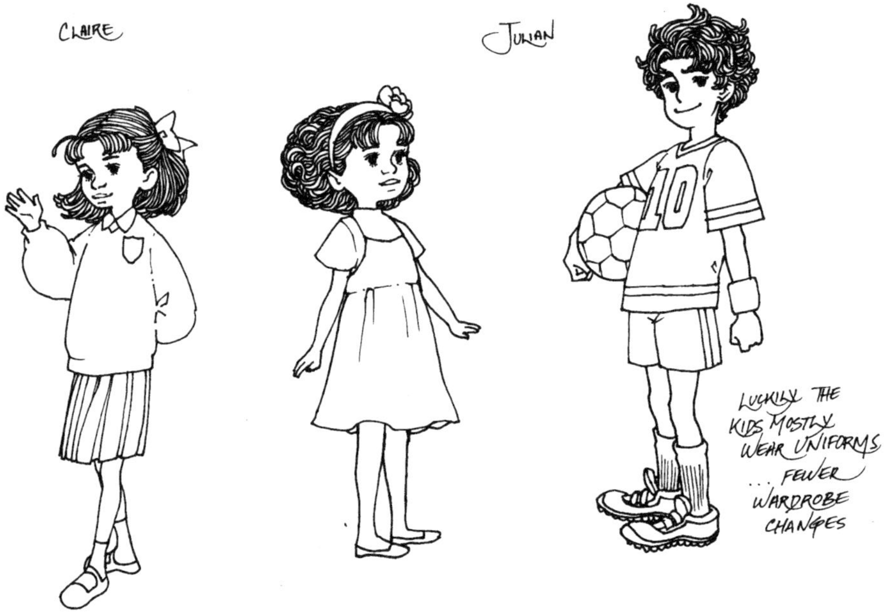
CLAIRE
JULIAN
LUCKILY THE KIDS MOSTLY WEAR UNIFORMS ... FEWER WARDROBE CHANGES

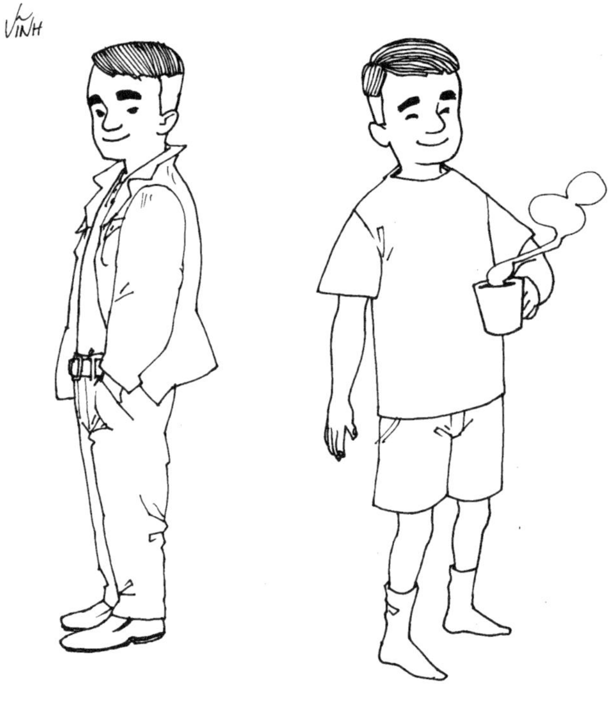
VINH

Character Concepts

These character drawings were more for my benefit than anyone else's. I actually started drawing the book before I made these. At some point I realized that it would be easier to have a drawing of these characters pinned up somewhere than to keep referring to finished pages.

Unfinished Page

The trouble with working traditionally is
that sometimes you get too far into a
drawing before you realize it doesn't work.
I did this a few times before I decided to
switch over to digital drawing to help hit
my deadlines. I really loved this image of
Alera dancing with the prince, but I had
composed the page in a way that didn't
work with the speech balloons.

Tulip Dress

For "Tattercoats," I looked at a lot of contemporary gowns. This was another way for me to practice interpreting real fabrics in a drawing where I was restricted by a rigid line weight. After this drawing, I felt more confident approximating fabrics with nothing but dots and lines. This dress is based on a Dior dress from the fall 2011 couture collection.

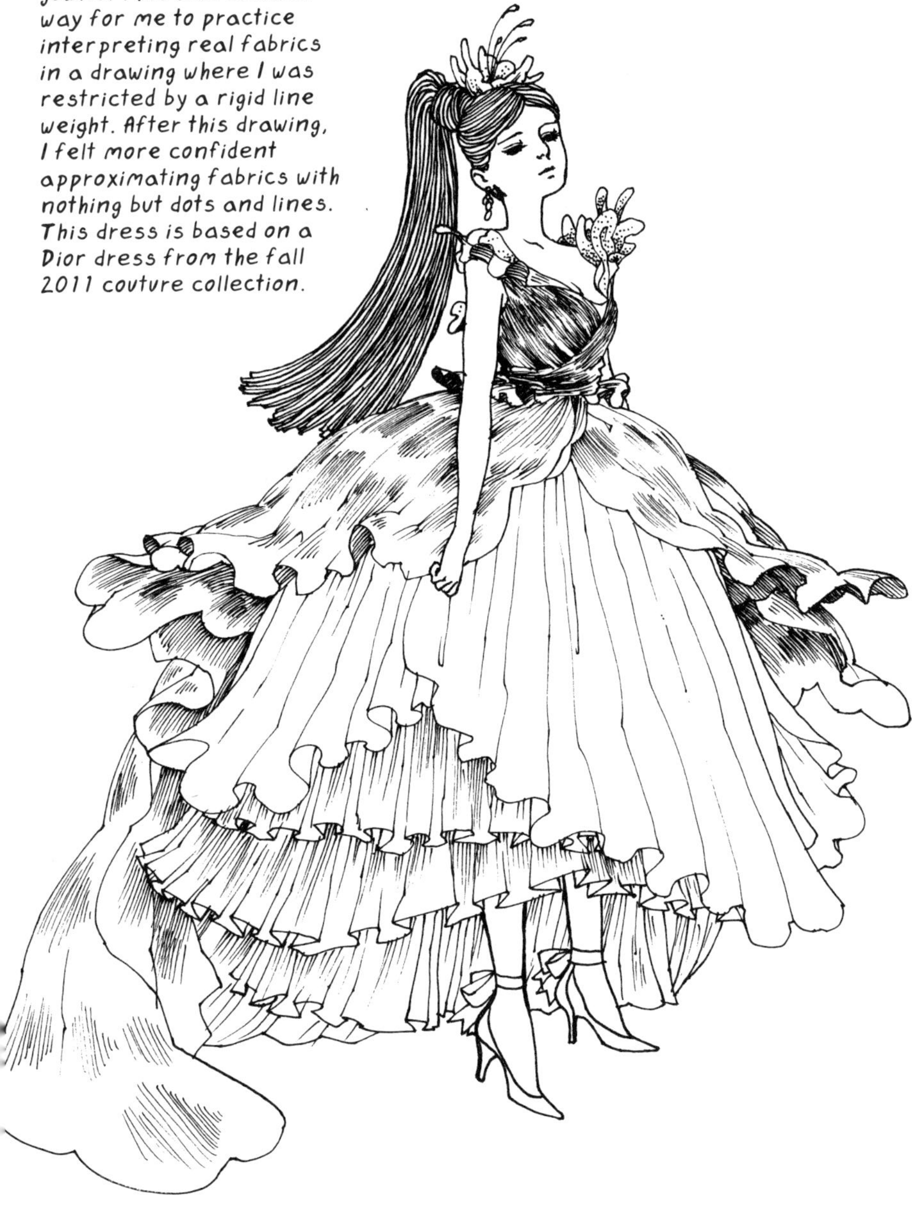

Dress of Midnight and Dress of Starlight

These two images were made once I had finalized the look of two of
Alera's dresses. I needed images to reference for the book that would
stay largely consistent, so I drew these. The background frames
are loosely based on some of the architecture from the Basilica of
Santa Croce in Florence, Italy. They were drawn almost entirely
traditionally, and then I cobbled them together digitally.

YOUR NEXT FAVORITE GRAPHIC NOVEL

The Magic Fish
by Trung Le Nguyen
How can Tiến talk to his parents about being gay when they're struggling with English and he doesn't know the words in Vietnamese?

Witchlight
by Jessi Zabarsky
Lelek's life is plagued by secrets. . . . Can she and Sanja work together to uncover her past and restore her magic?

Suncatcher
by Jose Pimzienta
Beatriz needs to write the perfect song to save her grandfather's soul—but what will she have to give up in exchange?

The Montague Twins
by Nathan Page and Drew Shannon
Pete and Alastair Montague are just a couple of mystery-solving twins living an ordinary life. Or so they thought.

@ RHKIDSGRAPHIC
RHKIDSGRAPHIC.COM